A Novel

By

Don Hess

To Catch a Fox

To Catch a Fox
Published by
Winter Hill Publishing, LLC

Publisher's Note
This is a work of fiction. Names, characters, places and incidents either are the product of the author's imagination or are used fictitiously. Any resemblance to actual persons, living or dead, business establishments, events or locales is entirely coincidental.

Creation date 2005
Cover design by Adam Perry

Printed in the United States of America

I dedicate this book to the following people.

To my wife Pat, who always supports me no matter how crazy my ideas.

To my "kids" without whose technical advice this book would have been impossible.

Finally I dedicate the book to Kate Orban Ed D who waded through the rough draft and made the manuscript presentable.

To each of these I owe my humble thanks.

To Catch a Fox

A note from the Author

To my readers: This story is a work of fiction. In some instances I have utilized real physical locations and in others I've simply made them up. I have used real towns and cities, but moved street locations or used fictitious addresses. In some scenes I have utilized the names of establishments and organizations as they existed within the time frame that this story takes place. In other scenes the timing of actual events has been altered to accommodate the story.

To my friends I post a warning. Sometimes when my creativity failed me I borrowed some familiar surnames. Some of my characters are a bit unsavory and they speak and behave as you would expect. If I bestowed your last name on one of them it by no means is a reflection of my feelings toward you. I thank you for helping me when I experienced a mental block.

All of the situations, companies and characters in this book are the product of my imagination. Any resemblance to real people or actual events is pure coincidence, as stated above this is a work of fiction. As your humble storyteller I hope that it provides you with enjoyment and a chance to escape reality for a bit. I had fun writing it.

Take care, God bless and thanks for choosing to read my book.

Don Hess

To Catch a Fox

Mr. Hess resides in Quarryville Pennsylvania with his wife Patricia. They have two grown children and three grand children. Mr. Hess states that "To Catch a Fox" was written in the evenings during his many nights alone in hotel rooms while traveling on business. He attended Franklin & Marshall College and Lancaster Theological Seminary. His career in the cabinet industry spanned 32 years beginning as a cabinet maker and working his way up through several corporations in Service, Sales and as an executive. That industry is the background for this book. Upon his recent retirement Mr. Hess determined that it was time to have the book published. As an "insider" to the industry Mr. Hess brings realism to his story telling that few could replicate.

To Catch a Fox

List of Characters

William "Mac" McLode – President of Fox Cabinetry an operating division of Atlantic Corp
Crystal Harrison Rankin – Daughter of Mary Johnson Harrison, adopted by the Rankin family
Foster Harrison – Ex husband of Mary Johnson Harrison
Mary Johnson Harrison – Deceased mother of Crystal Harrison
Trevor Mason – CEO of Atlantic Corporation owned by Wellbon-Smith Holdings, LLC
Abe Rueben – Lawyer hired by Trevor Mason
Denton Wellbon III - Grandson of the founder of Atlantic and Wellbon-Smith
Mary Justice Wellbon – Denton Wellbon III's mother and vice chairman of Wellbon-Smith
Carlton Smith – Current chairman of Wellbon-Smith
Tony Conocenti - V.P. Marketing, Fox Cabinetry
Carroll Brubaker - V.P. Manufacturing, Fox Cabinetry
Dale Hershey – CFO Fox Cabinetry
David Elliott – V.P. Customer Service, Fox Cabinetry
Sarah Frazer – New V.P. Human Resources, Fox Cabinetry
Dennis Morton – Retiring V.P. Human Resources
Brady Miller – Executive Secretary of Fox Cabinetry
Blair McManis – Tony Conocenti's girl friend
Sean McLode – William McLode's father
John Hogg – CFO of Atlantic Corp and close friend of William McLode
John Malicki – Mid West Regional Sales Manager for Fox Cabinetry
Glenn Glen and Mark Markel – Partners in new Fox flagship showroom in Chicago
Mitchell Green – Union Organizer
Andy Bevilacqua – Owner of Andy's Diner
Sam Grabowski – Detective Lieutenant NYPD
Harry Siegfried – Senior FBI agent, New York Office
George Smith / Mr. Jones – Mysterious person who contacts Crystal Harrison
Milissa Kensington – Major shareholder in Wellbon-Smith
Donald Kensington-Cramer – Milissa's nephew
Mr. Roberts – Major investor in Futures Unlimited, an investment company
Raymond "Don" Luca – Crime family boss

List of Characters continued

Tom Luca – Senior partner in a "Big Six" accounting firm and Raymond Luca's son
Jerome Jefferson – President United Federation of Millwrights International
Clint Matthews – CEO of Cab Corp
Albert Benard – Baltimore private investigator
Tom Erving – Manager of Fox Cabinetry's Las Vegas plant

To Catch a Fox

Prologue: June 1999

Foster Harrison sat in the atrium restaurant of the Savannah Marriott. It was seven in the morning and the early riser tourists and business types were beginning to filter in for breakfast. He had a cup of black coffee on the table before him and he took his first sip of the day. That would probably be the first of many sips.

Foster was a man in his early forties. He was tall and thin with thinning sandy colored hair and a high forehead. If someone told you that he was a college professor you would certainly agree that he looked the part. In fact he was a "road warrior," a territorial sales manager for a large West Coast Corporation. His home base was San Francisco. His sales territory stretched from San Diego to Seattle. He covered all the Pacific Coast states for his company. He sold drugs for a major drug and chemical company to pharmaceutical supplies distributors. At this moment he was in Savannah Georgia for a seminar.

As he sat sipping his coffee he watched as a huge container vessel slowly made its way up the Savannah River. The hotel sat on the riverfront at the end of River Street. He was not thinking of the ship however, nor the upcoming classroom sessions that would begin later in the morning. At this moment he was reflecting on his past. Many years ago when he was a younger man he made his home in Savannah. He was married to a girl that was somewhat younger and they had a daughter. Then he left not only Savannah, but also his wife and daughter. He had never returned until now. He would not have returned at all except his boss told him that this seminar was mandatory. It concerned new government regulations that the sales force had to be familiar with. While he wasn't fond of returning to the site of the "sins of his youth," he believed that he would be able to come in to town, attend the seminar and leave unnoticed by the end of the week. It was not to be.

The evening of the first day of classes he returned to his room to find the message light blinking on his phone. When he retrieved the message, he was shocked to discover that it was his daughter, Crystal Harrison. She wanted to meet him this morning for breakfast. She said simply that she would be in the atrium restaurant by 7:15 AM at the latest. If he wished to see her after all of these years, he should be there. That was it. The entire message was three unemotional sentences. Foster didn't want to go.

He had never contacted either his wife or their daughter after he left. All dealings that he did have he managed to keep between their lawyers. He kept tabs on them and was faithful in sending alimony money after the divorce, but he never again made personal contact. Now, for some reason that he couldn't explain, he was sitting here in the restaurant waiting, for what he didn't know. What would she be like? Why did she want to see him? Would she be angry and resentful? Of course she would. This could not end well. He knew the question that would burn from her lips: "Why?" He wondered if he could answer. He was a grown man and he was terrified at the prospect of facing his daughter. He had nightmares about this moment.

Suddenly she was there, standing at the hostess station waiting for someone to seat her. She was scanning the room searching for him. Maybe she wouldn't recognize him. After all she was only five when he left. He had changed a lot in twenty-one years. He recognized her immediately. At twenty-six she was a news anchor on a local television station. He saw her smiling likeness and name splattered all over billboards and the sides of buses ever since he stepped off the plane two nights ago.

Then she stopped looking. She was staring right at him. The hostess arrived at her arm to seat her, but she said a couple of words and brushed the woman aside. She was coming straight toward him. Foster rose awkwardly to meet her. He didn't know what to do so he offered her his hand. "Crystal Harrison I assume?" his voice crackled and his mouth felt dry.

She stopped directly across the table. Her eyes locked onto his. He couldn't look away. He couldn't even blink. My God she's beautiful he thought! She's the image of her mother! Some old emotions and memories stirred within Foster. Her face betrayed no emotion.

"Yes I'm Crystal Harrison...and you would be...my father." Her voice was as emotionless as her face. But her eyes, they were a blue blaze, and Foster felt as if they were burning into his soul. She was smaller than she appeared on television. Especially when you realized that she was wearing high heels. She had a trim figure with shoulder length auburn hair. Her determined face had a pale complexion with freckles showing faintly through her make up. She looked very professional in an expensive gray pin striped business suit. She made no move to reciprocate his proffered hand, leaving him standing awkwardly with outstretched arm. He quickly dropped it to his side.

“May I sit down?” she asked.

“Oh! Of course! Please do!” He fumbled to move around the table in time to help her be seated, but was too late. She seemed to pull the chair from the table and glide into it in one quick fluid motion. Foster paused behind her long enough to catch the subtle trace of expensive perfume; he then moved apprehensively around to his side and sat down. They stared at each other. She said nothing. While her face betrayed no emotion her eyes held his in a decidedly icy stare. Finally Foster regained his voice and attempting to keep the nervousness from it he said; “I don’t know how to start this…or what to say.”

“I imagine it is extremely difficult,” was her curt reply.

Foster was saved from having to respond by the waitress who arrived to take their order. “Just coffee, black please,” said Crystal. Foster agreed and asked the waitress to bring them a pot.

“How did you know that I was in town?”

“I’m a reporter. I have contacts all over the country. I tracked you down several months ago. I knew that your company was having a seminar here and I figured, by the nature of the seminar, you would probably have to attend.”

“You tracked me down?” He knew it was a mistake as soon as he uttered it.

“Yes, that’s what you have to do to find a father that deserts you and your mother when you are only five without any explanation or a forwarding address.”

“Is that what this is about?”

“Of course that’s what this is about. That and the fact that I wanted to see you face to face.”

To Catch a Fox

"I'm sorry Crystal. I don't know what it is you want from me. I fail to understand what good it does for us to meet after all these years," an exasperated tone, triggered by the tension, was creeping into Foster's voice.

She closed her eyes and tilted her head back slightly, her breasts rose as she took a deep breath. When she opened her eyes again he thought that they appeared moist for the first time. She exhaled and appeared to be imposing an iron hand of restraint on her very being. She had run this scenario through her mind a thousand times and had conjured up just as many things to say to her father when they finally met. All of them escaped her at the moment. "You don't even care do you?" she finally blurted out.

"Yes I care. I sent alimony checks all those years. I sent them willingly! When I could I sent your mother more than I was required to send. After she died I continued to support you through the foster family that you were living with. I only stopped after they adopted you."

"Why did I have to live with a foster family? Why couldn't I have come to live with you? Why did you allow me to be adopted?"

"It was too late then. I had remarried. My second wife didn't want any children. I had my own life then and I figured you did too."

"Oh I had my own life alright. What a dandy life it was. I had no idea why my father didn't want me. My mother never got over the fact that you left her. It haunted her until she finally committed suicide!" Crystal's eyes finally over flowed with tears. Her voice had dropped to a menacing whisper. "I was ten years old and was shuffled about from one foster home to another before the Rankin's took custody of me and, thank God, gave me a loving home. That's more than you ever did!"

"Crystal, you don't understand…."

"Of course I don't understand! How could I understand? Mom never understood! You never even cared enough to write me a letter and at least make an attempt at explaining! You never picked up a phone to ask how your daughter was doing. You never did anything!"

"It's all too complicated. You were just a child. I felt so betrayed." Foster was staring out at the river. He could no longer look his daughter in the eye.

“You felt betrayed? How do you think we felt? Well in case you haven’t noticed I’m not a child anymore. I’ve a college degree, top third of my class at Auburn. I think I can probably comprehend it now. Give it a try. Why did you desert me?”

“I really don’t want to talk about this Crystal. It serves no purpose now. It will only hurt both of us all over again.”

“I’ve never stopped hurting.” Her voice was now almost a plea.

Foster closed his eyes as though in deep painful thought. Crystal sat staring at him. This was her father. The man she knew only by the few pieces of information that others had told her over the years and by what she had pieced together on her own. This was the mystery man that had haunted her entire life. After he left, her mother could never bring herself to talk about him. She hurt that much.

Crystal thought of her mother. Even as a little girl she only clearly remembered her mother and her together. Her father was a dim memory shrouded in mist. Crystal was nine before it hit her that there seemed to be no other family for them to turn to for support. No grandparents, no aunts or uncles, no other immediate family available to help them. Her mother explained to her that she was an orphan and had grown up in a series of orphanages. Crystal’s father was the only real family that her mother ever had. This was why she had been so devoted to her husband. Her mother said that the three of them had been so happy. Then for no apparent reason, her father deserted her mother and her. Crystal had longed to know what she; Crystal could have done as a child to cause this. It had to be her fault as her mother claimed that they had been so happy and no amount of therapy could change her mind on that.

Now she was wondering why she had ever decided to meet her father in the first place. It was obvious that he couldn’t say anything to make up for the last twenty-one years. The waitress brought the pot of coffee, and pretended not to notice the tear tracks on Crystal’s make up. “Just call me if you want anything else,” she said and then quickly disappeared. But there were things that Crystal had to know and this was the only man that could tell her. She decided to take a different tack. She forced her voice to sound calm again.

"Have you noticed that I have taken your name as my professional name? I'm Crystal Harrison on the TV, not Crystal Rankin, the sir name of my adopted parents."

"What…? Oh yes. I thought that maybe your producer thought that it sounded better or some such thing."

Crystal smiled for the first time. Foster noted with a sidelong glance that it was a beautiful white smile. "My producer didn't know what my name was. I have always used Harrison as my professional name. My 'real' name is Rankin since the adoption went through, but I have used your name since I cut my first audition tape."

Foster turned to face his daughter once again. "Why is that?"

"I don't know. I guess I still want to have some link with you. No matter how tenuous it may be."

Foster didn't know what to say, so he said nothing.

Crystal pressed on. "I'm sorry for my outburst. I promised myself over and over that if this day ever came I would not allow that to happen. But when I saw you I just lost all my self control."

"It's okay. I'm not behaving well either."

"Can we begin again?" asked Crystal.

"Yes, yes we can." Then Foster opened the gate. The gate that he knew in his rational mind should never be opened. "What do you want to know?"

Crystal decided to touch the peripheral questions first. "I know that Mom was an orphan, but if I couldn't come live with you after mom…died, why couldn't I go live with my grandparents on your side?"

Foster blinked. "What did you just say?"

"Why couldn't I have gone to live with your parents? I've never met my grandparents you know."

"No, no, what did you say about your mother?"

Crystal looked puzzled. "I said that she was an orphan. That's why I have no family on her side."

"Who told you that your mother was an orphan?"

Crystal was really confused now. "My mother, she told me."

Foster shook his head. Your mother's family lives in Maryland, near Baltimore. They always have. Your grandfather on your mother's side may have died or perhaps he's still alive, I don't know. About a year ago I heard that he was suffering from some sort of cancer. Your grandmother was still alive the last I heard. Your mother wasn't an orphan. She was an only child, but she certainly wasn't an orphan."

Crystal was stunned. "What are you saying?"

"I'm telling you the truth. I told you this would hurt more than it helped."

Crystal's mind was reeling. She was only barely listening to Foster now. Foster continued. "The reason that my parents didn't take you in is because…" Foster stopped. He looked at Crystal's helpless expression. She wasn't taking the news of the existence of her mother's family well. She would never accept what he was about to tell her. Why did he ever allow this meeting to take place? She was better off before. Up until now she only hated him.

Crystal shook her head. She had a dazed look in her eyes. Her eyes focused on Foster once again. "Go on," she said. "I'm listening. What about your parents?"

Foster took a deep breath. What the hell he thought, after today she would probably never want to lay eyes on him again. She should know the truth. "My parents couldn't claim you."

"Why not? I don't understand."

Foster unconsciously bit his lower lip. "After I relinquished my rights they couldn't claim you even if they wanted to, because you are not their grand child and there were relatives in Baltimore."

"But that can't be. If it were, then I wouldn't be your daughter."

Foster stared at the table. "That's why I left," he answered softly.

"No! I don't believe you!" Crystal threw her full cup of coffee at Foster. It splashed all over his face. Luckily it had cooled considerably since the waitress poured it or he would have received some serious burns. With that she sprang to her feet. She glared at him, tears welling up again. "Why did I ever think I wanted to meet you? You are the same cad that you were twenty-one years ago when you left us. She's dead! She's dead and you still want to belittle her memory!"

Foster wiped his face with a napkin. They were the center of attention in the restaurant now. "I've told you the truth. There may be no excuse for the things that I've done in the past, but today I told you the truth."

Crystal turned and stormed out of the restaurant leaving a wake of gawking patrons behind. "Isn't that the girl on channel 3? It certainly looked like her." Foster finished wiping his face. He inspected himself and looked at his watch. He would just have time to go up to his room and change cloths before the first session. He paid the bill, apologized to the hostess for the disruption and headed for his room.

Across the restaurant sat a large man in a well-tailored dark suit. He had entered the restaurant just behind Crystal Harrison. He was eating a western omelet and was casually observing the father and daughter confrontation while only being mildly concerned about his immediate calorie and cholesterol intake. When both had departed he reached into his inside jacket pocket and removed a cell phone. After punching in a number, he waited for a few seconds and began talking.

"Yeah they finally met. By the reaction I would guess that Foster Harrison told Crystal some things that she didn't want to know about her family. What do you want ME to do?" The big man listened for a few moments more. "Okay boss. I understand." He closed the miniature cell phone and returned it to his pocket. He was in no hurry to follow either Crystal or Foster. He knew exactly where they would be. Crystal had to be at the television studio within the hour. No matter what tragic event she was dealing with in her personal life she would continue to work and function. She was tough. The big man had a lot of respect for her. She had to be tough with the hand life had dealt her, but she would survive. Foster would return to his room in the upper levels of the hotel, change cloths and attend the next session of his seminar. The big man had no respect for Foster. What a jerk he thought. He knew that Foster would botch this encounter. He didn't even have to over hear what transpired to know that he was correct in this assumption. He leisurely finished his breakfast.

To Catch a Fox

PART 1

CHAPTER 1

Trevor Mason stood staring out of the twenty first-floor windows of his up town Manhattan office. It was 8:00 PM on a warm rainy evening in June of 1999. He was watching the rivulets of rain streak down the pane. He could hear the wind faintly whistling outside. Normally, by this hour, he would have been drinking a martini in his Connecticut study. Tonight he had important business to conduct; the kind that he did not wish to conduct during normal working hours when too many eyes and ears were lurking around the office. He looked at his watch. Denton should be arriving with their visitor any minute now.

Trevor was a large, physically powerful man. He was not tall, as he was only five foot eight inches in height, but wide and squat. He was not fat as he continued to work out three times a week. Indeed, his body fat ratio was less than twelve percent. The workout regimen was a habit that he had developed in college during the off-season. It was only in recent years that he cut back to only three times per week. This was partly because with his business travel it became increasingly difficult to exercise every day and partly because as he reached middle age his muscles needed some time to recuperate between sessions. He simply grew tired of being constantly sore.

Trevor attended Michigan State on a football scholarship. He played several positions all on the offensive line. Trevor was an excellent player and would probably have been drafted by a pro football team had he not severally damaged his right knee in the next to last game of his senior year. Everyone, family and friends thought that he would be devastated by the news that he could never play football again. Trevor surprised them all by taking the news exceptionally well. Trevor's father was a self-employed electrician. Trevor had always admired the fact that his father ran his own business. Few knew that Trevor planned on running his own business some day, only Trevor planned to run a much larger business than a small residential electrical firm that only employed three electricians. Trevor's plans for the future were much bigger than that. Football only provided the vehicle for Trevor to go to a Big Ten college. He was serious about his studies and graduated in the top twenty percent of his class with a degree in Business Administration. If he could have signed a pro football contract for big money he would have done it, but he viewed this as only a stepping-stone to his goal. The fact that he would not have a big bucks football contract only meant that he would not have the funds to begin his own start up business after a football career. If the truth were known, after midgets, high school and college, Trevor was weary of football. He was ready to begin working at a large corporation and work his way up the corporate ladder. Trevor still walked with a slight limp thanks to his knee, but the knee had not slowed his career progress one iota.

Trevor's thoughts moved to Denton. Denton Wellbon the III, grandson of the late founder of the Atlantic Corporation of which Trevor was the President and CEO. Denton Wellbon, the "ski" was dropped by the intrepid immigration agents at Ellis Island upon Denton's arrival in this country, founded an import business in the late 1890's in the City of New York. He was highly successful; though there were always rumors of illegal contraband making its way into this country through the auspices of Denton's company. Rumors and allegations only, nothing was ever proven. Wellbon detractors hinted that the reason that no charges could be filed was because Denton had several well-placed police, politicians, and more than one judge on his payroll. In any event, Denton Wellbon was the epitome of the hard driving rags to riches story. His ruthless personality spawned many an off the cuff tale in several prominent boardrooms even today. The old man was the stuff from which corporate legend is made.

Denton's son, Denton Wellbon II, was every bit as ruthless as his father was, albeit far more subtle and sophisticated. Blessed with both wit and charm, attributes that his late father never possessed, he was accepted in New York society. It was often said that Denton Wellbon II had the unique ability to tell someone to "go to Hell" and have him or her look forward to the trip. It was this Denton Wellbon that turned the Atlantic Corporation, and its holding company Wellbon – Smith LLC into the conglomerate that it is today. Denton Wellbon was every bit the hard driving dictator, and unlike his father who lived to be ninety, died relatively young in his late sixties of a massive heart attack. He collapsed at one of his own board meetings after threatening to replace all the members for having the audacity of considering the stockholders interests over Denton's ego and refusing permission to stretch their finances to the limit by acquiring yet another company. His death forced the reorganization of the company and thrust the current Denton Wellbon into the spotlight. Young Denton was twenty-eight years old at the time.

To Catch a Fox

Ah yes, thought Trevor, Denton Wellbon III. When you stepped off the elevator on the top floor of this office building, which served as world headquarters for Wellbon – Smith Holdings, L.L.C. the first objects that your eye was drawn to were two massive portraits of the first two men named Denton Wellbon. It was uncanny how they resembled each other and even more uncanny that the current Denton Wellbon was the spitting image of both. Spitting image in appearance, but somehow he was woefully short on the drive and courage of his immediate ancestors. Trevor smiled to himself, thank God for small favors. If the current Denton had been half the man his father and grandfather had been, Trevor would not be sitting in the chair of the President and CEO of the Atlantic Corporation.

Upon the second Denton's death his wife, Mary Justice Wellbon, reorganized the corporation with the help of the second Denton's lifelong business partner and friend Carlton Smith. Wellbon – Smith became the Limited Liability Corporation that now acted as the holding company for its flagship, the Atlantic Corporation, and several other conglomerates of which it either owned all of the stock or held controlling interest.

Mary Wellbon, like all mothers, loved her only son but was also an astute businessperson in her own right. She told the board that her son at age twenty-eight lacked the experience to succeed his father. The board members smiled and agreed. They all knew that the only reason young Denton was accepted to and graduated from Princeton, was because his father funded one of the most ambitious building programs in the history of that institution. While young Denton Wellbon III was not stupid, neither did he distinguish himself during his academic career. He was regarded as a willing worker, and pursued his career in business with what was best described as a lack of urgency. Mary spared them the embarrassment that having to vote against her wishes would have caused had she attempted to impose her son on the board. With great relief the board elected Carlton Smith to the unusual dual role of President of Atlantic Corp. and simultaneously to the position of Chairperson and CEO of Wellbon – Smith. In a gesture not only of gratitude but recognition of her abilities, the board elected Mary Wellbon Vice Chairperson.

The year of Denton Wellbon II's death and subsequent reorganization of his business was 1979. Mary wished to spare her son as much embarrassment as possible for not inheriting his father's chair so she and Carlton Smith arranged for young Denton to become a junior vice president in Atlantic Corporation.

Mary hoped that Denton would learn to master the world of his father and grandfather and eventually take his rightful place, but it was not to be. Even under the watchful tutelage of family friend Carlton Smith the current Denton failed to grow. Things remained in this state until February of 1995.

Both Carlton Smith and Mary Justice Wellbon were younger than Denton Wellbon II. Mary, born in 1931 was sixteen years her husband's junior. Carlton, born in 1929 was her peer. Carlton was now in his seventies and Mary was approaching that mark so it was soon time to consider handing the reins of their empire over to younger hands. Mary still enjoyed attending and contributing to the monthly board meetings of Wellbon – Smith, but Carlton lost his wife two years prior and was losing interest. In February of 1995 Carlton requested that he be relieved of his dual responsibilities as president of Atlantic Corporation and Chairperson of Wellbon–Smith Holdings. The board reluctantly accepted his resignation from Atlantic, but managed to persuade him to remain as Chairperson of Wellbon – Smith until a successor could be groomed. As this position did not require his daily presence in the city, Carlton agreed.

Trevor knew that Denton Wellbon III, at that time forty-four years of age, expected to be elevated from junior vice president to the position of president of Atlantic. He saw this not only as his birthright, but also as a stepping-stone to becoming chairperson of Wellbon – Smith, his father's old job. He was to be disappointed once again. His mother, accurately appraising her son's abilities, abstained when the nominating committee contacted her for suggestions. Carlton Smith suggested that perhaps the company, whose profits had been sluggish since Carlton became distracted, would be best served if someone from the outside were to be found to give a fresh perspective. The nominating committee found Trevor Mason, the son of an electrician who had worked his way through Michigan State on a football scholarship, and had moved up through the ranks of several increasingly larger companies. Trevor demonstrated an interesting ability for "cutting through the bullshit" as he put it, and solving problems that had stymied many "more qualified" executives. To Denton's shock, Trevor Mason was voted in as president of Atlantic Corporation on a unanimous vote, with his mother abstaining. In a second vote Denton was elevated to executive vice president and therefore second in command to Trevor. He found this to be of little consolation.

Trevor turned from the window and looked at the large antique grandfather's clock that stood in the corner of his office. 8:15 PM, one thing Denton could boast of was his punctuality. He was supposed to have Abraham Ruben at Trevor's office at 8:00 PM. Knowing Ruben, it was his fault, even in bad weather and heavy traffic Denton would have allowed enough leeway to still arrive on time. Trevor knew that Denton would be having fits. That thought made Trevor smile.

When he arrived at Atlantic, Trevor Mason expected Denton to be a thorn in his side when he was told of Denton's history, but he soon discovered why Denton had been passed over twice. To Trevor's surprise, Denton simply and meekly "rolled over" and made no attempt at sabotage, revenge, or even put up a fight. To Trevor's further surprise, Denton made an excellent assistant. He was meticulous to a fault, had a good understanding of math and accounting, and could be counted on to put in long hours without a complaint when it was required.

It was required quite a bit. Trevor, upon his arrival at Atlantic, immediately improved Atlantic's profitability. He forced all of the operating division presidents to reduce inventories. If possible, they were instructed to stock as much inventory on consignment as they could force their vendors to accept. For those who refused this concept, the divisions were instructed to "twist the vendors arms." for shorter delivery times. If an Atlantic Company could not stock inventories on consignment, then they were instructed to use their suppliers as their own warehouse. Trevor Mason verbally bludgeoned his division executives until they could all boast of a minimum of twelve inventory turns per year. Considering that when Trevor assumed control of Atlantic the average was two turns per year, this was real progress. He also made it corporate policy to extend payment of accounts payable to sixty days, and then still required his divisions to take the cash discount. If vendors didn't like these terms they could take a hike, and the Atlantic companies would find other vendors. Because of the purchasing power of the seven operating divisions, most vendors grumbled but were accommodating. All divisions were required to reduce receivables to an average of twenty-eight days. These tactics produced screams of protest from the vendors, distributors and division presidents alike, but all soon discovered that they best comply or they too could be invited to "take a hike." All this sat well with the board of Wellbon – Smith as Trevor Mason improved the bottom line of all of the Atlantic Corporation businesses, and reminded them nostalgically of the founder and his son.

To Catch a Fox

Trevor's next project was improved quality. Trevor's approach was simple. No matter how low the returned goods and warranty costs were at an Atlantic company, Trevor gave them twelve months to reduce the number by half. One division president failed to hit this mark and he immediately accepted Trevor's offer of early retirement. While none of this increased Trevor Mason's popularity with his division presidents, he was acquiring a reputation for success among his peers in other Wellbon - Smith controlled conglomerates.

Through all of this Denton Wellbon III became Trevor's efficient and trusted assistant. Indeed, Denton who had never received much respect from the division presidents or his peers in New York suddenly was given new respect and even deference. Denton was now Trevor Mason's right hand. He had the ear of the boss. He delivered both the messages of praise and rebuke from the dreaded "Mace" as Trevor was called behind his back. Denton was sought after for advice on how to "get along" with Mason, and how to escape "certain corporate death" when goals were missed. In short the meek and mild mannered Denton basked in the shadow of fear that Trevor Mason cast wherever he went, and Denton found that he enjoyed it.

Those who witnessed this unexpected relationship were at a loss to explain it. Mason's reputation as a hard driving accepts no excuse S.O.B. preceded his arrival at Atlantic. Everyone expected Trevor to "eat Denton alive" or put it on the line with Carlton Smith and Mary Wellbon that if they wanted to provide Mary's son with employment that was fine with Mason, but do it somewhere other than Atlantic Corporation. This did not materialize.

8:30 PM, Trevor was becoming concerned; this was far too late for Denton. He should have called by now. Just then the phone on his desk buzzed. It was the security guard in the main floor lobby. Denton and their guest were on their way up. Trevor was relieved, he was about to begin the biggest gamble of his career and he didn't want any unnecessary problems.

Trevor thought again of his assistant. He knew that no one expected them to work well together let alone actually get along. Trevor was even surprised himself. On the surface, the meek and mild Denton was not the kind of person that Trevor had ever had anything in common with or any patience for. However, early on in their relationship, along with Denton's other skills, Trevor became impressed with Denton's near photographic memory. The man was a virtual library of information concerning the companies that he had grown up with.

To Catch a Fox

Denton's only problem was that he had no idea how to use all of this information. Trevor did. He used it to develop policy, procedure and, more importantly, to defeat anyone who offered resistance to the freight train that was Trevor Mason. Blackmail and intimidation were no strangers to Trevor Mason. Indeed, they were his comrades in arms, during corporate warfare. Denton Wellbon III became the most valuable resource that Trevor possessed and he didn't even realize it. He was simply happy to be Trevor's confidant. In addition there was Denton's best and previously unrecognized virtue; he was completely loyal and could keep his mouth shut.

Denton Wellbon III carefully opened the door to Trevor Mason's office. He entered cautiously in an attempt to determine the exact mood of his mercurial boss before allowing their guest to enter. Now seated, Trevor looked up from the papers on his desk.

"Is Ruben with you?" he asked.

"Of course Trevor, I apologize for our tardiness, but Mr. Ruben insisted on dropping off some files across town on our way here. I assure you that had I known in advance..."

"That's okay Denton, what's important is that you're here now. Bring Ruben in."

Abraham Ruben entered the plush office of Atlantic Corporation's President. In contrast to his well-tailored hosts, Ruben was wearing a rather ill fitting suit. His tie revealed his choice of soup at lunch and his shoes hadn't seen the benefits of polish in months. All in all he appeared out of place, but the confidence of his stride spoke otherwise. Against his better judgment Trevor Mason rose from his chair, walked around his desk and offered his hand. He was well aware that Ruben was one of the least known but most financially successful lawyers on "the street." He also knew the risks involved in dealing with him. Abraham Ruben could be a very dangerous man. Ruben accepted his hand and returned a rather limp handshake. It was not at all the type of grip that Trevor preferred.

"Long time since we've seen each other Trevor," said Ruben. Denton's eyes widened. He wasn't at all certain why they were meeting with this rather distasteful appearing person and now he was surprised to learn that Trevor had made his acquaintance before this evening.

“Yes it has been a long time,” answered Trevor.

“I told you when we last met in Chicago that sooner or later you would be in need of my services when you moved to New York.”

“That you did Rueben. Let’s get down to business. Would you care for a cigar?” Trevor Mason opened a desk drawer and revealed a handsome cherry humidor filled with illegal Cuban Cigars. Denton was even more shocked that Trevor would offer one of them to this individual. He hoped that his surprise did not register on his face. He had come to expect anything from his boss over the past four years. Ruben accepted the cigar and allowed Trevor to trim the end and light it for him. Following Trevor’s gesture, he found his way to a leather sofa accompanied by two matching leather easy chairs near the grandfather clock. They all sat down as Ruben opened his battered brief case and extracted a rather thick manila file.

CHAPTER 2

William MacLode, known as "Mac" to his associates, sat at his desk at Fox Custom Cabinetry. Maclode was a tall, distinguished man in his mid fifties. He had short, thinning gray hair, a "salt and pepper" mustache and a neatly trimmed beard. Everything about him was either neatly trimmed or tailored. He had just returned from a mentally and emotionally exhausting trip and had come straight from the airport to his office. It was late in the evening and the offices of Fox were deserted. In spite of the lateness of the hour and the fact that he had been seated on an airplane for the best part of the day, MacLode remained sharp and meticulous in appearance. A phenomenon that his business associates admired but could never explain.

Fox had been a part of the Atlantic Corporation since 1978. It was the last company acquired by Denton Wellbon II before his untimely death. Denton had closed the deal with the owner and founder of Fox, Elias Fox, just months before Wellbon died of a heart attack. Elias was a highly talented cabinetmaker who started his business in his garage some forty years ago. Like most entrepreneurs, Elias was constantly in debt. His exceptionally high quality product was in high demand by both young wealthy professionals and the guardians of "old" money. As his network of distributors grew, Elias constantly had to borrow money to expand his manufacturing facility to meet the increasing demand. He was primarily a cabinetmaker and therefore lacked the sophistication to raise money in any other manner such as going public and selling shares of stock. Had he even considered this concept, he would have rejected it as out of hand. This was his company, he created it and he would control it!

The company employed about five hundred people and sold its product, primarily custom kitchen cabinets along with specialty cabinetry for other rooms, through a network of dealerships that operated in thirty-five of the lower forty-eight states when it became too much for its founder to cope with. That's when Elias became acquainted with Denton Wellbon II. Denton had recently purchased some of Elias' cabinetry from a New York dealership. He was impressed with the quality and the fact that this company did an amazing volume while custom fitting every design to the individual whims of the purchaser. After a visit to the factory located in southeastern Pennsylvania in the heart of the Amish country, Denton wooed Elias with the skill of a seasoned Romeo persuading a reluctant young girl to give up her virginity. It was however a good deal for both. Elias was finally out of debt, not to mention fairly wealthy after the sale, and he was still young enough to enjoy his new found wealth having turned fifty just two weeks prior to finalizing the deal. Denton Wellbon II acquired what he had always coveted, a company that manufactured an expensive product that bore a prestigious name. Elias' cabinetry was nearly handcrafted and bore a price tag that insured that only people of the stature of Wellbon could hope to afford it. Atlantic finally owned a business more exciting than the import business, and the dreary metal stamping and machine firms that Denton and his father had acquired that previously defined its image. As should always be the case, both men departed the lawyer's office in Manhattan with smiles on their respective faces. Elias promptly retired to a condo in Key West Florida. A few months later Denton Wellbon II died of a heart attack. Elias made the trip north to New York City to pay his respects.

Carlton Smith, after the second Denton's death, proceeded to evaluate all of the companies in Atlantic's portfolio. He quickly discovered that their most recent acquisition, Fox Cabinetry, was somewhat less than a star performer. Fox generated large volume with very slender profits. Upon Elias' exit, a gentleman named Daniel Martin was elevated to President of the Fox division. Daniel was previously Elias' sales manager. Because Fox was a new acquisition, Carlton had little knowledge of its people. He possessed only the monthly numbers and the history that Denton had obtained before the purchase. As is the situation with most entrepreneurs, Elias trusted no one but himself to watch his money, therefore Fox had no controller on staff. Carlton immediately tapped a promising young CPA named William MacLode to move to Pennsylvania and assume that position with Fox. MacLode, like everyone else at Atlantic, had no knowledge of the cabinet business. He was however, one of the fast rising stars on the staff of Wellbon – Smith. MacLode had been extremely helpful in the restructuring of Wellbon – Smith, and had been instrumental in setting up several tax shelters.

Upon MacLode's arrival at his new position he soon discovered that Elias Fox promoted hard working people as a reward for their hard work and not necessarily because they were qualified for the positions that he promoted them into. After a year of observing Daniel Martin and his staff commit a series of mistakes and missed opportunities, MacLode was left no choice but to submit a confidential report to Carlton Smith on the reasons that he believed that Fox was financially a poor performer. Soon thereafter Carlton flew to Lancaster Pennsylvania and paid "Mac" a quiet visit.

Smith and MacLode met at the Lancaster Airport over breakfast in the airport coffee shop. Carlton gave Mac a letter to deliver to Daniel Martin. The letter contained Martin's dismissal and a very generous check as his separation compensation allowance. Mac MacLode remembered thinking that Daniel, at his present age, would never have to work again and wondered if he were ever in the same situation if Atlantic would be as generous. In addition, to Mac's surprise, he was promoted to fill Daniel's vacant position as division president of Fox Cabinetry. Smith also authorized him to make whatever changes he saw fit in management and elsewhere at Fox. Smith finished his modest breakfast and boarded the next plane back to New York leaving the stunned MacLode to his thoughts and realizing that he would have to present the letter to Martin.

William "Mac" MacLode was born near a small village in the Scottish Highlands in 1946 and came to the United States to attend college at New York University in 1965. He never intended to remain after graduation, but he received a job offer from Wellbon-Smith that he couldn't refuse. After enjoying success, both personal and financial in his new position and realizing his potential for a profitable future Mac finally resigned himself to his new home and after passing the tests, became a citizen. Mac was not a sentimental man. While he empathized with Daniel Martin and his staff, he immediately removed all of them except for Carroll Brubaker, the Vice President of Manufacturing. Carroll was a cabinetmaker like Elias. Mac MacLode was an accountant who knew nothing of the trade. Mac did know how to find qualified people and make money for his owners. Mac needed Carroll and Carroll was smart enough to realize that he needed Mac.

MacLode quickly interviewed replacements and within six months had managed to attract a competent staff of professionals. He achieved a nice mix of locals and professionals imported from other parts of the country. Under Mac MacLode Fox Cabinetry grew to over one thousand employees working in two manufacturing plants. The original remained in Lancaster County Pennsylvania, and a new plant was erected near Las Vegas Nevada. The new plant was designed to more economically service the West Coast. Fox was a consistent performer for Atlantic with the operating profit line generally finishing the fiscal year between 12% and 14% of net sales. This had always pleased Carlton Smith and Smith and

MacLode maintained a good relationship.

Then came 1995 and the arrival of Trevor Mason; in Mac's opinion Mason had but one goal in mind, the rapid promotion of Trevor Mason within the corporate world of Wellbon – Smith, regardless of the cost. Where Carlton Smith had always taken the long view of the Atlantic companies' strategic plans Mason wanted results now! "To hell with the future!" he often ranted, "I only care about lining the owner's pockets now! I'll worry about the future when the future is the present!" As this was diametrically opposed to the strategies that had always been successful for MacLode, the two had been working under a strained relationship since Mason's first visit to Fox headquarters in Pennsylvania.

On this evening Mac was catching up with the latest e-mail from the corporate offices in New York City. Most of them were standard housekeeping, but the final one made him groan. Trevor Mason was moving the date of all of the division's annual strategic presentations forward by a full month. For Fox that was the first week in September. It was always a struggle to prepare the annual book in the time frame allowed without having one less month to work with. This made it all but impossible. He bowed his head and rubbed his closed eyes in thought. It is what it is he concluded and authored his own e-mail to his staff. Two of them, Tony Conocenti and Carroll Brubaker were out of town at the moment. Tony, Mac's Vice president of Sales and Marketing was in Chicago attempting to finally fill a long time gaping hole in their marketing plan. Carroll was at the Las Vegas plant trying to solve his own set of problems. Mac's e-mail would summon both sooner than they expected. He looked at his watch today was Thursday he'd give them tomorrow for arrangements and travel. That would get them here in time for a 9:00 AM meeting on Saturday morning. Carroll would have the most time zones to cover but Tony would be the loudest one to protest. Mac smiled, as different as they were these two were more responsible for Fox's success the past few years than anyone else. The remainder of the staff: David Elliott V. P. of Service and Transportation, Dale Hershey V. P. of Finance, and Dennis Morton the soon to be departing V. P. of Human Resources, could begin work with Mac in the morning.

Mac finished proof reading his e-mail and clicked "send." That should do it he thought. He then rose from his chair, ran his fingers through his short thinning gray hair, stuffed his brief case full of reports that he would have to review before meeting with those present on his staff tomorrow morning and walked out the door. He soon returned and switched off the light in his office. If Brady, his secretary for the past fifteen years, came in tomorrow morning and discovered that he had forgotten to turn off the lights there would be hell to pay.

***

The next morning Tony Conocenti awoke in his hotel room in the Holiday Inn at the Mart Plaza. This is the hotel that is at the top of the building directly across from the Chicago Merchandise Mart. Tony had spent the entire day before negotiating with the Mart people for a long term lease on a showroom on the tenth floor. It had been a long and exhausting day, made all the more tiresome because Fox Cabinetry's potential partner and newest dealer in this venture seemed to be vacillating between enthusiasm and cold feet. Tony stared at the ceiling for a long time and then rolled over to gaze at his bed partner. Blair McManus wrote for the Chicago Tribune. She specialized in articles concerning style, the home and home furnishings. She worked closely with the publicist at the Merchandize Mart planning special consumer day events at the Mart that the Tribune cosponsored. She was average height, Tony guessed about five foot four, cute figure, and beautiful. Her long red hair streamed out over the sheets in tangled strands as she slept. At this moment Tony knew that she was naked under those sheets and the thought of her the night before excited him all over again. Then Blair snored and Tony wasn't as excited as he had been just a moment ago. It's probably best that you make love to someone that you have a casual relationship with before one or the other of you falls asleep he mused. He stretched, rolled out from under the sheets and ambled toward the bathroom.

Tony was average in height; just shy of six feet tall, possessed a lean, tan, muscular frame that he exercised religiously to maintain and inherited a trait from his Scandinavian mother that was difficult to explain with his Italian surname, blond hair. After tooth brushing, a cold shower and a shave Tony emerged clad in one of the hotel's warm terry bathrobes. Blair was awake by now, sitting up in bed watching the Today Show on television. To his disappointment she was discreetly covered. "Good morning" he said as he sat on the edge of the bed and kissed her.

"Good morning handsome," she purred. "What's on the agenda for today?"

"Well I have the contract with the Mart nailed down. All they have to do is have their lawyers look it over. I'm picking up a copy at their offices at nine, and then I am meeting with our new dealer and his partner in the space we just leased on the tenth floor. I'm attempting to get them to sign the dealer agreement that I've rewritten for the sixth, no make that seventh time since I've been in Chicago. I'll take it along home with me on Monday so our lawyer can look it over along with the Mart contract. That should only take me until ten this morning, no make that eleven, my dealer will no doubt have had another anxiety attack overnight and I'll have to reassure him again before I dare to leave. After that I'm free to spend the weekend with my favorite redhead!"

"Doesn't your boss expect you to return today? It is Friday you know."

"Mac? Hell, I've been here all week! He doesn't care where I am or how long I stay as long as I return with the results he expects. Besides, I think that he's out of the office all week. He left for somewhere last Thursday. He was rather tight lipped concerning his destination and his purpose for traveling. He may not have returned."

"What about your wife?"

"You know that we've been separated for over a year. I expect the divorce papers to be final within the next couple of months. I think we're finally finished fighting over visiting privileges." Tony felt a pang in his stomach. It still hurt to think about his pending divorce. He knew exactly whose fault it was. It was his. In his efforts to make Fox the premier cabinet line in the United States he had spent far too many weeks on the road. He was proud of the fact that while they were together he had never once cheated on her. During their marriage there had never been any nights like this past night. In the end it was Sheila who found someone else and announced that she was leaving him. How could he blame her? She was a young woman who had been neglected by her husband for years. He never denied that he was the primary cause of their separation. He put up very little fight once he realized that there would be no reconciliation. He gave her the house, the car, and set up a trust fund for their daughter Sharon's education. The only point of disagreement was how often he could visit Sharon, the duration of those visits, and how far away he could take her during those visits. But before he departed for this trip to Chicago his lawyer contacted him to say that arrangements he was certain Tony could live with had been reached.

Blair was someone that he had a strictly professional relationship with in New York several years previous to his divorce. She had worked for the New York Times then as a research associate for one of the Times columnists. Tony met her through a friend that handled Public Relations for the Architect and Design

Building in Manhattan. Fox had its New York flagship dealer, "The New York Fox of Cabinetry", located in that building. They crossed paths several times as Tony spent considerable time in the city and Blair was assigned to the Style section of the Times. New York City was a benchmark territory for Fox. Blair then received the offer of her own column in the Chicago Tribune. She jumped at the chance, left her live in boy friend of four years behind and moved to Chicago. Tony lost track of her at that point as Fox's marketing strategy in Chicago was in a shambles and it depressed him to even set foot in the town. It was one of his few glaring failures nationally.

Then John Malicki, the Fox sales representative in the Western Great Lakes Territory, territory six as it was known at the office, found Glenn Glen. Tony still recalled the day that John returned to Pennsylvania looking like the proverbial cat that swallowed the canary. John took a seat in his office and proceeded to tell Tony about the new account that he wanted to open in Chicago. Tony was skeptical; nothing had worked in Chicago before. When John came to the candidate's name Tony could be quiet no longer.

"Come on John! Glenn Glen?" Tony exclaimed. "That can't be his real name."

"I think he had it legally changed."

"Why, is he hiding from a bad debt, the cops, the mob, a woman, what?"

"Trust me Tony, this guy isn't hiding from any women. He might be hiding from some guys if you get my drift."

"Okay, okay, he won't be the first gay designer male or female that we have selling for us. It matters not to me. Most are excellent designers. The question, is Glen any good? Does he have a track record?"

This was John's moment. He had eagerly anticipated dropping this "bomb" on Tony from the moment that Glenn Glen had first contacted him. "He's worked as a designer / sales person for the past seven years for George," replied John with a satisfied grin on his face.

"George Peterson? You're kidding the George Peterson?"

"The very one," replied Malicki as he settled back in the chair in a self-satisfied pose. This was quite the feather in his hat. George Peterson owned the biggest kitchen cabinet dealership in Chicago. With five thousand square feet of Design District show room, (Big by industry standards.) fifteen designer sales people, and annual sales in the millions at wholesale value, George Peterson owned the custom market in Chicago, The Gold Coast, and The North Shore. The only problem from Tony's vantage point was that he wasn't a Fox dealer. He carried Fox's rival line Country Quality Cabinets as his "high end" line. Tony had long ago given up on switching George to Fox. He was loyal to Country Quality to a fault. Tony only wished that his own dealers were that loyal. Now, Tony had a chance to open a rival dealership with one of George's own people. If Glenn Glen or whatever his name was lasted for seven years at George's, he had to be good. George did not tolerate amateur designer / sales people.

This all conspired to bring Tony back to Chicago on a regular basis as he attempted to work out a business agreement with Glen and a lease with the Merchandise Mart that wouldn't give Mac MacLode a heart attack. During one of these excursions he met up with Blair. They talked about old times, had lunch, had dinner, and made arrangements to see each other again the next time that Tony was in town. What the heck thought Tony, Sheila had already left him for good. One thing led to another and soon they were making dates for his next trip and sleeping together. But it wasn't serious Tony reminded himself. This was the same Blair that ran out on her "serious" boy friend back in New York. Indeed, Blair was the one who kept the relationship from moving beyond casual sex. So Tony felt no particular obligation toward her, but had to admit he looked forward to going to Chicago like he never had in the past.

Blair had Tony hand her the other hotel robe and disappeared into the bathroom. Tony, for the first time all week put on casual clothes. All week long he was in suit and tie, "full battle dress", as he liked to call it. Today the battles were all but won. He put on Dockers and a golf shirt with loafers. No wingtips today. He would pick up copies of the lease, have Glen and his partner sign the dealer agreement, and meet Blair for lunch.

"How about meeting me on the Navy Pier for lunch?" he yelled through the bathroom door.

"Sounds good to me," was the reply through the sound of running water in the shower. "I already told my boss that I would be leaving the office early today."

To Catch a Fox

"I'll meet you at the entrance about eleven thirty." Tony felt this would give him enough time to get Glen over one more imagined crisis.

"What?"

"Eleven thirty! I'll meet you at the entrance to the Navy Pier at eleven thirty!" Tony yelled the reply as he was getting his laptop out of his brief case. He should probably send Mac an e-mail and give him an update. As Blair emerged from the bathroom in the robe and a towel wrapped about her head Tony was plugged into the data port on the phone and was logged onto the office. He was working his way through his e-mail. The last one to be read was from Mac.

"What? Son of a Bitch!"

"What's wrong Hon?" asked Blair as she put her arms around his neck. Tony was staring at the screen in disbelief.

"I can't believe it! Read this!"

"NEW YORK HAS MOVED THE DATE OF OUR STRATEGIC PRESENTATION FORWARD BY ONE MONTH. THOSE OF YOU IN THE OFFICE WILL MEET WITH ME AT 9:00 AM FRIDAY MORNING. (WE WILL SEND OUT FOR LUNCH.) TONY AND CARROLL, I WILL EXPECT YOU BOTH TO BE PRESENT FOR THE SATURDAY MEETING THAT WILL BEGIN AT THE SAME TIME.

SORRY GUYS. DON'T MAKE ANY PLANS FOR THE WEEKEND."

"MAC"

"Does your boss know that when you e-mail in capitals it means you're shouting?" Blair asked in her innocent little girl voice.

"He knows. He was shouting." Tony's voice was disheartened. "Do you know how much I was looking forward to spending the weekend with you?"

"Me too," Blair kissed his ear. "I understand. You're lucky that I'm a corporate girl. Those little Miss Suburbs wouldn't know why you couldn't just say 'no.' I know about these things. I will expect you to be as understanding if this happens to me sometime in the future."

Tony turned and looked into her large emerald green eyes. "You're great, do you know that?"

"I sure do, and you better never forget it!"

Tony caught his breath for just a second. Had he just heard something different in her voice, saw something in her eyes, what if anything was it? He suddenly had the sensation that they were somehow closer at this moment then they had ever been before, even closer then he felt last night. This was somehow different. Blair held his gaze for just a second, and then broke it off with the faintest grin playing at the edge of her lips. She turned and began to get dressed.

"I have time to change your flight arrangements this morning if you want me to. That way you can go and do your thing with your dealer and the Mart."

"That would be great! Thanks." Tony was still trying to determine if he had just imagined something or if something basic had changed between them.

"You'll have to trust me with your credit card number."

"I trust you." He replied. She laughed an ornery little laugh that suggested that just maybe he shouldn't be so trusting.

They finished dressing, packed their bags, (Blair's was only an overnight bag.) and went down the elevator to the lobby. The lobby was on the fifteenth floor. Their room was on the twenty-second. The remainder of the building consisted of hotel conference rooms on the fourteenth floor and offices from there down to the ground floor. Blair had to change elevators to reach the ground floor. Tony had to check out. She caught him by the sleeve as he moved quickly in the direction of the main desk.

"I'll arrange for the electronic tickets. Just check your bags and get a boarding pass. I have to get to work now. Call me when you get home."

Tony turned to give her a kiss, but she was already staring at him from a crowded elevator. "Hey…" he began. She blew him a kiss as the elevator door closed. Tony stood in the lobby for a long moment. He was sure of it. Something had happened between them, he just wasn't certain what. But he thought it was good. He looked at his watch. He knew which flight Blair was going to attempt to get him on. If there were a problem she would call him on his cell phone. He found that he was hoping for some kind of problem that would strand him in Chicago for the weekend. Fat chance! He turned toward the desk. He didn't agree with the charges that he saw on the TV screen when he attempted the electronic check out.

***

Carroll Brubaker jogged into the lobby of the MGM Grand Hotel in Las Vegas. He was tall and fit with a thick shock of brown hair. He had the ruddy complexion of an outdoors man. He achieved this quite naturally as in addition to his position of VP of Manufacturing at Fox Cabinetry; he owned and operated a rather large farm in Pennsylvania that he had inherited from his father. Actually his son and daughter-in-law ran the farm. His job permitted him little spare time to do anything but play gentleman farmer, but he got outside and walked the fields as much as possible.

Carroll broke stride and walked past the imposing statue of Leo the Lion, the MGM mascot whose image graced everything inside the massive complex. He was dressed in his sweats and boarded an elevator for his room. He had already read Mac's e-mail and quite frankly he didn't object to the opportunity to head home early. He was originally scheduled to remain until next Tuesday and was scheduled for weekend meetings anyway. The meetings were designed to determine accurate production projections for the very strategic plan that Mac was summoning him home to help create. This would mean that he would have to instruct his "Vegas" managers to work out the numbers on their own and forward them to him even sooner than he had told them just yesterday. His reason for being here in the first place was that last year's numbers were way too optimistic and Carroll had extreme difficulty in making production quotas in his western plant.

There was another reason that he was anxious to escape. Tom Erving, the Las Vegas plant manager, had privately approached him with some troubling news. It was a bolt from the blue and one that Carroll had never even considered as a remote possibility. Tom attempted to assure him that it was only suspicion on his part, but Tom had experience in these situations and his suspicions had to be taken seriously.

To Catch a Fox

Carroll left the elevator and walked down the maze of hallways toward his room. He was staying in the "Oz" tower; therefore he was walking and living among murals depicting scenes from that classic movie. They were all tastefully done, and Carroll rather enjoyed them. That particular classic was the first movie that he had watched as a child, and he had a warm place in his musings for it. He came to the room and entered to see the message light on his telephone blinking. Upon retrieval he found the message was from the travel agency that Fox utilized for all corporate arrangements. He was booked on a United flight to O'Hare in Chicago. It left in two hours. That was no particular problem as he had packed before he left the room to jog and the airport at Las Vegas was visible from his room. He would change out of his sweats, shower and put on jeans and a tee shirt. He never traveled in anything but extremely casual clothes. Flying on commercial airlines had lost its glamour over the years and now was more akin to riding the bus.

Carroll picked up the phone and dialed the factory that lay twenty miles to the east out on the desert. It was too early for Erving to be in his office so Carroll explained his departure and left specific instructions for Erving and his staff on voice mail. Tom was a good man. He would follow directions and get the job accomplished whatever the challenge. That was the reason it was so unlike he or his people to miss production quotas as they had done last year. However, Tom's suspicions may provide the explanation. Carroll toyed with the idea of calling Mac and sharing Tom's comments, but he thought better of it. Better to inform Mac of this in private, in person. Carroll began to remove his clothes. He would grab a coffee at the airport and the message from the agency assured him that breakfast would be served on the plane.

To Catch a Fox

CHAPTER 3

It was early in New York on the morning after the meeting between Trevor Mason, Abraham Rueben, and Denton Wellbon III. Denton had called Susan, his wife of fifteen years, around eleven o'clock the previous night and informed her that he may not be home until morning. This unfortunately was not uncommon in the years since Trevor Mason had taken the reins at Atlantic. Susan was very understanding. She was just grateful that the man she loved so much finally felt a sense of purpose. She did not care much for Trevor Mason, but he had done something that in her opinion not even Denton's mother had done. He gave Denton meaningful work. After Denton had gotten over his disappointment of being passed over yet again, he began to have new interest in business, his family, and life in general. All this occurred because Trevor had taken Denton into his confidence and truly made him his second in command at Atlantic. If that meant that sometimes Susan had to be alone for an evening, then it was a small price to pay.

She never feared of another woman. Even before Trevor Mason had discovered it, Susan knew that one of her husband's strong points was his strict sense of loyalty. She knew that he would never consider cheating on her. It was simply unthinkable. After hanging up the phone with Denton, Susan called her twin sister. Shana lived out on Long Island and was married to a doctor. She too spent many evenings alone, as her husband was one of the most sought after neurosurgeons on the East Coast. The two could wile away countless hours on the phone talking about "nothing" as she explained to an amazed Denton. Denton, as an only child, had no comprehension of the bond between his wife and sister-in-law. This presented no problem. It wasn't essential that he understand. He was simply happy that she had someone to share the hours with when business kept him away.

After the meeting Denton accompanied Mr. Rueben to his home via a company limousine. Upon dropping his passenger off the driver assumed that Denton wished to go home, as it was nearly five in the morning. Denton surprised the chauffeur by asking to be taken to one of the city's small all night restaurants.

To Catch a Fox

This one happened to be near The Fulton Fish Market.

"Are you certain that you want me to leave you here sir?" asked the concerned chauffeur.

"Oh yes. I'll be quite all right. I come here rather frequently in fact." Denton smiled at the expression that he saw in the mirror. This was in fact an establishment that his father had taken him to as a boy. The neighborhood was even more hostile at that time, but the owner was somehow a friend of Denton's father and the senior Denton had helped him out financially a time or two. Denton never asked as to the relationship believing that if either of the two individuals had wished him to know more they would have told him. Denton continued to frequent the establishment after his father's death and Denton and the older gentleman who owned it had developed a friendship of their own.

It was still raining, although the wind had fallen, as the limo pulled up to the curb outside the restaurant. Denton climbed out and walked around the accumulating puddles on the sidewalk and through the front door. The chauffeur, feeling uneasy about leaving the executive vice president alone in a strange neighborhood, never the less did not wish to risk his boss' displeasure by ignoring his wishes. He reluctantly pulled away from the curb and headed toward his own home.

The man behind the counter looked up as Denton entered. "Hello Mr. Wellbon!" he exclaimed. "You're out and about at a strange hour. Are you on your way home or on your way to the office?"

"Surprisingly on my way home Sid." Sid was the owner's chief cook. Andy the owner would not be in until eleven in the morning. They both worked twelve hour shifts. Eleven to eleven as Andy often stated. Denton had no idea how they arrived at this particular method of dividing the day, but he knew that he was just grateful that he didn't have to work those hours. After a moment of reflection, Denton realized that in another fifteen minutes, it would be twenty-four hours since he last slept. Perhaps the all night restaurant business wasn't as bad as he had imagined.

Denton found that his favorite booth in the back was vacant. Indeed, there were quite a few people in the diner. Many of them had to be at work on the docks by seven and stopped in here for their breakfast every morning. More than a couple nodded to Denton in recognition. Denton smiled to himself. If Trevor or for that matter anyone at the office knew that not only did he frequent this establishment, but was fairly well known here they would have been shocked out of their Gucci's. Denton removed his raincoat, settled into the booth and gazed out the rather cloudy window at the dark Hudson River. Just up river from here were the docks that serviced the ships of the numerous cruise lines that made New York their departing point for Bermuda and numerous stops in the Virgin Islands.

A young girl with dirty blonde hair approached Denton. Her white apron had multi colored stains that the laundry service had failed to eradicate in numerous attempts. "Good morning Mr. 'W', what can I get for you?" Denton thought that she would be rather attractive if she would only have her hair done occasionally and apply some make up. However, it didn't seem a concern to her or the numerous longshoremen who, Denton observed flirted with her on a daily basis.

"Good morning to you also Connie, I'll have two eggs over easy with bacon and toast. Oh, and bring me coffee and a small glass of orange juice." Denton usually ate rather sparingly and very carefully as he watched his weight and his cholesterol. However, there was precious little on Andy's menu that fit into Denton's diet, so he treated these little excursions as a sinful escape from his normal regimen.

"Comin' right up Mr. 'W'!" and with that cheerful reply Connie was off to take the order of another customer.

Denton was left alone with his thoughts. He could see his reflection in the window. He was a little man with straw colored hair and a rather stark thin face. He too thought it strange that he bore such a strong resemblance to his father and grandfather but they seemed to be strong in their appearance while he only conjured up images of a Casper Milquetoast. He was well aware that the newly found respect that he enjoyed around the Atlantic "empire" was only out of the knowledge that he had the ear of Trevor Mason and was Mason's confidant. Trevor struck fear in the hearts of everyone that he came in contact with except, strangely, Denton. Denton knew the reason. He was almost ashamed to admit it even to himself. No matter what happened to Atlantic. No matter what Trevor may decide to do to him in the future, Denton Wellbon III was rich! His father had set up several trust funds for him that he inherited upon his father's death. Although his mother could disinherit him from her sizable fortune, which he knew that she wouldn't do, he would still be rich even if she did. The trusts were ample to begin with, but Denton oversaw their investment and he had steadily and cautiously made shrewd investments in mutual funds and the market that allowed the trusts to grow to a sizable fortune in their own right. Denton also realized that they were probably his curse as well. With this security he was never in a position that forced him to succeed to survive.

Denton's thoughts turned to the meeting that occupied most of his night. He knew that Trevor was ambitious, but he had never suspected that he was this ambitious. What Trevor was proposing was against the corporate by-laws of Wellbon – Smith and indeed may be illegal period. Denton would have to check. He also did not approve of that grubby little lawyer Abraham Rueben. At several points in the conversations Denton thought that any lawyer worth his salt would have jumped up and informed Trevor in the sternest possible fashion that what he was proposing was unethical at best if not against the law of the land. But Rueben to the contrary not only failed to sound the alarm; he proceeded to explain just exactly what they would have to do to be successful.

At one point when the hour was nearing two in the morning, Rueben requested a break. After he left the office, Trevor opened his wet bar for the first time and poured three glasses of Scotch. He took one for himself, left one for Rueben upon his return and handed one to Denton.

"You're disturbed by all of this aren't you?" Trevor asked.

"If I understand exactly what you are proposing, yes. I am to say the least, uncomfortable." Denton found that his mouth was suddenly dry.

"Why are you uncomfortable Denton?" Trevor's voice was so flat and totally lacking in emotion that Denton for the first time in their relationship felt the hairs begin to rise on the nap of his neck.

"We are discussing my mother's company Trevor."

"Yes, but it not only belongs to your mother, it belongs to numerous other people as well. People that have not always treated you with the respect owed to the grandson of the founder. Am I wrong on this point?"

"No, you know that you are correct."

To Catch a Fox

Trevor continued: "People that have on several occasions made you look bad not only in your circle of business associates, but in your social circles as well. For example, those articles a few years back that not only appeared in the Post, but in the Times' gossip columns, concerning the reasons that you have been passed over not once but twice to run this company. It was attributed to unnamed sources within the corporation. Do you really have any doubts that it came from individuals that serve on the board of Wellbon – Smith?"

"Those are the only people who would have had the knowledge of the conversations that were quoted. You are again correct Trevor."

Trevor downed his Scotch in a single gulp. "People who thought nothing of publishing your rumored final grade point average at Princeton and who had no qualms about speculating that perhaps your father may have exerted some influence with the faculty to have your final grades tweaked just a bit."

"That wasn't fair! I was not a bad student! I was simply young and lazy. I did pass my courses at Princeton and even though my grades were far from the best I did not cheat nor was it necessary for my father to intervene for me to graduate! The college refuted those allegations the very next day."

"Calm down Denton, your face is becoming flushed. I know that what you say is true. I know what a smart man you really are. If you weren't smart do you think I would have kept you as my right hand? No I would not! But I also know something else. For whatever reason, jealously, whatever, these people do not want you to succeed. They fear you even now. Especially now as they see that I have made you a powerful man within this company. They thought that they had you buried but I brought you back. I brought you back! Don't forget that one fact! Not your mother, not Carlton Smith, but me, Trevor Mason brought you back from a certain corporate grave!"

"I realize that Trevor and I will be eternally grateful to you. I truly enjoy working with you."

"I know that you do Denton." Trevor's voice softened to the point where Denton actually thought that he heard genuine affection in it. "And I enjoy working with you. But realize something. Because you now present a problem once more to certain people they are already plotting against you."

To Catch a Fox

"But why, why do I present a problem? Whom have I ever presented a problem to?"

"To whom do you present a problem? Really Denton are you that naive? Who stood to benefit most by you not replacing your father as chairperson when your father died? Your mother didn't benefit."

"Carlton Smith replaced father."

"Precisely, because you were deprived of your birthright he and his cronies have had the opportunity to run this corporation for years. If you had been appointed to the position would you have chosen the same people that he did to fill the top positions in the holding company? To fill the chairs like the one that I sit in as president of one of Wellbon-Smith's mini-conglomerates? I don't think so. Did Carlton really give you a chance to grow here at Atlantic? Did he really spend time with you and teach you everything that he knew, or did he simply allow you to waste your time on meaningless tasks while he periodically reported to your mother that sadly young Denton just isn't growing in the job?"

"That's what Susan has always insisted was the case, but I always thought of Carlton as my friend, indeed I thought of him as an uncle. Has Susan been right all of these years?" Denton was considering the case that Trevor was making.

"I think so," replied Trevor as he considered refilling his glass.

"All right, I will concede that what you are saying could have been true, but now Carlton is ready to retire. Even after four years he remains heartbroken over the loss of his wife, and he really has little interest in the business at present. In fact he is becoming irritated at the board for, as he perceives it, dragging its feet on selecting his successor. What does he have to fear from me now?"

At this point Denton's reverie was interrupted by the arrival of his breakfast. "Here you go Mr. 'W'." said Connie. "Enjoy!" She placed the generous helping of bacon, eggs and toast alongside the coffee and juice that she had brought immediately after she took his order. Denton thought that it smelled wonderful. He began to eat. He found that he was very hungry.

While devouring the cholesterol-laden meal Denton returned to his thoughts. He remembered that Trevor was silent for a long moment while he concentrated on pouring himself another Scotch. Denton was always amazed at the amount of liquor that Trevor could consume without any visible effect. When his glass was full again Trevor finally replied. "He's not concerned for himself anymore, but he has a lot of his younger lieutenants putting pressure on him. Each of them wants to replace him as Chairperson, and he has his own preference as to his successor. The board is dragging its collective feet because it wants to avoid deciding between Carlton's top lieutenants. Trust me my friend you are not on either the long or short list."

"To be honest Trevor, since you arrived and have had such stunning success with Atlantic, I've rather ceased my desire to become Chairperson of Wellbon – Smith. I have witnessed what you have accomplished in a short time, and I confess that I would never have known how to do half the things that you have done. Susan and I have discussed this and we believe that perhaps the best place for me is as a number two. Besides, you have been so successful that I just assumed that the Board would choose you to take Carlton's place when he steps down."

"No, they will never consider me. I am too abrasive; I'm not a member of the club that has been in existence here since your father died. Indeed, Carlton wanted an outsider to come in, make Atlantic profitable again and because of the lack of seniority the individual was expected to shut up and be grateful for what he had. It was never in the plan that this individual would be considered for the top post. I have been too successful. I have made the other conglomerate presidents nervous. If I was elected to the chair they would be reporting to me and they certainly don't want that." Trevor permitted himself a smile. "They see how popular I am with my division presidents," he said facetiously.

Trevor turned again to face Denton. "That's what this is all about Denton. This will not hurt your mother one bit. It will not even hurt Carlton, although I think he deserves to be hurt a little. It will hurt no one except those who aspire to be Chairperson when they do not deserve to be either because of their lack of ability or by birth. It will help us! You and Susan are correct! You are the best number two in the business. I am at once happy that you are, but saddened by the fact that you do not possess the skills to run Wellbon – Smith. That is a fact that I am proud of you for facing. Help me complete this plan that we are discussing and I have a proposition for you."

Trevor paused and filled Denton's glass. Denton was surprised to find that he had emptied it. Trevor replaced the bottle to the cupboard and locked his gaze onto Denton's. "My proposition is simple. If we execute this plan successfully we, you and I, will control the majority of voting shares in Wellbon-Smith. At that point we will disband the nominating committee and place your name as the only name on the ballot for the position of Chairperson!" Trevor paused to allow this statement to have its full impact on Denton.

Denton's brain was reeling. The prize that he had dreamed of all of his life, the prize that had been denied him twice, the prize that he had given up on ever attaining was now being offered to him!

Trevor continued: "There is one catch. Because you, Susan and I recognize the fact that you cannot run Wellbon-Smith alone, you will immediately appoint me as Vice Chairperson. In that capacity I will run the corporation in my usual manner while you enjoy the recognition, influence and prestige that you have always deserved because of your family connection. That my friend is even better than being president of Atlantic Corporation!"

Denton told Trevor that he made a strong argument and that he would take the plan under serious consideration. Trevor took a step toward Denton, "One more thing to think about while you are taking things under consideration. Your friends on the board are aware of the embarrassing little situation that your father bailed you out of with that very young girl you met at your fraternity's frat party. They are prepared to go public with the information if they for one moment think that you have even the remotest chance to ascend to the chair. I don't imagine that either Susan or your mother know of that incident."

Denton's mouth dropped open. This piece of information caught him totally unprepared. "No! How could they know? No one knows!"

"I know, but I'm your friend. Your secret is safe with me. But if I know they know and can use it against you. As it is they feel that they have us both under control. They feel that there is no need to use what they know against you. They expect nothing. You really have no choice Denton; we must strike now while they have no suspicions. We must act quickly before they can react. After you become chairperson if they would go public with their knowledge, it will only appear to be sour grapes at having lost control of the company. However, as Chairperson I'm convinced that you can prevent them from leaking the story. After all they will then have to depend on you to keep them in the positions that they now hold. But even if they should go public you can control the situation so that no one will seriously consider it to be true. Your father did an excellent job of covering up your tracks; it would be difficult for them to prove anything beyond innuendo. After you are elected Chairperson it would simply be your word against their word. But don't take too much time deciding what to do. To have this unfortunate incident leaked to the press before you become Chairperson puts it in an entirely different light. It would damage our plans and your happiness immensely. The timing is everything. I can't do this without you and you can't afford not to do it."

Denton sank in his chair. He was stunned, all of these years Denton believed that no one knew his secret. Obviously he had been wrong. How could anyone know now? But Trevor was correct. If Trevor knew others may also. Distasteful or not, Denton had to consider Trevor's plan. Almost as if on cue Abraham Rueben returned to the office and gratefully accepted the Scotch that Trevor had poured for him. The meeting resumed as Denton finished off his second glass.

Denton's thoughts returned to the present and he finished his third cup of coffee. The darkness outside the little diner had given way to a gray dawn with overcast skies. The rain had ceased. He found that sometime during his recollections Connie had silently cleared his empty plates away. She obviously realized that he was in serious thought and did not disturb him. His bill lay on the corner of the table. Denton reached inside his breast pocket and pulled out his wallet. He left a generous tip on the table and proceeded to the cash register. Sid took his bill and money. "How was everything Mr. Wellbon?"

"Just fine as usual Sid."

Sid gave Denton his change. "Andy was just speaking of you the other day Mr. Wellbon."

"Really?"

"Yeah, he told me that if you came in here when he wasn't working to tell you that he needs to talk to you next chance that you get."

Denton was surprised by this unexpected request. Andy had never proposed anything other than the normal good-natured banter that they indulged in during Denton's visits to the diner. He fumbled in his wallet and extracted one of his business cards. "I'm at his service," said Denton. "Tell Andy to call me at the office. I will make time to talk to him at his convenience."

Sid, obviously impressed at Denton's accommodation, took the card. "Thanks Mr. Wellbon. I'll give this to Andy as soon as he comes in this morning."

Puzzled, Denton waved good-bye to Connie and exited onto the street. He was carrying his raincoat over his arm. It was going to be a hot muggy summer day in New York City. Denton estimated that the temperature was already in the upper eighties and it wasn't quite seven o'clock in the morning. He loosened his tie, something that he seldom did, and began strolling slowly the few blocks toward The Fulton Fish Market. The Fulton Market had become quite the tourist attraction in recent years. Denton was still puzzling over Andy's unusual request. Perhaps he would finally receive an explanation of the relationship that his father and the proprietor of the diner enjoyed. Denton suspected that Andy needed money. If so, Denton would take care of him, as he believed that his father did in the past; for what reason Denton did not know.

Once again Denton's mind turned to more serious matters. Wellbon-Smith was a limited liability corporation. That meant that it was basically a privately held corporation that enjoyed the benefits of a partnership. Like a partnership Wellbon-Smith, as an entity paid no corporate taxes. All of the shareholders received either dividends or statements of loss, whichever situation applied, at the end of each fiscal year. The corporation filed copies of those statements with the IRS. It was then the responsibility of the individual shareholders or partners to report the income or loss on their tax returns and pay the appropriate taxes. This differed from other corporate entities where the corporation paid taxes on profits and the shareholders also paid taxes on dividends. One level of taxation was avoided while still retaining the veil of corporate protection for the owners.

Trevor's plan was simple. Buy outright or through coercion get signed commitments to purchase within six months thirty-five percent of the outstanding shares of Class 'A' voting stock in Wellbon-Smith. Then either through alliance or coercion acquire an additional 16 percent of the shareholders to commit their proxies to Trevor. In that manner Trevor would control 51 percent of the voting stock and therefore control Wellbon-Smith.

All of the shareholders knew that current "published" value was an arbitrary number. It had been determined previous to the time of Denton's father's death. Since Wellbon-Smith shares were privately held and not traded on any of the exchanges there was no real way to put an accurate market price on them. In addition the entity of Wellbon-Smith, in its role as a holding company, either owned all of the stock or controlling interest in numerous corporations such as its flagship Atlantic Corporation, some of these stocks were traded publicly and therefore their value was known. Others were not traded on the public exchanges making their value the stuff of speculation. It was common knowledge that the published per share value was extremely low.

Denton stopped in his musing long enough to hail a cab. Climbing into the back seat he gave his Park Avenue address to the driver, settled back, and looked thoughtfully out the window. His mind really wasn't "watching" what his eyes were seeing. His thoughts were exclusively on the requirements of Trevor's plan.

The situation was complicated even further by the fact that each of the corporations that Wellbon-Smith acted as a holding company for were also mini holding companies. Wellbon-Smith held all or most of the stock in Atlantic Corporation, Sterling International Inc., Williamson Manufacturing, Global Industries and Pfeiffer International Trading Corporation. Each of these mini-conglomerates in addition to their core business operated a collection of smaller companies. Some such as Thompson Tool and Die Inc. located in Rhode Island had one hundred percent of its stock issue held by Williamson Manufacturing. Others such as Fox Custom Cabinetry in Pennsylvania had no shares issued whatsoever. Fox reflected the thinking of Denton's father and grandfather. Upon purchase companies like Fox and several others were simply absorbed into the "parent" or holding company and ceased to be separate entities. In Fox's case it became an operating component or division of Atlantic Corporation. There was no Fox stock in existence; there was only Atlantic stock. Wellbon-Smith had built its empire on small companies scattered all over the world. Depending on the situation a company may be an "E" corporation, an "S" corporation, or an operating division of the parent. They could also be a limited partnership or a limited liability corporation. Whatever proved to be the most beneficial type of entity for its peculiar tax situation. On paper there wasn't a company worth more than twenty million dollars in the entire group. Therein were simultaneously the beauty and the Achilles Heel of Trevor's plan.

Several problems had to be overcome for Trevor's plan to be successful. First and foremost was the value issue. There were originally one million shares of stock issued for Wellbon-Smith L.L.C. At a predetermined value per share as the minimum that a shareholder could expect to spend upon purchase of his shares. One hundred fifty thousand shares were purchased back from their owners at this price and designated as treasury stock previous to the reorganization that took place after Denton's father's death. This was accomplished when several shareholders complained that they had held their shares for many years and wanted to cash in on the perceived appreciated value. The same problem as to the determined value existed at that time also. To satisfy those shareholders that wanted to cash in all or some of their shares, the board of Wellbon-Smith had a team of bankers and appraisers tour the companies, review their financials for the previous three years and set a value on each based on expected future earnings. Actually they "camped out" in the home offices of the major corporations that made up Wellbon-Smith: Atlantic Corporation, Sterling International, Williamson Manufacturing, Global Industries and Pfeiffer International Trading Corporation. The "home offices" of each were located on a floor designated for their use in the Wellbon-Smith Building on Fifth Avenue, so the travel expenses for the team were minimal.

At that time a purely arbitrary price of 135 percent of the appraised value determined by the team was set. In the absence of more concrete data this seemed to please the shareholders that wished to sell their shares. Wellbon-Smith itself purchased the shares with funds that they raised by selling high interest "junk" bonds that they issued at the time. "Junk" bonds paid high interest to the investors because they were unsecured by any real assets. While more complex they bore close resemblance to promissory notes. Most of the shareholders took advantage of this opportunity to "line their pockets" while retaining much of their stock. Because all of the shares purchased by the company were retired as treasury stock, most minimized their loss of position within the partnership in relation to the other partners.

Then a strange turn of events occurred. Several Wall Street traders were charged with fraud involving the sale of "junk" bonds. This triggered the fears of investors who had speculated on the unsecured bonds and the market for "junk" bonds crashed. The holders of these bonds had to settle for pennies on the dollar from the issuer as no one else would buy them. The board of Wellbon-Smith was presented with the unique opportunity of buying back their debt at a mere fifteen cents on the dollar. Chase Manhattan Bank was delighted to finance this purchase as Wellbon-Smith had an excellent credit rating. The board was able to easily pay off this loan in only a couple of years.

This made the whole arrangement appear to be something akin to legalized theft. The corporation assigned an inflated value to the shares. The corporation itself purchased the shares from the individual shareholders allowing them a healthy profit. The corporation paid the shareholders with money raised from selling unsecured "junk" bonds. The "junk" bond market crashed allowing the corporation to pay off the bondholders at a fraction of the value of the original debt that the bondholders were owed. The corporation employed traditional financing in the form of a bank loan at prime rate to pay off the bondholders. All this spelled large capital gains for nearly all of Wellbon-Smith's shareholders. Denton had to admit that he had some ethical problems with the whole affair. It appeared to him that Wellbon-Smith had created wealth out of thin air and paid off the debt at a reduced price with the 'blood" of the bond speculators. Mary Wellbon's lawyers put his mind at ease. It was all very legal and above board. In addition his mother told him, with the air of an aristocrat, "This was capitalism at work. The bondholders were quite willing to take the risk when they anticipated big profits. Where there is the possibility of big profits there is always the possibility of big loss. Especially when trading in unsecured paper. If they couldn't stomach the risk then they shouldn't get into that type of market to begin with!"

So problem number one was to affix a current value to the shares that would tempt enough shareholders to sell. Problem number two concerned the manner in which the Corporate By-laws stipulated that shares might be sold. As with most privately held corporations, Wellbon-Smith desired to know the identity of its partners. All of the existing partners had to sign off when a new person or group was invited to purchase stock. If a new issue of stock was required every shareholder was to be given a fair amount of time to invest more money in the corporation in order to hold his or her position, as it was not the practice of the board to dilute the shareholder's positions. The need for a new issue in the parent company was reserved for extreme cases when it was desirable to raise "new" money. When this was the case the board usually had one or more potential investors ready to present to the existing shareholders.

The most common type of stock transaction in a privately held corporation such as Wellbon-Smith was when one shareholder wished to sell to an existing shareholder or if a shareholder wished to sell to an outsider, someone who did not already own shares of Wellbon-Smith. All of these transactions required the approval of a majority of the shareholders. There was the major problem with Trevor's plan. His plan required secrecy and all transactions of this type were required in the by-laws to be made public to the board of directors. If the board became aware of Trevor's plan it would be obvious that his intention was a hostile takeover and they would halt it in its tracks.

When Denton raised these issues to both Trevor Mason and Abraham Rueben during their all night meeting, Trevor explained that he had an answer to both the problem of value and the problem of disclosure. Several of the current shareholders were again making requests from the board to the effect that it may be time for the corporation to buy back some of the outstanding shares of stock. These shareholders correctly determined that the value of their shares now far exceeded the published value per share that was determined years ago at the time of the last buy back. They wished to reap what they perceived as overdue financial benefits from their holdings in excess of the moderate dividends that Wellbon-Smith issued annually like clockwork.

Here the makeup of the body of shareholders could possibly work to Trevor's favor. The shareholders of Wellbon-Smith were a rather diverse international group of investors whom Denton's father had assembled. There was no one left from grandfather's era, but several of those investor's heirs retained their inherited stock. Those latter shareholders were the owners that were pressing the loudest for the corporation to buy back some or all of their stock. The reason for their request being that the stock was valued at the time of their ancestor's death so any capital gains would be figured from that point forward. The capital gains would not be figured from the time that their relative purchased the shares. In addition, Wellbon-Smith had a policy of reinvesting eighty percent of its profits, if there were profits and there usually were. This made the annual dividends relatively small, much to the chagrin of these shareholders.

Because Wellbon-Smith was an L.L.C. it was permitted to value its shares on a changing basis. In theory if money was reinvested or losses were recorded this changed the basis for the valuation of the corporation annually. Again assuming that there was profit and eighty percent of each year's profits were reinvested into the corporation, this new number (old value plus the addition of the reinvested money) was utilized to establish a new per share value at the time of sale of the shares. This minimized the capital gains and therefore the taxes that a shareholder would owe the government. This gave even more incentive for the disgruntled shareholders to sell.

As Trevor gleefully pointed out, because of the diverse and complex structure of Wellbon-Smith and all of its subsidiaries, short of liquidating the entire company it was nearly impossible to determine the exact value of the corporation at any given time. This meant that anyone's educated guess could be viewed as reasonable. Trevor hoped to arrive at a number that would allow the shareholders to reap a substantial gain and appeal to their greed while not incurring an excessive amount of capital gains taxes due the IRS. In addition it had to be an amount that he and Denton could hope to raise.

Trevor then proceeded to run through a complex formula that he had devised that considered the reinvested profit, any accumulated loss and the rate of inflation from the last date when a per share value was determined. Although the formula produced a per share value of nearly 185% of the previous number, Trevor determined that they could persuade enough shareholders to sell at 125% of published value to execute their plan. Denton's personal stock, Denton's mother's shares and the relatively small amount of stock that Trevor had accumulated through his options during his tenure at Wellbon-Smith, accounted for sixteen percent of the outstanding shares. Mary Wellbon alone controlled twelve percent making her the largest single shareholder. That left an additional thirty-five percent of the total shares of voting stock that had to be controlled in one fashion or another by Trevor and Denton in order for them to account for fifty-one percent.

With one hundred fifty thousand of the original shares retired that left eight hundred and fifty thousand shares still in shareholders hands. Mary Wellbon, Denton and to a very small extent Trevor accounted for one hundred thirty six thousand shares. The hard math came to two hundred ninety-seven thousand five hundred shares that had to be either purchased or controlled. This would give them control of four hundred thirty-three thousand five hundred shares total or fifty-one percent of the voting stock. Denton did some rapid mental math. At 125% of the published price that came to just over 200 million dollars. "Good Grief!" exclaimed Denton aloud.

"Did you say somethin' Bud?" asked the cabby.

"No just muttering to myself." Replied Denton quickly, not realizing he had spoken out loud. This wasn't the first time in the last six hours that he had contemplated this number. Trevor had done the math during their meeting. Somehow every time that Denton thought it through, it appeared more and more impossible to finance. But Trevor had an answer for that too, along with the need for secrecy.

The cab pulled up in front of Denton's co-op building. Denton gave the cabby his fare and a generous tip and climbed out. He checked his watch, just a little past seven on Friday morning. He should have been exhausted but he discovered that he didn't feel a bit tired. He decided that he must have been running on adrenaline. The doorman greeted him warmly as he held open the door. Upon Denton's passing the doorman pressed a button that opened the security lock on the lobby doors. The doormen had to recognize the occupant and allow them to pass into the lobby. If a visitor came calling the doormen would call up to a resident on the intercom and get permission for the visitor to proceed.

Denton was popular with the building staff. He and Susan always stopped to talk and took an interest in each employee's personal families and problems. Susan in particular always inquired as to children and grandchildren's health and individual fortunes. If the wife or child of a building employee was sick for any extended period of time it was not unusual for the individual to receive a card, candy or flowers from the Wellbon family. In addition there were generous gifts at Christmas time and the appropriate Jewish holidays.

Denton crossed the lobby and entered the elevator. He pushed the button for the fourteenth floor. Denton wondered if he should tell Susan about any of this. He decided against it for now. He had to sort it all out in his own mind before he could hope to answer any of the questions that he knew she would have. The elevator door opened onto a small hall. There were only three co-ops on this floor. Denton's door was directly ahead as it was one that faced Central Park. Denton punched his security code into the keypad beside the large double oak raised panel doors that opened into his foyer. Upon entering Denton saw that the apartment was still dark. Only the weak morning light was penetrating the sheer curtains that hung between the tall elegant drapes on the massive living room windows. This co-op had two floors with a spiral staircase connecting them. As Denton recalled it had about two thousand five hundred square feet of living space. It was very spacious. Susan had decorated it in subdued good taste. All appointments and furniture were very expensive but understated. Denton approved of all her selections. He enjoyed their home immensely.

Denton quietly removed his jacket, tie and shoes and slipped into his favorite reading chair with a view of the Park. He knew that Susan was still sleeping upstairs and he didn't want to wake her. He suspected that in his absence she and her twin sister had spent hours talking on the phone. Denton heard a door close quietly in the rear of the apartment. That was where the large eat in kitchen was located. Margo the maid came out of her quarters with a cup of coffee in her hand. She spied Denton sitting in his chair.

"Mr. Wellbon, I didn't hear you come in.," she said quietly. Although she was dressed in her work clothes she did not have to begin until eight AM. "Can I get you some coffee?"

"No thank you Margo, I already had breakfast."

"You certainly are working strange hours."

"Yes, yes I am" replied Denton somewhat wearily.

Margo could see that her boss was not in the mood for small talk so she quietly left him and returned to the kitchen.

Denton continued his review of Trevor's plan. First Trevor noted that they really didn't have to come up with all the money immediately. In fact, he believed that the shareholders would prefer to have installment payments for a period of at least four years to spread out the tax burden. This reduced the amount that they would have to pay out within the next six months. Trevor believed that they could strike deals with the shareholders that were anxious to sell that allowed them to acquire the proxy voting rights immediately with a promise to pay them twenty-five percent of the agreed upon sale price after six months from the signed agreement, still a tremendous sum of money to come up with. Trevor had an answer for that also. Strike a quiet deal with a bank to bankroll the initial payment, promising to sell two companies within the next twelve months and use that promise as collateral. Trevor believed firmly that if you could get an accurate value on all of the individual Wellbon-Smith operating divisions the real value of the stock would be far in excess of three to four times the published value. Denton at this point had to question all of this.

"Let me see if I understand Trevor" he began. During their meeting this was the second instance that Denton raised a question with Abraham Rueben in the room. "We approach a bank and promise to sell two or however many companies is required within the next twelve months. We convince them that we will be able to get enough for these selected companies so that the bank will feel comfortable in loaning us millions now so that we can make the first installment out of four annual installments. We must strike this deal with enough shareholders so that we attain the necessary voting proxies immediately upon signing the deal. That will allow us to control fifty-one percent of the voting stock within the next six months. Six months being crucial because it coincides with our annual end of the year board meeting."

"Correct so far Denton," answered Trevor.

"Then what," asked Denton?

"With our own stock and the voting proxies for the shares that we just purchased we have enough votes to bring several suggested changes in the corporate by-laws to the floor. As the remaining board members and shareholders will not know how we obtained these proxies, they will be forced to hear and consider the changes that we have proposed. They will want to bury them in a committee to investigate the ramifications; we will not allow that, as we will control fifty-one percent of the voting shares so we'll be able to stop dead any stalling tactics that the board attempts. Before they realize what is happening we will approve the changes we want to the corporate by-laws after which we install ourselves as Chairman and vice Chairman."

"Among those changes I assume will be wording that allows us to purchase stock in the fashion that we have just completed?" asked Denton.

"Correct again Denton!" smiled Trevor. "The others will smell a rat, but they aren't lawyers and some of them aren't very bright. They will protest, but in the absence of hard facts they will be forced to accept what we do until their personal lawyers have an opportunity to review what has taken place."

At this point in the meeting, Abraham Rueben spoke up. "The beauty of all this Denton is that when your father needed to raise capital beyond what any bank would offer him he decided to set up Wellbon-Smith. This allowed him to invite investors to put money in his holding company so that he could purchase more companies. Your grandfather did not approve of bringing in outside investors. Your grandfather believed that the family would lose control. Your father was a smart man. Only by writing up a very vague set of by-laws that frankly allowed many loopholes could your dad convince your granddad that he could maintain control. One method was by ignoring the issues of proxy votes altogether. While selling of one's shares without the Board's approval is a violation of the bylaws, there is no mention of approval for acquiring proxy rights."

How do you know this?" Denton asked Rueben.

"I know this because as a young man the law firm that I had just joined upon successful completion of the State of New York's bar exam, was the firm that handled the formation of Wellbon-Smith. It has since become a limited liability corporation for tax purposes but the by-laws have remained essentially unchanged since your father conceived them."

"The investors put money into this holding company even after having their lawyers read the proposed by-laws?" Denton was wondering why he hadn't noticed this ambiguity himself.

"They sure did and don't give lawyers too much credit. Many of them, me excluded, don't know their ass from a hole in the ground," continued Rueben. "Your father did an excellent job of picking investors that, if you will excuse me, had more money than brains. In addition, your grandfather and father could demonstrate that the original business entity, Atlantic Corporation, was hugely profitable and had made them both extremely wealthy. Greed won out over common sense. When a potential investor raised too many questions your father would lay it on the line: 'Do you want to be a part of this or not? I'm giving you the opportunity to own a piece of the vehicle that made me rich. Do you want to acquire more wealth or would you rather I make this offer to one of your friends so you can watch them benefit from it?' This was usually enough to bring out the checkbooks. If they chose to decline, your father didn't want anyone that smart to own shares anyway."

Rueben continued. "They all made money off the deal but none ever made the huge profits that your grandfather and father made from the old Atlantic Importing Company. I believe that was the original name. It later became Atlantic Corporation."

"You are correct concerning the original name, but I must inquire as to why the investors never realized the profits that my father and grandfather realized previously?" Denton was a bit disturbed that this stranger was implying that he knew more about his father's company, indeed more about Denton's father than Denton did.

"I said earlier that your father was a smart man. I meant every word. He correctly determined that with the introduction of outside investors the operation would have to go straight. By that I mean that they would have to abandon all the illegal operations that fueled their growth for all those years. The presence of investors forced them to go straight. But in the long run it gave them access to large amounts of capital that they could not have attained legally any other way. It was time for a change and your father realized it. While the immediate profits were not as large, the long-term results were well worth it. In addition the risk factor was far less. Your father figured out how to steal from the government legally by constructing Wellbon-Smith and all of its subsidiaries so that they could take advantage of every tax loophole in the book. While many of those loopholes have now been closed you must agree that even today, Wellbon-Smith is a master at avoiding taxes or pushing the obligation into the future."

It was seldom that Denton raised his voice. It was even less frequent that Denton lost his temper. Abraham Rueben had inadvertently managed to arrange for both to occur. Denton turned to Trevor. "I object to the implication that this so called gentleman is making! He is implying that my family was dishonest! Not only that but he is seated in the office building that my family's company owns and drinking scotch and smoking cigars that the company has paid for while he is doing it!" the outburst was so unlike Denton that even Trevor Mason was taken aback.

"Calm down Denton" Trevor's voice was unusually soft. He really needed Denton to be on board for this plan to work. He had never once imagined that Denton could possibly be ignorant to a situation that virtually the entire city of New York accepted as gospel for years. True no one had any proof, but that was only because Denton's original two namesakes were very smart. No one had any proof that is except for the "so called gentleman" as Denton had put it seated here tonight.

Rueben allowed Denton to regain his composure. "I'm sorry Mr. Wellbon" he began. "Believe me the last thing that I desire to do is to upset you." Abraham Rueben was also aware of how essential Denton was to the plan. He did not want to face Trevor Mason should he be responsible for Denton deciding to decline. He was however prepared for just such an occasion. On this subject he had perhaps more history on Denton Wellbon III than did Trevor Mason.

"You see Mr. Wellbon" Rueben continued. "I eventually became the senior partner in the law firm that I referred to a minute ago. At the time that I joined, your father was setting up Wellbon-Smith as a new holding company. Years later

I was going through some of the old files in the basement of our office building. I came across a series of thick folders bound in leather. They were unmarked. I brought one page with me for you to look at in the event that you doubted what I am telling you. Do you think you would recognize your father's handwriting if you saw it?"

"I believe that I would" Denton answered cautiously. He was beginning to get a sick feeling in the pit of his stomach. First Trevor had informed him of a conspiracy against him that seemed to be bent on keeping him from the chairman's position. A conspiracy coordinated by a man that Denton had always respected as a personal friend and a friend of the family. Now he feared that the paper that Abraham Rueben was removing from a folder would indite his father as having involvement in who knows what beyond the law. Denton hesitated to take the paper from Rueben's out stretched hand. Finally he summoned the courage and took it. He hoped that Trevor and Abraham Rueben failed to notice that his hand was shaking. Denton's sick stomach got worse. He wasn't certain what he was looking at but it was definitely his father's distinctive flowing style.

"What you are looking at is a hand written manifest. It is for a shipment of whiskey and liquors entering this country illegally from Ireland to avoid U.S. import taxes. Stolen and counterfeit tax stamps and seals were affixed to the bottles and they were then sold at cut-rate prices to distributors, hotel and tavern owners who asked no questions. Without the expense of import taxes all made windfall profits. There was even some evidence that the whiskey was stolen from the distilleries to begin with. Even then the Atlantic Importing Company controlled enough individual companies as to make money laundering and obscuring the trail of the contraband easy tasks. Showing large profits becomes much easier if you eliminate the major expenses in your business." Abraham Reuben paused to allow all of this information to register with Denton. "Do you recognize the hand writing Mr. Wellbon?"

"I'm not certain. It could be my father's." Denton lied and his mouth felt so dry that he was afraid that his words might sound slurred. It was unmistakably his father's handwriting. "But you said that my father was a smart man. If this is what you claim and my father did author it, it seems to me that wasn't very smart."

"He had to have the proper tax stamps available when the shipments arrived. Speed and keeping the product moving from ship to warehouse to customer was the secret to not being caught. This required a manifest for him to work from. He could not afford to wait until the whiskey was on U.S. shores to begin producing the tax stamps. Your father did exhibit one personal weakness in this situation. There were no practical computers in those days and your father abhorred using a typewriter. He did place himself in jeopardy by writing this document himself. However by doing that he did avoid the need to involve anyone else. That was where he was brilliant. While others became lazy and had helpers take care of the 'grunt' tasks your father kept those who could turn evidence on him to a minimum. He and your grandfather handled most of the illegal work personally." Reuben paused again.

"How did you come by this document? Efficiency was my father's trademark. He would have destroyed this as soon as the need for it expired." Denton was looking for anything to distance his father from this offense.

"I suspect that someone, perhaps a senior partner in our law firm stole it and other incriminating documents. You see, your father and grandfather always utilized the somewhat less than scrupulous firm that I joined to aid them in illicit tasks. Crooked lawyers are not hard to find, but good crooked lawyers are. My firm was good. Lawyers are necessary to cover tracks in any major illegal endeavor. As there is little honor among thieves I suspect that my firm wanted some form of protection to hold as a sword over your father's head in case the relationship soured. I'm certain that you know what I mean. Of course after the formation of Wellbon-Smith the company's activities became totally legitimate and the need for anything but the normal legal services ceased. The firms that carried out these services for your father came to the forefront and my firm was simply kept on a generous retainer. When I took control of the firm I of course saw to it that all illegal activities ceased" Ruben reached out and relieved Denton of the document.

Somehow Denton doubted the accuracy of that last statement. "I do not intend to sit here and argue this claim with you. Let's move on." Denton had regained his composure and a degree of his dignity.

Trevor was relieved. He was afraid that they had lost Denton or that he would fail to understand the underlying message that He and Ruben were attempting to communicate. First, the only way for Denton to become chairperson was to join them in their plan. Second, if he did not join them, not only could personal secrets be revealed but also the confirmation of generations of rumors concerning

Denton's family would finally come to light. It is one thing to hear rumors but it is quite another to have them confirmed in public. The best example of this was Denton's reaction.

Trevor continued: "The next question is how to keep all of this quiet. As you can both imagine, if word of what we are doing leaks out before we have the voting proxies for fifty-one percent of the voting shares, those who would oppose our taking control could stop us cold and even force us out of the company. We can do nothing; change nothing until we control the votes. I suggest that this isn't as difficult as it sounds. First we must be very careful to choose the correct targets. We must select only those shareholders whose personal income isn't dependent on Wellbon-Smith. By that I mean strictly investors who are neither employed by the company or serve on its board of directors. Those people who have only an investment that they wish to unload or can be persuaded to unload for a generous profit. Those who do not concern themselves with form, function or the letter of the law; in short those who are greedy and self interested enough to keep their mouths shut!" Trevor couldn't help but accentuate that point.

"I'm sorry Trevor, but this involves a lot of people to keep quiet for the extended period of six months. Is this reasonable to expect?" It was now well into the wee hours of the morning, Denton was becoming weary and he really didn't want to offend his benefactor. But this was very frightening business that they were discussing. The consequences of failure were enormous.

Trevor stood up and walked slowly, thoughtfully around the room. His limp was only slightly apparent. Contrary to his steady demeanor his mind was racing. Denton feared that if he had the benefit of Trevor's thoughts he would have felt even more frightened than he already was. This was it. They were now at the moment of truth. Trevor's face expressed concern. Denton suspected that he was about to discover exactly what role he would be expected to play. He wondered if he had what it takes to play this role. "This is where you contribute your part of the plan Denton." Trevor's voice was quiet and serious. "You are the lynchpin of this entire operation. Rueben and I will see that all of the necessary shareholders are contacted discreetly. You have but two tasks to accomplish. It is first and primarily your responsibility to secure your mother's vote, either by proxy or by guaranteeing that she will vote with us."

"That could well be impossible Trevor! You know mother, she is strong-willed and is quite content with the way things are operating!"

Trevor continued: “I will assist you with this task, but in the end it is you whom she trusts and you must be the one to convince her. I do have some suggestions for you to gain her cooperation. We will discuss those at a later date. Your other role does not involve personal contact but is every bit as crucial. You know the characters involved in this company better than anyone other than your mother, and I’m convinced that you know these people better than she does because you have been an observer from the inside all of these years. That’s a much better view than the one from the boardroom.”

“Where are you going with this Trevor? I don’t understand” was Denton’s response.

“Simple Denton, you have been blessed with a near photographic memory. We need you to remember and recall any bit of ‘dirt’ that you have knowledge of, be it rumor or provable fact. We need some insurance that goes beyond greed to keep these people’s mouths shut. I believe that you have that knowledge and I also know that this group of investors that your father assembled is no choir of angels. You tell all to Ruben and me and we will do the rest. I need to know where all the skeletons are hidden and where the proof may be buried if indeed some form of proof exists. There is an ancillary benefit that you need to consider Denton. If the skeletons are dreadful enough, then the owners of those skeletons may just be willing to part with their shares at a reduced price to keep them hidden. This would make our task much less expensive.”

“But… but, that’s blackmail!” Denton had now reached his limit of emotion for the evening.

“Damn right!”

“I…I need to think about this Trevor. This is too much for me to make a snap decision on.”

Reuben was about to speak as Denton stared off into space, but Trevor waved him off. “Of course you do Denton. I would never ask you to make a decision of this magnitude without time for consideration. I must allude to the time factor though. We have less than six months until the annual shareholders meeting. Can we have your decision by Sunday morning?”

"Sunday…Sunday morning? I…I suppose so Trevor. Sunday morning."

"Denton, before you take our friend Abraham home let me say one more time that we must strike first and fast. There is really no option for you. You cannot allow your enemies to expose your private affairs and you of all people deserve to finally take your rightful place at the head of this company. Remember that Denton."

Denton noticed that Reuben didn't question what Denton's private affairs were. Did he know, or was he just being polite?

"I'll give you my decision on Sunday morning Trevor."

"Thank you Denton. I know that you will make the correct move." If Denton had access to Trevor Mason's thoughts at this precise moment he would have been more uncomfortable then even he expected. If you don't thought Trevor, I will have to force you to make the correct decision. This piece of information was not available to Denton as he considered the meeting of the previous night from his living room. However the possibility that he may have as much or more to fear from Trevor than any of his reported "enemies" was beginning to dawn.

"Good morning handsome." Susan greeted him from the spiral staircase. Denton returned to the present. As he considered his wife he thought that she looked very alluring in her bathrobe and slippers. "Should I have Margo make us both breakfast or would you prefer to go straight to bed?"

Weary as he was, Denton desired the company of his lovely wife at this precise moment. "I've already eaten but I will have coffee with you while you dine."

"Great! I'll have Margo put some on."

Denton watched as she left for the kitchen. Susan was the perfect New York socialite. She came from an old respected family with old money. She was beautiful, with shoulder length auburn hair. Her small delicate features disguised the fact that she participated with relish in numerous outdoor sports. If the truth were known she was a bit of a tomboy underneath that very proper but disarming demeanor. She was open and outgoing while Denton had difficulty relating to people. She was in many ways just the opposite from Denton who sometimes wondered what she saw in him. She certainly had no need for his money as she had plenty of her own. He loved her with all of his heart. She was the best thing to happen to him in his entire life. The best part was that for reasons still mystifying to Denton, she loved him with equal devotion.

They had met as children as their parents belonged to the same country club. Indeed their parents were involved in several of the same social and charitable organizations so their paths crossed rather frequently. They attended different private schools of course, Denton to an all boy school and Susan to an all girls. During one of the Christmas holiday breaks from college Susan's parents held a gala party at their home in the Hamptons. It was at this party that they began to see each other as adults for the first time. Denton summoned all of his courage and asked if he could take her to dinner and a Broadway show later that week. To his surprise she accepted. Denton's surprise was due to the fact that Susan seemed to have a constant entourage of handsome young men at her beck and call. He couldn't to this day understand why she accepted. He was eternally grateful that she did as the relationship blossomed through the ensuing year. Finally, during graduation week, Denton popped the question and was again astonished when she said "yes."

The only sorrow in their relationship was that they suffered through two miscarriages. After the second the doctor recommended that it would be wise and far less threatening to Susan if they stopped trying to have children. To Denton's amazement, Susan recovered from this disappointment far sooner than he did and she was the one who pulled him out of depression.

Through it all they became soul mates. Denton made no decisions before consulting Susan and vice versa. Denton took a deep breath; this was one decision in which he definitely could not include Susan. This made him extremely uncomfortable, as he knew that this would most likely be the biggest decision of his career if not his life. Susan returned and her bright smile as she offered him a mug of coffee only emphasized the gravity of what Trevor was proposing.

CHAPTER 4

Sarah Frazer pulled her vintage Pontiac Trans Am into one of the visitor parking spaces at Fox Custom Cabinetry. She was aware that her first official day at work wasn't until Monday, but Dennis Morton the V. P. of Human Resources suggested that she come in this Saturday to meet some of the "principle players" as he phrased it. Dennis was retiring after twenty-five years with the company and Sarah had been chosen from a long list of candidates to be his replacement. Dennis explained that the company was very busy at this time and not only would the plant be working on Saturday but many people would be in the office as well. He felt that the casual Saturday morning atmosphere was conducive to introducing her.

Sarah was fifteen minutes early. She sat in her car and looked at her new work place. Fox was headquartered in a quaint Cape Cod style building with dormer windows on the second floor and a cedar shingle roof. It sat well out in the country in a small village named Goodville. The village was named after the pioneer settler who established it in the very early 1700's. It sat at the eastern edge of Lancaster County, Pennsylvania. This put it approximately sixty miles west of Philadelphia.

The office was very deceptive in appearance. The combination showroom and office sat just off the main street on the crest of a ridge that ran for miles from west to east. The main road, state route 23 that ran through Goodville followed this ridge. The entire village itself straddled the crest with back yards and open fields falling away in either direction. There was only one main street with secondary streets that quickly turned into country roads running perpendicular to it. The Fox factory sat behind the office on the south slope of the ridge. It was barely visible from the road and gave the appearance of the entire establishment being contained in this single semi detached "L" shaped building. The "L" surrounded the parking lot on two sides, the east and the south. The main street bordered on the third that was to the north, and a small rural elementary school was next door to the west of the parking lot. The only clue to the near two hundred thousand square feet of manufacturing space that was the Fox factory further down the slope was the flat roofs that were barely visible down the driveway.

Sarah was very pleased to be accepted at Fox. The green rolling hills and pastureland of Lancaster County vaguely reminded her of her homeland in Scotland. Sarah had come here as a foreign exchange student at the age of eighteen in 1978 to attend college. She lived with a local family, to whom she became very attached, while attending Franklin & Marshall, a local liberal arts college. Upon graduation she returned to her native land. After attaining her master's degree at Cambridge she worked at what she considered several rather mundane jobs that were not up to the level of her qualifications. After a rather dreadful divorce coupled with the tragic death of her parents in an auto accident, there was no longer any reason to remain in Scotland. When she received the invitation from her exchange parents to return to the States and live with them she jumped at the chance. Correctly or not Sarah perceived that there was more opportunity for an educated woman in the United States than there was in the British Commonwealth.

Since her return she kept seeing the articles in the local papers on this most eligible of bachelors who happened to be the president of Fox Custom Cabinetry. She was not interested in him from a romantic perspective, as she believed him to be an aging playboy, but the fact that he was a fellow countryman who just happened to settle at the same geographical location as did she fascinated her.
When the opportunity to apply at Fox materialized, Sarah couldn't resist. In the first place it was her chance to become a corporate vice president and department head. Secondly it was a substantial increase over her current salary and finally she would be able to throw this in the face of her "naysayer" friends' back home that thought that she was crazy to leave Scotland in the first place. In addition and only as a secondary factor, she would be on the senior staff and report directly to that other Scotsman that she had read so much about. Sarah, who was frankly surprised to be chosen by this male dominated firm in conservative Lancaster County, was eager to get started and show these men just what a woman could do when given the chance.

Sarah checked her watch, two minutes before eight. Morton had told her to arrive "around eight in the morning." Sarah wanted to let him know early on that punctuality was one of her strong points. She got out of her car and headed across the lot to the front entrance. Once inside a young woman greeted her dressed in jeans and a sweatshirt. Martin told her that they were very casual on

To Catch a Fox

Saturday mornings. Sarah was casually dressed but not that casual.

"Ms. Sarah Frazer for Dennis Morton," she said.

"Is he expecting you?" asked the girl.

"Yes he is," replied Sarah.

The girl picked up the receiver from her console and pressed a button. After a moment she said "Sarah Frazer to see you," paused and hung up. "He'll be right down."

From the two previous interviews that Sarah had been subjected to she had determined that the showrooms full of beautiful cabinetry were located on the first floor and the executive offices were on the second floor. She was not certain what lay down the short hall and to the right of the receptionist's desk, but she had the impression that there were more offices back there. Who was housed there she had no idea. Her speculation was interrupted by the sound of footsteps coming down the open stairway to her left. She recognized the comfortably disheveled figure of Dennis Morton. He was a small wiry man with gray unruly hair and a bushy mustache.

"Good morning Sarah," he greeted her with a slight smile. At least Sarah thought he was smiling as the mustache nearly hid his upper lip making it difficult to determine. "I trust you had no trouble finding us."
"No trouble at all," answered Sarah politely. This was their third meeting and she had become accustomed to silly questions such as this. Of course I had no trouble finding you, this is my third time here, she thought! The first time she was subjected to one of these questions she was offended. Did he think her some airhead bimbo? The next time she wondered if he was altogether present from a mental perspective. Perhaps he should have retired sooner, but finally after listening to him talk on the phone to an OSHA inspector that he couldn't keep waiting, she concluded correctly that he was sharp as a tack but was not very good at small talk. Apparently Dennis Morton had certain opening lines that he used continually to help make a new acquaintance, or anyone that he wasn't familiar with, feel at ease. Perhaps they also served to make him feel at ease.
"Good, let's go meet the remainder of the senior staff."

"I'm looking forward to it."

With that Dennis remembered to introduce Sarah to the receptionist after which he led the way back up the open staircase. At the top he opened a door off the landing. Upon entering he turned left and proceeded down a long hall. At the first open door on the left he entered. At a desk behind a counter sat a middle-aged woman. She was stick thin with her hair up in a tight bun and a dour look on her face.

"Brady Miller I want you to meet Sarah Frazer. Sarah is going to be my replacement when I retire in three weeks."

"Hi Brady, I'm pleased to meet you," offered Sarah.

"Good morning Ms. Frazer. You do prefer Ms. do you not?" The question did not have a friendly sound.

"Yes I do thank you."

"I noticed that you used Ms. extensively in your resume and later on your application. I handle all of the staff's paper work." Brady quickly added apparently suddenly feeling the need to explain her access to confidential documents.

"I'm sorry, does it offend you?" inquired Sarah not really concerned with the firm's paper flow.

"Offend me? No it doesn't offend me. I just want to get things correct. Too many people around here don't pay attention to detail. I'm not one of them, of that you can be assured. This is a lean organization. Mr. MacLode wouldn't have it any other way. I act as Executive Secretary for the entire senior staff. That will include you when you take over for Dennis. I just want to be correct from the start as to how you desire to be addressed as I will be typing up all of your letters."

"Oh, I see. Well yes I want to be addressed as Ms. on all of my formal correspondence but I only want to be addressed as Sarah by the people that I work with. I'm afraid that I have presumed quite a bit. I apologize. May I call you Brady?"

To Catch a Fox

For the first time Brady looked into Sarah's eyes. They were large, brown and friendly. Brady's tone softened slightly. "Everyone calls me Brady and so may you Sarah."

"Thank you. I look forward to working with you Brady."

Dennis appeared to have that slight grin on his face again as he gently took Sarah by the arm and led her through a door off Brady's office to an office on Sarah's right. Assuming a gruff tone Dennis continued with his introductions. "This scoundrel is Tony Conocenti, our V. P. of Sales and Marketing. He doesn't do much around here, so he's always flying off to who knows where. He claims that he's pushing the sales force to get more orders in here. Some of us suspect that the dealers know how good a product we make and the sales would come in even if we didn't have a high priced sales force traveling around everywhere. Tony this is Sarah Frazer, my replacement."

"I'm pleased to meet you Sarah." Tony rose from behind his desk and extended his hand. "I overheard your conversation with Brady so I know that it's okay if I call you by your first name. I hear every subject that Brady preaches on. I have no choice as you can see the close proximity of our offices. That is one of the reasons that I travel so much. Between Brady's sermons on striving for perfection and the bull that this old wind bag Dennis spews forth, I wonder how I keep my sanity."

"Let's show a little respect in there for the people that make you look good Anthony." Brady's reply came from her desk as she was typing at her computer. Sarah noted the speed with which her fingers were tapping on the keys. She also noticed that there was no pause while she responded to Tony's comment.

"Please call me Tony. Brady is the only one anywhere that calls me by my Christian name."

"Tony it is. I'm pleased to meet you and look forward to working with you." Sarah accepted Tony's hand and gave him a polite nod.

"You're coming in at a great time. We need all the help that we can get putting together our annual strategic plan. For some reason, corporate is in a big rush this year."

To Catch a Fox

"I'll do whatever you need."

"She comes with a 'can do' reputation Tony. That's why we hired her," said Dennis.

"Good! With the way Mac is pushing us we need some 'can do' attitude around here."

"Now that Sarah's here that will make two of us." interjected Brady while her fingers continued to fly across the keyboard."

"Welcome aboard Sarah."

"Thank you Tony."

Dennis led the way out of Tony's office across in front of Brady's workstation to an open door off the other side of the room that Brady occupied. "This is Mac's office. As you can see we have a rose between two thorns. This is a three office complex. Tony on one side, Mac on the other and Brady's desk is in the middle where she struggles to keep them both on track. Our boss isn't in just yet, but he will be soon as he's called a meeting for 9:00 AM. He's very punctual. I'll introduce you to him then."

"If he's punctual he and I will get along just fine," commented Sarah. Sarah also noted that her new boss' desk was strewn with papers, file folders and binders of every color that you could imagine. Secretly she was glad to see his desk looking as if a tornado just hit it. She never really trusted people with neat orderly and especially clean desks. Either they had little to do or they had something to hide.

"Yes I've noticed that about you Sarah." As he spoke Dennis led her back out into the hall again. "Come on, we'll see who else is hanging around this place on a day when they should be at home with their families catching up on their chores. Come to think of it, maybe that's why so many are hiding out here."

A small bespectacled man with a balding forehead and thin wispy hair rounded the far corner of the hall and was heading toward them with his head bowed over a thick open file. As he approached he noticed that he wasn't alone and stopped reading long enough to look up and smile. He had one of those round good guy faces and as he came closer Sarah noticed that he might be short in stature but underneath his open at the neck dress shirt and slacks he was powerfully built. She suspected that at some point in his youth he had played American football. It seemed that he was in a hurry and was going to attempt to simply smile and pass on his way, but Dennis stopped him.

"Want you to meet someone Dale," said Dennis in his rather slow cadence. "This is Sarah Frazer. She'll be the new V. P. of Human Resources when I retire. Sarah this is Dale Hershey our controller and V. P. of Finance."

"Well hello Sarah. I may call you Sarah?" Dale's face opened into a wide friendly grin. Sarah thought that it was a nice open trustworthy face, a distinct asset for a controller.

"You certainly may if I may call you Dale."

"Done deal, welcome aboard. Are you staying for this special Saturday morning meeting that Mac pulled on us?"

"It's not necessary Sarah. You really don't begin until Monday…"began Dennis.

"Think nothing of it Dennis, I wouldn't miss it for the world." Sarah interrupted. "It will give me some idea what I've gotten myself into."

"Your choice." replied Dennis. You'll get to know Dale real well. He keeps a close watch on everyone's budgets. He'll know if you're over budget before you will."

"That's what a controller is supposed to do Dennis. I keep telling you guys that but none of you listen." Dale turned to Sarah. "I'm not as bad as I am sure he'll make me out to be after I leave. Leave I must, I have to have copies of these financials ready in time for our meeting. See you later Sarah." With that Dale was off down the hall.

"You still have to meet Carroll Brubaker the V. P. of Manufacturing and Dave Elliott V. P. of Service and Transportation. Carroll's office is down in the plant, Dave's is down stairs but I know that he's not in just yet. I'll show you around the office. Most of the troops that really do the work in this office are home this morning. Back in this area we have accounting." The tour continued with Sarah taking in every possible detail

To Catch a Fox

***

It was Saturday morning and William MacLode was not only frustrated but he just didn't understand. When he failed to understand he became angry. This morning Mac was well on his way to becoming angry. When he logged onto the corporate web site with his laptop there was a long and involved message awaiting him from Trevor Mason. It was loaded with additional requests for information concerning Fox Cabinetry. All of this information was to be included in the annual strategic report. What is he up to? Is he trying to make this impossible? Moving the presentation date forward by one month was bad enough with the usual information, market studies and projections that were required, but now this. What possible reason could he have for wanting all of this information included in the strategic report? The only way that anyone could need this much information is if they were planning to purchase the company and Atlantic already owned it.

Mac's heart skipped a beat. You would also need this information if you were planning to sell it! No, that couldn't be the reason. In spite of Mason's best efforts to keep each company's results secret, Mac had friends at corporate and he was in possession of data that demonstrated that Fox was one of Atlantic's most profitable companies. In fact, Fox was one of the most profitable companies in the entire Wellbon-Smith Empire. Why would Mason want to sell it? Mac stared out the window of his suburban living room. There are only two reasons why you sell a company. If it's losing money and you want to cut your losses or if it's making money and you want to make a "killing."

Mac logged off and settled back in his chair. At this point in time Atlantic would certainly be able to ask top dollar for the company. Given a little time they may even be able to get twenty million for it. Why? What are they up to? What is Trevor Mason up to? He would have to get permission from the Wellbon-Smith board to sell one of the companies. Just as a CEO from any of the groups would have to ask permission to acquire a company the inverse was also true. Would they give permission? In their entire history there was only one company that Wellbon-Smith had ever divested itself of and it was bleeding red ink so badly that the only buyers that showed any interest was the management team that had allowed it to run into the ground. After weeks of haggling over the price, the management team picked it up at fire sale prices.

Mac checked his watch and picked up the phone. He knew that his call would not be welcome at this hour on a Saturday morning, but he decided to make it anyway. The phone rang several times without answer before an answering machine was activated. He left a message requesting a return phone call as soon as possible. He left his home number, cell phone and his private extension at the office. After downing a second cup of coffee he fed his two pet cats and prepared to leave for the office. Bernie, a striped tiger cat and Slater a gray tabby, were the only cohabitants with which Mac shared his house. Mac was a confirmed bachelor.

This did not mean that Mac had a boring social life. Indeed, the opposite was the case. Nearly every year Mac's name appeared on the local newspaper's "most eligible bachelor" list. Mac was constantly seen escorting any number of attractive females to local events. As Fox under Mac's insistence was a strong supporter of the local arts, Mac was photographed frequently at openings of local theaters, art shows, and charity functions. His name appeared regularly on the local society pages.

Mac triggered the automatic garage door opener and backed his black restored '57 T-Bird out of the driveway. It was a beautiful morning and he had decided to remove the top and let the classic see the light of day. The T-Bird was his passion. He had restored it over a period of five years and only took it on the road when the weather promised to be perfect. This morning's forecast saw no precipitation until the middle of next week, so Mac felt safe in taking it out. He normally drove a top of the line Buick Aurora. The Buick was a company car. Corporate policy set in New York allowed division presidents such as him to choose from a top of the line Buick, Oldsmobile or Pontiac for their personal car. Mac resented that the Mercedes, Jaguar and BMW's were reserved for the New York cadre exclusively. Mac's reasoning was that the New Yorkers, as the far-flung divisions referred to them, did little or nothing to contribute to corporate profitability so why did they merit the best cars. As with all division presidents, Mac felt that he did far more to contribute to a healthy return on investment than did the boys at corporate.

Mac lived approximately ten miles from the Fox plant. This gave him ample time to think while driving. Should he attempt any explanation to his staff concerning the additional work that he was about to assign them? Yesterday's session with the partial staff had been testy to say the least. Even in a foul mood they had all accomplished far more than Mac had expected without everyone's participation. With all of his vice presidents present this morning they would want to know why corporate were making these demands. Should he simply make light of it, shrug his shoulders, and reinforce their suspicions that not only did corporate not know what it was doing, but that it had too much time on its hands? He decided to make light of it until he had more time to discover Mason's motives, if he could discover them.

With that decision made Mac's thought's returned to the trip that he had completed to his homeland earlier this past week. Mac received word that his father was rushed to the hospital early on the Thursday morning previous to the one just past. He quickly made arrangements for the earliest available seat on the Concorde and arrived in London's Heathrow Airport a little after six AM local time Friday morning. As the Concorde has its seats reserved for months in advance, Mac had to utilize his resources as an officer in Atlantic Corporation to get a seat on such short notice.

Thankfully Mac's friends in the corporate offices in New York checked the companies travel records and discovered a contact in one of the travel agencies that the Wellbon-Smith conglomerates utilized. This savvy individual always kept one or two seats on the Concorde reserved just in case one of his upper echelon corporate customers required rapid passage to Great Britain or Europe on short notice. This was of course a risky and expensive proposition for the individual, but he was well connected with the financial powers on "The Street" so that he was seldom stuck with a ticket. Fortunately with a sympathetic telling of Mac's emergency and a little bribery, the travel agency officer was able to secure a seat for Mac. Mac thanked God for the timing of the Concorde's schedule and for friends who knew how to work miracles.

After the Concord landed in London Mac traveled as quickly as possible to the Scottish Highland. His transportation consisted of a shuttle plane and a car that his father's chauffeur had waiting for him at the local airport. Mac made it to the hospital before his father died of coronary arrest, but unfortunately the old man had already fallen into a deep coma. Mac was unable to do anything except sit by his bedside caressing his hand until he passed away. Mac remained with him through the day and into the long night listening to his father's labored breathing. Failing to convince him to go out to the cafeteria and get some nourishment or to take a break the hospital attendants eventually brought him some food and a blanket as he began to nod off during the early morning hours.

At around two-thirty A.M. the commotion of the doctor and nurses gathering around his father awakened Mac. For the past seven months Mac's father had been suffering from a rare incurable blood disease. Mac had trouble even pronouncing the name. It remained a mystery as to what caused it. While incurable, it was possible with drugs to sometimes beat it into remission for months or even years. Sean MacLode had put up a valiant fight, but in the end the inevitable had overtaken him.

Several months ago the elder MacLode in concurrence with his son, had laid out the conditions for his death. He had no desire to become "a living corpse" as he referred to the condition of life sustained by machines and not the brain. Therefore he gave strict instructions to his doctors that when his blood oxygen content slipped below eighty-eight percent for more than 20 minutes, the point at which brain damage was likely to occur, they were not to take extraordinary means to prolong his life. When this condition presented itself, Mac and the caregivers watched as his father slipped peacefully into eternity.

In spite of the great distance that separated them, Mac and his father had been close. As a boy his father had spent considerable time with him on the family landholdings teaching him to hunt and fish. In addition his father helped hone his skills on the links so that Mac could hold his own on the golf course with any business associate or client. If the truth were known Mac could best nearly all of the competitors that he invited to a round. In addition to the formidable skill sets his father had armed him, he also instructed the young lad in the wisdom of knowing when it was far wiser to lose a round than it was to win. Mac was talented enough that no one ever suspected him of losing on purpose.

Mac's father, while visiting his son in the United States several years earlier, had the opportunity to join him on the links with one of his son's dealers. After observing a nip and tuck match through seventeen holes, the old man witnessed his son skillfully miss a putt on the final green to lose the match and one hundred dollars to the rather mediocre talents of the customer. After the winner had departed, Mac and his father hoisted a pint in the clubhouse bar and discussed the day. The old man upon hearing his son explain that winning the match and the "C note" would guarantee that the dealer would exceed his sales quotas for at least the next year had but one comment. "Aye it makes me proud laddie that I raised a duffer that is even more skilled at losing than he is at winning!"

To Catch a Fox

Even though an ocean had separated them Mac and his father were in regular contact on the phone. Initially, while Mac was attending college, Sean MacLode had trouble remembering the five-hour time difference. Mac could easily be the recipient of a phone call at four in the morning with his father greeting him: "Nine o'clock in the mornin' an yer not up yet?" Eventually, being an intelligent and well-read man, Sean made the connection and they began scheduling their conversations for hours that worked for the both of them. "I know about the blasted time zones," he exclaimed! "It's just that when I want to talk to my son, I want to talk to him now!" Their relationship became even closer after the death of Mac's mother four years ago. The old man never really got over it. The two had been together "through thick and thin" as Sean described it for just over fifty-one years.

Sean MacLode, like most people who work away from home, felt guilty for the extended periods of time that he had been away from his family as a member of the House of Commons. Sean was a member of the Conservative Party. He lived in what was considered a safe seat for the Tories and he served for many years representing his constituents. Try as they did, the Laborites could never unseat the elder MacLode. Sean not only bore the favored politics of his district, but he was a popular gentleman who always took time to listen to the people's problems. He listened even when the problems were a tad on the silly side or when serious, there was little else that Sean could do. All of this conspired to keep returning Sean to office. It mattered not if the Prime Minister felt secure that his party would be returned to power and requested Her Royal Highness to dissolve Parliament, or the Opposition was able to muster a vote of "no confidence" and force a general election, Sean survived. Whether the Tories were ruling the country or were out of power and playing the Opposition role, Sean MacLode maintained his seat and even increased his margin.

While the House of Commons was in session he would only make it home from Westminster in London on the weekends. Sometimes he stayed over depending on the issues and the backlog of legislation. Never wishing to play a central role in either the government or the "shadow government of the Opposition", Shawn was content to reside on the backbench for his entire career. From there he served his friends and neighbors well. After the death of his wife it seemed that Sean's lust for politics diminished and he soon resigned his seat.

As Mac was an only child, both father and son used their relationship as a link to mother and wife. When they were talking on the phone or were together during the now more frequent visits, they would always get around to sharing their memories of her and for that brief period of time neither missed Emily MacLode nearly as much. Now Mac would have to learn to live without them both.

After Mac had attended to the hospital paper work he and his father's chauffeur drove the car out into the country to his father's only surviving sister's house. Sean's long time chauffeur had long since ceased to be an employee and was considered by all as one of the family. He was standing vigil in the room with Mac at the time of the elder MacLode's death. The poor man was so overcome with grief that Mac felt it would be better if he drove. When they arrived at Mac's Aunt's picturesque country cottage, Mac dreaded going in. This had been his favorite Aunt over the years and she had always been close to his father and mother. Now he would see her for the first time in months and had the task of giving her the sad news.

Ian, the chauffeur remained in the car. Mac thought that best as the little man had finally regained his composure and Mac feared that if his Aunt broke down it would only pull Ian down with her. Mac knocked gently at the door. The drive out to the country had taken the best part of an hour and so the first light of a gray dawn was now creeping across the meadows and hills. Mac shivered, was it cool or was it just the circumstances? He raised his hand to knock again when the door opened and his Aunt Anna MacGregor stood before him.

"Aye mornin' to you William MacLode," she muttered. "Forgive me. Me heart's usually filled with joy to lay eyes on me wayward an only nephew, but I fear it's sad news ya bear this visit. Come in! There's tea an scones on the stove if you've a hunger."

"What are you doing up so early love?" asked Mac gently.

"I've not been able to sleep well since yer Daddy went to the hospital lad." She led him down the hall to the kitchen. "Sit down!" she ordered and bustled about fixing two cups of tea. Mac watched her in the dim light. The combination of the early hour and the small divided light windows keep the room dark. Being frugal Anna wasn't about to waste electricity once the new day had dawned. Mac knew that the act of preparing the tea prolonged having to hear the news that she knew he bore.

To Catch a Fox

The steaming tea was poured in their cups, the pot returned to the wood burning stove that his Aunt refused to part with and she finally settled in a chair across the table from him. “Well?” she nearly demanded.

“Dad died at about two-thirty this morning,” he said softly.

“Did he though?” her voice was low and sad. She suddenly appeared older than she did just a few moments before. Her normally square shoulders seemed to sag. For the first time she looked old to Mac. He suddenly realized that she had never appeared old to him before. She always seemed to be somewhere in a nether state. Neither was she young or old. Age seemed to be irrelevant when it came to his Aunt. She was simply Aunt Anna MacGregor, his spunky, feisty; don’t cross her path, widowed aunt. Suddenly he felt silly. She was two years older than his father was and his father had just turned eighty-one three days ago. Of course she was old. He wondered if this woman that he loved and admired so much could muster the strength to overcome the death of the sibling that she was so close to.

After a long moment she seemed to come back from wherever her mind had transported her upon receiving the news. “Ya know laddie, I’ve now out lived three brothers, yer mom my sister-in-law, and a husband. I loved them all. Two o’ ma brothers were lost in the war with that bastard Hitler. Lost in His Majesty’s service they were. My husband was wounded in that war, but he came home to live a few years more before the after affects of the wound took him. Then a few years ago your mom passed on and now, now yer dad. Tis’ hard to believe, I’m all alone now.” She took a sip of her tea. “Yer dad was the only one to come back from the fightin’ without a scratch. He always was lucky.” She paused in thought and her eyes seemed to be seeing more than the rustic old kitchen that hadn’t seen change in at least a hundred years. Then she was back. “Yer Daddy saw some terrible fightin’ too, terrible, terrible…” she bowed her head as she shook it slowly back and forth almost in disbelief at the horror she knew that her brother had seen. “He was wit em durin’ the Great Invasion at Normandy. Aye…he was. ‘D’ Day the Yanks called it. The Scots, the Brits, the Yanks, didnta matter who they were on tha day, they all got cut to pieces. ‘Cept yer daddy…cept yer daddy. Aye he was the lucky one he was.” Her voice trailed off and she appeared lost in her memories again. “Tis all the foolish ramblins of a old woman it tis. Yer knowin yer daddy’s histry wells me…wells me.”

Mac sipped his tea not knowing what to say. His aunt seemed oblivious to him for the moment. “Will you help me with the arrangements auntie?”

"Wha? Oh…oh sure. Yer daddy was always good ta me. Sure, it's the least I can do. You'll want the Vicar to do the service in the chapel I imagine?"

"Of course, Dad wouldn't have it any other way. The family has been buried at the chapel for centuries, except for those black sheep that the presiding head of the clan wouldn't allow." This brought a smile to Anna's face.

"An a lot o them there were!" laughed the old woman. "We've been a rowdy clan over the years ain't we?" Her face broke into a broad smile revealing surprisingly strong healthy teeth.

"If you and the Vicar would put the service together, I'll attend to the other arrangements. I'll meet with the funeral director later this morning."

"I'll ring up the Vicar after it's light a bit." She sipped more tea. "Yer daddy was some man, some man indeed William. Servin' the people all those years in Commons. Never servin' for himself. He never sought a seat in a "sittin" govement. No sir! He was there for the people! An they knew it too! That's why they kept sendin' him back it was! Ya can be proud of 'im William. Proud indeed."

"I am proud of him auntie. I always have been." Mac felt his eyes become moist and he choked back the tears. Suddenly he realized that it wasn't important that he know what to say it was only important that he was here for her. It was important that they were there for each other.

Ian's voice called from the hall. "Canna come in mam?" Mac realized that it was a mistake asking Ian to wait in the car. He needed to be a part of the family grieving too.

"Is that you Ian? O course ya can. We're owt in the kitchen." Aunt Anna rose and busied herself with another cup of tea. Ian entered and sat down at the table. With Anna's back turned toward them, Ian gave Mac a quizzical glance. Mac simply nodded his head to let Ian know that for the time being at least, Anna was doing okay.

When Anna had served Ian she sat down with the two men. "Anna," began Mac. "Will you consider moving over to Duncan Hall. It's what dad would have wanted you know. I'll need both you and Ian there to look after it for me when I'm back in the States. Over there you have dad's household staff to help you. Here in this cottage, you have to do everything yourself."

"I moved owt o the castle when I married my Tommy I did. I danna hav no reason ta move back now."

The castle was just that. Duncan Hall was an old fortress overlooking a beautiful lake. It had been in the family for centuries. Mac's father inherited it upon the death of his two older brothers. Mac grew up in it and loved it dearly. In recent years his father and mother had turned it into a rather oversized bed and breakfast, as the Yanks would call it, so that they could offset the cost of the taxes and pay the fairly large staff it required to maintain it. "It's good she's built solid," Sean would say. "'Cause she's a break even proposition at best wit owl a lot o major repairs." Somehow they managed to keep it. Mac knew in advance the contents of his father's will. He knew that his father had left the entire estate to him and like generations before him, he would find a way to keep it in the family. Of course, being an only child, that meant that Mac would have to form a family so that there would be a MacLode to leave it to.

The chapel that Aunt Anna had referred to was within the castle's eight-foot thick stone walls. Generations of MacLodes had been christened, confirmed in the faith, communed, married and finally buried in the small ancient cemetery within the courtyard.

Mac wasn't going to push the issue just now with his aunt. "Just consider it. For me, love," he added.

She looked him straight in the eye with one of her hard glassy stares. Then her eyes softened and became moist. "Yer daddy would be sayin' the same. 'Tis the truth ya speak William MacLode. For you laddie I'll consider it."

After sitting with the old woman long enough to determine that she would be all right, Mac and Ian prepared to take their leave. Aunt Anna delayed them until she phoned the Vicar. Upon being informed about Mac's father the Vicar promised that he would come over to the cottage within the hour. After some warm embraces and a few tears Mac and Ian got into their car. Ian insisted on driving Mac to the castle, and having convinced Mac that he was okay, Mac allowed it.

To Catch a Fox

The next several days saw Mac tending to all the arrangements; picking a casket, reviewing the service with the Vicar and his aunt, putting relatives and family friends arriving for the services up at Duncan Hall and a million other details that you never think about until you have to do them. He was grateful for the help of the local funeral director who also happened to be a lifelong family friend.

His mood was a strange combination of grief for the loss of his father, enduring grief for his mother and joy at seeing distant clan members and friends. He hadn't seen some in months and others for years. Then there was the service in the ancient chapel.

The day broke clear and found Mac roaming aimlessly through Duncan Hall in a tee shirt, jeans and bare feet. His feet were cold as he walked over the combinations of ancient stone and wood, but he barely noticed. He was lost in his memories. He strolled slowly through the great banquet hall where his father and mother had held countless parties for friends, relatives, and the local political powers. He fondly remembered the Christmas Eve parties that they threw for the house staff and their families. The parties, whatever the occasion, seemed always to involve plenty of food, spirits and singing. He spent some time in his father's study. Books, papers, ledgers and files lay strewn where the elder MacLode had left them before entering the hospitable. Mac knew that he must go through them, but he couldn't bring himself to tackle that task just now. He knew that neither Ian or any of the household staff would presume to do it and that meant that if he didn't force himself this trip, the chore would be waiting for him his next time home.

He reflected on the amount of time that it could take to settle his father's estate. While he knew that the will was relatively simple and that he was the executor and essentially the only heir, the distance involved and the demands of Fox Cabinetry back in the states would complicate matters immensely.

Mac continued roaming through the ancient halls and his personal history, his mood melancholy at times and grief stricken at others. Ordinary sights sounds and even smells seemed to evoke an endless stream of memories. Finally Ian found him out on one of the parapets and coaxed him inside to join he and the cook for morning tea in the kitchen. It was summer and Duncan Hall had its share of tourists in residence, but the household staff had done an admirable job of keeping them separate from Mac and the family while not impeding their customer's vacations. Mac was grateful for the tea and company of two people that he had known all of his life. Two people that understood and shared in his sorrow. The three lingered over the tea and shared memories. Mac was normally a very private and nearly introverted person when it came to his emotions and affairs, but he began to understand the need to share times such as this no matter how painful it may be. In fact he found that talking with “Cookie” and Ian actually buoyed his spirits and prepared him for the day ahead. “Cookie” Thomas-Smyth was originally hired as a combination nanny and cook by his parents after Mac’s birth. Mac’s father had discovered her in London and convinced her to move to the “provinces” as she termed it. “Cookie,” Mac now wondered if he had ever heard her actual first name, was a short slightly overweight gregarious person. Nothing, not even the death of her beloved employer of all these years could keep her spirit down for long. Even on this solemn morning Mac and Ian found themselves laughing with her as she recanted fond tales of Mac’s father. When he outgrew the need for a nanny his parents kept “Cookie” on the staff because, like Ian, she had become one of the family. Besides Mac’s mother was a terrible cook and the elder MacLode had no intention of returning to a “continual state of heart burn,” as he termed it.

Ian not only was the chauffeur for the family, but he also oversaw the operation of the house. The entire staff reported to him. Mac knew that at the reading of his father’s will, Ian would discover that the old man had generously remembered not only Ian, but also Mac’s Aunt Anna and the entire household staff. Mac received everything else. Duncan Hall and the substantial acreage that went with it along with whatever other assets Sean MacLode had accumulated. Mac had no idea how much this amounted to and really didn’t care. He had been successful in his own right. He imagined that outside of the landholdings that had been in the family for centuries it was a modest amount. However, he had been mildly surprised when his father told him the contents and terms of the will that the old man could give so much to Aunt Anna and his loyal staff. No matter, Mac was only interested in Duncan Hall. It was likely that the old castle would be more of a burden than a benefit but in the end it was his home and he loved it.

At ten AM the clan processed from the main hall across the courtyard to the small stone chapel on the south wall. With all the family, friends and political associates that had come to pay their last respects all but the family and closest of friends had to stand outside. The funeral director, anticipating Sean’s popularity, had a temporary public address system installed in the courtyard so that all could hear the service. Fortunately the weather remained clear and slightly cool for the season.

To Catch a Fox

As the Vicar delivered a very uplifting service that was more in celebration of Sean MacLode's life than it was a memorial service, Mac felt his spirits rise. The Vicar and Aunt Anna had put together exactly the type of service that Sean MacLode would have wanted, full of fond memories and most of all hope. There were no eulogies. Mac's father had strongly insisted before his death that there would be "no such foolishness at his funeral!" The elder MacLode often remarked on the grand eulogies that he had been forced to listen to even at some scoundrel's passing. He vowed that no one would have to lie or stretch the truth at his. He was content for all to keep their own memories of him. He desired that at least in the sanctity of their own minds they would truly remember him as he was.

At the close of the service everyone filed out behind the casket to the ancient cemetery in the rear of the chapel. The late morning sun shown brightly as the pallbearers placed the casket over the grave site. The crowd gathered around as closely as they could. Mac, Aunt Anna, Ian and "Cookie" sat in the folding chairs provided in the front row. The Vicar committed Sean MacLode's body to eternity and after a prayer stepped back. As Sean had served in the army during World War II a flag was draped over the casket. The local veterans group had provided an honor guard. After a six gun salute echoed over the hills the honor guard crisply folded the Union Jack and presented it to Mac. It was at this point that Mac's emotions finally welled forth and he cried.

At the close of the service the crowd retired to the banquet hall where the household staff had prepared a huge buffet lunch for all the visitors paying their respects. Mac spent the afternoon moving about the gathering, listening to stories about his father and mother. Some he knew by heart while others he was hearing for the first time. All present desired to speak a few words to the new master of Duncan Hall. The mourners stayed far longer than anyone expected and at four PM when Mac walked with the last group to the front door, he was exhausted.

Cookie realized that he had not partaken of the lunch himself and she had prepared a plate for him in the kitchen. To his surprise Mac found that he was starved and gratefully devoured the mini-feast, after which he joined Ian in the library for a brandy and then climbed the open staircase to his private bedchamber. He collapsed into bed and slept the best he had since his arrival. No one woke him the following morning and he discovered that it was ten o'clock when he finally rolled out of bed.

To Catch a Fox

Mac had to return to the States as soon as possible. He saw his relatives off the next day and then instructed his father's lawyer to begin the legal proceedings to probate the will. The lawyer felt that they should meet personally as Mac was speaking to him on the phone. "Is there a problem?" asked Mac.

"No, none at all, it's just that I will need some instruction. You will have some decisions to make. There are a lot of things to attend to."

"We're not insolvent are we?" asked Mac.

"Heavens no!" came the reply. "I just don't like doing these things without you."

"Well you get things started and I will return as soon as I can. I must get back to the States."

"I'll see you in a fortnight then?"

"Twice that long, but I promise no longer." That seemed to satisfy his lawyer, so Mac hung up and proceeded to make flight arrangements. This time he had to travel more conventionally. He dreaded the long sub sonic flight back across the Atlantic. Even the Concorde took approximately three hours and forty minutes and conventional planes much longer. But with no connections on this side he would have to travel as the masses did. At least he would give himself the luxury of a first class seat. That would be uncomfortable enough during the long flight. Ian drove him to the local airport and with mixed emotions Mac gave him a fond good bye and left Duncan Hall in his charge.

Mac's thoughts returned to the present. He was surprised to be approaching Goodville. Shocking he thought how you can be lost in thought and your mind drives a car on "automatic pilot" over roads that you are familiar. As he drove into town he turned on his right turn signal and swept the classic T-Bird into his parking spot in front of the office. He checked his watch, eight fifty-five, perfect he thought. He had called the meeting for nine AM. He was not looking forward to this morning's session. As he got out he noticed a strange car in the lot. He believed it to be a 1989 Trans Am GTA. It seemed to be in good condition. Not a classic in the vein of his T-Bird, but worth preserving. He wondered to whom it belonged.

To Catch a Fox

CHAPTER 5

The rear deck looked out over the five acres that made up Trevor Mason's Connecticut estate. The five wooded acres were meticulously manicured by a contract gardener who at this moment was making his rounds on a red tractor pulling a gang mower. The large expansive deck was attached to an equally large colonial "salt box" style white clapboard home. While the style terminology was correct it certainly seemed incongruous to a home of this size to refer to it as a "salt box." Trevor's maid had just cleared the breakfast dishes away from the large trestle table at the corner of the deck. Trevor's wife Julia enjoyed the quiet Saturday morning breakfasts on the deck. It was one of the few times that she could force Trevor to take his mind off business. This morning however was an exception. Julia finished her coffee and turned to the rather unpleasant little man who was their breakfast guest. "I know that you and Trevor have business to discuss so I will excuse myself and allow you to do so. It was a pleasure meeting you Mr. Rueben." Julia lied and extended her hand.

Abraham Rueben accepted her hand but did not rise to his feet. This did not surprise Julia. "The pleasure was all mine," was his return. To Julia it sounded automatic and not at all sincere. She was glad to escape the deck this morning. Rueben had impatiently devoured his breakfast while hardly speaking a word. Indeed he barely acknowledged Julia's attempts at small talk. At one point she caught Trevor's eye and gave him a sharp questioning glance. Trevor simply winked at her while Rueben had his face bent close to his plate of eggs Benedict, the better to shovel it into his mouth Julia suspected.

Julia retired to the large book lined study that she and Trevor shared. Whatever the reason Trevor felt he must do business with this individual was not sufficient for her to feel any obligation to make him a friend of the family. Julia returned to the task of planning a large dinner party that she and Trevor were hosting two weeks from this day.

The maid refilled the men's coffee cups. Trevor stared out over his property and took in the warm June morning sun. The weather had cleared just in time for the weekend. Trevor decided that he would play a round of golf later this morning, as soon as he dispensed with the business at hand.

Rueben was the first to speak. "I have concerns about Denton," he began.

"Don't! Allow me to handle Denton. He really has no choice and he is far too intelligent not to understand that fact."

Rueben took a sip of the steaming hot coffee. "Forgive me, but you seem to be the only one that holds that view of Denton's IQ."

"That's because I'm the only one who has ever taken the time to learn to know him. All the others simply wrote him off. I on the other hand refuse to write off someone who owns that much stock in a company that I plan to take over." Trevor was watching the Gardner disappear into the woods, his aging tractor puffing white smoke as he gave it gas and shifted to a higher gear.

"You're running this show Trevor. I will abide by your judgment. Do you wish me to wait until you receive Denton's answer before making any contacts?"

"Absolutely not, you begin immediately as soon as you return to your office this morning." Trevor reached into his shirt pocket and extracted a piece of folded tablet paper. "Here is the list of the first to contact. These are people that we do not require Denton's help with. I have already supplied you with detailed files concerning all of these names. I expect a report from you as to the outcome of these conversations by Monday afternoon."

Rueben looked over the list. There were only four names on it and he was familiar with the contents of the files. All lived within a fifty mile radius of New York City, so allowing that they were not out of town for the week end, it should be easy to contact them. "I don't expect any of these to be a problem. I'll be in contact with you by four o'clock on Monday afternoon. How would you like me to make contact?"

"Use my cell phone number and the code that we discussed. Never refer to any of the targets by name or to any details of the plan over the phone." Trevor stood up and opened the brief case that he had placed on an unused deck chair when they first came outside. He removed a large brown envelope. "This should cover your initial expenses," he stated as he laid the envelope in front of Ruben. "Your final payment will be in stock as per our agreement." Abraham Rueben opened the envelope and counted the very large bills that were stuffed into it.

"This will do nicely," he smiled. "As per our agreement the final and largest payment will be in Wellbon-Smith shares at the completion of the takeover." Rueben rose and shook Trevor's hand. Even though he had not finished his second cup of coffee he knew from previous experience that their business was completed. Trevor did not spend an excessive amount of time indulging in useless conversation. "I'll find my way out Trevor, and thank you for breakfast."

Trevor watched the small man leave without comment. It was not difficult to find greedy lawyers who had no aversion to bending their ethical standards, but it was difficult to find one who was also skilled at not getting caught in the process. Rueben had lodged no protest when Trevor had suggested that he come out to the house on Saturday morning. For the amount of money in the envelope the short time spent at Trevor's home in relation to the trip was well worth his while. Soon he heard the sound of Rueben's car leaving the driveway. Trevor smiled to himself. Finally it has begun he thought. With that he picked up his cell phone and called his country club for a tee time.

***

It was one thirty Saturday afternoon. Everyone was tired and ready to go home. Tony Conocenti looked up from the pile of papers and notes in front of him and stared at his boss. Mac, as always, appeared as fresh as he had at the start of the meeting. At this moment he was reviewing the individual assignments that either each member of his staff had volunteered for or he had assigned. He appeared lost in thought and oblivious to the hour. Tony looked around the conference table. Dale Hershey was checking over some obscure numbers on a massive computer spread sheet with his calculator. David Elliott, V. P. of Service and Transportation looked bored as he stared out through the second floor window at the beautiful day that was going to waste.

David was in his fifties with salt and pepper hair. He was tall; a very big man who weighed far in excess of two hundred pounds, but who carried it well. Tony mused that if he lost any weight he would probably look emaciated. He was a paragon of patience with a deep soothing voice. He had to be because it was his job to make all the unhappy customers and dealers happy when something didn't quite live up to the Fox reputation. Dave and his staff did an excellent job of fulfilling this task. Tony wondered if he would have the patience to remain in good humor as Dave did after listening to complaints day after day and wrestling with the problems. He suspected that he would not.

Dennis Morton was nodding off. Sarah Frazer the new member of their team was taking in everything. Tony caught her grinning at Dennis. Carroll Brubaker sat to Tony's immediate left. He normally had a comment on every subject, but today Tony thought him unusually quiet. Tony poked Carroll with his elbow. "Smile Mr. Brubaker," he said. Carroll looked at him with a start, and then he smiled.

"Sorry Tony, I was lost in thought," he replied.

"I'm amazed that anyone can still claim to be able to complete that exercise," responded Tony. Carroll smiled his answer and glanced at the boss, Mac was still studying the assignments and the time line that they had worked out.

Tony turned to Mac. "It was bad enough that you called Carroll and me home early before we could finish our assignments, but it's even worse that you've kept us here well after lunch time on Saturday boss." Tony's voice was tired but more playful than the words implied. As an afterthought he added: "There's golf to be played man!"

Mac looked up from his papers, a faint grin on his face. "I'm sorry did you say something Tony?"

"You know damn well what I said. It's time to get the hell out of here!"

"I suppose it is if you're a quitter and you really insist," responded Mac. The grin grew larger.

"Mac it's only the fact that we have a lady present that is keeping me from recommending a particular course of action that you should personally take at this moment," replied Tony.

Sarah looked directly at Tony and with a heavy Scottish brogue that, up until now, they had not heard said; "Dona let me stop ya, if you wana to tell im to 'go pound sand' you go right ahead laddie." The men burst out laughing, taken totally by surprise. All morning they had been strictly business. Sarah suspected that her presence was keeping them on their best behavior and she knew that if she was ever to be considered one of the "boys," this was the first obstacle she had to cross.

With a brogue equally alien to the five other men seated at the table Mac replied. “Aye lass, ya use the lang age of a highlander ya do. Ma dear departed mum couldnta said it any better. Tis thata where ya hail from?”

“Nei, um a city dweller aye um lad. Ba I cum from the docks ya see, so um well versed in all the variations o the king’s English I um.”

Dennis Morton looked confused. The laughter had brought him back from his nap with a start. He looked around and then joined in although he had no idea what everyone was laughing about.

As the laughter died down, Mac with a broad smile on his face returned to his “normal” refined and very slight accent. A British accent as the locals erroneously described it. “I suppose you are correct Tony. It is time to cease and desist. I suspect it will only go downhill from here. Gentlemen…and lady,” Mac remembered at the last moment. “We stand adjourned. I want to thank you all for the tremendous amount of work that you accomplished today. We are much further along than I ever expected to be when I returned to the office the other night and read my e-mail from ‘Mace’.”

“If I may be rude and interrupt chief, just where the hell were you last week? I know that you don’t have to answer to us, but you left so suddenly and without a word that we were all worried.” Tony was perhaps the only one of the Fox vice presidents that would be quite so brazen as to speak the question that was on all of their minds. He was also the only one who could get away with it as Mac genuinely liked him and admired his moxie.

Mac paused, the smile still on his face. “It was personal, but I thank you all for your concern."

Mac continued: “If we all complete our assignments according to this schedule we should have about a week to spare. That will give us ample time to have several dress rehearsals before we make the actual presentation. In addition I want to welcome and thank the newest member of our team. Sarah, it hardly seems fair, even before your first official day we’ve conned you into volunteering for several assignments on this list. It is appreciated.”

“I’m happy to tackle it. I will require a lot of help from all of you, but I find that the best and quickest way for me to learn to 'swim' is for me to jump right in. I thank you for the confidence that you've shown," answered Sarah with an appreciative nod in Mac's direction.

"Anything else? If not…" Mac began to gather up his papers.

"Well yes, there is something else that you all should know," said Carroll. His voice contained a serious edge that no one could miss. The sound of the shuffling papers and the chairs being pushed back came to a halt. Sarah looked about. By the expressions on everyone's face she realized that something was up. She also observed that when this man who had been relatively quiet all morning spoke, everyone else listened. She discovered earlier from Dennis Morton that Carroll Brubaker was the staff member with the longest tenure. He had earned a lot of respect from the others over the years. Even from the boss.

"What is it Carroll?" asked Mac. In all the years that Mac had known Carroll he tended to take things in stride and was normally the master of understatement. The tone of his voice now foretold something serious.

"You all know that I was out in Vegas this past week. Trying to understand why we missed our production forecast at that facility by such a wide margin last year. Well in private conversations with our plant manager Tom Erving I might have discovered the reason." Carroll paused as if he did not wish to speak the next words.

"Go on Carroll," urged Mac.

Carroll took a deep breath. "Tom thinks that there's a union trying to get in the door."

To Catch a Fox

CHAPTER 6

John Malicki entered the Hubbard Street Grill in downtown Chicago. Normally he was happy to be here. When in Chicago he liked to entertain clients in this restaurant. It was located barely a block away from the Merchandise Mart and it had an excellent luncheon and dinner menu. In addition it was a sort of casual festive place that was just noisy enough to insure that the table next to you could not eavesdrop on your conversation while not forcing you to yell to be understood at your own table. John waited near the hostess' station for someone to acknowledge his presence. When the perky young lady arrived he explained that he had a table reserved for five o'clock, but he was about a half an hour early. After checking his name in her book she queried: "That's for a party of three?"

"That's correct, but I imagine that my guests haven't arrived as of yet," answered John attempting to survey the rather dark dining room.

"No one has asked for a table under your name. Would you like to wait at the bar until your guests arrive?"

"Yes that will be fine. Will you come get me at five o'clock even if they have not yet arrived?"

"Certainly sir," with that she was on to the party that had just entered the door behind John.

John walked up the four steps that took him to the bar level. It was a huge oval shaped bar that allowed seating the entire circumference while the bartenders operated inside. John positioned himself so that he could see the hostess desk and look down into the dining room without turning around to do so. There was only a half partition with planters that separated the bar from the dining room. The bartender approached, "What can I get for you sir?"

John wanted a Canadian Club on the rocks but he thought better of it. Whatever

To Catch a Fox

Glenn Glen and his partner wanted to talk to him about on a Saturday night he had better keep a clear head. He decided to go easy but indulge himself a bit. After all it had been a hard week and he was staying in the Holiday Inn at the Mart tonight rather than attempt to drive back home to Wisconsin. "Give me a white Zinfandel."
"Coming right up sir."

John reached into his inside breast pocket and extracted a pack of cigarettes. He selected one and lit it up with a disposable lighter that he located in another pocket after rummaging about. He couldn't believe that he was back in Chicago. He had left Friday at noon to miss the horrendous traffic that would begin spilling out into the suburbs after three o'clock. Driving had been pleasant and he was actually looking forward to working in his lawn Saturday morning. John made excellent time and the trip home to Wisconsin had only taken three and one half-hours. He and his wife had planned to go out for dinner that evening. As a "road warrior" his wife accused him of getting to eat out all the time while she came home every evening from her elementary teaching job and cooked her own dinner over the stove. John didn't have the heart to tell her that by Friday evening he was ready to be home and share some of her excellent cooking. However, Ellen had been his "girl" as he called her for the last twenty-seven years and he enjoyed making her happy. When he returned home Friday after a week of travel it had become their custom to partake of dinner at different neighborhood restaurants. This Friday was no exception.

As it turned out they had an exceptional meal and both were in good spirits. Ellen had experienced a satisfactory week with the "school kids" as she called them and John felt good about having helped his boss Tony "nail down" the Mart lease. In addition they finally got Glenn's signature on a dealership agreement. This was a major accomplishment. With a Fox Flagship Showroom coming on line in the Chicago Merchandise Mart, John's income and bonus should be greatly enhanced in the next year or two. With their own children now out of college and married, John was concentrating all of his financial efforts on their retirement funds. This Chicago Flag couldn't come at a better time. John and Ellen decided to celebrate.

It developed into the perfect evening until they arrived home and the message light was blinking on the telephone. John had switched his cell phone off during his time with Ellen. This was a rule that John never violated. Ellen had set it shortly after John had acquired the "infernal" device as she called it. John debated the wisdom of taking the message tonight, but was afraid that one of the "kids" may have an emergency. He reluctantly pressed the button marked "play."

John groaned: the message was from Glenn Glen. He was having another anxiety attack. His voice was almost desperate as he explained that he had to talk to John in person as soon as possible. Ellen raised her eyebrows. "I told you that we need a separate business line. That way you would know if it was a family emergency or just business." She shook her head and went to the kitchen to make them coffee. He knew that she was right and he cursed himself for not taking the time to have a separate line run in. John picked up the phone, hit Glenn's auto dial code and called him immediately. It rang several times and for a brief moment John thought that he might get away with just leaving a message on the answering machine. Then Glenn answered.

"This is John. What's up Glenn?"

"I've just heard something very disturbing!" was the breathless reply on the phone.

"What?"

"I don't want to talk about it on the phone!"

"I have a private line. You have a private line, tell me what you heard."

"No not over the phone, I need to talk to you in person tomorrow!"

"Tomorrow is Saturday Glenn!" Ellen heard John raise his voice even though she was in the kitchen. It was seldom that she heard John raise his voice, especially to a customer.

"I have to talk to you tomorrow. I only have three days by Illinois law to verbally retract my signature on the dealer agreement!" The voice was rising to unexpected levels.

"What do you mean retract? This is the best thing that has ever happened to you in your entire career!" Suddenly John could see the patient work that he had completed over the last six months begin to crumble before his eyes.

"Not if what I heard is true! You get right back to Chicago tomorrow and I'll meet you then! If not I will call Pennsylvania the first thing on Monday and cancel my agreement regardless!"

John gave an audible sigh. "Okay, okay, I'll meet you at five o'clock tomorrow evening in the Hubbard Street bar and grill. Will that work for you?"

"Why so late in the day?" asked Glenn. The question was asked in the closest thing to his normal voice that John had heard since making the call.

"It's Saturday. I've got to make a three and one half hour drive to get to Chicago and I thought you might permit me to sleep in just a bit tomorrow."

"Oh, well I guess that will work. I had plans for tomorrow night."

"You're going to make it work Glenn!" for the first time in his twenty plus years as a salesman he actually considered hanging up on a client. John counted silently to ten. He needed this particular individual and the deal he represented. After a pause he inquired, "So we have a date?" John made a serious though only partially successful attempt at sounding friendly with this question.

"Well. I guess, but if you could make our appointment earlier in the day it would work better for me."

It was as if he hadn't heard a word that John had just spoken. With conscious effort John replied in a very controlled voice, "No Glenn, I'm sorry, I can't make it any earlier in the day. I'll see you tomorrow at five. Good bye."

That thought John, was how he wound up driving all the way from his home in Wisconsin to Chicago on a Saturday. Making Ellen understand the necessity of the trip proved to be a challenge in itself. But in the end she was a teacher and dealing with parents understood that when people are upset or afraid they sometimes cease to be rational. She still didn't like losing her husband on Saturday.

The bartender brought him his glass of wine and an ashtray. John nodded his appreciation as he took a sip of the wine. It tasted good. His thoughts returned to the reason for the trip. Six months of work could be hanging in the balance during the upcoming conversation with Glenn Glen and his business partner

To Catch a Fox

Mark Markel.

Six months ago John Malicki made one of his twice a year futile visits to George Peterson's showroom in downtown Chicago. He made the trip on the outside chance that George would have had some disaster with his long time vendors and would be in the right mood for John to suggest a switch to Fox. It never happened, but to keep his boss Tony Concenti happy back in Pennsylvania, John made his biannual attempt. The high-end cabinetry business was almost a cottage industry. There were probably no more than one thousand people that actually ran the industry in the whole country. Those one thousand were involved with the major name brands that occupied the upper price range, semi-custom cabinets to high priced total custom. In this small environment everyone seemed to know everyone else. They also thought that they knew what everyone else was doing at any given time and most of the time they were correct. Secrets were almost impossible to keep in this business.

The major brand names barely controlled forty to forty-eight percent of what was defined as the high-end market. Some suspected the percentage was even less as the remainder was controlled by the small local cabinet shops with twenty employees or fewer. These shops came and went without leaving any trail. They certainly never contributed any statistics to the trade publications or the NKBA, National Kitchen and Bath Association. The bottom end semi-custom and stock or "box" cabinet manufacturers were small by comparison to other industries but large compared to the custom houses. These were sold by the "big box" mass retailers. But because of the much lower prices their sales volume in dollars was considerably larger than that part of the market controlled by the high-end custom manufacturers. It was however the top name national brands like Fox that gave the less expensive manufacturers some quality "rub off" to their image. Or so the custom houses would like everyone else to believe. If the truth were known, the average consumer remodeled the kitchen no more than twice in a lifetime. With this infrequency of purchase and the relatively limited size of the advertising budgets of even the largest manufacturers, no cabinet manufacturer could ever expect his name to become a household word. As cabinetry for the home, more often kitchen cabinets as opposed to cabinetry for "other rooms," was a seldom-made purchase the consumer was ignorant of respective construction and quality levels. The level of public knowledge of available product was nowhere near that of the consumer when he decided to purchase an automobile. In the expensive custom market this made the choice of a dealer to represent the product crucial. The dealer had to begin the education process with an outstanding web page on the internet. In the last year of the 20th century only a small minority were truly savvy on using the internet effectively to promote their business.

To sell product at the level of the cabinetry manufactured by Fox a dealer had to "hit the bricks." The days were long gone when a small retailer in the custom cabinetry business could afford to sit in his showroom and wait for the business to walk in the door. To be successful he must pay regular visits to architects and designers in his territory. He must listen to their problems, ask questions, and offer to help support them with their clients in any way possible. In short, he must cultivate credibility, confidence and trust in his abilities to the level where the professional designer / architect felt comfortable to recommend the dealership by name in their specifications. At this point in time the average kitchen remodel utilizing Fox cabinetry could exceed $100,000. The cabinetry alone could account for sixty percent of this cost at retail pricing. Glen and Markel were both registered professional interior designers who had independently developed loyal followings in chic professional circles. They dealt with clientele on the Gold Coast and North Shore. For John to get the two of them to form a dealership headquartered in the Merchandise Mart was a miracle indeed. He could not believe that his miracle could fall apart now.

George Peterson was the name among retailers in the Chicago market. Over the years John had developed a friendly if cordial relationship with George. It was on his last visit to George's showroom that John finally hit pay dirt. As is often the case it did not come in the manner that he had always fantasized it would. George accepted John's invitation to lunch. They went to a favored tavern close to Peterson's showroom where once again John enthusiastically made his pitch for Fox cabinetry. George as always listened politely and then proceeded to tick off the reasons why he was electing to stay with Country Quality Cabinets. He admitted, as he always did, that Fox quality was "slightly" better than Country's and the field service offered by Fox was second to none, but he liked the people at Country and had a long term relationship with them that he just couldn't bring himself to terminate. There was the rub. It was long standing policy of both Fox and Country not to enter a showroom that displayed a rival brand. Both would tolerate a dealer carrying brands that did not compete with them directly on price and quality, but neither would sit in direct competition with a rival. If George elected to carry Fox, Country Quality Cabinets would drop him like a hot potato. Fox would do the same if the situation were reversed. Barring a change in policy by the manufacturers that would allow him to carry both George would not take on the Fox line. So ended another pleasant but useless lunch.

But then something different, although seemingly innocent, happened. George Peterson had an appointment with an architect at two o'clock. As it was across town and he was running late he asked John for a favor. George had forgotten that he had some drawings in his brief case that Glenn Glen would need. He asked if John would be kind enough to stop by the showroom on his way out of the city and give them to Glenn. John agreed but thought it ironic. Fox had such poor representation in Chicago that George Peterson wasn't afraid to give the competition drawings for a job that he was bidding. He knew that Fox had no hope of stealing it.

Back at the showroom John found Glenn working in his cubicle. He gave Glenn the rolled drawings and explanation then turned to leave. Glenn caught his arm. "I'm glad I got this opportunity. I need to talk to you," he said in a low conspiratorial voice.

"Sure, what can I help you with?"

"Not here!" Glenn whispered, "Somewhere else, after work."

"Okay, how about the Hubbard Street Grill. I assume that you desire a place where your boss and co-workers don't frequent, and I've seldom if ever seen any of them there." John matched the low secretive tone.

"Good, good, tonight after work? Six o'clock?"

"I'll make the reservations. Just the two of us?" asked John.

"Yes. I'll see you then." With that Glenn returned to his computer screen.

John had not planned on staying over in Chicago that night, but he was curious to discover what Glenn Glen had in mind. He was only aware of Glenn as a top-notch designer of long tenure with George Peterson's organization. John left the building and quickly made all the arrangements outside on his cell phone. As he was not leaving Chicago today he had to call several of his appointments and reschedule. John disliked having to do this, but all were accommodating as John was a popular sales rep in his territory. John returned to his hotel room and spent the remainder of the afternoon catching up on paper work and talking on the phone.

It turned out to be more than worth it. Glenn Glen believed that George Peterson wasn't giving him enough of the credit with the clients for his "superior designs". He was "sick and tired" of George being hailed as the "Chicago design guru" at the annual Kitchen and Bath Show awards presentation. He wasn't going to stand in George's shadow any longer. It was time to let the world know who the design genius was and who wasn't. That is what led him to decide to form a partnership with fellow designer Mark Markel, and go into the kitchen cabinet business for himself. Glen wanted a competing line. He was convinced that Fox was the only line that offered a comparable product that he could do direct battle with Peterson for the Chicago market.

John was delighted. Even though he highly doubted that the loss of Glen from George's staff would force Peterson to file for protection under Chapter Eleven. It was common knowledge within the industry that George had several designers with equal talent to that of Glen on staff. A fact that John suspected Glen would vehemently dispute. He was aware that Glen accounted for a hefty percentage of Peterson's business. The loss would at least temporarily hurt Peterson's sales. In addition, Glen had a following with the design and architectural community that catered to the wealthy elite that were potential Fox customers. Competition within a dealership was a common reason for designers in the business to look elsewhere. John often characterized designers in the kitchen business as "M & M" people, mobile and mercenary.

After that evening meeting there were many more. John was introduced to Mark Markel. John had Tony Conocenti fly out to meet them both and look for the ideal location for their new showroom. All agreed on the Merchandise Mart, after which the long negotiations between the Mart and Fox began. Which of the available suites and which was the best floor for their product? The floor that the Mart wanted to put them on was not acceptable to Tony.

After many discussions, Tony personally met with one of the leaseholders on the home furnishings floor. The location Tony desired. Tony convinced the individual that he would increase his sales if he moved down two floors to the all-purpose level. This floor had sporting goods stores, camping equipment and clothing. This was where the Mart wanted to locate Fox Cabinetry because the home furnishings floor was full. Tony offered the man $10,000 cash on the spot if he would agree to sign the new lease for the space on the all purpose level, with an additional agreement to allow Fox to take over the lease on his current showroom. The man happily signed the agreements.

The Mart wasn't too pleased with Tony's style of negotiating because the lease that Fox had just taken over had provisions for the Mart to pay the expense of moving the showroom if the owner took another location within the Mart. Tony claimed that since Fox had only taken over the old lease and not purchased a new one the clause was still in force should it ever become necessary for the Fox showroom to move. This would be a very expensive proposition for the Mart as they were well aware that Fox planned on installing very elaborate totally functional displays. Eventually a compromise was reached. The Mart put a cap of $15,000 on moving expenses. This was fine by Tony, it was $15,000 dollars that he normally wouldn't have for a move.

So Tony managed to get the space he wanted, just as you got off the elevators, on the floor that he wanted. What more could Glen and Markel desire? Quite a bit more as it turned out, from this point forward there were constant negotiations concerning exactly how much money Fox would invest into the showroom either in cabinetry or cash. Fox had never before invested more than the cost of displays, the upfront money for the lease, and the guarantee for the lease if a flagship owner should default. Fox expected flagship owners to take out a small business loan to finance the remainder of the enterprise. The demand that Glen and Markel were making amounted to an interest free loan up front. Trips back and forth between Pennsylvania and Illinois became commonplace. Tony finally insisted that the $10,000 that Fox had given to the leaseholder for the space would be the total additional cash involvement. In addition, Glen and Markel would not be expected to pay this back.

The length of time that Fox claimed title and depreciation before the initial displays were fully owned by the two designers, terms for replacement of the original displays when the originals became obsolete, all required negotiating. Designs for the fully functional displays were proposed. Drawings were made and the plans rejected. For a while it seemed that Glen and Markel would never agree on any designs. Tony had the Fox staff designers developing plans based on the sales history of the Chicago territory. Glen and Markel correctly pointed out that Fox had never sold enough in "their" territory to know what sold and what did not. Finally after many discussions, many compromises by both sides and the fifteenth revision, Tony declared that enough was enough. This was the design that would be built. Surprisingly everyone went along without any dissension. Being a part of these negotiations gave John greater respect for both Glen and Tony as hardnosed businessmen.

This past week John was relieved when Tony finally got the final details of the lease worked out and signed. But more important, Glen and Markel finally signed their dealership agreement. John went home feeling great! Now here he was sitting in the Hubbard Street Grill little more than twenty-four hours later waiting to hear about another in what seemed an endless stream of problems. Whatever it was he would handle it and make certain that Tony and the guys in Pennsylvania never caught wind of it. For the first time John wondered if George Peterson was smiling to himself when he heard that Glenn Glen was jumping ship and going with Fox.

John saw his two guests enter the front door and climb the short flight of steps to the hostess station. He paid for his glass of wine and left a generous tip for the bartender, and then he moved resolutely to meet Glenn and Mark. He greeted them with a cheery "Good to see you"; John shook their hands not mentioning that they had just parted company yesterday after spending a marathon week in meetings. The response was subdued and serious. John ignored their demeanor as he had become accustomed to the grave face that they placed on every problem. The hostess took them to their table.

Silence basically ruled as drink orders were taken, the menus studied and dinner selections placed. The waiter disappeared. John sipped on his second glass of wine for the evening. He allowed the tension to build. Glenn and Mark avoided making eye contact with him, as they each appeared to be more interested in other events around the room. When they were struck by one of these anxiety attacks the impression that they always left was one of 'we know that you are trying to screw us.' John was becoming all too familiar with this routine and he wondered if they really believed it or if this was just a negotiating ploy. If it was a ploy it was wearing thin.

"What's the problem guys, what have you heard?"

"Don't feign ignorance with us John," as always it was Glenn who replied. Mark took the passive role and followed Glenn's lead. John knew that Mark had opinions and was very smart. He was always mystified at his silence.

"I'm not feigning anything as you put it. What is the problem?" He resisted the temptation to add 'this time.'

"You know very well what the problem is John." Glenn was almost sulking.

John Malicki breathed a big sigh and fumbled for another cigarette. He took his time in lighting it. After a long drag he decided to take a mild gamble. He was tired of the dramatic games. John was a large man, slightly overweight with balding reddish hair and a neatly trimmed beard that was more gray than red. His face was open and friendly; the face of a loving grandfather, which he was. One of the elements of his personality that made him a successful salesman was the fact that he was extremely slow to anger. But at this moment he was getting very angry.

"I'm not playing twenty questions, guys. I don't know what you are talking about. I don't like traveling all this distance on a Saturday to talk to you and then have you play silly games. If you don't answer my question immediately and politely, not only am I outta' here right now, but you can pick up the tab and on Monday I'll call Tony Conocenti personally and inform him that you are no longer our Chicago dealer."

"Well…well…I've never been treated so rudely!" sputtered Glenn.

"Neither have I retorted John, except by you two! I'm leaving! You're not worth the mental anguish!" He pushed back his chair and rose to leave.

"Wait John, we really need to talk." Glenn placed his hand firmly on Malicki's arm.

John glared down at him as he slowly settled back into the chair. "Then talk. Let's really talk. No dramatics, no insults, just plain simple talk with no hidden meanings or agendas; talk that's clear and to the point; talk between equal partners, what is your problem?"

Glenn released John's arm and looked nervously at Mark and then around the room, as if he thought that everyone in the building was eavesdropping on this conversation. Typically Mark remained passive. After completing his "security check" Glenn leaned his face in close to John's. "We've heard that Fox Cabinetry is for sale," he nearly whispered.

John was taken aback. If you would have asked him just five minutes before to speculate on what the reason for their concern would be this would not even have entered his mind. He didn't know whether to laugh or not. "Where did you hear this?"

"That's not important, is it true or not?"

"Of course it's not true, now where did you hear this?"

"We think it is true. Our source is impeccable."

"No games! Where did you hear this?"

"Promise not to tell anyone?"

"Have I ever broken a confidence with you?" was Malicki's retort.

Glenn and Mark looked at each other as if they were seriously considering this question. When they saw the look of sheer disgust on John's face they quickly retreated from speculation. "No you haven't John."

"Damn right I haven't! Now I'm only going to ask one more time, where did you hear this?"

Glenn Glen was a small man, barely five foot four, with meticulously trimmed white hair. He possessed a fair complexion that was highlighted with freckles that seemed to stand out when he was excited. At this moment they seemed more predominate than ever. Mark was of even smaller stature but was very dark in complexion with a thick shock of unruly black hair. They were both dressed, as always, in variations of the black "official" designer's "uniform." Tonight's version was black slacks and tee shirts. Glenn was wearing a black sport coat while Mark had no coat. This was so Mark could show off his sculpted biceps that he was constantly pumping iron to develop. Malicki was jealous and unconsciously sucked in his gut. Both were gay, but they were not involved with each other. Their relationship was strictly as friends, professionals and business partners. Glenn had a steady relationship that had remained constant for the last ten years. Mark had just broken off a two-year relationship and was looking for the one person that he would feel compatible with for the remainder of his days. He was weary of the dating scene. Both were in their forties.

To Catch a Fox

"My boyfriend told me," said Glenn in a quiet voice.

"How would he come by information like this?"

"He works for Bertrum and Bertrum the big investment bankers and business brokers here in Chicago."

"And…?" John felt a hollow spot in the pit of his stomach. He was becoming uneasy. He wasn't at all sure how he was going to answer this charge.

"Friday morning while we were with you and Tony signing our dealer agreement, Ronnie, he's my boyfriend, Ronnie's boss gave him the task of researching one of the Atlantic Corporation's companies. As Bertrum is involved in many aspects of investment banking and brokerage services, Ronnie asked what the purpose was for the research. Ronnie's boss said that Atlantic was considering putting the company up for sale. The company was Fox Custom Cabinetry." Glenn's voice became nearly pleading. "John, you must not, I repeat, you must not tell anyone from whom you heard this information. It would cost Ronnie his job with Bertrum. Please, please promise me."

"Of course I promise Glenn. I have no desire to hurt Ronnie."

"Is it true? Is Fox Cabinetry for sale? Have we just entered into agreement with someone who is about to be sold?"

John attempted to keep a poker face. He had no way of knowing if this tidbit of information was accurate or not. The last thing he wanted to do was feed Glenn and Mark's fears. They seemed perfectly capable of doing that on their own without any outside help. He considered his answer carefully. Glenn and Mark were now silent and peering directly at him. The waiter arrived with their appetizers. This provided a break in the tension and allowed John a little more time to consider his answer. After he took a couple thoughtful bites of his smoked salmon and capers, he answered their original quarry in as soft, as calm, and as reassuring a voice as he could muster.

"I've always been honest with you and I'm going to continue to be so. I have no knowledge of what you are saying. No one in Pennsylvania has ever, ever suggested to me that Atlantic is considering such a sale. You know that I have access to the entire senior staff in Goodville. I speak with them on a weekly basis. I travel back to the factory frequently and they come out to travel with me in my territory. No one has ever even speculated on this possibility to me."

John couldn't help noticing that the look of apprehension was still clearly visible on their faces. He pushed onward. "Let me ask you this. How often have you had to deal with or even come in contact with Fox's parent Atlantic Corporation?"

"In our short tenure with Fox that has never happened, we have always dealt with the people at Fox."

"In my much longer tenure with Fox it has never happened," was John's reply. "In fifteen years as a Regional Sales Manager for Fox, I have never had any personal dealings with or contact with Fox's holding company. So even if Fox would be sold to another holding company, what are you afraid of?"

"We're afraid that the new owners won't honor our agreement!"

"If someone is going to purchase the company they will also be purchasing all agreements too and they will be legally bound by them. I suspect that you wouldn't know the difference. Life would go on as usual. For all practical purposes the fact that Fox is owned by a holding company, no matter if the name is Atlantic or the "XYZ" corporation has little if any effect on you or your business." John sat back and finished his appetizer. All conversation ceased as Glenn and Mark thoughtfully joined him. Soon the waiter brought the salads.

Glenn was the first to speak after the waiter departed again. "But why would they put Fox in the hands of a broker? Aren't they making any money off Fox?"

John slowly began eating his salad, his now calm outward demeanor disguising the fact that his mind was racing. "Let me answer your second question first. I see the numbers at our regular quarterly sales meetings and Fox is a very profitable company. In our industry there is a very tight margin of profit as compared to others. Fox is outperforming the competition in this respect. We show a greater profit as a percentage of net sales than the industry average. The answer to your second question is much more complicated and I will have to speculate a bit. Companies use brokerage services for various reasons. First, they may really be considering selling Fox. More likely, in my humble opinion, they are looking for a source for more money to invest. By telling the brokerage house that they are considering a sale they will be assured that the firm will place the highest possible value on the company. The brokerage house would do this because they would expect to be handling the sale and they want to keep their commission as high as possible while still maintaining room to negotiate with potential buyers. With this number in hand it's possible that Atlantic may be borrowing money and using Fox and perhaps other of their companies as collateral. Remember, you asked me a month ago if Fox or its parent was traded publicly and I told you that they were privately held. Because they are they have to have some form of appraisal to determine their values."

Glenn affixed his thoughtful expression on his face as he mulled John's response over in his mind. John was familiar with the entire range of dramatic facial "props" that Glenn employed. "John, I gather that you favor the 'collateral scenario' over the 'for sale' scenario. Why is that?" asked Glenn.

"Yes I do and I'll tell you why. I only know of one other time in its history that Atlantic sold a company. That time the company in question had a performance level so bad that they felt that unloading it for whatever they could get was the only viable course of action. As I have just explained this is certainly not the same situation that we now have with Fox."

Glenn was persistent. "Could it be possible, that with Fox in such a profitable position Atlantic has decided to cash in? By that I mean they feel that they may never have the opportunity to sell at this high a price again? That this is as good as it gets?"

John shrugged. "Yes that is possible but what is their real business?" John paused and switched his gaze from Glenn to Mark and back. They looked puzzled so he proceeded to answer his own question. "They are a holding company. They buy other companies from which they expect to show better than average profits for their shareholders. When they have a company with a history of performance such as Fox has, why sell a sure thing and then turn around and purchase a company for which they have no experience? Why trade a known quantity for an unknown quantity? You know that their shareholders will not permit them to just sit on any cash that the sale of Fox would generate. If the investors desired a typical safe return on their investment they would place their money in CD's and not be exposed to risk. Their investors desire a better than average return. That's the reason they invested in Atlantic to begin with. So again I ask: Why trade a known for an unknown?"

Silence descended on the meal again. The salads were devoured and the waiter cleared the plates away. The entrees arrived. Hunger now took precedence over business concerns. All three dug into the delicious meals with gusto. John ordered a carafe of wine. As the meal progressed and more wine was ordered the mood became lighter. "Let me ask you this John," queried Glenn sounding much more relaxed than when the conversation had begun. "If Atlantic is planning to borrow more money to invest and is not planning on selling Fox, does that mean that they will invest the money in Fox?"

"Hard to say Glenn."

"But if they are using Fox as collateral…?"

"They can use Fox as collateral and invest the money in any of their other companies. More likely, they are planning to add to their empire. They may have found a start up high tech company that intrigues them. It could be that they have chosen to use Fox because they believe that it is so solid that banks will allow them to borrow more money against it than any of their other holdings. Maybe Fox isn't the only company that they are attempting to affix a value. They may have other brokerage firms around the country working on some of the others. That's the advantage of having a lot of far flung assets."

"That's interesting," mused Glenn and Mark nodded his head in solemn agreement.

The empty plates that the entrees were served on were cleared away and dessert menus were placed before the trio. Glenn and Mark ordered sumptuously fattening finales to their meals. John sadly settled for the black coffee. He had to start watching his weight. Being overweight was an occupational hazard of the corporate road salesman. Too many clients expected to be treated to an excellent lunch or dinner, combined with too many hours just sitting behind the wheel of a car. John envied the slender physique of Glenn Glen and the muscular physique of Mark Markel. Unfortunately he was aware that they both spent a lot of time exercising at the gym. A luxury that time did not afford him.

Over dessert Glenn changed the subject to the upcoming advertising campaign that would create the "big build up," as Tony Conocenti called it, to their grand opening. John was relieved that the conversation had moved away from the sale of Fox Cabinetry. He felt far more comfortable with this topic and the fact that Glenn introduced it into conversation meant that he was satisfied with John's explanation of the sale "rumor." The meal finished on a positive note with a toast to their continued partnership and success over after dinner drinks. John paid the bill and walked them to the curb. The valet service retrieved Glenn's car from a local city parking garage and John bid them goodbye. As they merged into traffic and disappeared, John pushed his hands into his trouser pockets and began the block long walk back to the Holiday Inn at the Mart. He had successfully allayed all of their fears. Now if he could only lay his own to rest.

John made a mental note to call Ralph Sinclair first thing in the morning before starting the journey home. Ralph was John's counterpart on the West Coast. Unlike John who was hired as a salesman, Ralph had been promoted to the West Coast Regional Sales Manager position three years ago after working at the factory in the Customer Service Department. Ralph had worked "on the inside" for an extended period of time and still had many friends and contacts in Pennsylvania. John and Ralph had become fast friends as Ralph had spent considerable time traveling with John in his territory. Observing John was considered on the job training before moving Ralph to the field. John was curious to know if Ralph had heard anything concerning the impending "sale." Lost in thought John Malicki returned to his hotel.

Chapter 7

Sarah Frazer lay awake in her bed staring at the ceiling. What a day it had been. She smiled to herself, as she was pleased with the outcome. She believed that she had taken a very giant first step to being accepted by the male members of the Fox management team. Taking a part in their special Saturday morning meeting before she was required to, volunteering to help with the burden of preparing their strategic plan, and even the risk of her rather crude comment to Tony concerning Mac. All seemed to take her beyond breaking the ice and work to her favor. She could hardly wait for Monday morning. Never had she anticipated a "first day on the job" as eagerly as she was anticipating this one.

In fact she could begin some of her research for her part in the strategic plan tomorrow. She would get on the Internet with her laptop and begin reading the web pages of Fox's competition and that of the NKBA to find whatever supporting information she could to back up the market share numbers that Tony wanted to include in the plan. This was going to be fun. She could hardly believe that she was about to become a corporate vice president.

Her thoughts turned to her new boss. He was not what she had imagined that he would be. The local papers focused on his status as a successful bachelor. As he seemed to have a new, usually young, female companion on his arm in every photo, she had a preconceived notion of an egotistical aging playboy. She expected Mac to be completely and totally absorbed with his own ego and attempting desperately to maintain the appearance of youth. She had prepared herself for the friction that would naturally develop between a domineering, chauvinistic male ego and a liberated woman. To her surprise her first experience of him was not at all as she imagined it would be.

Aside from opening the morning meeting and recapping the previous day's progress for those not present, Mac outlined what the group must still accomplish and turned the meeting over to them. He spent most of the session listening to his staff tackle the requests of their corporate masters and come to a consensus on how to answer those requests. He took copious notes. The entire group determined who would be responsible for which parts of the plan. Sometimes there were volunteers; sometime the group assigned a particular task to one of the members. Occasionally Mac would make comments, but only to express his opinion and open it for discussion. Never did he present his opinion as law that all others must adhere to no matter their own views. Mac's ideas were as subject to being dismantled and trashed by the staff, as were those of anyone else. A stranger coming into the room to observe and having no knowledge of the individual job titles would never have guessed that Mac was the president and CEO.

Sarah liked what she saw of the group dynamics so far. Mac seemed to be content to be the "first among equals" and at most play the role of the facilitator. The part of the experience that she appreciated the most was the air of respect that she was given when she asked questions. None of the veteran managers talked down to her. They all gave her questions their complete attention, answered them earnestly and to her surprise even asked her opinion as a newcomer on several topics. They told her that having someone present that brought no "baggage" to the table in the form of preconceived notions was extremely valuable. Only near the end of the session when Dennis Morton dozed off did her comments not receive one hundred percent of everyone's attention. But by that point Dennis wasn't listening to anyone's comments, including those belonging to Mac.

When Carroll Brubaker made his surprise comment concerning the possibility of a union getting into their plant out on the desert, the attitude of the group was not one of panic, but of concern and discussion as to what actions they could take. Why was this happening? Mac suggested that they contact Fox's lawyer and have him meet with them in private off site as early in the coming week as possible. He then suggested that with the knowledge of what they legally could and could not do, they put together a plan of action. Mac volunteered to contact the lawyer sometime during the remainder of the weekend.

Carroll Brubaker asked if it would be a good idea to fly Tom Erving in for that meeting. He could answer any questions that they may have at that time. All thought this was an excellent suggestion and Carroll volunteered to contact Tom before the day was out.

Sarah was impressed that Mac looked extremely fit, as he appeared slightly younger than the middle fifties that she knew him to be. However, he didn't seem to be making any attempt to hide his age. His close-cropped hair and neatly trimmed beard had considerable gray. There was no attempt to comb his hair in any fashion that would hide the fact that he was balding on the back of his head. His face had the lines and color of an outdoors man who had spent much time exposed to the sun and wind. His casual attire was simply the comfortable functional clothing of a man who is content with who he is and isn't attempting to make any statement. Most of all she was impressed with his quiet, almost humble demeanor and subtle self-depreciating humor. He was not at all what she imagined. Sarah was looking forward to working with her new boss and getting to know him better.

Somewhere in the midst of her analysis of the people and situations that she had encountered for the first time today, exhaustion overtook her and she drifted off to sleep.

***

Denton Wellbon III woke with a start and sat up suddenly. It was dark in the bedroom and it took him a moment to realize that he was at home and in his own bed. Susan's small body was curled next to him and she moaned softly in response to his sudden movement, but she did not awaken. Denton shuddered, his hands were shaking and his stomach seemed to be griped in cold dark panic. He took a deep breath of air and exhaled slowly. His hands stopped shaking. He felt cold but realized that he was perspiring profusely. Legs feeling weak he nonetheless pushed blankets aside and swung them out of bed. He sat on the edge of the bed and surveyed the darkness until he saw the glowing face of the digital clock on the nightstand beside the bed. It was 4:07 in the morning. His mind was groggy, what morning was this? After some consideration, he determined that it was Sunday morning. His stomach felt better, and the feeling of panic was subsiding, but it was being replaced with a sense of uneasiness that he couldn't explain. Suddenly his bladder felt full. He slowly rose from the bed and on wobbly legs found his way to the master bathroom just off the bedroom. There, after closing the door so as not to disturb Susan, he turned on the light. The sudden glare nearly blinded him. As his eyes adjusted to the light he found the commode and relief, after which he toweled off the perspiration.

Turning off the light he returned to the bedroom, but now he felt awake so he stumbled to the door and went out into the hallway. There were soft lights embedded into the paneling that lined the stairway where the spiral staircase circled down into the main floor of the co-op. These provided enough light for Denton to make it downstairs without ever being in any serious danger of falling. He padded across the large living room dressed in pajamas with nothing on his feet and made his way to the study. Sitting down in his large overstuffed leather chair he pulled the sheer drapes back and looked down on Park Avenue.

Denton was always amazed at New York City. Even though he grew up here it still fascinated him that no matter what the time of day there was always traffic on the streets. This morning was no exception. Even this far above the street he could hear the low rumble of the traffic. There was the "banging" sound of garbage trucks and the ever-present yellow taxis ducking in and out of lanes. The city truly never slept. It hardly slowed down.

It would not begin to get light for at least another hour. Denton allowed the sheer drape to fall closed. He leaned back in his chair and let out an audible sigh. His anxiety attack was subsiding, but he still had a sense of foreboding. Now fully awake he knew the reason behind his feelings. Today was the day that he had promised Trevor Mason that he would give him his answer as to his participation in Trevor's takeover scheme. He was not comfortable with the plan. He was well aware that several of the key shareholders would be "forced" into agreeing to Trevor's terms of sale. They would sell because of the threat of damaging revelations that he Denton could supply. It was blackmail there was no other way to look at it. In addition the secret promise of a stock sale without the prior approval of the board was in direct violation of the corporate by-laws. But if Denton failed to cooperate, Trevor had enough on Denton himself to force him out of the company and even worse.

Denton had no allusions concerning Trevor Mason. He was grateful to Trevor for treating him with respect and for being the first person to recognize his abilities and allowing him to play a truly key role in Wellbon-Smith. Not even his mother, whom he loved dearly, ever saw more than an insecure little boy when she looked at him. Trevor gave him real authority. Trevor gave him real responsibility. However, Denton realized that Trevor only did this for two reasons; he recognized that Denton could handle both and he recognized that he could use Denton in his takeover bid. Denton knew that if he stood in Trevor's path and failed to cooperate that there was no sentiment involved in their relationship. Trevor would destroy Denton just as quickly and ruthlessly as anyone else. Indeed, Trevor had made it clear in their meeting the other night that not only did Denton's "enemies" possess the knowledge that could destroy him, but so did Trevor. That was the not too subtle unspoken message of the entire meeting.

Trevor also recognized something that few other than Susan ever realized. Denton had a near photographic memory. Denton knew that not everyone had this ability, but remained unimpressed viewing his gift only as an interesting curiosity. Susan and Trevor both saw it as a unique tool. Susan saw it as allowing Denton to attain a unique knowledge base that would someday benefit him if he ever had the opportunity to run Wellbon-Smith. Trevor realized that all those years of "inconsequential" busy work that Carlton Smith had assigned him allowed the "mundane" corporate paper work to pass through Denton's hands. From this paper work an intelligent person like Denton was able to piece together a lot of diverse facts that ultimately added up to acts committed by numerous prominent well-connected people within the corporation. People who used the company illegally for their own profit and to avoid taxes, most of this profit coming from "sweetheart" deals between Wellbon-Smith and purchases from other companies of which were a clear conflict of interest for those involved. All of this profit came at the expense of the other shareholders that lived within the letter of corporate and public law. Denton being a detail person and an excellent speed-reader became privy to these acts and more importantly remembered contents of files and where they were kept.

In attempting to aid Trevor, Denton had informed him of several rather archaic facts that revealed Denton's gift. When Trevor questioned Denton, Denton produced various files that separately appeared innocent, but together produced a trail of damning evidence. Trevor immediately placed all corporate files that Denton designated as sensitive under tight security. Denton's memory became the index file and reference key. The total of the files was truly voluminous and would have taken years to categorize. Denton provided quick and accurate access. Denton was originally pleased that he could aid his new boss in this manner. He believed then and still believed that Trevor had been good for Atlantic Corporation and through its increased profits, Wellbon-Smith. Now he realized how Trevor ultimately planned on using his knowledge. This was the reason for the anxiety attack in the middle of the night.

Why, thought Denton, with this knowledge had he not gone to his mother years ago and "blown the whistle" on the guilty parties? Unfortunately he was now forced to face the reasons behind his silence, reasons that until now were too painful to face. Some of those files were incriminating to both Mary Wellbon and

Carlton Smith. In spite of the resentment that he may have subconsciously harbored over their treatment of him, they had been the only "family" he had known since the death of his father. He was loath to do anything to harm them.

Well that's it in a nutshell thought Denton. He really had no choice. If he didn't cooperate Trevor would destroy his career and even though remote, there was the possibility of jail. Unknown to Denton at the time the girl that Denton had the one night fling with was under age. What a price to pay for one stupid night as a youth! In addition, Denton still desired to protect his mother. How clever of Trevor thought Denton, he specifically told Denton that Mary Wellbon was to be his responsibility when the time came to secure her vote. He was really telling Denton that cooperation not only protected his own past mistake, but it would allow him to shield his mother as well. Trevor had set him up beautifully. The takeover plan had appeal on two levels. On one level, albeit as a figurehead, it was Denton's only hope of being chairman of his father's company. On a darker level, it was Denton's only hope of keeping shameful personal and family secrets, secret. Including what would pass as proof positive of the long circulated rumors concerning his father and grandfather's conduct of business.

How did he get into this mess he wondered? Until now, he always believed in his heart that he was a member of a socially prominent and upstanding family. He believed that the rumors that he heard whispered all of his life was the product of envious backstabbing people. Now it seemed that he could no longer ignore the truth. All of them, including him, were scoundrels. Well deserve it or not, he was going to protect the family's reputation. Who would get hurt in the process? Scoundrels, people who were willing to cheat and gain profit at the expense of their fellow shareholders. Denton smiled to himself. This is what it all comes down to. "I'm going to do everything that I can; including threatening to reveal other's shameful secrets, so that my family's shameful activities remain secret," he said to himself. He knew at that point that later in the morning he would place a call to Trevor Mason and confirm what Trevor knew from the start; that Denton would cooperate with the takeover plan.

Denton Wellbon leaned forward in his chair and pulled the sheer drape back for the second time. It was just beginning to get light in the east.

***

"Bernie" the cat lay contentedly on Mac's lap. The large house cat with tiger stripes really enjoyed Sunday mornings. This was his time with his owner. After breakfast Mac always took a cup of coffee and the Sunday paper into his den. Bernie always followed and after allowing Mac to get settled into his easy chair, Bernie would jump up onto Mac's lap and settle himself for an extended stay while Mac read the paper "around" him. Mac spent a rather long time reading the paper in a systematic fashion while sipping the hot coffee. This was fine by Bernie, as he wasn't planning on moving any time soon. The only interruptions were when Mac decided to have another cup of coffee. Bernie made no secret of his displeasure of these decisions, but he would wait rather grumpily by the chair until Mac returned. Then they both resumed their "assigned" positions. Bernie's cohort Slater, the equally large tabby gray, was content to lie nearby in a sunspot when available. He preferred to be in front of the large floor to ceiling windows that left the morning light flood into the den. This was pretty much Sunday morning around Mac's house. Mac looked up from his paper, took off his reading glasses and observed his two furry friends. "So this is the life of the county's most 'eligible bachelor,' Mac said out loud, "How exciting!" Bernie opened his eyes and looked up at Mac with a non-committal expression. "I don't want you telling anyone how boring I really am Bernie." Bernie closed his eyes. Done deal thought Mac.

Mac's wireless phone that he brought from the kitchen rang. Bernie laid his ears straight back in a disapproving fashion but he failed to be disturbed enough to open his eyes. Slater continued with his nap. He could care less.

"Hello, William MacLode," answered Mac.

"Well hello Bill. John Hogg here, how are you?"

"John Hogg my favorite CPA. How are things in West Chester County New York?"

"Things never change in West Chester Bill. You just keep selling all these rich people up here more and more kitchen cabinets."

"That's good for all of us Johnny."

"Hey I'm not complaining. You guys are having a hell of a year. If no one else will tell you, I will. Good job!"

"Thank you. I can assure you that you are the only person at corporate that has complemented us."

"Yeah, I know, but don't let it get you down. Trevor Mason never compliments anyone. I don't understand it. He's from the old school I guess. 'Don't spoil them with compliments.' Hey Bill I got your message on my answering machine yesterday. I'm sorry that I didn't get back to you before this. I was in the office all day. You guys at the division level aren't the only ones that Trevor cracks the whip on. What do you need?"

"Information, Johnny."

"Let me guess. You want to know why Trevor is piling so many extra requirements on Fox Cabinetry for the strategic plan."

"You got it."

"Honestly I don't know. You guys are the only company that he's making those demands on."

"I know Johnny. I called the other Atlantic division presidents last night. He's being his usual unreasonable self with the other guys, but this goes far beyond that. Is he that upset with me personally that he's taking it out on the whole division? Is he trying to keep piling it on until I just give up and quit? Is that what he wants?"

"No I don't think so. You don't kiss his butt like some of the other division CEO's, but he often uses you as an example to them on how they should run their companies. He would like you to grovel more but at the same time you get results and he likes the way that makes him look in front of the Wellbon-Smith board when he gives Atlantic's annual report. How are your people holding up?"

"Better than I expected. I had everyone at home this week except Tony and Carroll. When I first met with them on Friday there were a lot of complaints and I dreaded hearing Tony when he returned. Then yesterday when "Mace" added even more I expected Tony to go through the roof and Carroll to finally retire to his farm. He's been threatening to do that for the last few years you know. One of these days he's going to do it. But when I got the meeting started we had the unexpected presence of our new V. P. of Human Resources. She's also the first woman to be a member of an Atlantic Company Senior Staff. The guys listened to Trevor's newest demands and instead of bitching they dug right in and set up a schedule and made the commitment to get everything completed on time. I think they wanted to impress her."

"That's great! You got a bunch of good people there."

"Tell me about it. It would be nice for them to hear that officially from Mace sometime."

"Don't hold your breath, how's the new gal seem?"

"So far I'm impressed. Time will tell… Nice stalling Johnny. What do you really know? Don't hold out on me."

"I'm not holding out. I really don't know, but something is definitely going on."

"Why do you say that John?"

"Well, we got an estimate for some 'up front' contract work from Bertrum and Bertrum out in Chicago."

"Who are they?"

"Well hold on to your hat. Are you sitting down?"

"Come on Johnny! Who are they?"

"They're business brokers Bill. Trevor has them appraising Fox Cabinetry."

"You think he wants to sell us?"

"That hardly makes sense Bill. He could be getting an appraisal for a lot of different reasons. You know that as well as I do."

"That certainly explains all the information he's requiring us to assemble. It's Bertrum that's asking for it so that they can put a price on us."

"Got to admit, I think you're probably right Bill. But that doesn't mean that he's going to sell you."

"No it doesn't. I guess we play it by ear and wait and see. Sooner or later someone from this Bertrum organization will come around and ask for a guided tour. Just to be certain that the place actually exists. Perhaps then we will learn what Trevor's has up his sleeve...How's the wife and kids Johnny?"

"Great Bill, Jane's health problem this spring turned out to be nothing more than a small benign cyst that was a big relief. We're in the process of looking for a college for the twins. As you can imagine both girls want to go to the same place. Phew...talk about expensive! I'm glad I've got a good job! But then a bachelor like you has no idea about stuff like that."

"I'm jealous of you and Jane and you know it. All I have is my two cats."

"Two cats, a classic T-Bird, big house, pool, money in the bank.... Life's tough huh Bill? Say how's your dad? I know that his health wasn't so good the last time you were up here to golf."

"Well I'm sorry to have to tell you that we lost him last week." Mac proceeded to relate a condensed version of the past week's events to his old friend. Mac and John Hogg both joined the Atlantic Corporation right out of college. They both played a major role in the restructuring of Wellbon-Smith. During this period they worked closely together and a strong friendship developed. The friendship didn't diminish when Mac was transferred to Goodville and John was promoted to corporate V. P. of Finance for Atlantic Corporation. Mac always suspected that his close friend was the one who placed the "bug" in Carlton Smith's ear to make Mac president of Fox. John Hogg always denied that accusation. 'You earned that on your own pal. You didn't need anyone's help.' John Hogg remained one of the few confidants that existed in Mac's life. He was also the only person outside of family that called Mac, Bill.

Mac wound up the conversation. "That's life I guess John. We all have to go through losing our parents."

"That's too bad Bill. You know that Jane and I are here for you if you need anything. Why don't you come up and spend a long weekend with us next week? We'll fish, play some golf, the whole bit. Jane and the girls were asking me the other day when would we see you again."

"Can't for the next couple of weekends John, Trevor has seen to that. But I promise I'll come up soon. Thanks for calling, and thanks for listening. Give my love to Jane."

"Any time pal, I'll keep you informed if I learn anything."

"Thanks John. See you later." Mac pushed the "power" button and placed the phone on the end table. He stared out the window for several minutes, lost in thought. Suddenly he made a decision, picked up the phone again and punched in a set of numbers that he knew by heart. "Yes, this is William MacLode of Fox Cabinetry, I want to reserve some tickets for the earliest train to New York City tomorrow morning."

Bernie the cat jumped down from Mac's lap and decided to go check out the upstairs bedroom.

***

Fred Balderson was sitting on his patio in the Hollywood Hills overlooking Los Angeles. The city seemed to sprawl all the way to the horizon. He knew that the boundaries were not quite that extreme, but it certainly appeared that way from this vantage point. Fred, because of his recent divorce, leased this home perched high on an outcropping of the rugged hills. It was endowed with a spectacular view. He was hard put to determine which feature he liked the best. The large kidney shaped swimming pool or the low Spanish architecture. Of course there was also the pinkish stucco on the walls that surrounded the entire property. They afforded a level of privacy from the other homes that were situated above and below him, but he hated the color. As the owner of a kitchen retail showroom this was a bit extravagant, but the showroom wasn't his only source of income.

It was nine AM. Pacific Daylight Savings Time on Sunday morning. Fred was relaxing on a chaise lounge beside the pool, a Bloody Mary in his hand. He was wearing only his bathing trunks and was enjoying the warm sun. It had been unusually wet in LA this summer and Fred was planning to catch up on some "rays" while the opportunity presented itself. He placed the remains of his drink on a small patio table, leaned back in the chair and closed his eyes. He heard the phone ring. He ignored it. It continued to ring. He still ignored it. His answering machine picked up the call. After Fred's recorded message and the "beep," what could only be described as a frantic voice was heard. Fred could hear all of this because the phone was located just inside the open patio door behind him. When Fred recognized the voice he knew that the message would fill the tape. He just MUST program a limit on those messages.

The voice continued talking. Fred reluctantly got up; sliding the screen back on the patio door he entered the dining room and picked up the phone. "I'm here Glenn. What is it that the newest member of the Fox Chicago team wants of me? As near as I can tell, you just filled half my answering machine tape and so far I haven't heard you say anything!"

"Thank God that you're there Fred. I need to talk to you."

"Make it quick Glenn. I'm very busy."

"Oh, I'm sorry that I bothered you on a Sunday morning, but I just had to tell you what happened last night and ask your opinion. You have been a Fox flagship showroom for several years. I need to know what you think."

"You're repeating yourself Glenn. I may not have even one opinion, let alone two."

"What?"

"Forget it. I was just being funny," Fred had forgotten what a terrible sense of humor Glenn Glen possessed. Or perhaps he, Fred, wasn't as funny as he thought he was. Fred had met Glenn in person for the first time at the last Fox dealer meeting. He knew him by reputation only previous to their meeting. He now knew that he was a high-strung individual who Fred thought tended to make mountains out of molehills. Fred realized that he better just listen. Any interruption in his thought train and Glenn would start from the beginning again. "I'm listening Glenn."

With that Glenn Glen began relating, in excoriating detail, the meeting that he and Mark had with John Malicki the previous evening. "Glenn I don't care what you and Mark ordered for dinner!" At first Fred was only half listening while mentally making plans to call his girl friend and see if she might be "up" for tennis in the afternoon. Fred was currently between marriages, as his fourth was a disaster, and he had been seeing the current female companion for about two months. Suddenly Glenn got his attention and Fred was compelled to interrupt. "What did Malicki say when you told him you thought Fox was for sale? Uh huh, uh huh…so he didn't deny it?"

"No he didn't deny it! I had the distinct feeling that this was the first time he had heard anything about it. What are we going to do?" Glenn Glen had managed to work himself into another frenzy of emotion. The problem was that the emotional level was the same no matter if the steak he ordered was too well done or if he discovered that his home burned down.

"Okay, okay, calm down. The fact that Malicki didn't know anything could mean that the rumor is totally wrong. Are you certain the source is reliable?"

"I'd stake my life on it!" Glenn declared with too much emotion. He had not revealed his source to Fred.

"Glenn I want you to calm down. We aren't going to do anything. I am going to call Terry Barlow in Atlanta. She's the number one Fox flagship in sales right now and has always been in tight with Fox management. I'll see if she has heard anything. I'll let you know what I learn. Now go take an aspirin and lie down. You can give yourself a heart attack over stuff like this."

"Promise you'll call as soon as you know anything?"

"It's as good as done." Fred hung up and rummaged around the table looking for his address book. When he found it he looked up the phone numbers, both the home and showroom of Terry Barlow. He quickly calculated what time it was on the East Coast. Should be just after noon he thought. He wondered if he could locate her on a Sunday. He began punching in the numbers.

***

The Boeing 727 touched down at Atlanta's Hartsfield International Airport at precisely five forty-five PM on Sunday evening. David Elliott had a window seat and watched the busy scene pass by outside as they taxied to their gate. This was a totally unexpected trip. Mac had called him at home just before lunch. David had just changed into casual clothes after returning with his family from church.

"Dave, this is Mac. I'm sorry to bother you at home on the weekend but we have a slight emergency down in Atlanta."

"What's the problem Mac?"

"Antonio Reveria."

"You mean the golf pro that's interested in Fox supplying all the cabinetry for the condos on his new championship golf course?"

"That's him."

"What's the problem?" asked David cautiously.

"Well I don't know if there is one or not. I just got off the phone with Terry Barlow. She in turn just got off the phone with the architect and the designer for Reveria's golfing community. You know that Terry sold this project for Fox and she just took delivery on the cabinetry for the sample condo. Anyway Terry's installers were out working on the installation Saturday because the grand opening for the sample is only three weeks off. The designer and architect just 'reamed her out good,' her exact words. They claim that nothing is right."

"That's hard to believe Mac. Terry's meticulous."

"I agree. Anyway, Terry called her installers and told them what the architect told her. They were shocked. Seems everything is going smoothly from their point of view. They even claimed that both the architect and the designer paid the job site a visit last week and seemed to be quite pleased."

"Terry looked at the cabinetry when she took delivery?" asked David.

"She claims that she did and they looked fine to her. You know how picky she can be."

"Yeah if she thought they looked fine there can't be too much wrong with them. Anyway, what do you want me to do Mac?"

"I hate to ask this of you David, but this project is worth somewhere upward of $750,000 over the next three years to Fox. I don't want to lose it for either Terry or us. I need you to get on a plane today so that you can be on the job site with

Terry first thing tomorrow morning. With someone of your stature in the company making that kind of an effort we should be able to smooth over whatever is going on."

"I'll be there boss. You know I'll do whatever must be done to save this project."

"I know you will David. That's why I called you. By the way, you must be back by Wednesday. Our lawyer desires to meet with us first thing Wednesday morning at 8:00 in the conference room of the Hilton Garden Hotel to discuss our little problem out in the dessert. Have a safe trip my friend."

"Thanks." With that they both hung up. David began punching in the numbers for the travel agency that took care of Fox's travel needs.

David was not certain what he was getting into, but it wasn't worrying him at all. He had been doing this job for far too long to be worried about troubleshooting on problem jobs. No one would die as a result of his decisions. Cabinets were made out of wood. In the end every part could be replaced if necessary and he doubted that this situation was that extreme.

The plane was secured and the enclosed jet ramp moved against the outer hull. Everyone was jockeying to get his stowed luggage out of the overhead storage bins. David had his brief case as a carry on and one bag that he checked. He was only scheduled to stay one night and fly back late Monday evening to Pennsylvania. The travel agent was fortunate to get him booked on this flight at such a late date. It appeared that every seat was taken. He was forced to take a cramped seat in "coach." This did not work well for his six foot two inch tall "Oklahoman" frame. He was grateful that the Harrisburg, Pennsylvania to Atlanta, Georgia flight was a relatively short hop.

The afternoon had been one of mass confusion. As soon as the agent confirmed his ticket and hotel arrangements, David threw a few clothes and toilet articles in a bag and made a mad dash for the airport. He had just barely made the flight.

Now that David was in Atlanta he was in no hurry. All he had to do was pick up a rental car and go claim his hotel room. Following the hectic afternoon he was looking forward to a nice dinner and a leisurely evening watching television in his room. Tomorrow he would meet Terry Barlow at her showroom and the two of them would go to the job site. If there were any time left he would spend it making a goodwill visit with Terry, as she was Fox's current number one flagship dealer. Fox believed that their top dealers should get constant reassurance that the manufacturer still cared about them. David waited until the rush was over and then he strolled out of the aircraft and up the ramp to the gate. To his surprise Terry Barlow was anxiously waiting for him there. She waved and quickly rushed up to him. David, a tall mid westerner, towered over the slight attractive southern belle. "Terry, what a pleasant surprise, how did you know what flight I was arriving on?'

"I called Mac, who in turn called the travel agency you all use. I decided to save you all the hassle and expense of a rental car. I'll chauffeur you to your hotel. I can pick you up in the morning and we can head directly to the job site. No need to go all the way out to the showroom and then turn around and come back. The job site is out beyond Buck Head." David always found her southern accent charming. Charming she was, but underneath beat the heart of a cool calculating businessperson.

"I have one bag to claim at baggage," he said as they began to walk through the crowded airport. "Tell me, what is your take on the Reveria project?"

David was totally unprepared for Terry's response: "To hell with Reveria David! What's this I hear about Fox Cabinetry being sold?"

CHAPTER 8

"Leon Beatty from the Seattle showroom is on the phone. I have New York on hold, Boston on hold, Providence Rhode Island on hold and a list of at least twenty showrooms that I promised them personally that you would return their call today. In addition the entire sales force 'needs to talk to you immediately!' What should I be telling all these people?" Brady was not a happy puppy that was clear by the tone of her voice. Tony shifted the phone to his other ear, putting his hand over the mouthpiece so that the caller couldn't hear his response.

"How the hell should I know?" he answered. His tone was equally annoyed. Brady sniffed her disapproval of his language and his answer and returned to her station.

Damn Mac for leaving him to deal with this. Tony only found out this morning that Mac was off to New York on the early train. Why this quick trip to the city anyway? Brady usually knew everything. But she had sworn that she did not know Mac's whereabouts the previous week and she now claimed that she was not told the reason behind Mac's current exodus. She was probably telling the truth. No she was definitely telling the truth. Brady didn't lie. If Mac had bound her to secrecy she would have simply told Tony that it was "confidential." Confidential had always been one of her favorite words, especially when she was one of the few confidants.

Tony's home phone began ringing last night at around ten in the evening. The first call was from Ralph Sinclair, Fox's West Coast Salesman. He totally surprised Tony with his question: "Is Fox Cabinetry for sale?"

"Of course not where did you hear that?" Tony laughed. But Tony wasn't laughing for very long. One by one the sales force started checking in, all with the same question. By his own admission, the question had originated with John Malicki. During his call to Tony he had related the conversation that he had on Saturday evening with Glenn Glen and Mark Markel. He also acknowledged that his first call on Sunday morning went to his counterpart on the "Coast," Ralph

Sinclair. The sales force wasn't the big problem though. There were only twelve of them. It was the fact that Glenn Glen must have contacted at least one dealer in every sales territory to find out if anyone knew anything about this rumor. Each of those in turn called another dealer and so on. Now it was Monday morning and the phones were jumping off the hook. Dealers wanted to know if the rumor was true.

The really bad part was that Tony didn't know for certain if it was or wasn't. He was eighty percent positive that it wasn't, but he couldn't find out where it started. He called Glenn Glen and did everything short of threatening bodily harm in an attempt to discover where he heard it, but Glenn refused to divulge his source. Tony suspected that John Malicki knew Glenn's source, but Glenn had him bound by oath not to divulge it to anyone.

Tony was in the process of assuring the Saint Louis dealer that he was not aware of a sale when an attractive thirty-something-young woman stepped into his office doorway and leaned wearily against the jamb. Tony managed to get off the phone. "No more Brady!" he yelled.

"What should I do with the calls that are still holding?"

"Tell them I will either get back to them personally today, or they will receive an official statement from Fox management by fax no later than tomorrow morning."

"Is that for certain?"

Sometimes Tony really wanted to strangle Brady. "Of course it's for certain! Have you ever really known me to lie Brady?"

"I've known you to stretch the truth on occasion. But no, I have never known you to tell an out and out lie, just thought I'd check though."

Tony really suspected that deep down Brady was enjoying the discomfort that he was experiencing. He looked up at the striking young woman standing in his door. "Good morning Pam."

"Good morning Tony. It's barely nine o'clock and already I'm exhausted. The phones in Customer Service are nuts!" Pam Collins was Fox's Customer Service manager. She reported directly to Dave Elliott. At Tony's gesture she came on into the office and sank down into one of the easy chairs that faced Tony's desk. Tony thought again how beautiful she was. It's really a shame that she's happily married. Then he remembered her temper. It was a temper that she could strangely control on the phones with customers, but could unleash at a second's notice if someone "on the inside" innocently crossed her path. The dealers and indeed most of the sales force would not believe this simple fact if you attempted to warn them. For those who dealt with Pam on the phone knew her only as an extremely helpful and capable service person. Maybe, thought Tony, he should light a candle for her husband each night instead of feeling jealous.

"Let me guess, you are being inundated by dealers and our own sales force asking if we are for sale."

"You got it boss man. That's all I've heard since I got here this morning. It's all that my phone people are hearing too."

"What are you and your people telling them?"

"We are asking them all if they have talked to you or anyone else in upper management concerning this. They usually say yes. I then have everybody asking them what you guys told them. When they say that you either said 'no,' or 'you have not been told that we are,' we say then that's your answer."

"Good girl Pam. No wonder Dave guards you like gold and won't let anyone else in this place even think about stealing you away from him."

Pam smiled for the first time. 'Dave and I get along most of the time and he does take care of me salary wise."

"Now Pam, you've been doing this too long not to know that you had to give an answer that was in 'sync' with what I was saying while maintaining your department's credibility. You came up here to find out what the truth really is. Am I right?"

Pam's beautiful white smile got even bigger. "Right again boss man, my boss is in Atlanta this morning and I have no one else to bug. So what's the story? Are we for sale or not? After this morning I really have to tell my people something. They all have trusted friends out on the shop floor and the rumors are ripping around this place at the speed of light."

Just then Carroll Brubaker's lanky frame barged into Tony's office. "What the hell is going on Tony?" He caught himself as he realized that Pam was in the room. "I'm sorry Pam. Forgive me. I didn't see you sitting there."

Pam grinned up at him. "You don't have to apologize to me. I know all those words. It's a relief to find out that at least you know one of them. No one ever hears you swear."

"I really don't like to use that kind of language Pam. I really am sorry."

"Apology accepted Carroll."

Carroll turned again toward Tony. "What is going on? I've had at least twenty people on the floor this morning ask me if the place is up for sale. Is it or isn't it?"

"Why would I know more than you Carroll?" Tony knew he was being evasive, but his question was valid.

"Because your office is right here next to the boss', that's why. The rest of us have offices scattered all over the place. I thought you might have heard something."

"You think he tells me more than the rest of you?"

"I thought in this case he might have."

"Well he didn't. If he had I could have avoided being swamped with phone calls from panic stricken dealers and uneasy sales people. I could have put a good face on it. But to answer your question, no I don't think we are for sale. Mac may like to play close to the vest but he's never been in the habit of letting us hang out to dry. This morning Pam and I have definitely been hung out to dry."

Carroll settled into the other chair facing Tony. He silently reached over and pushed the office door closed so that only the three of them could hear the conversation. Quiet though it was, this move did not go unnoticed by Brady who was left on the outside.

To Catch a Fox

"Have you seen Mac this morning?" Carroll asked in a low voice.

"Mac's not even in the office this morning. I was unable to contact him by phone or e-mail last night. At least he didn't respond to either. Then I came in here this morning to have Brady tell me that he was on the early train to New York City but he would be back in time for our meeting with the lawyer Wednesday" Tony's eyes darted quickly toward Pam. Carroll hesitated. The purpose of that meeting required only the knowledge of the senior staff. Pam noted the pause and the slightly guarded expressions on the faces of her two superiors.

"We need to somehow make contact with him today," said Carroll. "This thing has gotten out of hand real quick. People do irrational things when they are faced with an unknown. We need to have Mac verify or deny the rumor and make a statement either way."

"I agree," said Tony. "At this point we not only need a statement from management to the employees, but also to the dealer network. We have a good year going I don't want anything to foul it up."

"So what can Carroll and I tell our people?" asked Pam brushing her long blond hair out of her face.

Carroll stared at Tony, "Yeah, what?"

"Yeah what you ask? Yeah what? You're the Senior Vice President and you're looking at ME?" A look of consternation appeared on Carroll's face. "Okay, okay, I'm sorry. That was uncalled for. I suggest that you Carroll call a senior staff meeting for eleven o'clock in the conference room. I will continue to attempt to track down the boss. Weather we do or we don't find him; we will come up with a statement for both employees and dealers alike. It will be as true and honest a statement as we can give them even if we have to get Trevor Mason himself on the phone to get it." That was a prospect that failed to appeal to Tony on any imaginable level. "Pam, tell your crew that we will issue a statement to them and everyone by three o'clock today."

"Right boss," she rose and left the room quickly. There were phones to answer and problems to solve.

After she closed the door behind her, Carroll stood up and walked to the dormer window behind Tony's desk. Tony swiveled in his chair to look at him. Carroll stared out at the parking lot. "Do you think we are for sale Tony?"

"So what if we are? You worked for Elias, the place was sold and you definitely benefited by it. We have a good track record why would any new investor, because that's all that they are, think of changing a winning formula? What does it matter if Trevor Mason is yelling at us or someone new is yelling? Heck, it might be a lot easier working for someone else."

"You sales guys are always optimistic aren't you? Yes you are correct. I wound up with a much better job than I had while working for Elias Fox and Daniel Martin. But remember, I was the only one of the original staff under Elias to survive for more than a year."

"Come on Carroll! That's because they were incompetent! You knew that, Mac soon found out after he came here, and Mac kept you while getting rid of the remainder. You're the only real manager that Elias Fox ever hired or promoted. Today we have a very competent staff, and unlike those days, we're making money. No one is going to mess with that. Believe me."

Carroll turned and moved to the door. With his hand on the knob he again faced Tony before turning it. "I hope you're correct Tony. Find Mac, and let's get to the bottom of this if we can." With that he was gone.

***

Mac strolled through the main concourse of Pennsylvania Station in New York City. After leaving his train he climbed the flight of stairs that took him from the track level to the concourse and eventually he would climb another flight to the street level. Madison Square Garden was overhead. The cavernous building reverberated with the mixed sounds of literally thousands of travelers, employees, shopkeepers and the ever present public address system that echoed nearly unintelligible train names, track numbers and destinations. Mac loved it.

He enjoyed the train trip over to the city; even the part where your train sits engine-less in the dark in the "catacombs" of Thirtieth Street Station in Philadelphia. There four trains per day traveling to New York and four traveling from New York sit and wait for the engine change to accommodate the switch from electric to diesel power and vice versa. This dates back to the days of the old Pennsylvania Railroad. Pennsylvania engines are run on electric power and the Jersey trains are diesel power. This has been going on for years but for some unknown reason it still takes from one half-hour to forty-five minutes to make the switch. As if no one at the station realizes that you are arriving and they must suddenly find the proper type of engine to accommodate the situation. During this period there is no power on the train as its power unit has rumbled off to God knows where in the "underground" complex.

So there you sit. No light to read, no air conditioning in the summer and no heat in the winter; for the time span of about forty-five minutes. This from the people of the United States of America, the one and only super power to survive the twentieth century, the people who sent men to the moon not just once, but several times. Mac nearly laughed out loud just thinking about it. This was one of the charming aspects of this truly free society that he had reluctantly adopted, but now had come to love. All this high technology and Mac could picture two engineers walking the miles of track hidden under Thirtieth Street station calling out: "Has anyone seen a diesel engine anywhere?"

Mac climbed the last huge staircase to the street level and emerged in the New York City morning. Except for midday New York was always in shadows because of the tall buildings. Mac looked at his watch. It was just about ten o'clock. Plenty of time he thought. No reason to rush. He could get to his hotel room, make contact, and go on line with his laptop and work on his portion of the strategic plan until time for his meeting.

Mac got in the line for the taxicab stand. When it was his turn the "cabby" grabbed his single overnight bag and placed it in the trunk. Mac kept his briefcase with his laptop in his possession and climbed in.

"Where to sir?"

"Short trip this time my friend, Marriott on Times Square."

"Marriott it is sir."

Mac watched from the back seat as the cabby muscled his way into the crowded street. Typical bumper-to-bumper New York City traffic thought Mac. He had grown to love New York while he lived here during his college days. He still was in the city frequently on business, but he also tried to get "over" on pleasure several times a year. During a good season, Mac enjoyed at least two Broadway shows a year. In addition a lady friend would sometimes accompany him. They would make a weekend of it and enjoy a shopping spree and taste the nightlife.

The cab pulled up at the entrance to the Marriott. This Marriott sat right in Times Square on the Broadway side, right where the fabled street began. Mac retrieved his bag, shouldered his briefcase and paid the driver. He hesitated in thought before entering. He hoped that this trip would enlighten him as to the future. Mac waved off the bellhop, he had a thing about carrying his own bags, and entered the lobby.

***

Tony picked up the phone in the conference room. Brady's shrill clipped voice was on the other end. "Mr. MacLode on the line for you," she said.

"Thank God! Put him on!"

"You'll have to hang up so that I can transfer him."

"Don't lose him Brady!"

"Really Anthony, if anyone around this place understands the correct operation of this phone system, it's me. I was the first one that the systems people instructed on how…"

"Damn it Brady, put him through!"

"Very well, you don't have to be rude."

Tony hung up and waited. The remainder of the senior staff was seated around the table. It was just two minutes after eleven, they had all gathered and were just getting settled. The room became quiet in anticipation. They waited for what seemed like a mini eternity. "I'll bet she's making small talk with him about the weather in New York," grumbled Tony. Finally the phone rang and Tony had the receiver in his hand before it had the chance to complete the ring.

"Mac! Good morning!"

To Catch a Fox

"Hi Tony. I'm sorry but somehow my cell phone must have been accidentally turned off. I just checked my messages and discovered that about twenty of them were from you. What's up?"

"Four were from me. What planet are you living on? What do you mean 'What's up?'" Tony's voice was impatient. He had been playing defense most of the night and all of the morning. Mac's usual calm voice was just a bit more than he could tolerate at the moment. "The entire sales force and dealer network have heard a rumor that Fox is for sale. They're in a panic. Pam and the 'kids' in customer service have been holding the lions at the gates all morning. In addition, Carroll can't get anything off the line this morning because everyone in manufacturing is standing around talking about the rumor that we are for sale. In their usual manner they have already identified the buyers as Japanese and are certain that the plant will be moved to Taiwan."

Mac laughed. "Never let it be said that Pennsylvania Dutchmen don't have an active imagination."

"Mac may I put you on the speaker so that everyone can hear what you are saying?"

"Who is in the room with you Tony?"

"Only the senior staff is here, including Sarah."

"Sure, put me on."

Tony pressed the "speaker" button. "Can you hear me Mac?"

"Loud and clear, are you able to hear me?"

"Yes we can," answered Tony.

"Hello everyone!" said Mac in a cheerful tone. "Good morning Sarah! It sounds as if we've had an interesting first day arranged for you."

"Good morning. Yes very interesting," was Sarah's reply.

To Catch a Fox

"Enough small talk Mac," interjected Tony. "What is the word on this rumor of the sale of Fox Cabinetry?"

"Well as always there is a grain of truth to it, but that's all, just a grain. It turns out that Trevor wants Atlantic to expand into high tech companies. That will require cash, a great deal of cash. It looks as if Trevor is planning on using Fox as collateral for any additional purchases. That's all.

"How in blazes did the dealer network find out before we did?" Tony avoided the temptation to ask Mac how he knew and failed to tell his staff.

"Who knows Tony? I only found out yesterday morning. Even then it was just a rumor that was circulating around corporate. Fortunately I have a few friends at corporate, even if Trevor Mason isn't among them." Reading "between the lines" of Tony's question Mac added: "I didn't want to pass on any rumors to you before I had the opportunity to confirm them. I guess I should have anticipated that corporate would be as sloppy and unprofessional as always in handling this."

"Is that why you are in New York this morning?"

"That among other reasons," as usual Mac's reply was non-committal and Tony knew from experience that it was not wise to push the issue any further.

Tony covered the answers that both sales and customer service were giving to the inquiries. Mac gave his blessing and complemented Tony on his handling of the situation. He agreed that the staff should issue a statement by three o'clock today to dealers, the sales force, and all employees confirming what Mac had just told them. He requested that they e-mail him a copy before sending it out.

"Do you want to approve it before we send it?" asked Tony.

"No I trust the judgment of the staff. I only want it in advance so that if I am asked I will be saying the same thing as you folks. Are there any other problems?"

Tony looked around the room; everyone indicated that there were no other pressing issues. "I guess that's it," answered Tony.

"If that's it I will see you all on Wednesday morning."

"Okay boss. Oh wait. Are you going to visit Richard in the New York showroom while you're in the city?" There was no response as Mac was already gone. Tony turned to the group. "I guess not," he looked around the table. "Why am I not reassured?"

Carroll looked up from the notebook where he had been absently scribbling. "I believe that Mac has told us all that he honestly knows. Therefore that's what we go with."

Tony paused and held Carroll's gaze. After a long moment he replied. "Okay, sounds good. How about this for a rough draft…?"

***

Mac closed his cell phone. He was seated at the small desk in his hotel suite. I hope that satisfies everyone he thought. He also hoped that it turned out to be accurate. With that he turned and began clicking the keys of his laptop. He had a lot to accomplish for the annual report and his meeting was not until late in the afternoon.

***

David Elliott and Terry Barlow stood listening as the architect, designer and general contractor yelled at each other. Danny Meck, Fox's Regional Sales Manager for the Southern States, met the two this morning. David had informed Danny of the problem on Sunday. As the yelling continued Danny busied himself inspecting the beautiful Fox cabinetry that was already installed. They were in the kitchen of the sample condo. It was a typical construction site. Plumbers, electricians, carpenters, carpet and tile people all were shuffling about in each other's way. All were attempting to complete their tasks before the grand opening. All were behind schedule. All were blaming the others as someone else was always to blame for the chaos. Terry's installers continued the installation appearing oblivious to the situation.

The architect, designer, and general contractor each had a set of drawings that they all had approved. Each set of drawings was slightly different. None of them had noticed until now. The soffit treatment did not match the drawings and the individual copies failed to match each other. Each believed he had the final copy although the revision dates varied. The architect had the most recent copy and insisted that he had sent this copy to everyone. Terry's copy agreed with the contractor's but no one else. She quietly unfolded her version and showed it to David, the cabinetry and accessories that she and Fox supplied matched her set of drawings. She didn't show it to anyone else.

Dave nodded as her finger pointed to the revision date. It was two days earlier than the version that the architect was claiming to be final. At this point she would not antagonize anyone further as the heat switched from her when it was discovered that the drawings didn't match. They had all but forgotten the three cabinet people as they argued among themselves.

Finally Terry could no longer endure the yelling. "I may have a solution to OUR problem if you could give me a chance to cover it with you," she said at the top of her voice. The bickering continued as if she were not present. She glanced toward Elliott and rolled her eyes. Elliott allowed himself an amused smile. She made a second attempt.

"Hey! Is anyone interested in solving this problem so that we can finish in time for the opening?" This time Terry was yelling as loud as the others. The shouting ceased. All eyes turned toward Terry. "I thank you all for your undivided attention," she said in her most aristocratic tone. "Now as I see it the problem lies with the soffit and the recessed area of the ceiling. We can argue forever over who has the final version of the drawings and who's at fault here or we can move forward so that this project is completed for the much-advertised open house. Would you all consider listening to my humble suggestion?" The three men standing before her glanced at each other and then acquiesced to her tiny but formidable presence; without hesitation Terry spread her copy of the prints out on the island counter top and began sketching her proposed alterations. The "rival" professionals gathered around her and became immersed in her creative solution.

David Elliott allowed himself another smile as he watched Terry wrap the three previously obstinate men around her finger. She combined creative problem solving, ego massaging and just the proper amount of compromise to come to a solution that was palatable. In addition, by the time that she was finished, each individual could claim part of the remedy. This was what made Terry stand apart from many cabinet dealers, the ability to solve problems and sell the solutions. David wished that some others representing Fox had her skill sets. Whether dealing with fellow professionals or with the retail consumer Terry would not be denied. She excelled at determining individual needs and meeting them. Unlike others who placed their own ideas over the desires of their clients, Terry's ego was satisfied when her sales exceeded those of the previous month. Terry would readily accept a client's suggestion over her own if it meant preserving the sale.

As the antagonism dissipated and the solution's details were worked out, Danny offering Terry support glanced toward David and winked. David knew with that wink that all would be well. Danny Meck was a pro that had nearly grown up with Fox. Like Terry he possessed his own unique skill sets. Danny had the ability to listen and offer support without appearing to manipulate. Danny had a sixth sense for when to be assertive and when to keep his mouth shut.

David strolled out onto the patio deck. He was greeted by a beautiful view of the ninth hole of a superbly manicured PGA class golf course. The golf pro Antonio Reveria personally designed the course. For the moment this seemed to be the only area in the condo where chaos did not prevail. David retrieved his cell phone from a pocket, and listened to his messages. Several were from Pam asking if he knew anything about Fox being sold. Several were from dealers asking the same question and one was from Mac requesting that he call a New York phone number as soon as possible. David called immediately to Mac's hotel room.

"Good morning Mac, its David."

"Good morning David, where are you?" was Mac's cheerful greeting.

"I'm with Terry and Danny at the Reveria project."

"Can you talk?"

"Yes Mac, at the moment I'm alone on the patio."

"Good. How are things going?"

"Terry and Danny are working out a solution. None of it is our fault or Terry's. I'll be called in shortly to determine how quickly we can manufacture some additional pieces. Probably not much more than a few feet of molding and paneling will be necessary. I'll call the factory and push it through. In addition, I think that we should supply the parts at 'no charge' just for the goodwill factor. This project is worth a lot to us over the next few years."

"I agree. Whatever you determine David," was Mac's reply.

"Mac there is one other matter…"

"Allow me to speculate. Terry asked you if the rumor that Fox is for sale has any truth to it."

"You got it boss." David wasn't surprised at Mac's reply. If the dealers and sales force were calling him, some would call Mac. David shuddered to think what Tony's phone calls could have been like this morning.

"What did you tell Terry?" inquired Mac.

"Nothing, I told her that I hadn't heard a thing, which was the truth, but I promised to call you and get to the bottom of it. I gather that this rumor has crossed the dealer network like wild fire."

"You're right on that score David." Mac then proceeded to give David the same answer that he gave to Tony and the staff just minutes before.

David countered, "Is this something that we should be concerned about? Once they determine the value it could be tempting to turn us into cash."

"Yes, they could be tempted, but I believe that their main interest continues to be growth and increased sales. Remember there is no quicker way to add to your sales numbers then to purchase another company. While they would certainly realize significant capital gains by the sale of Fox, they would reduce their total sales numbers by our number for next year. While nothing is ever certain, I think for the time being this is much ado about nothing. I'll tell you guys if I hear anything."

"Thanks Mac, that's all that we can ask."

"Will you be able to satisfy Terry with the explanation that I just gave you?"

David considered this for a moment and then answered. "Yes, I think so, but she will want to hear it directly from you."

"Very well, tell her to leave a message with Brady if she wants to talk and I'll call her this evening at home."

"Will do boss. I see that Terry is motioning for me to come inside now. I've got to go, anything else?"

"Isn't that enough?"

"Quite enough boss. You have a good day. By the way, why are you in New York?"

"I'll tell you when I see you on Wednesday and thanks again for making that trip. Now, go make Terry and her customers happy and give Danny my rumor explanation." Before David could reply Mac was gone.

***

He sat alone in a booth in one of the numerous restaurants in the MGM Grand Hotel complex in Las Vegas. He was only vaguely aware that the theme was vintage Hollywood. Murals of Cagney, Monroe, Taylor, Sinatra and the obligatory Presley were everywhere. The only important fact in his life at this moment was that he was on time for this clandestine meeting.

He glanced nervously at his watch. It was five minutes before the predetermined time of the encounter. He looked quickly around the room for what seemed like the tenth time. He verified again that there was no one present that would recognize him. After all, this entire place was for tourists and gamblers. He was a local and he was certain that none of his co-workers would frequent this establishment. What was he doing here? He was risking his job that's what he was doing. If the management at Fox Cabinetry's Desert Operation discovered whom he was meeting and the purpose he would lose his job and be on the street before he could blink. No! He mustn't think that way. He was doing the right thing. He had been over and over this in his mind. He had to go through with this meeting.

He glanced toward the entrance. A young couple had entered. He was expecting a solitary man. The hostess met them and he thought for an instant that the young man glanced in his direction. Then in response to a comment the man made the hostess also glanced toward him. A sinking feeling surged through his stomach. He looked at the couple more closely while trying desperately to appear as if he had taken no notice. Was this someone that worked at the Fox factory and recognized him?

The hostess pulled two menus from a nearby rack and began escorting the couple to a table. She abruptly turned into the section that he was sitting in. This can't be! I don't know these people he thought! But there was no denying that the hostess seemed to be looking in his direction. She walked the couple past several empty booths as the advance on his booth continued. He studied his menu more carefully not wanting to look up at the trio. Then they were at his side! He pulled the menu closer to his face so that they might not notice him! Then they were past! The hostess had seated them just beyond him. "Will this be alright?" she asked in a perky voice. He heard the young man acknowledge that it would be fine.

Buzz Olson breathed a sigh of relief. It was all his imagination. He didn't know that couple and they didn't know him. It was just a coincidence that they asked to be seated in the same section as he. He had to get hold of himself. He could not appear like a nervous amateur when his real contact arrived. This should be child's play. He wasn't doing anything illegal. In fact he was simply exercising one of his rights as a worker in the United States of America.

"You must be Buzz?" said the voice at his left ear as a hand gently touched his shoulder. Buzz nearly jumped out of his skin! He looked up to see the smiling face of the young man who the hostess had just seated. "May I join you?"

"YES!" replied Buzz much too loudly. "I mean yes, you certainly may," he restated as he forced his voice to take on a more relaxed tone. "I thought you would be alone." Buzz glanced across at the young woman. She was playing keno.

"Don't worry about her. She could care less why I am here."

"Okay, well how do I know just who you are? I was expecting…I'm not entirely sure just what I was expecting." Buzz thought that his voice quivered just a bit as he spoke.

To Catch a Fox

"You were expecting someone older," replied the man with a smile. He appeared to be in his mid twenties. His hair was cropped short and neatly trimmed. He was dressed casually in a blue tee shirt, brown silk sport jacket and Dockers. If Buzz would have been remotely interested he would have noticed he was wearing loafers with no sox. "My card," said the young man as he handed Buzz a business card. Buzz took the card and looked at it carefully. 'Mitchell Green Director of Field Organization' it said. In smaller letters underneath Mitchell's name was the name of Mitchell's organization. The United Federation of Millwrights International was emblazoned next to a logo. "I am the person that talked to you on the phone Mr. Olsen."

"Okay, I don't doubt you. I… I'm just a little nervous I guess. I've never done anything like this before. I'm …I don't know how these things are supposed to work." Buzz rubbed his hand nervously over the back of his clean-shaven head. Buzz was forty-two about five foot eleven and approximately one hundred eighty pounds. From a distance he appeared to be bald, but when you were close you realized that Buzz shaved his head. He was tanned and had a rough weather beaten appearance about him. Buzz worked with his hands, they were tough and callused with stubby strong fingers. He was a cabinet-maker and had worked for Fox ever since the factory out on the desert opened its doors. He was at the top of his trade. Fox designated him as a cabinet-maker grade "A."

"You're not supposed to know how these things work," answered Mitchell. "That's my job to advise you. That's why we are meeting. Now, answer a couple of questions for me if you will, and don't feel you are betraying your employer. Trust me; your employer never includes you in the discussions when deciding to lay off your fellow workers. Does he consult you when he is setting pay levels? He certainly doesn't discuss staffing requirements with you does he?"

"No, we are not included in any of those things. We only become involved in the results."

"That's right. That's the way that it always is Buzz. The only reason that business has been able to get away with these things in recent years is because a little while ago companies put the unions on the defensive by talking about the Japanese threat. They correctly convinced us that we had to become more productive or all of our jobs would wind up on the Pacific Rim. Well the American Worker rose to the challenge! He did as he always has done when presented with a challenge; he rolled up his sleeves and put his mind and muscle to the task and pushed the United States right back to the top of the productivity list! He beat back the Japanese threat! Beat it back to the point that Japan was pushed into a recession that they are only now beginning to recover from. But what happened? What was the American worker's reward for this miracle? Reorganization! Downsizing! Under staffing! That was his reward. When he looked around for help he discovered that in the glare of unprecedented prosperity the traditional defender of his rights, the union, had been pushed out of the work place. Business had deceived the younger members of the work force and convinced them that the unions were the cause of America's falling behind and not business skimming excess profits off the top rather than modernizing their factories. But now in the face of mergers, under staffing, reduction of benefits and pay increases that are shameful when compared to the obscene salaries of CEO's the union is prepared to make a comeback."

Buzz listened intently. Mitchell certainly touched upon some of the issues that he and his fellow workers were concerned about. Under staffing, long hours, reduction in benefits, Fox had just informed its employees that Fox's "matching" contribution to their 401 K plan would be cut in half next year. In addition the employees would soon be expected to pay a greater share of health care. While Fox remained an excellent place to work with a very low turnover rate the workers were concerned about the trend that seemed to be emerging. Now there was talk about a new compensation program based on something called pay for performance. The company said that this would allow them all to make more money, but the feeling on the floor was that this was really a pay cut in disguise.

This morning a new and disturbing rumor swept the floor. The word from back east was that Fox was going to be sold. This could either be a scare tactic employed by management to get them to submit to the pay for performance compensation plan or if true, the work force would be subject to the whims of new owners who could be far worse than the Atlantic Corporation. The feeling was that the workers would be far better off if the new owners were also purchasing a contract with a union, something that they did not have the benefit of now.

Buzz swallowed hard. He had always enjoyed working for Fox and he really didn't want to work for anyone else. Fox offered a pay and benefit package that was superior to any other in this industry. The last thing Buzz and his co-workers wanted to see was a reduction in the very benefits that had lured them here to begin with. "Okay, you've touched some nerves. How do we get started?"

"Well to begin with you have to present your employer with enough signed cards requesting a vote on a union to force Fox to hold an election. At the same time you inform the National Labor Relations Board that you've done this. The clock starts ticking and sometime between 45 to 60 days later the NLRB oversees a secret ballot to decide if there are a majority of workers at Fox that want our union to represent them. You have to circulate the cards because until you have enough signed to request the vote we, the union, cannot set foot on Fox property."

"I'm listening," replied Buzz as the two ordered coffee and burgers and hunched together over their task. The young girl that accompanied Mitchell Green to the restaurant was alone in her booth happily playing keno. She seemed oblivious to Buzz and Mitchell.

***

Trevor Mason's cell phone vibrated. He reached into his inside breast pocket and removed the small device. The tiny screen revealed a familiar phone number. He chose to ignore it and looked at his staff as they were seated about the large oak table in Atlantic's conference room.

"Excuse me for a moment," he said as he rose from his chair at the head of the table.

"Sure Trevor," replied John Hogg. As Trevor left the room Denton Wellbon III, John Hogg and the three other executives that made up Atlantic Corporation's executive staff continued their discussion of the monthly numbers that the operating divisions had just turned in.

Trevor Mason strode down the carpeted hallway toward his own office. The number on his cell was that of Abraham Rueben's cell phone. Trevor looked at his watch. It was two-thirty Monday afternoon, Abe was early thought Trevor. As he passed his secretary he gave instructions that he not be disturbed. He entered his office, closed the door behind him and punched Reuben's number into his own cell phone and waited.

"Abraham Rueben," the voice said at the other end.

"Trevor Mason," was the curt reply.

"All four horses are in the stable."

"Good, any problems?"

"None, these horses are hungry and are open to any suggestion of a 'free' meal."

"As I expected, in addition all hands are now on board." Trevor was referring to Denton. "Move on to more difficult pastures. Do we need to meet?"

"Not for the next several horses, but after that I will probably require some of that special hay that you were speaking of to coax the remainder of the herd into the stable."

"Call me with progress reports and let me know when we need a face to face.'

"Of that you can be certain Trevor, good afternoon."

Trevor hit the power button without replying. He gazed out over the city and permitted himself a smile. After savoring the moment he turned to the phone on his desk. He hit the intercom button. His secretary responded immediately. "Yes Mr. Mason?"

"Call my wife. Tell her I'll meet her at her favorite restaurant about five o'clock. I'll make the reservations."

"Right away Mr. Mason."

Back in the conference room Denton Wellbon, John Hogg and company were mildly surprised when Trevor's secretary entered and informed them that their boss had left the office for the day and they were instructed to carry on without him. "Is there anything wrong?" inquired John.

"No, he said that he and his wife were going to celebrate tonight."

After the secretary's departure Trevor's staff looked at each other in disbelief. Trevor never left early. "Must be a personal event," said John as they returned to the business at hand. "You all have Williamson Manufacturing's monthly report.

Anyone see a solid reason as to why the margin should have dropped off as much as it has?"

***

Mac entered the dark restaurant and waited to be seated. He told the hostess he would be expecting a guest. In addition he requested a table in a dark corner. She flashed him a dazzling smile. She was a beautiful young Italian girl with long black tresses and a skirt that was much too short even when compared to Mac's somewhat liberal criteria. Mac followed her dutifully to his corner table while finding it extremely difficult to remove his gaze from her shapely legs.

The restaurant was formerly an old warehouse in the heart of New York's Little Italy. The brick walls had been left untouched except where they had to be "pointed" or risk falling down. The woodwork, where there was woodwork, was white oak with a clear natural finish. These elements, brick and natural oak, combined to give the old place some warmth and charm. Mac picked up the menu. It was loaded with delicious pasta dishes. He made his selection in advance and then turned to the wine list. Here Mac's preference was purely Californian. He much preferred the California wines to the Italian and French. Australian wines were a second choice.

Mac looked up to find the proprietor of the establishment hovering at his elbow. "Gueto my friend, do you remember me?"

"Of course I remember you, you a friend of Tony's, you Tony's boss!" Tony Conocenti grew up in Little Italy. On one of their numerous joint business trips to New York Tony brought Mac to this establishment so that he could taste real Italian as Tony had described it. Mac wasn't certain if it was real Italian or not, but it certainly was delicious. "My girl, she say that you expecting a guest. Can I get you something to drink while you wait?"

Mac chose a bottle of his favorite Merlot. It would go well with the dish that he was planning to order. Gueto scribbled on his pad and was gone in a flash.

Each time Tony traveled through Little Italy with Mac he would shake his head and lament, "The place just isn't the same anymore." First neighboring Chinatown had been steadily growing and encroaching on the old neighborhood shrinking Little Italy. Second the fading power of the New York crime families.

To Catch a Fox

They provided an exciting alter ego for residents of Little Italy who were born, raised and worked there. Tony did not support organized crime, but he liked the "romantic mystique" that accompanied it in literature and the movies. The harsh reality was something that was best forgotten. Ironically it was that harsh reality that brought Mac to this place on this evening.

Mac's bottle of Merlot arrived. The proprietor had sent his brother to do the honors while he was off personally greeting another guest that he deemed worthy of his attention. The man expertly removed the cork and presented it to Mac. Mac sniffed it and nodded his approval. A splash of the wine was apportioned to Mac's glass. Mac raised the glass, swirled the deep red liquid about, placed the glass under his nose and inhaled the bouquet. He then sipped the liquid, swished it about in his mouth and swallowed. It tasted excellent and Mac again nodded his approval. With Mac's signal of approval the smiling gentleman now poured more into Mac's glass and with a flourish placed the opened bottle on the table. Still smiling he made a positive comment about Mac enjoying the meal and was off to help with the ever-growing number of customers.

Mac as always was amused by the entire procedure. Mac suspected that the wine steward was smiling because he believed in their ignorance his customers wouldn't know a great wine from sour grape juice. Mac in his lifetime encountered one and only one bottle of bad wine. He didn't know if he was just lucky or if the industry standards for bottling were simply exceptional in modern times. The interesting part of that occasion was that another individual at Mac's table had put the wine through the same test and accepted the bottle. The wine had turned and the first sip that Mac had taken nearly ended in his spewing it out of his mouth. So much for the sophisticated taste buds of the American consumer.

Mac's reverie was disturbed by the young lady in the all too brief skirt approaching with another customer in tow. This customer had a familiar face that was smiling at the sight of Mac. Mac rose to offer his hand as the gentleman arrived.

"Tom! Good to see you again!"

"You too Mac, it's been far too long!" answered Tom Luca.

Tom was an old college friend of Mac's. They had shared their first off campus apartment. Over the years the periods between visits had sometimes grown long, but their friendship developed that rare quality of being able to pick up right where they left off whenever they got together.

Tom was short and fit with thick curly black hair and a dark complexion on his slightly pox marked face. Mac offered him wine to which Tom accepted. After a sip, Tom nodded his approval. "I see you still have excellent taste old friend." Tom's voice had a constant mild rasp. After you realized that he wasn't just "hoarse" from a slight cold, it sort of grew on you in an odd way that Mac couldn't describe.

"I try. How are you? It has been too long."

"Yes it has." With that the two lifelong friends began to catch up on their recent activities. Tom graduated with Mac and earned a bachelor's degree in accounting. He went on to become a Certified Public Accountant and joined one of the "Big Six" accounting firms. After surviving the traditional internship and third year "cut" Tom began a steady march up through the corporate ranks. Along the way he earned an MBA. Today he was one of the partners and it was rumored that he would soon be offered one of the exclusive senior partnerships.

Salad came followed by two large dishes of excellent pasta. The talk was by turns somber, as Mac briefly discussed recent events in Scotland, and jovial as the two shared a humorous story. More wine was ordered as seconds on the pasta were brought to the table and set upon with gusto. The hours drifted away as main course led to dessert and finally after dinner coffee and liqueur. As they slowly sipped the drinks there was a lag in the conversation. Tom Luca smiled at his friend. "You call me at the office and ask me to meet you for dinner. Then all through the meal I have the distinct feeling that there is something you want to ask, but aren't. We can talk more about your father if you want."

Mac smiled, "You always could read me like a book."

"One of the few who could, now what is it?"

"It's not about my father. That hurts and will hurt for a long time, but I'm dealing with it. No there is another problem. Let's call it a corporate problem. I need your help Tom. Not only do I believe that my own job may be at stake, but the jobs of other good hard working people. Perhaps the very essence of what Fox

Cabinetry has become is at stake."

Tom looked puzzled. "This doesn't sound like the hardnosed 'it's just business no more no less' William MacLode that I know."

Mac took a deep breath and another sip of his drink. "No it doesn't. Maybe I'm more under the influence of my father's death than I want to admit. Maybe I'm getting soft and sentimental in my approaching old age." Mac's glass was empty. He glanced at Tom's and it appeared to be in the same condition. He looked around and caught the attention of the young girl in the short skirt. Mac ordered another round for them both.

"You obviously feel that you and your company are being threatened. There's nothing wrong with pride in what you helped create. You have concerns for your employees and believe that the possibility it could be destroyed is very real. Nothing wrong with any of those reasons Mac. That's no sign of weakness. It's to be expected. Let's look at your problem together. What's going on?"

Mac smiled. "Are you certain that you didn't also take a major in psychology?"

Tom grinned in return. "No psychology, but my uncle is a priest."

"Only your one uncle," was Mac's retort. "All the others are 'family' members."

"Shhhhhh" Tom placed a finger to his lips. "Now don't go spilling secrets."

Mac began with recent history. How Fox and Atlantic Corporation functioned under the benevolent hand of Carlton Smith. Mac observed that in a remote sort of way Smith had been his mentor and benefactor. How all of that changed with the arrival of Trevor Mason.

"Whoa. Hold it right there. Is this the Trevor Mason from Chicago?"

"Yes. Why do you ask? Do you know him?"

"I know of him. If he's who I think he is."

"What do you know Tom?"

"I know that he managed to sell off all or parts of the last two corporations of which he has been an officer. In all cases he was also a stockholder and benefited immensely from the deals."

"There's nothing illegal in that."

"No, not on the surface, but I heard that there were some shareholders in the last company that felt that he went beyond the boundaries of their corporate charter to insure the sale."

"What kind of boundaries and how far beyond them did he go?"

"Some thought it odd that three of the large shareholders were attacked by muggers and wound up in the hospital one week before the crucial vote on the sale. The muggers were never caught and the victims were very uncooperative with the police."

"You're saying that he used strong-arm tactics?"

Tom shrugged as the waitress brought them fresh drinks. Upon her departure he continued. "By some coincidence all three chose to assign their proxy to Trevor Mason so that he could vote as he saw fit in their absence. This occurred after the attacks. Previous to these unfortunate events all three had expressed negative opinions concerning the sale of their company and a similar distaste at the sight of Mr. Mason."

"Then they suddenly had a change of heart concerning both their opinion of the sale of their shares and their feelings of trust for Trevor? Their change of heart was so drastic that they gave their proxy to him?" Mac was incredulous!

"From the relative discomfort of their hospital beds, yes. Keep in mind that the sale of this company was far from a cordial unanimous decision among the shareholders. It was privately owned and the shares were spread among senior managers and three families. The debate leading up to the shareholder's meeting was nasty at best. In the end it was a close vote, the motion to sell carried by only fifty shares. The three proxy votes that Trevor gained in the final weeks made the difference."

"Incredible!"

"Yes it was and for some strange reason there were no law suits. It almost seems as if everyone was afraid." Tom drained his drink in one gulp.

"The police didn't uncover anything in their investigation?"

"Oh they were suspicious. The attacks were in a part of Chicago with a very low street crime rate, but when the victims insisted that they couldn't identify their assailants or even describe them and it was obvious that they didn't want publicity, how far could the police go? Just like here in New York, police are very busy people. The 'road' ends when victims fail to file complaints."

Silence ensued as Tom observed Mac contemplating this news. "Please continue. I'm sorry that I interrupted. But I thought you might want to know the type of person that you may be in business with."

"You could verify that for me?"

Tom nodded in agreement. "Let's hear the rest of your story."

Mac continued with the unreasonable demands that Trevor Mason placed on all of the Atlantic divisions, but in particular Fox. "This isn't just your opinion?" asked Tom.

"No, not at all, several of the other division presidents have made it a point to contact me and ask what I did to 'piss Trevor off?' answered Mac."

Mac concluded with the events that have culminated in his belief that Mason now plans to sell off the Fox division. "I'm certain Tony had a few choice names for me when the rumor leaked to the dealer network and I wasn't in the office to help stem the tide of insecurity. I can't believe that Trevor was that stupid as to allow word to get out."

Tom reached into his breast pocket and extracted a silver cigarette case. He opened it and offered one to Mac. Mac declined. "I've quit thanks."

"Since when?"

"About a year ago, no that isn't correct, one year two months and, let me think, ten days. I can give you the hours and the minutes if you give me a chance to think about it."

Tom laughed. "It has been too long since we've been together. Congratulations! I wish I could do it. Would you prefer that I don't?"

"No, please go ahead. I have to be around people that smoke every day. If I can't watch you smoke without joining you then I haven't really quit."

"Okay." Tom began to light up, but then thought better of it. "I'll forgo it tonight. Maybe this will be the start of something. Now where were we? Who is this Tony you mentioned?"

"Tony Conocenti is my Sales and Marketing VP"

"Oh yes, I remember you speaking of him before… Maybe Mason wasn't stupid. Maybe someone doing the appraisal was stupid or maybe Trevor himself arranged the leak. Remember, if he's looking for a quick sale he wants the word on the street without making it official. If he doesn't release it he can always officially deny it. That won't stop the potential buyer from inquiring."

"You think it is part of the plan?"

"Could be, let me ask you something. Why do you care?"

Mac thought about this for a moment, "Probably for all the reasons that you pointed out at the beginning of this conversation."

Tom looked his old friend straight in the eye. "What makes you think that being sold is the worst thing that could happen to Fox? You made mention earlier this evening that you fear the start of a labor union out in your Nevada plant. I would think that is of more concern than who owns you. With everything that you've just told me it's hard to imagine you getting a harder person to report to than Trevor Mason. Your life could get better with Fox sold to the right owner." Tom paused and lowered his voice. "You're not afraid of change are you Mac?"

Mac raised his eyebrows. Those words were the kiss of death to modern managers, sort of a litmus test. The popular thinking was that change is a good thing, if you aren't constantly changing then that's not a good thing and your abilities and motives are suspect. Mac and his team had introduced a lot of changes at Fox during his tenure. Based on the results he believed that the changes were for the better. However he had been careful to leave certain elements intact, both physical and cultural, that he believed attributed to the success of Fox. He had witnessed several of his peers at other Atlantic divisions' institute what he believed was change for the sake of change only. Change to draw attention to them. Change instituted with only one purpose in mind, to appear progressive and with the popular trends. Mac observed that if the change was not carefully thought out in terms of its long-term impact, then the basic culture of an organization could be changed for the worse. In these situations there was usually an initial surge of success followed by a mysterious long-term reversal of fortunes. Usually a key part of the organizational culture was changed that had long been quietly contributing to success, but now was missing. No Mac was not against or afraid of change, but he knew that these things could not be made up as you go along. The spontaneous appearing change required long and thoughtful planning by those closest to the organization and its cultural base.

"I'm waiting for your answer old friend."

"No," Mac smiled, "I'm not afraid of change. However, you are well versed in my views on the subject and they haven't changed if I may use that word."

"I know and I generally agree with you. But I think that even though Trevor Mason is a son of a bitch, you have learned how to deal with him and you are comfortable with that. You just told me how you were impressed the way your team has pulled together and to your surprise you believe that they will be ready with their annual strategic plan on the accelerated schedule. You put that team together and you are the motivator. This has been the key to your success. You are not happy with having to figure out yet another boss during your career. Look at me! Look me in the eye! Trevor Mason is really only the second person that you have had to report to since college! First Carlton Smith who you just described as your mentor and now Trevor Mason. Do you realize how rare that is today? You're spoiled Mac!"

"It's good that you are one of my best friends or I wouldn't let you get away with that." Mac's voice was even but not hostile.

"I know that. But that's why we're sitting here tonight isn't it?"

Mac smiled. "I suppose that it is. But you yourself have just introduced a new element. This guy Mason may be a very dangerous person. How do I deal with that?"

"It's doubtful that with the relatively small amount of Wellbon-Smith stock that you and your fellow managers have accumulated through the bonus plans that any of you will be the target of strong-arm tactics. I don't think that you need to fear that."

"I would agree, but I still believe that I'm an ethical man and I can't work for a person like that. Even putting that issue aside, as I have no real proof of his brutality, Trevor may have just coldly caused damage to Fox with the rumor of its sale that could take years to repair. Kitchen dealers like all retailers can be a skittish bunch. They fear being 'orphaned' by the manufacturers that they are affiliated with. This could push them to align themselves with other factories and dilute their sales effort on behalf of Fox. I do fear that kind of change. That's an example of self-serving and reckless change. It threatens not only my future but the future of all those hard working people at Fox who reasonably expect to retire from there."

"You could afford to retire right this moment," was Tom Luca's retort. "You have no dependents. You've never been married. Hell, you don't even have an ex-wife like some of us intent on bleeding you dry. You've made a hell of a good living for a lot of years not to mention your impending inheritance. Am I right? Why are you afraid for yourself?"

"I guess that I'm not really afraid for myself. With my father's death there is certainly a need for me to return home and take care of the family's affairs. I suppose I could envision myself as a country gentleman like my father."

Tom smiled. "I think we are at the heart of the matter. I agree you aren't afraid for yourself. Neither are you afraid of change in general, but you don't trust the likes of Trevor Mason to determine the future of the people that you have worked with for so many years and have become dedicated to preserving their jobs and futures."

Mac finished his drink. The melting ice had diluted it considerably. "I suppose you may be correct."

"I may be correct? I may be correct that the 'Great Loner' that I have known for most of my adult life actually cares for people? There are a few of us, a very few mind you, that you have allowed inside that fortress of your personality long enough to discover that you are really a warm and caring human being. You fail miserably at broadcasting that fact to the outside world, but it is fact none the less." Tom paused and his voice and eyes softened. He really liked this man and valued their friendship. "What can I do to help?"

"You've already begun with your knowledge of Trevor Mason's past," replied Mac.

"I will verify that we are talking about the same person, but I'm nearly positive that we are."

"Okay. In addition to that I need you to impose on your family members and pull a few strings. If I'm going to fight this, I have to know everything about Mason, his strengths and his weaknesses, everything and anything that I might be able to use."

Tom smiled a wry smile. "You're implying that my blood relatives are members of a greater 'family'?"

"With the exception of your uncle the priest, you know that they are. Remember whom you're talking to Tom. This is Mac. We both know that the FBI watches your relatives and is on a first name basis with them."

"Yeah, you're going to make me pay my entire life for that one indiscretion that weekend I took you along home from college. Could you try to remember that my mother was never involved with the family business, and that my father is now retired and a respectable citizen? In addition, my father never spent a day of his life in jail. Nor did he ever permit my brother and me to become involved. And keep your voice down!"

"Only because they could never prove anything, and you know that I love your father dearly. I just don't want to know any more than I do concerning his business career."

"Hey Mac, don't you read the papers? The 'families' are not what they used to be. They're going to hell in a hand basket. 'The Teflon Don' is away for good.

The Scarfo family down in Philly is in total disarray. Things aren't that way anymore."

"Because of my lifetime association with a certain Big Six accountant, I also know what few people know. There has been a split in the organization. There are the Don's that you mentioned that their time has passed. The old violent ways just don't make it anymore and they chose not to change. There are also the men like your father that were glad to split with them. They run very discreet operations. Sophisticated computerized operations behind legitimate businesses, they keep a low profile and they don't gun down people on the street corner anymore. These guys have education and class. They put their kids through college and a few of those kids become successful like that accountant I was in college with. Don't tell me that your family no longer has power and influence. Can I count on you to get me the help I need?"

Tom was silent for a long moment. He exhaled a long soft sigh. "Okay, no bullshit. I'll talk to Pop. We'll get you what you need. I'll explain the situation to him. He likes you, and he really enjoyed spending time with your father during his visit to this country a couple of years ago. It will be done."

"Thank you Tom. I knew that I could count on you." Mac was relieved. The information that Tom Luca could supply would be crucial if he were to have any chance at all to block Trevor's plans whatever they may be.

"Mac, there's just two things you need to remember."

"What's that?"

"Just because my father's business appears to be legitimate and you don't see his name or the names of his associates in the news like the others that we just mentioned. Just because you happen to be a friend of my father and also a friend of mine, none of this means that my father won't expect you to repay this favor in kind some day. You understand that don't you?"

"I understand," said Mac. His voice sounding more certain than his stomach suddenly felt. "What's the other thing I need to remember?"

"You said that they don't gun people down on the street corner anymore and you were correct. But people that owe a debt of a favor and then turn their backs on the friend that performed the favor for them when it's time to reciprocate..." Tom paused unnecessarily for effect. "Those people, how shall I explain it? Those people become non entities."

"I will remember Tom. Thank you very much. You are a loyal and trustworthy friend." Mac didn't understand exactly what his friend meant by a "non entity" and he was strangely afraid to ask. He just knew that he would make certain that he never became one.

Tom decided to change his mind concerning the cigarette. He retrieved one from his silver case and lit up. After a long drag that he exhaled noisily he looked at Mac and smiled. "I enjoyed our dinner and the conversation immensely. I'm also flattered that you came to me for advice and help. Most of all I'm glad that I can help. Your friendship means a lot to me Mac."

"Our friendship means a lot to me also Tom. It is one of my prized possessions."

Tom held Mac's gaze for a long moment and then spoke in a low tone. "I have a suggestion."

"That being?"

"Why don't you round up some investors and buy Fox yourself?"

Mac was stunned. He had never once entertained that possibility.

To Catch a Fox

PART 2

CHAPTER 9

Mitchell Green was seated aboard a Boeing 737 that was bound for Harrisburg, Pennsylvania. He looked at his watch and smiled to himself. At this very moment Buzz Olsen was passing out cards and soliciting signatures from Fox employees in the Desert Rat bar. The Desert Rat bar was located in The High Plains Industrial Park approximately twenty miles east of Las Vegas. At least twenty-five companies including Fox Cabinetry had decided to build factories within its confines. Mitchell was confident that all would go well. He and his union had been researching Fox Cabinetry and several other companies in the Atlantic Empire for the past several months. It was not because these particular companies were easy targets; indeed there were no easy targets for union organization. It was because of the actions of one man. His past record had come to the union's attention while he was involved with a Chicago based company. That individual was Trevor Mason. Mason had developed a method of operation that appealed to the union organizers. Not because they approved, but because of the opportunity that his actions ultimately presented. Mason had gained a reputation as a "turnaround artist." Simply put he had made his reputation by taking charge of marginally profitable organizations and turning attractive profits quickly. His methods were harsh but effective. No matter how efficient a company's managers were, Mason through fear and intimidation forced them to take actions that cut expenses and produced greater profits. Admirable achievements in this day in age except for one tiny flaw in the theory; Mason assumed, as do most modern managers, that all business is alike. Particularly if you are considering manufacturing operations, a widget is a widget is a widget. It matters not what the product may be because the same principles apply to all, all that is except the work of artisans.

The United Federation of Millwrights International (UFMI) was essentially a union of artisans. Millwrights, pattern makers, wood workers of all stripes. Increasingly they had been pushed out of the shops where mass production techniques could be easily applied. This included the semi custom and stock cabinet manufacturers in the kitchen industry and nearly all furniture manufacturers of any size. The reason being that these companies basically produced a lot of units that were the same or similar. Because of this, mass production techniques that included software and robotics systems could be applied. The requirement for true tradesmen in these shops was becoming less and less. These companies could implement piecework or pay for performance systems that allowed the worker to make more money as an individual then as a union member. The union's traditional "protection" of all workers actually reduced the earning potential of the extremely quick and creative laborer in these environments. The truly custom end of the cabinet and furniture industry, that industry within an industry, still stubbornly resisted automation. This was a labor intense industry where no two "units" moving through the factories were alike; indeed the fact that they were different was the very niche that these companies were striving to fill. Thus the need for artisans to make up for the lack of automated systems.

This subtle difference was lost on people like Trevor Mason and the management of holding companies like Atlantic Corporation. They would tour installations such as Fox and determine that they could increase the margins dramatically by simply applying the principles of automation that the current managers were too ignorant to apply. This seldom worked and forced the front line management to boost the margins by making cuts in the budgets. Those cuts were invariably expenses associated with direct labor. Those were the cuts that a union organizer could "get his teeth into."

Mitchell Green's union had looked long and hard at Fox just a few short years previous to this and decided that there was no hope in organizing the work force. They came to this conclusion because the long time Fox president, one William MacLode, was not only a good businessperson, but also very shrewd in his methods of organization and his dealings with people. MacLode had come to the conclusion that a plant that employed five hundred people or less was hardly worth the time, expense and sheer manpower that a union would have to expend to organize and maintain it. MacLode was correct in this assumption.

Acting upon this belief MacLode, upon assuming control of Fox, immediately began to look for a site to locate an additional plant. He chose the industrial park just east of Las Vegas. This solved two problems. First it allowed Fox to have two factories with five hundred or less employees. Second Fox was expanding its market to the West Coast and the costs associated with delivery from Pennsylvania were high. In addition MacLode raised Fox labor rates to the highest in the custom industry. He could afford this because of the Fox reputation. The consumer expected to pay considerably more for their product. This fact allowed MacLode to absorb these increased costs into the higher "sticker" price.

As soon as the Fox factory in Pennsylvania employed over seven hundred people MacLode exercised the option that he held with the High Plains Industrial Park. When the new plant was complete, he offered generous relocation bonuses to nearly two hundred of his skilled craftsmen to move to the Nevada plant. With this number of seasoned personnel in place and tight production procedures, Fox was able to achieve what no one in the industry before them had accomplished. Fox opened a second plant without any noticeable difference in the level of quality. Today there were nearly five hundred employees at each plant. Mitchell Green's sources confirmed that with sales growing and Fox tentatively looking at the Pacific Rim for additional markets, MacLode was now scouting the Pacific Northwest for a possible future additional manufacturing site. The addition of plants served to lower delivery costs while giving better service and because of the relatively small number of employees at each and the diverse geographical locations, the strategy succeeded in keeping the unions out.

Because MacLode's previous boss, Carlton Smith, was satisfied with this strategy, he was able to incur the necessary expenses. Now with Trevor Mason's push for greater profit margins, Fox was pressured to increase its performance. Maclode soon found that the only way that he could achieve Mason's expectations was to cut costs. He attempted this through two very different avenues. First, MacLode was convinced that with the advent of new programming languages it would soon be possible to begin incorporating many of the automation techniques that have been successful in the "bottom two thirds of the industry" into the totally custom segment. Two years ago, he hired two programmers to create a new order entry and manufacturing software package to bring as much science to this custom art form as is possible. This project, while still maintaining MacLode's support, was well behind schedule and over budget. Rumor had it that MacLode had so far hidden this expense within the Fox operating budget so that Mason could not readily see how expensive it truly was.

Secondly Maclode reluctantly began cutting benefits. First he asked the employees to increase their share of expense for the company insurance plan. In addition, MacLode found it necessary to decrease the company's percentage of "matching" funds to the 401K programs. Neither of these decisions was popular and for the first time Mitchell Green's union believed that Fox was vulnerable.

To Catch a Fox

The rumor of the sale of Fox was an unexpected gift. Nothing instills fear in human beings faster than contemplating the unknown.

The real beauty was that Fox management would be totally oblivious to the union effort until it was too late. They would remain secure in their belief that by splitting the operation in two at either end of the continent the economic situation for the union would remain prohibitive. In this they would be correct. The economics were atrocious! What Fox failed to realize was that the UFMI had a tentative offer to merge with the much larger Consolidated Trade Unions of America. The CTU of A placed one condition on the merger after all operating issues had been negotiated. The UFMI had to come to the "marriage" with a minimum of one hundred thousand members. At this moment they were but a few thousand members short. Fox, with its potential for growth, along with two other relatively small companies in different industries would provide just enough membership for the two organizations to consummate the marriage. When this occurred, the merger would be announced. Mitchell Green's union had been on shaky financial grounds for more than a decade. The merger would allow them to survive. Much was riding on the organization of these few companies.

Mitchell Green looked out the window of the airliner. It was dark now and they would soon begin the decent into Chicago's O'Hare. The lights of the towns below were getting brighter and much closer together as they moved east. He smiled again to himself. The operatives that he had placed within the Fox rank and file had paid off. At this moment he felt as if he knew as much about the inner operation of Fox as did William MacLode. He looked forward to negotiating with this formidable opponent.

***

It was nearly eight o'clock in the evening and Tony Conocenti was waiting impatiently in the nearly deserted main waiting area of the Lancaster Railroad Station. The large high ceiling turn of the century building had been beautifully adorned with that era's opulent décor. Tony mused for a second on how they would explain "turn of the century" architecture after next year when civilization entered the 21st Century. He guessed that it would then become the "turn of the 20th century" architecture. No matter, he wasn't waiting here to give a critique on the architecture of landmark buildings within the boundaries of the City of Lancaster Pennsylvania. No, he was waiting with great anticipation for the surprising arrival of Blair McManus.

Earlier that afternoon Tony was in his office when the phone rang. Brady's business like voice welcomed him when he picked it up. "Call for you Anthony. It's a woman, but she wouldn't give me her name. She claims that you will know her. Do you wish me to brush her off if she refuses to identify herself?"

"No I'll take it."

"She probably is one of those brokers trying to sell you the 'hot stock' of the day. Are you certain you wish to talk to her?"

"I'll risk it Brady. If you're correct, I'm pretty good at brushing people off myself."

"I would respectfully disagree with that statement Anthony. You tolerate telephone salespeople far too long."

"Brady, I could have brushed her off by now. If she hasn't given up already, please put her through."

"Very well Anthony. Hang up and I'll transfer the call."

A second later the phone rang again, "Tony Conocenti speaking."

"Hi Tiger! How are you this afternoon?" Tony was delighted to hear Blair's voice.

"I'm great now that I'm talking to you!"

"That's the kind of attitude I like tiger."

"Where are you? What are you up to?"

"Surprise I'm in New York! My boss sent me here late yesterday to meet with a renowned interior designer from Europe and do an article on him. It seems that this guy has just been commissioned to redecorate one of the Queen of England's country homes. Everyone expects his work to be trend setting. Problem is that he's a bit of a recluse and seldom grants interviews. I requested that on the condition that I get the interview, could I take a couple of days off after filing the article? My boss said yes, and I just e-mailed it to him. He was so ecstatic not only with the interview, but with the fact that I even got to meet with this guy, that he told me to take the entire week off. I don't have to be back in Chicago until next Monday."

"Good for you! How did you manage to convince the designer to see you in the first place?"

"I sent my photo to his hotel and promised him sex."

"You're kidding right?" There was a naughty little laugh on the other end. Sometimes Blair wasn't funny thought Tony.

Breezing right by Tony's inquiry Blair continued, "The reason for my call is this: Could an out of town girl come and shack up with you for a couple of days? I won't be any trouble. I promise."

"Of course you can!" Tony found that he was delighted. He noticed that the stress of the day suddenly seemed to evaporate. "I won't be able to get off work during the day to entertain you though. We have a few emergencies going here right now." He held his breath and hoped that this news wouldn't discourage her. Damn! What's going on here? He discovered that he was crossing his fingers!

"That's okay. I didn't expect that you could. I plan on doing some shopping at those outlet malls you have down there and perhaps a little antiquing on the side. I would prefer your company in the evenings though. Do you think that you can manage that?"

"You bet I can."

"Great! I'll be on the last train from 'The City' to Lancaster tonight. I think it gets in about eight. Can you meet me at the station?"

"Sure will. I'll confirm that schedule."

"See you then. Love you." she was gone!

Tony slowly replaced the receiver in its cradle. Did she actually say 'love you?'

he thought she did, or did he hear wrong? As was typical with Blair, things happen so fast that you have to regroup to determine what actually took place. No he was certain that was what she said. Was it just a substitute for a friendly 'good bye?' Did it actually mean what the English language meant it to mean? Blair had never spoken those two words to him previous to this conversation. Of that he was certain. That feeling he had the other morning in Chicago returned. He was becoming convinced that something fundamental had changed in their relationship. He found that he was gripped with a simultaneous feeling of elation accompanied with an underlying fear. He wasn't over the emotional residue of his long-term marriage. Some nights he wasn't certain that he would ever get over it. Was he prepared to venture into a new relationship? Especially a relationship with a free spirited individual the likes of Blair.

Tony gave a long sigh. He couldn't deny one fact. He suddenly found that he was extremely relaxed, excited and happy. Yes happy. He admitted to himself that he hadn't truly felt happiness in more than a year. Best not to over analyze this he thought. Blair would be the first one to instruct him to 'go with it and have a good time.'

Tony punched the intercom button on the phone. "Brady can you call Amtrak and find out the exact time that the last train from New York City arrives at Lancaster tonight?"

"Right away boss," was Brady's reply. Tony suddenly realized that he felt resentment toward that unnamed European designer that Blair had interviewed. He better not have touched her! Whoa! What was that, jealously? Tony shook his head. Damn Blair! This was all taking an unexpected turn.

"Last train arrives at eight fifteen tonight Anthony."

Tony checked his watch. He had time to work about a half-hour longer, then head for his apartment, freshen up and change clothes. He and Blair could grab a late dinner. He was definitely certain of one thing. He didn't want to be late meeting her.

Tony's thoughts returned to the present as the long silver train glided into the station. Upon announcement of its arrival, Tony had left the upper level and proceeded down the outside staircase to the boarding platforms. The cylindrical "tubes" slowly came to a halt. The doors opened and the late travelers began emerging onto the platform. A few other "greeters" were standing with Tony as he looked up and down the length of the train. He found that he was holding his breath in anticipation. The late train was never as crowded as the earlier editions. Suddenly there she was pulling with her a single piece of wheeled black luggage. Her long red hair streamed out behind her in the slight evening breeze. She wore jeans, a white blouse, and a lightweight hooded denim jacket. Tony thought she looked great. She waved a cheery hello. Tony found that he covered the distance between them in short order. Her arms opened and she gave him a hug and a kiss on the lips. Was it slightly longer than usual? Did she hold him closer and tighter than before?

"Hi Tiger it's great to see you! I'm starved. Could you take a weary girl to a nice quiet restaurant for some much needed nourishment?"

He was captivated by her dazzling white smile. "I've already made reservations."

They stood there in silence for a long moment looking at each other, as Blair's ornery little grin held him trance like. "We ain't left yet?" she inquired.

"Oh! Yeah… let's go. We don't want to be late." Tony took her bag and led her up the stairs. Her hand slipped into the crook of his arm.

***

It had been a long day. Mac looked around the table in the hotel conference room. His staff all appeared to have glazed eyes. One of the lawyers from the firm that Fox kept on retainer was droning to a close. "That's pretty much it," he said. "There are a lot of things that you can do to prevent a union from coming into your plants, but I can't emphasize enough that you have to play by the government's rules. Do you have any questions?"

Mac leafed through one of the bound folders that the two lawyers had provided for each of his staff. He looked up. Hearing no questions, he guessed that his troops were by now too "brain dead" to even think of anything intelligent. "Thank you gentlemen for your fine efforts I think we all have to review this book of guidelines and formulate a strategy. At that point we will no doubt have questions and we will be certain to run any counter moves that we come up with by you for your opinion." Mac began packing his briefcase. "That's all people we meet back here tomorrow morning at eight sharp. I have this room for another day. The hotel will provide pastries, juice and coffee for breakfast." He turned to the lawyers. They were both specialists on labor law. "As an afterthought, would it be possible for one of you to be here tomorrow? I want to be proactive in this and we will need your immediate opinion on our defensive strategy. I definitely don't want to run afoul of the law."

"I can be here sir" answered the youngest. Mac was grateful that the younger of the two responded with a positive answer, as he was the least boring.

"Thank you," said Mac as he shook their hands.

Everyone was slowly saying their goodbyes and heading toward the exit. The only exception was Tony. He usually remained behind after an offsite meeting and had a drink with Mac, but tonight he seemed in an unusual hurry as he nearly bolted out the door. As Sarah Frazer passed Mac he turned to her. "Could I see you for a few minutes after the others leave?" He asked quietly.

"Certainly" she replied. With that she placed her briefcase on the table and busied herself with the bound hand out that had been provided. She was surprised by Mac's request and found that she was slightly apprehensive.

When everyone else was gone Mac turned to her and smiled. "Can I hold you here a bit longer while we talk a little business?"

"As long as you need" Sarah answered.

"Good. I don't know about you, but after all of that I need a drink, something stronger then the warm sodas that are left from this afternoon's break. May I buy you something in the hotel bar?"

Sarah smiled. "You certainly may."

They left the meeting room and walked side by side down the hall toward the bar. Sarah noted what her new peers often marveled at; Mac appeared as neat and pressed as he had the first thing this morning. She wondered how she appeared. She noted that a long strand of her auburn hair was dangling in front of her face. She attempted to push it back in place before it was noticed. Mac turned into the dimly lit lounge. They surveyed the arrangement of tables. A piano player was playing softly to the few patrons that were sitting at the bar. A hostess came to seat them. Noting that no one was seated at the tables Mac inquired if that was permitted this early. The hostess affirmed that it was and led them to a table in the corner.

When they were settled and the waitress took their drink order Mac turned and smiled at Sarah. "This is quite a first week that we arranged for you Sarah. We introduce you to the unrealistic expectations of the Atlantic Corporation. You hear along with all of us that the company may be for sale, and if that wasn't enough, we face the possible threat of a union organization of our labor force. Are you bored yet?"

Sarah laughed. She found again that her new boss' demeanor was not only disarming, but the twinkle in his eye was especially charming. "No I'm definitely not bored."

"Any regrets? You left a very secure and respectable job to come on board with us."

"No regrets. This is exactly what I was looking for. I want to be where the action is and you certainly seem to have an abundance of that."

"No argument there," was Mac's reply. He paused thoughtfully as if he was trying to decide what to say or more accurately how he wanted to say what he was thinking. "Sarah, at this particular time, faced with this particular situation, I'm very glad that we have you here with us."

Sarah was pleasantly surprised by this comment. She could not suppress a smile. Just then the waitress brought their drinks. Sarah was having a glass of Chardonnay and Mac was having a Scotch on the rocks. Sarah noted for future reference that he preferred Dewars as he requested it by name. When the waitress placed a bowel of "munchies" in front of them she departed. "I'm not sure what to say. I certainly appreciate the comment but perhaps you had best wait to determine the quality of my work before you pass judgment too quickly." Was that the correct response? Yes, she felt that it was.

"In the short, let me say extremely short time that I have had the pleasure of your acquaintance, you have voluntarily attended a Saturday meeting before you officially started to work for Fox. In addition you volunteered for some pretty heavy research work in support of Tony's portion of our strategic plan, and you have already turned in some of that research to Tony. Research I might add that Tony expressed an appreciation for the quality contained within. He couldn't even find any serious grammatical errors with it. You are not aware of it, but Tony Conocenti is a real stickler for good writing. He is so good that I have him proofread many of the more serious letters and reports that I author. When did you find the time to do it? You must have worked all day Sunday."

Sarah smiled "Pretty much. I had the laptop 'smoking' while I searched the Internet for facts to support Tony's contentions."

"You'll be happy to know that Tony agrees with all the data that you found."

"That's a relief. In the short time that I've known him, I find him to be very exacting and intimidating."

"He can be, but deep inside he's a real cream puff. He would kill me if he heard me talking like that concerning him." Mac paused in thought while he sipped his Scotch. Sarah sensed that the subject was about to change. "I'm still surprised that we have union activity out in the desert."

"Why is that?" queried Sarah.

"Well, it's a matter of economics. We purposely kept our two plants far enough apart and small enough so as to make them unappealing, or rather not cost effective enough to be worth a union's efforts."

"These are not the best of times for unions."

"That's true. Perhaps we in management aren't as smart as we believe ourselves to be. It's possible that there is an element to all this that we have either overlooked or are ignorant of. Whatever, I trust Erving's opinion therefore we must act. That is the second reason that I'm glad you are with us at this time."

Sarah smiled a quizzical smile but held her tongue. She was learning that patience and silence has its dividends with this man. Mac's soft but very direct gaze was bearing down on her. Sarah held his silent stare. Mac took another sip of Scotch. Sarah sipped her wine.

"Don't misunderstand what I'm about to tell you Sarah. When you hear, you will understand why I'm going to ask you not to repeat it... Dennis Morton is a fine hard working man. He has done a yeoman's job administering our various benefit plans. Our insurance, 401K and in addition he keeps us from running afoul of the law in the form of OSHA (Occupational Safety and Health Administration), DER (Department of Environmental Resources), and all the other labor and environmental departments to which Fox is subject. But this challenge of a labor union is beyond him. The Human Resources Department, soon to be your department, is the department that should head up the counter effort. Dennis has less than a month until we throw his retirement party. Not only is this out of his realm of experience, but also his interest in company problems is waning. Please understand I'm not faulting that. Dennis is slowing down. He's run the good race for Fox. He is ready to pass the baton to you. I want you to take that baton right now this instant. I noticed in the meeting today that you gave Dennis a great deal of deference. I appreciate that. He deserves it. But from this moment forward I am putting you at the point position in Fox's battle with the unions. Can you handle it?"

Sarah didn't hesitate. "Yes I can."

"Good!" Mac looked up to see Tom Erving entering the lounge. "Tom over here" he called. Tom acknowledged his boss' call and approached their table.

"Yes Sir Mr. MacLode?"

"Good lord," said Mac. "No one calls me either Mr. or Sir. Please, just call me Mac."

"Okay Mac." Tom smiled an easy smile. Sarah was impressed with Tom's knowledge of labor law during the meeting today.

Mac gestured to an empty chair. "Please sit down and allow me to buy you a drink." Mac caught the waitresses' eye and soon Tom was both seated and had ordered.

"Now Tom," began Mac. "You were extremely positive in the meeting today when I asked of your certainty concerning union activity at your plant. Now that it's just the three of us here. By the way, I've just asked Sarah to head up our efforts against the union. That probably means that she will be working very closely with you Tom." Tom nodded his head in both approval and understanding. "Now, what makes you so positive?"

"Simple Mr.... uh Mac" Tom stumbled. "I didn't want to say this in front of our lawyers, but the fact is I have an informer on my payroll."

"A spy that works for you?" asked Mac.

"Yes sir, I mean Mac. I didn't know if that was legal or not."

"Probably not, but I'm glad that you have one. I don't think I want to know how you pay him Tom." Mac smiled. "Can you depend on his information?"

"What makes you think it's a he?" asked Sarah.

"I stand corrected. You are quite right. Forty-five percent of the Fox work force out in the desert is female. Thank you, Sarah." Sarah smiled and nodded.

"In fact," continued Tom, "she is female, and I have never found her information to be wrong. You should know that I never solicited her. She approached me one evening after work. She works second shift and I happened to be walking the floor during second that week. I like to switch around and be visible to all of our employees. Anyway, it seems that she had a very bad experience with a labor union at her previous place of employment. That has translated into a real fear of them. She was hearing rumors after we announced the cut backs in benefits. She believed that some of the employees were considering contacting a union for organization information. At first I listened politely but discounted what she claimed."

"Why did you initially doubt her?" asked Sarah.

"Just like here in Pennsylvania we have an extremely low turnover rate at Fox in Nevada. I've always assumed that this means that the work force is basically satisfied."

"Just because they are happy with the place where they work doesn't mean that they are always pleased with the policies. They may view policy changes as a 'threat to paradise' and their actions are only the normal human reaction of defending one's home and not an act of disloyalty. Management takes a narrow view of these things at their own peril."

"That's an interesting observation Sarah." Mac was becoming even more impressed with his new staff member.

Tom Erving continued: "Then she began to inform me on specific conversations from specific people. Each seemed to coincide with some specific event of discontent. For example, the work cell where the people that she mentioned worked began to fall off in productivity for no apparent reason; no reason except that they were becoming discouraged, voicing their discouragement to each other and as these things develop, they feed on each other's discontent and the whole event spreads and becomes exaggerated."

"I don't suppose that she has any knowledge of a union attempting to recruit on the premises?" Mac knew that he was looking for a long shot. One of the things that they heard during today's session was that this specific act was illegal. The union could not set foot on company property until a sufficient number of cards had been signed, the NLRB was informed and a vote was scheduled to consider union membership. After it was established that enough of the rank and file desired to consider a union, the preferred union could then enter the property and openly campaign for approval to represent the workers. At that time the company could also campaign to keep them out.

"No Mac, she has never mentioned any knowledge of unauthorized people on the property. I believe our security to be better than that anyway. We would know if someone not employed by Fox was on our grounds."

Mac was thoughtful for a long moment. "I wonder if we have unknowingly hired a ringer?"

"A ringer?" asked Tom. "I'm not familiar with the term."

Sarah replied, "A ringer is a person that, while not employed by the union, is specifically sent to a place of business by the union to seek employment and then to surreptitiously lay the ground work for the rank and file to request that the said union represent them." Sarah was at this moment very grateful for her previous experience working at a union shop.

"Very good Sarah," was Mac's comment.

"I never considered that possibility," said Tom.

"Sarah," said Mac, "tomorrow first thing call into the office and have Julia, she's your clerk, pull the files of all personnel hired by Tom's people out in the desert for the past twelve months. Get her to compile a list on each of the last two places that they worked. Tom has your informant speculated on which union may have an interest in us?"

"Oh yes, she believes emphatically that it's the United Federation of Millwrights International. She claims that this is the union that the more militant discontents have contacted."

"What am I looking for in these personnel files Mac?" Sarah believed that she knew where Mac was going with this, but wanted him to be specific.

"I want to see if any of Tom's people came from companies where the UFMI was the representing union."

"I can have my people in Nevada do that for you Sarah. After all they are the people that did the hiring and have the original folders." Tom volunteered.

"No Tom. I thank you for the offer, but I think that Mac wants to keep this little investigation as far away from your plant as possible."

"Right on Sarah in addition I need you to do the crosscheck personally. I trust Julia, but in this situation the fewer people that know what we are doing the better." Mac was thoughtful again. "I hate to say this but we should have Julia pull the same folders for the new hires at Goodville too."

"I agree Mac." Sarah was hoping that Fox didn't require too many 'new hires' at its facilities this past year. This would be pick and shovel work.

"I'm sorry to have to do this to you Sarah, I'm aware of the potential size of this project and the time that it will require. Did I also say that we must have this information as quickly as possible?"

"I understand completely Mac. Don't worry I'll give it my full attention."

Mac turned to Tom again. "I know that I just told you that I didn't want to know how you were paying your informant, but just for the record is she receiving any additional reward, consideration, or compensation for the information that she brings to you?"

"None, as I said, I have never solicited this information from her."

"Good, we have to stay on the correct side of the law in this. That's good enough for me," said Mac. He then turned his attention back to Sarah again. "I'm not intending to put you on the spot Sarah, especially after the long day we just put in, but what measures would you recommend that we take immediately to attempt to counter the union?"

"That's easy. Tom stated in the meeting that the work force was especially upset concerning the cuts in the matching 401K funds and the greater share of the insurance expense that they were asked to absorb. I think that under these circumstances we must restore both to their original levels."

Mac shook his head. "I didn't want to make those cuts to begin with. It was as if we were going back on our word with them. Unfortunately it was the only way that I could get even close to Trevor Mason's profit margins. Yes I agree that's what we must do!" Mac was emphatic. "In addition, I not only want to restore the matching 401K funds to the original level, but I want to increase it by one percentage point."

Sarah and Tom both smiled. "That gives me some ammunition boss!" said Sarah.

"The troops in the desert will be happy to hear that boss," commented Tom.

"They should be," was Mac's response. "Those two changes are going to cost hundreds of thousands of dollars."

"I assume you have already calculated the costs?" asked Sarah.

"Yes." Mac was contemplating the remainder of his Scotch. "Sarah, how soon do you think we should announce these changes?"

"Immediately."

"I agree" said Tom.

"Okay, I want the two of you to be on a plane tomorrow morning for Las Vegas. When you arrive, call me on my cell phone. By that time I will have run these numbers by the remainder of the staff. Sarah, you should know that I'm not in the habit of ramming my will down their throats."

"I'm already aware of that, and I appreciate that you don't."

"This is a desperate situation. Fox cannot afford to allow a union in the door. When you call me I expect to be able to give you the approval of the entire staff."

"Do you think anyone will object?"

"No Sarah, I really do not, but this will place a great burden on Tony and Carroll and you too Tom. Tony will not only have to sell more product then the dealers have projected for the remainder of the year, but he'll have to sell an unexpected middle of the year price increase. I will have to pay for this somehow. Carroll will be putting pressure on you Tom and your counterpart here in Pennsylvania Marty Shultz, to get me the most that you possibly can in productivity gains."

Silence fell on the trio as they contemplated the impact that their decisions would have. They all finished their drinks. Mac looked at his two young associates, "Anyone for another round?"

Both declined as they decided that they best make flight arrangements and then prepare for the flight tomorrow. They decided to travel together. Sarah volunteered to make the arrangements. After Mac thanked Tom for making the trip from Nevada, Tom departed to his room upstairs. Mac opened his briefcase and gave Sarah a copy of his estimation of the cost of what they were planning. "By the time you call me from Vegas, I'll have accurate numbers from Dale Hershey for you." Mac paused and smiled at her. "Welcome aboard Sarah. I think you are indeed where the action is."

Sarah smiled as she took the computer printouts. "I agree and I couldn't be happier."

"Call me from Vegas," said Mac.

Sarah nodded and left the lounge on her way to her car and home. Mac watched her go. By god, he thought, I believe Dennis managed to hire a gem for us as his encore performance. The waitress returned to clear the remaining glasses away. "Anything else for you sir?" she asked.

"Yes, I'll take a refill and then bring me the tab."

"Yes sir."

Mac finished off the remaining Scotch in his first glass. The melting ice had diluted it somewhat, but it still tasted good to him. This is all very interesting he thought. The dealers may revolt against a surprise price increase, especially when it will mean that Fox has far exceeded the annual inflation rate. It might then be possible that the strong sales of the first half will vanish by the end of the second half of the fiscal year. Fox may not be able to hold the margins that Trevor is demanding, and he, William MacLode may be out of a job. The waitress brought him a fresh Scotch. "That was a Dewars?" She inquired.

"Yes it was, thank you," replied Mac as she gave him the check. Mac sipped his Scotch and closed his eyes. Tomorrow was Thursday. He hoped that the strategy meeting would not take the entire day. Friday, he must leave for Chicago and he needed a little time to prepare for that trip. Life was never dull he thought.

CHAPTER 10

The attractive young woman's face filled every television monitor in the control room. Three rows of men and women, fifteen people in all, sat before computer consoles watching the monitors and taking direction from another woman standing in the rear of the room. She was the producer of the "News Live at Six on Three" and "News Live at Eleven on Three" television shows. The producer dominated the very intense scene, giving orders through her headset while listening for the voices of reporters at remote locations, network signals, updates and information passed on to her by people in this very room and on the set outside.

"Switch to camera three for close up. Prepare to roll tape one of the high school football summer camps…"

"Tape one punched up," was the response.

"Roll tape one in three, two, one, now! You're out Crystal. The weather's up next. Sam you ready? Sam, damn it, the tape is only forty-five seconds! Punch up weather backdrops!"

"Weather backdrops ready!" answered a voice from the consoles.

"Trouble with Sam's mike!" another voice materialized.

"Get him another! Crystal you may have to fill if Sam's mike isn't ready. Why do we wait till the last second to rig his mike?"

"He doesn't like to wear it," was the response.

"To Hell he doesn't! I want his ear plug in and his mike working at the top of the broadcast!"

"Tape one ends in ten seconds!" yet another technician weighed in.

To Catch a Fox

"How's the mike? Talk to me!" The producer's voice was urgent but there was no trace of panic.

"In six, five…" a new voice began the countdown to the tapes end.

"Mike's a go!"

"Go right to Sam, Crystal! I want Crystal on three!"

"Two, one…"

"You're on Crystal. Get ready on camera two."

Crystal Harrison's smiling face returned to the monitors. "It looks like we're in for an exciting high school football season this fall. Now here's Sam Calhoon with the weather. Sam?"

"Sam on two! You're out Crystal!"

"Looks like a hot one tomorrow Savannah…"

All this was part of a typical evening news show at WSAV Channel 3 in Savannah, Georgia. This happened to be the eleven o'clock addition. This producer and crew would soon turn the reins of the station over to the morning shift that was already preparing for operations.

The only thing that was even slightly out of the ordinary this night was the presence of a visitor with a priority clearance tag in the control room. These tags were usually reserved for visiting dignitaries or network types. What was strange about this individual was that no one from the station manager on down seemed to know him, what he represented, or where he came from. During the pre show briefing the station manager informed the production crew that an unnamed visitor would be present for the eleven o'clock edition. Beyond that he knew nothing about the individual. The priority pass came from corporate headquarters in Atlanta. Atlanta was the home of the Southern Communications Company; an entity that owned Channel 3 and seven other local television and radio stations in the Carolinas and Georgia. This unusual presence was the seed for numerous rumors that were now working their way through the station.

To Catch a Fox

The man with the priority pass appeared ten minutes before broadcast time. He was introduced as a Mr. George Smith. A name that no one, including the station manager believed, but all were at a loss to explain. He was a large man, at least six foot one in height and probably about two hundred sixty pounds, with short black curly hair. He wore a dark expensive and excellently tailored suit. He was polite and pleasant enough although he only spoke when someone was introduced to him or someone else spoke first. He did exactly what he said he would do observe and stay out of the way.

"...And we're out! Good show people! Switch to network uplink at the end of this commercial!" The producer turned to her mystery guest. Removing her headset she smiled and asked "That's how it's done. Can I answer any questions?"

The large man smiled an easy friendly smile. "No, thank you, it's all very interesting. I've enjoyed it immensely."

"Is there anything that I can do for you? We all wish to accommodate you, but frankly we don't know what it is that you are looking for or why you are here. How may I help?"

The large man chuckled. "I suspect that I am the source of multiple rumors, you don't need to be concerned. Your owner has not sent a 'spy' into your midst. I just work for an organization that did a favor for your principal owner some time back and in return he has allowed me to fulfill this small dream. But since you ask, there is one thing that you could do."

"Anything that is within my power, what is it?"

"Could you introduce me to Crystal Harrison?"

"That's easy enough. Follow me."

With that the producer led the man out onto the set where the on camera personnel were disconnecting themselves from their electronic hookups and briefing the morning people. She stopped in front of the desk that Crystal Harrison was preparing to leave.

"Crystal, there is someone here who would like to meet you."

To Catch a Fox

Crystal rose from her seat and smiled at the large man. "I'm Crystal Harrison."

The producer turned and presented Mr. George Smith. "Mr. Smith, Crystal. Crystal, Mr. Smith."

"How do you do Ms. Harrison? Please call me George."

"You may call me Crystal."

"Thank you. I've been a fan of yours for some time. It is indeed a pleasure to finally meet you in person."

The producer excused herself as she had a meeting to attend. After she left, Crystal turned to Mr. Smith. "Well---- George, what may I do for you?" she paused, tilted her head to one side and frowned slightly. "Do I know you? You look slightly familiar to me."

Smith smiled. "I'm sort of generic Ms. Harrison, large, slightly overweight man in his fifties. There are a lot of people on the street that bare a strong resemblance to me." The large man's face turned serious. "Actually, you and I have some very personal business to discuss."

"Personal business?"

"Yes, concerning your family."

"My family? What could you possibly know about my family?"

"As it turns out I know more than you do."

A frown crossed Crystal's face. "Recently I've felt that many people must know more than I do concerning my family, but I can't imagine that you, a stranger, could know more than me."

"But I do. In addition I know more than your father Foster knows."

"You know my father?" Crystal was surprised and perplexed.

"Not personally, but I am extremely familiar with who he is and his, excuse me, rather despicable past as it concerns you. I'm also familiar with your mother's history."

"I don't know who you are Mr. Smith, I'm sure you mean well, but I've about had it with my family. Recently everything I thought I knew about them has been thrown into question. I don't know what the truth is, and suddenly I no longer care. I'm Crystal Harrison-Rankin and from this point on I'm going to forget the past and make my own life. You're not somehow related to my adopted family are you?"

"No. No I'm not. But I do know that your mother's name was Mary and she has family in Baltimore Maryland. You really should talk to me Ms. Harrison. How about if we get out of here and you allow me to buy you a cup of coffee at an establishment you choose."

Crystal wanted to tell this mystery man to 'go to Hell,' but something inside kept her from doing so. His soft gentle manner led her to believe that she had nothing to fear physically from him. She considered him suspiciously.

"Please Ms. Harrison. I really think that it would be in your best interests. What can it hurt? How could anything I have to say hurt you more than you have already been hurt?"

"I don't know. Every time I think that I've been hurt as much as possible, something else occurs." Crystal unconsciously wrinkled up her nose. "Okay, I'm out of here in ten minutes. Meet me at the blues bar above the Pirate House Restaurant."

"The blues place? Just up the hill from the Marriott Hotel?"

"That's it. You're not from Savannah are you?"

"No, I'm not."

"I am, and I love the blues and I love the food at the Pirate House. I'm also hungry, so you can plan on spending more than a cup of coffee on me. Do you think that you can find the place George?"

The large man smiled his easy smile once more. "I'll see you there Ms. Harrison and thank you." The man most recently known as Mr. Smith continued to smile pleasantly; He turned and walked out of the studio.

Crystal watched him walk away. Her expression was a mix of concern and confusion. "Yeah, you're welcome I guess," she mumbled half to herself.

***

Denton Wellbon III sat in his Manhattan study going over a file that Trevor Mason had requested. Actually Trevor did not request this specific file. What he asked was that Denton review Millissa Kensington's "history of activity with Wellbon-Smith." Denton knew exactly what that meant. Millissa Kensington was a large shareholder in Wellbon-Smith. She was on Trevor's list of investors that could be "persuaded" to pledge her proxy or sell her shares to Trevor.

From brief comments that Trevor made to him, Denton determined that Abraham Rueben was having an impressive level of success in his meetings to date with targeted shareholders. Just today Trevor commented that the plan was progressing well and that one should never underestimate the power of human greed. Denton translated that to mean that all those contacted to date saw an opportunity to make a windfall profit and they could care less about the corporate bylaws. Rueben was collecting commitments to sell stock to Trevor and Denton with every meeting. Denton wondered just how much cash they were on the hook for already.

Millissa Kensington's name had struck a familiar note in Denton's memory. He immediately pulled several folders from the files that Trevor had consolidated and secured. All but one of those folders was stacked about on the floor beside his chair at this moment. The other he was reviewing. As individual files none of the folders contained anything out of the ordinary, but when read together they spelled out a pattern for fraud. This is what Trevor was looking for. Kensington was rich and would not roll over and play dead because of greed, so she would most likely require some encouragement. Her favorite nephew was the target of this trap and Denton would be the only individual within Wellbon-Smith that could remember the different instances well enough to gather the diverse incriminating evidence. Here was the evidence, strewn about Denton's easy chair.

To Catch a Fox

Denton laid the folder down and rubbed his eyes. This was the beginning of his distasteful role in all of this. Millissa Kensington would have to be forced into selling her stock or at least assigning her proxy. She would not do this willingly. But, she had willingly been a party to fraud; at least she turned a blind eye to it if she didn't actually commit any illegal acts personally. But she had knowledge of and failed to protest the fact her nephew held down various jobs in various Wellbon-Smith Corporations at various times. Nothing wrong with that except that he collected the extremely hefty paychecks and never once showed up to work or perform a service for any of the companies that paid him. In addition to that, while on the various payrolls he apparently took several trips to attend seminars in exotic locations. Of course he always chose a young attractive secretary from the corporate steno pool to accompany him as his assistant. Many of the legitimate attendees reported to Human Resources in the various companies that he was "working" for that he and his assistant never attended any sessions. It was easy to deduce that Donald Kensington-Cramer was collecting salaries, having affairs on company time and expensing everything. This is a clear case of fraud, but the various HR directors' reports appeared to "get lost" once they reached the corporate headquarters, because everyone was fearful of attacking a relative of a powerful Wellbon – Smith shareholder. The "theft" amounted to nearly one million dollars over a period of a few years. Denton had to admit that none of this could have taken place without the approval and the complex arrangements to avoid detection made by Carlton Smith.

Denton knew Millissa Kensington. She was not a close personal friend, but Susan had served with her on the boards of several charitable foundations. What he knew of her he liked. But why, thought Denton, did so many wealthy people believe that they had a right to bend the rules? Kensington's nephew had always been the black sheep of the family. Millissa had no children of her own, as she had never married. It seems that she decided to take this lad under her wing. She could have performed a far greater service for him if she would have forced him to get a real job, instead of concealing his lazy habits from the world.

So in reality were the people like Ms. Kensington to be pitied? Pitied because someone like Trevor Mason decided to take advantage of them by using the fact that they were cheating their follow shareholders against them? Denton didn't know. What he did know was that he was becoming just as low as these other pirates by working with Trevor. One set of pirates stealing from another set of pirates.

To Catch a Fox

The worst part was that the longer Denton considered Trevor's plan and thinly veiled threat to expose Denton's own past, the more he realized he was just another pawn in this grand scheme. Would Trevor honor his promise to put Denton in the chairman's seat or would Trevor find a way to discard Denton when all the cards had been played?

Denton lost himself in thought when suddenly the phone beside his chair rang.

"Wellbon residence, Denton Wellbon speaking."

"Mr. Wellbon, I'm sorry to bother you so late at night in your home. This is Andy, Andy from the diner."

Denton sat up straight. This was the last voice that he had expected to hear when he picked up the receiver. "Yes Andy! How good to hear from you! I trust that you are well?"

"Yes sir, Mr. Wellbon. Quite well thanks. Again I apologize for calling you at home and at this hour."

"Not a problem Andy. Really, I'm glad that you called. Sid informed me the other day that you desired to speak with me. How can I be of service to you?"

"Actually Mr. Wellbon, it's really me who can be of service to you."

Denton was puzzled. "How may that be Andy?"

"Not something we should talk about on the phone Mr. Wellbon. I think we need to sit down, just you and me."

"Okay. I was planning on coming to the diner for lunch sometime next week…"

"Forgive me Mr. Wellbon, but that's really not soon enough. You need to hear what I have to say as soon as possible."

Denton was nearly speechless. He didn't know what to say. What could Andy possibly have to tell him that was this urgent?

"You still there Mr. Wellbon?"

"Yes, Andy. I… I was just thinking about my schedule."

"Mr. Wellbon please listen and trust me. I was a close friend of your father's."

"I know that Andy, he always spoke highly of you."

"And I had the highest regard for him in return. Your father trusted me without question. If he needed me he called and I came. No questions asked, Likewise if I needed him. That's the kind of respect we had for each other. Now it's time for you to trust me in the same way as your father did. It's time for you to step up and take over for your father."

Denton could not comprehend what Andy meant by this last comment, but he correctly perceived that this was not the time to ask questions. Denton cleared his suddenly dry throat. "When do you want to meet?"

"I got the night shift at the diner tonight. Its quarter after eleven now. I just came on. I expect to be pretty busy early on. The diner's nearly full right now. I should get a break around three in the morning. Let's meet then, here at the diner. I got an office in the back. No one will hear us there."

It was obvious to Denton that this was not a request. "I'll…I'll be there Andy three tomorrow morning." Denton looked at his watch. "That's not a very long time from now."

"No it isn't, but that's great Mr. Wellbon."

"Andy please call me Denton."

"Okay Denton. I like that. It's like old times. Your father always insisted that I call him by his first name too. I'll see you at three… Oh Denton. Take a cab. Don't drive your big Beamer. It would draw too much attention down here at that time in the morning. Okay?"

"Okay."

"See you then." Andy hung up without waiting for a reply.

Denton replaced the receiver. He sat in mystified silence, the folders and files that were strewn around his chair now forgotten. The phone call that just ended was an unexpected bolt from out of nowhere. What could Andy possibly wish to tell him? The mystery of his father's relationship with Andy was even deeper now and suddenly, Denton realized, rather foreboding. Other details began to sink into his awareness. How did Andy get his unlisted home phone number? The business card that he had given Sid to pass on to Andy only had his office phone number printed on it. In addition, Denton realized that he had never driven the big BMW to the diner. How did Andy know about it?

Denton shook his head. He was obviously at a disadvantage and the only thing that he could do at this point was to go along and play the entire situation by ear. He made an audible sigh. He would have to give Susan some explanation as to why he was leaving their home at that hour in the morning. Thank God she trusted him. A jealous suspicious wife could not have lived with Denton in the time since Trevor Mason came to Atlantic Corporation.

His thoughts returned to Andy and his late father. Suddenly their relationship seemed far more complex than he had ever imagined. Now after all these years of curiosity he may receive the answers to some of his questions. Suddenly he felt trepidation toward this long time curiosity. Suddenly he was not certain that he really wanted to know more concerning his father and Andy.

***

Crystal Harrison and Mr. George Smith listened to the last set of blues songs in the dimly lit upstairs bar above the Pirate House Restaurant. The music and the food had been excellent. The late evening meal with this charming soft-spoken stranger had been extremely relaxing. The waiter approached and when Crystal declined desert Mr. Smith ordered appropriate after dinner drinks.

Crystal sat staring at the large man that was treating her to this unexpected evening. She looked at her watch; it was one-thirty in the morning. She was grateful that she had been moved to the late shift at the station and did not have to return until three in the afternoon. The drinks arrived and Mr. Smith proposed a toast: "To unexpected interludes," he said as he touched her glass with his. "To unexpected interludes," Crystal returned. They both took a sip of the liqueur.

"Now Mr. Smith, I'm sorry, George; you are a very charming companion and this has been pleasant, but you've managed to spend our entire time together without even once broaching the topic that lured me here to begin with. This wasn't all an elaborate scheme to get a date was it? I hope that you're not planning on hitting on me. If you are, allow me to give you some advice: don't." Crystal allowed a coy smile to play at her lips as she administered this mild admonishment.

"Well you are certainly beautiful and enticing enough to make a man consider going to such lengths to enjoy the pleasure of your company, but I fear that I am here for the purpose that I originally stated."

Crystal's expression and voice became more serious, "then let us begin," she said.

"Very well, Crystal what I am about to tell you may be difficult."

"I've recently been introduced to a new level of difficult by my father, thank you. I suspect that you will have a hard time surpassing that."

"I would agree, if you are referring to your recent and only encounter with him since he deserted you and your mother."

"How do you know about that?"

"My dear Crystal," said Mr. Smith with a gentle smile, "anyone who was present in the Marriott's restaurant that morning knows about that encounter."

"You were there?"

"Yes, I was having breakfast across the room."

"Why were you there?"

"More important than the reason for my presence I believe that I know what your father told you that upset you so."

"What is it that you think he said?"

"I believe he implied that contrary to what your mother told you all your life, he is not your father. That is what upset you. This is the man whose rejection you have been attempting to understand since you were five years old. A man you truly believed was your father. It's no wonder that you threw your coffee in his face."

"Why do you think that this is what he told me?"

"Because Crystal, it's the truth. Foster Harrison is not your father."

Crystal touched her fingertips to her forehead. Her eyebrows pinched into a frown and her eyes became misty.

"I'm sorry Crystal. I know that however Foster Harrison has hurt you and your mother you still wanted to make things right between the two of you. That was based on your belief that he truly is your father. He is not. However, he was married to your mother and because of that you were his responsibility. There was no excuse for him to turn his back on you at that tender age." Smith shook his head slowly back and forth. "At least for an old fashioned guy like me there was no excuse for his behavior."

"But that means that my mother was lying to me all those years. I didn't just assume that Foster was my father, she referred to him constantly as my father." Crystal found that she was once again fighting back the tears.

"Yes, she did. Right or wrong she had a reason for doing that. She believed, correctly I think, that it was truly for your own good."

Crystal was trembling. She tried to speak but words would not come. All she could mutter was: "Why?"

"That does require some explanation. I will attempt to explain as much as I may. Your mother did deceive Foster when they were dating. They had been intimate and your mother became pregnant with you. Foster obviously knew that they had been intimate. On a frequent basis I might add, so when your mother, Mary, told Foster that she was pregnant, he had no reason to doubt that the child belonged to him. The problem is that you weren't his child. Your mother had an extremely brief affair with another man. You are that man's child."

"How could she know?"

"Blood tests, they proved beyond any doubt that the father of her unborn child was the man with whom she had the brief affair."

"Why didn't she confront this 'other man' and marry him?"

"She did confront him. He was well aware that she was pregnant. He was the one that insisted on the blood test. He discovered that your mother had a steady boy friend just previous to him and he wanted to be certain that the child was truly his. Your mother had broken off with Foster Harrison after she met this other man who is your true father. Foster was always, how can I put it, Foster. Your mother realized that she wasn't in love with him when she met this other man. As I said, a brief and torrid affair ensued from which your mother became pregnant. When she discovered that she was pregnant, there was no doubt in her mind who the father was and she was correct."

"So my real father rejected me too? This is just great! I was wrong there are new levels to which I can be hurt!"

"Hear me out Crystal. I believe that your real father truly loved your mother. For what it's worth your mother never doubted that he loved her either, but there were insurmountable reasons that prevented them from getting together. I suspect it was the fact that she had to live knowing that she and her true love could never be together is the real reason that she took her own life. I really doubt that it had anything to do with Foster deserting you. It would have been better for both if they, your mother and your real father had never met. However, if they hadn't, I wouldn't have the pleasure of your company tonight."

"What sort of reasons? What kept them apart?"

"I am not permitted to tell you that."

"What do you mean that you are not permitted to tell me? Oh, that's right. I must listen carefully to your use of the English language. You did say in the beginning that you would 'attempt to explain as much as you may;' you did not say that you would tell me as much as you can!"

"I'm sorry Crystal, but please allow me to continue."

"Why not?" Crystal's voice had an edge of sarcasm in it. She wasn't certain anymore who she was angry with. Was she angry with her mother, the man who for all these years she believed was her father, this new mystery father, or all of them? Maybe she didn't even care anymore.

Mr. Smith finished his drink. "With it being impossible for your mother to marry the man she loved, she believed that her as yet unborn child deserved a father. She returned to Foster and asked him to forgive her for breaking up with him, slept with him again and then announced that she was pregnant."

"Dear Lord above" said Crystal in a voice of disgust.

"Don't be too harsh on her, or your natural father for that matter."

"Assuming that this is all true, and may I point out to you that anyone could spin a tale such as you just have, why should I not be upset with my mother and my supposedly real father? Both you and the person that I was told is my father for nearly all of my life portray her as a slut. The portrait that you paint of my mysterious natural father is one of an individual who can't manage to overcome some problems to be with the woman that he loves. The woman who is the mother of his child! With the personal ethics that all of these actions point toward, why should I not be harsh in my judgments?"

Mr. Smith ignored the anger in her voice. "Where did you live during your childhood Crystal?"

"Here in Savannah."

"Exactly where did you live, in the poor section of the city?"

"No, mother managed to rent an apartment in the historic district."

"Not a low rent district."

"No."

"Where did you go to school?"

"I was in the public school system until I started third grade. At that point mother enrolled me in the local parochial school. She was a lifelong Catholic and felt that that's where I should be."

"Private school that's not inexpensive. Where did you go to college Crystal?"

"Auburn University, what are you driving at?"

"Did you attend Auburn on a scholarship?"

"No, I'm afraid that I was not a very serious student in high school. I finally wised up in my freshman year in college. During my college years I buckled down and became a decent student. With my high school record, there was no way I could qualify for a scholarship"

"How did your mother pay for all of that?"

"She worked very hard. She held down two jobs. She was a beautician during the day and she worked behind the meat counter in a local grocery store at night. Please remember that she died when I was only ten. My adopted family helped keep me in parochial school and put me through college."

"Yes your mother was a very hard worker. That's one of the reasons that I have a lot of respect for her; and you were only ten when your mother committed suicide?"

"Yes, I was ten."

"How old were you when you went to live with the Rankin family?"

"Eleven. Why do I believe that you know all the answers to these questions before you ask them?"

"Because I do know the answers to these questions, but I want you to put all of this together in your mind before I tell you what I really have to say. How did the Rankin family, your adopted parents, manage to put you through parochial school and Auburn?"

"My adopted father, Joseph, was a hard worker."

"Yes he was and he was a decent honest man. He worked twenty-five years at a local feed and grain store in the small town that you lived in just south of Savannah. In that time he never made more than thirty thousand dollars a year. That by the way was his best year. He worked a lot of over time that year. Did you have any adopted brothers and sisters?"

"I think that you know that I did. The Rankins had a boy and a girl of their own when they adopted me."

"The boy is older and the girl is younger. Is that correct?"

"Yes." Crystal was beginning to sense where this was going. How did this stranger know so much about her life?

"Did your adopted brother and sister go to college?"

"Yes, they both went to state universities and no they didn't go on scholarships either."

"So how did your mother put you in private school and pay the rent in an exclusive neighborhood? In addition how did the Rankins keep you in private school and manage to put you through the far more expensive Auburn when they couldn't afford those kinds of institutions for their natural children?"

"My mother had a trust fund which she could use to help support us."

"Where did that trust fund come from?"

"I don't know. Mother was always vague concerning that, and I was only a child when she…died, so I really didn't question it."

"What happened to it when your mother died?"

"I'm not sure. I believe my adopted parents were allowed to use it for my education and to help supplement the expense of raising me."

"Your mother told you she was an orphan?"

"Yes, but now my father, or whatever Foster is to me, claims that mother has family that are still alive in Maryland." Crystal was not certain why she hadn't just walked out on this Mr. Smith or whatever his name really was. Perhaps it was because his manner was gentle and sympathetic. Somehow he seemed to convey a sense of caring.

"So where did this 'trust fund' come from and what happened to it?"

"I don't know where it came from, but my adopted father told me that we were fortunate that there was enough left in it to put me through college. I believe that it was exhausted paying my tuition."

"Who administered this trust fund?"

"I don't know. I assumed that the state did after mother died. Occasionally they sent a man around to talk about it with my adopted father."

The waiter reappeared and inquired if there would be anything else that he could get for them. It was obvious that the bar and restaurant was ready to close as it appeared that Crystal and Mr. Smith were the last patrons still on the premises. Mr. Smith requested the bill. Upon receiving the bill, he left enough cash on the table to cover everything and reward the waiter for the excellent service.

"Let's allow these people to close and go for a walk down on River Street. I think you really want to hear the remainder of what I have to tell you."

As Smith helped Crystal on with her coat she decided to challenge this gentleman one more time. "Why should I go for a walk with you? You seem nice and all that, and I'm not afraid of you, but why should I listen to anymore of this story without proof?"

Mr. Smith smiled his gentle smile, "Because the State of Georgia did not administer your mother's trust fund after her death. For several years I was that man that came to discuss the trust fund with your adopted father."

Crystal stared at him. "Let's go for a walk," she said.

***

Dale Hershey was accustomed to working late, but seldom like this. He was tired, bone tired. Assembling the numbers to support all of the other vice presidents strategies for the strategic plan was bad enough, but now there was this union thing. Initially Dale believed that he would play a secondary supporting role in the battle. After this evening's phone call from Mac, that changed. Dale had barely arrived home after the daylong "union seminar" when the phone rang. "Dale, this is Mac. Sorry to disturb you at home, but I need a favor." With those words Mac launched into his plan for restoring and increasing the 401K "matching" benefit and once again reducing the employee paid insurance contribution. Dale agreed that the strategy had to be accomplished immediately. He also agreed with Mac that they had to demonstrate how they intended to pay for it. There was no way around it. Fox would have an unprecedented middle of the year price increase.

Mac had made an educated guess as to how much the increase would be. He came up with 3%. When placed on top of the purely inflationary 2% increase that Fox had announced in the spring, both Dale and Mac agreed this would be intolerable to the dealers. In the "kitchen business" as it was called; it was traditional to have one price increase per year. The dealers liked this arrangement because of the long sales cycle between the initial consumer visit to the showroom and the final design approval and contract. No one wanted to explain a price increase after months of design proposals and changes.

Mac gave Dale the task of analyzing each department's current budget and requests for next year to determine where cuts could be made allowing a smaller price increase while accommodating the increase in benefit costs. "Oh yes," reminded Mac. "Don't forget, we have to hold the overall gross margin somewhere between 30% and 32% and at least look like we are moving toward a 14% operating profit."

"How can I forget Mac? Your buddy at corporate, John Hogg asks how we are doing on that score at least once a week. "

Mac laughed, "Don't let John bother you he's really a big fan of Fox."

"It's not John that worries me. It's his boss, Trevor Mason. I've worked for some unreasonable people before but this guy takes the prize."

"Let me worry about Trevor, Dale. You just give me numbers that I can defend."

"I'll do my best Mac. Have you run this past Tony?"

"Not yet, he'll hear about it tomorrow morning along with the rest of the staff."

"He's going to go through the roof. It's going to be a tall order to sell to the dealer network when none of the competition is raising prices. Tony is going to want time for the dealers to close the jobs that they currently have in progress before the new prices kick in."

Mac gave a long audible sigh. "I know. I also know that the added expense of increasing the benefit package will begin immediately."

"Tough for us to attain Trevor's operating line that way Mac."

"Tell me about it."

"Mac you've done a superb job at Fox, don't let this be the excuse that Trevor needs to ax you."

"Dale I appreciate the comment. I really do, but I've always done what I believe to be right for Fox. I never worried about what corporate thought in the past. I can't change the way I operate now, Trevor Mason or no Trevor Mason. Can you have these numbers by the eight o'clock meeting tomorrow?"

"I'll have them for you Mac."

"Thanks Dale, I'm sorry we have to move so quickly."

"No problem Mac. See you in the morning."

Dale finished reviewing the numbers. He was working at home in his den. The numbers were the numbers. They would not be as good as corporate would like, but they were realistic. Dale printed them out, folded the copies neatly and placed them in his brief case. He looked at the clock on the wall, two-thirty in the morning. He had to be back at the hotel by eight. Dale headed upstairs to bed. He was definitely getting too old for this.

***

Denton Wellbon emerged from the taxi just up the street from Andy's Diner. He could see the "ancient" orange neon light announcing that fact from here. Denton paid the cabby and watched him speed away. It was a dry night with a cool breeze coming off the river. Denton shivered, not from cold but from anxiety. He found himself looking up and down the street. Why am I acting like I'm afraid that someone is watching me? Who could possibly be interested in the fact that he was paying a visit to an old friend of his father's at this hour in the morning? Still he remembered Andy's warning: "Don't drive your big Beamer, it would draw too much attention down here at that time in the morning." In addition he remembered that Andy suggested meeting in Andy's office in the diner because "no one can over hear us there." Denton assured himself that no one was observing him. In fact it appeared as if the entire street was deserted.

Denton checked his watch. Twenty-five minutes past three in the morning. Denton took a deep breath and walked toward the diner. Ironically Denton had always imagined that someday this meeting would take place, but not exactly in this fashion. He had always supposed that someday Andy would call in need of a favor of some sort. Denton assumed that Andy would require money and enlighten Denton as to how his father had always bailed him out in the past in return for some ancient favor Andy had performed for his father. Denton imagined himself assuring Andy that he would continue his father's largess and Andy being forever grateful. Somehow the tone of Andy's voice and the authority that it expressed set the stage for a very different encounter.

Denton entered the diner. Connie the waitress was 'ringing up" a transaction for a departing patron on the cash register. "Hi Mr. Wellbon!" was her cheery greeting.

"Good morning Connie." Denton stood to the side as the patron received his change and departed.

"Do you want your regular booth?"

"Not just now Connie, I need to see Andy. Is he available?"

Connie looked mildly surprised. "Sure. Follow me he's back in the office."

Connie proceeded to lead Denton through the kitchen, an area of the diner that he had never seen before. He was rather surprised to see that it was spotless and equipped with the latest of commercial equipment. Several cooks in white were busily working over the hot grills. There were customers to feed and they paid little attention to the well-dressed man that was moving through the midst of the activity. Denton suddenly had the impression that it was not rare to see strangers come through here to visit Andy. Somehow he had always believed that he was much better off not seeing the kitchen as he suspected that it struggled to pass the City's periodic Department of Health inspections. Apparently nothing could be further from the truth. At the rear of the long narrow room was a portal with the word 'private' neatly lettered on the upper cross rail of the six panel colonial door. Connie knocked softly.

"Yeah!" replied a voice from within.

"Mr. Wellbon is here to see you Andy."

"Send him in!"

Connie opened the door and stepped aside for Denton to enter. She closed the door quietly behind him and returned to her duties out front. Denton found himself in a small room with a large desk dominating the center. Andy sat behind the desk in a large leather chair. Denton thought that it rivaled in size and quality the chair that Trevor Mason had in his spacious corporate office. The walls were lined with filing cabinets; a computer screen glowed on a small table behind the desk to Andy's immediate right. The table had a shelf between the legs that contained a printer, and what looked to Denton to be a scanner. There was one small window high in the wall behind Andy's back. Andy was going over some printouts with an intense look on his face. He was absently smoking a large cigar. Without looking up or stopping in his study of the numbers on the computer paper, Andy removed the cigar from his mouth and placed it in an ashtray on his desk. It continued to fill the room with a rather putrid smoke.

Andy was a man in his sixties. He wore a white tee shirt and blue jeans. Denton could see that Andy had on a white apron over his jeans. Andy was no stranger to the grill when the diner was busy. He had gray slightly frizzy hair around the sides and back of his head. The top of his head was completely bald. Andy cultivated a large bushy moustache that seemed to always be in need of a trim. On this particular morning the remainder of Andy's face also required some attention from a razor.

Suddenly Andy looked up from his work, rose out of his chair and extended a large callused hand. His face broke open in the familiar friendly smile that Denton was accustomed to seeing. "Denton! Welcome! Good of you to come on such short notice." Denton took Andy's hand and winced slightly as his hand was pumped vigorously in a vise like grip.

"My pleasure Andy," Denton was slightly more at ease after the tone of this welcome.

"Grab a chair and make yourself comfortable." Andy gestured in the direction of two chairs that were squeezed into a corner. Denton pulled one in front of Andy's desk and was seated. Andy sank into the leather of his much larger chair and smiled again. He motioned toward the printouts on his desk. "Damn Y2K 'bug,' I don't want to be caught short. I'm running the tests on my system now. Can't afford to have the diner shut down, but we can run it with paper and pencil if we have too. No it's the loans, rentals and mortgages that I have out that concern me. I have enough trouble getting paid on time without having my monthly billings screwed up. I guess big time operators like you know all about that stuff huh?"

Denton was afraid that his face showed surprise. "You have a lot of mortgages Andy?"

Andy's smile grew bigger. He motioned to the filing cabinets lining three walls of the office. "Only what's in those."

Denton observed that they were the large five drawer models. He also noted that except for a few drawers each drawer had but a single letter of the alphabet on it. Some letters required more than one drawer. They all appeared to be sagging slightly under the weight of their contents.

"Course that's just the paper backup, I got it all on disk now. Probably should throw all that away as I 'back up' the computer every night and take the disks home with me to be on the safe side. I suppose that's the old geezer in me. Don't trust these computers unless I can put my 'paws' on some hard copy."

"If you need help in becoming Y2K compliant, I can get you some software that we are using at the office to test our systems and make the necessary repairs."

"Well Denton I really appreciate that. What a nice gesture for you to make; it's so like your father. I just may take you up on that offer." Andy's big gravelly voice filled the room. Denton was beginning to feel a little more at ease.

Andy picked up his cigar from the ashtray. After a few puffs he seemed to have it fired up again. “I guess my phone call sort of surprised you huh?”

“Sid told me that you wanted to speak to me several days ago.”

“Yeah he gave me your card. Sid was impressed that a high-powered corporate guy like you would be so accommodating. I told him that’s how your father and I always did business and I believe that like father like son. Huh?”

“I try Andy.” Denton wondered what type of business Andy and his father did together. He briefly remembered the shocking hand written cargo manifests that Abraham Rueben had revealed to him.

Andy’s gregarious smile disappeared. “You got trouble Denton, but true to the promise I made to your departed father. I’m here to help you out of it.”

“What kind of trouble?” Denton was almost afraid to ask.

“That girl, you know the minor you boinked at the frat party while you were in college.”

Good grief thought Denton. Was there no one that didn’t know of this one foolish indiscretion?

Andy saw the shock on Denton’s face. “Relax Denton, I’m the guy your father came to when he wanted your ‘tracks’ covered. You could have been in real trouble my friend. You were a big wealthy Ivy League College boy. You were twenty-two years old at the time. You were a legal adult. She was only what, sixteen or seventeen? Her Daddy could have had you thrown in jail for statutory rape!”

“I know I know…I’m sorry Andy, Dad never told me of your involvement.”

“I know that, your Dad and I decided that the less you knew of what we had to do the better.”

Denton took a deep breath. He was afraid to ask this next question, but he had to.

"Just exactly what did you and Dad have to do?"

"Huh!" Andy smiled again, "like we always did, make certain that everybody kept their mouths shut."

"Forgive my ignorance Andy, but precisely how did you achieve that?"

"No problem Denton. Like I said your Dad and I purposely kept you ignorant of the details. But now you need to know. Your Dad knew that this time would come. That's why he made me promise to stick by you no matter what had to be done. Your Daddy loved you a lot Denton. He wasn't very good at showing it but he did."

"If I had any doubts about that, I believe that you are in the process of erasing them. You need to know that I was not aware of the girl's age. She looked much older and she somehow got invited to my fraternity party. I assumed that she was of age. I know that was stupid."

"Hey, you were a kid! Don't beat yourself up! You had desire and hormones working against you. You were that age. She had hot pants and she was out looking for excitement. She found it at your expense!"

Denton was not at all certain that he agreed with this throw back chauvinistic opinion. It seemed to him that he should have been far more concerned about the impact of his actions. True he did not know the age of the girl, but he never attempted to find out either.

"It was 1973. It was a different time Denton."

"Yes, I guess that it was."

"Anyway, your father had me check into the girl's background: Who she was, who her parents were, who her daddy owed money to, where he worked, any skeletons, all the usual stuff. We got lucky. We found plenty."

"Like what?"

"Wait till you hear, seems that her daddy worked in the main office of the Coastal Savings Bank. At that time they had operations all through the Middle Atlantic

States."

"Coastal Savings, why does that name sound familiar?"

"That's the real beauty of all this. Sometimes you just can't beat coincidence. American Bank International bought Coastal out ten years ago. You made a killin' on it. Coastal was one of the stocks in your trust's portfolio. The trust your daddy set up for you." Denton wasn't about to ask how Andy had knowledge of the contents of his trust's portfolio.

"Anyway, as I said this girl's father worked in the main bank. 'Seems when I started checking up on him the bank was also conducting an internal investigation. He was one of their accounting staff, and they suspected him of embezzlement; as it turned out this guy had pocketed about $100,000 over the course of three years. Before they finalized their investigation, banks are so cautious that they move like molasses, I told your father what I found out. Well your father immediately acquired enough of the bank's stock that they were forced to offer him a seat on their board. Your dad asked to see the results of any internal investigations that they might be conducting. I suspect they were curious as to how he knew that they had an investigation in progress. When they showed him the results, and I might add that there was no doubt that 'our boy' was guilty. Your dad insisted that because this man had a spotless record previous to this offense that he be allowed to confront him before the bank took any action. That included making the crime public. That's when your dad had me pay the gentleman a visit. Isn't life funny? As it turned out, because you screwed his daughter and he stole from the bank where he worked were the only reasons that your father bought a major interest in that particular institution. Later on that stock winds up in your trust fund and you get a windfall profit when a larger bank buys it out!"

"Had he made any move toward reporting my indiscretion with his daughter to the authorities?"

"When he found out who you were, and how old you were, he had his lawyer contact your father. They threatened to press charges against you for rape unless your dad coughed up a million bucks. It was blackmail plain and simple. If he hadn't of done that your dad would have probably made some reconciliation with him, your father never felt that you were an innocent lamb in all of this. But the one thing no one ever got away with was threatening your dad or any member of your family."

"Dad never told me about any of this. He told me to go back to school, not to worry about it, and never, ever do anything like that again. He said this was the only time he would bail me out of a mess like this."

"He meant it too," said Andy. "I never knew your dad to bluff. Anyway, I paid this guy a visit. He wanted to have his lawyer present. I told him I wasn't a lawyer and I was certain that he didn't want anyone else to hear what I had to say. He reluctantly agreed. I put it on the line. If he or any of his family; I told him he was responsible for keeping his daughter's trap shut. If they ever told anyone about your little excursion with his daughter, the evidence that we had on him concerning the bank money would be sent to the state bank examiner and the local District Attorney immediately. You should have seen his face. He turned pale as a ghost. He had no idea that anyone was on to him. Then the dumb shit had the guts to ask me if this meant that 'he wasn't going to get any money from your dad?' I broke his nose just for asking! I told him he already got the money to keep his trap shut! It was the hundred grand he stole from the bank!"

"Your father convinced the bank officials to keep him in their employ, only at a less responsible position, one that he couldn't steal from. Your father also told the bank that this joker had agreed to pay back the money. Actually your dad replaced the money in small payments through another account that couldn't be traced back to him. I administered that account for your dad."

"Why did Dad do that? This guy already had the hundred thousand?"

"I asked your Dad the same thing. He said the only way to keep the bank from prosecuting was to guarantee them that this jerk would pay the bank back. In addition, your Dad wanted to keep this guy close, where we could keep an eye on him. Your Dad also wanted this guy to realize that not only did he owe your Dad for keeping him out of prison, but also he owed every paycheck to the fact that your father went to bat for him with the bank's board. The few members of the board that knew of the embezzlement thought of your Dad as a kind and forgiving person. They of course had no knowledge of your roll under the sheets. I think that your Dad enjoyed that. It was not the image that most people had of him. Your Daddy was a smart operator."

"I'm beginning to realize a lot about my father that I didn't know."

Andy continued: "Back in '79 when your dad died, I made it my business to pay this joker another visit. I didn't want him to think that just because of the death of your father, our little deal was null and void. He got the picture. He's been a good boy. Lived up to his end of the bargain, and retired from the bank a few years ago. Why they had a party for him and everything."

"I truly thank you for all that you have done on my behalf Andy."

"No problem, your Dad helped me out a lot of times."

"But you said that after all of these years I am now in big trouble again on account of this. How is that?"

"My associates and I got wind over a month ago that somebody was poking around. Some guy was looking up and talking to your old college frat house buddies concerning that night that you left the dance with the girl. Then they started checking up on the girl. We're afraid that someone is putting two and two together."

"How could they even know what to look for let alone where to look?"

"Only one way, there was a law firm that your father and grandfather used a long time ago. Let's just say that in that day things were a little more freewheeling at the Atlantic Corporation then they are today. Because they were kept on a large retainer, your father occasionally utilized them when he desired to keep his activities out of the main stream. This firm was very good at doing things and not asking too many ethical questions. I believe that they are the firm that helped set up the dummy accounts that I administered to pay back the embezzled bank funds. Could be that someone in that firm has decided to check up on you for one reason or another? If so they probably got the girl's family name from the bank."

"To your knowledge have they contacted the girl or her family?"

"At this point I'm not certain. I don't think so, but I have some of my associates checking up on that right now. I want you to know one thing Denton. The current senior partner in this firm is one Abraham Rueben." Andy paused and watched Denton closely. "He's a very dangerous man. He is licensed to practice law in the state of New York and the State of Illinois. He has offices in both New York and

Chicago and he done work for both the New York and Chicago families in the past." Andy paused. "You understand who I'm referring to when I mention the New York and Chicago families?"

"You mean crime families?"

"Yeah Mafia, Costa Nostra, you got the idea. Anyway, he's not real popular in New York at the moment because of his work with the people in Chicago."

"Crime families."

"That's right."

"I thought that they were almost a thing of the past."

"Some aspects are just about out of business. Those are the groups that the FBI likes to crow about their demise. But some, the one's smart enough to keep a low profile, are extremely healthy."

Denton was wondering if one of the healthy segments included a diner near the Fulton Fish Market.

"Denton the point that I'm making about Rueben is that this man decides to go looking for dirt on you or your family, he may have access to some old forgotten and extremely sensitive material. He's also clever enough to take unrelated pieces of a puzzle and determine what the puzzle should look like."

Denton swallowed hard. This is how Trevor found out about this whole fiasco. Abraham Rueben had already put two and two together, and Denton himself confirmed it to Trevor during their recent late night planning session. He felt his ears burning with embarrassment.

"Denton, I know that your boss Trevor Mason used Rueben's services in Chicago. I know that he has recently retained his services here in New York. People were hurt in Chicago. Hurt badly. Some are only now recovering from long hospital stays."

"Physically hurt?"

Andy sighed. Denton's father had kept his son too well protected from the reality of the world that his father and grandfather chose to live in.

"Yes. Physically hurt. Let's just say that Abraham Rueben has enough contacts that he can provide a 'full service' law firm." Andy grew silent while he watched Denton closely. This last bit of information had visibly shaken him. Andy had watched young Denton Wellbon III grow up. His father had brought him into Andy's diner from the time that he was about eight years old. His father often talked about his son even when the boy was off at school. The elder Denton's pride in his son knew no bounds. A pity thought Andy. The son didn't seem to realize that. But now it was time again for a member of the Wellbon family to take control of the company that his family built from nothing. This Denton Wellbon had to face his legacy and master it.

Denton broke the silence. "Has there been any evidence of anyone else over the years attempting to poke, as you say, into my back ground?"

"None."

"Never before?"

"No."

Then, thought Denton, there was no conspiracy among the members of the Wellbon-Smith Board to expose Denton's secret. Denton now suspected that Carlton Smith was also ignorant of his misadventure. If that was indeed the case, then Trevor Mason was Denton's only threat of exposure. "Andy, I have yet another question."

"Ask away. As I served your father, I'm prepared to serve you."

Denton was caught off guard by this comment. "Why thank you Andy. I must admit that until tonight, I was unaware of how extensive a relationship you and my father had. I appreciate your offer."

"It's not an offer. It's a promise. Your father helped me, I helped him, and he asked me to promise that when the time was right, and he trusted my judgment on that issue, I should begin explaining our arrangement to you and extend the same courtesies to you that I had to him. I believe that the time is now. He also promised me that you would continue the relationship with the same support for me that he had provided in the past."

"What kind of support did my father provide?" Denton's mouth was so dry right now that his voice was becoming hoarse.

"When I needed anything, no matter what, money, a particular service performed, no matter if it was legal or illegal, your father used the full extent of his power and wealth to provide it for me."

Denton closed his eyes. He didn't know if he should ask the next question or not. "How did the two of you come to this arrangement?"

"We owed our lives to each other. Someday, if you prove to be as loyal a friend as your father was, I will tell you about it. For now the fact that your father would make a commitment like that for you, after all that he had done for you should be all the reason you need to renew that commitment. Will you make the same commitment to me as your father made? I will make the same commitment to you!"

Denton took a deep breath. He knew that this man could be lying to him, but he truly doubted that was the case. First of all his father had constantly spoken highly of Andy. Second, Andy was too well informed concerning his family's affairs. Even before this meeting Denton was having doubts that he could fully trust Trevor. Nothing that he heard here made him comfortable with his relationship with Trevor Mason and certainly not Abraham Rueben. Yet everything that Andy told him was strangely in 'sync' with what he knew to be his family's history. In addition Andy seemed committed to protecting his secret, not making subtle threats concerning it. Denton made a split second decision. He would take a chance and trust this man. "I will make that commitment. You must understand that I am not as powerful a figure in the Wellbon-Smith Empire as was my father."

"You will be. You had another question."

Denton thought it wise not to follow up on Andy's last comment. "Oh, yes. Did my father ever include Carlton Smith in any of his dealings with you?"

"Only your father and grandfather ever did business with me. Carlton Smith wouldn't even know where to find this diner."

"There is no evidence that Carlton Smith has any knowledge of my unfortunate escapade with the under-aged girl?"

"Carlton Smith couldn't find his ass if your father hadn't kicked him in it and showed him where it is!" Upon hearing this comment, Denton allowed himself a faint smile. Andy continued: "Carlton Smith has had your mother buffaloed ever since your father died. She thinks that he's God's gift to business. If your Dad knew how he's been running things or the way he convinced your mother to treat you, he'd turn over in his grave."

"What do you mean by 'the way he convinced my mother to treat me'?"

"Exactly that, you should have been made top dog in Wellbon-Smith when your father died. It's what your father wanted and your mother knew it. The people were there to support you in the areas that you were weak. In addition, what the board had no way of knowing was that my associates and I would have been there to support you also. Unfortunately your father died suddenly before he had a chance to set things up so that you could take over. Carlton seized the moment while your grieving mother was vulnerable." Andy looked Denton hard in the eye. "Listen to me. Your father and grandfather believed that this company belonged to them and them alone. They never intended for someone outside the family to sit in the top chair. It's time for you to get your ass there and put a Wellbon back in control. It's time for you to start acting like a Wellbon!"

Denton took another deep breath and sat up straight in the chair. "Where do we begin?"

Andy's big smile returned. "That's what I like to hear. Even your tone of voice and the set of your jaw are beginning to sound and look like your Dad! Well, we both know who is employing Abraham Rueben now, your boss, Trevor Mason. Let me have some of my guys check up on Rueben's activities."

"I can tell you that Trevor, Rueben and I are attempting to buy up enough stock to get controlling interest in Wellbon-Smith." Denton was surprised that he spoke these words. Trevor would kill him! From what he just heard, that may be more than a figure of speech. But then, why not tell Andy? He had just made a decision to trust him. That could be no worse a decision than his father had made concerning Andy many years before. After all he had really known Andy far longer than he had known Trevor Mason.

"Really? That's great! Let me guess, their methods are somewhat less than ethical in your opinion and they got you to cooperate by hinting that they know about your problem with the girl."

"I'm embarrassed to say that you are essentially correct."

"Don't be embarrassed. It's important that you tell me everything. That's the only way that I can be of any service to you. You must promise me that we will have no secrets from each other."

"I promise Andy."

"Good! Keep involved with them and keep me informed. My guess was an educated one based on what I know of Rueben and the fact that he and Trevor always like to have something 'on' the people that they partner with. It's good insurance. In addition, you only have one skeleton in your closet. You and I now have two objectives. First to keep your life long secrets a secret and second; to make certain that your buddy Trevor doesn't screw you." Andy smiled at Denton. "Don't worry we'll be successful. I'll have one of my boys make certain that Rueben understands that it's not a good idea to expose a Wellbon's secrets."

"But Andy, you said that Abraham Rueben was very dangerous."

"He is, but don't worry, you're too valuable for him to risk harming you. We'll just let him know that it's dangerous to even threaten you. There's one more thing I should tell you Denton."

"What's that?"

"I'm a lot more dangerous than Rueben and I'm on your side!"

Denton contemplated this final statement. "Andy, may I make one request?"

"Certainly."

"Don't put any pressure on Rueben just yet. It's apparent that he and Trevor have no knowledge of you what so ever. I think that I would rather wait a bit before I play all of our cards."

"Okay Denton, okay. I like that. It sounds like something your father would have said. He always wanted people to underestimate him until it was too late. I'll wait for your word."

"Thank you Andy, and thank you for calling."

"It was time Denton."

Andy rose from his big chair and shook Denton's hand again. Denton rose in unison, it was obvious that the meeting was over.

"It's good to be working with a Wellbon again Denton."

"It's good to finally begin to understand my father's friendship with you. I hope that I can be as good a friend as Dad was."

"Don't worry. You'll do fine."

Andy walked Denton to the front of the diner. "Can't get you to stay for breakfast? It's on the house this morning."

"Thanks I'd love to, but Susan my wife was very worried when I left at such an odd hour this morning. I must get home and assure her that I'm all right."

"Of course, we'll give you a rain check on breakfast."

Denton said goodbye and left the diner for the street. Andy watched him go. He was well pleased with this meeting. His doubts about being able to do business with the young Denton had vanished. After Denton was gone, Andy returned to his office and picked up the phone. He punched in a number and waited. Soon there was a voice on the other end. "I just finished meeting with young Denton Wellbon…Good. Very good…I have no worries about him at all. I can see in his eye that he wants to sit in his father's chair… Yeah, it will be good to have the Wellbon alliance again… It's been a long time since we had those resources… It's been a long time since the Wellbons had our resources too… This will be good for both of us and it's just what his father wanted…Yeah, I'll talk to you later...Yeah, hey, I got a diner to run here... See you."

***

Crystal Harrison and the mysterious Mr. Smith walked slowly along Savannah's River Street. At three-thirty in the morning all of the shops and bars were closed. The street was deserted. The occasional police cruisers bumping along on the cobblestone street were their only companions. Cobblestone was a very loose description of the materials utilized in paving this street. During the seventeenth century, sailing ships used to use large rocks in their holds for ballast when sailing from England to the Georgia colony. When they returned, they were so laden with goods and raw materials that they no longer needed the additional ballast. They emptied the rocks from their holds to make room for goods. Something had to be done with all these rocks, so the citizens of Savannah decided to pave the streets with them. The only ones that remained in this condition were River Street and the few adjoining streets that worked their way up the steep hill from the waterfront to the city proper.

The two strolled silently, enjoying the cool air of the wee early morning hours, a welcome relief from the oppressing heat of the deep-south summer. River Street may have been asleep but the waterfront on the Savannah River above and below River Street was anything but asleep. Both up and down river the huge cranes with their crews were working under bright klieg lights. They were loading and unloading ships with containers, grain, concrete and just about any cargo that you could imagine that was passing through this major deep water seaport. Sandwiched between all these activities was River Street. This was the original waterfront area of this historic city. The city's dedicated historical groups saved the old cotton warehouses with their Proctor or Broker's offices on the top floor and the cotton storage on the bottom. They were converted into shops, offices, hotels and restaurants.

Against this historic backdrop Crystal and Mr. Smith found themselves on the brick covered wharf where two stern wheeler riverboats were finished carrying tourists for the day and rode quietly at anchor. Beyond the riverboats were the private luxury yachts that were tied up near the Hilton Hotel. Mr. Smith suggested that they have a seat on one of the benches near the riverboats.

"Savannah's a beautiful city Crystal," said Smith. They were both looking up at the brightly lit soaring suspension bridge that spanned the Savannah River between Savannah Georgia and South Carolina.

"Yes, I enjoy living here... Now stop changing the subject. Who are you and how were you involved with my mother's trust fund?"

"The first question that you need to ask is where did this trust fund come from?"

"Have you noticed how you never answer my questions?"

Mr. Smith smiled his pleasant patient smile. "I'm trying to tell you what you need to know."

"Okay, I'll continue playing the game. Where did the trust fund come from?"

"I'm not being difficult Crystal, but you have to understand all of the elements. What you don't know is that your real father comes from a very wealthy family. He realized that no matter how much he may have loved your mother, they could never be together. He felt a strong sense of responsibility for you and your mother so he set up a trust fund. Since he knew that he couldn't be present to control it he put certain restrictions on it. Your mother could request funds from it at any time for clothes, housing, or education for you both. No matter how foolish your stepfather might be at handling money your mother could always provide the essentials for you."

"Where do you come into this?"

"I work for the organization that your father chose to administer the trust fund. We monitor the financial firm that invests it and administer the pay outs."

"So if I understand this, mom could only use the money for food, shelter, or education?"

"Yes, for either you or her. The only 'catch' if you can call it a catch, was that your mother had to get our permission before we would release funds. Remember that your father may have loved your mother very much, but he only knew her for a short time and she was very young. He came from a family of astute business people. Your mother would tell us what she needed and where to send the money. We paid the bills. She never had to handle the money. The same was true of your adopted family. That's why someone from our organization would pay periodic visits."

"I'm getting the impression that my father was older than my mother?"

"Yes."

"So tell me more about my father. Who is he? Where does he live?"

"No, I'm not permitted to do that. I really can't say any more concerning him."

"Why? What possible harm could it do for me to know who my father is? I've already lost my mother, the man I thought was my father isn't, and now you tell me that you're not permitted to tell me about my real father?"

"It would do far more harm than you could imagine."

Crystal's shoulders sagged. She was emotionally spent. She shuddered.

"Are you all right Crystal?"

Crystal turned toward this strange man. If what he said was true he had in a few hours told her more about her life than anyone else ever had. At the same time he had raised more questions then she had ever thought possible. "No I'm not all right. I am so drained. I am so tired of all of this. Good lord, I can't even cry anymore." She stared into the large man's kindly face. "I don't understand. Why did you even come to see me? Did you think this would satisfy me? Did you think that learning a little would make me happy?"

"No Crystal, I didn't think that any of this would make you happy. As someone that has followed you and your achievements for the past several years, this was not an easy chore for me. I have a lot of respect for you Crystal. You have succeeded with the deck stacked against you and you have only just begun. Armed with a good education you have broken into the broadcasting field and are now considered the top news personality in the Savannah market. You have an excellent chance to move up to one of the major networks before you are thirty years old. But I have a job to do and now I must complete it. Crystal the reason that I am here tonight is because both your mother and your adopted family were very wise and conservative in their requests for funds to support you. They were never told the size of the fund so they were careful to only make necessary requests. In addition the fund's managers have been very successful in their investment decisions. The fund prospered and you have just passed your twenty-sixth birthday."

"What are you telling me?"

"The trust has been set up so that when you reached age twenty-six you are entitled to take over control of it yourself."

"There is still money in the trust? My adopted father told me that it just reached far enough to get me through college."

"He didn't deceive you. That's the impression that we gave him. Your natural father had given instructions at the inception that after college you had to have a chance to make it on your own. He believed that the only way for you to mature was to have to survive and pay your bills like everyone else. As his family's power and influence could never come to your aide because of the need to keep their identity secret, he decreed that if there were excess funds upon the completion of your education the fund managers would simply continue to invest them. When you reached the age of twenty-six, he believed that you would be mature enough to accept this responsibility and should be entitled to what was left." Mr. Smith paused to observe Crystal's reaction. She seemed puzzled, as if the night had provided more information then she was able to process at one time.

Smith continued, "There are two conditions though. You are never to attempt to discover your father's identity. If you do you will forfeit any money that is left. The other condition is that because of the outstanding job that they have done, you continue to seek advice from the money managers that have managed the trust successfully all these years. My organization will see that they are reimbursed for their services, so you will not have to 'waste' any of the remaining funds on advice. Other than that you may withdraw any portion of it that you desire at any time and use it as you wish."

"Suppose I wish to withdraw the money and use it to help me find my father?"

"There are papers for you to sign. Contractual agreements that you will enter into that specifically forbid any remaining funds to be utilized in such a manner. I would not advise you to get into a battle, legal or otherwise, with the organization that I represent."

"What is the name of this organization?"

"It is not necessary for you to know that."

For just an instant Crystal thought that she detected a hard sinister edge in his voice and a cold look in the large man's eyes, but it was gone in an instant. That instant made her shiver and for the first time she felt uncomfortable with him. But then his smile and gentle demeanor returned and she thought that it must have been her imagination.

The large man's smile broadened. "Aren't you curious as to the value of the trust?"

"Oh…Yes, I guess. There can't be too much. After all it paid for all that private schooling, your fees and the managers, which I suspect have been ample. It even paid all my expenses to Auburn for God's sake… How much?"

The large man laughed. "Three point five million," was all that he said.

***

Sam Grabowski waited for the vending machine to fill the paper cup with hot coffee. A buck for a tiny cup of coffee was totally unreasonable he thought. Thank goodness everyone back at the Precinct station agreed to chip in and buy a couple of coffee makers. He removed the cup from the machine and cursed as it burned his hand. Damn thin cups! For a buck they could at least supply cups heavy enough to protect you!

Lieutenant Grabowski of the New York City Police Department was at this moment in the New York City Federal Building. He was waiting to see an old friend, agent Sigfreid of the FBI. As Sam sampled his coffee and resisted the urge to curse out loud, a voice from behind caught his attention.

"Sam, how are you doing?"

Grabowski turned to greet a familiar face. "Good morning Harry. I'm fine and you?"

"Ah, you know how it goes. We're both in the same business. Long time no see! What can I do for you?"

"Can I talk to you in private?" Grabowski glanced around the busy office.

"Sure follow me." With that Sigfreid led the way to a small office with the faded letters that spelled out 'senior agent' stenciled on the opaque glass in the door. Upon entering the room Sigfreid offered Grabowski a seat and then settled into the worn chair behind the desk. Harry Sigfreid had a lot of respect for this veteran city policeman. While relations between the Bureau and local police departments were not always the best he and Sam had long ago surmounted the petty rivalries.

"What do you want to talk about Sam?" There was no need for small talk between these two professionals. They were both on the clock. Small talk could be enjoyed in a bar over a couple of beers after hours.

"Maybe nothing, maybe something, I don't know. Last night I was working the graveyard shift and on my way home I decided to take a detour and get some breakfast. Remember that old diner down by the Fulton Fish Market? Andy's is the name."

"Yeah, boy that brings back memories. I haven't been down there in years. At one time we thought it might have mob connections."

"That's the one. Remember that rich guy? Big time businessman that everybody whispered was crooked. He used to hang out down there. Nobody could figure out why."

"Sure. What was his name?" Sigfreid frowned.

"Denton Wellbon."

"That's it. You got a good memory Sam."

"Yeah, tell me about it. There's a lot of stuff I wish I could forget. Anyway, Denton and his father, I guess it was Denton Senior; they were legends in the City's business circles. Everybody claimed that they were big time smugglers of booze and anything else that there was a market for. At one time they were supposed to have half the police and judges on their payroll. Nobody could ever prove anything but that was always the rumor."

"Yeah, I remember now that you mention it. What was their company's name? Ah... Oh yes, Atlantic Importing or something like that. We investigated them from top to bottom but could never find anything to hang our hats on. Finally figured that, while probably not totally honest, they were no better or worse than a lot of other big companies."

"We also quit watching Andy's Diner."

"There was nothing there. With the changes in the federal racketeering laws and the ability to wire tap that gave us, we soon found out who was really who in the crime families. We no longer wasted our time with 'red herrings' like Denton Wellbon and Andy's Diner. That's why the so-called Mafia is in such a shambles. We got all the big boys behind bars."

"Are we sure? Are we really that positive?"

"What are you driving at old friend? Don't you watch the news? We won the war. Most of the big time bosses are either behind bars or waiting to be sentenced. Why even Gotti for God's sake."

"Yeah, I guess you're right."

"What is it Sam? I could almost hear the 'but' behind your last comment."

"Well, like I said, I decided to get breakfast at Andy's Diner last night. When I started down that way I wasn't even sure that the place was still open. Well it is. So I have a great typical diner breakfast and just after I get my bill and I'm digging in my pocket for a tip, guess what I see."

"What?"

"Comin' out of the kitchen is Andy himself. He looks to be in his sixties now, but he still looks like he could beat up an army of today's young punks and not even work up a sweat."

To Catch a Fox

"So our old 'buddy' Andy is still alive and still running his diner, so what?"

"So guess who's with him?"

"Well it can't be either of the Denton Wellbons. Both the father and son are dead."

"Remember how the son used to bring his boy along with him to the diner sometimes?"

"Yeah."

"Well the kid's a man now approaching middle age. He's the spittin' image of his father and grandfather. I'd know him anywhere."

"That's who you saw with Andy?"

"Yeah, weird ain't it? And guess what? They're looking real serious as if they were doing big business. Just like this kid's old man and Andy used to look. They shook hands and the Wellbon kid leaves. Far as I can tell he didn't have anything to eat at the diner either."

Harry smiled, "Just because there were no stains on his tie doesn't mean that he didn't have anything to eat. Some people are neater than the NYPD."

"That's enough of that my friend." The ribbing was good-natured. After a chuckle Sam shook his head and got serious again. "I told you 'maybe something, maybe nothing' maybe I'm watching too many cop shows on TV. I don't know. I just had this sudden feeling of déjà vu."

"I can understand that, but for all we know they are in business together. Maybe the Wellbon family is a silent partner in Andy's Diner. Who knows? There's nothing illegal with that. This is America, free enterprise, capitalism."

"Yeah, but you don't usually see some big time corporate society players like the Wellbons rubbin' elbows with the likes of Andy... What was his last name anyway?"

"I forget, but I know what you mean my friend and I sympathize, but their connection goes back a long way. Hell we aren't that much older than the current Wellbon. We were just rookies starting out when they had us watching Andy's place…Bottom line old friend, all the king's horses and all the king's men couldn't find anything wrong with their relationship in the past. God knows we tried. There isn't much future in looking again."

Sam sighed. He had forgotten the coffee in the cup he had been holding. Now it was cold. Damn! "You're right. I have been watching too much TV. It's just that after all those years I can't get it through my head that we finally got the mob down for the count. I keep thinkin' that maybe we only got the dumb ones. The ones that weren't smart enough to change. I keep thinkin' that maybe some of them wised up in time and went deep. So deep that now they're almost legitimate."

"If that's the case, then legitimate is legal and we have no business snooping around. Even if you're right, we got most of the big time crimes closed, so there would be no reason to keep looking for crimes that they might have pulled off that no one is complaining about."

Sam got up to leave. "You're right my friend. I'm sorry to waste your time."

Harry rose and they shook hands. "You didn't waste my time. Don't ever stop having hunches. Most important don't ever stop sharing them with me. You're right far more than you're wrong."

"Okay, got to go Harry. I have to go on duty again in a few hours. I need my beauty sleep."

"See you Sam."

After Sam Grabowski left his office, Harry Sigfreid sat lost in thought for a long time. Suddenly he picked up his phone and asked his secretary to check the computer files for anything on the Atlantic Importing Company. Sigfreid settled back in his chair. He had learned over the years that Sam's instincts were seldom wrong.

CHAPTER 11

Mitchell Green sat in a booth in an Italian restaurant named Portofino's. The restaurant was located on a side street in the City of Lancaster in Southeastern Pennsylvania. It was lunchtime. Mitchell sat alone but he was expecting a guest to arrive soon. While he waited he sipped on a glass of wine. Mitchell was tired. His flight had arrived in Harrisburg Pennsylvania at seven AM this morning. He spent most of the previous eight hours either on a plane or at O'Hara airport in Chicago. After his arrival, he rented a car and drove the approximately forty miles from the state capital to Lancaster, checked into a hotel and made phone calls until his lunchtime rendezvous.

This was an important meeting. He was meeting with his informant that worked at Fox Cabinetry's main installation in Goodville. Goodville lay well to the east of the city. In fact it was located on the very eastern edge of Lancaster County. That was why Mitchell had insisted that he meet with his informant in the city. This location was sufficiently far away from Fox so that the chance of someone walking in on them during a workday was almost nonexistent.

Mitchell may have been tired, but he was very pleased. One of the phone calls that he made earlier was to Buzz Olson. Buzz reported that the card signing had nearly enough names to force Fox to hold a vote of its employees to determine if they wished to be represented by the union. Mitchell reminded Buzz that the total had to include the same proportion of signatures from the plant in Goodville. It had to be representative of the total of Fox employees, not just the correct ratio from one plant. Buzz reluctantly agreed. In his enthusiasm he had forgotten that fact. Mitchell cheered him up and told him to continue to get as many cards signed as he could. He also suggested that he might get Buzz to take a few days vacation and fly back east to Pennsylvania where he could help Mitchell recruit. Mitchell assured Buzz that he could set it up so that no one in Fox management would know that he was helping to unionize. Mitchell also reminded Buzz that he was only exercising one of his rights as an American worker. The conversation ended with Buzz regaining his enthusiasm and vowing to get well over the number of signed cards that Mitchell had told him they required from

Vegas. Mitchell smiled to himself; events were progressing on schedule.

The tall slender female entered the restaurant. She moved slowly past the bar to the hostess station. Before the hostess could meet her she spied Mitchell and proceeded toward his booth. Mitchell rose to greet her. "Good to see you again."

"Good to see you also." They never used names when they were in a public place, just one more precaution on which Mitchell insisted.

She seated herself across from him. Her brown hair was pulled back in a plain no nonsense style and she wore no makeup. Easy to manage, no time wasted on vanity thought Mitchell. She was perhaps ten years his senior. When they first met, she struck him as plain, but over time, especially when she removed her glasses, he began to see her as attractive. In a different way than he had ever thought of "attractive" before. She was far different from the more conventional beauty of his girl friend in Las Vegas. It disturbed him. These thoughts were crossing his mind more frequently each time they met. In fact she was married.

It was through her husband that they first met. Her husband was an active union man in a local communications company. He was representing his local at a national convention in Washington D C when Mitchell, quite by chance, sat next to him at one of the seminars. During a break the conversation turned to his wife's place of employment. Mitchell was surprised to learn that she worked at Fox Custom Cabinetry. Mitchell informed her husband that he was researching Fox as a possible target for his own union. That's when the floodgates opened and her husband informed Mitchell of just how unhappy the employees had recently become. One thing led to another and Mitchell found himself seated opposite her ordering lunch. Mitchell told himself that he chose this restaurant because of the privacy of its layout and its remoteness to Fox and not because it was a very romantic setting.

She began the conversation. "I wish you wouldn't make me drive this far for these meetings."

"I'm sorry, but you know the reason I chose this location. We can't be too careful, especially when we are getting so close to our goal. My man in Vegas had outstanding success yesterday."

"I'm glad to hear that. But remember that I warned you that these 'Dutchmen' in

Lancaster County won't be as easy to convince as the people out west."

"You let me worry about that. When they hear that their fellow workers want the vote they will come around. You keep me in the loop on what you observe at Fox."

"Well you're not going to be very happy with what I have to tell you."

Mitchell tensed. "What are you talking about?"

"I think they know."

"How could they? What makes you think this?"

"I can only tell you what I have observed Mitchell…"

"Don't use my name!" He said more sharply than he intended. She sighed and the look on her face indicated her displeasure with all of this cloak and dagger stuff as she called it. Unlike Buzz Olsen, she had no fear of management hiding in every shadow. Mitchell wished she were more afraid. "I'm sorry, I didn't mean to snap. Please, tell me exactly what you know."

"A lot of activity, first MacLode has taken to leaving on mysterious trips without notice. He tells no one, I repeat no one, where he is going."

"Not even his secretary?" Mitchell raised a cryptic eyebrow.

"Not even his secretary. That may or may not have any bearing on our interests, he does play close to the vest, but he usually permits his secretary to know where to contact him. Instead he's taken to checking in each day from God knows where. But that's not all," she paused for affect.

Mitchell hated her sense of drama. He also hated the fact that she looked even more attractive today than he remembered. He was about to insist that she go on when the waitress arrived. Mitchell had already determined what he wanted and ordered. His companion on the other hand took a maddeningly long time to examine the menu before ordering the salad that she always ordered. She's enjoying this he thought. He took a deep breath and tried to relax. Her information was always sound, and she would share it with him eventually if he was patient. The waitress finally left them alone. "Please go on." Mitchell said in as calm a voice as he could muster. The Fox project was important to both his personal and the union's future.

"Top management held a special meeting off site this week. Usually when they hold an off site meeting there are agendas being circulated, topics of discussion, assignments, you know the routine. For this meeting there was nothing. They all were strangely vague when someone would inquire concerning it. As if they really preferred that no one knew. That's impossible in an office. Their staff managers have to know when they will be absent. However, other than the fact that they would be out of the office for a couple of days there was no information forthcoming; in addition they held it at a hotel here in Lancaster."

"Not the usual nearby hotel that they use for off site events, the one out near the turnpike exit?"

She smiled a sardonic smile. "What did I just say?"

He felt foolish, and he didn't like to feel foolish in front of her. "I'm sorry I apologize for asking the obvious. Please continue." He realized for the first time that she really could intimidate him.

Her smile softened into something that appeared to be a smile of concern. "I'm sorry for toying with your emotions. I know how important this is to you. It's important to me too."

"It's okay," he liked this new feeling that she might possibly have some concern for him. "Why do you think that they traveled out of their way to Lancaster for this meeting? Most of them live closer to Goodville than to Lancaster."

"Why are we meeting in Lancaster?"

He considered this. "Go on."

"It's who attended this meeting in addition to top management that caught my attention. There were two lawyers from the firm that represents Fox, but not the usual lawyers."

"Who were they?"

"It's not who but what were they. They were labor specialists. I did some checking around when I didn't recognize their names. They conduct seminars for local business on how to prevent unions from penetrating their companies. They also help devise strategies for companies when they suspect that a union is making an attempt to organize a work force."

Mitchell grew pale. There was a sick feeling in the pit of his stomach. He was no longer hungry.

"There's more," she continued. "Guess who else attended?" Mitchell refrained from commenting. "Tom Erving." This bomb exploded over Mitchell with maximum impact. He thought for a second that he would become physically ill. Union busting lawyers, Fox's Las Vegas plant manager, how could MacLode possibly know? They sat in silence with Mitchell staring into empty space, his mind racing, she, observing his reaction. The waitress brought their lunch.

His companion ate heartily while Mitchell considered the possibilities. The plan that had seemed to be working like clockwork when he entered the restaurant suddenly seemed to be coming apart. He returned from his thoughts. "Is there any more devastating news?"

She paused in her meal and looked him in the eye. "Are you certain that you can take it? You haven't touched your food and you really don't look well."

Mitchell flushed bringing color back to his face. "Yes, I can take it. I'm just surprised. There had been no indication that management was aware. What else can you tell me?"

"The new Human Resources VP returned with Tom Erving to Las Vegas on an early flight this morning."

"You think they are attempting a counterstrike?" Mitchell's mouth went dry.

"I think they are attempting a preemptive strike. Remember you don't as of this moment have enough signed cards to force a vote for your union to represent us."

"Do you have any indication what she and Erving are going to do?"

"None, but whatever it is it can't help our cause, remember this trip comes after a day's session with the anti union lawyers."

They fell into silence once more. Mitchell's guest finished her salad and asked for another glass of wine for both. Then at her insistence, Mitchell did make an admirable attempt at his BLT. It was good that he did, because having skipped breakfast the first glass of wine was beginning to "buzz" in his brain.

"Anything that you need me to do?" she asked.

With time to recover from his initial reaction, and the sandwich having a positive effect on his stomach, Mitchell reflected on her question. "Just keep doing what you are doing, observing. I can't tell you how valuable this information is..." Mitchell paused, "I think that we keep with our plan. We know that the work force is unhappy. We are now aware that they will attempt to change that attitude, but we are also aware of the pressure that they are under from Atlantic Corp. Have you been able to discover if Fox is really for sale?"

"No, other than the statement issued from senior management at Fox, there has been no more information of which I am aware."

"Okay then. Our plan remains sound. We just no longer have the element of surprise. We're going to be in a real war. But I remain positive that it's a war that we can win. It is now imperative that we speed up the pace. Let's not allow them to get the upper hand. Have you picked someone to get cards signed at Goodville?"

"I think I have someone. Do you want me to contact them to test the waters?"

"Yes do that, and let me know how it goes. You need to have someone else in case the first prospect gets cold feet."

"She won't, trust me."

"I do trust you, you know that. You are in the perfect position to pull this off."

"Yes, I am. I'm treated like furniture. I'm there and I'm dependable. I take care of their customers and solve problems but they forget all about me. It's the perfect position from which to spawn revolution..." She raised her glass in a toast, "To revolution."

"To revolution," Mitchell responded as his glass touched hers.

She smiled and held his gaze. He was quite handsome, a bit young, but quite handsome. She removed her eyeglasses.

***

Denton Wellbon III closed the folder that he had been reading for the last hour. It was a proposal from Sterling International, an Atlantic operating division, for permission to expand their plant. They had gone into great detail in their projections and the numbers seemed convincing on the surface. Denton's only problem was the same problem that Trevor would have. The company was only running one shift at present. Why would they want to invest in bricks and mortar to increase capacity when they weren't even close to using the capacity they possessed? Sterling's answer: There were not a sufficient number of skilled laborers in the area to support two additional full shifts. Trevor would ask. "Then how in hell do you hope to find the fifty percent increase in employees required after the plant expansion?"

Denton sighed. Why do seemingly bright executives make such ignorant proposals? This type of request would raise Trevor Mason's ire and he would pick up the telephone and "ream Sterling's president a new asshole!" But that was Sterling's problem. Trevor asked Denton to make a recommendation and Denton would. The management at Sterling would not like Denton's decision.

Denton was in his office just down the hall from Trevor Mason's. That morning he had delivered his verbal report with substantiating documents on the escapades of Millissa Kensington's nephew. He and Trevor had discussed the nephew's history for over an hour behind closed doors. Trevor was almost jovial. "This is great work Denton! Great work! Millissa will have no choice but to work with us. If she doesn't, we'll have her nephew charged with fraud so fast it will make both their heads spin."

"Not to sound less than positive Trevor, but what if she calls our bluff. What if she no longer cares what happens to her nephew? What if she decides to go public with our offer to her?"

"She will have no way to prove that we ever made such an offer. The others that have agreed to become a part of our little scheme will keep their mouths shut because they want to make a lot of money when we buy their shares. Millissa on the other hand will have her hands full defending herself. You've made an airtight case against her and her knowledge of her nephew's fraud. By the way, you realize that your mentor Carlton Smith had to have knowledge of this or it could have never taken place?"

"I realize that, but it's all circumstantial against Carlton."

"That's 'cause he's smarter than Millissa. He would never allow his fingerprints to be all over something as hot as this, but you and I know that it couldn't have happened without his silent approval."

"I fear that you are correct in that respect Trevor."

"Damn right I'm correct." Trevor reviewed the documents again. "Damn Denton, you're good. No one but you could have remembered all of this let alone actually put their hands on all of the unrelated documents that pull this puzzle together. My hat's off to you my friend."

As Denton watched Trevor glower over his work, he again wondered just how much of a friend Trevor really was. Denton felt betrayed by Carlton Smith, was Trevor Mason just another individual in Denton's life who was using him for his own means? But today for the first time Denton no longer felt that he was destined to be subject to the devices of others. For the first time he felt a sense of personal power. He hadn't felt this way since as a boy he accompanied his father as they walked around this very building. His father's building.

The reason for this sudden surge of confidence was his meeting at the Diner last night. Denton was still somewhat uncertain as to the exact relationship between Andy and his father, but he knew now that one derived power from the other. Now Andy was offering that same arrangement to him. He loved and admired his father immensely no matter what he may or may not have done. He didn't exactly know how, but he sensed that Andy could give him the opportunity to finally be like his father. What did Andy tell him on the phone? "It's time for you to step up and take over for your father."

Denton returned from his thoughts as the phone buzzed on his desk. It was his secretary. She was confirming an appointment for four o'clock this afternoon. When he hung up, he turned and looked out at the New York City skyline.

His father and grandfather both looked out from this building on the City. But when they looked out they knew that they were in command of Wellbon-Smith and the Atlantic Corporation that had spawned it. For the first time in his life, Denton believed that it would be possible for him to do likewise. In addition, he had this sense of kinship with his father and grandfather and believed they would approve.

Denton thought again of Trevor. He was no longer afraid. No matter how dangerous Andy claimed that Trevor and Abraham Rueben could be. If Trevor failed to live up to his promises, then Trevor had best be prepared for the fight of his life. Denton didn't possess the name Wellbon for no reason at all! Denton turned back to his desk and opened the Sterling folder once again.

***

Mac sat in the restaurant of the Holiday Inn in the Merchandise Mart Plaza in Chicago. He checked his watch. It was seven o'clock in the morning. The restaurant was on the lobby level of the hotel and was totally open. Mac could see the front desk, the elevators and the entire atrium that soared to the top floor. The open walkways on each level ringed the structure so that every floor had the rooms on the perimeter of the building while the walkways looked out on this central atrium. The occupants of the rooms could exit onto the walkways and look down to the lobby and restaurant below. The waitress brought Mac his cup of black coffee and inquired if Mac was ready to order breakfast. Mac explained that he was expecting company and would wait until his guest arrived. Mac sipped the hot coffee and looked about. No sign of Mr. Roberts, but then Mac always liked to be early for appointments and he did not expect his guest for another fifteen minutes.

As he slowly sipped the excellent hot coffee, Mac reflected on the previous day. The strategy meeting at the hotel back in Lancaster began promptly at eight in the morning. Dale Hershey, looking very tired, passed out copies of the financial projections that Mac had requested. All agreed on the general strategy. There was no question why the Fox employees were unhappy and no question as to what may have the best chance at restoring their confidence in management. The problem was in the details and the execution. As Dale had predicted the night before everyone agreed that the announcement of the restoration of benefits must take place immediately. Paying for this restoration was where the debate ensued.

Tony agreed that they had to be able to show corporate how they were going to finance these additional costs, but he was very concerned about announcing an unexpected price increase to the dealer network. Things just weren't done that way in the cabinet industry. Dealers expected the manufacturers to have one price increase per year and to give them several months advance notice as to the increase. The retailers viewed this as necessary.

Tony understood the problem with corporate and the margins on which Trevor Mason was insisting. However, as VP of Sales and Marketing he also had to look ahead to sales for next year and the year after that. The grip that any manufacturer in the cabinet industry had on its dealer network was tenuous at best. To convey the impression that their factory "partner" couldn't be trusted to give them advanced warning on price increases was inviting them to begin talks with other manufacturers.

But not even Tony could come up with a solution to this problem. The fear of dealing with a unionized work force presented the greater threat to the future of Fox Cabinetry then did an unexpected price increase. Eventually Tony acquiesced and the plans were approved with the one concession. That Tony could have one month from the date of announcement till the effective date of the increase. The announcement had to take place within two weeks of this meeting.

Everyone sprang into action. Mac got on the phone to Sarah and Tom in Las Vegas and gave them the green light to set up an employee meeting of all shifts for the next day. Tony and David huddled to determine how quickly they could call the sales force to Goodville for a meeting to provide an explanation of the price increase. Tony believed that the sales force required a 'face-to-face" before the announcement to the dealers.

Dale went over the details of the numbers with Carroll and Dennis. With Sarah in Las Vegas, Dennis would have to conduct the employee meeting that would take place tomorrow in Goodville. Carroll would back Dennis up when they opened the floor to questions. All looked to Mac to make the explanation to corporate. Mac said he would consider the timing of that task carefully and inform them when and how he would attempt it.

To Catch a Fox

The meeting officially broke up at noon with all returning to the office to proceed with their assignments; all but Mac who surprised everyone by arriving with a suitcase. Mac simply told them that he had to be in Chicago by morning. He volunteered no further explanation. He knew everyone would like to know the reason for this trip, but at this juncture he had to play out this hand alone. What they didn't know would not hurt them if corporate got wind of Mac's plans. Mac caught an afternoon flight out of Harrisburg to O'Hare.

Now Mac was waiting breakfast on a man that he had never laid eyes on before. This man, Mr. Roberts, could ultimately determine if Mac remained as president of Fox. This man could possibly determine if Fox Cabinetry continued in the form that it existed today. Just four weeks ago Mac would have never envisioned that he would be in this situation keeping this appointment. Life certainly was full of unexpected twists and turns he thought.

Mac noticed that a man was now speaking with the hostess. Mac had left his name with her for the benefit of Mr. Roberts. The hostess looked in Mac's direction and proceeded to bring the gentleman toward Mac's table. The gentleman was a tall portly man with only a very little white hair. He was dressed in an expensive albeit very conservative blue suit and a red "power" necktie with gold geometric designs. It became obvious that this was the man that Mac was to meet. He rose for the greeting. "Mr. Roberts?"

"Yes, and you must be William MacLode." The man's face broke into a broad smile as they clasped hands briefly.

"I am indeed, please be seated." Mac turned to the hostess and asked her to inform the waitress that they would soon be ready to order and to bring Mr. Roberts a cup of coffee.

"Make it with cream please," said Roberts as he took a seat at Mac's table and immediately began to study the menu. The waitress arrived promptly with Mr. Robert's coffee and a refill for Mac. Both were prepared with their choices and the orders were placed. After the waitress departed Mr. Roberts took a long sip of his coffee and studied Mac closely. He smiled. "So you want to buy a business."

"I want to explore the possibility."

"Good. Do you understand how my organization, Future Unlimited, operates?"

"I believe that I do. You are a group of chief executive officers of various companies in various industries scattered around the world. You in essence have created your own mutual fund, for lack of a better term, and with this fund you help other CEO's purchase the companies that they are running from the investors that own them."

"That's essentially correct. We of course hold stock in all of the companies that we help purchase and some of our members represent us on the board of directors that you form. Since we like our investment to give all of our members a good return, these board members are at your disposal for any advice that you may need and in addition they keep watch over our interests. We do like you to involve other key members of your current team in this deal as fellow investors so that we can be assured that the people who know the business best will stick around and help you operate the enterprise."

"Yes, I anticipated that and do not see it as a problem. I wouldn't want to invest my money unless the key managers were prepared to remain and continue to help me run the company."

"Good. Just remember that we achieve their commitment because they become fellow investors along with you. Have you approached any of them with this idea as of yet?"

"No I wanted to speak with you and your associates first."

"Just as well, I agree with you that it is probably too early for that conversation. My associates and I have studied the numbers that you sent to us. I must say that Fox Cabinetry is an impressive little business."

"You see backing me as a distinct possibility?"

"We certainly do. How much money are we going to have to supply?"

"A lot," said Mac. "I'm not a poor man, but this will require far more than I can come up with."

Mr. Roberts smiled. "That doesn't make you unusual Mr. MacLode. Let me ask you some questions that my associates and I came up with after reviewing your numbers. Then after breakfast we will drive across town to our office, I'll introduce you to some of my business associates and we can get them to help us decide exactly what Fox is worth and what kind of an offer we can put together"

Mac took a deep breath. This was a hell of a big step, "Sounds good to me." Their breakfast arrived and they began to sort out the numbers between mouthfuls.

***

"Fox Custom Cabinetry, Mr. MacLode's office, Brady Miller speaking. How may I help you?"

"Yes, yes you may help me," returned the heavily accented voice on the other end. "My name is Brian Hempstead Esquire and it is imperative that I speak with Mr. MacLode."

"Mr. McLode is out of town, is there something that I can help you with?"

"Oh dear, no, no I'm afraid there is nothing that you can do miss. Nothing at all, I really require Mr. MacLode."

"As I told you that is impossible, Mr. MacLode is out of town. If there is a message, I will be happy to relay it to him."

"No I'm afraid that I must speak with him personally. Is there a number that I could call to reach him at his 'out of town' location?"

"Mr. MacLode did not leave a number with me."

"Can you put me through to someone who might be in possession of such a number?"

"Believe me Mr. Hempstead, if I don't have the number, no one in this organization has it. I'm his secretary." Brady was becoming slightly irritated with the pace of this conversation. She had work to do. "I offer again to deliver a message to him."

"If you can deliver the message, does that mean that you have a number where you can reach him?"

"No, that is not what my offer implies. Mr. MacLode makes a practice of checking in with me on a daily basis when he is out of town. At that time I will deliver any message that you might give me. However, you have to give me the message in order for me to deliver it." Brady's voice was slowly rising.

"Oh, yes, yes, I see. Very well then, just tell Mr. MacLode to call Brian Hempstead."

"Does he know who you are and does he have your phone number?"

"Yes, yes he knows me very well, very well indeed. He has called me many times over the years. I was his father's lawyer for many years and now that his father is gone I am representing William in the settlement of his father's estate. There's been some unexpected business cropped up and I need William's decision as executor of the late Sean MacLode's estate."

Brady was astounded! "Sean MacLode is dead?"

"I'm afraid so Miss. I'm sorry to be the one to break the news to you. We're you a close friend?"

"No, no I never met him, but Mr. MacLode spoke of him often. When did he pass away?"

"Going on three weeks now."

That's where Mac was the other week. He went home to Scotland for his father's funeral. Brady could hardly believe it. Mac never said a word to anyone. She realized that this must be a severe blow to him, as he was very close to his father.

"So will you tell Mr. Maclode to call me as soon as it is possible? It really is an emergency."

"Yes, yes I promise I will tell him. You are in Scotland now?"

"Yes I am."

"Just to be on the safe side Mr. Hempstead, please give me your phone number, in case Mr. Maclode may have misplaced it." Mr. Brian Hempstead obliged as Brady scribbled the number on a piece of paper.

"Well thank you ever so much for your help. Good Day." Mr. Hempstead was gone.

Brady sat mystified. Suddenly she snapped back to reality. "Anthony! Anthony! I've got to tell you what I just learned!" Brady raced for the open door to Tony's office.

***

Sarah Frazer sank into the chair behind Tom Erving's desk. She looked up at his smiling face. "How did we do?" she asked. She and Tom had just completed a plant wide all shifts meeting of Fox Las Vegas employees. They held it at seven in the morning so that they could catch the first and third shifts as they came and left. The second shift was the only one that had to make a special trip. Sarah held the meeting in a nearby auditorium in the High Plains Industrial Park because the Fox plant had no meeting rooms large enough to hold all four hundred and ninety six Fox employees. In addition, to reward them for the effort and inconvenience, she had a catered buffet breakfast for them immediately following the meeting. She could hardly wait for Dale Hershey to see the bill. This would be an excellent test of her authority, as she had not sought anyone's approval.

"I could be wrong, but I think we hit a home run."

"Really, what makes you think that?"

"First after we announced the meeting on such short notice yesterday, the rumor circulated that we were going to announce that Fox had been sold. Everyone was apprehensive as they entered the auditorium, and everyone except twenty-two employees who are on vacation was in attendance. That's the best numbers we've ever had at an employee meeting. We got their attention. Then you surprised them by introducing yourself. I could see the nods of approval throughout the audience."

"Why did my presence as the new kid on the block bring approval?"

"Two reasons. First you bring no old baggage to the table and you must be aware of the second reason, the best reason."

Sarah frowned. "I must be stupid Tom, but I have no idea where you are going with this."

"Hey Human Resources lady, the population of the Las Vegas plant is forty-five percent females! You're one of them!"

"Oh. Yes, I forgot about that."

"It's forty-five percent in Vegas and now it's up to thirty-nine percent in Goodville. You're going to carry a lot of weight with them. They are going to look up to you for certain!"

Sarah had suddenly forgotten that the Fox management team was exclusively male until her arrival last Saturday. She smiled. Good for us she thought. Then she had a second thought. Is this why she was hired? Did Mac tell Dennis Morton to 'hire me a token female manager?' Is this why he placed her in charge of the union busting effort? She would have to think about that before she decided if she was angry with Mac or not. But for now, Tom's excitement was catching.

Tom continued with his view of the meeting. "Because people are terrified of change, the fact that you didn't announce that Fox was sold was good news. You didn't even make mention of it. This had been the number one topic on the floor for over a week. You just ignored it as if it wasn't there. Then you told them that Fox would return to the previous level of contribution to their health insurance. Surely you noticed the applause?"

Sarah was smiling at Tom's little boy enthusiasm. "I didn't miss that."

"Then, like a true pro, you saved the best for last. You went for the knock out. You told them that not only was Fox going to return to the previous level of 'matching funds' for their 401K, but we are going to increase the amount that we contribute. I know you heard the chorus of cheers."

Sarah was laughing as Tom's arms shot into the air as if signaling a touchdown. "It was very gratifying to hear the cheers."

"Now if that wasn't enough you put on a virtuoso performance during the question and answer period. You knew what you were talking about. You understood the programs and you made your answers clear and simple so that they understood. Then because of your advanced planning the aroma of pancakes, sausage, bacon and eggs was too much to resist. They cut the Q & A time way down and essentially said 'let's eat!' All this and you're beautiful too!" Tom suddenly realized what he had just said. His face flushed. This was a vice president seated before him! "I'm sorry Ms. Frazer. I…I got carried away…I didn't mean anything by that comment…I'm so sorry."

Sarah laughed. "I certainly hope you meant what you said Tom. I like to hear it when people think that I'm beautiful. Thank you very much! No offense taken… I am inclined to agree with you, about the meeting, not my appearance, she quickly added…I think we did score a home run. We're not out of the woods by any means, but as I moved around while they were having breakfast the comments that I received from individuals were very positive."

"Yeah, everything that I heard was positive too."

"When I did get a comment or a question concerning the possible sale of Fox, I simply referred back to the memo that we issued the first day that the topic raised its ugly head. That seemed to satisfy them."

"Your presence here as a member of senior management and your willingness to talk openly with them on a one on one basis concerning the speculation on the sale gave a lot more credibility to that memo. More than I could give it."

"Let's hope. Do you have a spare corner where I might work? I received the data from Julia this morning on the recent hires at Fox and previous employment. I expect Mac will be inquiring as to my progress the next time that we talk. We best check in with Goodville and let them know how we made out. I wonder if they also had success?"

"We can fix you up with everything that you need including a phone," answered Tom.

***

To Catch a Fox

Carroll and Dennis entered Tony's office all smiles. "You should have been there Tony." They had just completed their own version of the employee meeting. Giving the same message that Sarah and Tom delivered to the Fox employees out West. Dennis and Carroll decided to have their meeting at lunchtime and pulled all three shifts in to the local fire hall for lunch. They scheduled an hour lunch from twelve to one, in place of the normal half-hour from twelve to twelve thirty. The company supplied sandwiches, chips and soda for lunch. With the two-hour time difference between the two plants there was minimum risk of communication between employees in the two groups. Although Carroll suspected that by the more or less jovial attitude displayed as they entered the fire hall, that some of the office personnel had been talking with Fox folk out on the desert shortly after their meeting. Fox Las Vegas had their meeting at nine o'clock eastern daylight savings time.

Both Dennis and Carroll were pleased with the attendance. By choosing the lunch period for the meeting it was tough on the third shift people who would have normally been home in bed. But as Dennis pointed out, they had accommodated the first and third shifts with a morning meeting before. It was time to move a little closer to the second shift arrival time.

"I know. I know. I'm sorry that I was absent, but I have a very limited time to pull this sales meeting together. How did it go?"

"It went great," said Dennis.

"Yeah, I have to agree with Dennis," said Carroll. "The response was very positive and upbeat. The only time there was any apprehension was when someone asked if Fox was up for sale."

"How did you answer that?"

"We just basically repeated what our memo stated."

"How did that go down?"

"Pretty well, actually," replied Dennis. "Talking to them face to face always goes better than allowing them to read their own implications into a memo."

"Yeah I know what you mean. It's the same with us and corporate. Talking with them face to face is always better than reading e-mail unless of course it's Trevor Mason." Tony grinned. "The man's just a bastard. What can I say?"

Carroll smiled but then turned serious. He pushed the door to Tony's office closed. "Now that it's just the three of us, how much trouble do you think Mac's going to be in with Mason when he tells corporate what we've done?"

Tony considered their question. After some thought he answered, "I don't know. If he can convince them that he has taken the necessary steps to increase revenues enough to pay for the added cost and maintain Mason's margins and operating profit line, then I don't think that he is in much trouble at all."

"Dale's numbers support just that, but do you think we can achieve those targets?" It was Carroll that posed the question.

"That's up to us except for you Dennis. This time you're out from under the gun." Tony smiled at his elder.

"Suits me guys, but I don't envy your task one bit." Dennis shook his head.

Tony continued. "Carroll you have to make certain that your people will be more productive than they've ever been before. No small feat that."

Carroll sighed. "No it's not a small feat. I'm honestly not certain how we can make a group of artisans and craftsmen more productive than they already are and still maintain that handmade quality. That's what sells this product."

"You'll get no argument from me. In addition, I have to convince the sales force that a price increase is not the end of the world, so they will return to the field and 'sell' it with enthusiasm. Then I will probably have to personally convince our top ten dealers, all of the flagships for sure, that we have not stacked the deck against them by price gouging. If we can do those things while Sarah and Mac fight off the union, hey we may all still have jobs at Christmas. Except Dennis here, he'll be retired."

Dennis smiled. "Good luck boys. I mean it. I'm rooting for you." He placed his hand on the doorknob and started to leave.

"Hold up a minute please Dennis, I think I have some information that will interest you both." Dennis paused before opening the door. Tony looked solemn. He didn't know why, but he was uncertain how to say what he must say. Finally he just blurted it out. "Mac's father died about three weeks ago."

"What? When did you hear this?" Carroll was the most disturbed. When Mac's father paid him a visit a couple of years ago, Carroll had spent a day showing off his farm to the elder MacLode. As a good portion of the land that Duncan Hall was situated on was farmland the two had much in common and formed a bond during that visit.

"The old man's lawyer called Brady looking for Mac this morning. He said he needed to talk to him as soon as possible as there were decisions to be made concerning the estate. Evidently Mac is the executor."

Carroll was thinking. "Two, three weeks ago that's when Mac was gone for about a week and never told any of us where he was or why he went."

"That's what I was thinking too," said Tony. "Mac went home to be with his dying father and then to bury him."

"Why wouldn't he tell us?" Carroll's voice was frustrated and perplexed.

"You've know him longer than any of us Carroll. You tell us."

Dennis let out an audible sigh. "That's just the way Mac is my friends. Ever since I've known him he has always played close to the vest. It's like it just never occurs to him that you need to know any of his personal affairs. Too bad," Dennis turned the doorknob and moved to leave. "I've got work to do gentlemen." Both Tony and Carroll acknowledged him.

"Too bad is right!" said Carroll, obviously upset. "Why wouldn't he tell us? Why wouldn't he give us the opportunity to support him and express our grief?"

"It's too late to worry about. When he returns from Chicago I think we should all demonstrate sympathy and then respect his privacy."

"Okay, I don't understand why he didn't tell us."

"Nor do I. Ask him!"

"I'm going to."

After Dennis departed, the conversation returned to the union-busting gambit that they were attempting. Carroll looked at Tony. "This may be the hardest thing we ever tried to pull off. Blocking a union and keeping Trevor Mason happy all at the same time."

Tony leaned back in his chair and looked at the man who was his sometime ally and sometime adversary during their careers at Fox. He also knew that regardless of their opinions on different issues over the years, they had become full time friends. "God help us my friend."

"Amen," was Carroll's only answer.

***

Mitchell Green was on the phone in his room at the Hotel Brunswick in Center City Lancaster. "They did what?" He listened as Buzz Olsen described the employee meeting that Sarah Frazer and Tom Erving had conducted just a few hours before. "We know what Atlantic Corporation and Trevor Mason expect from them in financial performance. There is no way that they can afford to do that! You're certain that you understood correctly? They are increasing the amount that they will contribute to the individual 401K plans?" Mitchell paced back and forth in the room as if he were a caged animal. He couldn't believe what he was hearing. What was MacLode up to? This could cost him his job.

Buzz continued to chatter on the other end of the line. Mitchell interrupted. "Okay, okay, calm down and listen to me. Keep trying to get more people to sign the cards…I know…I know…But keep reminding them that no one has stated anything different then what the memo said concerning the possibility of Fox being sold…Remember, no one was satisfied with that answer. The threat is just as real today as it was yesterday…I don't care if some new chick in a short skirt comes out there and wows them…She still failed to say beyond a doubt that Fox isn't for sale… Keep hammering on that fact; play down what they are doing with the insurance and the 401K plans. Take the position that we have them on the run. It's only because they suspect that you are talking to a union that they took this action. Tell your fellow workers that if it weren't for us, the union, they would never have done this! It's because they are considering unionization.

That's the only reason they restored your benefits! That's the only reason that they sweetened the pot! Remember keep getting more signatures. What? No! No! Under no circumstances do you allow any of them to take their cards back…I don't care if they changed their minds. They have signed it and their name remains on that card! Do you understand what you are to do? Yes, yes, hang in there. We're going to be okay, we just have a real war on our hands now. I'm going to talk to my superiors down in Washington and we will work out a counter strategy. Yes. You do that. Keep your chin up Buzz. See you soon."

Mitchell hung up the phone and fell backwards onto the bed. He couldn't believe that this was happening.

***

Mac rubbed his forehead. He thought that he might just be flirting with a headache. He looked at his watch. It said six o'clock in the evening. He elevated his gaze from the calculator and the financial spreadsheets that were strewn on the table in front of him and looked about the massive oak conference table.

There were four distinguished looking men seated around the table with him. The man across from him was Mr. Roberts, whom he had met for breakfast this morning. After their initial "run through" of the overall numbers, Mr. Roberts escorted Mac to his waiting limousine. It whisked them silently and comfortably across down town Chicago to a high-rise office building where Mac was introduced to the others. These men were on the "investment" committee of Futures Unlimited. None of them were full time associates. They were all investors in Futures and were CEO's of other companies. Futures Unlimited was not only an integral part of each individual's portfolio, but it was also their hobby. They couldn't get enough of 'hands on' investing so they joined this elite group of business leaders that allowed them to pursue their passion while aiding other CEO's to purchase the companies that they were operating. In addition each expected a good return on investment.

Mr. Roberts looked up from his spreadsheets. "Gentlemen are we agreed on the number?" he inquired. There was a nodding of agreement around the table. "Well Mr. MacLode, I believe we have determined a workable number for you to offer Atlantic Corporation for Fox Cabinetry. Are you in agreement with our calculations?"

“I am.”

“Good, let’s recap. Mac we certainly appreciate the through back up documents that you provided. Thanks to those documents we all have a full understanding of the dynamics of your industry. As you are aware, it is difficult to achieve ‘double digits’ on the operating line with your product. For that reason we cannot value your company as highly as we might others with the same net sales.”

“I understand and I’m in complete agreement.”

“Good. At $45 million gross sales we are projecting a conservative operating line of $3.6 million. That’s only 8% of net sales. Because of this low profit before interest and taxes we cannot authorize an offer for any more than $18 million. That’s five times the operating profit. That’s a low number by today’s standards, but a fair number for a very labor intense low tech manufacturing operation.”

All murmured their agreement. The small man at the end of the table piped up. “You are in a tough business Mr. MacLode.”

Mac sighed. “Yes, I’m painfully aware of that fact.”

Mr. Roberts continued. “We are recommending Mr. MacLode that you and your associates come up with a minimum of $1.2 million and change as your minimum investment. I have the exact number calculated for you. We cannot finance you any further as you would be so highly leveraged that it would be impossible for you to survive. Even that number is dangerous so I would recommend that if possible your team comes up with more. However, with the low rates that we can arrange with our bank and the growth that you are projecting, we believe that it is doable. We will put up a great deal more of our own money in this venture than we normally would to keep the level of risk realistic. That way we can keep the bank’s participation to a minimum. For that money we will of course hold the lion’s share of class “A” voting stock.”

Mr. Roberts continued. “If you are successful in this acquisition we will give you the resumes for several of our personnel and you may select two of them to sit on your board and help you make a success of this venture. We believe this will be another profitable investment in our portfolio and you as the chief executive and your fellow class "A" shareholders will profit proportionally. Do you have any questions about the details sir?”

"No, you have explained every aspect quite thoroughly," answered Mac.

"And so have you Mr. MacLode. That is why we have complete confidence that you will continue to steer Fox to success as you have in the past. In fact, you and your team will now have an even greater incentive to do so. That being part ownership."

"Thank you for your vote of confidence gentlemen."

"The pleasure is ours," answered Mr. Roberts. There was another murmuring of agreement around the table. "Now Mr. MacLode, we will prepare the formal offer with our standard contingencies based on discovery that we will conduct after Atlantic's acceptance of our letter of intent and before the final settlement. I recommend that you start low in your offer. Who knows, they may be eager to sell?"

"I will most certainly proceed in that manner."

"We will also be at your side during the negotiations."

"I would certainly expect that you would."

"For all of those reasons we will not fill in the final number until we are prepared to sign a letter of intent. When do you anticipate opening negotiations?"

"I must now return home and apprise my team of our intentions. I will then discover who chooses to be part of the deal and who does not. I believe that we can make contact with corporate on this subject within the month, if that is satisfactory to you."

"Quite satisfactory," Mr. Roberts looked around the table. It had been a long day and rather than loose time breaking for lunch they had cold sandwiches and sodas brought up to the highly ornate board room. They were working in the Futures Unlimited old but beautiful Chicago office complex. Everyone looked weary. "Gentlemen I propose that we all celebrate our anticipated partnership with Mr. MacLode and his associates by having a quiet meal of prime rib in the company dining room downstairs. I took the liberty of telling our chef and his staff that you would all stay. Did I over step the mark?"

The little man at the end of the table spoke up once more in his animated fashion. "Not as long as you tell the wine steward that he must have Dom Pereone flowing."

"Here! Here!" came the chorus from the remainder of the table.

"I shall certainly do that gentlemen, let's adjourn to the dining room and celebrate!"

With that they took turns shaking Mac's hand, and wished him luck in persuading Atlantic to sell. Mac received their encouragement gratefully. As he followed them out of the boardroom he wondered to himself how he and his staff at Goodville would come up with $1.2 million dollars.

***

Tony Conocenti poured two black coffees and selected two Danish Pastries before returning to the small table where he and Blair McManus were seated. They were in the United Airlines Red Carpet Club at BWI. (Baltimore Washington International Airport) It was six thirty on Saturday morning. Blair had spent the entire week with Tony. During the days she went shopping, and antiquing. The evenings she and Tony spent dining out at different restaurants, going to shows and the few nightclubs that were available in Lancaster. The late nights were spent enjoying what to Tony was the most fantastic sex he had ever experienced in his life. When he made a comment to that effect, Blair gave him that coy little smile of hers and informed him that she "usually had that effect on men." Tony found these comments not only irritated him but also made him almost insanely jealous. For him at least this relationship was becoming far more serious than he had ever intended. He wished that he knew how serious Blair was.

"Thanks tiger," said Blair as she gratefully accepted the coffee and the Danish he had selected. She looked around at their surroundings. This was one of the airline clubs that was available to frequent flyers. It allowed the airlines' best customers to relax while waiting for or between flights in relative comfort compared to the hard plastic seats on the concourses. In addition there was a complementary continental breakfast, snacks available during the day, a pay as you go bar, and airline customer service attendants to help you with any travel problems. In addition to these amenities there was a full array of phone, fax and computer ports so that the traveling businessperson could keep up with events and be proactive even while in route to their next destination. Each of the major airlines maintained these clubs in the major hubs throughout the entire system. Tony longed for the good old days when business travel took you out of contact with the office for days at a time.

"I may have to join one of these," said Blair.

Tony tore his gaze from her and joined in surveying their surroundings. "Try to get your editor to pay for it. Unless you are a very frequent flyer the annual fee is a little salty. I'm fortunate that Fox pays my fees. I belong to two of them, this one and Delta's." It was necessary to show a membership card at the front door to gain admission.

Blair sipped her coffee and then turned her attention to Tony. Her deep green eyes immediately captivated him. "I really had fun this week Tiger. Thanks ever so much."

"Believe me the pleasure was all mine."

"When will you be coming to Chicago again?" she asked in what was almost a shy little girl voice.

Tony thought of his immediate future. He had summoned the sales force to Goodville for a briefing on the price increase next week. Then he would have to accompany the appropriate sales people to their respective flagship showrooms to help with "selling" the price increase. By the time he returned home from that round it would be time for the post labor day strategic meeting with corporate. After that came the annual Kitchen and Bath Industry Show (KBIS). Fox was planning to have a booth there. This year it would be held in Chicago at the McCormick Center. "I'll be in Chicago in about two and a half weeks. It's going to be a quick stop though. I have to sell our price increase to our new flagship dealer."

"Do you think we could get together then?" her voice was strangely tentative.

"I'll see to it if you really want to see me." Why was he baiting her like this? She had just asked him if they could get together. Why risk rejection?

"Of course I want to see you!" Then the ornery smile returned. "I just have to know when you are coming so that I can let my other men friends down gently. The male ego is so fragile you know."

Damn it! He thought. Why do I let myself open to these "zingers?" Why can't I just leave well enough alone? Why do those comments bother me so much?

Blair changed the subject. Partly because she didn't quite understand the strange expression that had suddenly appeared on Tony's face. "Did you take care of my packages Tiger?"

Tony came back to the moment. "What? I'm sorry."

Blair smiled a patient smile. "So soon into the relationship and already you're not listening to a thing I'm saying to you."

"No! That's not true I was just thinking of my nearly impossible schedule the next month or two. That's all. I'm sorry." Tony always had a strange feeling when he lied to her. He felt that somehow she knew when he was being less than truthful. The truth was he wasn't thinking of his schedule at all, he was trying to decide if her suggestive little comments made him jealous.

"Well we don't have to see each other when you come to Chicago if it's inconvenient for you," her tone was slightly miffed.

"No Blair. That's not what I meant at all. I will cancel something rather than miss an opportunity to be with you!"

"Really? Why Tony, you could make a girl blush. I'm flattered."

"I mean it Blair. I've never meant anything as much as I meant what I just said." What was he saying? He felt like this relationship was moving entirely too fast as it is.

"Awww, how sweet," Blair actually appeared to be getting misty eyed.

Tony smiled, somehow reassured. One minute he felt that they should definitely slow down and the next he was fearful that she was losing interest.

"Now to my original question Tiger, are you paying attention?"

"Yes ma'am!" He sat up straight and leaned slightly across the table toward her. "You have my full attention."

"You're cute. Did you take care of my packages?"

"Yes I did. All of the packages from your shopping excursions are going by UPS. The antique washstand that you purchased will be delivered to your door via a Fox truck the next trip to Chicago. I'm taking care of the freight charge for you. How much did you spend anyway?"

"It's my money so it's none of your business. You aren't responsible for me... yet." The "yet" was added late and so softly that Tony wasn't certain of what she actually said.

"No, you're right. It's none of my business. I'm sorry."

"Apology accepted tiger." The dazzling smile returned.

They sat sipping their coffee, enjoying the Danish, watching the sunrise outside and reviewing the great times that they spent together during the past week. Blair moved around the table to a chair next to him. Tony was overjoyed at the silent gesture. Finally Tony checked the departure screens and it was time for Blair's flight back to Chicago. BWI was in Baltimore Maryland and a longer drive for Tony than Harrisburg International in Pennsylvania, but the flights out of BWI allowed Blair to remain an additional night. Tony was extremely happy when she insisted on it. Even though it meant that they had to rise much earlier this morning to drive to Baltimore.

They departed the Red Carpet Club and strolled to the gate where Blair's flight was boarding. Just as they arrived the attendant announced boarding the first class passengers. Blair was holding a first class ticket. She kissed Tony on the lips, took her carry on off his shoulder and said goodbye. She took her place in line. Tony watched until she approached the flight attendant taking the boarding passes. Then he turned to leave. He had only taken a few steps when suddenly someone grabbed Tony's left arm and turned him back toward the gate. It was Blair. She had a strange look in her eyes, an intense look that Tony had never seen before. He didn't know what to say.

"I'm going to miss you!" was all she said. She hugged him tightly, returned to the line, handed her boarding pass to the smiling attendant and vanished down the walkway without looking back. As always with Blair, Tony was strangely happy and excited, but not totally understanding of what just took place.

***

It was Tuesday morning, four days after William MacLode's meeting with the Futures Unlimited people in Chicago. Abraham Rueben sat at a table on the eighteenth floor open-air patio of Millissa Kensington's Penthouse co-op in New York City. He and Ms. Kensington were having breakfast. The sunny and warm August morning made the breakfast and light conversation pleasant and amiable. Even Abraham Rueben appeared to be adequate company for Ms. Kensington's near non-stop dialog concerning her family and its colonial heritage. With someone new to tell her families' history to, she had no problem overlooking some of Rueben's cruder habits.

While it was general knowledge that Millissa Kensington was in her early seventies, she looked to be no more than in her late fifties at worst. This was attributable to numerous "secret" excursions to the West Coast where her favorite plastic surgeon did his best to aid her in the battle to retain her youth. Even with these Herculean and significantly expensive surgeries, each passing year forced Millissa to redefine the parameters of "youth." Presently "youth" maintained its upper parameter somewhere around age fifty-five.

The maid was clearing away the dishes and pouring them both more coffee as Millissa paused in her "history of the family" dialog. "Well Mr. Rueben, this has all been very pleasant, but you did say that you came here to discuss my holdings in Wellbon-Smith."

"That is correct Ms. Kensington."

"Well, let us get down to it Mr. Rueben. I have appointments to keep. I'm a very busy woman." The maid raised her eyebrow as she heard this statement. The truth was that Millissa Kensington had a lunch date with her sister later this morning and had nothing on her schedule for the remainder of the week. Millissa noticed the raised eyebrow and dismissed her servant. "That will be all Deloris.

Please allow Mr. Rueben and me to discuss this business in private."

Abraham Rueben opened his briefcase and began with a very professional presentation of the offer for the eventual purchase of her Wellbon-Smith class "A" voting shares. In return for the purchase, at what Rueben described as an inflated price, Millissa would assign her proxy vote to Trevor Mason before the annual shareholders meeting.

Millissa sipped her coffee and looked out over her excellent view of Central Park. Rueben wondered if she had been listening to a word that he had said. "Did I tell you Mr. Rueben that three separate generations of my family served three different Presidents and their administrations during our country's history?"

"Ah, no you did not Ms. Kensington. Could we discuss your Wellbon-Smith stock?"

"They served three Presidents and two different political parties."

"Yes ma'am, about your stock."

"Stock, Smock! I tell you this Mr. Rueben so that you realize that I did not come from a family of fools! My family has survived, prospered and served no matter what the popular politics at the time! That sometimes requires cunning and flexibility, attributes that my family possesses in abundance, including the present generation!"

The ferocity of her mood change took even Abraham Rueben aback. "I never suggested that you or any of your family were fools ma'am," was his surprisingly meek reply.

"The hell you didn't. You must suppose me a fool to make the suggestion that I promise my proxy to Trevor Mason on his word that he will pay me more than my stock is worth at some vague point in the future!"

Abraham remained silent for a moment as he too decided to take a sip of coffee; he needed a moment to regroup. Millissa returned her now cold stare toward Central Park. Abraham replaced his china cup in the saucer and attempted another tack. "Actually I was suggesting quite the opposite Ms. Kensington. I was appealing to your excellent business sense, suggesting that you would recognize this as an opportunity to make a windfall profit from your Wellbon-Smith investments. If you will allow me to go into the details of the agreement, you will find that we are discussing very specific dates of performance by my client and the interests that he represents."

"How would I know if it were a windfall profit or if you just screwed me? The only way that anyone can know for certain what Wellbon-Smith stock is truly worth is to liquidate the damn corporation and all of its subsidiaries!" Now she was leveling a lethal stare directly into Abraham Rueben's flickering eyes. The little pipsqueak, she thought, can't even look me straight in the eye. For a moment she wondered how any man could have five o'clock shadow at nine in the morning.

"I assure you ma'am that we have done our best to be fair to people like yourself who must by now be a little tired of mediocre year end dividends."

"Fair? You're telling me that Trevor Mason is concerned about being fair? I doubt it! What's in this for him? Do you think that I don't know that your proposal to purchase my stock and my proxy is a violation of the company by-laws? Trevor is supposed to inform Carlton Smith and the board of his desires and they, if they approve, contact me on his behalf. Then and only then do you, representing Mr. Mason, and I have this conversation. Because I have not been contacted by the board I think it is safe to assume that the board has no knowledge of this offer."

Abraham Rueben reached into his brief case and pulled out an additional folder. Trevor had warned him that the conversation would most likely develop in this manner. He decided that he wasn't going to play games with the old bat. He decided to go straight for the jugular. "Ms. Kensington, I would like you to look at a few files that I brought along. Trevor and I think that you most likely would not like these to fall into the wrong hands." Rueben's voice had turned suddenly menacing. Millissa looked at him with suspicion in her eyes and after a long moment reached out and took the folder from him.

Silence ensued as Ms. Kensington scanned the files contained in the folder. The furrow in her brow grew deeper the more she read. Rueben poured himself another cup of coffee. Finally she looked up and handed the folder back to Abraham staring him directly in the eye. "Would you like me to explain any facet of those files or their implication for both you and your nephew?" Rueben sounded as smooth as an old-fashioned snake oil salesman as he stared thoughtfully at the tablecloth. As an afterthought he reached into his briefcase once more and found his cell phone. While he awaited her reaction he punched a number into the phone.

"Do you really think that you can make those charges stick?" Millissa hissed.

"Indeed we do. As you can see by these copies, this is not a trumped up charge. All of these documents are copies of actual verifiable company records. The original documents Mr. Mason and I have safely secured and could be delivered to the board and the New York District Attorney's office within the hour. This is simply documentation of a scam that you and your nephew perpetrated on your partners in Wellbon-Smith. Oh yes, we can make them stick and Trevor Mason would become a hero to many of the minority shareholders for his vigilance." Rueben listened as the phone rang in his ear.

"Suppose I call your bluff? Suppose I expose this little scheme of yours to the board. I'm certain that they would be interested in why Trevor Mason finds it necessary to step outside the corporate by-laws in an attempt to buy up shares behind their backs. They would probably conclude what I have concluded."

"That being Ms. Kensington?"

"That being that Trevor is attempting to take over Wellbon-Smith!"

A voice answered Abraham's phone call. He handed the phone to Millissa Kensington and she placed it to her ear, a puzzled look on her face. The voice in the phone said "Hello, hello? Carlton Smith's office, Tricia speaking, may I help you? Hello? Is anyone there?"

"Tell Carlton Smith whatever you wish Ms. Kensington, but remember you have no proof of the verbal offer that I just made and I will deny that I ever made it. On the other hand, you have just read ample proof of the fraud that your nephew, with your knowledge, has committed over a period of years. To his substantial benefit I might add. How do you think that your fellow shareholders might receive evidence of your blatant fraud?"

The secretary in Carlton Smith's office hung up. The phone went silent in Millissa Kensington's hand. She looked at it for a moment, pushed the power button to "off," and returned it to Rueben. "Blackmailers!" was her only response.

"You could say that. I suppose that in the scheme of things it's no worse than what you set up for your nephew's benefit. Some would call that stealing Ms. Kensington. So here we are. You agree to the proposition that Trevor is offering you and you and your nephew can go merrily on life's way. Trevor on the other hand can achieve his life goal with the aid of your proxy. As an additional bonus, you get a windfall profit shortly after the first of the year…" Rueben was all smiles. "Do we have a deal Ms. Kensington or must this get very unpleasant?"

"Give me a pen," was her dejected reply. "I suppose that with smoke and mirrors you have the ability to somehow make this all appear legal."

"Why Ms. Kensington, you were correct in your earlier statement."

Millissa Kensington raised her eyebrows, "How's that?"

"There really are no fools in your family."

CHAPTER 12

Mitchell Green sat silently in his boss' office. They were meeting in the offices of the United Federation of Millwrights International. The union had its headquarters on 'K' Street NW in Washington D.C. Jerome McKinley Jefferson, president of the union, sat behind his large desk silently reading the report that Mitchell had submitted concerning the progress at Fox Cabinetry. At the moment the progress was arguably in regression.

Jefferson was an African-American who had made it to the top of a union with a basically white membership. Two years ago he achieved a landslide election by building a reputation for doing whatever had to be done to protect and advance the interests of his rank and file. He came to the union as an organizer just out of Michigan State University. He had been a star receiver on the football team and earned a degree in Social Science. He had worked as a Senate intern during the summers of his junior and senior years in college, all the time working out with weights to stay in shape for the football season. Many thought that he couldn't miss the summer practices and still make the team in the fall. Jefferson proved them wrong. Each season he started on the bench but by mid season had earned the starting spot by virtue of his determination and superior athletic abilities.

For whatever reason he was passed over in the pro draft, Jefferson saw this as a sign that his future path lay in a more serious direction. He returned to Washington D C and got a job with the United Federation of Millwrights International. It was not his first choice. He had somehow envisioned himself fighting for the rights of his own people. However, this was the organization that offered him a job with a wage that he could survive on. He suspected that because the workers in this union were predominantly white, that he was hired as a token.

That may have been an accurate assessment in the beginning, but the career that began as a token to satisfy the union's critics soon became a career heading straight for the top on its own merits. Jerome McKinley Jefferson had found his niche in life. He had a knack for organizing employees into a union and negotiating on their behalf afterward. A star was born and Jerome's rise had been meteoric. There was nowhere in the country that Jerome Jefferson would not travel to either organize a new shop or negotiate better benefits. Jerome was so successful at negotiations that he soon became a favorite with both management and the rank and file. Soon his name was being bandied around as a possible candidate for president when the aging president, Boris Walenski retired. When the opportunity to stand for election came, Boris' handpicked successor never had a chance. Jerome, a black man, beat a white contender in a predominately white union.

Now as Jerome sat reading Mitchell Green's report he saw the crowning project of his career slipping through his fingers. It was Jerome who approached the much larger Consolidated Trade Unions of America and proposed a merger. It was Jerome who convinced the CTU leadership that it was to their benefit to merge with the smaller UFMI. It was Jerome who after the proper time had passed, planned on becoming president of the combined union. Now that could all be in jeopardy if they failed to organize Fox.

Jerome McKinley Jefferson finished reading and looked up. His young protégé sat nervously before him. He liked this young man. He and Mitchell Green shared common ambitions and abilities. Mitchell had worked very hard on the Fox project. However, there was no denying that things had taken a turn for the worse.

"How do you think they found out that we've talked to their people?"

Mitchell Green had agonized over this question. "I don't think that either of my operatives, in Vegas or in Goodville would have spilled the beans, but as the cards circulated more and more people became aware and the word must have leaked to management."

"No. No there was not enough time for them to set up an emergency meeting with their lawyers from the instant your man in Vegas began circulating the cards and they began to act. They couldn't have moved that fast. No they already knew of our activity before we began the sign up push."

"So how did they know?" Mitchell was truly puzzled.

Jerome smiled. "They already had their own operatives in place before we even recruited ours. They have had people with their ears to the ground long before we arrived. You commented on how clever this 'Mac' McLode can be, well this is just another example of his craftiness."

"So as a matter of policy, they have their own informants on the floor of both factories?"

"Not official policy of course, but they must have loyal people that tip them off if any suspicious activity develops."

"So they know what we are doing almost before we do it. Where does that leave us?"

"Your report states that since the employee meeting last week your man Olsen has only been able to add a few names to the list. In addition your first efforts in Goodville haven't gotten off the ground."

"That's unfortunately correct. My operative in Goodville supplied me with an excellent young woman that works first shift on the factory floor. She is popular and respected and has a lot of social contact with employees outside the work place. Even with all that going for her the initial sign up attempts have had little success. Both she and my operative attribute this poor response to the employee meetings. No one is looking beyond his or her nose on this. They now have gained back what was taken away from them and feel that they were given even more. They are not putting two and two together and determining that it was the mere threat of a union that prompted management to act, and not a concern for the worker's well being."

"That's to be expected. People fear change more than anything else in their lives, they will put up with far more than you would expect just to avoid it."

"So where do we go from here?"

"I've been thinking about that ever since your phone call last week. You know, sometimes coincidence can have a greater impact on events than all of the planning in the world." Jerome smiled.

"What coincidence are you referring to?" asked Mitchell.

"A coincidence in my personal history that may work in our favor, I know how Trevor Mason thinks."

Mitchell frowned, "How so?"

"I played football with him at Michigan State, but don't you concern yourself with that just now. I have an important task for you."

"That being?"

"I want you to get on a plane as quickly as you can make arrangements and pay a visit to our old friend Clint Matthews out in St. Louis."

"The chairman of Cab Corp?"

"Yes and here's what I want you to propose to him." The two men huddled together and spoke in low tones as Jerome outlined the proposition that he wanted Mitchell to present to Mr. Matthews.

Mitchell smiled upon hearing Jerome's idea, and then a slight frown creased his forehead. "This isn't exactly legal is it?"

"Does that bother you Mitchell, because if it does I'll get someone else on it right away."

Mitchell considered this for a long moment. "No. No it doesn't bother me. The work force at Fox will be far better off if we represent them. We must also assure our merger in order to survive. If we don't survive then what happens to the workers that already depend on us for representation?"

"So you'll do as I have proposed?"

"Yes. I'll do what has to be done," Mitchell smiled. "Just as you have always done Mr. Jefferson."

"You're a good man Mitchell Green! Just be certain that you meet Matthews alone in a public place where you can't be overheard. Do not allow him to bring anyone with him. We don't want any witnesses to this proposition. Someday we may have to deny that we ever suggested it."

The two men shook hands. The unionization of Fox Cabinetry did not look nearly as hopeless as it had when Mitchell handed Jerome his report.

***

Mac folded the computer printouts that he had been poring over ever since he had come home from the office. He still wasn't certain how he was going to make this deal work. He could cash in several of his own investments and come up with $500,000. If he sold some property that he owned in North Carolina he could maybe come up with another $150,000, $200,000 at best. That still left him slightly over $200,000 short of what Futures Unlimited required of him. The people at Futures had suggested strongly that he make this opportunity known to the remainder of his senior staff. At this point in time he had not mentioned a word to them. He didn't want any of them risking their life savings out of loyalty to him. But he really had no choice. If he didn't include them he would have to liquidate his retirement funds and he had taken a vow never to touch them.

There was always Duncan Hall, but Mac knew that when the estate was settled any money that was remaining would have to be invested as a hedge for years when expenses out stripped revenues. Duncan Hall was a break-even operation at best. Of course he could sell it, but the number of people that would be interested in an old drafty castle could fit into a small closet, besides having the old estate leave the family was unthinkable.

Mac removed his reading glasses and rubbed his eyes. Tomorrow he would have to reveal his idea to his staff. They were adults. They would have to determine according to their own circumstances if they could afford this enterprise. Success or failure could not be on Mac's conscious. This was America, the land of free enterprise and opportunity. What received less publicity was that it was also the land of high stakes and high risk, a land where for every success story there were three or four failures. Oh well, they must decide.

The phone rang and Mac picked it up. "William MacLode."

"William, so good to finally catch you, I'm just so amazed direct dialing across the Atlantic. Why I remember when the cable…so noisy it was…"

To Catch a Fox

"Brian! Brian Hempstead, is that you?"

"Good Lord yes old boy. Forgive me. Where are my manners? I was just so taken aback when I finally heard your voice. I've been attempting to contact you for over a week now, so glad, so glad to finally reach you."

"I'm sorry Brian. This is entirely my fault. Brady told me that you called. I have been remiss in not showing you the courtesy of a return call. I won't be a bore and make you endure all the details, but suffice it to say that my life is in a bit of turmoil on this side of the pond."

"Quite all right old chap, quite all right. It's not necessary for me to know your life's story William…I say, isn't this direct dialing amazing? Purely amazing!"

"Brian, its eight o'clock in the evening here, so it's one in the morning where you are."

"Quite right old chap, quite right. I've been sitting here watching the telly until I thought that you might be home. I say that Bean is funny isn't he? Do you get him in the colonies?"

"I've heard that the show is on public television, but I've not had time to catch it."

"Too bad, too bad, you must see it some time."

"I will Brian. I must remind you old chap that these international direct dial calls are a bit expensive even on the off hours. I believe that you probably have some estate business that you wish to discuss. As you are probably on my 'clock,' we best get at it. Don't you think?"

"Oh, yes…yes, we really should old boy. Your father would be proud. You remain true to your Scottish blood. I say, no one could squeeze a 'ha pence' like old Sean…No one indeed."

"Brian the business at hand please."

"Oh yes…Well for one thing you are still on that side of the Atlantic. You promised me after the funeral that you would return by now."

"I know Brian and I am truly sorry for that. I apologize. But you have my legal authorization to act as the chief financial officer for Duncan Hall. You are paying Ian and the household staff, are you not old boy?"

"Oh yes indeed William. The staff lacks for nothing. They are working their way through a right prosperous tourist season I must say. That makes meeting our commitments much easier."

"That's good to hear."

"Yes, and I'm pleased to tell you of it also. However, William, there are a lot of documents that require your signature, or I'm not going to be able to get the probate of your father's will off and running you know. Besides, you haven't even read it!"

"He didn't cut me out did he?"

Of course not! You are aware of the accommodations for your Aunt Anna?"

"Yes for some time before my father's death."

"For Ian too?"

"I'm aware of the arrangements for Ian and the household staff."

"Good, good I must say. Your father took care of his affairs in a right proper manner…So William, when may I expect you?"

Mac knew that this question was coming and indeed Brian was correct. He must attend to his father's affairs. The seemingly innocent thought hit Mac like a sledgehammer. These affairs were no longer the affairs of his father they were his affairs now. He must attend to them as promptly as possible. "I, I can't leave the States for another couple of weeks Brian…Listen, send the documents by special courier to me. Hand delivered, I sign for them after I prove that I am William MacLode. I'll pay for the extra expense."

"Well I suppose that we can attend to some of them in that fashion William, but that will only be a temporary solution. You will have to be here in person to attend to many of the affairs."

"I understand that Brian, but if you could buy me a few weeks by sending the documents that I can dispatch with in this fashion, I will be extremely appreciative."

"Very well William. Very well, I will attend to this affair tomorrow morning. Oh! It is tomorrow morning as far as I'm concerned. Very well, I will attend to this as soon as the sun comes up."

"Thank you Brian."

"No problem really, your father was a good friend and he thought the world of you William. I was indebted to him for a number of favors. This is the least that I can do. I do understand that you have many pressing things William. Really I do."

"Thank you again Brian."

"Oh William!"

"Yes Brian."

"Most of the documents that I'm going to send you will require some sort of witness to your signature. What do you call it in the States?"

"Notarized, I will have to sign them in the presence of a notary public. That won't be a problem. We have a notary working for us at Fox."

"Good and one other thing William."

"Yes Brian," said Mac wondering just how much this call was going to cost.

"I don't have the chap's name…Must have left it in my office…No, no, that was the strange thing, he wouldn't give it to me. So sorry William," Brian Hempstead stopped talking as if he was finished.

"What of this nameless chap that you are talking about?"

"Well your father had several investments that my office administered for him."

"What type of investments Brian?"

"You know, investments, but these were different."

"How were they different Brian?"

"Well he, your father, didn't want his name to be associated with them."

"Why not?"

"That's a long story and should be discussed face to face old chap, definitely not over the phone."

Mac was truly puzzled by this last statement. "Okay Brian, again I ask; what of this nameless chap."

"Oh! Oh yes. I'm sorry; memory's not what it used to be. Anyway, this chap has been calling for you at our London office. I'm sorry he's actually been calling for the administrator of your father's investments, the investments that I just mentioned."

"Didn't he know that my father is dead?" Another long pause, Sometimes Brian could be maddening to talk to thought Mac.

"Oh, yes well remember I just told you that Sean didn't want his name associated with these investments."

Mac was not following this at all. "Did he say what he wanted to talk about?"

"No, he was not forth coming with any such information. I explained that my firm was representing the holdings and that the owner was out of town and not available, but that wasn't good enough for him I'm afraid."

"Did he leave any number that you can contact him?"

"Yes, but he said that it was a sensitive matter and he only wanted to discuss it with the owner in person."

"Did you explain that I do plan on being in Scotland in a few weeks?"

"Of course William, of course, but I don't recommend that you meet with him personally."

"Then you didn't give him my name or number Brian?"

"No, mercy no William, your father wouldn't want your name associated with this, just as he kept his a secret. I need to talk to you first. I was not comfortable giving out your name and number to a chap that refused to give me his. In addition, I know that old Sean wouldn't approve."

"Brian I haven't a clue as to what you are talking about, but I quite agree old chap. I've enough problems just now without some bloke I don't even know contacting me and talk about investments that I don't understand. Hell I didn't even know I had them! I have enough problems without adding one more to the list. You did the right thing Brian. I suspect that his topic isn't all that sensitive. I suspect that he's simply trying to sell me something."

"I suppose William… I suppose. However, I do know that your father kept his distance from these particular investments. Quite profitable they are though..."

"Brian what are these investments?"

"Good talking to you William. I look forward to your visit in a couple of weeks."

"And I too Brian, go to bed. It's soon time for you to be up and in your office." Mac gave up on getting any more out of Hempstead over the phone and he didn't feel like discussing it any longer.

"Quite right you are, quite right, good day lad!"

Mac hung up the phone. The financial obstacles that he was facing in his attempt to buy Fox Cabinetry were forgotten. Instead Brian Hempstead's phone call had pulled emotions concerning his father's death to the surface. His eyes misted up as he thought of both his father and his mother. His father's passing seemed to also bring back the grief that he felt when his mother died. It was as if he was mourning the loss of both of them simultaneously for the first time. Slater the cat strolled over and rubbed up against his leg. Mac reached down and picked up the large gray and white tomcat. "How did you know that I need to hold a cat in my lap Slater?" Mac asked.

***

Abraham Rueben sat behind the desk in his New York office. It was seven forty-five in the evening and the remainder of the office staff and Rueben's partners had long since left for home. It was not unusual for a member of the firm to be working late. What was the main function of a law firm? It was to generate billable hours thought Rueben. That task Rueben's firm accomplished with a vengeance. They helped their clients with all manner of service. Services other firms would pass on because of questionable ethics. Because they valued the services and the veil of secrecy, the clients rarely complained about inflated hours. Ethics and morals were not a problem for Rueben's firm. From the days of its creation during the Depression, the firm of Murray, Marx and Rothmere was far more dedicated to showing a profit then getting bogged down in ethical discussions. In those days it was a matter of survival. The only people and organizations that had any money to spend were those that were operating "on the south side of the law" as old Mr. Marx would say. By the time the country was approaching World War II, the pattern of operation and the nature of the clientele had been firmly established.

Abraham had joined the firm out of law school. He came from a poor background and although he had been warned about Murray, Marx and Rothmere, he was attracted by their reputation of making associates who "played ball" rich in a short period of time. No one ever accused Abraham of not displaying an ability to "play ball." His reputation soon grew from one who "played ball" to one who "played hard ball." He became one of the firm's young stars and rose rapidly from associate to junior partner, to partner and now he was the senior partner. He also fulfilled his other ambition and became very rich in the process.

Abraham sensed that he was about to become even wealthier. This project with Trevor Mason was progressing nicely. In fact, they were having more success than originally expected. So much so that during their afternoon conversation Mason suggested that if Rueben could keep things going at this pace, they may be able to "strike" before the annual meeting. Nothing would please Abraham more. This could be the crowning deal of his career. Upon successful completion he planned an early retirement to his condo on Grand Cayman Island with plenty of cash and valuable Wellbon-Smith stock in his portfolio.

A strange noise caught Abraham's attention. He looked up from his desk and listened more closely. He thought that he heard it again. "Who's there?" He called out. There was no answer and he heard the noise no more. He knew that there was no one in the outer office. Just my imagination he thought. The firm had a security guard on the front desk down stairs, so no one could get into the building after hours. He returned to the file that he was working on. The file concerned the next Wellbon-Smith shareholder that Trevor instructed him to contact.

The noise was back. There was no mistaking it this time. Long years of working "on the south side of the law" had prepared Abraham for a moment like this. Instead of calling the security guard, he reached quietly into his desk drawer and removed a Ruger nine-millimeter semi automatic pistol. Being a veteran in dealing with dangerous people, the pistol had been purchased some years ago from an anonymous "dealer" on the streets. It was without a doubt stolen, and the serial numbers had been removed so that it was totally untraceable. Abraham touched a button on a device that resembled the "remote" for a television set. This locked his office door and extinguished the lights. He placed the device in his jacket pocket, silently rose from his chair, moved swiftly across the room and positioned himself behind a large potted plant that sat on the floor against the wall that contained the door. He knew now what the noise was. It was the sound of various office doors opening and closing, as if someone was searching for something or someone. The noise sounded strange because it was a noise that one heard hundreds of times during the course of a day. It was so familiar that no one took notice. Now in the night, when he knew he was to be alone, the rather common sound had an ominous affect.

The lights from the high-rise buildings outside the window were now the only source of light in the office. There was a strange matrix of shadows covering the floor. Abraham heard another sound. This was the faint sound of weight being applied to the hardwood floor just outside his office door. Abraham eased the safety off on the pistol. He sensed that the doorknob was turning in the dark. Abraham was relieved. He now knew that this was not a professional "hit."

A professional hit man would have sprayed the room through the door with a silencer equipped assault rifle. The hit man would already have been familiar with the layout of the office and would have known that he could "cover" ninety percent of it by shooting through the door. This would greatly increase the probability of success and lower the risk to him when he finally entered. Not to mention that he would be able to see through the remains of the door before he kicked it in. What a would be hit man would not know is that Abraham had already reinforced the center core of his office door with heavy gauge steel that would require armor piercing ammunition to penetrate.

Abraham had made numerous enemies within the New York underworld when he defected to work for the Chicago "families." He had been careful to cover his "tail" by not revealing any of New York's secrets to the Chicago people and discreetly informing the proper people of that fact. While New York suffered no injuries because of his actions, suspicion remained. Ever since, he had been on his guard. Business was business. His firm's work in New York had peaked and the Chicago people had plenty of tasks for a lawyer with his skills.

Abraham knew that it was impossible for his visitor to open the door with the knob. There were ½" thick steel slides that slid through from the doors interior to the jambs when Abraham had activated his remote. He swiftly turned and slid to the side a deceptively permanent looking bookcase. It was actually on ball bearing runners and revealed a secret exit. Passing through a small "alleyway" between his office and the next Abraham prepared to enter the main office area and confront the intruder. Behind him he heard the mystery person attempt to force the door. This emboldened Abraham further as he realized he was dealing with a rank amateur.

Abraham opened what appeared to be a utility closet door and stepped out into the main office. Just a few feet to Abraham's right the intruder was trying to force open his office door as quietly as possible. It was almost amusing except that the individual was holding a gun. The mystery person had his back to Abraham as he was pushing mightily against the office door. Abraham leveled his Ruger on the grunting figure. "You move another muscle and I'll kill you."

Even from the back it was obviously a man. He froze leaning against the door. "That's good," said Abraham. "Now drop the gun on the floor." The individual hesitated for a moment and then dropped the weapon. "That was very smart of you," said Abraham. "Now with the foot closest to the gun, kick it directly behind you." The intruder obeyed. The gun slid across the floor toward Abraham who took a step forward and picked it up by the barrel, never taking his eyes off of the individual or allowing his pistol to point anywhere except toward the man's back. He glanced quickly at the revolver he now held in his left hand and noticed that the safety was on. What a jerk he thought. Abraham stuffed the revolver in his belt. "Now step away from the door…that's far enough." With his free hand Abraham pulled the remote from his jacket pocket and aimed it at the door. The hidden steel bars retracted from the jambs into the core of the door. Abraham was still standing behind the individual. "Now open the office door… good. Put your hands on top of your head and lace your fingers together… Now walk through the door." The intruder obeyed and entered Abraham's office. The lights had switched back on simultaneously with the unlocking of the door. Abraham followed a safe distance behind. "Now keep your hands on top of your head and turn around."

The man was nearly a foot taller than Abraham, much heavier and younger. Abraham guessed that he was only about thirty. He had a round baby face with sandy colored hair slicked back to reveal the beginnings of a widow's peak. Abraham had never set eyes on him before in his life. "Who are you and who sent you?"

"You don't know me." There was anger and frustration in the voice.

"No shit! That's why I asked you who you are. Rule number one don't irritate the man who is pointing a loaded gun at you! Now answer my question and don't be a wise ass!"

The man looked around the office, an exasperated almost wild look in his eyes. "I'm waiting," said Abraham.

The young man looked down at the floor his hands remained on top of his head. He was wearing sneakers under dark brown slacks with a tan cloth jacket. "My name is Donald Kensington-Cramer."

"Melissa Kensington's nephew?"

"Yes," his gaze was affixed to the floor.

"Do you know who I am?"

"Yes, you are Abraham Rueben the lawyer that works for Trevor Mason. You're the bastard that is blackmailing my aunt, the aunt that I love like a mother!" In spite of the emotion in his voice his eyes remained focused on the floor.

"Why did you come here with a gun?"

"To kill you."

"To kill me…your aunt is a smart lady, obviously smarter than you. She made a deal and because of that deal you and she can live happily ever after. No problems, you can do your own thing as long as it's not at any of the Wellbon-Smith companies. Your ass is out of the fire boy! Killing me would put you in more trouble than your past scams ever would!" Abraham paused, something wasn't right about this guy but he couldn't put his finger on it.

"Auntie told me today what you did," the voice had become low and just barely audible.

"She told you…Great! Maybe she's not as smart as I thought."

The young man looked up abruptly. "Don't you say anything against my aunt!" The anger in the voice had become more menacing. The look in the eyes had become wild. Abraham Rueben realized what wasn't right about the young intruder. He had seen that wild look before. He was crazy! It was probably drug induced, as there was no odor of alcohol, but he was crazy nonetheless. Crazy was dangerous, Abraham would have to be careful.

"Now look son…"

"I'm not your son!"

"Shut up and listen! I know you're not my son!" Abraham's eyes and face hardened as his voice rose. This kid could be a big problem. He made up his mind to fire the security guard's ass as soon as he finished with Donald… "Now you listen and you listen good. If you really knew who I am you would never have come here tonight let alone have plans to kill me. I can be a very dangerous man Donald. Very dangerous indeed! I'm most dangerous when I lose my patience and I'm losing it very quickly with you! I'm also pointing a gun at a man that I caught breaking and entering my office! A man that I can prove I never met before tonight! A man I could tell the police I was forced to protect myself from! You know why Donald? Because you brought a freaking gun with you! Do I make myself clear? "

For the first time a trace of fear crept into Donald's voice. "Yes...Yes you make yourself very clear." His tone was not nearly as belligerent now.

"Good! Now here's what's going to come down Donald, right here! Right now! For starters, I'm keeping your gun with your fingerprints on it. You are such an amateur that you were handling it without wearing gloves! You bring a piece to commit murder and you leave your prints on everything! Doorknobs, gun, everything! So understand this, just in case you do something sometime in the future that pisses me off. I'll see to it that your gun with your prints turns up in the worst place you could imagine."

"Your prints are on it too...now. Besides, I was going to wipe mine off." There was an almost childlike tone to the reply.

"Yeah, on the tip of the barrel, I plan on removing my prints as soon as I'm finished with you...Next you're gonna walk out of here with me behind you like a good boy and you're never coming back and you're never telling anyone that you were here. Not even dear old aunt Millissa...You got that?"

"Yeah, I got that Mr. Big Shot Lawyer!"

"Don't make me think that you're getting brave again Donald." Abraham wasn't certain if Donald was still high or he was beginning to come down. He was guessing he was high. Either way he was dangerous. "By the way, just how did you get past the security guard down stairs?"

"I went around to the freight entrance and found a door that was unlocked."

That's just great thought Abraham. I pay all this money to screen people to be guards so that this office has tight security and this bungling kid not only finds a door that no one locked, but apparently no one was watching the security cameras when he came in. I'll fire all their asses!

"Okay Donald, do you understand the situation you created for yourself? It was bad enough that I have proof that you, with your aunt's full knowledge, were bilking Wellbon-Smith out of money that you did nothing to earn. Now you came here to kill me and failing that you have given me a revolver with your prints all over it. I will now keep that revolver in a clean safe place. If you ever do anything that causes Trevor Mason, Wellbon-Smith, or me a problem, I will send you to jail for fraud and frame your ass for whatever I can think of with that pistol. Be certain that you are completely clear on this Donald. From now on I own your ass!"

"Yes Mr. Big Shot Lawyer. I'm clear on everything Mr. Big Shot Lawyer."

"Don't get smart with me. You're in no position to get smart with me."

Donald Kensington-Cramer said nothing, but the "crazy" look in his eyes was even more intense.

"All right Donald, keep your hands on top of your head and start to move toward that opening over there beside the bookcase." Abraham pointed toward the still open passageway that he had recently utilized. "I will be a few paces behind you. Do not look back and do not speak. When you enter that passageway we will turn left." That was just the opposite from the direction that Abraham had recently turned. He had no intention of taking Donald through the outer office and down the main elevators. The elevators, along with the stairwells, were covered with hidden surveillance cameras. Since he managed to get in undetected, it was better that no one ever knew he was here. "At the end of the passageway there is a small private elevator, my private elevator. We will use it to go to the ground floor." There were no cameras in this elevator. Abraham was thinking he would have to move his private office elsewhere in the building and change his security procedures and escape routes, all because of this crazy drugged up kid.

Now what to do with him? In spite of what he had just told Donald about 'owning his ass' the fact that he was obviously a druggie meant that Abraham couldn't count on him thinking like a normal person. The threat of jail and blackmail would only work until he was on a high rage again. Who knows what he might do. Well Abraham knew what he had to do. He would take him to Duke right now. Duke was an all-purpose clean up specialist and hit man. Duke could take care of any messy situation. Abe had utilized him many times in the past. This kid had to be disposed of and it had to look like an accident... "Hey!"

For just an instant Abraham had become over confident and careless. He was thinking of eliminating this problem and not the business at hand. Donald, in a mad drug induced rage had spun on him and grabbed Abraham in a vice-like grip around the throat. Donald's full weight had struck the smaller Abraham Rueben and they both fell to the floor with a crash. The impact combined with Donald's superior weight, knocked the air out of Abraham's lungs.

"Now you're gonna die you Big Shot Lawyer!" Donald, suddenly mad, screamed as loudly as he could.

Weak, a searing pain in his chest and Donald's large fingers digging deeper into his throat, Abraham attempted to, wanted to, rip Donald's fingers from his neck! Somehow force him to let go! But he couldn't. With no air in his lungs, no way to breath with the increasing pain, all Abraham could do was flail with his left arm. His right arm seemed to be partially pinned. Don't panic! Don't panic! If you panic you're dead! Dead! Abraham thought of his weapon. Upon the impact of hitting the floor it slipped from his right hand. The nine-millimeter lay just inches away. He now realized why he could only marginally move his right arm. Donald's knee was on it just above the elbow. With Donald's bulk on top of him and in his suddenly weakened condition, it was impossible for him to reach the pistol. He was getting dizzy, his lungs screaming for air! Do something before you lose consciousness! He fought the pain that was now wracking his whole body and raised his left arm. If this failed he was dead! With all of his remaining strength he forced his finger hard into Donald's right eye! Donald screamed and released his grip as he jammed his hand over his injured eye. Abraham, with every ounce of strength left in his body heaved Donald off and rolled to the side. He was gasping for breath, as the air rushed into his lungs he thought that he might have a broken rib. That could puncture a lung if it hadn't already. His head was spinning, but he had to get up and reach his gun. Donald was writhing around on the floor screaming something that Abraham couldn't make out. Abraham crawled to the weapon and clutched it in his hand. There was a small table beside him. Abraham grabbed the top and pulled himself up into a half crouch. He tried to steady himself. He felt the room spinning. He dare not pass out. Donald's injury may not deter him for long.

Suddenly Donald was coming screaming at him again, in what looked like a headlong tackle! Abraham braced himself, dodged slightly to one side and with both hands and all the strength he had left he brought the barrel of the nine-millimeter crashing down on the back of Donald's head! Donald gave out a grunt and dropped to the floor like a stone.

To Catch a Fox

***

Abraham Rueben was sitting in a dark pit. At least he thought it was a pit. He wasn't certain. He wasn't certain how he got here. He couldn't see or feel any walls around him but he knew that they were there. He could sense that they were there. He wasn't afraid even though he didn't know where he was. That was strange he thought, under these circumstances even a tough "cookie" like him should be afraid. He remembered reading something sometime about how all of us if placed in a totally alien environment could be reduced to uncontrollable fear. But he wasn't afraid. Not even close to being afraid.

He thought he heard a faint noise in the distance. It seemed to be a rushing sound, like air rushing through a metal duct at high speed. He looked up. It seemed to be coming from up there. Up where that tiny light was shining. Abraham focused on the tiny light. Was it getting larger? It was! The light was getting larger! As the light got larger the sound of rushing air was getting louder and louder. The light got brighter too. Suddenly a sharp pain pierced his chest and his head! Ow! The pain wouldn't stop! Stop the pain!

Abraham Rueben opened his eyes and found that he was staring at a light in the ceiling of his office. He felt like hell. Chest pains with every breath, headache on the scale of a migraine, a wave of nausea passed over him but he fought it back. He raised himself up on one elbow and looked around. The bookcase was pushed to the open position revealing his "escape" route. The small table beside it, the one with the antique lamp on it was knocked over and the lamp was shattered. Oh well, he always thought that the lamp was ugly. He noticed that his Ruger was lying on the floor beside him. He must have passed out. What happened here? Then he saw Donald lying on the floor and it all came back to him. He grabbed the Ruger and stumbled to his feet. That kid might come around any moment and this time he would shoot him. Abraham was unsteady but he managed to walk the few feet between where he had been lying and where Donald Kensington-Cramer was still motionless. Donald was face down with a bleeding head wound. Damn! Thought Abraham, now I have to get new carpet! "Donald! Hey kid! Get up!" Donald didn't move. Abraham reached down and rolled him over on his back. His eye was already turning black where Abraham had poked him. He opened up the eyelid. There was a cut on the eyeball, but it wasn't severe enough to blind him. "Imagine that, I thought I probably gouged his eye out. I must have been even weaker than I thought." Abraham mumbled to himself. He stepped back and leveled the pistol at Donald. He wouldn't make the same mistake twice. “Get up punk we’re taking you down stairs now. Just like we were doing before I let you surprise me. That won’t happen again. I promise.”

Donald was motionless. Abraham reached down and felt his neck for a pulse. There was none. He stood back up. “Damn!” he said out loud. He looked around. The office door was still open to the outer office. As before, he and Donald were the only two on the floor. He closed it anyway. There was no surveillance camera in his private office. Because of carelessness the security guards weren’t even aware that Donald was in the building. That could turn out to be a lucky break thought Abraham. Abraham checked once more to convince himself that Donald was dead. He was. He inspected the wound on the back of Donald’s head. He hadn’t intended to kill him, at least not here in the office, now it was self-defense.

Abraham went to the wet bar in front of the huge windows looking out on the city. The sheer drapes allowed you to enjoy the view but afforded a large measure of privacy. He was comfortable that if anyone else were working late in a neighboring building, they wouldn't have seen anything. He leaned against the bar to steady himself. He was pleased that no matter the recent events and the way he felt, his hands didn’t tremble as he plucked ice from the ice bucket and dropped it into a glass. He took a bottle from the cabinet and poured a Canadian Club on the rocks. Closing his eyes he took a large gulp. The cold whiskey stung his throat as he swallowed.

Self-defense, thought Abraham, how ironic. I had decided to kill him and it turns out to be self-defense. The big oaf not only broke in with the intention of killing him, but after he had been disarmed he was still crazy enough to attack. However, at this time in this office with this individual it was really inconvenient. He looked at his watch. How long was he unconscious? He calculated that it was no more than ten minutes. Now he must think, should he call the police? There was no panic in Abraham Rueben as he moved unsteadily away from the bar and settled himself in his chair behind the desk. He had killed before, although this was the first time that it wasn’t intentional.

Abraham sipped the whiskey slowly. It tasted good. He felt a sharp pain in his side. He wondered if he really did break a rib. He sat there for a long moment breathing in and out very slowly. It hurt, and he determined that a rib might be cracked or broken, but he had not punctured a lung. Then he began considering all aspects of the situation.

Turning in his chair to the credenza behind him, he took some paper tissues from a box and carefully wiped any trace of blood from the barrel of the Ruger. He then replaced the Ruger in the drawer. After that he cautiously removed Donald's pistol from his belt, careful to touch only the end of the barrel. He rummaged around his desk drawers with the free hand until he found a plastic baggie that was left over from a sandwich that he brought to the office. After wiping his own prints off the end of the barrel, being careful to preserve Donald Kensington-Cramer's he placed the firearm in the plastic bag and laid it on his desk. He would determine later what to do with it.

Even though it was self-defense, merely having to explain why a man he had never met suddenly decided to attack him in his office would greatly complicate the Wellbon-Smith deal. His only connection to Donald Kensington-Cramer was through his client Trevor Mason and Donald's aunt Millissa. This was not the time to deal with those questions. No there was only one thing to do. Abraham picked up the phone and punched into an outside line. He glanced at his watch; it was now ten minutes past nine. He pressed a series of numbers into the touch pad. He knew this number by heart. The phone rang several times in his ear.

"Yeah," said the voice on the other end.

"Give me Duke," was Abraham's response. Abraham heard the sound of the receiver being laid down. He waited. He could hear faint music in the background. The bar across town was gearing up for another late night.

"This is Duke." The voice was deep and subdued.

"Abe Rueben, Duke."

"Hey Abe, what can I do for you?"

"I need you to clean up after me again Duke."

"Again? You're getting sloppy in your old age Abe."

"People don't understand me."

"Ha! That's a good one…is this a messy one? Is disposal involved?"

"It's a little messy. I'll need you to have your personal remodeling contractor here at the office by six in the morning. I need new carpet and the old has to go to the incinerator. As for disposal of the 'package' I really need it transported to the proper address. Its rightful owners should find it. It should look like an accident."

"How tough an address is this?"

"Mid town apartment building and the package has to be found first thing in the morning." Abraham knew Donald's current address because of the excellent research that Denton Wellbon had turned in with Millissa's file.

"It will be tough, but we can do it. Those buildings all have doormen and security. This one is going to cost you Abe."

"I know that. When has that ever been a problem?"

"Never, that's why I like doing business with you Abe. You understand value when it comes to my customized services. You also seem to require my services quite frequently."

"One more thing Duke, when you deliver the 'package,' you will have to leave quickly."

"Why is that?"

"I want you to deliver it to the apartment in the conventional manner. The apartment will be empty. Then I want the fastest possible delivery back down to the ground level. I only tell you this now, so that you can be prepared when you get here. Do you understand?"

"I get the picture Abe. I'll bring the boys right over. I suspect that the longer the package lies around the 'stiffer' this situation gets."

"You got it Duke."

"See you soon Abe." There was a click on the other end as Duke hung up the receiver. Abraham was glad that he had this line checked for bugs this week. He finished the whiskey, then taking the plastic baggie with Donald's gun in it he rose and walked a bit more steadily over to a picture on the wall. Behind the picture was a wall safe. Quickly spinning the dial he opened the safe and secured the firearm inside. This was not a good place for permanent residence, but it would do until he could find a better location.

Reaching into his pocket he again removed the all-purpose remote control that he used earlier. He aimed it at the fireplace in the far wall and pushed yet another button on the small panel. The gas fireplace sprung to life behind the fake log. Moving slowly over to the fireplace, because he remained in rather severe pain, he took the tissue that he had used to clean both firearms and deposited it carefully among the flames. Abraham Rueben watched as the fire consumed it. He carefully rubbed his side. First thing in the morning he would have to see a doctor. He returned to his desk, stepping over Donald on the way, and picked up the phone again.

"Security," said the voice. Abraham refrained from making any comment. He had decided to wait until this little problem blew over before he fired anyone. Besides, their lax performance was going to be very helpful in this situation. However, it was their ineptitude that caused the incident to begin with.

"Yes security, this is Abraham Rueben. I have to transport several large boxes of files for a case that I am working on. I have ordered a delivery service to send over a van. They will be arriving tonight at my private exit. I will identify them so you need not be concerned. I have to have the files over at District Court by tomorrow morning so we are going to load them tonight."

"No problem Mr. Rueben. Thanks for informing us."

"You're welcome," Abraham hung up. "Stupid bastards," he muttered to himself. They probably wouldn't have noticed Duke's van!

There was one more problem. Until Duke arrived, Abraham would busy himself by removing the surveillance disk from the camera covering the door and stairway where Donald entered. Abraham had always kept up on technology. That's why he had digital cameras installed for surveillance. He would insert a new disk to cover from this time forward. He would give the original to Duke. Duke had a multi faceted operation. He would be able to clean the original version of Donald's image, fill in the background and merge it into the new disk that Abe was inserting. Then he would "dupe" the merged disk so that it would appear to be the original. The disk would probably never be needed, but you couldn't be too careful.

***

The large man in a well-tailored dark suit, who was known only as George Smith in Savannah Georgia, was now known as Ed Jones in New York City. As George Smith in Savannah, he came complete with a full set of identification: Drivers license, social security card, credit cards, everything that he might require to convince someone that his identity was truly that of George Smith. As Ed Jones in New York City he was equally equipped to prove that he was Ed Jones. At this particular moment, ten forty five in the evening, he was parked in a large black Mercedes sedan directly across the street from the law offices of Murray, Marx and Rothmere. He was watching with interest a succession of innocent appearing events. As he was now observing one Abraham Rueben, Mr. Jones was suspicious of anything even remotely involving the object of his attention.

Earlier after the office personnel had long departed for home, with the notable exception of Mr. Rueben, a car located a space and parked along the street some distance behind where Mr. Jones was parked. A young man possibly thirty at most, heavy set with light hair got out of the car and walked past Mr. Jones' location. After moments of apparent indecision he crossed through the New York traffic and walked down an alley between Rueben's office building and the office building next to it. Mr. Jones never saw him emerge.

Just a short time ago an unmarked delivery van had approached and turned into the private parking garage that opened onto the street and disappeared underneath the office building. The van currently remained in the parking garage. Earlier, Mr. Jones had determined that there was only one entrance and exit to the underground garage so he knew that whoever was driving the van was still in the building. Suddenly the digital phone on his console buzzed. He picked up the phone.

"Jones here… Yeah they're still in there… I don't know… Old delivery van, no markings and I couldn't get a plate number from this angle… I'll get it when they come out… Yeah… Yeah I know… I walked back and checked out the car that the heavy set guy got out of… I'm a big man; he's heavy set… Make sure you know the difference… High priced set of wheels… Porsche Boxter… Yeah I got it… New York vanity plates, 'DON WAN'… I don't know if he fancies himself a romantic or if 'DONONE' was taken…Wait a minute… More activity… Now that's strange… A trade van with 'Queens Carpet Mart' on the side panels just went into the underground garage. Odd hour for someone to be laying carpet… Okay, you're probably right; I've been away from New York too long. I forget that some of these building 'regs' insist that work like that take place when the office force is at home. Could be nothing… Got to go, the delivery van just came out of the parking garage… Yeah I'm going to follow it… I'll get the plate number…you're not working with an amateur here… I won't miss anything if I don't stay with Rueben… Hey, maybe he's in the van… Trust me I'll call you as soon as I know… See you boss."

Mr. Jones turned the ignition key and the big black Mercedes sprang to life. Jones left just enough distance between himself and the van to insure that he wouldn't be detected and neither would he lose them. He eased out into traffic.

** *

Denton Wellbon III was enjoying his breakfast. Because of the long hours that he had been putting in and because Trevor was exceedingly pleased with the work he had accomplished with the Millissa Kensington matter, Trevor told Denton that he didn't want to see him in the office before noon. For the first time, Denton took Trevor up on his offer. Susan was delighted to have Denton present for breakfast. In the last week she sensed a change in his mood. Did he seem more relaxed and confident? She wasn't certain, but whatever the change, she approved. They were sitting in the breakfast nook, the television was on, Susan was listening to the morning news and Denton was reading the financial page of the Wall Street Journal.

Suddenly the female anchorperson on the television said: "This just in! Police were summoned to the exclusive Brandon Towers apartments this morning." A body identified as that of bachelor jetsetter Donald Kensington-Cramer was discovered in the courtyard of the exclusive building just after midnight. It appeared that he had either fallen or jumped from the patio of his fourteenth floor co-op. Police would not comment if it was a suicide or an accident. They remain on the scene conducting their investigation. Mr. Kensington-Cramer was the nephew of prominent New York society dame Milissa Kensington. Donald Kensington-Cramer had previously been in trouble with the law when in 1997 he was arrested for possession of a small amount of cocaine. Because of the small amount and his willingness to submit to rehab, Mr. Kensington-Cramer was sentenced to eight months of community service. It is not known if Mr.

Kensington-Cramer was still struggling with his habit. We will bring you updates on this story as we know more. In other news…" Denton looked up from his paper when he heard Donald Kensington-Cramer's name. He stared at the television, his face suddenly ashen.
Susan had her hand to her mouth. She turned to Denton. "We know Milissa! I served with her on the Fulton Children's Hospital fund drive last year…The poor woman…Her poor family." Denton folded his paper and pushed back from the table. He was no longer hungry.

***

Trevor Mason was pleased with the way traffic was moving on the Cross-Bronx Expressway this morning. He had been listening to the traffic reports on the radio of his big Lincoln Navigator. Trevor, like many a veteran New York commuter had several alternate routes that he utilized depending on the flow of traffic. It was kind of a game for him each morning when he left his home in Connecticut and started down Interstate 95. He would listen intently to the traffic report on the all news all the time station and try to guess the best route before he was committed. The Cross-Bronx was either moving at sixty miles per hour or it was nearly stopped. There was no in between. This morning he guessed right, the Cross-Bronx was moving well.

Suddenly he caught the news flash concerning Donald Kensington-Cramer. Trevor immediately pressed the auto dial on his digital phone. Trevor had the phone hooked to a speaker so that he could talk while maintaining both hands on the steering wheel. The phone rang several times until a voice responded. "Abraham Rueben."

"Abe, Trevor Mason."

"Good morning Trevor."

"I'm not certain about that. Have you heard the news this morning?"

"You mean the news concerning Milissa Kensington's nephew? Yes I've heard."

"How does that affect us?"

"It doesn't Trevor."

"How can you be certain? With her nephew dead she may no longer be willing to play ball with us."

"She has to protect herself. She was as involved as he was."

"Yes, you're right. I guess I'm just afraid that in her grief she may get a loose tongue."

"Let her! She can only hurt herself. Remember I have signed commitments... Trevor, as you have pointed out to me in the past, we should discuss this in private. Not on the phone."

"Yes, you are correct my friend. Be in my office at ten o'clock this morning." Trevor hung up.

***

Sam Grabowski got off the elevator at the fourteenth floor. All was confusion. His men had cordoned off Kensington-Cramer's apartment as a possible crime scene. Sam was a squad commander in homicide for the last four years. Homicide always investigated apparent suicides just in case they turned out to be something more. Sam seldom went out to the scene when suicide seemed this apparent, but there was something that clicked in the back of his mind when he heard the name. At this point he couldn't put his finger on it, but something in the name Kensington rang a bell. He crossed under the tape that was strung across the hall outside Kensington-Cramer's apartment. Several of the upscale neighbors were gawking nearby. Sam decided that no matter what the income level, death seemed to hold a strange attraction to people.

"Lieutenant, good morning to you," detective Peter Herman greeted his boss. Peter was around forty, slender, with straw colored hair and a very pale complexion. Sam knew him to be a pretty thorough cop.

"Morning Peter, what have we got here?"

"Could be a suicide, or maybe the guy was so drugged up that he thought he could fly."

To Catch a Fox

"Find a note?"

"No."

"I heard that this guy had a drug problem at one time."

"Yeah, we've been talking to some of the neighbors. They either don't want to comment or they are willing to tell us every bit of dirt that they know. Seems the neighbors were either neutral toward him or they hated him."

"Which ones hated him?"

"Those who live on either side or above and below him, apparently he liked to throw big expensive, noisy parties. If you lived at the other end of the building and only crossed paths with him in the elevator you thought he was an okay guy."

"So what kind of dirt did you dig up?"

"Well of those that comment, it was pretty much the conventional wisdom that the guy was a real druggie."

"So you think it was an accident?"

"I'm leaning that way Sam."

Sam looked around the apartment. Donald Kensington-Cramer had very expensive tastes. "Next of kin must have been yanked out of bed. You guys were called out here pretty early this morning."

"Yeah, the call came in from one of the building security guards just after midnight."

"Did he see him fall?"

"No one saw him fall. The guard discovered him lying in the courtyard."

Sam moved through the open patio doors to the balcony and looked over the railing. It was a long way down. Peter had followed behind him. "I expect that he was banged up pretty bad?" asked Sam.

"Yeah, he hit hard."

Sam looked out over the city. The morning was clear with a light breeze blowing. "Why does the name strike a chord with me Peter?"

"His aunt is some big shot society dame."

"Yeah, that's what I heard on the news. Hear how she's taking it? Not good I suppose."

"Polly went out to tell her. Polly is good at that sort of thing. She said the old lady was pretty broken up. Apparently he was like a son to her. Parents were divorced and the father lives somewhere else. He apparently has had little to do with his son since a fight they had years ago, about the time that the son was picked up for possession of illegal drugs. Mother has been dead for over twelve years. She was a sister to our famous Ms. Kensington. The aunt and her one surviving sister are the only family in the City. Polly said the old lady called several people while she was there. Finally she told Polly that everyone that needed to know had been informed. Polly got the impression that she is the matriarch for the whole family."

"Okay, humor me Peter. The place looks pretty clean and it's only been our people in here so far."

"We haven't touched anything boss."

"Good, did the CSI people do the apartment?" CSI stood for crime scene investigation.

"No they just did the body and the point of contact. They told me to have our guys, homicide, do the apartment if we wanted more."

"Okay I know downtown won't be in a big rush for an apparent suicide, but get the print boys out here to go over the apartment and when they arrive, make certain they don't rush it. I want this very thorough."

"Are you looking for something in particular Sam?"

"No, just don't let them rush to judgment on this one."

"Okay boss."

"Also talk to everybody. I mean everybody. I sure would like to find someone that might have seen this. Also find out if one of those neighbors might have hated Donald enough to take drastic action. "

"We are Sam, we are. I won't let them rush it. I promise."

Sam turned and smiled at Peter. "I know you won't. I'm glad that you pulled this one. Listen, I guess the body is at the morgue already?"

"Yeah, it left here as soon as the CSI people had all they needed and the photos taken."

"It sounds like they've already made up their minds on either suicide or an accident."

Peter shrugged his shoulders. "I told you I'm leaning that way myself."

"Okay, I'm going to have a look downstairs and then I'm off to the morgue."

"Sam, why are you taking a personal interest in this apparent accident suicide?"

"I don't know Peter. Maybe I just have a feeling on this one." Sam left the apartment and boarded the elevator for the ground floor. He wanted to look at the spot where the body had fallen. Outside in the courtyard he approached the area where the chalk outline of the body was. Sam turned to one of the patrolmen

guarding the integrity of the area. "Did the CSI people clean up some of the blood before they removed the body?" No sir, they examined the body, took pictures and then had the body transported to the morgue."

"This is all the blood there was surrounding the body?"

"Yes sir, I was one of the first officers on the scene and I haven't left since my arrival."

“Okay thanks,” Sam had seen a lot of jumpers in the past. If Donald Kensington-Cramer was alive when he went over the side there should have been a lot more blood on the ground. Sam couldn’t wait to see the autopsy results on this one.

***

It was nine in the morning. The large man known as George Smith in Georgia was now known as Ed Jones and sat in a restaurant near a window so that he could observe the office building across the street. It was a professional building that housed a myriad of doctors and lawyers. There were many of these offices in Manhattan. It was into this particular building that Abraham Rueben had disappeared slightly less than an hour ago. The file on Rueben told him that this was Rueben’s doctor’s office. He wondered if there was any connection between this visit and the events of the night before. The large man finished his warm sticky bun. He caught the waitresses’ eye and requested more coffee. He needed coffee. He had not gotten any sleep the night before.

It had been an interesting night. He had followed the unmarked delivery van across town to the Brandon Towers. The Towers was an upscale co-op on the East Side. It occupied nearly half a city block. The two towers faced on different streets and there was a courtyard in the center between them. Mr. Jones waited in his car as the driver of the van stopped briefly at the main entrance to speak with the doorman. Then the van was off around the corner to the freight elevator. Jones pulled around the corner and parked his Mercedes. He got out and cautiously walked to a point near the freight elevator. Standing behind some dumpsters the man now known as Jones was able to discern that there were at least three men unloading a rather large crate. Jones observed that there was no one from the building supervising this operation. That was standard procedure in the more affluent and security conscious co-ops. It was not unusual for deliveries to take place at odd hours in the night, but it was unusual that a building would allow a delivery to be taken up on the freight elevator when occupants would most likely be asleep. That task was normally limited to the daylight hours when many residents were at work. The purpose was so that distracting noises and commotion in the hallways would occur at a time least offensive to the residents.

The unloading was completed and the three deliverymen rode the elevator along with the crate to the upper floors. Jones returned to his car and timed the operation. The men were gone about twenty minutes. When they returned the crate was still with them. They returned it quickly to their truck and sped off. That's unusual thought Jones, to make a delivery and then take it back. Unless they unloaded the content of the crate somewhere in the building, but to retain the empty container seemed highly irregular. Jones decided not to follow the van any longer. He had written down the license plate number and phoned it into his boss early in the pursuit. His boss had sufficient resources to trace ownership.

Mr. Jones returned to the law offices of Murray, Marx, and Rothmere. After parking his car along the street again, he walked past the entrance of the parking garage that descended several levels below the ground floor. You could always count on the ego of people like Abraham Rueben. In spite of Rueben's near obsession with security it was obvious that the parking spaces near the door on the first level were the spaces that were reserved for the "bosses" of the firms that leased space in this building and the owner of the building himself. As Rueben's firm owned the building this was a status symbol that even Rueben couldn't pass up. There was his Lexus, still in the first space from the end, just inside the entrance. It occurred to Mr. Jones that if he were planning a "hit" on Rueben, he would not have to penetrate the tight security that Rueben's building was famous for. He could simply wait out here for the proper time and "pick him off" as he entered his car. It was not necessary to cross any of the security "trip wires" that Rueben had planted.

Jones returned to the comfort of his car. It was nearly two in the morning before the van from the Queens Carpet Mart left the garage. Shortly afterward, Rueben's Lexus emerged. Mr. Jones followed the Lexus until it arrived at Rueben's apartment building. Mr. Rueben was in for the night.

Just then the digital phone in Jones' console buzzed. Mr. Jones answered. "Jones here... Donald Kensington-Cramer owns the Porsche? Who's Donald Kensington-Cramer? His aunt just happens to own stock in Wellbon-Smith? Imagine that. Does Kensington-Cramer match the description that I gave you of the man that entered Rueben's office tonight? He does? Well you should know that everyone else has left and his car was still parked out there on the street when I left to follow Rueben home. What about the van plates? Yes, yes I know that establishment. It's a front for another business... I know who the man is that operates the other business... No I'm certain that the police don't know... He owns a small bar across town... No he's an independent contractor and he specializes in the kind of services that Abraham Rueben just might require... Curious, I may just stop over there and look around... Okay boss... I'll check in tomorrow."

Mr. Jones alias Mr. Smith drove across town. He made great time. In the "city that never sleeps" it was still easier to get around at this hour in the morning. He decided to skip the "front" business and drive directly to the "real" business owned by a man known only as Duke. Jones took up a position just down the street from the bar and settled in. It occurred to him that this was how he spent most of his time. Sitting in a car, albeit a very nice car, watching a building for strange people to enter or emerge from.

There were rewards. The large man known by numerous names during his career was very well compensated for the services that he provided. Every now and then there were rewards other than monetary. Getting to know, and finally meet Crystal Harrison was definitely an assignment that he enjoyed. Watching her grow to adulthood and become successful while overcoming the obstacles that life had placed in front of her was especially rewarding. He was also the one to give Crystal Harrison her inheritance. That was just fun. He would keep track of her because that was his job, but he also wanted to help insure that things turned out right for her. That was why he was sitting on this street at this moment. Crystal reminded the big man of his own daughter… At about this point in his revelry three men emerged from the bar. Why didn't it surprise him that they were the same three men that he had observed making their delivery at the Brandon Towers earlier that morning?

After watching the three depart their separate ways, Mr. Jones returned to his watch outside Abraham Rueben's apartment. Fortunately he had the rare opportunity to sleep long and well the night before. His "friend" Mr. Rueben was a bit of an insomniac and was prone to leave his apartment quite early even after late nights. After the events of this past night, Mr. Jones didn't want to miss out on Rueben's activities the following morning.

That was how the large man known currently as Ed Jones came to be sitting in this restaurant across from Abraham Rueben's doctor's office. The morning news filled in the blanks from the night before. For some unknown reason Donald Kensington-Cramer felt the need to meet with Abraham Rueben. The meeting must have degenerated into a confrontation. Perhaps it started as such given Kensington-Cramer's known drug abuse. It obviously didn't end well for the young man. Rueben called in the cleanup crew. They paid off or had previous connections with the Brandon Towers' security people and probably used the victim's own key to enter his apartment. Quick trip to the ground and the police, even if they discover that Kensington-Cramer was probably dead before he took the dive, will never be able to trace the deed back to Rueben's office.

Mr. Jones now understood the need for new carpet. Things like this tend to leave stains. He suspected that the original carpet had already made the trip to one of the cities' incinerators. Probably a small contractor who could keep his mouth shut and was willing to do small jobs for big fees and not ask any embarrassing questions. Ah, free enterprise.

It was a neat tidy package, but the large man was a true professional. He saw one detail that had apparently been overlooked. Mr. Jones alias Mr. Smith had observed Donald Kensington-Cramer's car was still parked on the same block where Rueben's office was located. He knew that it was locked, as he had looked it over carefully when he had recorded the license plate number. That means that Donald Kensington-Cramer, barring something utterly stupid like Kensington-Cramer losing his keys between his car and Rueben's office, should have been in possession of his car keys at the time of his death. How could Rueben and his boys not notice this? Whatever, Rueben had apparently come to the conclusion that the victim had arrived in a cab. That was dumb, thought Jones. However, the discovery of the car alone would not be enough to tie Rueben to Kensington-Cramer. The police would have to discover more than that and perhaps Rueben's boys decided to take the chance rather than run the risk of some one noticing that a different person other than the one that arrived in it, drove Kensington-Cramer's car away. Jones finished his coffee as Rueben emerged from the doctor's office. As he left the restaurant and walked to his car Jones smiled. Some day the police might truly enjoy looking at all the photos that he had been taking the previous evening with his digital camera.

***

Abraham Rueben sat quietly on the large leather sofa in Trevor Mason's office. His ribs hurt. He refused to take the time to go to the hospital for x-rays as his doctor had sternly suggested. After a heated argument he had agreed to go later in the afternoon. In the meantime, since he made it abundantly clear that he would not miss or postpone his meeting with Trevor Mason, his doctor reluctantly told him that his best guess without x-rays was that his ribs weren't broken but were most likely severely bruised. At Abraham's insistence the doctor gave him some pain pills but informed him, with his nurse as a witness that he could not be responsible if Abraham refused to immediately do as he suggested. Abraham assured the doctor that he wouldn't sue him if his ribs were broken and he happened to puncture a lung before getting treatment. Now he felt miserable as he watched Trevor pace back and forth. He wondered if those were really pain pills that his doctor had given him, or if they were simply sugar pills to humor him.

The farthermost thing from Trevor's mind at the moment was Abraham's discomfort. He stopped pacing and turned again toward Rueben. "You think that she can't say anything that would possibly hurt our campaign to take over Wellbon-Smith?"

Abraham was losing patience. "Trevor, listen to me. I don't care if Millissa Kensington stands naked at Rockefeller Center and tells the world what we are doing. How would she prove it? I kept all copies of the pre-dated documents that she signed. I have all copies, much to their chagrin, of all documents that her fellow shareholders have signed. The reason that I am able to get away with this is that they are all greedy bastards and they realize that they are violating the corporate by-laws. They are playing ball with us because they want to cash in and make a killing. They do not believe that they will get that opportunity by playing by the corporate rules. To rat on us is to destroy all hopes for windfall profits! As for Millissa, she still has liability for her actions concerning her nephew whether he is alive or not. She doesn't want to go through a trial for fraud! She doesn't want to risk spending her remaining years in jail! She and her nephew embezzled a million dollars for god's sake!"

"But if she did talk, it would alert Carlton Smith and his allies that they may be threatened. Even on suspicion alone Smith may act to protect his interests. He's no fool you know."

"I'm aware of that. I'm also aware that we are very close to having enough proxy votes to pull this off. If we continue on schedule, and I believe that we can, there is precious little time for Smith to make an effective counter move. We are in a far different position than we were just a few weeks ago. If the worst would happen I could always pay Carlton a visit and let him know without really saying it, that we could make a circumstantial case against him in the Kensington affair. That may just slow him down enough for us to complete our coup. A few weeks ago I wasn't aware of this situation. I didn't know that we had this ace to play."

To Catch a Fox

"We have Denton to thank for the ace… I suppose that you are correct Abe."

"I'm your lawyer, trust me on this."

"The fact that you have all copies of all documents and won't turn them back to the signers until after the vote, thereby making the predated agreements legal, there is really no way for any of them to prove anything."

"Precisely, and the signers are not looking to disrupt this in any way. Trevor if you still have concerns about Millissa, then I think that we need to pay our respects at her departed nephew's funeral if you get my drift."

"Just subtly remind her of our deal?"

"Yes very subtly, she's no fool either, as she took great pains to point out to me."

Suddenly the door to Trevor's office burst open and Denton Wellbon entered. Trevor noted with some surprise that this was very much out of character for the mild mannered Denton. Trevor's secretary followed closely on Denton's heels explaining that she had informed Mr. Wellbon that Trevor was in a meeting and did not wish to be disturbed.

"It's all right. Mr. Wellbon is welcome in my office anytime." Trevor dismissed his secretary with a wave of his hand. After the door was closed behind the secretary Trevor turned his attention on Denton. "What is it that you want Denton?"

"What happened to Donald Kensington-Cramer?" Denton's voice was tight, as if he was struggling to control it.

Trevor looked toward Abraham who responded. "I have no idea Denton. Trevor asked me the same question. From the gossip I am hearing this morning I suspect that Donald's drug habit caught up with him. He fell into depression and decided to end it all because in spite of his money he was a worthless human being or he simply fell from his balcony in a drugged stupor. I suspect the latter."

"You don't think that his death had anything to do with your visit to his aunt?" Even though the question was for Abraham, Denton did not look at him but kept his gaze leveled on Trevor.

"Could have, so what if it did?" Abraham's ribs and head were throbbing now and he had little patience for explaining things to Denton who was involved in a game of hardball but had no stomach for the results.

"So what if it did? My god man, have you no feelings? If the threat that we made of exposing his scam on the corporation drove him to take his life, do you feel no responsibility?" Denton had now turned to face Abraham.

Abraham Rueben slowly rose from the sofa to stand toe to toe with Denton Wellbon III. Even standing as straight as he could manage with his sore ribs Denton was still at least six inches taller. "I do not feel any responsibility Mr. Wellbon. I feel no responsibility because Donald Kensington-Cramer and his aunt Millissa consciously decided to defraud your company. The company that even now has your family name on the door. I feel no responsibility because he was stealing. He knew that he was stealing and if discovering that someone had found him out was too much for him to bear then too bad! Neither you, nor Trevor, nor myself are to blame if Donald Kensington-Cramer took his life...Got that Mr. Wellbon?"

Denton felt his face flush. He truly disliked this little man but he had to admit that Rueben was correct. He turned back toward Trevor. The belligerent tone in his voice and the tense expression on his face disappeared. They were replaced with a look and tone of resignation. "Very well I stand corrected... Trevor, I will have the research complete on the next subject by tomorrow at nine in the morning."

Trevor eyed Denton closely. "Abe's correct you know."

"I'm not arguing the point Trevor. I apologize to you both for this intrusion and outburst."

"Denton, do you still want to sit in your father's chair? Think carefully before you answer." Trevor's voice was very low, almost threatening.

"I don't have to think about it Trevor, the answer is yes."

"Good. Remember that Donald Kensington-Cramer brought his fate on himself."

To Catch a Fox

Truer words were never spoken thought Abraham as he listened to Trevor pull Denton verbally into line.

"I'll remember Trevor. If you'll excuse this interruption I'll get back to work."

"Of course Denton, our success depends on you as much as anyone."

Trevor and Abraham watched Denton closely as he departed. When the door was once again closed Abraham turned to Trevor. "You know that I never have felt comfortable with Denton."

"I know but he's essential to the plan."

"I understand, but just in case you have more trouble than you expect with him I have some information that I think you will find useful." Abraham reached into his briefcase and extracted a folder. Trevor received it and began examining the contents. A smile began to cross his face as he read. Before he finished he looked up.

"You discovered her identity! The under aged girl that Denton had the fling with."

"Yes, and it wasn't easy. Denton's father hired good people. But read on it gets more interesting."

Now a slight frown crossed Trevor's brow as he returned his attention to the documents. "She's dead?"

"Yes, she committed suicide some years ago."

Trevor returned to the documents in the folder and turned a page. "My god, there was a child!"

"Yes, I told you this information would please you."

"Crystal Harrison-Rankin. I see that you even have a photo…Attractive girl."

"Yes she is, attractive and successful."

"She has no knowledge as to the true identity of her father?"

"Not as far as I can determine."

"In your opinion Abe, do you believe that Denton is ignorant of the existence of a child?"

"I think that his father pulled so many strings to keep the girl's family quiet that 'Pop' felt it safer if even Denton didn't know that she was pregnant. It's entirely possible that the girl "vanished" and her parents weren't aware either. No, I don't believe Denton is even remotely aware of where she moved or that she is dead and that there was a child involved."

"Why didn't Denton's father just set up an abortion?"

"Not the way a Wellbon would operate. You have to understand the 'animal' you are dealing with. Remember this child Crystal is blood, family. Even if they could never claim her, Denton's father would never allow a grandchild of his to be abandoned or aborted before birth."

"How could he arrange all of this and cover it up so completely that not even the participants, not even his son whom he was protecting could know everything?"

"After tracking this down Trevor, I just want you to be very grateful that you are dealing with the grandson and not the father and grandfather. I never realized how powerful Denton's ancestors were until I got into this. I told you that the old man hired good people. That's an understatement. Whoever they were they were in a league by themselves. I never saw tracks so well covered. In the end I got lucky."

"What do you mean 'whoever they were'?"

"Just what I said, I have no clue as to the identity of the people that set this up for Denton's father. Whoever they are they are the best and they are so 'deep' I don't think we could ever find out their identity."

"You just said 'are' as in present tense. Do you seriously think that, whoever they are, they are still looking out for this bastard Wellbon girl? Even all these years after the man that hired them, Denton's father, died?"

"I don't know Trevor, but the way doors slammed in my face whenever I tried to discover what happened to young Denton's under aged fling, someone is still out there covering for her."

"You're absolutely certain that our own Denton Wellbon is ignorant of all this?"

"Absolutely I think daddy whipped his ass for getting into trouble and then sent him back to school and told him to keep his mouth shut and everything would be handled."

"Does the girl know who Denton is?"

"No."

"Thank you Abe. I think this will keep Denton loyal to us if he should get another attack of guilt."

"I agree. Not only would the mere existence of a child be a shock to him, but he certainly wouldn't want his dear wife and mother finding out about little Crystal."

Trevor laughed. "Just about the time that I think that I pay you too much you pull a rabbit out of the hat!"

"Believe me Trevor I'm worth even more than you pay me."

"When this is all over, we'll talk about a bonus Abe."

"Thank you Trevor. Now if you will excuse me, I have an appointment at the hospital for some x-rays."

"Yeah, go take care of yourself. You've earned the rest of the day off… Oh Abe!"

"Yes Trevor?" Abraham had almost escaped through the door.

"I'll let you know when and where Kensington-Cramer's funeral will take place."

"It will be a few days. The police will perform an autopsy. They always do in cases like this." Abraham waved goodbye and closed the door behind him before Trevor could think of anything else. He had to get to the hospital. His ribs and head were both becoming unbearable.

Trevor Mason read and reread the documents that were in the folder that Abraham Rueben had just given him. This was it. This was the piece of the puzzle that nearly insured success. Trevor would not hesitate to reveal the contents of this folder to both Denton and his mother if it became necessary. They would quickly do his bidding to keep this information out of the papers. He closed the folder and locked it in his briefcase. Wellbon-Smith was nearly in his grasp. All he had to do now was arrange the financing to pay for all the stock and proxies that Rueben was accumulating.

As he placed the briefcase beside his desk a feeling of uneasiness came over him. Who could Denton's father have hired to cover his son's screw up? Abe sounded nearly in awe of the job they did and awe was not natural for Abe. Equally important was the question of whether they were still out there operating, unknown to Denton, on his behalf. If they were who controlled them and would this affect his plan? Trevor settled back in his chair. He had come this far and he wouldn't allow anyone to stop him. Not even these mysterious operatives.

To Catch a Fox

PART 3

CHAPTER 13

Mitchell Green sat across the table from Clint Matthews. They were seated at a corner table at "Charlie's Restaurant on the Hill" in St. Louis. It was two o'clock in the afternoon and the lunch crowd had just departed. Except for a few individuals that remained at the bar in the next room the restaurant was nearly deserted. Even popular restaurants like Charlie's were subject to the same daily cycle. Mitchell had purposely chosen the after lunch "down" time to meet with Clint Matthews. He wanted this to be a conversation held away from Clint's office and remain as private as was possible. The fifty-dollar bill that he slipped to the hostess to insure that no one was seated close to them didn't hurt either.

Charlie's was a popular pasta place and was supposedly a hangout for the local powers behind the city's labor unions and the remnants of the St. Louis crime families. At the moment there was only one representative of labor and one from the ranks of management in the restaurant. No one represented organized crime. Those two were Mitchell and Clint. Both ordered the lunchtime special, a salad and a small plate of cheese ravioli. Both added their individual choice of wine. After the greetings and placing the order, both men settled into small talk until lunch arrived. Then over food the conversation turned serious.

"Okay Mitchell. I know that you're a messenger for your boss Jerome. None of my companies' labor contracts are up for at least two years. So let's get something straight before we even begin: I'm not going to be strong-armed into any concession while we are in the middle of a contract! If you have anything even remotely resembling a proposal to alter, or add to the terms of any of the contracts at any of my companies, forget it! You better ask the waitress to put your lunch in a doggie bag and get back on a plane to D.C. Because my friend, we've got nothing to talk about."

Clint Matthews was a hard driving corporate "M & A" specialist. "M & A" stood for mergers and acquisitions. Clint left the financial institution where he had risen to the vice presidential level ten years ago. That company had taught him how to assist other companies to acquire businesses and how to merge businesses together. Clint decided to take what he had learned and create his own empire. That he did successfully in an amazingly short period of time. He was now the Chairman and CEO of Cab Corp Corporation. The name was an acronym for Cabinet Corporation Incorporated.

Clint utilized his knowledge and contacts in the world of finance to acquire five furniture and cabinet companies. He did this in a series of both friendly and hostile take-over bids. After the acquisitions he standardized and automated many of the operations and materials used in the various companies. By doing this he created a situation where all of them manufactured to similar standards using similar techniques. This allowed them to have one central purchasing division that could nearly dictate the prices that they paid for raw materials because of the volume that they required. Clint reaped the profits, while his critics claimed that he had destroyed the uniqueness of the individual products and lowered the quality level of all of the companies. Clint could not have cared less. Unlike his competition in the furniture industry he avoided having to move off shore and he was getting very wealthy. He counted on volume therefore he purposely downgraded the quality level and simultaneously the price level of some of the companies he acquired. This put him right in the "lower middle class" markets. By standardizing production procedures he was able to take all of the factories to a level of automation that they had never "enjoyed" before. Clint also inherited the United Federation of Millwrights in the process.

Mitchell never felt any particular kinship with the Cab Corp Chairman. The nature of their adversary roles prevented that, but Mitchell also viewed Matthews as a self styled "cowboy." Indeed Matthews cultivated that persona. From the expensive "Texas made" cowboy hats to the equally expensive cowboy boots, to the abundant silver hair and handle bar mustache, Clint Matthews looked the role. True thought Mitchell, he could lay claim to that heritage as he was born on a ranch near Dallas Texas, but the whole "look" turned Mitchell off.

"No Clint, I'm not here to suggest that we renegotiate any of your contracts. I agree, it's too early for that and besides the rank and file are reasonably happy at this point."

"They should be you guys all but robbed me blind the last time."

"Hardly Clint it was time that you shared some of those excess profits with the people whose skills made you rich in the first place."

"Huh!" snorted Matthews. "There is no such thing as 'excess profits' and you know it." He speared some ravioli with his fork and shoved it into his mouth. In between chewing and draining his wineglass he asked; "So what is it you want to talk about anyway?"

"Jerome and I think that we have an opportunity for you."

"You do huh, and what might that be?"

"Surely you've heard the rumor that Fox Cabinetry is for sale?"

"Yeah, I didn't take it too seriously though. Atlantic has owned Fox for a lot of years. I made them an offer some time back for it but they had no interest. Said that they were very happy with Fox and intended to keep it for the 'glamour image' that it maintained for their company. It's privately held stock so there was no way I could make a tender offer and force a hostile takeover."

"Did you make that offer to Trevor Mason?"

"No, it was before he came to Atlantic. What was that guy's name anyway, I can't think of it just now? He struck me as a real New York pompous ass… Oh yeah, it was Carl… Carl… Carl Smith! That's who I made the offer to."

"His name is Carlton, Carlton Smith."

"Yeah, that's right… Carlton, how can you take a good solid name like Carl Smith and turn it into something that sounds like you think your ass weighs a ton and they should name a cigarette after you? People should be fined when they think up names like that for their kids. Affects their whole life it does. It's probably the main reason that Smith turned out to be the jackass that he is."

Mitchell smiled. He had never met Carlton Smith, but from the stories that he had heard he could imagine how the meeting between Manhattan bred Smith and 'cowboy' Matthews must have gone. "Jerome and I think that Trevor Mason may just be a lot more receptive to an offer now."

"You think that the rumor is true?"

To Catch a Fox

"Jerome is reasonably positive."

"Why? What makes him so certain?"

"Jerome has friends in one of Chicago's big investment banks. In addition to banking they have a merger and acquisition division."

"Which M & A outfit?"

"Bertrum & Bertrum."

"The big international outfit, yeah I know them well. They helped me finance my last acquisition. Keep talking."

"Jerome called his friends at Bertrum & Bertrum after hearing the rumor. While they would not confirm the rumor officially, they left him under the impression that it could very well be true."

"Other than having friends there, what made Jerome call Bertrum & Bertrum?"

"In our research on Fox and its parent company, we discovered that Atlantic Corporation utilizes Bertrum & Bertrum quite extensively."

"Your research on Fox, Fox isn't union to my recollection."

"No it's not."

"Oh, I see. You think you can organize it."

"We would like to."

"Could be tough, Atlantic picked a shrewd manager when they picked... Ah what's his name?"

"William MacLode."

"Yeah, that's it, MacLode. Irishman, Scotsman, something like that."

"He's a Scot."

"Why are you telling me this? Aren't you afraid that I might just call up my old friend and fellow manager Bill McLode and warn him?"

"First of all the mere fact that you referred to MacLode as Bill tells me that you've never met him, no one that knows him calls him Bill. His nickname is Mac. Second, we have a suggestion for you."

"I'm listening."

"We think that it would be a nice fit into your woodworking empire."

"Let me guess, organizing Fox has proven to be more difficult than you originally supposed."

"Yes it has."

"Since you already have all of my companies in your pocket, you believe that if I made a successful bid to Atlantic for Fox you could have me 'insist' on their membership shortly after the acquisition. My motive would be so that I could continue to deal with my union as if it represented one large company as opposed to having this one odd ball."

"That's sort of the gist of it, yes. You could at least only put up token resistance."

"I have to ask you, exactly what's in this for me? I may just like the idea of acquiring Fox and having it independent. I may use it as a thorn in your side."

Mitchell looked about the room to be certain that there was no one within earshot. Then leaning across the table he and Matthews drew closer to one another. "We need to add Fox to our 'stable' in the worst way. We want you to make an offer that they can't refuse."

"You want me to out bid everyone else no matter how much it costs? That's generous of me. Why would I do that?"

"How much would it be worth to not have any union troubles for the next five years?"

Matthews inhaled sharply and stared at Mitchell. "You're serious?"

Mitchell nodded his head in the affirmative. Matthews thought about this for a moment as he contemplated his empty wineglass. He then caught the waitress' eye and motioned for a refill. As the restaurant was nearly empty she returned quickly with a fresh glass. She was about to leave when Matthews called her back. He handed her the original empty glass. "Could you remove that please darlin'? I don't like to get them stacked up too deep on the table. Makes casual observers think I'm a drunk."

"Certainly, I'm sorry about that." She took the empty and headed for the bar.

"It's okay darlin." Matthews took a sip from the fresh glass and returned his attention to Mitchell. "Five years from now or do we begin counting when the next contract runs out?"

"We could live with five years from now."

"I bet you could," replied Matthews. "I could live with five years from when the next contract runs out. I'm already good for two more years without spending any money."

Mitchell winced, but this was not unexpected. "Mr. Jefferson said to tell you that if you have to go over twenty percent of what Fox would be reasonably worth we would consider those terms."

"No union troubles at all of my companies for five years after the current contracts run out. That could be worth quite a bit. What are they asking for Fox?"

"They haven't received that opinion from Bertrum & Bertrum as of this moment, but we expect that they will have a number within the next few weeks."

Matthews' eyes narrowed. "I'm guessing from what I've heard that Fox does something in the realm of $30 million in gross sales a year. Atlantic has always claimed that they were good 'earners' for them so let's assume that they make at least 10% on the operating line. At least 10%! That's 3 mill on the operating line. At ten times earnings that's $30 million! 10 % over that number is over $33 million! No way I go to 20% over! I might, repeat might go 10% but not without a promise of five years from the end of the next contract and you hold wage increases to 5% total over the life of the new contract."

"Can't do that Clint." Mitchell expected a counter offer and Jefferson had given him a counter to the counter. "First the custom cabinet business isn't like the furniture business. Let's assume you're wrong about the operating line. This is far more labor intense than anything that you are involved with. I'll give them the benefit of the doubt and say 9% on the operating line max. That's 2.7mil and because of that narrow margin even with a good will allowance they won't get any more than 5 times earnings in that industry. That's 13.5 million. Look, if you have to go 10% over the fair market value then we guarantee five years peace from the end of the current contract, but we can't guarantee what the total or incremental increase will be. You know that will depend on the mood of the rank and file. Keep your workers happy and you may just get away with a cost of living increase every year."

The two fell silent as Matthews thought this proposition over. Mitchell finished his lunch while watching his companion stare into space while making mental calculations. "I'd consider working with you guys on a project of that kind… It would be really something to own the almighty Fox Cabinetry… Yes it would… It would also be great not to have to worry about you guys for the next seven years. I've got some expansion plans and I want to keep my costs down."

"That could all be arranged… Do you wish to continue discussing the details of a deal like this?"

"No strikes, no goofy walkouts because one of their members was denied a promotion or other such bullshit for five years and you try damn hard to hold wage increases to cost of living. In addition, I want the current health care package and retirement package to stay just as they are now for that five-year period."

Mitchell and Jefferson had expected the health care and retirement to become an issue. What surprised Mitchell was that Matthews wasn't asking for the packages to be reduced in value. This was the line that they expected him to take. With other companies either reducing these packages or pushing more of the expense onto the employee, they could almost sell maintaining the status quo to the rank and file as a hard fought victory. This was better than either he or Jefferson had anticipated. "You drive a hard bargain, but I think we could live with that."

To Catch a Fox

Clint Matthews locked his gaze hard on Mitchell Green. "You of course realize that what we are discussing is highly illegal?"

"I do Clint, but understand that if we go down this road only the two of us and Mr. Jefferson must be the only people on earth that are aware of this. We, you and the two of us, are putting ourselves in equal jeopardy."

"You and Jefferson think that you can truly deliver on this promise?"

"Yes."

"Five years from the end of the current contract no matter what I pay. Understand that if I buy Fox and you and your boss don't come through then I'll be the toughest son of a bitch that you ever had to deal with."

Mitchell smiled. "We always thought that you were a son of a bitch."

"I'll ignore the fact that you left out the word tough. Let's get to it!"

***

William MacLode stood at the rear of the hotel conference room. Sarah Frazer had accompanied him from the office and stood silently beside him. They had quietly entered unnoticed by the gathering that was assembled in this room. They were in the Holiday Inn just off the turnpike exit only a few miles from the Fox factory. Standing at the front of the room was Tony Conocenti. Tony was addressing the Fox field sales force. All thirteen of them had been called in from their individual territories on short notice so that Tony could announce the impending price increase. It was not going well. Not unexpected the sales force were shocked that Fox would surprise their dealers with an "off season" price hike. Mac and Sarah intended that their presence be as observers only, but Mac was beginning to expect that Tony may soon look to them as reinforcements.

The sales force had arrived at the meeting expecting to receive compliments concerning the record first half that their territories had registered and indeed they did. Tony was very generous with those comments. However, the surprise of the unexpected price increase had them moaning that the second half would be a disaster as none of Fox's competitors was hinting at an increase. The Fox senior staff wanted to avoid discussing the possibility of a union if possible. Fair or unfair union shops had a bad image of slipshod quality in the eyes of the dealers and the sales force. Tony felt that some dealers might jump ship at the mere suggestion of a union. In the end, they decided to "play it by ear" and left the final decision to Mac as to whether the threat should be revealed. Tony was dealing with the tough questions as best as he could, but by avoiding a direct answer Tony sounded unusually evasive. The mere fact that Tony had a reputation for direct answers to tough questions was fueling the fears.

John Malicki asked to speak. Tony gave him the floor. John was the Fox sales force "elder" statesman. He was well respected by his peers and when he asked to speak all of the side conversations stopped. "Tony you know that I always try to be a good soldier. I try to do whatever you guys back here at the factory ask of me." Tony nodded in agreement. "I certainly have no complaints you have gone to extraordinary measures in helping me set up a flagship showroom in my territory. For that I am deeply indebted to you." Tony nodded again as John continued. "I believe that I can sell this price increase if I have some logical reason to give to my dealers. But the other manufacturers with whom they deal are not making any claims that lumber prices are going up and with inflation at record lows, this is going to be a tough sell. We're going to come off looking just plain greedy. Is there any solid reason you can give us? We're not fighting you we're just looking for a fig leaf here." There was a murmuring of agreement from the others.

Tony was standing facing the rear of the room while the sales force was seated facing him. He saw Mac and Sarah enter. He looked to Mac for help. Mac glanced at Sarah, raised an eyebrow, and started toward the front of the room. "I suppose this is my cue," he said. At the sound of his voice the group turned in Mac's direction. His presence surprised and pleased the "road warriors." Tony exchanged knowing glances with him as he approached. Tony and David Elliott were conducting the meeting from a table set up to face the sales force. Tony was standing next to a podium and David was seated at the "head" table. Mac seated himself casually on the table.

"You've asked honest questions and you deserve honest answers. I heard someone ask if we were under pressure to produce more profits or be sold. Let me assure you that we are always under pressure to produce more profits whether or not the company is for sale. However that's not the main reason for the increase. Allow me to introduce someone that I brought along for you to meet. I was only going to introduce her to you, but now I believe that you may want to hear what has been occupying her time since she joined Fox Cabinetry. Gentlemen, I give you Sarah Frazer our new V. P. of Human Resources."

Sarah came forward. She was dressed smartly in high heels and tailored gray suit with a plain white blouse. This was not unexpected. She and Mac had discussed the possibility early this morning in Mac's office. "Gentlemen, it's good to meet you," she began. All became deathly silent as they wanted to hear what she had to say and they were a bit taken aback by her sophisticated beauty. Sarah and Mac had agreed that they would opt for full disclosure. Sarah began her explanation with the request that what she was about to tell them would not leave this room. She and Mac were well aware that everyone there would tell at least one confidant but the request had to be made. She then began with Carroll Brubaker's surprising revelation of a few weeks ago.

***

Sam Grabowski read the coroner's report for the second time. Finally he looked up at the doctor that handed it to him. Her name was Janice something; Sam couldn't remember her last name. The New York City Coroner's Office had an entire staff of doctors working for it. Over the years Sam had dealt with all of them many times over. It didn't matter if he couldn't remember her name. "So doctor, what's all this about 'pooling blood' in 'inconsistent areas' of Donald Kensington-Cramer's body?"

"It's quite simple lieutenant, when the heart stops beating there is no longer any force, as in a pump, to push the blood out of the heart or force it back into the heart."

"Okay…your report states that there is 'pooling in areas that are inconsistent with the areas of trauma'… What exactly does that mean?"

Janice looked a bit impatient with the pace of Sam's comprehension of her report. "It means that severe trauma such as the type that the body experienced with a fall of that magnitude would have broken and ruptured blood vessels in numerous areas of the body. Such ruptures would be severe enough and numerous enough to cause massive internal bleeding even though the heart had stopped upon the moment of impact." At this precise moment Janice reminded Sam of a schoolteacher that he had in high school. Fifty something and single, at least Sam saw no ring on her finger, and a level of smugness that struck at Sam's very core. He hated that teacher. She always played twenty questions with him, as if she wanted to test him constantly to determine how much knowledge he possessed. When he failed the test she always looked at him in her condescending manner. That was exactly the feeling that Sam was experiencing now. Why not just come out and tell him what she was stating in veiled fashion in this report? Like his teacher, Sam could rapidly learn to hate Doctor Janice.

"Okay, okay, I'm stupid! I've already waited two days for this report and I still don't understand what the hell you're trying to tell me. What killed him?"

Janice looked a bit indignant, but she remained smug and calm. It never occurred to her that she might instigate these outbursts. "As I said lieutenant, it's quite simple, the blood normally pools where the wounds are in this type of death. In this case the blood had pooled in areas that had not even suffered damage and there was very little in areas that were severally damaged."

"You're telling me?"

"I'm telling you that he died from a blow to the back of his head. The injuries that he suffered as a result of the fall suggest that he landed face first. It's awfully hard to die from a single blow to the back of the head when you hit the pavement belly down!"

"You mean the fall wasn't the cause of death?"

"That's what I mean lieutenant. Because of the pattern of pooling blood and other factors I believe that he died at least an hour before the fall." The look of self-satisfaction on her face was enough to make a weaker man throw up thought Sam. "In addition to that the wound in the back of the skull appears to have been made by a blunt object, a small pipe like shape."

"When you made this rather startling discovery you never thought to call our office to inform me that I'm possibly looking at a homicide investigation?" It took all of Sam's will power to control his anger.

"My dear lieutenant do you realize how many autopsies we do here in a day? If the cause of death is not an obvious homicide, we may be a day or two behind in writing the reports. In that length of time, without you people placing a specific hold on it, the body may already have been released. May I remind you that this body came in as a possible suicide or accidental death?"

"You haven't released the body have you?"

"We released it to the family right after I completed the autopsy."

"On whose authority?"

"I knew that you would be asking that so I attached the release papers to the end of the report. Please check the authorization. I believe that individual has the authority to release a body to the family."

Sam found the release form. The document was signed by the Chief of Police. If Sam's memory served him the Chief was an old friend of the family of Melissa Kensington, Donald's aunt and society dame.

"That was two days ago?"

"Yes, that's the date on the release form. I told you if you people on the force don't place a specific hold on a body."

"Yeah, yeah, it's my fault! May I have this copy?" he asked more out of courtesy than any sense of obligation.

"Of course, I have a copy of the obituary attached also."

Sam quickly scanned the obituary. Good god he thought; the funeral is this morning!

With that Sam turned and burst through the doors and out of the morgue. The CSI investigation had turned up nothing. But this autopsy was in sync with his personal observation of a lack of blood at the impact point. He suddenly wanted very much to see who turned up at Donald Kensington-Cramer's funeral. Doctor Janice looked after him in disgust. Crude bastard she thought. He didn't even thank me.

***

The late morning sky was overcast as the funeral procession pulled into the high walled cemetery overlooking the Hudson River north of the city. The plots in this particular cemetery had been sold out for more than a quarter of a century. Only old and prominent family names from New York society adorned the elaborate tombstones. Few knew of the existence of this place, as the people who supported it desired privacy above all else. The cemetery was nondenominational and was not maintained or owned by any particular church. It was owned and maintained by a privately held organization whose members all had plots there. It had been in existence for over one hundred and fifty years.

The black Cadillac hearse wound through the rows of impressive monuments and mausoleums. It finally pulled to a halt next to a row of old intricately sculptured monuments with the name Kensington engraved in several of them. The procession halted close behind. From a nearby knoll Sam Grabowski stood leaning against a willow tree. He was unable to make it to the church in time for the memorial service but the obituary from the Times listed the place of internment so he came straight to the cemetery. He had no idea what or who he was looking for, but he hoped that he hadn't missed anything by not being present at the church. Damn that doctor, what's her name? Janice! He was certain that had the Chief known all of the implications he would have been slow to release the body.

The cars, mostly high priced luxury models, began empting out as the mourners approached the open grave site that was sheltered from the threatening sky by a green tent. There was a cool breeze blowing and it felt as if it could begin raining any moment. Suddenly Sam was startled as he realized that someone was approaching him from behind. He turned to recognize Harry Sigfried his friend and senior FBI agent. As Sigfried stopped at his side Sam greeted him, "What brings you out here Harry?"

Harry Sigfried smiled and contemplated his old friend. "I might ask you the same."

"Just curious as to who might show up."

Sigfried looked at his old friend. "So an NYPD homicide lieutenant decides to 'just see who shows up' at the funeral of a suicide?"

"Now I might ask you the same. What's the FBI's senior agent from the New York Office doing at a suicide?"

To Catch a Fox

"Somehow I don't think you believe it was a suicide."

Sam gave a deep sigh and looked back at the people gathering under the green tent. "It wasn't a suicide. I just came from the coroner's office."

"How can you be sure?"

"He was dead before he took the dive."

"Interesting, you have any motive or suspects?"

"Neither."

"You think the killer is down there?"

"Who knows? You know as well as I do that most murder victims are killed by people they know." Sam turned and looked at his old friend again. "You never said why you're here."

"I called your office to talk to you and they told me you had just called in and told them you were coming here. I decided to come on up here and talk to you in person."

"About what?"

"About that," Harry nodded toward the funeral service getting underway down the slope from them, "and about what we discussed in my office the other day."

Sam looked up with a start. "Go on, what did you come here to tell me?"

"It might be something or nothing."

"Let me be the judge of that," Sam answered trying to keep the anticipation out of his voice.

"Your victim down there, his Aunt's name is Melissa Kensington."

"Yeah, I know, so what?"

"Melissa is a major shareholder in Wellbon-Smith Corporation."

Sam's eyes narrowed, "The same company that was founded by Denton Wellbon I?"

"The same one."

"You have more?"

"No."

"I don't get it. What are you telling me?"

"I'm telling you that it may be more than coincidence that you notice an apparent renewal of an old alleged underworld alliance only a few days before Melissa's nephew is killed…as you so aptly stated, most victims know their assailants."

Sam's mouth drew into a wry smile. "Weren't you the one who just a few short days ago reminded me that there was never any proof that the Atlantic Corporation, or whatever they call it now, was ever linked to the mob?"

Harry returned the smile. "I was."

"So how do you explain this change of opinion?"

"I don't. Let's just say that Senior FBI Agents can be on the job so long they too can have unsubstantiated gut feelings."

The two old friends once again turned their attention to the service under the tent.

After a few silent moments Harry spoke again. "How come you released the body?"

Sam snorted in disgust. "Let's just chalk it up to a bureaucratic snafu."

"Aren't you going to need it if you want to prove homicide?"

"I got the coroner's report that should be enough."

To Catch a Fox

"Those are powerful people down there Sam."

"I like a challenge."

The immediate family was seated on the padded folding chairs under the tent. Melissa Kensington, her sister, and Donald Kensington-Cramer's father sat stoically while the Pastor offered a few final words of comfort. Then he delivered the prayer, benediction, and dismissal. The Reverend McIntire came forward and clasped the hands of the family and departed. Melissa rose, turned and embraced her sister for a long moment. She then turned to Donald's father. The heavy-set man with pale blue watery eyes stood up and began to shift uncomfortably from one foot to another as Melissa turned her attention on him.

"Thank you for coming Ralph."

"He was my son."

"Yes, he was. It is unfortunate that you chose to stay away."

"We, we had differences…"

"Yes, I know. Great enough that I had to persuade him not to legally change his last name to his mother's maiden name after you fell out." She turned as if she was about to dismiss him, and then had second thoughts. She turned back to him, her face a mask. Then a look of resignation passed over her. "Well it matters not now. Come back with us to my penthouse. My cook is preparing lunch for the family and friends."

Ralph Cramer couldn't conceal the surprise he felt. "Thank you Melissa. Thank you, I'm, I'm grateful, very grateful."

Melissa turned and began receiving condolences from the small group of friends that she had invited to the private graveside service. When they were all but dispersed two men in dark suits approached. They had been standing just outside the circle of mourners. Melissa stiffened as she recognized them.

"Ms. Kensington, allow me to express my heartfelt sympathy." Trevor Mason extended his hand.

“May I add my sympathy to those sentiments also?” Abraham Rueben was accompanying Trevor.

“I don’t recall inviting either of you to this service.”

“Forgive us Melissa, we were too late for the open service at the church and we did want to express our support for you. We were hoping that you wouldn’t object.” Trevor allowed his unaccepted hand to drop to his side.

“I have no time for either of you. You are the two that are responsible for pushing Donald into such deep depression that he committed this tragic act.”

“Forgive me Ms. Kensington,” Abraham began, “but neither of us told Donald of our mutual business deal. If Donald became depressed it’s because you must have informed him that we had knowledge of the activities that he had engaged in. In addition, it was the two of you that decided to perpetrate that little escapade not us.”

“You’re saying that I’m responsible for my nephew’s death?” Melissa’s voice was but a hoarse whisper. Her throat had suddenly gone dry. She felt as if she had to push the words out.

“Now, now Melissa,” Trevor’s voice was low and soothing. “Let’s not make this any worse than it is. No one knows why a human being takes his own life. It is the culmination of a series of incidents that finally become too much for the individual to cope with.”

“Why are you really here?” Melissa had regained control of her vocal chords.

“As I just stated, our purpose is to give you our sincerest condolences.”

“And for what other purpose did you come?”

“We simply wish to express the heartfelt feeling that as tragic as Donald’s death is, this does not need to become even more tragic.”

Melissa’s stare had locked onto Trevor’s in a test of wills. Neither would flinch from this challenge. "What does that mean?" she inquired.

"It simply means that you don't need any more grief in your life Melissa and no one wants you to have to endure any more. Right now our business deal will move to fruition and none will be the wiser of what really took place during Donald's tenure with Wellbon-Smith" Trevor's voice remained quiet and comforting.

"In other words, I should be very careful so that nothing bad will happen to me."

"We truly wish you no harm Melissa. You've suffered enough." Abraham's eyes narrowed slightly. Not only did it make him seem more menacing but his ribs were still extremely tender and the mere act of speaking and moving about made them sore.

Trevor spoke again; "We appreciate you welcoming two uninvited guests Melissa. We will be going now and leave you to mourn with your family and friends. Please call me if there is anything that you need."

"I'll keep your phone number close at hand Trevor," she said sarcastically.

Trevor and Abraham nodded, turned and walked back toward Trevor's vehicle. To the immediate observers the entire conversation appeared to be like all the others that Melissa Kensington had engaged in that morning, family and friends expressing their grief and support. Melissa alone knew that it was all a thinly veiled threat

Unnoticed by the mourners the two police officers remained further up the slope among the trees. Sam Grabowski was watching the events through a small set of binoculars that he carried for just such a purpose. As the two men in dark suits got into their car Sam Grabowski handed the "glasses" to his friend Harry Siegfreid. "Know either of those guys?"

Harry gazed through the binoculars, "Huh, how about that."

"What?"

Harry dropped the glasses from his eyes and handed them back to his friend. "Maybe there is something to 'gut feelings' when veteran gumshoes have them."

"You know those guys?"

"One of them, the short guy is Abraham Rueben, big time mob lawyer. He was once the darling of the New York families until he took up with the Chicago boys. I'm surprised that he has the nerve to show his face in this city."

"Who's the other one?"

"Don't know." Harry was reaching into his inside pocket to get a pen and note pad. He scribbled a series of numbers on the pad. "I got the license plate number." Sam pulled out his cell phone, and called the number in as Harry held the pad so that he could read it. They watched the remaining mourners drive away as they waited for a response. Sam's phone buzzed and he snapped it open. "Yeah this is Grabowski…Okay, thanks."

Harry watched as his friend placed the phone back in his coat pocket. He knew better than to push Sam for information. After all it was Sam's investigation the FBI had no reason to be looking into a possible homicide, unless of course there was racketeering involved.

"Thought you told me that the mob was almost dead?"

"I told you that 'we won,' that they were only a ghost of what they once were."

"Well we may have been watching a ghost in action. That SUV is registered to the Atlantic Corporation. It's listed as having one Trevor Mason, president, as the primary user." Sam paused and smiled, "Denton Wellbon's old company, just like old times eh my friend?"

Harry smiled and started for his car. He looked back over his shoulder at his friend. "Remember, we could never prove any connection. Keep me informed. Okay?"

"You know it." replied Sam.

***

Tony Conocenti emerged from the jet way linking his just arrived flight and

To Catch a Fox

Chicago's O'Hara terminal. It was 8:00 AM Central time on a Monday morning. Tony had taken the earliest possible flight out of Harrisburg International Airport in Pennsylvania. Tony had coffee and the airline equivalent of breakfast on the flight. He was on a seven day four state sweep of the Fox flagship dealerships. His stops included Chicago, Los Angeles, San Francisco, Seattle, Atlanta and New York in that sequence. It wasn't the easiest or most efficient route to take, but he was making the visits in the order of difficulty. He had scheduled the most difficult visits first and the easiest last. His mission was to "sell" his companies midyear price increase to his largest dealerships. The exclusive "flags" accounted for a full 25% of Fox sales. Tony's success or failure on this trip would have a lot to do with the success of Fox in the last half of the fiscal year. Fox's fortunes during that period would almost certainly dictate the personal fortunes of Fox senior management. Tony took a deep breath and scanned the people waiting to greet the arrivals. He quickly spotted John Malicki's smiling face.

John approached and shook Tony's hand. "Thanks for coming here first Tony. You know that I'll have my hands full and I'll need all the support I can get."

"No problem John. We've both worked too long and hard to get a Fox presence in Chicago to allow one price increase to kill the deal. How soon can we meet Glenn and Mark?"

"I've set up a mid morning breakfast meeting at the Holiday Inn restaurant across from the Merchandise Mart. I know that you are staying there and all our boys have to do is walk across the sky way from their showroom in the Mart and take an elevator up."

"Sounds good, what time must we be there?"

"Ten o'clock. That gives us about two hours to get your luggage, drive into the city and check you in. We should be fine."

"Good. Excuse me just a minute John I must make a phone call before we pick up my baggage. Are you in your SUV?"

"Yeah I drove in last night. I'm staying in the Holiday too. I didn't want you to have to deal with taxi cabs with your tight schedule."

"Thanks John I appreciate that." Tony reached into his inside suit coat pocket and pulled out his cell phone. He punched in Blair McManus' phone number. After four rings he got her recorded message. 'Hi, this is Blair and you must be one of my very close friends or else you wouldn't have this number. I regret to inform you that my paper has sent me to the Coast on a special assignment and I won't be back until next Sunday. You may leave a message after the beep. Have a good one!" Damn! She didn't mention this when I called her two days ago! Thought Tony, then there was the beep. "Uh, hi Blair, this is Tony. It's Monday morning and I just landed in Chicago. I'm only here overnight and was hoping to see you. Guess that won't happen now. I assume that you check your messages so give me a call on my mobile phone when you get the chance. You know the number. I'll be out in L.A. tomorrow night and up in the Bay Area by Wednesday evening. If you're anywhere close maybe we could meet up somewhere and have dinner. Call me. Uh, this is Tony. Bye."

John Malicki was standing nearby pretending not to be eavesdropping. When Tony returned the phone to his jacket pocket John looked up; "Ready to go?" he asked.

"Yeah, let's get going. We have important business to accomplish." Tony hoped that his voice failed to convey the disappointment he felt.

***

William MacLode sat at the head of the highly polished cherry table in Fox Cabinetry's conference room. He had gathered about him his entire senior staff with the exception of Tony Conocenti. Tony was in Chicago at this very moment on the first stop of what promised to be a difficult assignment; to convince the Fox flagship dealers that the coming price increase was justified. Mac didn't envy Tony this task, but if anyone could be successful, it would be Tony. Mac would call Tony this evening and fill him in on the content of this meeting.

Mac looked around the room. He had just dropped a bombshell on them. He had made the proposal that as a management team, they should present an offer to the Atlantic Corporation for the purchase of Fox Cabinetry. There was a deathly silence in the room. Mac studied each of the faces closely. Carroll Brubaker had a rather strange but intrigued look on his face. David Elliott, arms folded across his chest, was staring intently at the ceiling. He appeared to be deep in thought. Mac sincerely hoped that David was considering the possibilities and not just avoiding his gaze. Dale Hershey was punching the keys of his financial calculator. He had begun this task shortly after he perceived the gist of what Mac was telling them. Sarah, the newest member of the group and the one that Mac knew the least about, had a quizzical look on her face. This must be heady stuff for a brand new young vice president who, in her short tenure was thrown into the fray of a union battle and now was being propositioned by the division president to risk not only her savings, but possibly her future as well.

Mac broke the silence. "It isn't necessary for you to answer now. However, if we are going to make a move it should be made fairly quickly. I want you to understand that I have been truthful with you. I honestly have not heard that Fox is for sale, but what I have just shared with you concerning the activities of the merger and acquisition experts Bertrum & Bertrum on behalf of Corporate is accurate…Do you have any questions or comments?"

Dale Hershey was the first to speak. "Your numbers look to be correct Mac." Dale was looking over his copy of the spreadsheets that Mac had provided for each of them. The numbers were the numbers that he and the Futures Unlimited people had come up with in Chicago. "I must also say that you are contributing far more than the remainder of us will be required to come up with."

"It's good that he is," said Carroll. "I suspect that if he didn't we would fall considerably short."

"This is my idea and therefore I should be the one to risk the most."

Silence again. Mac didn't know how to read his staff. This was totally new territory in their relationship. Then David Elliott spoke for the first time. "I think it sounds good Mac. It would sure be great to get Trevor Mason off our backs."

"Understand that the Futures people would be present on our board of directors and they will be just as insistent as Trevor on Fox showing a profit." Mac was glad to have positive signs from both Dale and David.

"I think that we all understand that, but the big difference as I see it is that the Futures people will be our partners and not our employers."

"That's correct David. When I was in Chicago they took great pains to emphasize that difference."

"There is another change that this would bring about," it was Dale speaking again. "If we succeed with our offer for the first time we, as part owners, would have to go personally to the financial community to acquire operating capital. At the present time the corporate financial people headed by John Hogg assume this task for all the divisions in the Atlantic Corporation. We all have to become sales people for our business plans. This can be time consuming and often demeaning."

"Dale's correct, for all of our complaining about corporate they do assume a great deal of the dirty work of business. This has freed us to concentrate on the day to day proposition of manufacturing product and selling it," Carroll chimed in for the first time. "However I think that everyone at this table is up to the task."

David Elliott grinned, "Tony always tells us that he's the world's premier salesman, we'll let him deal with the bankers." Everyone laughed and Mac was glad to see the silence broken with honest comments and a trace of excitement.

Sarah initiated her first comments, "I think it's a great idea and I'm all for it, but I'm afraid that at this early stage of my career I'm not in a solid enough financial position to join you in this venture."

Dale looked at the newest member of the team and smiled, "Don't worry Sarah, we'll figure out some way for you to participate as a shareholder. We're not about to disenfranchise the newest and perhaps brightest addition to this group." Hearty agreement was exhibited from everyone around the table, to Sarah's delight and embarrassment as she blushed slightly.

Carroll looked around the table. "I say we join our leader in this venture. I don't need any more time to think about it. Let's give him that assurance now, take the next couple days to examine our own financial situations, and meet again on Friday morning to nail down this offer. Is everyone in agreement?"

All gave enthusiastic comments of agreement and turned smiling faces toward Mac. Mac caught his breath. He had not expected this kind of sudden and overwhelming endorsement of his idea. He was momentarily speechless. "I…I don't know what to say, thank you."

"You don't have to thank us," replied Carroll. "I think I speak for nearly everyone at this table when I say that over the years you've been right in your direction far more often than you've been wrong. That's why we feel that you've earned your position as our leader. It goes beyond the mere fact that corporate has placed you in that position. We're with you on this."

Sarah spoke again, "I realize that I haven't been here with all of you to share the problems of the past, but you have all made me feel very welcome and a part of this group. I want to be a part of this next phase of Fox Cabinetry."

Dale looked at Mac with a mischievous grin on his face. "Make certain that Conocenti comes along for the ride with us."

"I'm almost certain that he will, but his impending divorce may complicate things for him," replied Mac.

"He'll find a way," commented David. All nodded in agreement.

With that Mac rose, thanked everyone again and set the time for the meeting on Friday morning. After the group had filed out of the room, Mac sank into his chair again and began to contemplate the full impact of the events that he had just set in motion. For a moment fear gripped the normally stoic CEO. There was no turning back now he thought.

***

Trevor Mason swirled the Scotch whiskey around in his glass as he contemplated Abraham Ruben silently. It was late at night and they were in Trevor's luxurious office in the Wellbon – Smith Building in midtown Manhattan. Ruben waited for the implication of his last words to have their full impact. He was seated across the massive desk from Trevor. His own glass of Scotch, as yet untouched, was sitting on the edge of Trevor's desk. Without speaking Trevor turned his chair to the credenza behind him, opened a drawer and removed a paper napkin. He passed the napkin to Rueben and Abraham knew that he was expected to place it under his glass so that Trevor's highly polished desk would not have to suffer the indignity of a water mark. Abraham smiled to himself; he secretly loved to irritate the many foibles of his egotistical client.

Trevor concentrated his gaze again on his diminutive lawyer. "Let me see the signed commitment papers that you acquired today."

Abraham reached into his inside breast pocket and removed a document. He passed the paper across the desk. Trevor took it and put on his reading glasses. He scanned the document and a wide grin spread over his face. "Do you realize what this means?"

"Yes we need only one more commitment."

Trevor laughed. "You're wrong Abe we're looking good but not that good. There are four, but three of them are long time institutional investors that should be easy to get a commitment from and the other is Denton's mother. We're almost there."

"I must caution you that these last signatures could be the most difficult to obtain."

"Nonsense, didn't you hear me? I said one of them is Denton's mother."

"My point exactly, haven't you noticed that Denton is becoming more independent by the day?"

"Relax Abe. Denton is just beginning to feel like he's really going to move into his father's old chair. Remember, we're in control, we know about Denton's past secrets. When faced with those revelations Denton will convince his mother to sign our commitment. What about the other prospects?"

"Correction Trevor, the other prospect is singular."

"What are you talking about? There are three institutions and Denton's mother."

"As it turns out boss the three institutional investors are held by an individual."

"A single individual holds them? I don't remember any individual's name connected with those institutions on the list that I gave you, much less a single individual that controlled all three institutions."

"There wasn't any name on the list in connection with the institutions but apparently the original purchaser set up three funds as investments. It appears that he is a citizen of the British Commonwealth, or so said the lawyer that contacted Wellbon-Smith. He was also pretty shrewd at avoiding Her Majesty's taxman. These are all "off shore" funds in relation to the British Empire. Apparently he has totally ignored these funds until recently. Last week Wellbon-Smith was informed by a lawyer from a firm in London that from now on they will represent those shares which are held by the funds."

"Who is this individual?"

"We don't know."

"How can we not know?"

"The shares were sold to the institutions by none other than Denton Wellbon II."

"Really," Trevor began to feel uneasy. "You think this is a problem?"

Ruben was thoughtful for a moment. "I don't know. It could work to our advantage. After years of neglect, the respective funds never even sent in a proxy vote, this law firm has been assigned this task for some reason. It just could be that they intend to cash in. Maybe they want to settle quickly and walk away with cash."

Trevor sighed, "Up until now every shareholder has been reasonably predictable. That's why we selected them. Now this element of the unknown crops up."

Abraham Rueben finally took a sip of his Scotch. "I don't see this as the threat that you do. What I see is one individual or group to deal with in place of the three that we expected."

"But we expected three institutions that had a history of disinterest in these shares. Now we suddenly have an individual or a single firm that is suddenly taking notice to the shares that they own." Trevor paused in thought. "How many shares do these 'funds' own together?"

Rueben hesitated, "35000 shares."

"Only Denton's mother owns more. Together they are nearly equal to the single largest shareholder in the corporation."

"Remember we're dealing with all three funds combined."

"That's right… Well this may work, how long have the shares been in these funds?"

"Since 1964."

"That was before the last official valuation. Let's see, thirty-five years ago, what must he, for argument's sake we'll assume that this is a 'he' we are dealing with. What must he have paid?"

"Fifteen dollars per share, I checked the records."

"That's $525,000 thousand dollars! Even in 1964 the shares were selling for more than twice that price. How did he buy in at that price?"

"Actually the Board of Directors was selling shares at $75 per share in '64."

"So how did this investor purchase shares at $15?"

"Upon special hand written order from Denton Wellbon II. I have a copy here."

Trevor Mason snatched the photocopy from Rueben's hand and looked it over for a long moment. "No explanation. Not even the name of the buyer. Just an order to sell three blocks of shares to three funds listed as: Southern Cross Investments, Caribbean Funds and Commonwealth Fund for the price of $15 per share." Trevor gulped down the last of his Scotch, then rose from his chair, moved to the wet bar and poured himself another. He offered the bottle to Rueben who declined. "Damn Abe, Denton's old man must have been paying off a debt. It's anybody's guess who we may have to deal with here." Trevor leveled his gaze at Rueben. "It's also anybody's guess as to how dangerous this investor is. We know that Denton's father and grandfather would have dealt with the devil himself if they thought that there was a profit to be made!"

Rueben turned in his chair so that he could meet Mason's gaze more directly. "You're right but let's not forget our last venture together in Chicago. We have muscle behind us if we need it."

"I know." Trevor was reluctant to acknowledge this fact even to Abe Rueben. He preferred to remain ignorant of the methods that his lawyer sometimes employed. After the grave site visit to Milissa Kensington, Trevor wanted no more knowledge concerning her nephew's death either.

Abe took another sip of his drink. "Are there any other share holders that we could squeeze?"

"No, the others are loyal to the corporation and besides, we require these last large blocks of stock that these funds and Denton's mother represent." Trevor paused in thought and gazed out the window at the city skyline.

Rueben decided it was time to comment. "Trevor, I can do the math. Since we are actually dealing with only one investor with these off shore funds, assuming we have Denton's vote we are down to two signatures: the mysterious 'Limey' and Denton's mother."

"I never believed that you were mathematically impaired Abe, what's your point?"

"We only need one of them to gain control of the board. You know how I feel about Denton's dependability when it comes to signing his mother. If we get the Brit's signature we don't need Mrs. Wellbon."

Trevor continued to stare out of the window. Denton was becoming more independent. He still wanted both signatures for security, just in case someone else got cold feet between now and the annual meeting. But if he could secure this one mystery owner's support he would only need Denton's vote and could avoid having to deal with his mother. The vote would be closer than Trevor planned, but they could still prevail. Independent attitude or not Trevor remained confident of young Denton's support.

"Without Mary Wellbon's vote we still need Denton plus Carlton Smith. We always assumed Carlton would vote with Mary like he always does. Without Mary we need Smith for a majority."

Ruben smiled, "We have more on both Denton and Carlton then we have on Denton's mother. She's older and richer now. She may not care about her family's reputation."

"She cares about her son. Okay, call this lawyer that's running these funds and offer him $100."

"That's the price that Wellbon-Smith bought the stock back from investors when Denton II died. Do you really think he'll settle for that?"

"Let's try. He bought at rock bottom; he's going to make far more in capital gains then any of the other investors. Maybe, just maybe this lawyer will think that is reward enough, especially if he's in a hurry to collect his fee."

"You're the boss. I'll have to go to London to meet this lawyer."

"Go to Hell if you have to Abe, just return with those signed commitments."

Abraham Rueben rose from the chair. He winced slightly as his ribs were still very sore. Trevor Mason had already returned to the papers on his desk and never noticed. Rueben turned and left the office without a word.

As soon as the door closed behind Rueben, Trevor picked up his phone and dialed Denton's extension. He knew that Denton had already left for the night, but he wanted to leave a voice mail for him. "Denton, this is Trevor. I need to see you in my office first thing in the morning. I need to probe your memory. Thanks." Trevor hung up the phone and settled back in his chair. Good old Denton. He always checked his voice mail before he left home in the morning. Trevor was still confident that he could control Denton and by extension Denton's mother if need be. His thoughts returned to this unexpected wrinkle. However, if Abe was successful in London there would be no need to get any more signatures. They could blackmail the remainder into voting with them. He was so close to realizing his dream! He wouldn't let anything stop him now.

***

Crystal Harrison rode silently in the back seat of the cab. It glided along interstate I-195 leaving Baltimore Washington International Airport behind and heading for Baltimore. She was filled with apprehension. Not because the man that she knew as Mr. Smith had warned her against this very action, she was not concerned about losing the money in her trust. Indeed she had not touched a cent of it. After long consideration she decided that the guardians of "her" money could do with it as they pleased, it was more important to her to follow the trail of family history to the end. No matter what or who she found at the end of that trail. The morning was crystal clear and just a little on the cool side for this time of year. A subtle reminder that there were not many days left in this final summer of the 20th Century. The cab turned north onto I 95 and finally selected an exit off the Beltway that led toward the suburbs near Glen Bernie.

Crystal's position as a local news anchor had provided many connections to people through the network. Because she was easy to like, she quickly made friends with other anchors around the country. The Baltimore anchor recommended a local private detective that had retired from the Baltimore Police force. With the rather scanty information that she was able to give him he checked birth records, brazenly bribed a few people and came up with the names of a retired couple that lived in Glen Bernie. But it was not as easy as it sounded.

"There's something strange here Crystal," the detective told her. "This is more than just people wanting to protect their privacy. Someone had removed your mother's birth records from the local files. The birth records that I traced from your birth certificate indicated that your grandparents on your mother's side were deceased. However, with a little checking I discovered that those names while truly deceased never had any children. The records were falsified. If I hadn't known one of the people in the county records department personally, I would have never been able to locate your grandparents. I put a lot of pressure on my friend, based on the information that you gave me suggesting that your mother's parents lived in Baltimore. My friend discovered the records, 'misplaced' in the wrong archives. We had to bribe a courthouse supervisor to pull some strings and allow us to search the archives."

"How can that be? Could they have been misfiled by mistake?"

"Files are misplaced everyday but when you combine that with the other falsified documents and the story that you related to me, I think it's more than a coincidence."

Crystal had to agree. Who was her real father anyway? How much power and influence did he have?

To Catch a Fox

The cab came to a halt in front of a tidy white Cape Cod home in a middle class neighborhood. Crystal paid the driver and slowly got out. The cab pulled away and left her standing on the curb. The lawn was neatly manicured and Crystal could see colorful flower gardens in the back yard. Suddenly she was gripped by fear, did she really want to pursue this? She briefly considered turning and leaving, but then she gathered up her courage and walked up to the front door. After all she had come this far, she may as well discover the truth, whatever that truth may entail. She rang the doorbell. After a moment Crystal heard shuffling inside and her heart began to race. Soon the door opened a crack and a small kindly looking white haired lady peaked curiously out through it.

"Yes, may I help you?"

"Perhaps you can," Crystal's voice quivered. "Is your name Alice Johnson?"

"Yes."

"Is your husband named Howard?"

"Yes he is. Who are you?"

"I'm Crystal Harrison, Mary Johnson-Harrison's daughter."

The little white haired lady placed her hand over her mouth. "Oh my," was all she said.

"I believe that Mary Johnson, my mother, was your daughter."

The little lady opened the door, "You best come inside she said."

***

Tony Conocenti sat alone in a restaurant and bar on Pier 39 on the San Francisco Bay. In the distance he could see Alcatraz but his mind was not thinking about the old prison turned tourist spot. Yesterday he arrived in L.A. after a tense albeit successful meeting with Glenn Glen of the Fox of Chicago showroom. After much discussion, he and John Melicki were able to convince Glenn that the midyear Fox price increase was justified and that it would in no way hinder his ability to make sales. Tony viewed this as the first and the most difficult of his meetings. John and Tony had been extremely pleased at the results. In addition, it appeared that the Chicago showroom would be open soon after the first of the year. They parted discussing plans for a "New Millennium Grand Opening."

To Tony's surprise his meeting in L.A. with Fred Balderson was much more difficult. Fred was a businessman, unlike Glenn Glen and Mark Markel who were first and foremost designers. Fred brought his accountant along to the meeting that Ralph Sinclair, Fox's Regional Sales Manager for the West Coast set up at Melrose Place. Melrose Place was a very chic restaurant on Melrose Avenue and was not to be confused with the TV show of the same name.

Murray, the only name that Fred ever used when referring to his accountant, brought along a brief case full of spread sheets designed to prove to Fox management that this price increase would not only damage the profit picture at Fox of L.A. but may even eventually force the showroom out of business. Tony and Ralph were prepared for these arguments as they had heard them each time that a price increase occurred. This time however, probably because the increase was a surprise, Balderson and Murray were harder to convince. In fact they were downright adamant that this increase was intolerable.

The meeting began over drinks during "happy hour," continued through dinner followed by one of the restaurant's famous dessert concoctions, and finally concluded with after dinner drinks and coffee. By this time Tony had convinced Fred that several new door styles that Fox planned to introduce along with some "other room" individual furniture piece designs, would add sufficient value to the entire line to justify the increase in the eyes of the consumer. Tony brought along a portfolio of these designs that "had not yet been seen by any other dealer, but as Fred's opinion was valued by Fox management Tony was permitted to show them to Fred only!" Fred was visibly pleased by this revelation. Tony also pointed out that the average consumer made this type of purchase only three times in a lifetime, five times for the average Fox consumer. Therefore the buyer had no idea what Fox was selling for yesterday when he walked through the showroom door tomorrow. Tony also promised to honor any jobs that Fred had in "quotes" at this moment, providing that he sent a list of the names to David Elliott first thing in the morning. Tony knew that Mac would give him royal hell for that arrangement. By rights Tony now had to make the same offer to the other flagship dealers unless he could justify compensatory pricing. Which he could not! As the "flags" sold far more volume than the other dealers, Tony did not have to make the same offer to them. He could simply set the volume necessary to “earn” that consideration at the level of sales of the smallest Flag Ship Dealer there by shielding Fox from a series of lawsuits. Possibly he could get away with making the offer’s “floor” the exact sales figure that the L.A. flag was hitting.; thereby eliminating all the flags except L.A., Atlanta and New York. Tony wasn’t certain. He would have to discuss this with Dale Hershey as soon as time permitted.

The meetings ended on a high note with Fred committing to a 5% increase in sales for the second half of the year. Murray remained skeptical, but then Tony and Ralph had never seen Murray in any other state of mind. They all had another celebratory drink to toast the continued future success of Fox of L.A. and Fox Custom Cabinetry. Tony graciously declined to visit Fred’s excellent showroom in the Los Angeles Design Center citing his and Ralph’s commitment to meet with Bonnie and Brad Klein tomorrow up in San Francisco. Bonnie and Brad were the owners of Fox of San Francisco.

Fred understood that Tony and Ralph would be making the same pitch to the Kleins as he just received. He did take pains to underscore that he truly expected to be the only Fox dealer to have an advanced showing of the new styling. Tony assured him that he had the exclusive preview, and truly hoped that it would not be necessary to use that tactic again.

Early the next morning Tony and Ralph Sinclair caught a commuter flight out of LAX for San Francisco. As the MD180 climbed out over the Pacific the steward served the first class passengers their choice of Starbucks coffee, orange juice, or a Bloody Mary. Tony chose the coffee and Ralph ordered the orange juice although if the boss hadn’t been with him he would have selected the Bloody Mary. Hell, if the boss hadn’t been with him he would be back in coach so he supposed that it all balanced out.

They were on the ground at SFO, San Francisco International Airport, by 9:30 AM and soon had their rental car headed for the design district. Instead of the meetings getting easier as Tony had expected, the resistance seemed to be getting stiffer. Brad and Bonnie were relatively new to the ranks of Fox dealers. They were “standard” Fox dealers for two years before Ralph Sinclair recommended them for exclusive flagship status. Fox defined “standard” as a multi-line dealer. Flagship dealers were exclusive to Fox.

Bonnie was the designer and was responsible for the showroom's sales force while Brad supervised the installation of the cabinetry. Bonnie made the business decisions while Brad sort of went along. Bonnie was incensed. Ralph had told her that Fox "never" raised prices more than once per year and in her experience with Fox they never had until now! If this is the way Fox kept their commitments, "she might as well be a dealer for any of the other lines!"

Tony explained that Ralph hadn't deceived her but this was an extraordinary situation. Bonnie responded that she believed that the only thing extraordinary about this situation was the desire for Fox management and their corporate "fathers" in the Atlantic Corporation to "line their pockets with excess profits!" Bonnie then demanded to know just exactly what the extraordinary circumstances were. Tony hesitated and glanced at Ralph. Ralph's round "good fellow" head moved back and forth ever so slightly indicating that he preferred that his clients were not aware of the union threat. Ralph was a short heavy set albeit muscular individual. He had come up through the ranks in the Fox Customer Service Department before being promoted to the position of Regional Sales Manager for the West Coast. Tony possessed a deep respect for Ralph's ability to judge people and situations.

"Nothing could be further from the truth Bonnie," Tony replied. "I'll tell you exactly what the extraordinary circumstances are." Ralph Sinclair tensed wondering if Tony had missed his ever so subtle signal.

"The truth is Bonnie, we in management made a mistake." Tony let the impact of his words sink in. It was not often that senior management in this or any industry ever acknowledged a mistake to their customers.

"We cut back the level of benefits that we offered to our employees. We thought that they might appreciate larger increases in their hourly rates over the next few years. We were wrong."

"Whatever made you think that?"

"It's irrelevant really, but since you asked, the dip in the average age of our work force. We've experienced a large number of people reaching retirement age of late and we thought, incorrectly as it turns out, that we could continue our high level of appeal to young recruits by offering higher starting wages. The only way that we could do that was by cutting back slightly on benefits and our contribution to their 401 K plans."

"I thought that you offered the highest level starting rates in the industry?"

"We do, but we wanted to have an even greater edge."

"What made you realize that you were wrong?"

"Our employees, let us know in no uncertain terms that while they always desire higher wages, we were more than competitive and that even the youngest of their group came to us because of the superior benefits. In fact they felt that if any change was to be made it should be to increase the benefit package rather than the hourly rate. We heard and we reacted. As we had no desire to retract the larger than usual hourly increase that we had already awarded them, we restored the benefits to their original level and allowed them to keep the raise. That's the price that we paid for our mistake."

"So now you expect the Fox dealers to pay for your mistake."

"The reality Bonnie is that the customer pays for everything! However, look what this will do for you the dealer. Fox now has by far and away the best wage and benefit package in the industry. That means that we will maintain our extremely low 1% annual turnover rate. Everyone else in the industry experiences an employee turnover rate of 10 to 15% or greater. That's one of the reasons why you can guarantee your customers the consistent Fox level of quality that you and they expect and deserve. Must I remind you that our annual returned goods and allowances numbers are consistently less than 1.5%? That's a low for the entire high end industry."

Ralph Sinclair was both relieved and pleased. Bonnie was softening; he could see it in her eyes. Tony was making progress and he was accomplishing it without bringing up the threat of unionization. Ralph was uncertain how Fox's battle with the unions would play out here on the "left coast." Back east there would be a fear of a loss of quality if the work force unionized, but here there could be a lot of sympathy for the plight of the working individual. Tony was scoring on two fronts; first admitting a mistake and second demonstrating concern for the workingman and workingwoman.

Tony too sensed that he was winning Bonnie over. "Now Bonnie allow me to explain how Fox is going to help you pay for an advertising campaign that will not only promote your dealership, but also Fox quality and the reasons for the continuation of that quality through a satisfied and dedicated work force."

"You're going to assist me in additional advertising?"

"That's right, with a co-op advertising plan designed specifically for you. We will probably introduce it to all of our flagship dealers after the first of the year, but because of your meteoric rise in the dealer network, we wanted you to have the benefit of it first!"

"Wow, how about that Brad an advertising co-op program just for us?"

"Sounds good to me honey anytime that the factory offers to help with our expenses it's fine with me."

Tony continued, "Of course Bonnie we will expect you to be the primary salesperson for this program with a presentation to the other flags at our first group meeting next year."

"Oh, my, yes of course Tony. I would be honored."

Ralph smiled. There was no limit to the ego stroking that Tony was capable of utilizing in tough situations. From this point on it was all easy conversation. They toured the Klein's beautifully appointed showroom. Next came lunch, paid for by Tony and the factory, and an afternoon filled with planning the Klein's fall advertising campaign. Tony made several phone calls to Fox's advertising agency in Philadelphia for suggestions, pricing, and print schedules.

All this finally brought Tony to the restaurant on Pier 39. Tony managed to contact Blair after arriving on the West Coast. His plan was to meet her this evening at this restaurant for a relaxing evening before he left for Seattle in the morning. Blair sounded truly disappointed as she informed him that she would have to remain in L.A. for the remainder of the week to complete the interviews for the article on which she was working.

"Oh Tiger, I'm sorry. Believe me I'd like nothing more than to meet you for dinner up in Frisco, but I'll be meeting with one of the subjects that I'm interviewing that evening. When will you be back in Chicago? I'll be home by the end of the week to file my story."

"Sorry doll, I'm off to Seattle next and then New York and Atlanta. After that I'll be heading home to the factory in Goodville. Things are pretty critical in my business life right now."

"Can you tell me about it? Is it good or bad?"

"Not over the phone and it could go either way I'm afraid."

"I wish I could be with you to give you support." Her voice was soft and sounded genuinely concerned.

"Not to worry, I'm a survivor, I'll be okay."

"You sure Tiger? You sound tired."

"Yes I'm sure and yes I am tired, but I'm okay. It's nice that you're concerned."

"Of course I'm concerned!" she paused, "You're the only Tiger I have."

"Really?"

"Yes really silly! I wish I could talk longer, but I've got to go. Duty calls."

"I can understand that. I know all about duty." Replied Tony

"Keep in touch Tiger."

"I will." And with that she was gone.

Now Tony sat forlornly in the restaurant where he had planned to spend the evening with Blair. The problem was that he was waiting for Ralph Sinclair to return from the men's room. How romantic he thought. Ralph returned and seated himself. He nodded toward the television that was mounted above the nearby bar. "Not much on tonight. No sports, only some motion picture awards dinner."

"Doesn't matter, let's order." Tony motioned for the waiter to come to their table.

After the two had ordered and the waiter returned with a carafe of wine that Ralph had selected, the conversation inevitably turned to their meetings of the past two days. "Boss you certainly know how to bring reluctant, no I have to say rebellious, dealers around to your way of thinking."

"I've always said that this job really doesn't require a degree in marketing but rather a degree in psychology," was Tony's reply. "By the way, I truly hope that it's our way of thinking and not just my way."

Ralph smiled. "Field sales people always want better quality, faster delivery and if possible lower prices. We never hope for a price increase."

Tony returned the smile. He liked Ralph. At first he had resisted David Elliott's recommendation of Ralph to replace the previous West Coast rep. Tony had to fire Ralph's predecessor for lack of performance, but since Ralph had taken up residence on the "Coast" the territory was not only growing but also thriving. The only thing that Ralph did that slightly annoyed Tony was play very close to the vest. The answer Ralph just gave him really didn't say to Tony that he was 100% in agreement with the new pricing. Whether he was or wasn't really didn't matter. Ralph had expressed his reservations back at the sales meeting in Goodville, but once out in the field Ralph would support company policy. Indeed, Tony had received enthusiastic support from Ralph at both of the meetings they held these last two days.

"There's one lucky dog," Ralph was saying.

"What?" Tony returned from his thoughts.

"Dirk Andersen," Ralph was pointing toward the awards show on the TV. "Not only is he nominated for an Oscar, has a top show on TV, but check out that babe on his arm."

Tony turned to stare at the television. There was a ruggedly handsome young man waving to the cheering crowd as he entered the awards dinner with Blair McManus on his arm! Tony almost choked on his wine.

"Now there's a broad that you wouldn't mind warming your bed on a cold evening!" continued Ralph. Ralph had never met Blair, and was not even aware that Tony was dating again.

The announcer was commenting that no one on the crew or set knew who this glamorous mystery lady was that Dirk had selected to accompany him. Since Dirk's breakup with his second wife he hadn't been seen with anyone. Everyone was speculating as to whether this was his new love. Tony poured himself another glass of wine and took what could only be described as a large gulp. He felt as if a sledgehammer had just struck him in the pit of his stomach. He was afraid he might be sick.

CHAPTER 14

Abraham Rueben sat in a quaint little English Pub on Harrow Street in London. His brow was furrowed in thought. He had just ended his meeting with a lawyer from a local firm. The young man referred to himself and the firm as barristers. Rueben got the distinct impression that the young man who met him was a very junior member of the firm. It was very evident that neither this individual nor the firm that he represented was prepared for the offer that Abraham was making to the respective funds that were their clients. Indeed, it seemed that the young man's primary purpose was to reiterate that their firm now represented the joint funds and would be taking a more active interest in the reports issued by Wellbon-Smith. The young man seemed puzzled as to why Rueben had made the trip at all. Upon hearing the proposal the young lawyer / barrister became noticeably nervous and excused himself. Abraham guessed that he sought distance from the table where they were consuming pints of ale so that a call to his superiors could not be overheard.

When he returned he relayed his instructions to Rueben. "I'm to ask you if you have a written proposal in your possession."

"I do" was Abe's reply.

"I'm to take it with me and our firm will notify you after we review the documents with the principle."

"How long will that take? I'm not planning to be in your country for more than a couple of days."

"Oh dear, I'm afraid that we may not have an answer for you for several weeks."

"Several weeks?"

"Yes, our client is out of the country on business just now and may not return during that length of time."

"Surely you can contact him wherever he may be?"

"Perhaps, I'm not really certain. I only know that the administrator of these funds is very secretive. I don't know him myself in fact I've never met him or talked to him personally."

"I want to talk to someone in your firm that has met him and is familiar with his preferences."

"That may not be possible as I'm not certain that any of the partners or their associates have ever met him."

"You've never met your client?"

"I certainly haven't and I'm told that no one else in the firm has either" The young man's voice quivered slightly reflecting his heightened level of tension.

Abraham Rueben took a deep breath and exhaled noisily, attempting to convey his annoyance and disdain in one efficient action. As he observed his counterpart glancing about as if he was looking for an exit through which to escape, he wondered if the gesture was lost on him. "Look, I'll be in London for one more complete day. Take this proposal back to your boss and tell him this is extremely important and confidential and that I must have an answer by tomorrow at five o'clock. I expect you to hand deliver it personally. Do you understand?"

"Yes sir."

Rueben removed a large sealed manila envelope from his briefcase. Pulling a pen from his inside jacket pocket he scribbled a brief message on it. As he handed it over to the young man his voice became menacing, "I have written on the flap that this envelope was sealed by me. If the recipient, whom I assume will be your superior, discovers that it has been opened then he will have to assume that he has a nosey junior partner in his firm."

"Oh I'm not a, what did you call it, a junior partner sir I'm merely an assoc…"

"I don't give a rat's ass as to what you are! Just do as I tell you!"

"Yes sir."

Rueben pulled a business card from his wallet and wrote the name of the hotel in which he was staying along with the phone and his room number on the back. He passed it to the young barrister. "This is where your boss may contact me." The young man took the card and stuffed it into his pocket. They sat there staring at each other for a long moment.

"What are you waiting for? Go!" growled Rueben. Without another word the young man cradled the envelope in his arm, gathered up his briefcase and beat a hasty exit through the pub's front door. Then he was gone leaving Abraham in his present mental funk.

The proposal that he had sent along was the standard that he and Trevor Mason had been utilizing for all of the stock acquisition deals to date. It was perfectly legitimate, but left a few tantalizing questions to be answered. This was designed to open the door for an "off the record" conversation. Should any of this come to light before or during the annual shareholders meeting, both he and Trevor had perfectly plausible and more important legal explanations for the subtle lack of detail on some critical points, not to mention an explanation for the existence of the documents to begin with. Wellbon-Smith as an entity was never mentioned on these preliminary proposals, although it was obvious to the recipients whose stock the proposal was referring. In spite of his apparent irritation, not being able to meet with a more informed member of the law firm was not the primary reason for his impatience. The prospect of not being able to return to the States with an answer was. Rueben wanted desperately to wind up this phase of the takeover. Trevor's assurances notwithstanding, Abraham did not want to have to depend on the current Denton Wellbon to complete this deal by delivering his mother's proxy signed and sealed. He seriously doubted that Denton could deliver the old lady. The problem in circumventing Denton by getting this mysterious investor to agree to sell his or her holdings was that unlike the previous individuals that Abe approached, there was no "secret sin" to threaten to expose. There was only the unanswered question of why Denton's father had sold the stock to this individual at such a sweetheart price. If he knew the answer to that he may have the leverage required to force another agreement. He lacked that answer and it placed him at a great disadvantage.

Abraham signaled the waiter that he required a refill of ale. When that was accomplished he decided to remain for dinner. "Give me one of those meat pies that you have on your menu."

"Which of them would you prefer sir?" Inquired the waiter in what only could be described as a Cockney accent.

"I'll have the lamb please."

"Very well sir."

As the waiter left to place the order with the kitchen, Rueben reflected on the type of contingencies required if they were forced to rely on Denton and he failed to deliver. The secret contracts that he had put together were legal and binding. If they failed to acquire the necessary votes to complete the takeover, he and Trevor would not be able to make good on their payoff commitments. In this situation they would not be liable to be charged with fraud. The purchase of the stock was contingent upon them being able to control enough shares to take over the company. Once they had the votes they could complete the takeover and sell off enough companies to meet the payoff. If they could not acquire the requisite number of shares the contracts to purchase were null and void. However, if they failed people might question their tactics. Most of the shareholders who had agreed to sell would be disgruntled at the failure to turn huge profits, but would maintain silence; not wanting Mason and he to reveal their dirty laundry. Trevor would probably be dismissed for violating the corporate by-laws by secretly negotiating to purchase stock and Rueben himself might be called before the New York Bar for ethics violations in aiding and participating in Trevor's scheme. But that was not a violation of civil law. It was however unacceptable to him to risk losing his license to practice law in the State of New York. That alone made failure of this project unacceptable.

***

Crystal Harrison sat in the rental car across the street from Andy's Diner near the Fulton Fish Market in New York City. It was six fifteen in the morning. She left Baltimore late the night before and drove up Interstate I-95 to New York. She had no sleep from the time she left the Johnson household until now. Her visit with her mother's parents Howard and Alice Johnson, she still had trouble thinking of them as her grandparents, was emotional and informative. It was becoming clear that her mother had led a very secretive life. Howard and Alice had never met her real father. As with Crystal herself, they claimed his true identity was unknown to them. They did know more than she did however and it painted a frightening picture.

Howard was in the final stages of a losing battle with colon cancer. He was already under the care of Hospice volunteers. It was hoped, but was in no way certain, that he could spend his final days at home. Alice took Crystal into the bedroom that had become Howard's world. Crystal thought that the room had the odor of death in it. It smelled of medicines, hospital equipment and the stale odor that the human body gives off when a sponge bath is all that can be administered. When Alice explained to him who Crystal was, Howard broke down and cried. Crystal was so overwhelmed that she found herself hugging him and sitting at his bedside holding the frail hand of the grandfather she had never met. She came prepared to be angry. Why hadn't they made some attempt to contact her? Why hadn't they been available as her mother struggled to raise her only child and apparently their only grandchild? But now, confronted with the ailing presence of this sobbing old man Crystal's anger dissipated. She decided to give these people the benefit of the doubt.

Alice told Crystal of her mother; Mary Johnson was an attractive, bright young woman with above average grades in high school. "I'm not just saying that because I'm her mother mind you, others said the same." She was very active as a cheerleader, worked on the staff of both the school newspaper and the yearbook and was extremely popular.

"She was a good girl and a joy as a daughter," said Howard. He squeezed Crystal's hand weakly and then began to cry softly again.

At this point in her reflections Alice paused and turned with a worried look to her husband. Howard nodded his head to her, "Tell her everything 'mother,' she deserves to know. They can't do anything more to me now than what this cursed disease is doing." With that Alice seemed to concur and continued with her narrative. Maybe because Mary was so popular, especially with the boys, they should have seen trouble coming. But Mary had always been truthful with them and they trusted her completely. During Mary's senior year she began dating another local boy, Foster Harrison, "Your father."

"No!" Crystal's response was much sharper than she had intended. "I'm sorry, but Foster vehemently denies that. That's part of the reason that I am here now. I want to know the truth."

"Tell her everything mother!" Howard raised his voice as much as he was able.

"Yes dear I intend to, but even with all his faults and even though he walked out on Mary and Crystal, Foster was more of a father to her than her biological father ever was." There was an aspect that Crystal in her anger with Foster had never considered. After an awkward pause Alice continued with her story. It became apparent to Crystal that her grandparents, unknown to her, had been in contact with her mother far more than she was aware.

"Wait, wait," Crystal interrupted. "Why did my mother tell me that she was an orphan?"

Alice pulled a tissue from the box near the bedside and began to dab her eyes. "Your mother was protecting both you and us."

Crystal closed her eyes and slowly shook her head, "Explain that please."

With that Alice turned to Howard. "Tell her everything mother," was Howard's only reply.

Alice launched into the story of how Crystal's mother was on a four-day high school field trip to New York City and was invited to a college frat party even though she was still in high school. Several weeks later they found out about that night when their daughter tearfully informed them that she was pregnant to a college boy that she met at the party. From there the story moved to the terrifying contact with the emissary from the boy's father, the revelation about Howard's stealing from the bank where he worked and the promise from the emissary that his debt to the bank would be paid and if he and his family kept quiet about all of this Howard would never have to go to jail and would always have a job. "You see dear," said Alice. "The boy's father was afraid that we would press charges because the boy was over twenty-one and Mary was under-aged. That was statutory rape. Right or wrong, we were afraid. We traded one jail sentence for another." By now tears were streaming down Alice's face. "We made the deal as a family. Mary agreed to the arrangement along with us. Both families kept their word, ours and the boy's."

Crystal had been silently listening to all of this. Now she chose to speak. "May I ask a question? Even though it would have meant that I would never have been born, did you ever consider abortion?"

"Our family did not then and does not now believe in abortion. While this was legally rape, Crystal was consenting so in our minds this was not rape. The man that the boy's father sent made it clear that if there was a pregnancy abortion wasn't an option."

"If there was a pregnancy? You already knew that my mother was pregnant."

Alice glanced at Howard, "We never revealed that fact to the man that your father's family sent. We were afraid of him and thought that if he knew of this you may be in danger or your real father might try to take you away from our daughter. Your mother had already told us that she was going to give birth and raise you. We all thought this to be best."

Crystal found this piece of information intriguing; "Then you do know who my real father is?"

Howard and Alice stared at each other for a long moment. Howard shook his head at Alice and spoke. "No, no we only had contact with the man that the boy's father sent. We never talked with the boy or his father."

Crystal thought about this for a moment. Things weren't making sense. She decided to make another inquiry. "Was this man, who represented the boy's father, a large heavy set man, Caucasian, dark complexion with a large round face and dark curly hair?"

Alice and Howard glanced at each other before Alice spoke. Both looked puzzled. "Why no dear, when we first met him he had long sandy colored hair that was pulled back in a ponytail. He was Caucasian yes, but his skin was fair. He was very muscular but I wouldn't call him heavy set. He had a large rather unkempt moustache."

Howard began to speak, but then began a coughing spell that appeared to cause him great pain. When the coughing subsided he began again. "We saw him one more time years later. Apparently the boy's father died and this gentleman came to make certain that we understood that our agreement remained in force. We had no clue that the man had died so we assured him that we intended to keep our side of the bargain."

"We didn't want him to strike your Grandfather again like he did the first time," interjected Alice.

Howard nodded his head in agreement. "I was very much afraid of him. He was an extremely violent man. Anyway just like us he was older by this time. He had become bald on the top of his head and instead of a ponytail his remaining hair was now gray and was all frizzy around the sides. He still had that awful bushy moustache though."

This revelation of a new character involved in her life puzzled Crystal. She decided to probe a bit further. "When and who set up the trust?"

Alice and Howard appeared perplexed. "What are you talking about dear? What trust?" asked Alice.

"You didn't know about the trust fund that was set up to help Mom raise me and provide for our shelter and my education?"

"No, no this is the first that we've heard of this. We always tried to help as much as we could, but your mother always returned our checks and assured us that she was doing fine. We began sending the checks to her after Foster left you both. We always were puzzled as to how she was supporting you."

"You were in constant contact with her?"

"Yes, until she... until she died." Tears began welling up in both Alice and Howard's eyes. Alice got up and went into another room. When she returned she carried an old photo album. Crystal opened it and found page after page of photos of her and her mother. Inside the back cover were old yellowed pieces of paper. Crystal opened them to discover many letters dated through the years from her mother to her grandparents. She scanned some of them quickly; all spoke affectionately of her grandparents, all over flowed with joy when she spoke of Crystal.

"I don't understand," said Crystal, her own eyes welling up with tears. "Why didn't she tell me about you two? Why didn't she bring me to visit? Why didn't you come and visit us? You were in constant contact and I didn't even know that you existed." There was a sorrowful edge of resentment creeping into Crystal's voice.

"I know it doesn't seem fair, and it wasn't. Your mother and I spoke often about it on the phone, but we were afraid. Afraid not only for ourselves but also for you, right or wrong we all believed that the only way we could insure your safety was to keep you ignorant of everything and permit you to grow up and lead your own life."

Howard spoke up. "We didn't know who your real father's family was, but it was obvious that they were very powerful and we believed, on the strength of our contact with the man who worked for them, they were ruthless."

"We were certain that we were being watched, although we could never prove it." Alice trembled even now at the thought. "Neither your mother nor I wanted to see your grandfather go to jail or worse."

Howard stared into space. "Crystal, your mother made an adolescent mistake. My act, my sin was far more serious because I deliberately allowed greed to motivate me. I've not only had to pay for that sin my entire life, but my wife, my daughter and my only grandchild have also paid for it." Howard grasped Crystal's hand again and squeezed it as hard as he could. "Forgive me darling, please forgive me!" he sobbed and then broke down totally, crying in both pain and grief. Alice came over to the bed where Crystal now cradled the grandfather that she had only met but an hour ago. Crystal, tears streaming down her own face embraced them both. They sat silently that way for what seemed like a long while. When they all regained their composure Crystal asked another question.

"Why do you think Mom took her life?"

"Lord I wish I knew," Answered Alice. "I've asked myself that same question a thousand times. We had no clue that it was coming. She was always upbeat on the phone and in her letters, even during the divorce."

"Everything happened before we even knew what was going on," exclaimed Howard.

"It's true," continued Alice. "By the time that we learned of your mother's death, she had already been cremated and her ashes placed in the memorial garden of the parish that she was attending. Foster had been informed as next of kin even though they were divorced by then. The authorities assumed that he would inform the rest of the family. Foster apparently made all of the arrangements and never told us. He lived on the west coast by then and we tried to contact him but he never returned our calls or letters. Mary must have told him that we were aware that you were not his daughter and he never forgave us. We never did find out how Foster discovered that fact unless your mother either unwisely or unwittingly told him."

In spite of all the shocking revelations about her life, Crystal was finding some solace in the fact that Foster Harrison was not her real father. She could really learn to despise him. No wonder he feared their meeting that morning in the hotel. His every action appeared to be solely for the benefit of his own selfish and vengeful interests.

Alice continued; "That's the first time that we became aware that your real father's family knew of your existence although we have no idea how they found out. At the same time that we learned of your mother's death we were informed in a phone call from a man whose voice I had never heard before that you were well taken care of and you were going to be adopted by a good family. We should not worry, but we were also forbidden to attempt to try and locate you." Howard's voice was now filled with anger. "But we tried Crystal believe me when I tell you that we tried!"

"Yes we did try to find you darling, but we had few resources and the people that protected your real father were wealthy and powerful. Powerful enough to completely hide you and the family that you were placed with. We were soon forced to give up." The sadness in Alice's voice could not have been greater. "We had no knowledge until now of any trust fund that was set up for you and your mother. That explains how she was able to make ends meet after Foster divorced her."

"I suspect that I've met that 'voice' that called you with news concerning my future. Then my coming here today is the first you have heard of me since the day you learned that my mother took her life?"

"From the time that we were informed that you were being adopted, yes child."

Crystal was overwhelmed. After a long silence she began filling them in on her life: Her life with her mother, her conflicts with Foster, her adopted family whom she loved and respected, her college days and finally her current job in television in Savannah. They were amazed and happy for her. Together they spent the rest of the day talking, sharing memories of Crystal's mother and getting to know each other. In the emotions of the day the topic of the trust fund never surfaced again and Crystal decided not to burden them with yet another mystery. She did make it clear that she was financially secure and that she would help with any medical expenses that they might encounter that they could not cope with. Finally it was time for Crystal to go. While she was very grateful that she had found the courage to meet these people, she also couldn't shake the feeling that she had encountered a dead end in her search for her maternal father's identity. After kissing and hugging them both one more time she promised that she would remain in touch. They exchanged phone numbers and then Crystal asked just one more question. "You have no clue as to even the identity of the man who contacted you on behalf of my father's family?"

Again Alice gave a worried glance toward Howard. "Give her the card mother," was Howard's reply. Alice shuffled off into the room where she earlier went to retrieve the photo album. When she returned she was holding a small yellowed business card. She handed it over to Crystal. On the face of it was an advertisement for "Andy's Diner"; the address was near the Fulton Fish Market in Lower Manhattan. Crystal had paid a visit to the Fulton Fish Market the last time she was in New York for a network affiliates meeting. She was familiar with the area.

"The last time that the man with the moustache paid us a visit he must have dropped this. We found it on the floor after he left. We often talked about going to the police, but as we told you before, we were terribly afraid."

Howard spoke up. "Don't go there darling. These are dangerous people. If you do anything let whatever sources you have in the TV business check into it for you. Now promise me!"

"I promise you…granddad." Crystal was overjoyed at the large smile that spread across Howard's face upon hearing her call him 'granddad'. "Besides, this is probably just a place where he stopped to eat one day." Crystal used her cell phone to call a cab, they said their goodbyes and when the cab arrived she was off.

As the cab disappeared Alice returned to the bedroom where Howard lay. "All these years of fear, grief and living a lie and our granddaughter arrives unexpected on our doorstep. This was truly a miracle! What bothers me now is that we still weren't completely honest with her."

Howard sighed, "You mean about the identity of her real father's family and my attempt at blackmail?"

"Of course that's what I mean," her voice was merely stating a fact. There was no anger in her tone.

Howard sighed; "I guess I still feel the need to protect her. It was hard enough admitting that I was an embezzler I couldn't bring myself to tell her that I had stooped so low as to attempt blackmailing her real father's family. I can't believe that I was so opportunistic and motivated by greed in my youth." Howard began to weep again. Alice held him in her arms. "Everyone in her life seems to have shortchanged her, cheated her out of the very love that she is entitled to receive. The worst part is that we were all part of her family!"

Alice stroked Howard's head as he softly sobbed; "But we gave her the business card."

"I believe that she is correct about that. It's probably just a place where that awful man stopped to eat at some time. She'll follow it of course and it will be a dead end. Then she will believe that the trail truly has come to an end and go on with her life. A life I hope that will include us for whatever brief time I have left and for the remainder of yours." Alice sat on the side of Howard's bed and they held hands and cried together. For the first time in years these were tears of joy and hope.

Now Crystal sat in the rental car staring at Andy's Diner and watching the sun come up. She was unaware of her grandparent's conversation after she departed. She should have been exhausted but the adrenalin was flowing again as she watched the early breakfast crowd of dockworkers go in and out. Now that she was here just what was it that she intended to do? What did she expect to find? This business card that she clutched in her hand was dropped years ago. Did she really think that the man that had terrorized her mother and her mother's parents would magically be seated inside this establishment calmly eating his breakfast? Could she really identify him by the rather sketchy description that Howard and Alice had given her? And what if she could? And what if, by some miracle, he was at this place right here right now! What was she going to do, stride up to him and confront him? What would his reaction be if she did? Would he laugh? Would he deny all, tell her she was crazy and threaten to call the police? Would he threaten her? Would he harm her? Following this train of thought Crystal remembered the answer that Alice and Howard gave her to one of her questions. Abortion was out of the question for her real father's family. That meant that either her father or her father's family wanted her to be born. In addition to that there was the matter of the mysterious Mr. Smith and the trust fund that she now had access to and which had made her a very wealthy young woman. No, she would not be harmed. Whatever his identity the person who hired the man that had threatened her family wanted no harm to come to her. That person went to great extremes to see that she was provided for. Indeed that she remains provided for. No matter how violent this mysterious "emissary," as her mother's parents called him might be the person or persons who pay him want her to remain safe. How ironic thought Crystal, both her mother's family and her real father's family lied, committed acts of violence and even broke the law to protect themselves and her. To think that she wound up at the center of this sordid affair without even knowing about it was simply incredible. With that thought Crystal got out of the car, locked the door and walked slowly toward the diner.

As she entered through the small door she had to squeeze past two towering dockworkers that were leaving the establishment to, she assumed, go to their daily jobs. She ignored the stares that she received. She had not considered how she appeared. She was dressed in casual albeit expensive cloths with designer names. Being a lone, well dressed young woman in this early morning blue collar environment must have certainly seemed a bit unusual to the regular patrons. Upon entering Crystal was confronted with a typical crowded diner. The counter and most of the booths were nearly full with patrons. She could not help but notice that except for the waitress Crystal was the only other female in the entire establishment. A man was working behind the counter and the waitress was serving the tables and the booths.

The waitress approached. "Hi, I'm Connie, let me help you find a seat. It's a bit crowded here in the mornings."

"Thank you," murmured Crystal as she followed Connie around the side of the counter and into the rear room. The building was much larger than it appeared on the outside. Upon being seated and picking up a menu, Connie inquired as to what Crystal would like to order. With the overwhelming smell of bacon, eggs and all manner of breakfast foods in the air, Crystal realized that she had not eaten since lunch the day before. She quickly perused the menu and ordered a western omelet, toast, orange juice and coffee. Connie scribbled on a pad and left. She soon returned with the coffee and the juice.

"Your order will be up in a minute." Connie cheerfully announced.

"Thank you." Crystal drank the juice and began sipping the hot coffee. It was robust and good. It seemed to recharge her. After several slow sips, she began observing her surroundings. In spite of the crowd there was a hush over the entire scene. A morning hush thought Crystal. Everyone seemed intent on the food that was placed before him. The limited conversation that did occur congealed into a low murmur. People were slowly waking and accepting the first sustenance of the day. The most prominent sound was the clatter of silverware on the heavy diner style plates and saucers. The crowd was definitely blue collar and was slowly preparing itself for the coming labor.

Crystal began examining every face intently. She made a slow but thorough circuit of the entire room, at least the room that she now found herself occupying. She was unable to see the room through which she had entered the establishment. With that her breakfast arrived. Connie arranged the heaping plates on the table, laid the bill nearby and offered to be at her beck and call if there was anything else that Crystal might desire. Again Crystal thanked her and allowed herself to depart from her task of observation long enough to appreciate the aroma of her meal and the amazing speed with which it was dispensed. Determined as she was to continuing her mission, her hunger now overrode all else and her attention was consumed with satisfying it.

When she had finished eating she sat in the booth for a long time. Connie the waitress filled her coffee cup at least twice. She watched the patrons come and go but none of them bore even the faintest resemblance to the man that the Johnson's had described. Crystal finished her coffee and looked out the window at the river. It was a bright sunny morning. What was she doing here anyway? Chasing ghosts she thought, ghosts from the past, ghosts that were haunting the present. For what purpose she asked herself? What if she found her real father? What would she ask him? What would she say to him? Did he even know that she existed? Crystal stopped short in her revelry! What if he really didn't know that she existed? Everything she had heard from the Johnsons indicated that the boy's father was the one who had instigated all of the cover up. What if the cover up also included her father? Would she confront him? What if he was happily married with a family? Would her appearance ruin the lives of another woman and their children? Did she have the right or even the desire to continue on this path?

Suddenly Crystal was very tired. What was she doing in New York City? She was a successful young woman with a promising career to return to in Savannah. In addition to that, with apparent thanks to her real father's family, she was now very wealthy. She wanted to go home. She wanted to return to the South where she was born and raised. She looked around one more time. She didn't belong here. She decided to drive uptown and get a room at one of the swank hotels and pamper herself. She would request a large room with a view and expensive sheets. There she would collapse and sleep as long as she needed. When she awoke she would call her station manager in Savannah and inform him that her brief sabbatical was over and she would be home by the weekend. That would make everyone down home very happy as they kept in constant contact always asking when she planned to return.

Crystal got several bills out of her purse, left a generous tip for Connie and headed for the register in the front room where the counter trade was eating. She waited briefly until the man working the counter was able to free himself long enough to accept her money. The crowd had definitely thinned since her arrival. "Everything all right," he inquired?

"Everything was fine."

"Okay then, your change is a dollar twenty six cents." He placed the bill and coins in Crystal's outstretched hand. "You have a nice day miss."

"Thank you."

Crystal moved toward the front door. Just then a muscular man in a white tee shirt and blue jeans pushed through on his way in. He was bald on the top of his head and the hair on the sides was gray and frizzy. In addition he possessed a rather bushy unkempt moustache. As Crystal was in his direct path both were forced to halt face to face. Crystal caught her breath, their eyes met for a long second. His eyes were cold and hard and Crystal had no idea what her eyes were revealing about her in this moment of recognition. Fear struck at the pit of her stomach. "Excuse me," Crystal stammered.

"Sure," the man replied and stepped aside.

Crystal hurried out the door and ran for her rental car parked across the street. Andy, the man with the moustache, turned and watched her go. Recognition suddenly crossed his face. "My god!" he exclaimed under his breath and he quickly ran outside on the curb to see Crystal fumbling with her keys. She finally got the car door unlocked; scrambled in and as fast as she could start the car she drove quickly away. Andy watched her go as he memorized the license plate on her car. After a long moment he returned to the diner. "Sid!"

"Yeah boss?" replied the man at the register.

"Call Denton Wellbon, tell him I've got to talk to him right away. Have him call me on the private phone number I gave him. If it's busy tell him to keep trying until he gets through." Andy retreated to his office. He picked up his private phone and punched in a number. After a few seconds there was a voice at the other end. "This is Andy. Remember Mary Johnson? Yeah, that's the one. Well someone that is the spitting image of her was just here in the diner. Of course I know she's dead! How could I forget what she looked like? Remember who you're talkin' to. I'm telling you, this gal looked enough like her to be her daughter. Yeah, yeah, I got her license plate when she was leaving. It looked like a rental, but we can still trace it to be certain. Yeah, okay I'll find out what she's doing here and how she got here. No. No. I got a call into Denton Wellbon. Yeah I'm sure, but I'm gonna talk to him to find out if someone is starting to put pressure on him. Someone may have hired a ringer. You don't think she just stumbled in here on her own do you? She even acted like she recognized me! Yeah that's what I thought too. Yeah, I'll keep you posted." Andy hung up the phone.

None of this made sense. If someone hired a ringer to blackmail Denton, the ringer would have to be the same age as Mary would be today. Besides, it would then be time to tell Denton that she was dead. Why would she come here? How would she know to come here? The only way this would make any sense would be if, if there really was a daughter! Well wouldn't that just complicate things?

***

Tony Conocenti sat in his office at Fox Cabinetry. He had just returned from what could only be referred to as a hugely successful tour selling the price increase to Fox Cabinetry's largest dealers. These dealers accounted for more than twenty-five percent of Fox's annual sales. In addition to convincing these sometimes skeptical independent business people that the increase was not only justified but would not harm their sales, Tony managed to get most of them to commit to calling the multi-line dealers in their territory and selling the idea to them. Tony correctly concluded that if the "big time exclusive to Fox" dealers were not fearful of the increase, it would go a long way to easing the fears of the smaller dealers. What Tony and Mac were especially sensitive to and what everyone else often overlooked, was that the smaller multi line dealers accounted for seventy-five percent of sales. In addition, they had other product sitting in their showrooms. If they became disillusioned with Fox for any reason, it was a simple matter to switch the consumer to another manufacturer even if that manufacturer was not of the same quality as Fox. It was all in the mindset of the dealer and how he approached a consumer who was generally ignorant of the details of what constituted quality and what did not in this industry. But the successful conclusion of his trip was not what was occupying Tony's mind at the moment. "Mac" Maclode sat across Tony's desk from him. A slight smile playing at the corners of Mac's mouth as he waited for Tony's reaction to the proposition he had just presented.

Tony stared at Mac for a long time. "Well," quarried Mac, "are you in or do you require more time to think about it? I apologize for not approaching you sooner. I was going to call you the day I spoke to the others, but then decided this was better done face to face."

"No problem. It was better that we meet privately for this. We would own Fox Cabinetry?"

"We would own part of Fox Cabinetry. Futures Unlimited would own the remainder and sit on our Board of Directors. So that you don't get the wrong impression, Futures would own nearly seventy percent of this company at first, but we would have the opportunity to gradually buy them out with a portion of the profits that we hope to generate. Eventually the goal of both the people at Futures and the management team at Fox is for we in Fox management to become the majority and the Futures people to be the minority shareholders."

"Wow, that's pretty exciting!" A smile was playing at the corners of Tony's mouth as he contemplated the idea. In his wildest dreams he had wished for the opportunity to own at least a part of Fox, but never thought it possible. Those greedy bastards at corporate would never consider sharing with their division managers. Now here was Mac, the man he admired most in his business career offering him at least the chance. Tony's smile broadened. "You bet I'm in! I have no idea how I'm going to raise the money with my recent divorce settlement and all, but I'll find a way! I can cash in some of my retirement investments, I still managed to retain title to a small piece of land that I always thought that I'd develop some day, I can borrow money against that, or even sell it."

"Whoa, whoa," said Mac. "I don't want you jeopardizing your future."

"Look Mac, don't worry about me. You know that because of my divorce I can't go into this as heavy as I'd like or even as heavy as the others, but there's no way I'm going to pass up this opportunity. You know how much I love Fox Cabinetry and the good people that work here. You know that my main goal in sales is to keep all these craftsmen together and employed and that Atlantic Corporation's profits are secondary. I understand that they have to have those profits or none of us is employed, but my primary goal is to preserve these jobs for a great bunch of hard working people."

Mac smiled, "I know that Tony. Better than anyone else around here. I just don't want to be responsible for any of you losing your hard earned savings on what may be a farfetched dream of mine."

"Mac, everybody on your staff is a business person, they know the risks involved in a capitalist venture in a capitalist society. They know that three out of every five new enterprises fail within the first two years of their existence and that only one of the remaining two survives after five years. For all of our talk about our love as a people for an entrepreneurial society, we as individuals aren't very good at it. But even so it's created the most fantastic economy and standard of living in the history of man. Don't play Daddy to us kids Mac. We are big boys and girls. We know the risks. All I ask is for a chance to take those risks and you're giving us that chance. Without your personal funds going into this the rest of us couldn't come up with enough to get in the game. So don't worry about us. I think your entire staff would agree with me when I say that win or lose I'm grateful to you for the opportunity. Oh yeah Mr. MacLode, I'm in!"

Mac rose and reached across the desk to offer his hand. Tony's grasp was firm and sure. "We have a deal then and I promise you I'll play 'Daddy' no more."

With that Mac left Tony alone and once more closed the office door behind him. He had closed it upon entering knowing that Brady Miller would be listening intently if he allowed it to remain open. Tony sat silently reflecting on what had just transpired and the opportunity that it presented. He smiled to himself, if they were successful, this would be a dream come true. He picked up his phone to begin making arrangements to acquire the funds necessary to pay for his part of the deal, but decided to listen to his messages first. There was the usual and then a voice came on that made his stomach muscles tighten.

"Hey Tiger, what's wrong? I've left several messages since I came home and haven't heard a word from you. Your secretary told me you were still traveling, but you haven't answered the messages I left on your cell phone either. I know that you faithfully pick up your messages so I have to assume that you chose not to answer. What gives? Did I do something to piss you off? Is this a brush off? I deserve an answer. Call me!"

Tony hung up the phone. "You deserve an answer? I deserve an answer!" he muttered to himself. Then he realized that unlike her he had never asked the question. He had been unable to bring himself to call her since that night in San Francisco when he saw her on television. Just to think about it made his stomach churn. Why is that? They had no formal arrangement. Except for Blair's cryptic use of "love you" neither had professed that emotion to the other. What was he so upset about? She had never agreed to see only him, nor had he made any such commitment to her. There was a knock on the door.

"Come in," Tony responded and Brady entered. She was her usual self, with brown hair pulled tightly back, crisp white blouse, dark blue skirt and 'Plain Jane' glasses. She wore clothing that totally down played what appeared to be the attractive figure beneath. It almost seemed as if she was imitating a spinster schoolteacher, attempting to look as plain as was possible. Tony knew that she was married and had met her husband numerous times at company functions. He was an interesting outgoing man, in total contrast to Brady's stern demeanor. He often wondered how they met and what attracted him to her? If she ever left that thick mane down and threw those glasses in the trash she could be rather attractive in an earthy sort of way thought Tony. "Yes Brady?" Tony wondered if she had her ear pressed to the wall while he and Mac were meeting.

"Anthony I just put a call on your voice mail. It was that woman again. Once again I lied for you and told her that you had not yet returned from your travels.

You know how I feel about lying. I'm not doing it anymore. The next time she calls I'm putting her directly through to you. I don't know why you're hiding from her, but even though I know nothing of your private life she probably deserves better." When she lectured him Brady's voice grew even lower and throatier.

"You're right of course. I don't want you to lie. I should never have asked it of you in the first place. I'm sorry."

"Apology accepted. Just deal with it." With that she returned to her desk in the outer office. Yeah thought Tony, I've got to deal with it no matter how much it hurts. Because of the time of day Tony assumed that she was at work. He picked up the phone and with a deep sigh punched in Blair's office number.

***

Trevor Mason settled back in the comfort of a first class seat on the "red eye" from Los Angeles International to Kennedy International. The flight had just taken off. His mission to the West Coast had been successful. He had met secretly with two directors from the Bank of Taiwan. They agreed to finance the first payment to the shareholders that had signed over their proxy votes to Trevor. The bank made this agreement subject to Trevor producing signed Agreements of Sale for two of the companies that were owned by Wellbon-Smith. Second Trevor met with some European businessmen who had interest in purchasing Thompson Tool & Die in Rhode Island. He had acquired a letter of intent from them that was to be finally executed after Trevor's takeover of Wellbon-Smith. The offer had come as a pleasant surprise to Trevor as he had not commissioned Bertrum & Bertrum to do a book on Thompson. Apparently the Europeans had interest for some time and were content that conducting due diligence in addition to their own research would suffice. As Trevor was only violating corporate bi-laws and not violating any of the Securities and Exchange laws, neither of these entities had any problems with agreeing to participate. Thompson had a shaky bottom line but Fox Custom Cabinetry was very profitable. Trevor would have rather not sold Fox, but he had to offer a company that held appeal for investors and would sell quickly or the deals would never take place. Besides, in comparison to gaining control of the Wellbon-Smith Empire Fox and Thompson were easy sacrifices. The Europeans would probably strip Thompson and move operations across the Atlantic. Most of Thompson's employees would lose their jobs. But that's just business thought Trevor and it troubled him no more. With a tentative agreement on Thompson, that left only Fox to unload.

Trevor had some concern with Fox; before leaving for L.A. John Hogg had given Trevor the rough preliminary quarterly projections on the Atlantic operating Divisions. Fox's profits had dipped slightly. He had not had the time to investigate, but he had already informed John Hogg that they would be meeting on the subject upon his return. Trevor wasn't certain what MacLode was doing. Fox had been a top performer but Trevor felt that the employee compensation package was far too generous. Trevor also viewed with distaste Fox's extremely low turnover rate for its employees, less than one percent. Trevor disagreed with MacLode on both of these closely related issues. Trevor felt that the need for such highly skilled craftsmen was a symptom of Mac's softhearted reluctance to automate and modernize his plant. The proof of this in Trevor's view was the low turnover rate. Most of the Atlantic divisions averaged between ten and twelve percent. Fox's ridiculous one percent demonstrated a lack of will to kick out the mediocre performers. MacLode insisted that in the price range where Fox had found its niche, the handcrafted product was more of an art form to produce than a product that lent itself to automation.

Trevor had toured the Fox plant several times. While the so-called standard cabinetry was cut and assembled on several assembly lines according to the construction type, this remained ninety percent handwork. Then there was Fox's "specialty shop," where the one of a kind cabinetry was produced. Here a craftsman labored on one cabinet from start to completion. Even the finishing department, the most automated of all, involved extensive hand application and rubbing of stains and hand sanding. All of this produced an extremely labor intense product. A successful and profitable product, but a product that Trevor was convinced could be made even more profitable by cutting labor costs. MacLode obviously had other views on the subject and this led to constant tension between the two.

Trevor held Mac in high regard. MacLode owned the best record of all of the Atlantic Division managers. The Fox Division under William MacLode had shown a profit for seventeen of the twenty years that Mac had served as division president. On the other hand, twenty years was a long time to be a division president. All of Mac's contemporaries when he assumed the position had either been promoted to the corporate level within Wellbon-Smith or had taken more lucrative positions in larger corporations. Mac on the other hand seemed content to manage the small company that Atlantic had entrusted him with. In Trevor's view this was a severe character flaw. Mac wasn't ambitious enough. To Trevor he lacked desire, he wasn't hungry, and he was too content with himself and the operation that he managed. Trevor felt that in spite of his outstanding record Mac was becoming a liability, if Atlantic were to retain Fox Cabinetry he would have to be eliminated. But with Trevor's current plans to sell Fox, Mac became an asset. To the investor interested in purchasing Fox, Mac's stable record was reassuring, a safety valve against future failure. It would take the new owner some time to realize that Mac was beyond his prime as a manager. Trevor smiled to himself, Hell the new owners would probably offer him stock in the company to be certain that he remained during the transition. By selling Fox, Trevor was doing Mac a favor, extending his career as a division president by a couple of years.

Trevor's thoughts grew darker; if Fox's profits dipped in the third quarter and made Fox difficult to sell Mac could make a shambles of Trevor's plans. To the investor it would look like Trevor had a successful division that had developed a problem and he was trying to unload it. The end of the year corporate meeting would be fast approaching and there wouldn't be time to prepare a "book" on another division let alone quietly put the word out that it was for sale. It was a lot easier to sell a company whose profit picture fit the historical norm for the company. In this specific case the third quarter was traditionally strong for Fox, any drastic deviation from the relevant range would signal trouble.

The steward arrived for Trevor's drink order. He ordered a Scotch on the rocks then gazed out the window into the darkness. Yes, his meeting with John Hogg upon his return to New York was of immense importance. The drink arrived and Trevor sipped it slowly. The cabin lights dimmed, pillows and blankets were passed out. The passengers were settling in for the long flight. Trevor remained awake staring out at the passing ground lights far below. As the plane moved eastward the clusters of lights became sparser as the population centers grew farther apart. Eventually Trevor finished his drink and closed his eyes in sleep.

***

Abraham Rueben was preparing to leave his office to meet with Trevor Mason at Trevor's home in Connecticut. He had returned during the early morning hours from his unsuccessful trip to London. Going straight from the airport to his co-op on the Upper East Side he had just collapsed in his bed when the phone rang. It was Trevor. He was on board a red eye in California awaiting take off. He estimated that he would land in New York at around 7 AM Eastern. He wanted to meet with Abraham for a late lunch, say 2 in the afternoon at his home.

"I'm barely in the door after my trip to London."

"I know, your point being?" was Trevor's reply.

"Do you ever sleep?" inquired Abe.

"Not when there are deals to close!" snapped Trevor. "I'll sleep during the flight. That's what I expect you did while crossing the Atlantic."

"I can't sleep on planes."

"Not my problem. See you at two." The phone went dead. Trevor was gone.

Now it was a little past noon and Abraham was in his office stuffing a few pertinent files into his briefcase before leaving for Trevor's house when his secretary's voice came over the speakerphone.

"There's a call for you sir."

"Who is it?"

"All he would tell me was that he is an old friend of yours in Baltimore." Abraham's secretary had been with his law firm for twelve years. She had long since become accustomed to phone calls for her boss from people who refused to give their identity to her.

Abraham checked his watch. He still had time for a quick conversation. Besides, considering who was on hold, this could be important. "Put the call through."

Abraham picked up the receiver, "Yes Albert. What have you got?"

"Mr. Rueben?"

"Yes Albert, go ahead." Albert was a retired policeman in Baltimore who now made his living as a private detective. Albert believed that he was forever in Abraham's debt because years ago Albert was involved in a less than "clean" shooting while on duty. Abraham was conducting business with the victim at the time. Indeed, unknown to Albert, it was Abraham's anonymous tip that sent policeman Albert to the scene. As the victim was involved in illegal activity he pulled what turned out to be an empty automatic weapon on Albert. Albert shot him dead only to discover afterward that the gun was empty. Albert, whose record wasn't spotless was suspended from the force and expected to face manslaughter charges. Abraham contacted Albert and represented him during the investigation. He never questioned Abraham's interest or the fact that Abraham was able to locate another weapon of the correct caliber in the alley where the shooting took place. The weapon even had the slain man's fingerprints all over it and had been fired recently. This after the police had searched the scene. No one ever found the slugs that were supposedly fired at Albert, but Abraham made a convincing enough case of self-defense so that Albert was reinstated just long enough for him to take early retirement. Albert truly believed that Abraham saved his life. Abraham knew that by shooting the victim Albert had removed a problem for him.

"Remember that woman, Mary Johnson Harrison that you had me checking out a few weeks ago?"

"Of course I remember. You're the only one that could uncover the fact that she had a daughter. Valuable information that was Albert, I'm in your debt."

"No sir Mr. Rueben, I'm forever in your debt."

"What do you have for me Albert?"

"The daughter showed up."

"When?"

"She first called me a couple of weeks ago. Gave me her history and what she knew of her grandparents and asked if I could find them. Of course I had already found that information for you, but I waited a couple days to make it look like I had to do some digging."

"How did she come to you?"

"Remember she's an anchor on the local news down in Savannah. I did some work for the local affiliate on a story that began in Savannah. I got to know her when she came to Baltimore to follow up on the story. The conversations I had with her then meshed with some of the things that you were looking for at the time. That's what led me to check her out. Anyway, she seemed to like my work. I guess that's why she called me. I had no clue as to her identity until she gave me her history. It was at that point that I realized that she was Mary Johnson Harrison's daughter and that her grandparents lived in Baltimore."

"Did you give her the information?"

"Shouldn't I have?"

"No, no reason not to," Abraham lied. "What did she do with it?"

"She paid her grandparents a visit."

"When?"

"Yesterday."

Abraham was trying to guess how this unexpected information was going to impact on the Wellbon-Smith situation. "How did it go?"

"Well when she arrived I followed her from the airport, she never saw me she went straight to their house and stayed several hours."

"Several hours?"

"Yeah. When she left they hugged her."

"Hugged her?"

"That's what I said."

"Where did she go after that?"

"Rented a car and drove to New York."

"The City? She's here?"

"Yeah."

"Where are you now?" asked Abe.

"Right here in New York. I'm sitting in the lobby of the Gramisey Hotel, the elegant old place off Gramisey Park."

"I know where it is."

"I followed her here. She checked in earlier this morning and hasn't left since. I think she may have called one of the big places and they sent her here when they were booked full. They often do that. It's a pretty neat old place."

"Does she know you've followed her?"

"I'm better than that Mr. Rueben."

"Of course you are. She drove to New York City and went straight to the hotel?"

"No, it's the damnedest thing. She went straight as an arrow to a diner near the Fulton Fish Market and had breakfast. That's not exactly the part of town I would expect a sophisticated lady like her to head for."

Rueben closed his eyes as a furrow crossed his forehead. "Albert, was the diner called Andy's?"

"Yeah Mr. Rueben, how did you know?"

"Let's just say I know this City. Now listen to me Albert. As of this moment you are on my payroll. You stick to her like glue. Don't give her a clue that you're following her. Keep in near constant contact with me. I want to know what she's doing even if it's nothing. Understand?"

"You can count on me Mr. Rueben."

"I know I can Albert."

To Catch a Fox

"There's one more thing Mr. Rueben."

"Yes?"

"When she left that dinner she ran out like a scared rabbit. She looked like she'd seen a ghost. Could hardly make her fingers get her car keys straightened out and all she had to do was point the remote at the car. She was that scared."

"What do you think she was running from?"

"A big guy, balding on top with frizzy gray hair came out of the diner after she did, but then she got in the car and drove off like a bat. It was all I could do to keep up with her, and she doesn't know the city that well."

"You know what to do Albert. Keep me informed."

"Yes sir."

Abraham hung up the phone. He paused in thought for a long moment. The boys did a good job he thought absently as he looked around the office; the carpet, the paint, no one could tell that anything out of the ordinary happened here. Damn! Andy knows she's here. If Andy knows it means that he knows too, old enemies all. But it didn't add up. Andy and his associates were good, but not on the level that this secret had been kept. If Albert hadn't had some serious dirt on the woman in the Baltimore Court House Abe would not have known of this young women's existence. Who were these people that protected Denton's secret? How did Crystal Harrison know about Andy's Diner? He would think about these aspects later. Right now it was imperative that he talk to Trevor and that they make some serious contingency plans. Combined with his recent setback in London the presence of Crystal Harrison in New York was a ticking time bomb.

***

Denton Wellbon III slowly closed the file folder that lay on his desk. It was a review of the past business quarter and profit projections for the third quarter for Fox Custom Cabinetry. John Hogg asked him to review it before Trevor Mason returned to the office. Trevor had been to the West Coast for a few days on business and returned on the "red eye" flight early this morning. John said that Trevor called upon his arrival at JFK and informed John that he was heading home to catch up on some work. John also stated that Trevor was not happy with Fox's projections and that he wanted to review them with Denton and John the following morning.

Denton had just completed his review. Fox remained profitable but the profits were off compared with previous third quarters. It seemed that Fox had not only reinstated the benefit package that they had reduced at Trevor's insistence, but that they also increased wages. It was not MacLode's nature to declare across the board increases. He paid his employees well, but preferred increases on an individual merit basis when recommended by their supervisor rather than painting with a wide brush. With these large wholesale changes the result was reduced profits in a period that historically Fox set records. Trevor would not like that one bit.

But Denton was having a hard time concentrating. As he was preparing to leave for the office this morning he received an urgent phone call from Sid at Andy's Diner. Sid told him that Andy had to talk with him "right away!" Denton hadn't a clue as to what Andy might want, but he immediately called the number that Sid instructed him to call. When he finally got through to Andy, Denton sensed the urgency in Andy's voice. Andy wanted to know exactly where Trevor Mason and Abe Rueben were and what they were up to. Denton explained that Trevor was on the West Coast meeting with some Far East bankers and he hadn't seen Abe in several days. Andy paused, apparently in deep thought. "They haven't pressured you to bring home your mother's vote?"

"No, not yet, why do you ask?"

"Cause I think they are about to do just that."

"What makes you think that?"

"Just a hunch."

"Could you share that hunch with me?" Denton quarried.

Andy considered Denton's question for a long moment. "Yeah, I saw a person this morning that might have connections with Ruben. If I'm right I expect that you may come under increasing pressure. That's all that I want to say right now. Even on this phone."

"You believe that he is considering using physical force against me?"

"I said that is all I'm going to say on the phone. Now listen to me, you call me at the first sign that they might put the pressure on. Understand?"

"Of course Andy."

"Look I'm sorry that I can't be more specific, but I needed to know firsthand if anything was coming down. You know that we can't speak of these things on the phone."

"I understand Andy and I appreciate your concern."

"Keep me informed of everything that's going on Denton."

"I certainly will." With that Denton heard Andy hang up. Denton reflected on the phone conversation that he held earlier. Andy was not a man to over dramatize. The individual that he referred to in the conversation, whoever it might be, was important enough to warrant that brief but unsettling phone call. Andy definitely believed that Trevor and Abe were about to make their final moves, the moves that would involve Denton's and his mother's stock. Denton closed his eyes. He remembered the stories concerning Abraham Ruben's ruthlessness. Suddenly he felt sick in the stomach. For the first time he feared for Susan. Up until now he felt that he was the only one with any possibility of being in danger. Now he wondered if he should send Susan to their condo on St Croix? What about his mother? Good lord, what had he gotten himself into? Then a strange feeling of security came over him. After all he did have his father's old ally Andy, the very Andy who called to warn him that something might soon be coming down. Still it might be prudent to suggest to Susan that she and her sister take a late summer vacation down in the islands. Having made that decision Denton allowed himself to relax a bit. If he was ever to take his father's place in this company he must, like his father, be fearless.

After checking the corporate jet schedule for available times he called home to Susan proposing that she and her sister spend the remainder of August at the condo. She was delighted with the suggestion, but disappointed that Denton could not accompany them. Denton told her that this would be a girl's vacation. It would be a time for Susan and her sister to spend private time together enjoying each other's company. Susan did extract a promise from him that he would join them if at all possible during the final week of their stay. After returning the phone to its cradle he felt much better. With that Denton reopened the Fox file and began to review the numbers once again.

***

Jerome Jefferson stared at the report that Mitchell Green had written. Mitchell stood pensively on the other side of Jerome's desk. Finally Jefferson looked up. "For all practical purposes the card campaign is dead?"

"Yes, ever since Fox announced that the benefit package was restored and the pay increases will remain intact, the sign up rate has been reduced to a trickle."

"That means that without the proper percentage of workers requesting it we can't approach the NLRB for permission to enter the property and conduct a representation election."

"Yes sir."

"MacLode has outflanked us."

"It appears so."

"Damn! We have to have Fox or the merger will never take place!"

"Yes sir, I'm aware of that."

Jefferson allowed himself a weary sigh, turned in his chair and gazed out the window. In the distance he could see the Washington Monument at the one end of the Mall. He had worked hard to get to this position and his ambition was pushing him to go further. He wasn't prepared to accept defeat. With his back to Green he inquired about Clint Matthews. "Has Matthews made a move as of yet?"

"Not as of yesterday. I haven't talked to him since."

"Call him now. We'll both talk to him. If he diddles around much longer someone else will get Fox and we'll be forced to start over or look for another company. We don't have the time for either."

"Yes sir." Mitchell picked up the phone and began punching in Matthews' number, a number that he now knew by heart.

***

Trevor Mason sat behind his desk. John Hogg and Denton Wellbon sat quietly across from him waiting for him to finish reviewing Fox's numbers. "What the hell is MacLode doing down there?" growled Trevor.

"It appears that he has reinstated the benefit package and kept the pay increases in place," John Hogg replied. "Other than that the numbers aren't bad."

"I know what he's done, I want to know what the hell he thinks he's doing defying me like this? 'Other than that the numbers aren't bad?' What the shit are you talking about John? That's exactly what is making them bad! He's suddenly turned a 14% profit on the operating line into a 9% profit. That translates into a piss poor 3% bottom line before taxes! What am I supposed to tell the Board, that we thought the shareholders wouldn't mind if CD's looked like a better investment than our interest in Fox?" Hogg's face reddened but he said nothing. He knew the dangers of engaging Trevor in a pointless argument. "When's our review of Fox?"

"Next week. We fly down Sunday afternoon and meet with them first thing Monday morning at the Fox offices." It was Denton who replied, taking Hogg off the firing line for a moment.

"I've a good mind to call him right now and can his ass!"

John Hogg swallowed hard and spoke again, "Trevor, we should at least listen to his explanation. He's not stupid. He has always worked for the long term good of Fox. There may be a good reason." Hogg knew that he was on very thin ice at the moment, but he also knew that firing Mac would not sit well with the Board. Mac had made Wellbon-Smith a lot of money over the years and he needed to be on record urging caution. It was good that Denton was here to witness this exchange. Denton was a bit of a wimp in Hogg's opinion, but he was honest and would back him up with the Board if it came to that. Denton, with his family connections, was perhaps the one person that Trevor couldn't fire. Trevor looked up at Hogg over the top of the half-glasses that he used for reading. His glare was icy cold. There was a long silence. John met his gaze and held it. Denton Wellbon and John Hogg both held their breath. Finally Trevor spoke.

"All right John, I'll wait till we review them next week and listen to Mac's explanation in person." Trevor's voice was low and threatening. "But if he tries to bullshit me, even a little bit, I'll fire his ass so fast and so hard that he won't even want to hang around long enough to clean out his desk." Trevor returned his gaze to the reports in his hand. Both Denton and John Hogg simultaneously breathed a sigh of relief. They waited for Trevor's next comment. After a moment that seemed like an eternity Trevor looked up again. He glanced at both of them. "We're done," was all he said. As they both approached the door Trevor called Denton back. "May I have a moment Denton?" It really wasn't a request.

"Certainly," replied Denton. John Hogg left quietly. When he was gone and the door firmly closed behind him Trevor again looked intently at Denton.

"Denton whatever Mac's doing down there we can't allow him to scuttle Fox's numbers now. We need to get every nickel we can out of Fox when we sell it to cover the commitments we've made. We can probably finance the rest based on the meeting I just came from on the Coast. I have received a letter of intent concerning Thompson, but we have to sell Fox too because that is the contingent the boys from Taiwan have placed on us. If we get in a bind later on we'll just spin off another company, but right now the only one that we have a book on is Fox." The book was the confidential report that Bertrum & Bertrum assembled at Trevor's request to be distributed to any potential buyers. A serious deviation from the numbers that Bertrum had projected would effectively erode the value a potential investor might place on Fox.

"It's good to hear about the offer for Thompson Tool and Die. That's an unexpected windfall. Thompson's long-range profit picture is a bit uncertain anyway. I take it that your meetings went well?" Denton wanted to change the subject. William MacLode was always highly regarded within the Atlantic Corporation and the parent Wellbon-Smith. Denton was deathly afraid that Trevor would assign him to do the dirty work of terminating Mac. Not only did he personally admire Mac's record at Fox, but also did not want to be the one responsible for firing him. If the Board viewed that as a mistake it was possible that not even his holdings or his family could save him.

"Yes they went very well thank you. Better than Abe's meeting in London." Trevor then explained to Denton what Reuben had discovered about the mysterious holder of the shares that Denton's father had sold at fire sale prices some years back. "Denton do you have any clue as to who this investor might be and why exactly your father nearly gave him a block of shares almost as large as your mother's?"

Denton paused in thought for a moment. "You inquired concerning this before, nothing came immediately to mind then and after considerable thought I'm still drawing a blank."

"If you think of anything, no matter how obscure, I want to know about it. Without those shares your mother's vote in our favor becomes essential. I don't have to explain the math to you Denton. With the commitments that we have we need the combination of either your block of stock and your mother's or your block and the off shore funds to make a majority."

Denton's mouth went dry. "I was hoping that we might not have to ask her. You know how much she thinks of Carlton Smith."

"To hell with her regard for Smith! I want you to start talking to her immediately. Your mother was always a shrewd businesswoman, appeal to her instinct for personal profit and point out to her the value of having you in the chairman's chair. I'll give her a call this morning and fill her ear with compliments concerning your growth as an individual and as an astute businessman since I arrived at Atlantic."

Denton wondered how sincere those compliments were. "I'll talk with her as soon as we can get together Trevor." But not before he called Andy to update him on the current events thought Denton.

"Good man, now go." As Denton approached the door Trevor called to him again. "Denton, I won't be lying when I speak to your mother concerning you. I want you to understand that."

Denton turned back toward Trevor; he was a bit taken aback by Trevor's sincere tone. "Thank you Trevor, thank you."

To Catch a Fox

Trevor Mason nodded silently as Denton closed the door behind him. Poor bastard he thought, he's so starved for compliments it makes him an easy target for manipulation. With that Trevor picked up his phone. Regardless of what he had said to Hogg, he would call MacLode later. He knew that John Hogg probably called Mac immediately upon leaving Trevor's office. Hogg and MacLode went back a long way and both tried to warn and cover for each other in the face of impending danger. Right now he had a more important phone call to return. There was an interesting message awaiting him on his voice mail this morning. He put Mac temporarily out of his mind and punched in another set of numbers. He waited while the phone rang. "Clint Matthews please." Trevor stated to the female voice that answered. "Matthews, Trevor Mason. I have a message that you wish to talk to me."

"Yes I do Mr. Mason. I'll get right to the point. I want to buy one of your companies."

"Any company, or do you have one in mind?"

"You must know that I'm in the cabinet and furniture business."

"You're the man that put together the Cab Corp Corporation, one of the biggest in the cabinet and furniture industry, so I guess I'm to assume that in the interests of synergy you must have your eye on Fox Cabinetry."

"You assume correctly sir. Do you have interest in selling Fox?"

"I'll sell any company for the right price, but let's not discuss this over the phone, what works for you?"

"I could be in New York next week."

"Sorry Matthews, I'm taking my management team on the road next week. We're conducting our annual reviews of all of Atlantic's operating divisions. We will be meeting at all of their home offices. It will take about four weeks. After that we will be in Chicago for the Kitchen and Bath Industry Show. Fox will be one of the exhibitors."

"So will I Mason, my cabinet companies will be exhibiting. How 'bout if I meet you there?"

"Okay, call me when you get into town, I'll be in whatever hotel the Fox people have reserved for me. Let me give you my cell phone number. Trevor rattled off the numbers. Did you get that?"

"I got it Mason."

"Oh and Matthews, bring your checkbook and be prepared to write big numbers. Fox is one of our most profitable companies."

"I always write big numbers if the deal and the balance sheets make sense, so bring more than just big talk Mason."

"I always back up my talk Matthews. See you in Chicago."

"I'll be there Mason."

***

It was the morning following Trevor Mason's return from the West Coast. Mac sat in his office at Fox Cabinetry reviewing July's final numbers and the third quarter projections with Dale Hershey. "I expect to hear from Mason any time now and it won't be good," he said.

"No it won't, but he may wait until next week when he and his staff arrive for our annual review."

"Could be, he would enjoy chewing me out in front of my staff."

"He may direct it at you, but any threats he makes will be for all of us."

"I suppose, but I'm not afraid of him."

"He's a dangerous man Mac. He operates on ego more often than on common sense. He could fire you in the blink of an eye."

"Even if he does we will still make our offer, although if his ego dictates terminating me, it may also dictate turning down our offer."

"When do you plan on making our offer?"

"I'll do it during our review next week."

"That's probably a good time, our home turf, your staff and potential partners here to back you up."

"That's what I thought, but we have to get through the certain negative reaction to our projected numbers."

Just then Brady's voice came over the intercom, "Mr. Hogg on line one Mac."

Mac exchanged glances with Dale and then punched line one and the speaker button. "Hi John, I expect you want to talk about numbers?"

"Hi Mac, am I on the speaker?"

"Yeah, Dale Hershey is here with me. He knows the numbers better than either you or me."

"That's not a problem, hi Dale."

"Hi John."

"Okay guys you can expect a call from Trevor shortly. He's not happy with your projections."

"That's not unexpected John."

"Mac, you better have a damn good reason for reversing your position on the benefit plan and then maintaining the increased pay scale. Trevor threatened to fire you in our meeting this morning."

"One word John: union."

"What?"

"You heard me John someone's trying to organize our work force."

"But no one has filed a card check with the NLRB."

"I know, we think that we got it stopped before they collected the required number of signatures."

"Who?"

"We're not sure, but there are only a few possibilities."

"Listen Mac, Trevor's calling for me on the other line. I've got to go. I'll try to break the ice for you concerning the union before you have to talk to him. It might cool him down. He's got fire in his eye Mac. Be very careful what you say when the two of you talk. Don't, I repeat don't get into an argument with him. Agree with him no matter how crazy he gets. We'll both work on him later when he's calm. You have to stay employed for the good of Fox. Understand?"

"I understand John. I don't like playing games with an egomaniac though."

"Just do what I'm telling you Mac. Hell, apologize if you have to, he'll cool down after a while. You have to remain president of Fox!"

Dale placed his hand on Mac's shoulder "Its good advice Mac, take it."

"John Hogg could hear what Dale was saying over the speaker. "Listen to us Mac! I mean it."

"Okay, you've convinced me. I'll behave when Trevor and I speak."

"Thanks Mac, I've got to go." With that Hogg was gone.

Dale smiled thinly at Mac. "You knew that this would be rough."

"Yeah, this is no surprise but remember Trevor threatens to fire one of his division presidents at least once a week. I'll be fine. Since we're going to make him an offer for the company I promise you personally that I won't do anything to jeopardize our offer. It will be like him to accuse me of killing the bottom line just so we wouldn't have to pay as much to purchase Fox."

"You can't control that Mac. He's going to believe whatever he wants to believe." With that Dale opened the door to the outer office. "I've got work to do. If you need me when Mason calls, just yell."

"Thanks, Dale."

Mac spent the next thirty minutes reviewing the numbers looking for a way to make them better. The only hope was that Tony's strategy worked with the flagship dealers and that would filter down to the remainder of the network. Maybe, just maybe Fox wouldn't take the dip in sales that these numbers projected because of the price increase. If they could get a five percent increase as opposed to the five-point decrease that Dale and he had projected, over Tony's protestations, they would be all right in the third quarter.
The intercom buzzed again. "Mr. Mason on line one," was all that Brady said.

"Thanks Brady," and with that Mac put Trevor on the speaker. "Good morning Trevor."

"Good morning Mac, how the hell are you?" Mac frowned, as Trevor sounded almost jovial. "I was just talking to John he tells me that you think you might have a union sniffing around."

"It sure looks like it Trevor."

"Tell me about it."

With that Mac launched into a recount of the last month's events, he spared no detail, giving Trevor their full battle plan and the results so far. When he was finished he expected the explosion to encompass not only the projected numbers, but also how Trevor would have handled the situation. No doubt his way would be far superior to Mac's and also show a larger profit margin instead of the decrease that Mac was projecting. Instead, Mac got a big surprise. After a long pause Trevor spoke in a subdued tone.

"Sounds like you covered all the bases, at least all that you legally can. Good job Mac."

MacLode nearly fell out of his chair. "Why thank you Trevor."

"It sure explains your projection for the quarter. You think Tony can smooth down the dealer's ire about the unexpected price increase?"

"I certainly hope so. He's good at that sort of thing."

"Yeah, he's a real smoozer," Trevor chuckled. "Tell him I said that."

"I will." Mac was still incredulous; he was on pins and needles waiting for the other shoe to drop.

"You know Mac I should have had you with me at a company I worked for about ten years ago. The union got in on me there. Maybe if I had used some of your techniques it never would have happened, I don't know."
"I may yet fail to keep them out Trevor."

"I don't think so. I think you got them back on their heels. Anyway I beat that union in the end."

"How did you do that?" Mac knew he was expected to ask.

"Beat them at their own game. With their first contract they got real carried away on safety. I let them go, never argued about anything that they wanted to add for safety's sake. Told them that we, management, would agree to the additional safety provisions as long as their shop Stewards would be responsible for policing them and management would accept a fine for any problem not corrected within thirty days. I also added that if it were something that fell inside the worker's responsibility the union would fine the worker if it weren't corrected by the next shift. They believed that this gave them the opportunity to line their coffers with company money so they agreed. Then I combined their safety rules with OSHA's (Occupational Safety and Health Administration), after that I took a notebook and walked through the plant every morning and noted any violation that I found. Of course the infractions that I found were always within the worker's responsibility. Then I would call a meeting of the Stewards and tell them in the name of protecting their members I wanted everything brought up to snuff by the end of the next shift. I did this for three months; you know you can find something every time if you look hard enough. By the end of three months the workers owed so much in fines that they were beginning to wonder if they weren't better off before they voted for a union. By the second half of the year there was a movement on within the work force to vote the union out. By the end of the year they were out of there. I loved it."

"That was very clever Trevor. I'll keep it in mind should I ever need it."

"You do that Mac. Say, I've been thinking. You guys have been working your asses off trying to get your annual review together to meet my accelerated schedule. My conscious sort of got to working on me about that."

"Really?" Mac wondered how that sounded on the other end the moment he uttered it.

"Yeah really," Trevor laughed. "I know you guys in the divisions don't think that I have one, but I do and occasionally it rears up and gives me a swift kick. You guys at Fox have always been one of my better performers, not that you couldn't do better mind you, but I have others that give me more problems. Now that I know that you've not only been sweating to get those reports and the five year plan, but you're fighting a union too, I think you need a break."

"What do you have in mind Trevor?"

"Let's push you guys from first to last in the order. That gives you four more weeks."

"That runs into the Kitchen and Bath Show."

"I know, I thought that we could have an abbreviated meeting in Chicago. You know, if you guys get the plan and the backup data to me the week before for my staff to review we could reserve a meeting room at the hotel that we will be staying at and wrap it up in about two hours. Think that would work?"

"Well yes, if you think we can take a meeting that usually lasts at least a day and condense it into two hours that would help us greatly on this end Trevor."

"Let's do it. Now that I've already had cardiac arrest over your third quarter projections, all you need to do is finish the five year plan, which you should have done now as we were meeting next week."

"It's complete."

"Good, if we wait four more weeks Tony may be able to tell us if he got the dealers over the price increase okay. We actually should have a better feel for where we will be."

"Okay Trevor, we'll make all the arrangements for you and your staff in Chicago. I can't tell you how much this will help us."

"Hey, we have to work together, right?"

"All the time. Ah Trevor, could you schedule a little time for you and me to meet privately at your convenience? I'd like it to be before Chicago if possible, but Chicago will do if you can't work me in. I'll travel to wherever works for you."

"Certainly Mac, but It looks right now as if it will have to wait for Chicago. What's up?"

"I have a proposition for you, but I want to present it to you face to face."

"Sounds interesting I look forward to it. See you in Chicago Mac!"

"Chicago it is." Mac punched a button and cut off the all-clear tone that sounded the second that Trevor Mason hung up. He immediately called Brady and had her call a meeting of his senior staff. They're not going to believe this he thought.

On the New York end of the conversation Trevor sat thinking. Looks like Chicago will be very busy and very interesting. Trevor decided to postpone the Fox meeting not because he felt guilty about the workload he had imposed on Mac's staff, but because he wanted to give them that much more time to improve the numbers. Union, union, could it be? Could Clint Matthews somehow be mixed up in this? He punched an extension button on his phone.

"John Hogg."

"Yeah John its Trevor, are you familiar with the Cab Corp Corporation?"

"A furniture conglomerate owned by a Matthews I believe."

"Yeah, that's the one. I want you to find out everything that you can about them. Drop everything else. I especially want to know what union or unions that they're saddled with. I need it by tomorrow night."

"Okay boss. You got it." John Hogg was totally puzzled by this request, but he wasn't going to argue with Trevor. Not after the morning they had. He also knew that this wasn't a reason to be late with the regular work that he was responsible for. He would have to get everything done by the time that Trevor Mason demanded. John sighed, remembered the fat salary that he collected and picked up the phone.

***

Sam Grabowski got out of his unmarked police car and walked toward the black and white unit that was double parked up the street. The two uniformed police that called him were standing beside a Porsche Boxter that had been stripped of nearly everything of value. Judging by the amount of dirt and grime on the windshield it had been parked along this curb for some time. As he approached, the two uniforms acknowledged him. "What have you got for me?" asked Sam.

"Downtown said that you've been looking for this," replied the female half of the team.

Sam walked around behind the expensive sports car and checked the license plate: DON WAN. "Yeah, I have. What do you know about it?"

"Nothing really sir," this time it was the male half of the duo that responded. "This is our regular beat. There are a lot of professional offices along this block and the next so it's not unusual to see expensive cars like this one parked along the street. But they never remain very long. It caught our attention this morning. It must have been stripped last night otherwise we would have noticed it before. Judging by the street grime it was parked here for a while. We became curious as to why it was not reported stolen, so we ran a wants and warrants on the license plate. That was when downtown told us that you were looking for a car registered to a Donald Kensington-Cramer. This is it."

"Good work. We've been trying to locate this car ever since we found the owner dead." While Sam was speaking several unmarked cars pulled to a stop near him. Sam turned to the detective from his squad in the nearest car. "You guys start knocking on doors. Cover every office and shop. Do all of you have photos of Donald Kensington-Cramer?"

“Everyone has them boss.”

“Good, I want to know if anyone in this area saw Kensington-Cramer before he was killed. If they have I want to talk to them.”

“Yes sir.” With that the cars pulled away looking for parking spaces. Sam looked again at what was once a beautiful piece of machinery. He resisted the urge to get inside and start looking for something. Anything! When he received the call that Kensington-Cramer’s car had been found he had immediately called for the crime lab to have it towed in for a complete forensic examination. Sam hoped that he was looking at the first break in this case.

***

Blair McManus slammed the phone down on its cradle. She was in Chicago sitting alone in her Lakeshore Drive apartment. She had been playing phone tag with Tony for the best part of a week now. She did not believe that it was an accident. He was avoiding her! He called at times when he was reasonably assured that she would not be home, and he called the office when he could be nearly certain that she would be out. His most recent recorded message both broke her heart and infuriated her simultaneously. She rose from her sofa, crossed the living room and slid open the sliding glass door that opened onto the balcony. Her apartment was on the eleventh floor of the building and looked out over Lakeshore toward Lake Michigan beyond. It was eight o’clock in the evening. Even now the days were beginning to shorten, but this evening daylight had faded quickly in the face of an overcast sky accompanied by a persistent drizzle. She felt the light rain on her face. The cold made her shiver. She folded her arms in an unconscious attempt to hold in her body warmth and resist the cold damp air. A fog was rising off the Lake. To the south she could see the Navy Pier, to the north the shimmering lights along the coast curved out into the gloom. Tony’s words on the recording continued to haunt her.

“Hi Blair this is Tony. Sorry that I keep missing you. It’s apparent that we’re both very busy. Hey I just wanted to say that you shouldn’t worry about us not being able to get together out on the Coast. I had things to do and people to see and so did you. We both have to live our lives, right? If neither of us is too busy the next time I’m in Chicago maybe we’ll get together. See you around.”

"Maybe we'll get together. See you around." What was that? After all they had been to each other the past few months, always making arrangements for the next meeting before the last ended. Was he ending it? Did he just brush her off? Just like that? Underneath that cool tone of his voice she thought that she detected a slight sense of, a feeling of what? Was he hurt? Yes, he sounded just a little hurt. Had she hurt him? If so how had she hurt him and when? Was he hurt because she had to work when they were both on the Coast? He was working too! If that's all it took to hurt him, good lord how childish!

The rain came faster and Blair retreated back inside. She knew that in a couple of weeks Tony would indeed be in Chicago for a trade show. If he thought he was going to dump Blair McManus without facing her, he was going to be in for a big surprise! Her anger erupted.
"Damn you Tiger! Damn you! Damn you! Damn you!"

She sank onto the sofa, surprised at the intense anger contained in her voice. An outburst heard by no one but herself. Suddenly Blair felt exhausted, overwhelmed, and helpless all at the same time. Her anger subsided and her eyes became moist. Blair McManus, Ms. Cool, always in control, especially of her emotions. But not now, not at this moment, not when a simple telephone message was reducing her to an emotional wreck. The dread and despair had been building all week from the time it became obvious that Tony was avoiding her. Now with this message the emotions spilled over. But why was this having such an effect on her? She had been through many relationships that ended badly. Most of the time she was the one that ended them. Was that the problem? Was it possible that she was upset because Tony was the one brushing her off and not the other way around?

No; no that wasn't it. She was disappointed when her editor told her to honor Dirk Andersen's request and accompany him to the Universal Club's annual Television Awards Dinner. Andersen was one of the celebrities that she had been assigned to cover. When Dirk initially made the request of her she told him that she could not be his date for the evening because she had a previous engagement in San Francisco. The previous engagement was her dinner date with Tony. Dirk never took no for an answer, so he telephoned Blair's editor and got him to strongly suggest that Blair go. "It will be the highlight of your interview with him." So Blair reluctantly acquiesced. No, she wanted to see Tony that night, more than he would ever know and until recently she was willing to admit. It seemed that lately all she thought about was the next time she would be together with him and now he was so cavalier concerning her. "If neither of us is too busy the next time I'm in Chicago." Well she wasn't going to be the one that was too busy when Tony came for his trade show. This time he was going to see Blair McManus whether he wanted to or not!

CHAPTER 15

It was two weeks to the day from the phone conversation that Mac had with Trevor Mason concerning the third quarter numbers and the rescheduling of the Fox Cabinetry annual meeting. It was just one day since Mac received a short phone call from his old college friend Tom Luca. "Mac? Tom. Remember the request you made of me when we met in New York a while back?"

"Yes Tom, I do." In truth Mac was afraid that Tom had forgotten.

"I got your answers. Listen carefully and do as I say. Be on the first train out of Lancaster for New York tomorrow morning, but only buy a ticket to Philadelphia. When the train stops for the engine switch in Thirtieth Street Station in Philly remain seated until you are contacted. Understand?"

"Tomorrow I take the first east bound train to Philly and when it stops in the Thirtieth Street Station I remain on the train until I am contacted."

"You got it."

"Will you be the contact?" asked Mac, but Tom had already hung up. So now Mac sat in a window seat of an Amtrak coach as the train slowed in its approach to Philadelphia's Thirtieth Street Station. It was one minute before nine in the morning as the train slid out of the sunlight and into the dark cavernous terminal. As his eyes adjusted to the dim artificial light he could see rows of pillars slowly passing. The pillars were the supports for the massive building overhead. Rows of shiny tracks ran through between the pillars. The trains entered and departed from this level under the terminal. Concrete islands that formed platforms linked the upper levels with this massive dungeon by means of wide metal stairways that rose out of sight from the platforms surface at train level. The train on which Mac was a passenger slowed to a stop along one of these platforms. When the ever slowing clicking of the steel wheels on the rails ceased, there was a long moment of silence as the morning commuter crowd strained to determine exactly where in the terminal they had stopped.

Soon the conductor was making his way down the aisle. "We'll be stopped here for about twenty minutes," he said. "For those of you remaining with this train you will have that much time to go upstairs and use the vending machines or rest rooms. Please return promptly, as we will be departing as soon as we switch to diesel power. Return by the stairway marked 'track 5'." He then continued to the next car to repeat his litany.

Most of the passengers rose and filed out of the train. Many had reached their destination while others would be returning to continue their trip, along with newcomers, to points in New Jersey and ultimately Penn Station in New York City. Mac remained seated, as Tom had instructed. Only a few people remained in the car. Silence again ensued. Suddenly the train was rocked as the electric engine uncoupled and began moving away somewhere up front. With the engine's departure the lights and air conditioning shut down, as it was the only source of power for the entire train. The car was in semi-darkness now with the only light coming from outside on the platforms. Mac stared out the window wondering what, if anything, he should be looking for. Suddenly Mac jumped! Another train was screaming past just inches away from his face on the next track! In his mind Mac knew that the passing train couldn't be going more than thirty five miles per hour inside the terminal, but his eye told him that it had to be doing at least sixty!

Mac turned away from the window to realize that a tall man in a dark suit was standing in the aisle next to him. Mac looked up but the man's face was partially obscured in shadow. "William MacLode?" asked the gravely voice.

"Yes, I'm he" responded Mac.

"Come with me." With that the man started toward the front of the car. Mac rose and followed him, suddenly feeling very uneasy. When they were young men in college and Mac discovered that his best friend Tom Luca came from a family that had mob affiliations, it had always seemed exciting. As he grew to know Tom's family better through ever more frequent visits to Tom's home on Long Island, he began to realize that Tom's father was a major figure within their organization. Only once on that fateful night when Tom and he both had too much to drink did Tom actually acknowledge his father's role. Tom's father and mother, indeed the entire family had always treated Mac as one of their own. With Mac's family living overseas Tom would often invite Mac out to the Island for long weekends. Mac had grown very fond of Tom's father and had a difficult time imagining the dignified gentleman doing the things that he had seen mob figures do in the movies. For his part Tom made vague references about his father splitting his "family" off from the more violent factions and attempting to "take them legit" as he called it. Even as the years passed and Tom's father managed to keep a low profile while others were being hauled into court and sometimes off to prison, Mac became aware that not every aspect of their family business was in fact "legit." But up until this moment it had all seemed very romantic. Now Mac followed the tall stranger and stepped off the train onto the platform. Somehow this no longer had the feeling of romance.

The man turned toward Mac and was, for the first time, totally visible in the light from the lamps along the platform. He was such a stereotype that Mac wasn't certain whether he should laugh or be very afraid. The dark slicked back hair lay above hard eyes that were set in a leathery face. There was even a scar running down his left cheek! No hint of a smile lurked in the pursed lips and Mac wondered if those lips had ever known a smile. The dark eyes surveyed the surroundings for a moment before the man turned and quickly climbed the stairs immediately before him. Mac followed closely and decided that this was definitely not an individual that it would be wise to laugh at. They emerged in the grand concourse with its gilded vaulted ceilings that gave the building that train station echo that seemed to be required of all major rail terminals. The man pushed through the crowd of morning commuters and found a revolving door that exited onto the street. Once on the sidewalk he stopped so suddenly that Mac nearly bumped into him. As they stood there a black Lincoln limousine pulled up to the curb and stopped. Mac felt as if he was in a grade 'B' movie, but he couldn't ignore the sudden dryness in his mouth. For the first time since he spoke on the train the tall dark man acknowledged Mac's existence. He opened the rear door of the limo and told Mac to get in.

Mac entered and settled down on the rich leather upholstery. Across from him was seated an elderly gentleman with thick silver hair in a dark business suit. Mac recognized him immediately although he had aged somewhat since their last meeting. Mac was strangely relieved and glad simultaneously. "Mister Luca, it's good to see you again."

The familiar friendly smile broke across the old man's face. "Mac, you know better than that. Call me Ray. When did you and I become so formal? How are you son? It's been a long time, too long a time." The deep soft baritone voice was as commanding as ever.

"Yes it has Ray, and the fault is mine."

"Ah we all get so busy in this life that we forget that family and friends are the really important things."

"That's so true," replied Mac.

"Mac, I was terribly saddened to hear of your father's death. We only met that one time but in that short period we formed a bond. Did you know that we exchanged letters frequently?"

Mac was surprised. "No, I wasn't aware of that."

"Yes, yes we did and I shall miss them greatly. Your father was a fine man Mac. He was so proud of you and loved you deeply you know."

"I know, it was sort of unspoken, but I always knew."

"That, unfortunately, is the way we men are," replied Luca. Mac realized that they were moving. The big Lincoln moved softly and silently. For some time the two of them rode through the streets and reminisced about Mac and Tom's college days, the weekends spent at Raymond Luca's house at the beach and Mac's father. Mac was reminded of many things that he had long since forgotten. He was amazed at the clarity and detail with which the old man recalled events long past. It was a very enjoyable conversation and the closeness that he had felt toward his friend's father during his college days quickly returned. Then Luca abruptly turned to business. "Some time back you requested some information from my son."

"Yes I did."

"I have it for you. I also have some additional information that you may find very helpful."

"Very well," replied Mac. This last statement was meant to tantalize and it succeeded.

"To answer your original question; yes the Trevor Mason that is your immediate superior is the same Trevor Mason that my son told you about. The Trevor

Mason of Chicago fame, but even more important is one Abraham Rueben that is working for your Mr. Mason. This Abraham Rueben also worked for Mason when he was a CEO in Chicago. We in New York are very familiar with Mr. Rueben, as he has performed certain services for us in the past. However, the services that he performed for the people in Chicago, I should say the information that he sold to the Chicago people has diminished his popularity with some of us here in New York. That's another matter, what you need to know is that he is a very dangerous man with plenty of resources at his disposal. He serves his clients well and is not afraid to break the law or the ethical code he is obliged to maintain as a licensed lawyer, as long as the financial reward makes it worth the risk."

"Is Mason aware of Rueben's tactics?"

"Mason keeps himself carefully ignorant of any unpleasant details."

"What is their current objective? I believe that they are attempting to sell Fox Cabinetry. Why, simply for profit?" Mac could not comprehend why Mason would require the services of such an unsavory character to assist in a legitimate business transaction.

"Selling Fox is simply an end to a larger objective."

"What is that larger objective?"

"Take control of Wellbon-Smith." The senior Luca reached into his inside breast pocket and extracted a silver cigarette case. He opened it and removed a cigarette. "As I recall you currently don't smoke, but if you've recently reacquired this filthy habit you are welcome to join me."

"No thank you."

"Do you object to my indulging?"

"Not at all, I always indulge your son."

Luca sighed. "Yes he's picked up several bad habits from me." The silver case went back into the inside pocket and a lighter emerged from a side pocket. Mac admired the sleekly tailored suit and guessed that it was custom made, probably in Italy.

"No disrespect Ray, but how is a take over possible? While some of the subsidiaries and divisions are publicly traded, Wellbon-Smith is privately held. In addition to that, any sale of the privately held stock must have the new owner approved by the other shareholders before it can be sold."

"If you play by the rules you are absolutely correct. But if you quietly strike enough deals with enough shareholders that are anxious to cash in at inflated prices, well…"

"There can't be that many shareholders that want to cash in."

"The Board has been a bit short-sighted when it comes to dividends. They have consistently voted to pay relatively small dividends in order to preserve a fat treasury and purchase more companies. This has made a lot of the shareholders wish that they had their money invested elsewhere. In addition, they aren't happy with the valuation that the board places on the stock. When you aren't publicly traded there is no market to set value. The board tends to use appraisers that keep the value on the conservative side whenever a sale comes up. So Mason and Rueben have made quite a few big shareholders offers they can't refuse."

"But all those sales have to be approved at the annual meeting."

"True enough, but the assigning of proxy doesn't require anyone's approval."

"So they're buying up proxy votes with the promise of paying inflated prices for the stock. They gain enough votes to control the outcome of any floor vote and use the proxy votes to catch the Board by surprise and put the chairmanship in play."

"Right on the mark Mac, with enough votes they will unseat Carlton Smith. Then with their man as the new chairman they will entertain a motion to approve the sale of stock from several shareholders. All of the sales will be to Mason and his cohorts. The sales will be approved because Mason will have enough proxy votes to gain approval."

"But it can't work."

"Why is that Mac?"

"Because old man Wellbon left the proxy loophole in the company's constitution in case he wanted to use it. He was safe because his family held the largest block of stock. They still do. They have enough voting shares between them that you can't accomplish anything without their consent. That's why it won't work."

The old man beamed. He loved this man almost as much as he loved his own son. He was very proud of them both. "Congratulations Mac, you are an excellent student of your company's history. The family's block of stock does protect against just such a proxy revolt, unless all of it votes with the proxies." Raymond Luca lit up his cigarette and took a long draw.

"Why would they do that? Carlton Smith is the choice of Mary Wellbon. She even put him in over her son."

Luca exhaled a cloud of smoke. He pressed a button in the armrest and an exhaust fan quietly drew the smoke out of the passenger compartment. "That's correct and even if the current Denton Wellbon voted his block of stock against his mother, Trevor Mason won't be able to get enough proxies to override her block and those that are loyal to her. Neither side could win."

"So he has to have Denton's and Mary Wellbon's vote to succeed which is why it won't work."

"That's also why he's been able to secure so many proxy votes without being detected. First because those selling their proxy to him wish the act to remain secret because if he's successful they will profit handsomely and second, the scheme seems so impossible on the surface that none of the Board is paying any attention. But he knows something that none of them know. He knows a secret that the Wellbon family has been keeping for years. At least a secret that Denton Wellbon III and his father have kept for years and a secret that Mary Wellbon would want to keep hidden if she ever gained knowledge of it." With that the senior Luca launched into the story of Denton Wellbon's youthful indiscretion. When he had finished Mac sat incredulous.

"They strong-armed the girl's parents so that the parents wouldn't prosecute young Denton for statuary rape?"

"That's correct. They did get lucky in that the girl's father was caught embezzling. They also got lucky in that the girl decided to marry her boyfriend and run off. I expect her father told her to get lost and never speak a word about the whole affair if she didn't want him to go to jail. Now there is no statute of limitations on rape, statutory or not, but with so much time having past there is almost no danger of Denton being prosecuted at this late date. Besides, the case would be nearly impossible to prove now."

"But compared to all of the other illegal acts that are rumored to have been committed by Denton's father and grandfather, this seems pretty tame. Yet your telling me that this one indiscretion is enough for Mason and Rueben to blackmail the current Denton Wellbon and his mother if need be? Forgive me Ray, but it doesn't sound like enough. This is 1999 and I really don't think that anyone will give a rip."

Luca took another drag and then blew a smoke ring. "I used to be able to fascinate Tom by doing that when he was a mere child.... Forgive me Mac but you don't understand either Mary Wellbon or her son. You also don't understand the society circles that they travel in. They were up from the docks immigrants. The first Wellbon was a self-made man. Not everything he did was legal but he was a tough son of a bitch who fought his way to the top. He also tried to fight his way into New York society. They rejected him because he didn't come from old money. Finally, his son and daughter in law managed to break into those circles. Not so much because they were accepted, but because by this time they just had so damn much money and influence that the society dames couldn't keep them out. Mary Wellbon is very sensitive to what her social contacts think of her. She has done everything in her power to put to rest the unproven rumors concerning how her husband and father-in-law made their fortune. She knows that she and her son are still held to a tougher standard than the so-called old families are. If she knew Denton's secret she would do whatever she had to do to keep it a secret. In addition Denton is head over heels in love with his wife Susan. Incidentally Susan's family happens to be one of those old money families. Denton will not gamble his marriage on Susan learning of this escapade."

Mac was silent for a moment. Luca stumped out his cigarette in one of the numerous ashtrays conveniently placed throughout the spacious passenger compartment. "So Mason is gambling that they can force the Wellbon family to surprise everyone and vote with them," asked Mac?

"That's correct. He already believes that he has young Denton's votes sewed up. He's promised Denton the chairman's office in return for his votes. I expect that Trevor Mason will be the real power behind the throne in that situation. It will be up to Denton to persuade mother. They don't care how he accomplishes this, just so he gets the job done. Of course they have knowledge of his secret to hold over his head in case he has second thoughts."

"I suppose that by selling Fox and perhaps one or two other of their undervalued companies they will be able to pay off the shareholders that agreed to give them their proxy votes."

"Simple isn't it, although I did neglect to tell you two important facets of this deal. You were correct when you said that there weren't enough shareholders that wanted to cash out to pull this scheme off, even with the Wellbon family in line. So the Wellbon family isn't the only ones that are being blackmailed. It seems that there are a lot of skeletons hidden in the Atlantic and Wellbon-Smith closets."

"That's why Trevor requires the services of Abraham Rueben."

"It violates your company's articles of incorporation but it's all very legal except for the blackmail and strong arm, two methods of which I have some knowledge myself." Luca's face was empty of emotion as he gave Mac a cold stare. Mac was caught off guard by the sudden hard edge in the old man's voice. He was suddenly reminded that this man too was capable of the same type of actions as Abraham Rueben if he felt that he would benefit from them. Mac also realized that the man who had been a father figure to him when he was in a strange land and far from his real father was probably capable of much more. Suddenly he felt a twinge of fear in the pit of his stomach as he met the gaze of the empty eyes that were seated across from him.

Mac regained his composure enough to speak. "You said there were two things that you neglected to tell me. What's the other?"

The cold stare and blank face continued to bore into Mac's soul. "I neglected to tell you that the girl that young Denton had his fling with has been dead for quite a few years."

"Dead how?"

"Apparent suicide."

Mac filed this bit of news away and determined that it would not be very smart to inquire as to how Tom's father came to have this knowledge. They rode along in silence for a bit and Mac wondered how long Luca could go without blinking. Apparently he could hold out much longer than Mac. Luca spoke again in the same flat monotone that he had suddenly switched to, "Young Denton is not aware that she is dead. Mason no doubt believes that it's to his benefit for Denton to believe that she could suddenly appear and wreak havoc." The old man finally looked away out the window at the passing landscape. It gave Mac a chance to assess him. He still retained the thick shock of silver hair that he possessed for as long as Mac had known him. The strong rugged yet dignified face, although showing signs of age, remained very handsome. He remained erect and even though he was sitting Mac determined that he retained his excellent posture. He looked like any other businessman except that his business could be very violent at times. Of course, from the information that he had just received it sounded as if Mac's business could have some violence in it also.

Luca looked back at Mac. His friendly smile returned. "Tom tells me that you are considering making an offer for Fox yourself."

"Yes, I have the financing lined up and expect to make the offer within two weeks."

"Good, good! Do you need anything, money, influence?" Luca's tone was one of sincerity.

"Thank you Ray, I really do appreciate that, but I think that I have things pretty well set up."

"Good, good! Just remember that if Mason wants more than what your backers will supply, call me. We can work something out."

"I'll do that Ray. Thank you again." Mac had no intention of ever becoming indebted for money to Raymond Luca. No matter how close they were. He knew that as far as their family was concerned, business was business and friendship shouldn't get in the way.

"A piece of advice Mac," The old man leaned forward and placed a strong but wrinkled hand on Mac's knee. This time he stared into Mac's eyes with fatherly concern. His voice was low but the hard edge was now gone. "Buy Fox no matter the cost and take you and your people out of the Atlantic Corporation. These people are playing a dangerous game. Make certain you don't get caught in the middle. I'll help you wherever and with whatever you may require."

"I'm touched Ray. Thank you again." Perhaps it was because of the recent loss of his father, but Mac truly was moved by the offer of assistance. This man was the closest thing to a surrogate father as anyone could become. Mac realized that they were slowing. He looked out through the tinted glass and saw that they were pulling into a restaurant parking lot. He had no idea where they were. He looked at his watch, eleven thirty in the morning. They had been riding and talking for nearly two and one half hours.

The limo stopped and Luca gestured toward the building. "This is the Morgantown Inn. As you may have realized you are not far from your factory in Goodville."

"I was so engrossed in our conversation that I had no idea where we were," said Mac as he did indeed recognize the old tavern. It was one of those places common on the east coast that could claim to have been founded in the 1700's.

Luca continued, a smile tugging at the corners of his mouth. "Your Thunderbird is parked over there in the corner of the lot. You'll need it to return to your office."

Mac located his classic car, there was a muscular balding man dressed in a white tee shirt and blue jeans standing beside it. "How did he get into my garage and get my car? I have a very expensive security system to protect it."

"Yes you do and it still works quite well. However, as you are not naive, you must realize that my family owns many businesses. The people that operate them for us are highly skilled."

"He broke into my garage even though the security system was on?"

Luca's smile widened. "Broke in is such a harsh description and it sounds like the process would be rather crude. No Mac, it's not necessary to 'break in' when you own the security company."

Mac could only shake his head as the elder Luca laughed. "Don't worry Mac, when you're with my security company most of the common thieves know better than to break into one of my customer's homes. We only turned your system off long enough to extract your car. Now get back to your office and heed my advice. We also took the liberty of returning your company car to your home so it's no longer parked at the Lancaster train station. Yes we picked the lock, no damage."

Mac smiled, opened the door and began to exit. "Thank you for the information. I truly appreciate your help and I enjoyed our visit."

"I too enjoyed our visit. As for the information, I'm certain that someday you'll be able to do me a favor."

Mac hesitated as he stooped to look back into the car. The old man was smiling pleasantly. He extended his hand. Mac took it and was surprised at the strength of the grip. "Take care of yourself Mac, and let's not wait so long between visits. I'm getting to be an old man." Mac was feeling a bit uneasy about the mention of a favor.

"One more thing Mac, I told you that I had information in addition to what you inquired about." Luca paused for dramatic effect and then continued. "Have you ever heard of Southern Cross Investments, Caribbean Funds or Commonwealth Fund?"

"No, no I haven't. Why? What are they?"

"They are offshore investment funds. I think it would greatly benefit you if you investigated them."

"All right, I will, but why?"

"Just do it Mac."

At this time the man in the tee shirt and jeans slid past Mac and got into the back of the limo where Mac had just departed. He closed the door and the limo drove back onto the street. As it headed east back to Philadelphia Mac saw that the man who escorted him from the train was riding up front with the driver. As the passenger compartment was closed off from the driver's compartment Mac was certain that their conversation had been private. At least that's what he chose to believe. Mac turned and walked to his Thunderbird. The keys were conveniently hanging in the ignition.

In the limo the balding frizzy haired man in blue jeans looked at his boss. "Will he be of any help to us?"

Luca smiled. "Yes Andy, he will be a great help to us. Especially after he checks out those offshore funds I mentioned to him."

"I don't get it. What do they have to do with our getting Wellbon-Smith working with us again?"

"You don't have to get it Andy. All you have to do is keep getting closely allied with young Denton Wellbon. We need the same type of 'I scratch your back if you scratch mine' relationship that we had with his father."

"He trusts me and I got the boys keeping an eye on him and his family to make certain that Rueben don't make no moves on them."

"Good. What have you learned concerning the girl that was in your diner the other morning?"

"Her name is Crystal Harrison-Rankin. She goes by Crystal Harrison professionally. She's a TV news anchor in Savannah Georgia."

"This doesn't ring any bells with you Andy?" Luca's voice had just a trace of irritation in it.

"It rings bells boss. Harrison was the name of that joker that Mary Johnson married. So I'm thinking that this really is her daughter."

"If Mary Johnson had a daughter, why didn't we know about her?"

Andy's face reddened slightly and some of the cockiness left his voice. "Mary never came back to visit her parents. We just figured that if there were any kids she would have brought them back. We were keeping an eye on the parents."

"The way you and Denton Wellbon II scared that family, it doesn't surprise me that she never returned to Baltimore. Why didn't we discover the daughter when Mary committed suicide?"

"She and Harrison disappeared when they left Baltimore. We figured that we had our finger on her father through the bank where he worked. That was enough. Besides old man Denton and I had everything under control. Everybody kept their mouth shut. We discovered that Mary was dead about a month after the fact. That seemed to end the problem because we knew her father wouldn't talk, he just wanted to stay out of jail. Remember we were scratching Wellbon's back. That's all. We had no other interest other than helping him. He certainly scratched our backs plenty of times." Andy was getting defensive. It wasn't healthy to have the boss upset with you.

"I know Andy. Relax. Where was Mary when she committed suicide?"

"Savannah." Andy replied rather sheepishly.

"Savannah is the town where Mary Johnson Harrison was found dead, the town where Crystal Harrison is a TV personality; the same Crystal Harrison that shows up in your diner and even seems to recognize you. Do you think that there's a connection Andy?" The sarcasm was heavy in Luca's voice.

Andy squirmed in the deep leather seat. "Boss listen to me when Denton's father heard about Mary Johnson's suicide he sent me down there to check things out. That dumb shit Harrison had already left her several years before she did herself in. Remember, we found out she was dead one month after she died. She was already buried!"

"Where was she buried?"

"Savannah. Actually she was cremated."

"I don't care how, who made the arrangements?"

"Harrison. He was living in California and had his lawyer return to take care of her affairs."

"Did Harrison have the girl?"

"No, there was no record of a girl."

"It seems that there is a girl now." They rode in silence for several minutes. The old man watched the countryside slide past then turned back to his long time lieutenant. "There was no daughter listed in the obits under survivors?"

"No boss. I got a file if you want to look at it." Silence again as the old man seemingly ignored this answer and examined the shine on his shoes.

"About how old do you estimate this young woman to be?"

"Uh, I dunno, early twenties I only saw her for a minute." Andy was watching his boss closely. He was afraid that he was beginning to sweat.

"Early twenties, mused the old man. I'm ruling out the possibility that Rueben has hired a ringer. As you pointed out the other day when she was in your diner, a ringer would have to be much older. She would have to be the age that Mary Johnson would be today if she were still alive." Luca paused. "She could be Foster Harrison's daughter or…"

"Or?" Andy held his breath.

"Or, my dear Andy she could be your friend Denton's daughter, the result of that one wild infamous night with Mary Johnson."

Andy sat staring at the old man. "No boss she can't be, old man Denton would have known. You know how he felt about family. If he thought he had a granddaughter… He would have told us and…"

"You would think that wouldn't you. But let's consider the alternative. Let's consider that the girl is Harrison's daughter. She should have gone to live with him after her mother's death. Did she?"

"I, I don't know boss. I told you there was no record of there ever being a daughter no matter who the father was. Hell there wasn't even a mention of a daughter in the divorce settlement. No custody hearings nothing! There was no reason to even suspect or follow up on the possibility of a daughter. The girl in my diner has the last name of Rankin. She was adopted."

"Very interesting, and being adopted it's safe to assume that she didn't go live with Foster Harrison. What about that Andy, do you think Harrison is smart enough to erase all trace, all records of the existence of a daughter? If so why would he do it? Not only would he have to be smart, but it would take a lot more money than he apparently has."

Andy snorted. "Hell no, He's a jackass!"

"Even if he was smart enough, and I agree with you that he isn't, we have no good reason as to why."

Andy sat stunned. "There's no reason."

"Precisely Andy, there is no reason for Harrison to hide the existence of a daughter, but there might be a reason for Denton's father to hide her. Denton Wellbon II was also smart enough and had the resources to do the job right and it looks like this was done right."

Andy shook his head. "If this girl is young Denton's bastard daughter, I'm certain he's not aware of her. Could be that for some reason old man Denton knew and determined to keep it secret. But why didn't he have us take care of it? That was the deal. We got to use his companies to launder money and sometimes use the trucks to transport contraband and in return we took care of his dirty work for him. Our relationship was built on trust and neither side ever broke that trust. Why didn't he trust us to handle this for him?"

"A question that must be answered; why remove all record of her existence? Regardless, why didn't he have us cover up the existence of the daughter, we took care of everything else and if we didn't who did? I tell you Andy, to do this good a job for this long a time, whoever did this is every bit as good as we are. Maybe better. Think of it. Crystal Harrison had to be supplied with a Birth Certificate and other documents even though there is no record of her in the courts! Her adoption had to be arranged. Someone made her vanish in the official records while having her live openly under the name of Rankin. It's astounding. We have to get some answers. Do we still have solid connections on the West Coast?"

"You bet."

"People we can trust?"

"No problem."

"Okay, as soon as we return to New York, I want you on a plane out there right away. Use the local talent. Find Harrison's home. Get in there and get photos of his private papers. I expect you just might find the actual divorce papers and maybe if we're lucky the original birth certificate. Get everything you can. The papers that are on file in the Savannah Courthouse were obviously faked. We have to find out if old man Denton was behind this, who he used and why he went to such extraordinary measures. Andy, I can't emphasize this enough. We need Atlantic and Wellbon-Smith. The relationship died with young Denton's father. But before we proceed we need to know exactly who those people are that covered this up. I want to know who I'm working against and who they're working for."

***

Sarah Frazer, Carroll Brubaker and David Elliott stood in the staging room at the Fox factory in Goodville. The staging room was normally utilized for auditing especially complicated jobs before they shipped. The auditing process allowed quality control to set the cabinets up side by side to make certain that it matched the dealer's order. This was not normally done with jobs of average complexity. The normal checking processes were sufficient for those. The auditing process was reserved for jobs with multiple colors, complex special cabinetry and pre built soffits that had to fit together precisely on the job site. But that wasn't what the room was being utilized for on this particular morning. This morning the three managers were looking at the show booth that Fox was going to set up at the Kitchen and Bath Industry Show in Chicago in less than two weeks. The booth consisted of four rooms under a hip style "roof" made of redwood rafters with no roofing or shingles covering them. They were open to the sky, or in this case the ceiling. Just as they would be open to the cavernous ceiling at McCormick Place in Chicago. The rooms were made for easy access from three sides of the booth. Three of the rooms contained beautiful designer cabinetry in various Fox door styles and artistic finishes. The fourth was made to look like a den / library. This room would be used as an office at the show to talk with existing dealers and potential new dealers.

Jake and Matt, Fox's two senior and most experienced field service technicians,

stood proudly to the side. They had assembled the booth from the designer's drawings. A booth designed to be disassembled and reassembled in Chicago.
The three managers wandered about the interior of the booth. The cabinetry and the installation were, as always, magnificent. The booth was truly equal to and representative of the exclusive reputation that Fox had built within the industry. The subtly sophisticated exterior walls were covered in semi-gloss sheet material of a silver gray color, discreetly trimmed in black, the new Fox Company colors. The advertising agency had suggested a change to give the venerable company a fresh look. The Fox logo, a contemporary more implied then defined face of a fox inside a delicate oval, was tastefully executed on all four walls beside the entrances.

Sarah was truly amazed. "This company has such a high level of collective talent. Our employees are truly artisans. Carroll you must allow an hour at the end of each shift for everyone to walk through this booth before it's disassembled for shipment to Chicago. Everyone must have a chance to see and appreciate what will represent their skills at the National show. They have each made an important contribution and they have a right to be proud."

"Well Sarah, that's three hours lost production."

"Everyone will be energized just by seeing this booth. I promise you that we'll make it up on the next day's production. Let them be a part of the finished project."

Matt spoke up from the corner. "It's not my place boss, but people are stopping me when I walk past the assembly lines and are asking me how the booth looks."

"It's definitely in 'your place' to make any comment that you feel is timely and appropriate to anyone of us in management," responded Sarah.

Carroll grinned. "Okay Matt, I guess Sarah is right, it's for the best. It's important that we allow our people to feel the pride of working here." Besides, Carroll had not forgotten that they had just narrowly escaped a representation election. Tom Erving informed them that his source on the "floor" at Fox Las Vegas told him the card drive was all but stalled, and Mac told them that it was dead here in Goodville. Carroll was a bit mystified that the normally cautious Mac would speak in such certain terms. "Forgive me Sarah, but Dennis just never suggested things like you come up with. I have to get accustomed to this new style of yours."

In the short time that she had been with Fox, Sarah had introduced several new programs all designed to both keep the employees informed and get them more involved. There were the bi-weekly meetings that she called "bull sessions." These meetings occurred on each shift just after break time in the company cafeteria. Management would brief the work force on sales, production goals, safety issues and company sponsored events, such as family picnics, holiday parties or any item of interest. In addition, Sarah had created various teams to address problems that might arise in the course of daily production. She even persuaded Mac, Carroll, David or any appropriate member of the management team to attend to encourage and support the teams in their work. The senior managers had agreed to allow the teams to try their suggestions as long as the suggestions could be measured and didn't violate any safety or labor laws. At the bull sessions the teams would give their reports. In addition, at the bull sessions employees had the opportunity to make comments, suggestions or ask questions of anyone.

Sarah smiled at Carroll. "No offense to Dennis, but he never left his office. Everyone with a problem had to go to see him. I'm not sure he has seen the factory floor in five years."

"Well you certainly have," piped in David. "You're out here as much as Carroll and I."

"More!" was the quick reply.

"She also dresses the part," said Carroll. This morning after their inspection of the booth she planned on spending time leisurely walking through the plant stopping and talking to the work force. She did this at least one time per week on each shift. On these days, she wore jeans and a denim shirt so as not to intimidate anyone. She had fast become a popular member of the management team. Mac and the others were certain that the women in the work force found it easy to identify with her. As far as the men were concerned they suspected that the tight jeans over her shapely hips might have had some influence on her popularity.

"Okay, that's enough of that," grinned Sarah.

"What" feigned Carroll.

“You know what, that politically incorrect tone of yours.”

“Well the fact that you are still smiling I suppose is a good sign. Please accept my apologies.” Carroll placed his hands together in a gesture of pleading and bowed his head.

“Oh stop it. You’re forgiven.” She then turned to Jake and Matt. “You guys have done a beautiful job in assembling and trimming the booth. I just stand in awe.”

Happy to receive the compliment, the two technicians smiled and glanced at the floor. “We just try to do our job,” said Jake.

“You do it well. We’re lucky to have the two of you on our team. When must you tear down and leave?”

“We load the booth on one of the trucks on Friday. The driver will leave on Saturday morning to be near the front of the line at the docks on Monday morning at McCormick Place. Jake and I will fly out Monday morning to meet the truck and start setting up,” replied Matt.

“Have a safe trip guys. I’ll see you out there later in the week.” With that Sarah waved to Carroll and David and was off to roam the plant.

By late morning Sarah was talking with one of the women that attached glue blocks to the inside of the cabinets as they progressed down the line. The blocks were to mount special drawer slides onto the cabinet backs. They were discussing the birth of the women’s first granddaughter when Sarah’s cell phone rang. “Excuse me Ellie.”

“Sure thing Miss Fraser,” said Ellie as she returned to her task.

Sarah flicked on her cell phone. “Sarah Fraser.”

“Sarah, good morning, it’s Mac.”
“Hi Mac, where are you, I thought you would be joining us to look at the show booth this morning?”

“I planned on it but I had an unexpected meeting in Philadelphia.”

To Catch a Fox

"Philadelphia, is that where you are now?"

"No, I'm in Morgantown at the Morgantown Inn. I was wondering if you could sneak out and join me for lunch. I have a couple of items I want to discuss with you before we head out to Chicago."

Sarah looked at her watch. It was eleven forty five. She had a busy afternoon, but you never refuse the boss when he offers lunch. "I'm down in the plant, but I can get away now if you like."

"Sounds good, I'll get us a table."
"Mac, I'm in a denim shirt and blue jeans."

"Not a problem, the Tavern is very casual at lunch time. See you soon."

"Bye," said Sarah. But Mac, as was his habit was already gone.

To Catch a Fox

Chapter 16

Brady peered over her glasses at the rather oddly dressed gentleman that had just entered her office. The receptionist downstairs had called and informed her that there was a man from the law firm of Smyth Hempstead and Dinkel who wished to meet with Mr. MacLode. Brady informed the receptionist that this was not a law firm that Fox was affiliated or familiar with and that he should state his business. The man answered this query by saying that his business was not with Fox but was a personal matter concerning Mr. MacLode.

"Anthony, she called toward Tony's open office door, "are you familiar with a law firm named Smyth Hempstead and Dinkel?"

"No, why do you ask?" was Tony's half interested reply. He was putting together his outline for the upcoming sales meeting to be held at the show in Chicago. He did not appreciate Brady's interruption.

Brady related that a gentleman from that firm wished to see Mac on personal business.

"When do we expect Mac to return?"

"Who knows?" responded Brady. "He never tells us anything anymore. He just mentioned to me yesterday that he had business 'out of town' today, but was rather vague when I asked when he would return."

"So far 'out of town' that you don't expect him to return today?"

"No, he expected to be back today, but gave no specific time."

"Tell him Mac's not here. If that doesn't discourage him I'll talk with him."

"Wait!" exclaimed Brady. "I remember now. This is the lawyer that is settling Sean MacLode's estate! I'll get him up here but you deal with him. I have work to do."

"As if I don't, but you've got my word on it babe."

"Don't call me 'babe.'"

Now Brady was face to face with Mr. Hempstead. "Mr. MacLode is not in the office today. However, Mr. Conocenti will speak with you."

Hempstead raised his left eyebrow. "Anthony Conocenti is your Vice President of Marketing, what possible help could he be concerning a private matter of Mr. MacLode's?"

Tony came out of his office to meet Mr. Hempstead. He was mildly surprised that this gentleman in a, yes it really was a bowler hat he was holding, knew his name and title. "I can try if you'll allow me."

Hempstead huffed, "That isn't possible." He turned to Brady again. "Mr. MacLode has indicated to me that you and you alone have a pager number that can reach him at any time. It is imperative that you use it now." If there was any doubt concerning the gentleman's country of origin it vanished as the thick British accent rolled off his tongue.

Tony laughed, "If that were the case I would have…" Tony stopped as Brady picked up the phone and punched in a number. He stared at her incredulous.

Brady shrugged. "If he knows about the pager number, he has Mac's confidence. I thought that I was the only one who knew about it."

Visibly dismayed by this revelation Tony regained his composure and turned to Hempstead. "Why don't you make yourself comfortable in Mac's office while we wait for his return call." After getting Hempstead settled Tony returned to his own office muttering under his breath about how Mac should surely trust him after all these years. Brady kept her attention on her computer keyboard as she suppressed a smile.

***

To Catch a Fox

Sarah Frazer entered the Morgantown Inn, a quaint old tavern, and was greeted by the hostess. "I'm meeting a gentleman for…"

"Of course, Mac's already here and has a table. Just follow me."

As the hostess, with Sarah in tow, approached a table for two in a secluded corner, Mac rose to greet her. "Glad you could get away Sarah."

"Me too," she said as Mac pulled out her chair for her. As soon as she was seated the waitress brought two glasses of Chardonnay.

"If my memory is correct, this is your preference."

Sarah smiled. "Your memory is correct. Have you taken the liberty of ordering lunch also?"

"No, no I've never dined with you before, I wouldn't be so bold. But I do recommend the smoked salmon plate accompanied with a Caesar salad. The Caesar dressing is excellent here and they still offer anchovies if your taste desires."

"That sounds delicious."

The waitress was standing by so Mac ordered the same for them both. When the waitress departed Mac turned to Sarah. "You're no doubt wondering why I invited you to lunch."

"Well yes, I was."

"Two reasons, the first concerns our recent union problem. Tom Erving informs me that the card check campaign by the union has stalled short of the required number at the Vegas plant. In addition I can tell you that the movement at Goodville has never gotten off the ground. So it appears that for the time being we've dodged that bullet."

"Carroll informed both David and I that this was your feeling this morning, but he was puzzled as to how you could be so certain?"

"Well you and I know Tom Erving has a spy on the plant floor. His information has been very accurate so I have little reason to doubt his current assessment. As for Goodville I have my own sources."

"You have your own paid spy?"

"Not paid Sarah. You make it sound so illegal. Over the years suffice it to say that I have inspired, I hope that's not too egotistical a description, a certain loyalty among some employees on the plant floor. They tend to bring information that they imagine will interest me. Most of what they bring is just factory floor gossip, but I listen intently to all that they offer be it useless or not. Every now and then something valuable surfaces and I make use of it."

Sarah took a sip of her wine. "Your source claims that the campaign never got off the ground in Goodville? Why do you suppose that to be the case?"

"A couple of reasons: First the local culture has never been predisposed to unions. That is in the process of changing as there are more people relocating to Lancaster County, people that don't have the local work ethic. In this case that ethic translates to mean that if you aren't happy with your present situation simply go work somewhere else. These folks, for the most part don't believe in changing the culture of the work place. They believe that they are free to work where they will and with the company that will hire them. They don't have much time for picket lines. For the most part our workforce has been born and raised here. In addition to that my sources tell me that the union made a strange selection when choosing the person on the floor to head up this card signing campaign. That person is neither articulate nor dedicated to anything. This is not a person who can proselytize."

"You're confident in this information?"

"My dear Sarah, as you know nothing is ever 100% certain, but I'm at least 90% confident that this information is correct. For one thing, now that you have me walking the factory floor even more frequently than before, I've noticed that since we've restored the benefits to their original level workers once again make eye contact as I walk through the plant. That is as it has been historically however during the time that we reduced the benefits few were willing to look me in the eye. I like what I now see and I believe it to be a favorable sign."

"I agree Mac. My travels to the plant floor have been very warmly received since we made the announcement concerning benefits. May I ask the identity of the individual that the union chose?"

"You may ask, but I'm not telling."

Sarah tilted her head. A puzzled look spread across her face. "Why would you not tell me?" The waitress interrupted this exchange as she placed their order on the table before them. When she had departed Mac replied.

"This has nothing to do with trust. I trust you implicitly otherwise I would not have included you in the group of managers that I want to be my partners in purchasing Fox. What it has to do with is prejudice." A frown appeared on Sarah's face in response to Mac's comment.

"Prejudice, I don't understand. You think I'm prejudiced?"

Mac continued: "Everyone is concerning some topic, it's only human. We both have degrees in business administration and have made our living in management. This doesn't qualify us as big fans of unionization. If we're honest with ourselves we probably hold a deep-seated anti union bias. As proof of that I offer our recent actions. We both placed our careers with Fox and the Atlantic Corporation in jeopardy with the actions we took to thwart the union. We put our company in a less desirable financial position but we did it because we believed, correctly I think, that this was less of a threat than was the union."

"Okay I'll buy that," responded Sarah. "I'm no lover of unions. And yes, I believe that we can restore Fox's prior level of profitability. I believe that we can create a more secure future for our employees and us. More secure than they would have had with the union. But forgive me if I fail to see what this has to do with my knowing the identity of the union's card circulator."

Mac sipped his wine then looked at the glass thoughtfully. "I like the taste of their house Chardonnay. I must ask the name of the vintner before I leave." He sat the glass down and returned Sarah's gaze. "If you know this individual's identity you will never forget that he or she once took part in an attempt to unionize Fox. That will influence every decision that you make concerning this individual from this moment on. If the individual's foreman brings their name to you for a possible promotion, you will remember. If a supervisor recommends disciplinary action concerning this person, you will remember. If their name appears on a list of potential people for lay off during a slow period, you will remember. I don't want this one action to have any bearing on this person's career at Fox. Remember they were exercising their rights under the law. Besides in an odd way we owe this person a debt of gratitude for being a bit inept."

The frown slowly disappeared from Sarah's face and was replaced by a slow knowing smile. "You don't believe that I can be objective but you believe that you can be?"

Mac gave Sarah a broad smile in return. "Still searching for that dark chauvinistic heart that you believe beats within my chest?"

"Well maybe. You have a certain reputation as a ladies' man that would suggest that you didn't found the local chapter of NOW. Usually a man that is as experienced as you are rumored to be holds certain opinions concerning women, even if he doesn't admit it to himself." She immediately wondered if she was being too bold. She had essentially changed the topic of discussion. After all he is her boss; no, better to determine the man's true colors now before they become business partners and it's too late to take action.

Mac remained unruffled, "As to whether I believe that I can be more objective and less prejudiced than can you the answer is: hell no! If anything I think you stand a much better chance of being objective than do I. I hate unions, especially where our company is concerned. That's a level of emotion that I don't believe you have yet reached. However, I came by this knowledge quite by chance. I did not seek the identity of this person. It was told to me in the course of conversation. I suddenly had knowledge. Now there is no forgetting it."

"So what will stop you from exercising your prejudice even if I wouldn't?"

"My dear Ms. Frazer, as V.P. of Human Resources you should look up our respective job descriptions. You are required to be involved in every decision that affects the career of every employee at Fox. As CEO, I am only involved with the careers of the senior staff. That way I'll never be involved with any decisions concerning this particular person and you have no knowledge of his or her identity. We will never be open to charges that we retaliated, as you won't take any action that you can't back up with legitimate reasons and I won't be involved in those actions."

Sarah considered this for a moment. "I'm forced to agree with your logic."

"But do you approve?"

"Yes,

"Good!"

They both began enjoying their lunch and for a period ate in silence. Then after the waitress delivered his second glass of wine without being asked, Mac inquired as to the brand of the wine they were drinking. Sarah realized that Mac must frequent this particular establishment. As always she observed that he was ever the gentleman and treated the waitress, as indeed he treated everyone, with the utmost respect.

Having his curiosity satisfied Mac picked up the conversation, "Now the next topic is indirectly related to the union. Let's assume that we are successful in purchasing Fox from Atlantic. Considering our recent union experience we must do everything to insure that our employee's benefits remain exactly the same as they are now without interruption. We can't afford to have them think that our only motive was to appease them until we completed the purchase of the company."

"I agree, but that's going to be a tall order. I've been thinking about this very topic. Atlantic negotiates deals with insurance companies, truck and auto leasing contracts; you name it with the strength of multiple companies behind them. Therefore they get preferential rates. We will be negotiating as an individual company and a small one at that."

Mac finished his lunch and pushed the plates slightly away. "I know and I really don't have any preference as to companies. I just want every employee to feel that new ownership has not harmed them in any way. That's why I want you and Dale Hershey working together to find the best deal for the employees with the equivalent coverage. As you know I'm meeting with Trevor Mason in Chicago in less than two weeks to make our offer. I don't expect it will be accepted without protracted negotiations and of course discovery, although we know where the skeletons are hidden. We've got to be ready just in case things progress in a favorable manor."

“I agree, I’ll get right on it with Dale as soon as I return to the office.” Sarah was excited. This was more important than anything that she had on her schedule for this afternoon.

“Remember the goal is benefits that are the equivalent of what the employees currently have. Dale is an excellent CFO but sometimes he gets too wrapped up in the numbers and forgets the people side. Tell Dale that we will figure out how to pay for this somehow.”

Mac’s cell phone rang quietly. He pulled it from his inside jacket pocket and stared at the screen with a slight look of surprise. Returning it to his pocket he hastily picked up the tab that the waitress had left on the table and placed a credit card in the holder. “I apologize,” he explained to Sarah. “I have to return to the office immediately.”

“Nothing serious I trust?”

“Not as far as the company is concerned. It’s personal and I suppose that I’ve been negligent with all that has been going on.”

On impulse Sarah inquired; “May I ask you a question?”

“Of course” replied Mac.

“Why didn’t you invite Dale to lunch with us as he is equally involved?”

“That’s easy to answer Sarah. I had yet another proposition to place before you today. When we are all in Chicago I want you to have dinner with me one evening. I know a great Italian restaurant. As I intend this to be strictly social I didn’t intend to invite Dale.” He had an amused smile on his face as he studied her reaction. “That was my last reason for lunch. What do you say?”

Sarah was taken aback and she knew it must be written all over her face. She knew that she should regrettably say no. It just wasn’t proper to have a date with your boss. It made no difference if he was upset with her or not. She had to stand on her principles! “Why yes. Yes I’d love to have dinner with you she replied.”

“Good I’ll let you know the day and time after we arrive in Chicago. See you back at the office." Mac left her to go pay the bill. Sarah moved rather slowly outside to the parking lot. What just happened here? She wondered.

***

Brady was attempting to appear as if she was typing on her computer while straining to hear the conversation that was going on behind the closed door to Mac's office. Mac had returned about twenty minutes ago and had sequestered himself in his office with Brian Hempstead. It was apparent from the greeting that they really did know each other. Brady also noticed that Sarah Ferguson had returned from lunch at nearly the same time, as did Mac. Brady decided that she would speculate on that observation later. The walls to both Mac's and Tony's offices flanked Brady's desk as she sat between them. There was no soundproofing but Brady was only able to hear bits and pieces of the conversation.

"Settle the estate…as the executor you must…"

"How do I do that…? What of the inquiries…?"

"Sell…?"

"It may be prudent…because of certain current opportunities."

"What would the proper sequence be…?"

It was driving Brady crazy, these bits and pieces of information that made no sense. She wished that the walls were totally soundproof. That way she would hear nothing. This way she heard only parts of the conversation and they were just enough to whet her curiosity.

Suddenly Mac burst through the door with Brian Hempstead close behind. Brady knew that she must have jumped. "Brady, is it too late to make the last train to New York City?" Brady quickly checked a train schedule that she had pinned to the corkboard on the wall beside her desk.

"The last train to the city for today left over an hour ago. The only New York trains for the rest of the day are returning from there."

"Damn!" exclaimed Mac.

"William!" Brady's low-pitched voice was clearly critical of Mac's language.

"Sorry Brady, but you may have to give me some slack this afternoon. Mr. Hempstead has brought some unexpected news."

"That's no excuse…"

"Cut me a break Brady!" Mac's tone and expression were intense and made it clear that his usual laid back approach to events was not in evidence this afternoon. "Tony, do you have the name and number of that charter plane service that we used the other year to take the entire staff to that seminar in Boston?" Tony's office door was open and Mac's overheard reply to Brady made it clear that the boss was in no mood for any banter. Tony quickly grabbed his PDA and began frantically scrolling through his contacts.

"Yeah boss, the one out at the airport. Got us up and back all in one day."

"That's the one." The urgency was palpable in Mac's voice. There was no panic, but whatever this involved it was important.

Relief flooded over Tony as the name and number appeared on the tiny screen. "Got it boss, it's…"

"Just give it to Brady. Brady call the number that Tony gives you and see if they have a plane and pilot available to fly over to New York this afternoon."

Mac turned to Brian Hempstead. "Where are you staying Brian?"

"The Holiday Inn at Morgantown, you know the one just off the turnpike."

"You obviously have a rental car?"

"Yes I do William. I flew into Philadelphia last night and picked up a rental to drive out here."

Brady was on the phone by now with Tony standing behind her. “William, they can have a plane and pilot ready to take off by five o’clock.”

“What kind of plane? There are only two of us.”

“I’m assuming it will be you and Mr. Hempstead?”

“That’s correct.”

“There are only two passengers.” She turned back to Mac. “How about a twin engine Piper Comanche?”

“Perfect, tell them we’ll be there by four thirty.” Mac turned to Brian again. “You can check out and make that?”

Brian Hempstead took a pocket watch out and studied it briefly. “I can be back here by three. Will that work?”

“That’s perfect. We’ll leave the rental here and I’ll drive to the airport. If you decide to fly back to London from over there I’ll see that your rental is returned.”

Brady was still on the phone. “William, are they to bill this to Fox Cabinetry?”

“No put it on my personal American Express card. You have the details just give them the number.”

“Very well.”

Mac turned to Brian Hempstead. “I’ll see you at three.”

“Right Oh old chap” with that Brian was gone.

Brady, having regained her composure while making Mac’s arrangements, queried Mac. “William there is no way that you can make it to your house, pack a bag and be back here by three. I’m assuming that you will be staying overnight?”

“You’re right we will have to stay overnight. I’ll send the plane back as soon as we disembark. That way I won’t be charged for the pilot’s hotel and meals. I’ll come back on the train tomorrow morning. Reserve two rooms on my credit card at the Marriott in Times Square."

"Right away, but what about packing?"

Mac surveyed his appearance. "Well how does this suit I'm wearing look?"

"Impeccable as always boss," Tony responded.

"Agreed, you look good William," was Brady's comment.

"Good, I'll hang it up as soon as I get in the room tonight and purchase some casual clothes for the trip home tomorrow before I leave. Now, I believe that the show booth is still set up down in the factory?"

"That's right Mac, if you're going down to check it out would you mind if I come along?" Tony had not yet seen the finished product even though he had been making periodic visits. As the events of the last few minutes sounded extremely personal, Tony wanted to offer any assistance that Mac might require, but he wanted to do it in private as they walked together to the plant.

"Let's go. I should have time to do this before Brian returns." Now that the arrangements had been made, Mac's normal demeanor returned. As Tony and Mac were exiting the door, Mac paused and looked back at Brady. "Look up Denton Wellbon's office phone number in the company directory. I'll need it after Tony and I return from the show booth."

"Denton Wellbon III? You never have reason to call him."

"I guess I do now Brady," was Mac's reply as he hurried to catch up with Tony.

***

Abraham Rueben kept the phone pressed to his ear. He did not want this conversation on the speaker. In addition, he made certain that this particular caller always called him on this "clean" phone. A private line that Rueben was certain had no "bugs" attached. He was speaking with Albert Bernard who was currently in Savannah. "Are you certain that you have enough people to keep her under surveillance around the clock Albert?"

"Yes sir Mr. Rueben. As soon as I got into town I put six of the best P.I.'s on our payroll. I hired enough so that I can rotate them. That way she won't notice the same people in her vicinity all the time. I hope that I'm not spending too much money, but you said to do the job right."

"I'm not complaining. Now tell me what she's doing."

"Nothing, absolutely nothing Mr. Rueben, I mean other than going to work. She works all the time at that T.V. station."

"She's a young attractive girl. What about boyfriends."

"She must keep them hidden in her closet because we never see any."

"She has no boyfriends? Albert, she's a local celebrity and she's making big money. Surely there are young men in pursuit."

"I didn't say she wasn't being pursued. There are a lot of guys both her age and older that are trying to hit on her, but none of them are having any success."

"Well that keeps things simple," mused Abraham to himself.

"How long do you want to keep this up Mr. Rueben?"

"Until I tell you to stop Albert, just keep me informed of anything that breaks her set routine."

"Will do Mr. Rueben," Albert hung up.

Abraham Rueben sat in deep thought for a while. He was planning contingencies. It was looking more and more doubtful that he would be able to get the proxy vote from the off shore funds. Although that London law firm did contact him this week and inform him that they were finally able to meet with the owner and would give him the answer by the end of the week. But if the answer was no, then there was no way that he and Trevor could pull this off without Mary Wellbon's vote. In spite of Trevor's confidence in his ability to manipulate young Wellbon, Abraham had his doubts about Denton's ability and will to convince his mother. If Trevor was right concerning Denton's abilities to capture his mother's support then all is well. But if Trevor was wrong and the "A" plan fails, then Abraham must have an alternate plan. That plan seemed certain to include Crystal Harrison.

Abraham's revelry was interrupted by his secretary's voice on the intercom. "A Detective Grabowski of the New York Police Department to see you Mr. Rueben."

Abraham paused and a frown creased his forehead. In his long career many police had interviewed him, but he usually expected them. This time he hadn't a clue. His mind raced. He was covered on Kensington-Cramer, hell even the building's security was unaware that Donald came calling. Could one of the shareholders that he and Trevor were strong-arming gone to the police?

"Mr. Rueben, are you there?"

"Oh yes, I'm sorry. Please send the gentleman in."

Sam Grabowski entered the plush office. Abraham rose to greet him. "Detective Grabowski, please have a seat. What can I do for you?"

Sam displayed his badge for Abraham to examine. "Homicide lieutenant Grabowski, what could possibly bring you here?"

Sam took the offered chair across the desk from Rueben. Rueben met his gaze and held it. There was no sign of panic in his eyes. From what Sam had found out about this man he wouldn't expect it either. "Well Mr. Rueben, I'm here about a Donald Kensington-Cramer. I believe that you knew him."

"What makes you believe that lieutenant?"

"Well you attended his funeral."

"I wasn't at the memorial service."

"But you were at the grave site."

"Yes I was."

"You gave your condolences to his aunt, one Melissa Kensington."

"That's what one usually does at the grave site lieutenant."

"I guess I'm interested in how you knew the deceased?"

"I didn't, but I happen to be the lawyer of record for a Mr. Trevor Mason. Mr. Mason is President and Chief Executive Officer of the Atlantic Corporation. The Wellbon-Smith Corporation wholly owns Atlantic. Ms. Kensington is a shareholder in Wellbon-Smith. In my capacity as Mason's lawyer, I've had occasion to meet Ms. Kensington. If you know that I was present at the grave site you must also know that I was with Mr. Mason at the time. We both felt obliged to pay our respects, as Ms Kensington is an influential person at Wellbon–Smith."

"So you didn't know Donald Kensington-Cramer?"

"No I didn't."

"You never met him?"

"Not that I'm aware of lieutenant. I'm curious, why is homicide involved with this, I thought the papers said it was suicide."

"The papers said apparent suicide. Turns out it wasn't." Grabowski was watching Rueben closely.

"Was there a note?"

"No, but that doesn't mean anything. Many times there isn't any note."

Rueben eyed the lieutenant. He didn't like this game they were playing and he didn't have time for it. "You think he was pushed off that building?"

"No."

"Why do I have the honor of this visit lieutenant?"

"Kensington-Cramer's car, a Porsche Boxter, was found just across the street from this building. It was apparently abandoned."

"And that brings you to my office because…?"

"Well it's rather strange. The victim had his car keys on his person at the time of death. It's nearly twenty blocks from this office to the victim's co-op. You would think that he would drive home. Also you were at the funeral. By your own admission you have a connection with the family, however loose. The car is found near your office building. We're attempting to piece together the victim's final hours. I thought you may have seen him sometime before he died."

"No lieutenant I'm sorry I can't help you. By the way there are other firms in this very building not to mention other office buildings on either side of the street. I assume that you are checking those also."

"We may, but there was a janitor working in the office building across the street that saw the driver of Kensington–Cramer's car come into this building sometime between seven and eight on the night he was killed."

"Did you talk with our security people? We have twenty-four hour security in this building."

"Yes I did, but your guard informed me that the night guard had no record of any intrusion that night and no one came to the door requesting entrance."

"Well it sounds as if your janitor is mistaken."

"Sounds that way doesn't it," replied Sam. As Sam expected, Rueben wouldn't rattle easily. "I asked your security people if you have any surveillance cameras and they said that you did. I requested the tapes for that night but your chief security man informed me that I needed a warrant."

Abe Rueben smiled. "He was just doing his job lieutenant. Tell you what. I'll save you time. I'll have them give you the tapes for that night for all the security cameras. They cover all the entrances and hallways."

Grabowski was surprised by this offer but he certainly wasn't going to turn it down. "I thank you for that. How soon can I get them?"

"Right now," replied Abraham and he picked up a phone and called his chief of security. When Abraham hung up he looked at Grabowski and smiled. "They'll have them at the front desk in ten minutes. That's the advantage of owning the building." Abe rose from his chair and extended his hand, indicating that the meeting was over.

Grabowski rose also and accepted the hand. "Thank you for your cooperation. I'll let you know the results."

"No problem lieutenant."

Rueben stared at the door as Grabowski closed it behind him. The car, I should have considered that there might be a car. However moving it would have presented its own problems. No, the police finding the car won't be the end of the world. A bigger mistake was leaving the keys in Donald's pocket. Damn Duke! How could he be so careless? It occurred to Abe that he hadn't checked Donald's pockets either, but he was walking around with a broken rib for Pete's sake! What was he paying Duke for anyway? If the keys were missing it might have appeared that the car was stolen. Hell, they might come to that conclusion anyway. Who else would abandon a Porsche Boxter except some kids who had hot-wired it for a joy ride? Another possibility is that Donald was high on drugs and forgot where he left it. That's it. Kensington-Cramer was a documented druggie. No problem. That's a better explanation than the remote possibility that he came to see Abe. Abe didn't even know him and there's nothing to indicate that he did. That cop is just fishing. He's got nothing! Abe checked his PDA to see what he had to attend to next.

***

Out on the street with the tapes in his hand Sam Grabowski thought about the brief meeting. It went pretty much as he expected. Rueben was a cool cookie; there was no way he was going to panic. He was surprised by the access to the surveillance tapes. That pretty much told him that they contained nothing. He would have the lab look them over closely anyway.

The interview with Melissa Kensington didn't reveal much more. Sam took Polly with him when he informed Ms. Kensington that they were changing her nephew's death from a probable suicide to homicide. She seemed shocked by this, but could give no helpful information. When Sam asked if her nephew had any enemies, she simply shrugged and asked if the autopsy revealed any drugs in Donald's blood? Sam told her that there was a considerable amount of PCP, angel dust, in Donald's system. "That was his enemy lieutenant. Perhaps you should attempt to find out who was supplying him. I did my best to get him to stop, but apparently I failed." With that she broke down and Polly suggested that they leave for now. Sam had to admit; with Donald Kensington-Cramer's history of drug abuse it didn't stretch the imagination that he may have run afoul of his supplier. But that theory didn't ring true. Druggies got in trouble with their suppliers when they couldn't pay. Kensington-Cramer died with more money in his accounts than Sam would probably earn in a lifetime. Suppliers want to keep users like that on the string not kill them and there was no credible evidence that Donald was anymore than a user. He didn't have to sell drugs to get rich, hell he already was rich, or at least his family was.

So what about Abraham Rueben? Was he a suspect or not? The only thing that Sam had to tie him to the victim was the victim's car parked across the street from Rueben's office, a questionable eyewitness that claimed that the driver of that car entered Rueben's office building the night of the victim's death. The "driver of the car"; the janitor couldn't even identify the driver as Donald Kensington-Cramer. The distance and the dark night were both too great. The fact that Sam had personally observed Rueben at the victim's funeral paying his respects to the next of kin was hardly enough to accuse him of murder. Everything could be explained or chalked up to coincidence. Hell a druggie like Kensington-Cramer, high on angel dust, could have forgotten where he left his car.

What was at the center of all this? The Atlantic Corporation and Wellbon-Smith, those companies formed the only link between Melissa Kensington, Donald Kensington-Cramer, Trevor Mason and Abraham Rueben. It even indirectly linked Denton Wellbon III, whom Sam had seen at Andy's Diner. Was he really looking hard at Abraham Rueben only because of his hunch about Atlantic and the mob renewing ties once more? That could never be proven the first time around.

Sam also noted the new carpet and paint in Rueben's office; so new that the odor of formaldehyde in both was still strong. That meant that there was probably no hope of finding any of the victim's DNA in that office. Sam laughed to himself. As if he had enough to get the DA's office to request a warrant for a CSI team to enter in the first place. Who was he kidding? They would laugh him out on the street. Maybe they should. He was ignoring the first rule of investigation. Just look at the facts. He was operating on hunches. First a hunch that the mob was making another big time move and a hunch that Kensington-Cramer was killed in Rueben's office. The facts didn't support either hunch. Hell the facts didn't support anything!

Sam got into his unmarked car and threw the security tapes into the back seat. He decided to invite Harry Sigfried to meet him at Clancy's bar on 46th street for a beer tonight after his shift. He still believed he was right.

***

Tony Conocenti sat at the bar of The Pub. He was waiting for David Elliott to arrive. The Pub was located in the village of New Holland near Goodville and happened to be on the way home for both. The two had made arrangements to meet after work. Earlier Tony had driven Mac and the mysterious British lawyer to the Lancaster Airport. Mac had belatedly realized that he was driving his classic Thunderbird and had no desire to allow it to be parked overnight in the airport parking lot. Tony took his company car and dropped Mac and his lawyer at the airport. David promised Mac that they would lock his T-Bird inside the factory.

While waiting for David the girl behind the bar brought Tony his usual drink, a CC on the rocks with a splash and a twist. She was cute and young and she had a terrible crush on Tony, but Tony never noticed. If he had he would have wisely decided that she was too young and immature for him. If she knew what she did accomplish, she would have been crushed. It was her misfortune to have the same color hair as Blair McManus. It reminded Tony of Blair. Not that he needed much to remind him. He took a sip of the whiskey, closed his eyes and thought of how much he missed Blair calling him "Tiger."

There were no bars in Goodville. The township that Goodville was located in was what was known in Pennsylvania as a dry township. Pennsylvania, being the epitome of home rule allowed each local municipality to determine if it would allow liquor sales or not. Ultimately the Pennsylvania Liquor Control Board through the issuance of liquor licenses regulated the sale of liquor. This method of controlling the sale of liquor was either heralded or condemned depending on your views of the matter. The village of New Holland was not dry therefore David and Tony had to travel here to have an after work drink. The Pub was a friendly neighborhood bar and grill.

David climbed onto the empty stool next to Tony. "Well you don't look like a man who just got great sales numbers for the past four weeks."

Tony turned to David and smiled. "They have been pretty good haven't they?"

"You must have done a hell of a job selling that price increase."

"I think we convinced a few major dealers that it wasn't going to hurt them, and the multi line dealers are scrambling to beat the deadline for the old prices. With these numbers the sales force is now convinced that all is not lost. With them behind us we can pull the dealers along."

"Mac tells me that you've been hammering the phones with the sales force and the dealers ever since you returned from your tour of the flagships."

"Well that's my job. So much of sales have to do with the attitude of the people selling the product. I know that Carroll and his people in manufacturing believe that it's all product and I will be the first to proclaim how important quality is, but if the people selling the product don't feel right about any aspect, you can go out of business sitting on the best product in the world."

Elliott ordered a glass of merlot. "Dale tells me that if we can sustain this pace we will almost pay for the increased costs of payroll and benefits. He said that once we pass a certain volume the 'economy of scale' kicks in and our profit margin greatly increases."

Tony took another sip of the whiskey. "We won't be able to maintain this pace for the remainder of the half but I think we'll be strong enough that we'll offset most of our increase in costs above the line and still maintain at least a 27% gross margin for the year."

"Corporate wants a 32% margin and 14% on the operating line."

"Well they can't have everything they want all the time. I think we'll finish at 27% and 9% on the operating line."

David smiled. "Are you prepared to explain that to Trevor Mason?"

"Of course I am. Besides the worst that he can do is fire me."

"Something he's been known to do Tony."

"Shit on him."

"Bold words from a man on a bar stool."

Tony laughed, "If Mac's plan to buy Fox works out we may not have to answer to Trevor much longer."

"That would be nice, and I'm optimistic enough to believe it can happen. Hey what was Mac's rush trip to New York about today?"

"Mac told me it was personal, something to do with his father's estate. The lawyer was from Britain. Apparently the old man retained a London law firm to handle his affairs. The only thing that I don't understand is Mac told Brady to get him the phone number for Denton Wellbon at corporate."

"Maybe the two aren't connected."

"Probably not, but I'm still curious as to why he would be talking to Wellbon."

David thought for a minute. "Wellbon is the number two at corporate, right under Mason."

"Yeah but Mac and the other division presidents always deal directly with Mason."

Both were silent as they sipped their drinks. Then David spoke up. "Not to change the subject but you really looked down when I came in. Something other than work bothering you?"

Tony was probably closer to David than anyone else on the senior staff, even closer than he was to Mac. Sales and Service had to work together to solve numerous problems so they just naturally spent a lot of time talking to each other during the course of the workweek. Be it face to face or on the phone as Tony traveled. What began with mutual respect grew into friendship. David was the only person at Fox that had any knowledge concerning Blair McManus.

"Yeah, something is bothering me. It's Blair."

"I thought things were progressing nicely between you two."

"So did I, we haven't had time to talk since I returned from my last trip."

"We're talking now."

"Dave, you have a wife and kids to go home to, you shouldn't be sitting in a bar with your divorced buddy."

"Clare and the kids are out shopping with her mother. She called me and told me they wouldn't be home until late. I told her I was meeting you for a drink and she suggested that I get something to eat while I'm here, so how about dinner and conversation."

Tony looked at his friend. "Honest?"

"Honest, I'm not making this up. I don't intend to get in trouble with Clare just to watch you cry in your beer."

Tony grinned, "You're a good friend. Okay, let's move to a table and order."

Over dinner Tony told David the whole story of the canceled date in San Francisco and the image of Blair on some movie star's arm at the awards dinner. He then launched into an explanation of the phone tag that he and Blair played after his return and the final message he left her.

"Has she called you back since?"

"No."

"I wouldn't expect so."

"What do you mean?"

"Well you made it pretty clear with the messages that you left that you were ticked about something and you were brushing her off. At the very least you sent the message that you didn't want this relationship to go any further for whatever reason."

"Damn right I was ticked. I had a right to be."

"Well maybe."

"What do you mean 'maybe'?"

"The problem that I see is you never told her why you were brushing her off, let alone give her a chance to explain."

"What explanation could there be?"

"Well I don't know but there may be a very plausible one. The trouble is you'll never know will you?"

"I guess the only way to find out is for us to talk about it."

"Yeah, well I bet with those phone messages you left you have her fur up. Getting her to talk to you after that may be hazardous to your health. She is a redhead you know."

Silence ensued as the waitress removed their empty plates. "Can I get you anything else?" she asked.

"Just regular coffee black," said David. Tony nodded in agreement.

Tony looked his old friend in the eye. "Did I screw up?"

"It all depends how important she is to you. If she's not that important, then who cares if she's two-timing you with a movie star? Hey she was a good roll under the sheets, time to move on. On the other hand if you find yourself having dinner in a bar with an old friend lamenting recent events concerning her, well I think you at least need to have one more face-to-face conversation. Even if it is hazardous to your health and even if it ends badly. That way you'll know for sure where the two of you stand. You'll also know if you screwed up."

The coffee came and they sipped it in silence. Finally David spoke. "When are you going to Chicago?"

"This coming Wednesday, I'm going out early as I have to get a lot of arrangements finished before the sales force fly in."

"Go out Tuesday."

"Why do you say that?"

"Go talk to Blair. Get this settled between you once and for all. And don't walk up to her with a chip on your shoulder."

"Suppose she never wants to see me again?"

"If that bothers you, then as I said before you really will know that you screwed up. If it's broken so bad that you can't fix it, well you've been through that before. You know it hurts but you also know that you can survive it."

"Wow, David you don't mince words!"

"Friends shouldn't mince words with each other. I hope you don't with me."

"No, you're right, they shouldn't. And if the situation ever presents itself I won't either. Dinner is on me. I owe you that much for listening and for the advice."

"Okay, I'll allow you to do that."

Tony paid the bill and they headed for the parking lot. Before parting David had one more thing to say. "Tony I want you to know that if this girl is what you want, I'm rooting for you."

"Thanks Dave. I'll keep in touch and let you know how things work out."

***

Mac and Brian Hempstead were sitting in an upscale restaurant called The Brasserie in the theater district in New York City. Neither of them had expected to be sitting here when they awoke this morning. Mac glanced at Brian who seemed to be enjoying himself immensely over a vodka martini as he listened to the shapely lounge singer sit on the piano and croon some favorites. "Brian, I have the utmost respect for you and your judgment. My father always spoke highly of you, but I do think you need to eat some pretzels and nuts along with that martini. Neither of us have had anything to eat since lunch and I want you to be sharp when Denton Wellbon gets here."

"I will take your advice William, but I wonder if your father ever told you that I could drink him under the table if I had a mind to?"

Mac raised an eyebrow. "No he failed to mention that fact Brian."

"Thought so."

Brian returned to ogling the singer and Mac reflected on the day. It began with the train ride to Philadelphia to meet Ray Luca. The drive back to Morgantown during which Mac found out exactly what Trevor Mason was planning. The unexpected arrival of Brian Hempstead, the estate lawyer, determined to force Mac to attend to important estate business. Incredibly that business meshed perfectly with the information that Ray Luca gave him and dictated the decision to make the flight to New York and meet with Denton Wellbon. Mac smiled to himself. There was one more item of importance in a very important day; Sarah had accepted his invitation to dinner in Chicago.

They took off in a chartered twin engine Piper Comanche at precisely 5:30 PM and landed at Kennedy around 6:30. Most of that time was spent in the Kennedy traffic pattern. It took nearly 50 minutes to travel by cab to the Times Square Marriott. Another 30 minutes to check in and freshen up. It was now nearly nine in the evening and they were sitting in the restaurant that Denton Wellbon III had recommended they meet. Mac had phoned Denton at his corporate office.

Mac ran through the conversation again in his mind. Denton's secretary put Mac through immediately. Mac had met Denton several times at their annual corporate briefings, but Denton usually sat in the rear and allowed the others to take the active role. Since the arrival of Trevor Mason, the remainder of the corporate staff seemed to join Denton as passive participants. Corporate meetings were now mostly a one-man show. At corporate social affairs Mac had found Denton Wellbon III to be a very pleasant and highly intelligent man. Mac failed to understand the persistent rumors of his ineptness.

Denton answered. “Mr. MacLode, what an unexpected pleasure.”

“Please Mr. Wellbon call me Mac, everyone else does.”

“I will only if you call me Denton. It’s not like we don’t know each other. We’ve been seated together several times at corporate dinners and I’ve always enjoyed your company.”

“Thank you Denton, and I’ve enjoyed yours.” Mac marveled at the sincerity in Denton’s voice. If he wasn’t sincere and trying his best to make you feel at ease, he was the best actor Mac had ever come across. “Denton I have a rather large and unusual favor to request of you.”

“Ask away Mac, I’ll do whatever I can for you if it’s in my power.”

“I need to meet with you tonight to discuss a subject of mutual importance to both of us.”

“Well I have to admit I wasn’t expecting that type of request. Let me check my schedule. Where are you now?”

“In my office at Goodville but I’ve made arrangements to charter a plane at my own expense to accommodate you tonight if you can fit me into your busy schedule.”

“This must be important.”

“It is or I surely wouldn’t bother you with it.”

“No Mac I don’t imagine that you would. I have a 6 PM appointment but that shouldn’t last more than an hour. I expect with traffic and all the later the better for you?”

“Yes, later would be better.”

“Let’s meet at 9 PM at The Brasserie. That’s a restaurant that my wife and I enjoy and I’m assuming that you desire to be somewhere that others from corporate seldom frequent?”

"You're very perceptive Denton."

"I'll fax the address down to your secretary immediately. I have your fax number, and let me assure you that this will be just between you and me."

"Thank you Denton, I really appreciate this. I will tell you that I will have my father's lawyer with me because he has information that is pertinent to what I wish to discuss."

"Mac you have really peaked my curiosity. I'm truly looking forward to meeting with you. Have a safe trip and I'll see you this evening."

"Thank you again Denton." The conversation ended and Mac truly hoped that he could trust Denton's discretion. While it wouldn't change anything Mac didn't want Trevor Mason to be privy to this conversation.

Mac was suddenly pulled from his revelry. The hostess was seating Denton Wellbon III at their table. Mac began to stand but Denton waved him down and offered his hand. "Please Mac we certainly don't have to be formal tonight."

"Very well Denton. It's good to see you again." Mac accepted and shook the hand that Denton had offered. The waitress had followed Denton and the hostess to the table and took their drink orders. Brian Hempstead ordered another vodka martini.

"It's good to see you also Mac." Denton looked at Brian Hempstead. "I assume that you sir are the late elder MacLode's lawyer?"

"I am sir and you must be the honorable Denton Wellbon."

Denton smiled, "I'm not certain as to the honorable part, but I am Denton Wellbon. By the way Mac, I'm deeply sorry about your father."

"I appreciate that Denton and I must thank you for the flowers and the nice note that you and your wife sent me concerning Dad. How did you know?"

"If you promise not to get angry I'll tell you exactly how I knew of your father's death."

Mac was mystified. "All right, I promise."

A small smile tugged at the corners of Denton's mouth. "Your secretary Brady called my office shortly after you arrived home from your trip to Scotland. She tipped me off. She said that she thought I should know."

Mac smiled. "Bless her heart."

The small talk flowed through the drinks and the ordering of the meal. Finally Denton looked at Mac. "What's so important Mac?"

Mac took a deep breath. He knew that when he started down this path there would be no turning back. "Brian is not only the lawyer that I'm using to advise me concerning the settlement of my father's estate but he was also my father's lawyer, advisor and confidant for many years. He has just revealed to me some details about my father's estate that may have an impact on us both."

Denton's expression was a subtle mix of surprise, apprehension and curiosity. "Please continue Mac."

"I think that I'll let Brian begin. I was ignorant of all of this before this afternoon."

Mac and Denton turned toward Brian. Brian, loving the dramatic moment, took another sip of his martini before beginning. "Quite a few years ago, when Mac here was just a youngster and Sean MacLode and I were young men, Sean was serving his first term as a member of the House of Commons. I was his lawyer and had managed his election campaign for him. Sean was seven years older than I. It had been a rough campaign. Sean was up against a veteran politician and…"

Mac interrupted. "Brian, it's a long enough story. Just stick to the pertinent facts."

"Oh yes, quite right, quite right, where was I? Oh yes. It seems that at that time a bill came before the House to repeal some rather steep export taxes that had been placed on whiskey during the war effort. World War II I'm referring to. It was quite a hot topic at the time as the taxes had their supporters because of the revenues they brought in. Removing the taxes had the support of the brewers as they felt that the taxes were an obstacle to exporting their fine products.

Anyway, it was shaping up to be a close vote with the House split nearly down the middle. At this very time there were several American importers in London contacting as many of the members of both parties as possible to lobby for the lifting of the taxes. Your father, Mr. Wellbon, was one of them. The interested parties were taking private polls of the members and the general public constantly. It looked like the swing votes belonged to two undecided backbenchers. One of them was Sean MacLode. The senior Denton Wellbon managed to meet with Sean privately just before the vote. He made his pitch to him, but old Sean told him he planned on voting for what he viewed as best for his constituents. The elder Wellbon pulled out a study of the number of Scotch Whiskey brewers in Sean's district and how much more of their products that the Wellbon-Smith company alone would import if the taxes were removed. He had calculated the number of additional jobs this would create for his district. He had everything worked out. The pros and the cons, naturally the pros outnumbered the cons by a wide margin.

Sean wouldn't make any commitment, but told your father that he would review his numbers and if they seemed accurate he would certainly take removing the taxes under consideration. Your father thanked him and took his leave. He then went to speak with the other member.

The vote was called in the House and both Sean and the other bloke voted to remove the taxes. The measure just passed by one vote. Because of the voting order Sean MacLode was in the position of casting the deciding vote. The export taxes were gone.

Your father's numbers were pretty accurate. Not only did Wellbon-Smith purchase vastly more quantities of whiskey, but other importers did also. So much so that new jobs were created and helped ease the unemployment problem in Sean's district. That probably contributed the heaviest toward Sean's reelection.

About three months after the tax was eliminated, a letter came in the mail for Sean. It thanked Sean for investing in Wellbon-Smith stock. It informed Sean that the stock had been placed in three funds that where headquartered and administered in the Caribbean. The names of the funds were Southern Cross Investments, Caribbean Fund and Commonwealth Fund. The letter was signed by

Denton Wellbon II."

Denton's mouth dropped open. He stared at Mac. "You...you have inherited the three funds?"

"Well I will when the estate is settled. Until then I control them as the executor of the estate," replied Mac.

Brian continued. "Sean didn't understand the letter. He had never authorized the purchase of any stock so he contacted your father personally to straighten out the apparent mix-up. Your father told him there was no mix-up. He was selling Sean the stock at exceptionally low prices as a gesture of gratitude for his vote. He informed him that he could sell back to the company immediately and your father would guarantee him a huge profit. Sean protested. He had not sold his vote. He had voted his conscious! This all looked bad. Your father explained to him that the stock had been transferred to the funds and that was that. The funds were in Sean's name. They were offshore so no one in the British government need ever know about them and as Wellbon-Smith stock wasn't publicly traded who was to say the price was a 'gift?' Your father then advised Sean that if he wanted to make certain that this deal would stand up to scrutiny he damn well better write a check for the price named. Sean considered the implications of the stock being a gift and decided to pay for it. He had to borrow the money to do so, but determined that he had to avoid the appearance of a bribe if the transaction was ever discovered."

"Your father evidently paid the low price but never attempted to cash in?" asked Denton of Mac.

"It would seem so," answered Mac.

Brian continued. "You're both correct. Sean paid for the stock and in order to avoid any appearance of impropriety he never sold it. No offense Mr. Wellbon but your father had a certain reputation and Sean felt that stock was like a curse over his head that your father could use as leverage if any other votes that held his interest came before the House. A brilliant move by your father, he anticipated that Sean was now in a pretty safe seat and would be a member of the House of Commons for a long time, brilliant, but a tad unethical. By never touching it or claiming any of the dividends Sean felt that even if the funds existence became known he would have at least some defense against scandal. It just sat there and became more and more valuable. I flew here to the states for two reasons Mr. Wellbon. One is that Mac believed himself too busy to attend to his responsibilities to the estate."

"Brian," Mac protested. "I'm the only heir. What's the rush?"

Brian ignored Mac. "The second reason is that we, my law firm that is, have been contacted by a party with an offer to purchase the stock that the funds are holding for a generous price after the upcoming Wellbon-Smith annual meeting. The only stipulation is that we sign over our proxy to these individuals before the meeting."

Mac studied Denton. "Brian I suspect that Denton is already aware of the offer. The only knowledge he lacked was the identity of the owner. Now he knows."

Denton and Mac stared at each other for a long time, each wondering what the other was thinking. None of them had touched the food that was delivered halfway through Brian's tale. Then Mac broke the silence. "Brian, forgive me but I'm going to ask you to move to that empty table over there with your meal. I'm sorry to be rude but there are things that Denton and I must discuss."

"Rather expected as much old man. No problem at all. I have a feeling that the two of you are about to discuss some topics of which I desire to be ignorant. Who knows, I may have to represent you later. Besides it's even closer to that lovely singer. Ta Ta!"

Mac gestured to the waitress and inquired if it would it be permissible for Brian to move to an empty table? He also gave her a twenty-dollar bill. She accepted and said that there were plenty of empty tables at this time in the evening. She did caution concerning the theater crowd that would be coming in later.

After Brian Hempstead had relocated Mac picked up the conversation. "Now Denton, tell me, was I correct? You did know about the offer that was made to the funds the other week didn't you?"

"Yes Mac, I had knowledge that an offer would be made."

"In fact the offer was really made on behalf of Trevor Mason and yourself. The go between, the man who met with one of the associates in Brian's firm is one

Abraham Rueben, a lawyer of dubious reputation."

Denton wondered how much Mac knew and how he knew. "You seem to be very well informed Mac."

"I'll take that as a 'yes' to my question. The funds are just one in a long list of shareholders that you have made generous offers to, all with the same condition. That if they give you and Trevor their proxy before the annual meeting, you will buy their stock afterward for a very handsome return on investment. I expect that the only reason that you would make these under the table offers is with the intent of a hostile takeover of Wellbon–Smith."

Denton sipped his drink and slowly began eating his food. Mac did likewise but his gaze never left Denton. He wasn't finished by a long shot. Meeting Mac's gaze Denton dabbed his mouth with the linen napkin. Good lord, how could he know all of this? Have Trevor and Abraham been this careless? If Mac, a division president for Atlantic knows these details how much must the Board know? Denton needed to find out. "You obviously believe that you know more Mac."

"Yes I think that I do. To begin with we both know that anytime a shareholder desires to sell his stock he must take the potential buyer before the Board to be approved. Wellbon–Smith is a very exclusive privately held club. If the Board fails to approve the buyer, then the Board has six months to either buy the stock back at book value or find another buyer the Board approves. If the Board cannot find another buyer then the shareholder may sell to the original buyer approved or not."

"We are both students of Wellbon–Smith's corporate by-laws Mac. Yes what Trevor and I are doing is in violation of those by-laws. We anticipate legal action from some of the shareholders after the meeting, but by then we can probably negotiate a settlement because we will control the company. I don't argue with your description of this maneuver as a hostile takeover, but I emphasize that we are not breaking any civil laws. Are you planning on informing the Board of our activities?"

Mac paused before plunging ahead. "On the surface you aren't breaking any civil laws and no I've no intention on ratting you to the Board."

"I appreciate your discretion…But?" quarried Denton, "You seem to be implying a 'but'." Denton wondered if Mac wanted a piece of the action?

"Yes I am. This Abraham Rueben that I mentioned before has quite a reputation. It's not limited to his ability to extract large settlements in lawsuits. In Chicago, advising one Trevor Mason on the sale of another company the rumor is that Rueben was behind the strong arm tactics that 'convinced' several of the reluctant stockholders to sell their shares, thus completing the deal. Did I mention that nearly all of them wound up in the hospital?"

Denton pushed his plate away. No longer hungry. He downed the remainder of his drink and signaled the waitress for another. "No one at Wellbon–Smith is in the hospital Mac."

"Not yet but that may be because I believe that you are a decent man and wouldn't stand for it. I believe that you have, in an odd manner, protected the more reluctant shareholders."

"What makes you say that? How do you think I accomplished this 'protection' that you speak of?"

"Denton, I'm only speculating now, but you have literally grown up in Wellbon–Smith and its Atlantic Division. If anyone knows where the skeletons are hidden I'd bet it's you."

"You're accusing me of blackmail?" Denton felt a minor wave of nausea pass briefly over him. What does this man want?

"No. No I don't believe that you would ever blackmail someone. I've always held the opinion that you are a man of integrity. I do believe however that you may have provided the information that others, I would imagine Rueben, have utilized for blackmail. With the knowledge of hidden secrets at his disposal, Rueben would have found that strong-arm tactics were unnecessary, at least so far."

"Well there's your problem Mac. I too like to think of myself as having integrity. If that weren't the case, why would I distinguish between brutalizing people and blackmailing them? Can't you just accept that Trevor and I believe that the by-laws are out of step with the times when we are only months away from the twenty-first century? Yes we are violating the by-laws, but don't imagine that there are bigger sins lurking."

"I think that you are being forced to supply the information." Mac allowed that comment to drop like an anvil.

Denton felt sick again. He finished his second drink. How much does this man know and how does he know it? There was no point in denying that they were violating corporate by-laws, Mac already knew that because of the offer made to his funds. But now Mac was moving into an uncomfortable area. "Do you believe that Rueben has threatened me with physical harm? If so you are mistaken. Mac this is a business deal. We're playing hardball but what business deal isn't hardball these days. From what I hear you've been playing hardball with the unions lately, and having some success."

"No Denton I don't believe that you've been threatened physically, although I don't think that to be impossible. I think that you've been threatened with exposure, just the way some of the other shareholders that have signed over their proxies have been threatened."

Denton swallowed hard and for the first time he appeared to be slightly nervous. "You're suggesting that I'm being blackmailed? Why is it that you think I could be blackmailed?"

Mac had turned his attention back to his meal. He remained silent as he finished it. Then looking up at Denton he asked, "Shall we have some coffee and discuss that point?"

"Yes let's," Denton sighed. There was no use rushing this. Denton had great respect for Mac. He also knew Mac to be an honest man so he knew that there must be some purpose to this. He couldn't possibly know about the girl, but then he has already demonstrated that his knowledge encompasses far more than you should reasonably expect.

The waitress brought two cups of black coffee. Mac sipped his while Denton stirred his cup for no apparent reason. "They know about that one-night stand you had in college with the under aged girl don't they?"

Denton had just raised his cup to his lips as Mac spoke. The cup slammed down on the saucer and coffee splashed over the rim onto the linen table cloth.

Suddenly Denton was very tired. He looked around the room at the other diners. Brian Hempstead had invited the lounge singer to his table during her break and they appeared to be enjoying each other's company. Denton wondered if there was anyone, anyone at all in this restaurant that didn't know of his "secret." Denton raised his cup once again and sipped the coffee. It was good coffee, very robust. "What are you talking about Mac?"

"You know what I'm talking about Denton. There are probably only five people in the world know your secret. They would be you, Trevor Mason, Abraham Rueben, me and the person who informed me."

"And who might that person be?"

"Sorry, I can't reveal that. Are you admitting that I'm right? You might as well because I know it to be true. Besides by telling me that person has your interests at heart."

Denton placed his head in his hands and rubbed his eyes. Mac was correct, Trevor Mason was blackmailing him just as he was blackmailing Melissa Kensington and the others. He slowly sat up straight and leaned back in his chair. "Assuming, just assuming mind you, that everything you said is correct; how does your knowledge of it work in my interest?"

Inwardly Mac breathed a sigh of relief. Denton was willing to listen. Mac had been afraid that he would simply storm out and inform Trevor Mason of this meeting. Who knows what would happen then? He may yet decide to do that, but at least for now Denton was willing to listen. He began throwing this idea together the moment that Brian Hempstead informed him of the off shore funds. He wished that he had more time to work out the details but he didn't. So this was it. "Denton it occurs to me that there can only be so many shareholders that want to cash in and fewer still that have secrets to hide. So Trevor must need the shares that my funds are holding to pull this off. I'm assuming that he is already counting your shares in his voting total."

"What makes you think he doesn't have enough votes to take over the company now?"

"Abraham Rueben is calling Brian's office every day to see if the 'mystery owner' made a decision to sell."

Denton suddenly leaned forward, a renewed sense of urgency in his voice. "Abe and Trevor remain unaware of your identity?"

"Of course, your father did a good job of layering the ownership to keep my father's identity hidden. He wanted to be the one to threaten to reveal the existence of the funds should he ever need another "favor" from my father. Turns out he never did. He also followed my college career and then had his people recruit me at graduation. It's been rather disappointing to learn of this today. I had always thought that Wellbon – Smith hired me on my own merits, not because your father wanted to keep my father indebted to him as a hedge against possible future needs."

Denton smiled a thin smile. "However you came to Wellbon–Smith you have proven your worth Mac. Regardless of what Trevor may say during one of his tantrums." So, thought Denton, Trevor wasn't lying when he inquired if Denton had any knowledge of the individual to whom his father sold shares at fire sale prices.

Mac was surprised to hear this compliment from this person under these circumstances. "Why thank you Denton."

Denton waved his hand and sipped his coffee. "You were counting votes."

"Yes, I'm assuming that he's counting on you to bring your mother's block of voting shares to the table. While I don't know actual totals it has always been conventional wisdom around the corporation that your father saw to it that even if you and your mother didn't hold a majority share, you hold enough to make certain that nothing can be accomplished without your consent. If Trevor doesn't need both blocks he at least requires one of the two. Either the votes I hold or your mother's. Am I correct?"

Denton was thinking fast. The funds had been sort of abstract until now. If they got the fund's proxy then they really didn't need his mother's vote. But if they failed Denton was expected to deliver his mother's block of votes. But if the two blocks along with his were united against Trevor he was literally screwed. Denton made a decision. "Your second assumption is the correct assumption. He must have one of the blocks, either the funds proxy or my mother's votes, along with my voting block added to the current list of proxies signed to him. That is the only way Trevor can possibly out vote the remainder of the shareholders. We have to assume that the remaining shareholders will vote their blocks to retain Carlton Smith."

Mac looked around. "If my educated guess is correct, there are enough votes sitting at this very table to thwart Trevor's plan assuming that your mother would never throw in with Trevor."

"What makes you think that she hasn't Mac? You are correct in thinking that Trevor is counting my block of voting shares as voting with him. Why is it so hard to imagine my mother joining us? I'm certain that a man as smart as you has already deduced that the price of my votes came high. I want to be the new Chairman of the Board."

Mac had considered the possibility that by now it was a done deal. However at this moment he had no choice but to gamble. "What makes me think that your mother hasn't moved to Trevor's side? Only these facts: Carlton Smith was her first choice as chairman. She even picked him over you. Why would that change now? Second, as I stated before, Rueben calls Brian's office in London every day."

Denton smiled for the first time. "Yes, you and I together could prevent anyone from getting a majority." Mac motioned for another cup of coffee as Denton contemplated the new math. "Amazing, with you owning those shares everything could change. Actually Mac, I think that you are underestimating the size of the block that I personally control. Together you and I could force a deadlock. If mother went with some other hypothetical group of shareholders and we split three ways between Trevor and his group, mother and the hypothetical group and us, no one could come up with the majority required to accomplish anything."

"But that's not what either of us want is it?" The waitress arrived and poured more coffee.

Denton was becoming extremely excited, though he tried not to show it. Suddenly Mac was presenting the possibility of an alternative course of action. One in which Trevor Mason wasn't able to pull all of the strings. "I've already made it clear what I want Mac. I want to sit in the chair that my father and grandfather sat in. I want to be the Chairman of Wellbon–Smith. I've thrown in with Trevor because he presents the only vehicle to date to get what I want. Both

Carlton Smith and my mother have failed me in this quest. Now what is it that you desire and what must we do to attain both?"

"We can put you in the chairman's job without Trevor."

"How is that possible? I need the votes that he has amassed."

"Not if you and I vote together and you convince your mother to vote with us. I'm only guessing on the totals, but you know the exact numbers. If I throw the votes held by my funds behind you and your mother I'm betting that we could put you in the job."

"Numerically that's correct, but mother would never agree to me in that position. She already expressed reservations as to my leadership skills when she endorsed Carlton Smith over me to run this company."

"Then prove to her that you are a leader in the fearless fashion of your father and grandfather." Mac was beginning to smell victory if he could only convince Denton to have some backbone. Granted it would require more than he had ever exhibited, but this was one of those defining moments in his life.

"How pray tell can I accomplish that?"

"Get your mother and your wife together, explain Trevor's plan and then confess your secret. Blackmail only works when you have something to hide. If it's no longer hidden then it becomes useless."

"No that would crush them. Susan would never forgive me. Mother would be disgraced in front of her friends. There's more than you know Mac. It's not just my indiscretion. There is written proof that my father and grandfather were smuggling contraband. Trevor and Abraham would expose everything to the world. If that wasn't bad enough the publicity may bring Mary Johnsonn out of wherever she has been living since that fateful night. Who knows what she may do. She may sue me and that would provide daily updates to the public on the front page of every New York paper and tabloid."

Mac took a deep breath. He was asking this man to risk his family life. A family that Denton knew intimately and Mac only observed from afar. But he had to continue. Denton must take this risk. "Denton listen carefully to what I'm about to say. First, this one-night stand took place before you met Susan. Am I correct?"

"Well, yes."

"So you weren't cheating on her."

"No you're correct. I wasn't cheating on anyone at the time. I was unattached."

"Good. Second who cares what your father and grandfather did a generation or two ago? They're both dead now. No one can prosecute them and you had nothing to do with it."

"But people still care. My mother…"

"Bullshit Denton. People already believe that your immediate ancestors operated outside the law. They don't need proof. It's accepted that they did these things. Right or wrong there are many a story that circulates in boardrooms concerning the audacity of both your father and grandfather in the lengths that they would go to for success. I expect that by now the legend exceeds the reality. What have you to fear from written proof? These people don't need proof they believe the stories already. If you had written proof to the contrary, proof that your family was innocent, they wouldn't believe it. With all of their looking down their collective noses, they admire your father and grandfather for their sheer guts and above all, their toughness.

As for your mother, she earned her way into those society circles a long time ago with her tireless charity work and generous contributions. Why we've even heard of her work in Goodville. There have been articles about her in both Time and Newsweek. She's at a point now when the so-called society dames want to be associated with her and not the other way around. She has nothing left to prove. She has outdistanced the people that she has been trying so hard to impress."

"But Susan's family…" Denton had a perplexed look on his face.

"Well you know Susan and her family. I don't. But I've observed one thing when I've seen the two of you together at corporate gatherings. The way she looks at you when you're talking with others. She looks at you like a man that she's deeply in love with. I envy that look. As someone still looking for a soul mate, I've not found anyone that I ever catch looking at me in that manner. Do you really think that this revelation from what is now the distant past would kill the solid relationship that you two have enjoyed these many years? Do you think that her family would disown you?"

Denton considered this for a long moment. "I suppose not. They would express disappointment, but disown? No, they love me like their own son. But if Mary Johnson would return, she could create havoc."

"She's not coming back Denton. She committed suicide several years ago. A few years after her ex-husband Foster Harrison divorced her."

"She married?"

"Yes."

"She's dead?"

"Yes. Trust me on this. My source is unimpeachable. As proof I give you what I know about you."

Denton appeared stunned as he allowed Mac's logic and this revelation to settle in.

Mac decided to go for the kill. "Denton let's consider what life will be like if you continue down this road with Trevor Mason. Tomorrow Brian Hempstead is going to contact Abraham Rueben and inform him that the funds owner has decided against their offer. He's going to inform him that unlike other years the funds are not going to automatically vote their proxy with the majority. He's going to tell him that this year, for the first time, the funds will send a representative to vote their interest. That means that Trevor will be after you to bring your mother's voting block to the table signed and sealed. You of course will have to comply no matter what lies that requires that you tell your mother. If you don't Trevor will reveal your secrets to the Times, New York Post, Channel 5 and whomever else he deems appropriate. Complete with documentation. He may lose Wellbon–Smith but you know that he'll take you down with him.

At the annual shareholders meeting, if you do what Trevor would have you do.

You, Trevor Mason and Abraham Rueben, yes Rueben will now be a part of the triumvirate; will successfully take over Wellbon–Smith. You will be installed as the Chairman of the Board. You will sell Fox Cabinetry and perhaps another of your many companies to pay off the shareholders that you struck your unholy deals with. You'll settle a couple of lawsuits filed by the disgruntled losers. 'Heavy rests the head that wears the crown' but that won't be your head, it will be Trevor's. Denton you may have the title and the office but except for holding court at cocktail parties, you will no more be running the Wellbon-Smith empire than will I. Every action that you want to take will have to be approved by Trevor Mason. Everything that Trevor wants to do you will do, whether you like it or not. You will have to because he will own your ass! He will own your ass as long as you are afraid that he will reveal your precious family secrets!

Eventually his enormous ego will demand that he have the title and the office to go with the power. Then he will find a way to push you aside and you will remain silent. He'll be able to do this because he owns your ass! He'll be able to do this because you will have allowed him to own your ass."

Denton just sat there staring at Mac. He said nothing. Mac wasn't able to read him. His face was pale, his expression blank, he seemed devoid of emotion. "Denton ask yourself one question. Is this the way your father and grandfather would have dealt with Trevor Mason and Abraham Rueben under the same circumstances?"

Suddenly Mac could hear the sounds around them again. The soft murmur of people laughing and talking, the clatter of dinnerware and glasses, the lounge singer was taking her place once more beside the piano. As she began to sing Brian Hempstead raised his martini glass in a toast to her and Denton Wellbon III just sat staring. They sat that way for what seemed like a very long time and then Denton shifted in his chair, straightened his tie and his impeccable dark suit jacket. He looked again into William MacLode's eyes. "So Mac, what is it that you want in return for joining forces with Mother and me?"

Mac smiled. "I want to purchase Fox Cabinetry. I have the financing set up and I and my associates are prepared to make you a fair offer."

"Do I know these associates?"

"They are my entire senior management team."

“I should have guessed as much. During our visits to Fox I’ve often noticed the camaraderie that you share with them. Yes, if we pull this off I will certainly recommend the sale of Fox Cabinetry to your team.”

Mac permitted himself a larger smile and the smile was returned by Denton. “Thank you Denton, I can’t ask anymore of you.”

“That’s strange, everyone else does. Mac you may have saved my life tonight. I don’t know how you came by or who gave you such detailed information. I hope that someday you feel comfortable enough to tell me.” Mac shrugged and Denton continued. “What we are talking about here will require strictly timed execution. It will require planning. I for one am very tired. This has been an exhausting day.”

“I’m feeling a bit that way myself.”

“Would it be possible for you to meet with me tomorrow morning and we can plan the details?”

“Wherever you suggest, Brian will be returning to London tomorrow, but he’s a big boy and can fend for himself.”

Denton thought for a moment. “There is a place I go for breakfast at times. I guarantee that neither Trevor nor Abraham will be anywhere in the vicinity. Do you know where the Fulton Fish Market is located?”

“I know the area.”

“Good, just a block north of the Market is a diner called Andy’s. Could we meet there around nine tomorrow morning?”

“Could we make it ten? This is the only set of clothes I have with me. I’ll have to buy something either tonight or first thing in the morning.”

“Ten it is.” Denton rose from his chair and picked up the check that the waitress left with the last coffee refill. “I’ll get this and the tip Mac.”

“I’m the one that requested this meeting, it should be mine.”

"Believe me Mac, if this comes together and I can become the chairman without beholding to Trevor, I owe you much more than this."

"Very well then, if you insist," Mac received Denton's extended hand it was a strong determined grip that clasp Mac's.

"Thank you Mac. I truly intend to finish this in a way that my father and grandfather would respect." With that Denton signaled the waitress and gave her his credit card. Mac gathered up Brian Hempstead at the other table. Brian looked at Mac cautiously.

"Did all go as you had hoped laddie?"

"Yes Brian. Thank you for the extra effort that you took by flying over to force me to deal with my own affairs."

"Don't worry lad, it will all be in my bill." With that they said their goodbyes to Denton Wellbon, headed toward the door and sought a cab. Mac would sleep well tonight, but he was well aware that his battle for Fox and the larger battle for Wellbon-Smith were not yet won. The irony was that most of the participants were not aware that a war was even engaged. Mac himself only fully realized it about thirteen hours before in Luca's limo. Then the surprise meeting with his lawyer Brian Hempstead and the information that Brian had concerning the very off shore funds that Ray Luca had advised him to look into. Luca obviously knew that Sean McLode's estate owned them. Had the old man told him as much during that one visit they had years ago? Ray did tell Mac that he had corresponded with Mac's father for years after that visit. He must have told him sometime during that period. They hailed a cab and headed for their hotel.

Chapter 17

Morning came quickly. Brian Hempstead and Mac met in the hotel restaurant for coffee. Mac had already found a men's clothing store that opened early on Broadway and had purchased a casual outfit consisting of underwear, a pullover, Dockers, sox and loafers. He also purchased a suit bag to protect his suit on the trip home. He just had enough time to change before meeting Brian. Brian informed him that he had purchased airline tickets on the Internet and would be flying home via British Airways at 11:00 AM. He had already arranged for a limo service to pick him up at the hotel and transport him to JFK in plenty of time.

They proceeded to discuss other transactions that had to be completed to settle Sean MacLode's estate. Brian carried with him what looked like a bale of documents for Mac to sign. Mac, keeping track of the time waded through them with the help of Brian's tutoring. Now that Brian had managed to sit down with Mac this morning and in Mac's office yesterday, he estimated that they may be able to have the estate completely settled by Christmas. This pleased Mac, as he despised loose ends.

Brian informed Mac that he would wait until he was at the airport before contacting Abraham Rueben with Mac's answer of no to sell his shares. Mac agreed with the timing. He knew that the negative response would immediately force Mason and Rueben to apply pressure on Denton for his mother's proxy vote.

After they completed their business the two men shook hands and went their separate ways. Mac checked out of the hotel and hailed a cab. He proceeded to the Fulton Fish Market and Andy's Diner. Mac carried his two pieces of baggage. He planned on taking the earliest train possible back to Lancaster.

Mac found the diner and entered. He looked around but failed to see Denton. Mac checked his watch. It was five minutes until ten. Connie the waitress approached him.

To Catch a Fox

"I bet your name's MacLode," she said.

"Why yes, it is."

"Mr. Denton is in the back, come this way."

Mac followed her into the rear of the diner. In his admittedly limited experience with Denton Wellbon III this was the last place that he would have anticipated that he would frequent. Denton was seated in a booth facing Mac. There was another man in the booth with his back toward Mac. Connie stopped and turned, "He's waiting for you."

"Thank you." Mac approached the booth. Denton saw him and rose in greeting.

"Good morning Mac. I want you to meet an old friend of the family. This is Andy, he owns the diner. Andy this is William MacLode, he's a business associate of mine."

Andy rose and turned toward Mac, a wide grin on his face, "Always a pleasure to meet a friend of Denton's."

Mac hesitated and then grasped the outstretched hand. He tried to conceal his surprise. Andy was the man that brought Mac's T-Bird to the Morgantown Inn yesterday morning and then left with Ray Luca. Not certain how to react, Mac tested the waters. Looking Andy directly in the eye he queried; "Have we met before Andy?"

"Nah, not unless you've come here to eat before, I practically live at the diner and seldom leave the city."

"As I've never been to your establishment until now I suppose you simply remind me of someone else." Mac understood all this to mean that Denton shouldn't be aware of the connection that Andy and Mac shared.

"I'd guess you to be right. Now I can tell when there's important business to be discussed so I'll leave you two alone." With that Andy left the booth and moved into the front room to greet some of the regulars.

Mac slid into the booth across from Denton. “Andy was an old friend and confidant of my father’s. I’ve known him since I was a boy. Believe it or not I find his advice invaluable on certain occasions. He is, in spite of his appearance, quite an astute businessman.”

“Are you soliciting his advice on our deal Denton?”

“Andy promised my father that he would look out for me. He is loyal to me as he was to my father. I have not made Andy privy to our plans, but if I did I know that he would approve.”

“Why is that?”

“Because I know you and Andy share the same opinion of Trevor and Abraham Rueben.”

“He knows of your involvement with them?” Mac was beginning to realize just how involved Ray Luca was with Wellbon–Smith even if Denton and the others did not. Mac suspected that Denton was not aware of the connection between Andy and Ray Luca, whatever it was.

“Yes he does, but they are not aware of him. That’s why I suggested meeting here this morning. This is a place where Trevor and Abe would never set foot and we are among friends.”

Mac looked around and smiled. “You amaze me Denton you are not always what you may seem to be. Yes I think that this place is perfect for our meeting.”

“Then let’s get started. I assume that your lawyer Mr. Hempstead is contacting Abe this morning with the news the funds aren’t going to accept his offer?”

Mac checked his watch. “That should take place in less than one hour. That means that Trevor and Abraham Rueben will have no choice but to bring pressure on you to deliver your mother’s votes. How will you handle that?”

“I’ve led them to believe that I have already opened a dialog with her concerning it.”

“Have you?”

"No not yet. I wanted to discover what the funds would do first. I was attempting to avoid discussing it with Mother if possible."

"How will you stall them? They realize that without your Mother's votes this is all for nothing."

"I've told them that I'm telling her I believe that I am now ready to take my father's place and that since Carlton Smith wants to retire this is a good time for her to throw her support behind me. I'm saying that I believe that the other board members would not support me and Trevor's plan is the only alternative for me to take."

"Do you think that they're buying that?"

"Not for a minute. Oh they believe that is my approach, but they both have serious doubts as to my ultimate success, especially Abe. And for obvious reasons, why would Mother change her mind now when she could have installed me as chairman originally? That is why they are keeping the possibility of blackmailing me open, no matter how subtle."

"Could she have done it by herself back then? Even with your votes she could have only prevented someone else from gaining the required two-thirds majority. Think about this Denton. That first time around, would anyone else other than your mother and you voted to put you in the chairman's chair?"

"I never looked at it that way. I suppose not. She couldn't even have counted on Carlton Smith."

"It's just possible Denton that your mother's decision to support Carlton Smith over her own son was an attempt to avoid a crippling deadlock that would have left the corporation leaderless at a time when someone had to step forward quickly to fill the shoes that your dynamic, forgive me, dictatorial father left vacant."

Denton's eyes widened. "Could it be that my feelings of betrayal and resentment have not been justified all these years?"

"Did you ever ask her about her vote?"

"No, no I did not. I know that must sound strange to you Mac, but I was always closer to Father than Mother. I assumed that she like all the others considered me a lightweight and believed that I couldn't be trusted to take the helm. I suppose that vote actually served to convince me that they might be right. I was so hurt and embarrassed that I never broached the subject with her. I never considered that as a practical matter she really had no choice."

"Whether she did or not that very argument if presented to Trevor may gain enough of his confidence to buy us some time to convince your mother to join us."

"Yes, I suppose that it might. It is logical."

Connie brought them two mugs of black coffee without being asked. They deferred on her offer of breakfast. She told them to call her if they desired anything and then left them alone. Mac sipped the coffee and then leaned across the table toward Denton. "We have several goals. They are: First stall Trevor and Rueben long enough for us to bring your mother on board with us. Second convince your mother that you are the man now to run your father's and her late husband's company. Third with your mother's votes in our possession convince Trevor and Rueben that she is actually going to vote her block with them on condition that you be installed as the next chairman as soon as your takeover is complete. Fourth prevent Trevor from entering into any under the table agreements in advance of the annual shareholder's meeting for the sale of Fox Cabinetry or any other Atlantic company."

"As to the last item on your agenda. I can tell you that as of this morning there is no agreement or offer on the table for the sale of Fox. But, I know that Trevor is meeting with one Clint Matthews at the Kitchen and Bath Industry Show in Chicago."

"Forgive me but who is Clint Matthews?"

"He's chairman of Cab Corp, the cabinet and furniture conglomerate. He is the only U.S. manufacturer of furniture remaining."

"You think Fox would make an excellent addition to his stable of wood-based manufacturing companies?"

"I do indeed Mac, and here's an interesting side note; all of the companies owned by Clint Matthews' Corporation are represented by the United Federation of Millwrights International."

"How do you know this?"

"Trevor had John Hogg do some research on Clint Matthews and his companies after he agreed to meet with him. Now Mac, to my knowledge you have never mentioned a name in connection with the union that is attempting to organize Fox. However there are very few candidates in the woodworking field, mostly because the manufacturers in your industry are considered to be too small to be worthwhile. But if someone like Matthews could acquire Fox and add it to his already unionized companies it would make perfect sense."

"You think Matthews wants to purchase Fox?"

"What other company would he be interested in? I'm sure he's aware of the book that Trevor had Bertrum & Bertrum put together on Fox. Are you aware of that evaluation?"

"Yes I am. So is our dealer base. That was the worst kept secret that Atlantic Corp. ever had. It nearly cost us a third of our dealers. Thanks to Tony and my staff they quelled those fears."

Denton gave Mac a wry smile, "Fallout of which Trevor is blissfully unaware. He allowed the possibility of Fox being for sale to leak in the hopes of snaring a buyer. I think he lined the pockets of someone at Bertrum."

Mac let out a guttural growl. "You think that there is a connection between the unionization effort and Matthews' desire to make an offer for Fox?" The concern was evident in Mac's voice.

"Trevor obviously does. He made the specific request of John Hogg to determine, in his words, 'what unions that Matthews was in bed with.' This happened the same morning that you revealed the unionization attempt and Matthews made an appointment to meet with Trevor at the show."

Mac stared out through the discolored window toward the river. "Would

Matthews believe that the presence of a union could devalue Fox?"

"In this industry it probably would, and he is already experienced at dealing with that particular union. Better the witch that you know."

Mac turned back to Denton, "But that's illegal."

Denton smiled, "Mac I'm not totally certain that all of your actions concerning the union have been strictly legal either."

"Denton I also have a meeting scheduled with Trevor at the show. At that meeting I'm planning on making an offer of my own to purchase Fox."

"That's good. I'm glad that you're prepared. I will do everything in my power to convince Trevor to accept your offer over Matthews. If Trevor thinks that Matthews is behind the union effort to decrease Fox's value it will piss him off. In addition Trevor played football at Michigan State with Jerome Jefferson the current president of the UF of MI. I gather they had quite a rivalry. But remember his primary interest is in selling Fox so that he can pay off all those proxy agreements. Pissed off or not that will be the ultimate motivating factor."

"Denton I'm assuming that your name is also on those proxy agreements?"

"Oh no, Trevor is giving me a 'free ride', but I know it's because he wants to own a significant block of shares himself when this is all over."

"How would Trevor end up owning that stock? He'll be using company money, the proceeds from the sale of Fox and possibly another corporation to pay for the shares. That stock should rightly return to company treasury."

"By having his newly appointed Chairman of the Board, eternally grateful for Trevor installing him in that position, allowing the company to loan Trevor the money to purchase the stock with easy payback terms."

"So what happens if your mother joins us and Trevor fails?"

"He's off the hook because the deal states that he has to be successful in changing company policy on the sale of shares. In other words he has to be successful in his takeover bid. Trevor is very clever it's a shame he feels he must resort to these tactics to get what he wants."

Mac noticed that Denton's smile was becoming more confident and that was a good thing.

"Mac if we succeed I will honor Trevor's obligations by selling Fox to you and one other company if I'm forced to do so. That will start me off clean and I'll retire those shares to the treasury. This will eliminate the unhappy shareholders and increase the advantage that Mother and I possess with the other shareholders."

"Spoken like a true Wellbon." Mac observed that Denton was very pleased with that comment. "Now Denton, we have to get your mother to back you by joining us."

Denton sighed, "I'm aware of that Mac."

"If I may be so bold, what is the state of your current relationship with your mother?" Mac hated to get this personal but it was past time to hold anything back.

"As it always was, Mother has always been a bit distant. She was always out working with various charities while a series of nannies raised me. I think that having a child was a bit inconvenient for her, but father wanted a son and heir." Denton smiled. "As you can see once again my father got his way. As I said before father and I were always closer, but he was busy too, at least he took me along to work on occasion. Mother was always working to prove herself to the other society dames. In some ways she worked longer hours than father even though she wasn't employed by anyone. I lacked for nothing except their time, but father was easier to talk with. Although he never actually said so it has become obvious that he really loved me. As for the present, I visit Mother at least once a week. She tells me about her charity work and I discuss issues that she will encounter at her next board meeting. It's all strangely formal now that I think of it, but it's the way it has always been."

"Denton, as I told you last night, you have to disarm Trevor. You have to tell your mother the secret that you and your father have gone to such lengths to suppress."

To Catch a Fox

"I've been considering it all night Mac."

"You have to do more than consider Denton. You have to act like a Wellbon. You must do whatever you have to do to regain control of your father's company."

"That means that I must tell Susan too."

"Yes, you must tell your wife too."

It was Denton's turn to gaze at the river. The seconds ticked away. To Mac it seemed an eternity. If Denton couldn't muster the courage for this then Mac's attempt to make an end run around Trevor Mason for the purchase of Fox would fail. If it did Mac would be left with only his original option. Now that seemed most likely to wind up in a bidding contest with Clint Matthews. In a contest such as that Mac feared he and his staff would come in second. Unless he became financially indebted to his old friend Ray Luca and Mac was not yet ready to consider that. Then Mac considered what would happen to Fox if Matthews was the successful bidder. The senior staff would almost certainly be replaced, perhaps not immediately but over time. While Mac was ignorant of Clint Matthews' identity, he was not ignorant of the quality of the products produced by the Cab Corp companies. There were some once respected names among them, but Matthews had reduced them all to run of the mill average quality products. He mentally cringed at the thought of that happening to Fox. Denton was still staring out the window. He almost appeared to be in a trance.

"Denton," Mac spoke softly. "Denton I thought that you made this decision last night."

"What?" Denton was pulled from his revelry. "Oh, yes, I'm sorry Mac. You are correct. I did make the decision last night and I'm going through with it. It's time for the truth to be told. I was just wondering how my dear, dear Susan will react."

"I honestly don't know Denton, but I know that a lie is never a better choice than the truth."

"No it's not Mac." Denton reached into his inside pocket and pulled out his cell phone. He punched up a number from memory and waited as it rang, "Mother? Denton. How are you? I'm fine, yes so is Susan. Mother I know that you are up in Boston until Friday, but I was wondering if we could get together Saturday morning at your place… No I'm bringing Susan along too. I have something of importance to discuss with you both… No I don't want to get into it on the phone, but it's imperative that we get together Saturday…Nine will work fine Mother…Yes, yes…Susan and I will see you on Saturday…Yes, good bye Mother and safe trip."

Denton returned the phone to his pocket. Mac smiled. "That took courage Denton."

"Not nearly as much courage as I'll need on Saturday morning."

"You'll have it. I know you will."

"Yes I will Mac you have nothing to worry about." Denton's cell rang in his pocket. He pulled it out again and looked at the screen. "It's Trevor." Denton took the call.

"Yes Trevor, Denton here…so, we don't have the funds proxy? I see…As a matter of fact I just got off the phone with Mother. She's in Boston but she will be home this weekend…I'm meeting with her on Saturday…Tell Abraham to relax, I expect to have good news for you after that meeting…Yes, it's going well…yes I'll keep you informed…I'll be into the office this afternoon…See you then Trevor."

Denton replaced the phone. "I think the die is cast. I have to be successful on Saturday. Mac I would appreciate it if you could be on hand Saturday morning to meet with Mother and Susan after I convince her to join us. She will need to meet you and then we can plan how to keep Trevor and Rueben under control until the meeting."

"I can't be in the room when you tell them everything. That should be private."

"No, you can wait somewhere nearby until you get my call." Denton smiled. "I'll call you when it's safe."

"Very well, I'll be catching a train home this afternoon, but I'll be back for the weekend."

Denton looked at his watch. "Its 11:30, but they serve breakfast here 24 hours a day. Will you join me?"

Mac grinned. "I'd be happy to Denton." He needed some food to go along with all the coffee he drank this morning.

In the back office Andy smiled. He reached under his desk and snapped the switch off to the intercom. At every booth the miniature microphones were hidden carefully in the bottom of each of the old jukeboxes. The customers thought that Andy kept them for nostalgia and they enjoyed playing them. Andy knew that they served a much more important purpose. The jukebox that Andy just now "turned off" was the one at the booth where Mac and Denton were seated. The hidden microphone allowed Andy to listen to their entire conversation. He picked up his cell phone and punched up a number. "Hello boss? Andy…Guess who's in my Diner meeting with Denton Wellbon?"

Out in The Hamptons Ray Luca sat in the study of his large beachfront home. Several of his "boys", the ever-present bodyguards, stood outside the study door in the hall. More were discreetly stationed at various strategic points around his walled and gated estate. Ray smiled. "Let me guess Andy, William MacLode."

"How did you know boss?" Andy was dumbfounded.

"Mac is a very bright man. With the information and the clues that I gave him yesterday he was bound to figure out how best to combat the gentlemen whose initials are T.M. I admit I thought it would take a little longer than this, but Mac is a fast mover. Did Mac recognize you?"

"Yeah, but he was cool and didn't let on to young Denton that we had recently met."

"Good, it's best if we make that connection for Denton at the right time. We need to keep him indebted to us. Give me the details Andy. I know that you have "access" to conversations in your establishment, just refrain from using names over the phone." With that Andy gave Luca as detailed an update as he could without revealing too much on the phone. When he finished, Luca thought for a moment. "I told you Mac would be very useful in helping us achieve our ultimate goal. Now listen carefully. This is where T.M.'s partner A.R. may become very dangerous. A.R. doesn't like to lose and seldom does. I'm certain he has plans for such a contingency. That's why we must be a step ahead of him. Young Denton and Mac will play by the rules, T.M. and A.R. won't. When are you leaving for the Coast?"

"Tonight."

"The sooner the better, see if you can't get an earlier flight."

"Right boss."

"When you get out there move fast. We've no time to waste by being nice. Use muscle if you must. You know whom to contact for muscle out there. Those people will cover the trail and they can be trusted. I have too much on them for them to talk. Find out if that girl in your diner the other morning is really connected to Denton. Don't come back until you know. Oh and Andy, if possible watch for anything that might tip us off as to who the mystery people are that covered all this up. I need to know who else is involved. Are you clear on everything?"

"Yeah boss, you can count on me."

"I always do Andy."

"Boss can I ask a question?"

"If you're careful, this is not totally secure."

"How did you know about the offshore stuff?"

"You forget I developed a long-term friendship with Mac's father. He confided that information to me not knowing that I was the one that suggested to Denton's father that the 'offshore stuff' as you call it be set up in the first place."

Andy laughed. "You're something else boss. You played both sides. You're the smartest"

"Don't you forget it Andy. Keep in touch." With that Ray Luca pressed the tiny button on the cell phone and hung up.

To Catch a Fox

Chapter 18

The morning sun streamed in through the floor to ceiling windows in the Upper East Side penthouse. The weather outside had suddenly turned to fall. Friday was a typical long warm late Indian summer day in September and now Saturday dawned abruptly with a chill in the air. Soon the leaves in Central Park would be turning into a blaze of color. Mary Wellbon stood looking out the window at the New York skyline against the clear crisp blue sky. Susan Wellbon sat silently on the couch. Denton was fidgeting apprehensively by the fireplace, the flames licking the gas log supplied ambiance and warmth. He had just finished his story and now he awaited the repercussions.

Susan spoke first. “Denton I have to admit I’m a bit surprised, knowing you it's hard to imagine you approaching a strange girl. But you were only a boy at the time.”

“I was over twenty one, I was a legal adult and I was drunk.”

“Denton, I’m not condoning what you did, in fact I’m shocked. It seems so out of character. But you’re certainly not the only frat boy to get mixed up with an under aged girl.”

“No, but I’m the only Wellbon to do it.”

Susan got up from the couch, walked over to Denton and put her arm around his waist. “I’m not going to hold a youthful indiscretion against you. It was a long time ago and I love the man that you are today.”

Denton leaned over and kissed her forehead. “I love you too,” he murmured.

“There are no legal implications are there?” The concern in Susan’s voice was evident.

“Not after all this time, it would be hard to prove. Besides, the poor girl, ah woman is dead now."

"Not because of this one night with you?"

"Well, no, her husband left her a few years before her death, but who knows why anyone commits suicide. I'm sure my escapade didn't help her ultimate self esteem."

Mary Wellbon turned back toward the living room. Her tall frame was erect and ramrod straight. The sunlight glistening off her snow-white hair, hair that had been white since it began turning from her natural dark brown in her early forties. No salon blue or imitation brown hair for Mary. This was authentic. What you saw in Mary Wellbon was what you got, even if it wasn't what you desired or were seeking. "How many votes is Trevor short in this attempt to take over the company?"

Denton and Susan were taken aback by the cold calculating tone of her voice. Denton had expected that her first concern would be the talk around town if knowledge of his indiscretion escaped. But her concern was solely focused on the company. "He needs either your block or the offshore funds block combined with mine and the proxies he's accumulated," was Denton's response.

"So he assumes your block is locked up."

"That's correct Mother."

"William MacLode controls the off shore funds?"

"Yes."

"We're certain that he'll vote with us?"

"Yes."

"We need to talk to him. How soon can we meet with him?"

"How about meeting with him now?"

"He's nearby?"

"Yes, we anticipated that you might wish to talk to him."

"Get him up here."

"Yes Mother," replied Denton. He pulled out his cell phone and punched in Mac's number. It only rang once and Mac answered. "Mother wants to talk to you," was all Denton said. Closing the phone he faced his mother, not knowing what to say. He found that he didn't have to say anything. Mary Wellbon spoke first.

"Denton, you said that you were drunk the night of the incident, how drunk?"

Denton sighed, "Pretty drunk mother. I didn't hold my liquor very well as a lad."

"No, you didn't, tell me exactly what you remember about that night."

An exasperated look crossed Denton's face. He wasn't too keen on covering the details with his wife and his mother. "Well I remember this stunning young woman that all the guys were drooling over. I normally just stayed on the sidelines during these affairs, but several of my frat brothers started betting me that I couldn't get her to go to bed with me. I don't know what came over me. I always suspected that the other guys had less than total respect for me because I didn't exude the macho image that others strive to attain. So I took their bets and approached her."

"You don't know what came over you? You were drunk, that's what came over you."

"Yes, well you're certainly right about that Mother. Anyway, I asked her to dance and barely halfway through the dance I… I still can't believe that I said it, but I asked her if she wanted to get laid. In just those words, I've never been so crude and disrespectful before or since. To my surprise she just grinned and said 'sure'."

"Was she drunk too?"

"Well she had been drinking, but she wasn't as drunk as I was."

To Catch a Fox

"How do you know?"

"Mother," it was Susan "Is it necessary to make Denton relive this?"

"Susan I love you as if you were my own daughter, but allow me to continue. This is extremely important. How do you know that she was not as drunk as you?"

"She had to help me to my car and then I gave her the keys, because there was no way that I could drive."

"So she got you in the car when you couldn't get there on your own power, and then she drove. Where did you go?"

Denton shrugged. "I don't know somewhere that we could be alone and do it." Denton could feel himself blush. He couldn't bring himself to look at Susan. It was difficult enough holding his mother's intense gaze.

"To a motel, a hotel, a park? Where?"

"I don't know, maybe we parked somewhere and did it in the car. Mother, I'm a grown man now. You're grilling me like a teenager."

Mary ignored the last comment. "You don't know? You don't know where you screwed her?"

"I was drunk!" Denton was getting angry.

Mary Wellbon folded her arms and looked at the ceiling. "Get me my purse Denton, it's in the foyer." Denton acquired her purse and handed it to her. Mary immediately opened it and retrieved a gold cigarette case and matching lighter. Extracting a cigarette she lit it and took a long draw, exhaling the smoke loudly. Denton and Susan were shocked. They had never seen her smoke.

"Mother, I didn't know that you smoke," stammered Denton.

Mary took another draw and leveled her gaze at Denton. "There's a lot about me that you don't know, and it's not your fault. Denton, if you had trouble walking and you couldn't drive I have serious doubts that you could screw." Denton and

Susan had never heard the Grande Dame talk like this. "In fact if there was any screwing going on, I suspect that she screwed you. Good lord, she probably raped you!"

Denton felt his face redden even more. This certainly wasn't the reaction that he had expected from his mother. He was about to speak but his mother was far from finished.

"No, I guess you weren't raped. Your offer to get laid sort of removes that element. Denton, do you remember anything about the act itself?"

There was a long pause and Denton found himself staring at the floor. He now realized that there was something worse than shame. Feeling stupid in front of your mother and wife was worse. "I remember riding around and then the next thing I remember was waking up in the back seat of my car. It was early the next morning and the car was parked in front of the frat house."

"You don't remember having sex?"

"Honestly no."

"So exactly what made you think you had intercourse with this girl?"

"Well my frat brothers made good on the bet because they said that Mary brought me back to the house and asked them to take special care of me because I was the best lover she ever had."

"Then of course her father contacted your father and attempted extortion."

"Yes, how did you know that, I didn't tell you, I only told you about me and Trevor Mason's veiled threat to reveal my secret."

Mary ignored this comment and continued. "And your father reacted as he and your grandfather normally did and had Andy at the diner solve the problem with brute force."

"You know about Andy?" Denton was approaching a total state of befuddlement.

"Oh yes, I know about Andy and Andy's boss. Andy reports to Don Luca, although he's too 'respectable' to be called that now."

Susan looked at Denton. "Who are these people you two are talking about?"

Denton could only shake his head while Mary continued to puff on her cigarette. Staring through the cloud of smoke she was generating she continued: "Don Luca is exactly what he sounds like, he's a mafia Don. He hides behind respectable businesses and lives in a respectable neighborhood out on Long Island. Andy runs a diner down by the Fulton Fish Market, but it's only a cover, he's the Don's right hand man, the Don's Number One. Your father made an unholy alliance with Andy and the Don many years ago. They supplied any muscle or clean up services that your father and grandfather thought necessary and in return your father provided the means to launder money, or supply interstate transport with one of our company's trucks when they required it. The arrangement worked quite well until your father died, then it sort of died too. Since you know who Andy is Denton I can only assume that the Don is attempting to revive our alliance once again." Mary Wellbon sat down in a wing back chair. "To address your previous comment, I was aware of the entire incident and your father's reaction to it. What you and nearly everyone else are unaware of is that your father spoke with me concerning everything that happened in our lives and businesses. We were real partners."

"Mother, you obviously know more about Andy than I. If you don't want this relationship revived I can…"

"I didn't say that. The Don and Andy can be quite useful at times. Just remember that they can be very dangerous and don't get personally involved in any of their escapades. Now does Trevor know about Andy?"

"No, no Andy is in fact advising me on how to protect myself against Trevor. He told me he had promised father that he would watch out for me and my interests."

"Good, then the Don correctly believes that you can run Wellbon–Smith without Trevor Mason and prefers it that way. I'm certain that what Andy told you concerning a promise to your father is correct. It sounds like something that your father would do. If Andy made that commitment then it also means that the Don is committed. They won't go back on their word. In a strange way they have their own twisted form of honor."

Denton had to allow that comment and its implications to sink in for a moment. Susan just sat back down on the couch in stunned silence. The intercom from the doorman down on the street broke the temporary silence as William MacLode's arrival was announced. Mary rose from the chair and moved to the intercom. She pressed a button and uttered a curt "Send him up."

***

Denton introduced Mac to Susan and then turned to his mother. Mary crushed her cigarette butt on a silver coaster and took Mac's extended hand. "No need for introductions Denton, while I've never met Mr. MacLode I know all about him."

Mac smiled, "I'm flattered Mrs. Wellbon."

Mary smiled and released Mac's hand. "You are one of our best managers Mr. MacLode. Fox Cabinetry has consistently shown respectable profits under your guidance. Except for '81 and '82, what happened those two years?"

"As you may recall we were in a vise between a recession and runaway inflation." Mary locked her gaze on Mac. Mac did not flinch. "Forgive me for being so bold, but how many other Wellbon–Smith companies lost money those years?" Mac maintained his pleasant smile as he posed the query."

Mary Wellbon permitted herself a faint smile. "An excellent question Mr. MacLode, however forgive me for sidetracking us as we have important business to discuss." Mary turned to Denton. "A bit of history Denton, in your abridged version of your 'incident' you did explain how Mac, might I call you Mac? I understand all your friends do."

"Certainly Mrs. Wellbon, I'm prepared to call you my friend."

"Please call me Mary."

"Very well Mary."

Mary Wellbon continued. "As I was saying, you have come into possession of these funds that are made up of Wellbon–Smith voting shares because my husband wanted to tie your father to our company under what some outsiders might have perceived to be payment for your father's vote in the House of Commons. Your father was in a bit of a predicament. If he sold the stock he would reap huge capital gains because my husband would only accept below value payment, and if he didn't pay for it, well it would look even worse. There was no way that he could return the shares. We wouldn't take them back. Your father did the only smart thing that he could do. He paid for it and sat on it, never taking a penny of the dividends. Exactly what my husband expected him to do. That way Denton could always have leverage on your father if it was ever required. It never was."

"Yes, my father's lawyer explained all that to me."

"Did he also explain that we purposely recruited you out of college to put icing on the cake?"

Mac's expression became serious. "Yes he did."

"Well your lawyer was wrong. We recruited you because you looked promising. Guess what, we were right. Now it is true that we arranged for you to be roommates with Tom Luca, the Don's son, while you attended college. Don't raise your eyebrow. My husband and your beloved 'godfather' out on Long Island had been 'business partners' for years before that. We didn't expect that the two of you would become such lifelong friends or that the Don would become so close to your father. But that was all good."

Mac was surprised at the level that the Wellbon family had manipulated his life. All these years and he had no clue. He didn't know how he felt about all this. The discoveries were coming too fast. But he did know that he wanted to own Fox Cabinetry and this domineering woman might be the key to realizing that dream.

Mary paused and looked carefully at Mac. "You aren't going to express your anger to me? You aren't furious at my family for the way we used your family?"

Mac looked briefly at the ceiling as he pondered his answer. Then he once again engaged Mary Wellbon eye to eye. "I'm very proud of what I've done at Fox. Your company has rewarded me handsomely for those results and had it not been for your family's machinations I wouldn't be standing here today with a block of voting stock."

"Ah a pragmatist, I like that. Let's get down to business." Mary summoned the maid who had just returned from buying groceries for the pantry and provided coffee for all. Then she gave her the remainder of the day off so they could continue their discussions in private. Denton and Susan were seated on the couch and Mary and Mac sat in opposing wing back chairs. Only after the front door closed behind the maid did the conversation continue.

"You're in a unique position of power Mac," said Mary.

"Not as powerful then are you and Denton. According to the numbers that Denton has provided me if any two of us determines to either vote with Trevor or against him, that's the way things will go. In fact as long as you and Denton agree to vote together you really don't require my votes. Trevor is assuming that he has Denton's vote locked up because Denton will not want the incident with Mary Johnson - Harrison revealed. Since my lawyer has informed Abraham Rueben that the offshore funds will retain current ownership and that they will vote as they see fit not selling their proxy, your vote has become crucial. As I'm certain Denton has informed you, he is receiving pressure to deliver your vote. Mason and Rueben are counting on their assumption being correct that you will share Denton's fears and will join them to protect your son and avoid scandal."

Mary had already calculated the numbers in her head after Denton had finished his revelation of the plan. She was far more familiar with who held the shares then she was given credit. "True enough, they assume that we will be so terrified at the thought of exposure that they will be able to control our voting removing the possibility of having to purchase our proxy. That's crucial to their plan. It's interesting that they were willing to buy out your funds Mac. That would have been a far larger commitment than they've agreed to until now."

"Not really Mary," Mac found that the informal method of addressing Mary Wellbon did not flow freely from his tongue. "The deal offered to me through my lawyer was distinctly different from that offered to the other shareholders. They were only offering to purchase one third of my holdings. Your husband, for reasons that we have previously acknowledged, forced my father to purchase the stock at a drastically undervalued price. They are aware of the purchase price and believed they could tempt me into granting them my total proxy for this one meeting by only purchasing a portion of the holdings. The capital gains would have been ridiculous and they argued that I could still retain stock and continue to collect dividends. Or I could redeem the remainder at a later date, one more convenient to them."

"Interesting, as you would expect they've given this a lot of thought," replied Mary. Then turning to her son she spoke sharply. "Denton, what's the plan?"

Denton nearly choked on his coffee. "Pardon me Mother?"

"Well Denton, we're here to determine how we are going to thwart Trevor Mason's plan to take over Wellbon–Smith. We have the votes, or I should say that we have nearly enough votes. As long as we stick together there is hardly any way that he can succeed, however there are implications behind every course of action. What we have to do is make certain that we are in control every step of the way and minimize any damage that Trevor may be able to do. Whether you go with Mason's takeover bid or remain with me you are planning on sitting in the chairman's chair. If you are to lead a billion-dollar enterprise I assume you have a plan. What is it?"

Denton regained his composure as Susan held her breath. Mary Wellbon had always been a loving mother-in-law hopelessly involved in her charity work. Susan found this newly revealed persona as corporate maven very intimidating. She only now began to see why Denton always seemed to react with a touch of fear whenever his mother's name was mentioned.

Denton cleared his voice and rose from his seat. "Yes Mother I do have a plan. I've discussed it with Mac and he is in agreement." Denton was pleased that his voice had the sound of confidence. Mary glanced quickly at Mac and he gave her a slight nod of approval. "First Mother, from the discussion we had before Mac's arrival that unknown to me you already had knowledge of the incident during my college days."

"That's correct and I want you to know that I wanted to fight it out then, but while your father included me in everything, he was strong-willed and decided to deal with the matter in a manner to which he was more accustomed. A much more violent manner I must say." She turned to Mac, "Are you aware of the actions that your friend the Don had Andy take?"

"If you're referring to Andy at the diner acting on behalf of your husband and Ray Luca, yes I'm aware. Denton filled me in."

No one noticed Susan's raised eyebrow. At this moment she was wondering how two apparently strong-willed people like Mary and Denton II ever got together let alone remained together.

Denton continued: "Also from our recent conversation I gather that you really suspect that the incident never took place?"

"I don't doubt that you did what you say you did, that is made an indecent proposal and then left the party with the girl, but I do doubt that in your inebriated condition you were able to perform. Especially considering your near photographic memory cannot recall the act."

Denton blushed and glanced at Mac. Mac gave him a slight noncommittal shrug. Denton moved on, "However Mother, we do have to consider that true or not Trevor and Abraham will reveal the story to the gossip columns and the tabloids. Can we live with that? You know there will be a sizable element of people not to mention collaborating witnesses that will assume it to be true."

"For God's sake Denton this is 1999, we have a sitting president that admits to an affair with a White House intern that wasn't much older than Mary Harrison at the time of your encounter. When and if it comes out we just deny, deny, deny. Mary Johnson – Harrison is dead. God rest her poor tormented soul. There is no statute of limitations on rape, statutory or not, but Mary's family will keep quiet because of the father's crime. Besides without Mary even her family's revelations would be hearsay. As for this family's standing and my charity work that clock will not be turned back. Besides, I give too much money to these organizations. They won't refuse me. To answer your question Denton; yes, I can live with it. Can you?"

Denton paused, "I feared revelation not for myself but because I believed that it would crush you and Susan. I now know that you have been aware of the incident all the time, so that leaves only one person." Denton turned to Susan. "Darling, can you live with this should it come out?"

Susan rose from the couch. She approached Denton and put her arms around him. "I love you. I've always loved you and I never thought you to be perfect. I told you earlier that this doesn't matter to me. I'll stand beside you no matter what."

Denton hugged her tightly. "I love you so much," he whispered. Then releasing her and turning back to Mary and Mac he said: "Yes Mother, I too can live with it."

Mary turned her attention to Susan, her voice suddenly soft. This was the voice that Susan was accustomed to hearing. "Susan darling, I know how shocking all that you've learned this morning must be to you. Because I know you so well I fully believe what you've just said. I do have to consider your family, your parents and sister. How would they handle this revelation?"

Susan smiled a defiant smile. "Mother Wellbon, I believe that they too are strong enough and supportive enough to handle this. But if they can't, understand that when I took your son's hand in marriage I became a Wellbon. I will stand with my family no matter what."

"Thank you Susan, your answer doesn't surprise me. When Denton told me he was asking you to marry him, I told him he would never make a wiser choice during his life."

"Thank you Mother Wellbon."

Denton reasserted himself in the conversation. "There is another factor that we haven't discussed at this point."

"And that would be? asked Mary.

"My incident isn't the only dirt Trevor has on our family." With that Denton proceeded to inform Mary and Susan concerning the vouchers obviously signed by Denton's father that verified the shipment of illegal contraband into the United States by the Atlantic Corporation. "Trevor will not hesitate to turn them over to the authorities. I know father and grandfather are gone, but I fear that there might be legal and financial repercussions in the form of fines levied by the government if the vouchers are verified to be authentic. Having seen them, I fully believe that the vouchers could be proven to be originals in court. Can we afford to be dragged through a high profile court case?"

Mary furrowed her brow as she weighed the consequences on her company. "Abe Rueben's law firm represented Atlantic during that time frame. Your father and grandfather selected them because they were not above helping smooth the way for transactions of questionable legality…that's how Abe acquired those documents." Silence hung over the room for a brief period. Mac was hoping that this bit of information would not spook Mary from her determined course of action. Then Mary spoke again, "To hell with them, better to be fighting with the government over long past sins then to have no fight with them and be sitting here with Trevor Mason controlling our company. If push comes to shove I'll take care of Abe Rueben concerning this matter!" Mac and Denton glanced at each other; both curious as to what Mary Wellbon's intentions were, but neither deciding to ask.

"Very well Mother, I just wanted you to be aware of all of the implications of opposing Trevor Mason. Next topic: the numbers aren't as certain as they seem on the surface. We are making the assumption that all of the other shareholders will vote along with us. An assumption that could prove as disastrous as Trevor's assumption that he has my vote locked up. Just because Trevor couldn't find any dirt on the remainder of the shareholders doesn't mean that they won't perceive an opportunity to sell some of their own holdings. They would demand capital gains equal to the gains of those shares that Trevor is committed to buy. While most of the shareholders can be counted as loyal to you mother; there could be some that will decide, without coercion, to vote with Trevor. They will do so making the assumption that once he is in control of the company they would have a much more advantageous position to argue that if they sold some or all of their holdings the price should be equal to Trevor's purchases. That's an argument that I would not have to entertain if we defeat Trevor."

"It's a point well taken," commented Mac to Mary.

"I believe you to be correct Denton." Mary was mentally reviewing the major players and attempting to determine who could be counted on and who couldn't. "There are those who will see through what Trevor is doing as soon as his control of proxy votes is revealed. They will deduce how he acquired them and seize on the opportunity."

"It would not take a huge number of defections Mother. Even with the total of voting shares represented in this room we do not control 51%."

"Correct, and again I ask what is the plan?"

Denton smiled, "Mac has an appointment to meet with Trevor at the Kitchen and

Bath Industry Show next week in Chicago. Mac will present Trevor with an offer to buy Fox Cabinetry. Mac and his senior staff along with an institutional investor have put together an impressive package of financing."

Mary interrupted, "Will it impress Mason?"

"Probably not, as I know how much Trevor needs to finance his purchase of proxies and shares," Denton answered.

"Is there anyone else making offers?"

Denton looked at Mac, "As I told Mac just a few days ago, I now believe there will be, probably at the same show. Cab Corp Corporation, one Clint Matthews, CEO. Trevor had John Hogg doing research on Matthews and his organization. What John found didn't make Trevor very happy. John found that the same union that is trying to organize Fox is the union that represents the employees of all the divisions of the Cab Corp Corporation. Trevor suspects that Matthews has struck a deal with the union to make trouble for Fox and drive down the asking price."

"I've never met Matthews and already I think him a son of a bitch," muttered Mac.

"That's only speculation on Trevor's part Mac."

"Trevor's not stupid Denton and I've noticed to my irritation that he's right more often than he's wrong."

Mary interjected; "your statement is accurate Mac, he is right far more often than he is wrong. It's truly a shame that he has become greedy and is attempting a takeover. He has a future here. He may be gruff and alienate people but he does get results…continue Denton."

"I propose that we have Mac keep his appointment, meet with Trevor and make the offer. Trevor won't accept on the spot. He doesn't have to as he's arranged financing with an Asian bank to pay for the proxies. No, he'll stall and attempt to get Mac and Matthews in a bidding war. If he can get enough for Fox, he may not have to sell a second company as was the original plan."

Mary turned to Mac, "you're certain that Trevor has no clue that you control the offshore funds?"

"Not even suspicious. Your husband did an amazing job of hiding the true ownership. I only discovered the fact myself this week and that because my father's lawyer revealed it to me as part of the estate." Mac suddenly wondered how Ray Luca knew. He now realized that Luca not only had intimate connections with his own family through Mac and his father, but Luca was deeply involved with the Wellbon family also. Mac decided it was best not to go there just now.

"I can vouch for that," added Denton. "There is no thought of Mac in connection with the offshore funds. Now while Mac is keeping up appearances mother, we need you to personally verify that you are reluctantly agreeing to throw your votes in with Trevor. I need you to personally call Trevor and express your displeasure with his methods but you agree to vote with him. Be convincing, make him a believer."

Mary smiled, "Worry not Denton, I can be convincing." Susan suppressed a smile behind Denton's back and Mary winked at her.

"Now Mother the important part of this plan involves Carlton Smith."

"What about Carlton?"

"We need his votes. Carlton's vote combined with ours makes it impossible for enough defectors to side with Trevor and override us."

"True enough, but why would Carlton vote with Trevor?"

"I have no idea Mother and Trevor and Abraham have not indicated that Carlton is in their camp, but we can't take the chance. Remember mother, Carlton is the one who brought Trevor Mason here from Chicago."

"That's true, I never considered that."

Mac had remained silent but now spoke. "Mary, we can't take the chance that Trevor and Abraham have been totally open with Denton. I'm certain that they still regard him as a bit of a risk."

Mary thought this over. "You're right we have to secure Carlton somehow, but how?"

"You Mother, you have to secure him. We have to gamble that he isn't working with Trevor. You have to approach him and use the long history you and father have with him and lay it on the line. He has to support us. If he has doubts, you have to convince him."

"Suppose he is aligned with Trevor, when I 'lay it on the line as you say' then he'll simply inform Trevor that we're bluffing about our voting with him."

"That's why you have to meet with the board's executive council as soon as possible Mother. You have to meet with the council before you meet with Carlton. In fact we have to hold the Carlton Smith meeting until the last possible moment. There are five members on the council. Can you safely say that you can trust three of them?"

"Why?"

"You must convince them to move the annual meeting up from the second week in December to the second week in November."

"Impossible Denton, Wellbon–Smith companies run on a fiscal year from October first to September thirtieth, they'll never be ready with the final numbers by then. The council will never agree to it."

"We'll tell them that they can go with preliminary numbers and the board will review the final numbers at the regular time. Are there three of the five that you think you could trust to keep our confidence?"

"But what reason can we give them for the move?"

"We tell them the truth Mother that someone is trying a hostile takeover of the company and we have to act quickly to thwart it."

Mac spoke up again. "By moving up the date it will make it more difficult for Trevor to buy or extort more votes. He will be counting on your votes and believe that he is home free. Then if you secure Carlton's votes we drop the surprise of a lifetime on Trevor at the annual meeting."

"What if I can't secure Carlton's vote?"

Mac deferred to Denton. "Then Mother it could get very close. Especially if there are defectors that place greed over the importance of the corporate by laws, personal gain over the principal of the board choosing management."

Mary fell silent again considering this. "Yes Denton there are three that will be loyal to me no matter what. They remember that they owe their jobs and current positions to my husband. They will keep our confidence."

"Is that three in addition to Carlton?"

"Yes Denton, three in addition to Carlton. I still believe that Carlton will stand with us, but I'll play it the way you want." Then she turned to Mac. "Forgive me Mac, but I have to ask. Why is it that you have chosen to stand with us? It sounds to me like Trevor offered you a pretty tempting deal. You could have had a measure of revenge against my family for the way that my husband attempted to keep your father under his influence."

Mac finished his coffee, rose from his chair and taking the coffee pot from the coffee table he replenished Mary's cup and then his own. Denton and Susan passed on Mac's offer. "The thought crossed my mind Mary, but several things influenced my decision. First, my father's initial vote on the whiskey issue was truly in the interests of his constituents. Second, while your husband did an excellent job of tying my father to him just in case he ever needed influence in the future, he never required that influence so a 'request' was never made."

"And if it had been?" Mary was studying Mac closely.

"My father would have told your husband to go to Hell!"

"But then my husband would have given an anonymous tip to the London press telling them how to unravel the complicated layers of ownership surrounding the offshore funds. My husband never bluffed."

"I view that threat the same way I view Trevor Mason's threats against you. Blackmail only works if the intended victim is afraid to have something revealed. You are not afraid therefore the threat is worthless. My father was not afraid, therefore your husband's threat, should it ever have been employed, would have been worthless."

"Again I'm impressed with your pragmatism. But I still don't see that as enough reason not to cash in."

"Your right, it's not. There are two other reasons, both more compelling." Mac walked to the huge windows and looked out into the bright late morning sun.

Mary waited for a few moments and then continued her pursuit. "I think we have a right to know those reasons Mac. Considering the circumstances we find ourselves. At the beginning of this conversation I commented that you are in a very powerful position. You disputed that statement on the basis that Denton's block and my block of stock made us virtually invincible. As our further discussion has shown, we are only invincible if most of the minority shareholders that have not sold out to Trevor vote with us. The other scenario is if Carlton Smith votes with us. But the bottom line is who makes up this 'us' to whom we are referring? Ironically it seems to me that it hinges on you Mac, and the stock that my husband made possible for you to control. Should you move into Trevor's camp all might be lost for Denton and me. Denton has wisely realized that the chairmanship as he would gain it with Trevor would only be a figurehead. With you joining us he would be the true chairman. I personally need to know those 'more compelling reasons' you've mentioned."

"Yes you do have the right and I'll tell you." Mac turned and faced Mary. "First, I want to own Fox more than anything else. If we win this battle I will demand to sit down across the table from you and your son and drive a hard bargain to acquire it. Don't underestimate me as a negotiator. I also expect you and Denton will do whatever is necessary to prevent Trevor Mason from signing a letter of intent to purchase Fox if offered by anyone else but me. Should you not make a good faith effort on my behalf I would have to reconsider my position."

"Sounds fair, I believe we can effectively deter the sale of Fox for that short period of time and I look forward to the exchange between us during the negotiations. What's the other reason?"

"I don't like Trevor Mason."

Mary smiled. "Those reasons are good enough for me."

To Catch a Fox

They all agreed with Denton's plan and determined that they would set it into motion immediately. By this time it was nearly noon. Mary bid them goodbye and Mac rode down in the elevator with Susan and Denton to the ground floor. They shook hands in the lobby and Mac left by the rear exit. It was not unusual to see Denton and Susan coming and going from Mary Wellbon's penthouse, but it would have seemed highly suspicious if certain people observed Mac leaving.

Alone in the penthouse, Mary Wellbon poured herself a glass of sherry from a decanter at the bar. She then carried the glass with the amber liquid into the combination den - office that she began using after her husband's death. Except for some cosmetic changes that gave the room a more feminine appearance, it was very much the way her husband had left it. Mary settled down in the big leather chair behind the Fox built solid cherry desk. She sipped the sherry and sat silently in thought. The room was bathed in bright fall sunlight.

Mary was thinking of her son. She was extremely proud of him. He was finally beginning to act like a Wellbon. He was prepared to stand up to Trevor Mason and risk embarrassing revelations to maintain control of the company that his grandfather had founded and his father had built. If they could see young Denton now she knew that they would both be proud. She took another sip of sherry and appeared to be totally lost in thought.

Then sitting the glass on a coaster, she opened a desk drawer and extracted a large book. The title "A Competitive Market Analysis of Fox Cabinetry" prepared by Bertrum & Bertrum of Chicago. Mary smiled a faint smile. After all, how could Trevor Mason know that Ted Bertrum, one of the founder's sons, once dated Mary while they were both in college? Obviously the romance didn't work out, but the two had remained friends. As soon as Ted realized that the business that was to be sold was Fox Cabinetry, and that it was part of the Atlantic Corporation owned by Wellbon–Smith he called Mary immediately. When she told him she wasn't aware of any plans to sell Fox, Ted offered to send her a copy. That was how she independently began to put the pieces of the puzzle together. This morning Denton and Mac had filled in those portions that had been missing.

Mary stared at the book for a long time and then picked up the phone and punched in a number. She listened to it ring until the call was answered on the other end. "Mary Wellbon here...Denton is finally going to fight...yes...Oh yes he quite possibly could win…he has a surprising and unexpectedly powerful ally…yes this changes everything…I agree, we have to change our plans in light of this development…yes, yes, let's meet tonight." Mary hung up the phone and finished her sherry.

***

They were there when Foster Harrison returned to his hotel room in Los Angeles. Foster was on a regular swing around his sales territory and ended in L.A. He was finished for the week and he was tired. He planned to catch a flight out of LAX for his home in San Francisco tomorrow morning but decided instead to check out tonight. He was scheduled to leave on a flight north at 10:15 PM. The reason for this change was a phone call that he received from his wife this afternoon. When she returned home from work she discovered that their home had been broken into. All that was missing were some personal papers that Foster kept locked in his desk drawer, but the house was completely ransacked. The police were looking into the matter.

Upon entering the hotel room Foster flicked the light switch, but the lights failed to come on. He moved toward the lamp on the small desk that was visible in the shaft of light provided by the open door. The blinds must have been pulled, as there was no late afternoon light coming through the window. Foster assumed that the maid had closed them because he was certain that they were open when he left that morning. As he approached the lamp the door slammed closed behind him putting the room in semi-darkness. As he turned to see what had caused the door to close he was roughly grabbed from behind, a towel stuffed in his mouth as he attempted to yell and was forcibly thrown to his knees. A hard cylindrical object was pressed against the back of his head.

"Now Mr. Harrison, it would be very, I repeat, very unwise of you to make even the slightest noise when I remove this towel from your mouth. Unwise because this is a nine millimeter Glock with a silencer that I have pressed against your head. Do you know what effect a nine millimeter slug would have passing through your head? Before you could finish yelling whatever it is you decided to yell, your brains would be splattered all over the carpet. If anyone even heard the extremely brief noise that you might make they would soon dismiss it as their imagination or as a curiosity. They certainly won't hear the shot. Now, you are going to remain on your knees put your hands behind your back and nod your head if you understand. If you cooperate we will soon be on our way and you will be none the worse for the ware. Are you going to cooperate?"

The voice was low and menacing. Foster had no doubt that the person behind the voice would do exactly as he stated. Foster nodded to the affirmative and placed his hands behind his back. His heart was racing and his mouth had gone dry with fear. Who was this and what did he want?

"Good, that's very smart on your part Mr. Harrison I'm sure we'll get along just fine. Now I'm going to remove the towel, for your sake don't disappoint me."

The towel slowly was taken from over Foster's face. The only sound that Foster made was that of his now rapid breathing. The room was still dark but his eyes were becoming accustomed to the dim light. He could hear the faint sounds of movement. Although he couldn't see anyone he believed that there were at least three people in the room in addition to him. One was holding him down, one had utilized the towel and still held the gun to his head and another was off to his left beside the bed. This was probably the one that closed the door. What could they want?

The voice again, "Understand your situation Mr. Harrison, you have information that we need. Our questions will be easy to answer. They are the kind of questions that you will not have to strain to come up with the answers. If you give us any trouble or if we even suspect that you might be lying we will kill you. Under different circumstances when we might have more time you would have the luxury of playing games. Then we could take the time to demonstrate several methods that we sometimes use to extract the truth from stubborn individuals. All of these methods would be extremely unpleasant for you and my associates here would truly relish your discomfort. But unfortunately we don't have the time to indulge ourselves. If this isn't enough incentive allow me to inform you that we have your home address in San Francisco. As proof of that I suspect that you are already aware that we paid your home a visit early this morning while your wife was at work. We then flew down here to visit with you. You live in the Haight Ashbury District do you not? You may nod your head if I am correct."

Foster felt sick to his stomach. He nodded in affirmation.

"If we don't like your answers and we kill you our next stop will be a visit to your wife to see if she might be smarter than you. Oh and we'll make certain that if we must visit your wife we'll have more time to ah, indulge our rather vicious and perverted methods. You may nod again if you understand."

Foster nodded.

"Good. First question: Did you and your first wife Mary Johnson Harrison have any children?"

Even in his terrified state of mind Foster was taken aback. This was the last question he expected. How to answer, how to answer?

"Silence is not acceptable Mr. Harrison." The gun muzzle was pressed harder against Foster's skull.

"My, my wife Mary had a daughter, but it wasn't mine!" stammered Foster. "That's why I left her! She told me it was mine! She lied to me! That was why I married her in the first place! But the girl wasn't mine! Honest, I'm telling the truth! Please believe me. Don't kill me! Please!"

Now there was silence on the other side and Foster closed his eyes tightly expecting the gun to go off at any second. He briefly wondered if he would hear or feel anything. Then the voice again:

"How do you know it wasn't your child?"

"Blood tests, the girl contacted an infection as a toddler and there were blood tests. I was suspicious so I had a sample taken of my blood and unknown to Mary I had a comparison done. Crystal wasn't mine."

"Who was the father?"

"I don't know. Mary would never tell me even when I confronted her with the proof. You've got to believe me!"

"Where's the girl now? She's gotta be an adult and on her own."

"She's the news anchor on Channel 3, W, W something… WSAV in Savannah!" Foster's voice was now a high-pitched wail.

"Savannah Georgia?"

"Yes, yes Savannah Georgia! That's where Mary and I lived after we got married. We moved there from Baltimore!"

"Does she know who her real father is?"

"I don't think so. She still believed that I was her father up until a couple of months ago."

"How do you know that?"

"Because I'm the one that told her I wasn't her father!"

"Where were these blood tests on the girl conducted?

"Atlanta General Hospital, at that time there was no facility that could deal with an unidentified infection in Savannah or Chatham County. We had to take her to Atlanta. Please let me go. I'm telling you the truth!"

There was a long silence and Foster began to weep softly. The voice spoke again but this time it wasn't speaking to Foster. "Whatda ya think?"

Another voice answered for the first time. "Seems to explain a few things but his story doesn't match the birth certificate we found in his desk or what's on file in the Savannah Courthouse."

"Should I kill him?" The voice was casual. Foster began crying openly now, tears streaming down his face.

"Please, I'm telling you the truth, please," Foster was now sobbing like a baby.

The person connected to the new voice stepped in front of Foster. "Keep your head down Mr. Harrison, don't look up." Foster did as he was told. It was still dark in the room but his eyes had completely adjusted. Through his tears he could see feet wearing sneakers connected to legs in blue jeans standing before him in the gloom. "How do you explain the birth certificate that lists you as the father and the divorce settlement that awards uncontested custody to Mary Harrison your ex-wife? We found these documents in your desk."

"I didn't want to shame her. I never insisted that the official records be changed; I just relinquished all claims to custody of Crystal. Mary was satisfied with that. That's why when Mary committed suicide I never attempted to seek custody again. That allowed Crystal to be adopted. She got a good home too…I mean she wasn't my child. Please let me go."

The new voice continued, "Why is it there is no trace of Crystal Harrison's existence in the birth records or your own divorce records that are on file in Savannah? Why don't your personal records match the official records? The only record is of the adoption of Crystal Rankin. Her supposed birth name was taken from the tombstone of a person that died in infancy. That took us a lot of time to figure out. How do you explain all of these discrepancies?"

Foster was at his wits end, terrified not knowing what to say. He had no clue that the records in Savannah were different from his own copies. He didn't know what these strangers wanted to hear. He didn't know what answer might save his life, so he did all that he could do, he told the truth. "I don't know! He wailed. I wasn't ever aware that the papers in Savannah didn't match mine! Please let me go!"

The sneaker clad feet moved out of Foster's view. Foster was certain that he was about to die when suddenly he was yanked to his feet. The menacing voice was next to his ear now the gun still firmly pressed to the back of his skull. "You just got terribly lucky Mr. Harrison. Your answers satisfy our friend, for now… If you attempt to go to the police, if you attempt to tell anyone including your wife about our little meeting we will find out and we will come to get you. Hell, you're not hard to find. We even found you in this hotel room while you were traveling on business and you know that we have your home address. Do you doubt what I say? Do you have any questions as to what is expected of you?"

"No…No, I'll keep quiet. I'll never tell anyone! I promise! Please just let me go!"

"There's one more thing Mr. Harrison." This time it was the second voice again. "Is there anything else concerning Crystal Harrison that you might want to tell us? Think hard. Anything at all that might be of interest to us."

Foster's mind was racing. Think damn it! Think! "Well just one thing that always puzzled me. I don't know if it's anything of importance or not…"

"I'll decide that, just tell me."

"I could never understand how Mary did it on what she made and what I was paying her in alimony."

"What do you mean?"

"She always seemed to have more than enough money. She lived in apartments that I don't understand how she afforded them. You know what I mean? She always seemed to be able to live better than what her income would allow, yet she wasn't in debt…that's all I can think of just now." Foster was ready to collapse. He didn't know if he had just helped or hurt his situation.

"What does Crystal look like today?" It was the second voice that inquired.

"If you know what her mother looked like she's the spiting image of her mother at that age."

Silence again, terrifying silence and then the second voice spoke once more. "Thank you Mr. Harrison that is the most valuable information you've given us today." There was another pause and then the second voice spoke to the first voice. "Explain to Mr. Harrison what will happen if we discover that he lied to us or failed to tell us everything he knows."

The first voice was right in Foster's ear again. "If we have to return because the information you've given us today is inaccurate, allow me to explain the procedure we will follow on our second visit…" Foster held his breath. "First my associates will stuff a towel in your mouth again. Then to demonstrate that we were not happy with the information that you gave us today and to emphasize that we mean business, while my associates hold you I will then take a very sharp knife and before I ask you any questions I will cut off one of your fingers! Because we are not heartless we will allow you to then take the towel from your mouth and use it to try to stop the bleeding while we ask you more questions. If we don't like the answers you give us I'll pull down your pants, take my knife and begin cutting on another part of your body until we like your answers! …But relax." The voice was now almost purring in Foster's ear. "I've seldom had to make that second cut. It's surprising how cooperative people become."

With that graphic explanation Foster was thrown to the floor face down. The three men stepped over him and left the room. Foster lay crying for a long time. Then he became violently sick and ran to the toilet and began throwing up.

***

The black Buick sedan slide effortlessly along the approach to LAX, Los Angeles International Airport. Two of the three men it carried were involved in uproarious laughter. "Did you see the look on his face when I threatened to cut his pecker off?"

"Yeah, I thought he was going to lose his lunch right there!"

"What a wuss! Cryin' and pleadin'; we should have killed him just for being so gutless!"

"He was so scared if we would have told him we wanted to bump off his mother he woulda drawn a map to her house!"

"He mighta tried, but his hands were shakin' so much I doubt if he could have made a straight line!"

"I'm surprised he didn't pee his pants. That would have been so funny!"

Again the laughter until the man with the balding head and frizzy hair who had been riding silently in the back seat spoke "Shut your traps! I'm trying to think!" Silence fell immediately upon the other two. Andy was from the respected New York family and their boss told them that he was personally indebted to Andy's Don. Their instructions were to do whatever Andy required.

Andy pulled out his cell phone and chose a number in the memory. Soon he was talking to Raymond Luca himself. Andy quickly and without mentioning names brought the Don up to date with what he had discovered. When he was finished there was a pause on the other end. Then the old Don spoke.

"Andy it sounds as if our suspicions were correct. There is a daughter and our mutual friend is her father. You're certain that he is unaware of this."

"As certain as I can be Boss."

"Then it had to be his father that provided the money and the professional cover up."

"That's the way I see it Boss."

"Where are you now Andy?"

"We're just about to pull into the short term parking at LAX. I called after leaving our acquaintance in his hotel room and booked a flight to Atlanta. I'll try to find those old blood tests. You got anybody that I could lean on or that owes you somethin' in Atlanta?"

"Very good Andy, I'm glad to see that you've learned a few things after all of these years. Yes, there's a doctor in Atlanta that had a gambling problem and got into trouble with our friends in Atlantic City. I bailed him out and have never asked anything in return. I think it's time to call in that marker. When you get to Atlanta call me, I'll give you everything you need to know. Good job Andy and in record time. You always could apply force judiciously." With that the old man was gone. Andy permitted himself a small smile. It never hurt to be on the Boss' good side.

The car was stopped and the two local "mechanics" helped Andy get his bags checked and saw him onto his flight. They wanted nothing but good reviews from this important man from the east.

Chapter 19

Abraham Rueben was walking along Fifth Avenue in New York toward the parking garage where he left his car. He had just been to a meeting with Trevor Mason and Denton Wellbon III. Denton was enthusiastically explaining that his mother had agreed to support them in their attempt to take over Wellbon–Smith. Trevor was pleased and felt vindicated in his efforts to manipulate both Denton and his mother. Abraham was skeptical. Everything that Denton said made sense. Indeed, Mary Wellbon called Trevor personally while they were discussing the vote. A well timed call indeed thought Abe. She was her normal haughty self. She cursed Trevor for his tactics and his audacity, but in the end she had no choice but to go along. Why wasn't he feeling in a celebratory mood? Mary Wellbon combined with Denton's support and the accumulated proxies all but assured their success. It no longer mattered that the offshore funds could not be brought on board. It would have been nice if they could have secured the offshore funds but in the larger scheme of things it was not necessary. Mary Wellbon's vote should mean that Carlton Smith would come along. It was nearly impossible to imagine Smith voting against the Wellbons.

Rueben wasn't certain what troubled him. Denton told them that it had been extremely difficult for him to reveal his secret to his mother. That made sense to Abraham. He could accept the fact that hard-nosed Mary Wellbon would only support her son because she was being forced to do it. After all had she wanted to she could have anointed him chairman years ago. However she chose not to do that.

Abraham was hungry and one of his favorite street vendors worked this block. He spotted the vendor's cart and got in line to order a hot dog. When it was his turn he ordered a foot long dog with everything on it. As he watched its preparation he made a mental note to call Albert down in Savannah and get a progress report on Crystal Harrison. As he paid for the dog he reassessed his feelings concerning Denton Wellbon. By the time he reached the entrance to the underground parking garage he had not only finished his hot dog, but he had made a decision. He would call his main "mechanic" Duke. Abraham had decided that they needed insurance. It was not necessary for Trevor to know the details. Abraham handed the attendant his ticket. He felt much better.

***

It was seven o'clock Tuesday morning, the week of the Kitchen & Bath Show. Tony Conocenti sat at a table near a window. He was in the Regency Club on the thirty-fifth floor of the Hyatt Regency on East Whacker Avenue in Chicago. The Regency Club was available to individuals that frequently stayed at the Hyatt Regency Hotel. A free continental breakfast was available in the morning, juices, sodas and alcoholic beverages were available all day and night and a hot buffet during "happy hour." Everything was "no charge" except the alcohol. That had to be charged to the room in which the guest was staying. As Tony recently chose to switch to the Hyatt rather than the Holiday Inn on the top floors opposite the Merchandise Mart he had become a frequent guest. He was not displeased with the Holiday Inn, but chose not to accidentally run into his two Design Center dealers on the ground floor of the Mart unless he intended to meet with them.

Tony sipped his black coffee and stared out the window. The morning sunlight reflected off the Wrigley Building, magnificent across the street in alabaster splendor. He had taken his good friend David Elliott's advice and flown out to Chicago on Monday, a day earlier than planned. He arrived in plenty of time to look up Blair McManus, but lost his nerve. After agonizing all day and half of the night he had decided to just let it die. He couldn't erase the image of her on the arm of that, that… celebrity! Why couldn't she tell him the truth that she preferred to be with a movie and television star rather than have dinner with him? Why couldn't she just tell him that it was over? Why did she let him discover her new romantic interest on the television? Did she think that there was no chance that he might see? Did she forget whom she was with and that they would be the center of attention when they walked up the red carpet? Why did she continue to call him several times after that evening? Why did her voice sound as if nothing had happened? Did she think that he was so hung up on her that he would be willing to continue their relationship as the second string? Someone to amuse her when she was on the East Coast or her new boyfriend was off making movies? What does she take him for?

Well that was it! He was finished with her and he didn't have to explain why to anyone! He would not be made a fool of. He would just let it die. After making that momentous decision in bed last night he finally succumbed to sleep.

Unfortunately this occurred when only about two hours remained until the alarm pounded into his ears. Now, sitting here on the penthouse level of the hotel, eyes bloodshot from lack of sleep, Tony could not think of anything else but Blair. With every thought of her his stomach jerked into a knot. This was not psychological, this was real pain and he wondered why, now that he had decided the relationship was over he could not stop thinking of her. How long would it take until this now ever-present pain would cease?

He attempted to put her out of his mind by turning his attention to a more immediate matter. He decided that he needed a Danish to accompany his coffee. He rose from the chair and moved from the lounge back the narrow hall to the room where the breakfast buffet was stationed. He walked to the counter, evaluated the various pastries that were pleasingly presented to him on a silver tray and selected a cheese Danish. Tony turned with the idea of returning to his table by the window when suddenly she was only inches from his face! "Blair!" he blurted, much louder than he realized. The numerous guests that had chosen this hour to partake of their breakfast all turned in the direction of the outburst. The spectacle before them was that of a tall handsome man looking startled and scared. Before him, standing as tall as she could in high heels so as to be eye to eye with him, was a strikingly beautiful redhead with long curly locks cascading over her shoulders, a set jaw and a determined look on her face.

Blair said nothing as she stared at Tony, her green eyes blazing. "Hi Blair, how did you get up here? This is a private club. How did you know I was here?" Tony knew his voice was trembling.

After a long icy pause during which her eyes seemed to grow even darker Blair replied in a low threatening voice, "I work for a newspaper. There are people on the staff of newspapers whose job it is to cover the conventions that come to town. They also determine who's in town in connection with these affairs and where they might be found. With you, my friends had an easy time of it. You are very well known in the kitchen and bath industry. I live in this town; it's my town. I know people, people who can get me one of these." Blair held up the plastic key card that members of the Regency Club were given at check in. Any guests wishing to take advantage of the club merely had to swipe the card through the reader in the elevator and then push the button for the thirty-fifth floor. The elevator would not go to that floor without the member's key. Blair was not a frequent guest at the Hyatt Regency, but apparently she knew a current guest that was.

By now Tony was blocking the path of the other guests to the Danish tray. Blair stood motionless staring at him while Tony fidgeted. Finally one of the hostesses at the Regency Club approached. "Is there a problem?"

"Yes" hissed Blair.

"No" stuttered Tony simultaneously.

The hostess looked at the two of them and decided it would not be wise to step between them.

"Could you both move into the other room so these guests can select a pastry?"

Tony regained a portion of his composure and taking Blair gently by the arm he began steering her toward the other room and the table. Looking back at the hostess he assured her that there would not be any trouble. When they were seated across from each other Tony once more noticed how beautiful she was. The fair skin with just the right amount of freckles sprinkled over her lovely cheekbones and delicate nose. The glorious red hair that now fell carelessly over her shoulders. She wore a white cashmere sweater with a boat neck that was fairly tight, tight enough to accent her soft full breasts. She wore a beige skirt that ended just at her knees with matching shoes and jacket. It was early fall in Chicago and a light jacket was necessary against the wind whipping off the lake. Tony caught his breath, the ever-present pain in his stomach even more acute. God she's beautiful he thought. Blair's expressionless stare was relentless.

"Can I get you anything, coffee, tea, something to eat?" Tony, the master of the sale didn't know what to say.

Silence, Tony left out a deep sigh and pushed his coffee and Danish to the side. "Okay Blair what's up?"

Her voice was low but intense. "What's up? What's up? That's your question to me? What's up?"

Tony returned her gaze and shrugged his shoulders. "Yeah, I guess that's my question."

"How about if I begin with some questions, why have you been ignoring me? Why haven't you returned my calls? Why are you brushing me off?"

"I returned your calls!" Tony was aware that his voice sounded defensive. Why he wasn't certain. He had nothing to defend or explain. She was the one that should be on defense.

"Oh sure, on my home phone when you knew I would be in the office and on my office phone when you were pretty damn certain I would be at home. Did you lose my cell phone number? You know I carry it everywhere."

Tony placed his elbows on the table and his head in his hands. "No I didn't lose your cell phone number. You're right I was avoiding you."

"For god's sake why, are you breaking up with me? If you are I would certainly like to know the reason. I deserve to be told in person, not shoved aside without explanation."

Tony now crossed his arms over his chest in a defensive position. "Breaking up, I don't know, were we ever an item? I don't ever recall us making it official."

"You didn't know that we were an 'item' as you call it? You didn't think of us as a couple? We made love every time we were together for god's sake! The last time I was with you in Lancaster you brought up the topic of my meeting your daughter when the time was right. But you didn't think of us as a couple? What do you think I am? Do you think I call other guys several times a week no matter where they are in the world or where I am for that matter? Do you think I have an intense relationship like ours every day with any guy that crosses my path?"

"I don't know, do you?" Tony's eyes suddenly hardened and his face became ashen. Blair was clearly taken aback and the surprise showed on her face. For a brief instant Tony felt satisfaction, but then he saw that he had hurt her and he felt terrible. Another long silence followed as they sat and stared at each other. Finally Blair spoke.

"I…I don't know what that means. I don't know where that's coming from." Her voice had lost the shrill edge. It was now strangely soft.

Well here it was. Tony decided to plunge ahead, "Dirk Andersen."

To Catch a Fox

"What?" Blair was incredulous.

"You heard me, Dirk Andersen."

"The movie star? What about him?"

"Don't play dumb with me. Yeah, yeah Blair I did think we were a couple and yes, I looked forward to every time we were together and every time the phone rang I hoped it was you. I believed, even though you were oh so coy, that this was going somewhere special...I believed that until that night on Pier 39 in Frisco."

"Pier 39? Isn't that where the restaurant is that you wanted to meet; when we were both on the coast...I don't understand, we never had that date."

"You're damn right we never had that date."

Blair shook her head, the puzzled look on her face growing more confused by the moment. "Okay, I remember, I had to work that night. I never left L.A...I explained that to you on the phone. You can't be this upset because I had to break our date. You've had to cancel on me several times because of your work."

"I have no problem with your reason for canceling. Me of all people understand that careers have to come first. Hell, that's what ruined my first marriage. Part of the attraction to you is that you understand that too. Unlike my first wife, you have a career and demands to meet just like me."

Blair threw her hands in the air, "I'm lost Tiger; I am freaking lost! I don't have a clue as to what you are upset about." Then suddenly, at that moment the truth began to dawn on Blair. Recognition began to cross her face. "Oh my word! Dirk Andersen! You think I dumped you for Dirk Andersen!" Blair's hand covered her mouth. She didn't know whether to laugh, cry or hit him.

"Yeah, that's what I think. Why shouldn't I think that? There I am sitting in the restaurant bar with my West Coast sales rep, a piss poor substitute for you, when who comes on the television? Dirk Andersen arriving at some Hollywood awards ceremony. And who's on his arm smiling for the camera? YOU that's who, I felt like a sledge hammer hit me in the gut!"

Blair just sat there with her hand over her mouth staring at Tony. Tony looked away and out the window at the busy street thirty-five stories below. There he thought it's out in the open. From that moment in the restaurant that he had just described until now he had imagined confronting Blair over this. This is where he should have felt triumphant, but he didn't. Instead for some reason he felt sort of, how did he feel, silly? They sat in silence again. Blair removed her hand from over her mouth and placed it on the table. "May I have a sip of your coffee Tiger?" she asked.

"What?" Tony's attention returned from the window.

"May I have a sip of your coffee?"

"Uh, sure, it may be cold."

"That's okay. Thanks." Blair took the cup and sipped it slowly. "Its fine," she said and cradled the warm cup in her hands. The silence returned.

Blair was uncertain how to approach this, but she had to make an attempt. This had to be settled, and not just Tony's misunderstanding of the situation. This went deeper than that. "Tiger, Andersen was my work, my assignment for the evening. He was the last on the list of celebrities for the style articles that I was writing for the Tribune. As you know I was out there all week with a camera crew interviewing celebrities in their homes for the style section of the paper. Andersen's home was the last photo op that I had to do. He met me for the interview earlier that week and we were supposed to go to his home the morning of our date, yours and mine. I figured that we could get the photos and I would still have time to fly up the coast and meet you for dinner. However, Dirk had other ideas. At the interview, he tried to hit on me. Weather you believe it or not I rebuffed him. He then asked me to at least accompany him to the awards ceremony on Friday evening. I told him I was meeting you. I thought that was the end of it until my editor called me the next morning. Dirk had contacted the paper and told them the deal was off unless I went with him on Friday night. My editor arranged for me to meet with a designer on Rodeo Drive to have a dress fitted and that he was ordering me to go with Dirk. I wasn't happy about it, but it's my job. I went to the ceremony and the parties afterward and then back to my hotel. Alone! The next morning, one day late, we went to Dirk's home and took the photos. I have not seen him or spoken with him since. I doubt that I ever will.

After the party he tried to hit on me again in the limo and I slapped him. He didn't like that much. I gather that not too many gals turn him down. That's it Tiger. That's the whole story. Do you believe me?"

It all made sense. Tony suddenly felt worse than silly. He felt stupid. He picked up his fork and took a bite of the Danish, avoiding her eyes as he did. Then he looked up and reached across the table for her hands holding the coffee cup. "May I have a sip?" he asked. Blair released the cup. Tony sipped the coffee and then set the cup down.

"Why didn't you tell me the reason when you canceled our date?"

"You sounded so tired and you explained that things were pretty rough for you just now. Your problems sounded worse than mine so I decided not to burden you with my details. I had to work. That was enough."

"Yes I believe you. I'm sorry I've been a real jerk. I was so, so jealous. Jealously makes you do stupid things."

"I'm sort of glad that you were jealous Tiger. It means that you care deeply and that makes me happy. I'm not glad that you didn't call me right away to tell me your fears and let me explain. I thought our relationship was based on trust among other things. Instead you jumped to your own conclusions and then built a wall between us to keep me out. All the while you judged me and passed sentence. You decided to send me out of your life without even talking to me. That doesn't make me happy at all Tiger."

Tony bowed his head, afraid to meet her gaze. How could he have been so stupid? "I'm sorry Blair, please believe me I'm very sorry."

"I believe that you're sorry, and I accept your apology. I'm also glad that you believe me. I don't think that I've ever given you a reason not to trust me. Have I?"

"No," was the whispered reply.

"But we have a bigger problem."

Tony looked up. "What might that be?" he asked tentatively. Blair took the fork from his hand and carved a bite of the Danish for herself. Then she popped it into her mouth and watched him closely as she chewed the morsel, her head cocked slightly to the side.

"You just stated that we both have careers. How you were happy because unlike your ex-wife I understand that sometimes the work must come first."

Tony wasn't following. "That's true I always know that you will understand."

"There's the problem Tiger. It's a one-way street with you. You always know that I'll understand, but when my work took precedent and you didn't like what I was doing, you were ready to punish me and scrap this special thing we're trying to grow."

"No, no, I was dead wrong, but this was different. I thought you were dumping me for another man."

"Yep, I know Tiger. It's all about you. You never considered what the demands of my job, my career might be. You never considered the compromises that I may have to make. Compromises that could affect you too, you just wanted me to be a working gal so that I could empathize with you. The trouble is that I'm more than a girl with a job. I'm a girl with a career, a career like yours. A career that is as important to me as your career is to you. Because of that you will have to accept that sometimes I'll be away and out of your sight and alone with other men. I know that you often take female dealers out to dinner as part of your job. I know that when that happens I may be thousands of miles away. But I'm okay with that because I know you and love you and trust you. Did you hear that? I love you and trust you. Now, when you can say for certain that you can do the same for me when my career requires another Dirk Andersen, well then maybe we can keep this special thing we have going alive and well."

"Blair, I…" Tony suddenly wanted to say so much but Blair cut him off.

"Don't answer me now Tiger. Take all the time that you need to think this over. I'm serious about this relationship, more serious than I've ever been before. But I want you to be equally serious or I'm not going to waste any more of our time." With that Blair rose from her chair, hesitated and then scooped up the remainder of the Danish and walked to the exit. She paused before pushing through the door. Looking back at Tony she said: "I'll be covering the KBIS for the paper.

"You'll be able to find me if you want to pick up this discussion. See you Tiger, have a good show."

Tony just sat for a long time staring out the window at the Chicago morning.

***

It was Wednesday morning and Mac and Sarah had just disembarked from their flight at O'Hare International Airport in Chicago. They followed the overhead signs to the baggage claim for their flight and found Tony Conocenti waiting there for them. "Good morning Mac." Tony offered his hand to his boss. Mac responded to the gesture firmly

"Good to see you Tony."

"Hi Sarah, I'm glad that Mac decided to bring you along."

Sarah returned Tony's smile and handshake. "Mac thought that the show would be a good place for me to learn more about the business and where Fox fits into the industry."

"I agree totally," replied Tony.

Tony turned back to Mac. "When are Dave and Carroll coming out?"

"This afternoon, I wanted them both to be here for our sales meeting tomorrow. Did you have a chance to check the numbers this morning?" This was the question that Mac and Tony above all others at Fox asked every workday. Pam Collins, who headed customer service and counted the incoming orders each morning, often told people that Mac and Tony didn't breathe until they received the incoming count. The numbers consisted of the unit count. The unit count was a complex formula that derived units of production time defined by material and labor from the number of cabinets that Fox received orders for each day. Currently Fox could produce 1800 units of manufacturing time per week. They needed to average 1500 units to make their original forecast, but it was imperative for them to now average 1650 per week to pay for the increase in costs that Mac's union busting strategy was forcing. Part of the increased cost was made up in the price increase and part of it had to be increased volume. So far the numbers were holding up. The capacity in Las Vegas was 800 units. This number was also holding up well, but they wouldn't get that number until later in the morning.

Tony smiled, "1700 Boss," was his reply.

"All right," squealed Sarah!

Mac grinned. "Good job Tony, the numbers are holding up and this couldn't come at a better time. Just before we meet with Trevor Mason."

"Don't thank me Boss, when times are good sales people get too much credit and when times are bad sales people get too much credit."

"So you tell me, but I know that if you and the sales force hadn't done a great sales job none of the dealers would have accepted this surprise price increase let alone exceed forecast."

"Take the credit when you can Tony," Sarah smiled.

"I'm glad to see you getting into it this much Sarah," replied Tony.

"You bet I am. This is the best job I've ever had and I love it!"

Mac smiled, "We're glad you love it. You've done so much for employee morale and relations. That as much as anything else will keep the unions out, we couldn't be happier that you're here."

"Thank you."

"Talk about timing," said Tony, "You came when we needed you most."

Mac grabbed his bag from the carousel and Tony took Sarah's. "I've got a rental car in the lot Boss, it's a thirty and change cab ride into Chicago. I figure that we can all use the car to get around the city if needed."

"Good, we'll check into the hotel and then go over to McCormick Center and check out the booth. How's it look?"

"Great, the guys are doing a terrific job."

"Are we on schedule, will we be ready for the show opening on Friday morning?"

"This year for the first time, we're ahead of schedule. That company that you hired to assist us with our shows has really done a great job. They somehow got our truck moved up in the line so that we could unload, when we needed some wallpaper touched up they found a local girl that is just terrific and if we need anything from shims to paint they get it for us pronto. But the best thing is that we've had none of the usual problems with the union workers. When we first came we were informed that we had to hire a union carpenter and electrician. We told the supervisor of the firm that you hired about this and he disappeared for a little while. Soon the union guy was back and told us that he made a mistake, and we didn't need any union people to do the work we were doing. I don't understand how that happened, but the show company that you hired had to have something to do with it. Who are these people?"

Mac smiled, the company that he hired specialized in assisting companies that participate in trade shows. They advertised that they take care of all the little details like registration, union requirements of the exhibition hall, unexpected material requirements or any problem that the exhibitor might encounter. What Mac wasn't going to reveal to Tony was that the company was recommended to him and owned by an associate of Raymond Luca. Mac strongly suspected that the modest price and excellent results were provided because the company was really a money laundering operation for Luca's family "business." That association and the fear, justified or not, that it generated allowed them to pressure everyone into cooperating with them and thereby give their clients the kind of service that Tony just described. The laundering that Mac suspected allowed them to provide this service for a modest price as their primary interest was not showing a profit but to clean the funds that the family business generated from other less legitimate enterprises. They were a legitimate business and Mac never asked questions. "A friend recommended them," was Mac's only reply.

As they headed for the parking garage the conversation continued. Sarah was glad that Tony was pulling her wheeled bag because she was having trouble enough keeping up with the two men with only her soft leather briefcase on her shoulder.

"Tony are you ready for the sales meeting tomorrow?"

To Catch a Fox

"Just about Mac, If you don't mind I'll let you and Sarah have the car after you check in at the hotel and you can go to McCormick Center and check out the booth. I'll put the last touches on my sales meeting presentation for tomorrow."

"Fine by me, has the sales force begun to trickle in yet?"

"Some are here, most come in tonight."

"Who's here that could help you get things together, you know, make copies get handouts ready at the hotel's business center?"

"John Malicki from the upper mid-west and Danny Meck from the southeast are the two that could be most useful to me."

"Good, they're both factory guys as opposed to the independent reps. Use them."

"I'm ahead of you Boss, they both checked in with me the instant that they arrived. I've already got them working on those things back at the hotel. When do we meet with Trevor and his staff for the annual review?"

"Tomorrow afternoon. By the way I read the report that you submitted for the review and it's excellent. Do you think that you can wrap up the semi-annual sales meeting in one morning?"

"So that's why you told me it had to be the Reader's Digest version. Yeah I figured on finishing by noon, afterward the hotel brings in a light lunch for everyone. I assume that we have the review in the same meeting room as the sales meeting?"

"Yes, that's why I had you reserve it for the entire day."

"Thank you for the compliment. I hope that Mason feels the same. When are you meeting with him to make our offer?"

"We're going out to dinner tomorrow night."

"Do you think we'll know tomorrow night?" Tony was always impatient.

"Oh my no, Trevor will have to negotiate and, if there is any other interest, he will attempt to use our offer to drive up the others."

"So what are our chances?"

"I think pretty good. There's a bigger game going on or Trevor wouldn't consider selling Fox. I think the bigger game favors us."

Sarah had been content to listen until now. "Care to comment on the 'bigger game' Boss?"

Mac smiled. "No."

They continued in silence until they came to Tony's rental car.

***

Sam Grabowski sat in the dark room looking intently at the oversized computer monitor before him. "I don't see it. What am I looking for again?"

The young computer technician beside him reset the computer copy of the surveillance tape again. "I'll run it by frame by frame. Watch the upper left hand corner. You should see an orange light reflecting off the wall."

"Okay," Sam watched as the seemingly identical frames slowly clicked by. "Hold it. I see it. Right there."

"You got it Sam. It's not very big and I almost missed it."

"So what is it?"

"That's what we need to know. It may be something or it may be nothing. It appears to be light from a source outside the hall where the exit door is."

"So what's the significance?"

"Like I said Sam maybe something or maybe nothing, but you wanted the surveillance tape examined thoroughly. Well to do that we have to explain what that orange light is and where it's coming from."

"Okay what was the time frame for that tape?"

"Eleven PM until seven AM and the orange light or whatever it is appears between eleven thirty and one thirty in the morning."

"Okay we'll find out what it is."

***

Tony Conocenti sat at a table in the room adjoining the room where the sales meeting was held. He shared the table with Ralph Sinclair, John Malicki and Danny Meck, three of his best sales people. They were partaking of the light lunch supplied by the hotel. The sales meeting was over and a success. All territories numbers were either up or on target to make forecast. The fear of the price increase was slowly dissipating and everyone was in a good mood. During the meeting Tony reflected on how seldom he had found himself in this situation. Tony could recall meetings in the past that verged on stormy. At various times quality problems, processing problems, low sales with management pushing for results had contributed to tense meetings. But oddly considering that they had weathered an onslaught by a union and the rumored sale of Fox he couldn't complain.

There had been discussion of the union situation and the rumored sale, but Mac had addressed both of these subjects in his usual low-key style that was both credible and assuring simultaneously. On the union Mac informed everyone that things were quiet for the moment but he did not think that the attempt to unionize was dead. He felt there would be another attempt in the future but for the moment management held the upper hand. On the sale of Fox, Mac stated flatly that when a conglomerate owns you, you are always for sale. Did he believe that Atlantic was shopping Fox? Mac said he had not been informed of any pending sale but he and his staff were meeting with the people from corporate this very afternoon and that would be a question that he would ask. Mac told them that if they were concerned about their future the best protection that they could have is to concentrate on doing their jobs to the best of their ability. Whether a new owner came along or not the sales force would be needed. Now was not the time to sit around and wring their hands, now was the time to continue to perform. Mac's speech along with his "no bullshit" Q & A period seemed to reassure everyone and produced the desired effect. He made no mention of the senior staff's impending offer to buy Fox. This information would only be shared if they were successful.

There were some minor service and quality complaints, but David and Carroll did their usual competent job by listening intently, taking notes and getting on their cell phones to the factory to address the problems. Even if nothing could be done immediately everyone knew that they would be addressed and an answer would be given. Even if nothing could be changed an explanation would be given. It was this kind of attention that endeared these two to the sales force and the dealers.

The three salesmen at Tony's table were discussing the booth-manning schedule. The schedule assigned times to each of them to be at the booth to talk to dealers and potential dealers. Tony wasn't listening. He was thinking about Blair. Was she right? Was he forcing her into a secondary role? Was he only thinking of himself and his career? Good god, was he making the same mistake as he did with his first wife by putting his career first? But was Blair being fair to him? A simple explanation as to the details of why she couldn't make their dinner date that night might have saved them both a great deal of anguish. Did she expect him to just accept any situation that she found herself in with no explanation? Should all inconvenient events, unusual circumstances or disappointments be automatically chalked up to career requirements? Suddenly it occurred to Tony that was exactly how he treated Blair. Thinking back, he seldom gave much explanation if any when he was forced to change or cancel dates that they had made. The now ever present knot in his stomach gave a violent jerk. Good grief, this was very similar to Sheila's complaints before their divorce. When he was served with the papers he remembered brushing off the charge of "irreconcilable differences." He felt in his heart that reconciliation was still possible, but his heart was wrong. Tony eventually credited the fact that Shelia found someone else with his failure to save the marriage. That the differences were truly irreconcilable no matter what Tony did to save the relationship had never occurred to him. Now he was beginning to wonder if he totally misunderstood what the complaint was about. Did Blair believe she saw this character trait already? A chauvinistic tendency that relegated women in his life to a secondary role to his own career needs. Was the same problem about to destroy this new relationship that destroyed his marriage? Perhaps a more important question was; could Tony truly accept a woman who saw herself and her career as equal to his?

A gentle hand on his shoulder brought Tony back to the moment. It was Mac.

"Tony, the people from corporate are arriving in the next room. It's show time. Are you ready?"

"Always Mac." With that Tony rose and excused himself to his sales people and followed his friend and boss into the next room.

***

The meeting with the corporate people was going amazingly smooth. Trevor had brought along Denton Wellbon, John Hogg and Betsy Michaels. Betsy was the Human Resources executive for the Atlantic Corporation. Each of Mac's staff gave their reports. Carroll on manufacturing explaining various successes and problems that they had encountered during the year and what must be done in the next fiscal year to improve productivity and meet Tony's forecast. Sarah did an exceptional job presenting the "people" programs that she had initiated and the complicated health care expenses that all companies must deal with. Mac was proud of her in her first corporate appearance.

Tony explained current sales and his forecast for next year. In addition his was the burden of justifying next years marketing expense and strategy. This elicited several pointed questions from Trevor as marketing wasn't his favorite expense, but Tony handled them quite ably. Dale Hershey, who had just flown in that morning, gave the financial picture for the five-year plan that they were required to submit. John Hogg was the obvious financial expert here and he and Dale got into some lively Q & A that both seemed to enjoy. Trevor finally put a stop to it by stating flatly. "Your questions are good John and Dale seems to be on top of all the numbers. Fox is going to make money and if their strategy works they will continue to make money so let's move on."

Mac finished with a sort of overall state of the company report. In this he addressed the union threat, his strategy to thwart it and the cost of that strategy. This is where Mac expected to receive the usual Trevor Mason upbraiding. When Mac finished the meeting had already gone three hours. If it had been held back in Goodville they would have broken for lunch and then Trevor would have indulged in his normal grueling inquisition during the afternoon. But it was already afternoon and this was supposed to be a reduced schedule because of the location and the need for everyone to finish preparations for the show. Mac took a deep breath and looking directly at Trevor asked if there were any questions.

Trevor leafed through the inch thick report that Dale had supplied to everyone in the room. He occasionally hesitated and reviewed a portion of a page, but then moved on. When he finished everyone in the room seemed to be holding their collective breaths. Trevor looked up at Mac. "Good job," he said.

Mac, surprised for the second time in less than a month by Trevor, simply replied "Thank you." But he braced himself for the other shoe to drop.

But it never came. Trevor looked directly at Mac and grinned. "If you hadn't been fighting a union and it appears that so far you are being successful in that fight. Probably I would fire your ass for disobeying my directive to cut back expenses, but you have a plan to absorb those additional costs and it appears that Tony's people are putting together the necessary sales, so my congratulations. You all have work to do. Meeting adjourned."

Everyone seemed to give a sigh of relief and a round of handshaking ensued. When Trevor took Mac's hand he asked, "We still on for tonight?"

"Definitely, I have reservations for Ruth's Chris Steak House for seven o'clock. It's over on North Cleveland Avenue so if we meet in the hotel lobby at around six forty-five it's a short cab ride."

"Sounds good Mac, I look forward to it." With that Trevor excused himself and left the room. When Mac turned back to the others Denton Wellbon and John Hogg were standing together smiling and giving him the thumbs up sign. Mac returned their smiles.

***

Mac had earlier asked permission of Trevor to bring along a guest to dinner. Trevor seemed mildly surprised but gave permission easily. Mr. Roberts of Futures Unlimited was already seated at their table at Ruth's Chris Steak House when Trevor and Mac arrived. Mac introduced the two, drinks were served and orders for the meal were taken. Everyone ordered steak as this was considered one of the best steak restaurants in town. Indeed wherever one of Ruth's Chris steak houses opened for business the opinion was the same.

"Okay Mac," began Trevor after a sip of his Merlot, "what is it you want to discuss that you had to bring along reinforcements?" Trevor's mood was jovial so Mac decided to get right into it.

"My staff and I want to purchase Fox from Atlantic. Mr. Roberts is here to assure you that we have adequate financing and can come up with the money."

The look of pleasant surprise on Trevor Mason's face was priceless. Trevor had speculated on the possibility of many topics for this dinner tonight but the purchase of Fox was not one of them. He thought that Mac wanted to either hit him up for a raise or request a position at corporate. But this and the perfect timing were too good to be true. Trevor had many questions and jumped right in: Yes he would consider it. How much were they considering offering? Mac and Roberts had agreed to start with 14 million. How would the deal be structured? Trevor made it clear that the entire sum would be due at settlement. In no way would the Atlantic Corporation consider leaving any money in the deal. There would be no upfront payment with a balloon payment five years down the road. Mac and Roberts assured Trevor that the deal would be complete at settlement. Roberts showed Trevor the financial statements that gave the details of the structure. He and Mac had documentation to demonstrate that the money from Mac and his team was assured and so was the money from Futures Unlimited. How fast could they put the financial package together? Roberts estimated that due diligence could be wrapped up in a month from the starting date and settlement could come anytime after that. And so it went, question after question and answer after answer, through dessert and into the coffee and after dinner drinks.

They had requested a table in the smoking section for Trevor's benefit and finally during the after dinner drinks Trevor pulled out his cigar case and offered Mac and Roberts one. Mac declined but Roberts accepted. "Cuban," said Trevor. "Don't ask how I get them."

"I wouldn't think of it," stated Roberts as he trimmed the end and leaned forward to allow Trevor to light it.

Both men took long draws and exhaled clouds of smoke. Roberts smiled as he considered the cigar, "Very good Mr. Mason, very good indeed. Thank you."

"You're quite welcome Mr. Roberts."

"So how does our offer look?" asked Mac.

Trevor hesitated. “Pretty good Mac. Pretty good.”

“Good enough?”

“I don’t know. I’m meeting tomorrow with another party that informs me that he’s interested in Fox.” Trevor paused to see what effect this would have on the two, but neither batted an eye. It crossed Trevor’s mind that they already knew of his meeting although he couldn’t imagine how except… Hogg or Denton! Damn, if he ever found out that those two leaked information to MacLode he’d…but that wasn’t important now. Pitting Mac and his friend against Clint Matthews to force a bidding war was what was important now. What luck this was!

Roberts took another draw on the cigar and pulled a contract from his inside breast pocket. “We’re prepared to put this into writing tonight. You’ll find everything in order here including a letter of intent. Naturally all terms of this contract are subject to the results of the due diligence that we will conduct.”

Trevor paged through the ten-page contract and letter of intent. “Everything looks in order, but the only hang up I have is the 14 million. I think that the guy tomorrow will offer more.”

Roberts smiled at Mason through a cloud of cigar smoke. “I expect that you’ll let us know if he offers more.”

“If you’re asking me if I’ll inform you if he upped the ante? Of course, I’ll give you every chance to beat him out.”

“We won’t guarantee that we’ll consider offering any more, but we would like to know the results of your meeting. That’s all we ask,” said Roberts.

With that they all shook hands and went their separate ways for the evening. But not before Roberts told Mac that they would talk in the morning.

***

The phone rang for the fifth time before Sam Grabowski was fully awake and able to answer.

To Catch a Fox

"Yeah, Grabowski here."

"Sam its Peter."

"Yeah Pete."

"I've been here in the alley at Rueben's office building for the entire time period that you requested and I've not seen any source of the orange light that you told me to look for."

"No orange light like I showed you in the tapes?"

"Not during that time frame."

Grabowski sat up in bed and put his bare feet on the floor. "What does that mean? Did you see an orange light or not?"

"I saw an orange light all right but not during the time span that you asked me to check."

"When and what did you see Pete?"

"Sam, the restaurant next to Ruben's office building has a large orange neon sign that would shine in the window at the exit door but the restaurant closes at eleven PM, therefore it couldn't be the source of the orange light on the surveillance tape."

"The restaurant turns the neon light off at eleven?"

"That's right Boss."

Sam sat thinking for a long moment. "Boss, you still there?"

"Yeah Pete…Hey good job, get yourself some breakfast on the department and go home and get some sleep. In fact does that restaurant serve breakfast?"

"Ah…yes it does and I think they are about to open up right now."

"Good, now listen Pete; go in and order breakfast and try to find out if there would be any way that light might have stayed on during the night that Donald Kensington-Cramer was killed. Find out if they turn it off and on manually or if it's on a clock. If it's on a clock find out if the clock has been malfunctioning lately. Got that?"

"Okay Boss, I got it. I don't know how good a job I did but it is what it is."

"Trust me, you did good. We'll talk later. See ya." Sam hung up but not before he determined that the first item on his agenda this morning was another visit to that computer technician at the lab.

***

Andy parked the rental car across the street from a very expensive home in Buck Head. Buck Head was a posh neighborhood in the northwest corner of Atlanta. Andy had arrived in Atlanta a couple of days ago. With the information that his boss had given him he had located the good Doctor Rouseau. During the initial visit the doctor was reluctant to attempt to access sealed records of over twenty years ago, Andy reminded him that his boss had saved him from financial ruin at the least and physical harm at most from the not so friendly boys in Atlantic City to whom he owed a great deal of money. Andy pointed out that Raymond Luca had never asked for a cent of the money back.

At the time of their first meeting Dr. Rouseau was at home alone. His wife was in Augusta visiting relatives. Dr. Rouseau explained that he was now very well off and though inconvenient he could pay the money back with interest and that's what he would prefer to do rather than look at files that were none of his business and protected under the privacy laws. After all the individual's files that Andy was requesting was a well-known T.V. personality in Savannah. The doctor just didn't want to be involved with this.

Andy had a pair of spiked brass knuckles in his jacket pocket. He slid his hand into them, pulled them from his pocket and slammed them through the plaster and drywall in the doctor's study. "We don't want your shitin' money doctor, we want results. Now how soon will you have copies of those records in my hand? I'd hate for the next thing I slam these into to be your face. You can see what kind of damage they can do."

The terrified doctor promised them by the following evening. Andy reminded the doctor that if he mentioned this visit to anyone, especially the police, it might not be someone as reasonable, understanding and patient as he who would pay him the next visit.

Now a day had passed and Andy returned. He rang the doorbell and in moments the doctor appeared. He was extremely nervous. “My wife is at home tonight.”

“Great I’d love to meet her,” was Andy’s smiling reply.

“That won’t be necessary. I have what you need in my study.”

The doctor quickly led the way through the entrance hall into the room where they had met just last night. As he walked through the hall Andy admired the open curved staircase that swept gracefully to the second floor hall. Andy decided that if he ever built a house he would certainly consider a staircase like this. In the study Andy noticed that there was already a plaster repair made to the hole he had punched in the wall. Andy smiled to himself as he imagined how the doctor explained the hole to his wife. Doctor Rouseau opened his desk drawer and pulled out a manila envelope. He handed it over to Andy. “There are copies of everything that you requested in there. Now please go.”

Andy took his time and opened the envelope. He slowly removed the contents and examined them. “You’re a smart man doctor. Everything seems to be here and in order.”

“Yes, yes, just please go. At the very least I could lose my license for this.”

“Is someone with you Roger?” The voice from the hall was that of a woman. When there was no answer a tall dignified and attractive middle-aged woman entered the study. “Oh, Roger you do have company, please introduce me to the nice gentleman.”

Roger stuttered, as he really didn’t know Andy’s name. Andy smiled and spoke up. “Andrew Bevilacqua pleased to meet you.”

“And I’m pleased to meet you also Mr. Bevilacqua. I trust my husband is assisting you in some way.”

“Yes, very well indeed, I’m a patient of his and I’m moving out of the country.

Your husband has been kind enough to give me copies of my personal files to take with me."

"Well I'm glad he could be of help. We usually have cocktails before dinner Mr. Bevilacqua, would you like to join us?" Roger Rouseau's face turned ashen.

"No thank you, that is most gracious, but I do have a plane to catch later tonight."

"So sorry that you can't join us, I wish you a safe flight."

"Thank you. I'll be going now."

"I'll see you out Andy." The doctor took Andy by the arm and led him to the front door. Outside on the veranda, when Andy and the doctor were alone, the doctor stopped Andy. "I presume that this squares up my debt with your boss?"

Andy smiled. "Dr. Rouseau, this is a payment. You aren't close to being paid up. Here's how it works. We may never need another favor from you again, if that's the case you will never see me again and you come out way ahead. But if we do need a favor, well you best cooperate. You have a lovely wife. She likes to visit her sister in Augusta. I believe that her sister lives at 534 Oak Lawn Avenue just outside of Augusta. Your wife usually goes there overnight at least once a month. You see we know a lot about you and your family. We even know more than that. The point is that as long as you cooperate with us, you don't have to worry about where your wife is. Do we understand each other Doctor?"

The doctor swallowed hard. He tried to answer but no words came out. He simply nodded in agreement. Andy smiled, "Look Doc, several years ago you owed the boys up in Atlantic City $50,000. They wanted the money now! You didn't have it, but a friend of yours recommended that you contact my boss. My boss bailed you out and when you asked how you could repay him he told you that maybe someday you could do him a favor. Well he may have meant more than one favor, but when you compare it to what would have happened to you if you hadn't taken his help…that's a rough crowd up in Jersey; they probably wouldn't have killed you, but you're a surgeon and need your hands to practice medicine. At least that's what I always thought. Let's just say that when they finished with you, you might have had to find another profession." Andy took the doctor's hand and shook it. "You have a good firm grip Doc; it's been a pleasure doing business with you." Andy left the veranda and crossed the street to the parked rental car.

There was a time when Andy thought his boss was crazy to help random people like the doctor and not take anything but the promise of a favor in return. But over the years he began to see the wisdom in having a number of people indebted to you. After checking to make certain no one had wired anything to the ignition, or that there was no additional objects attached to the frame of the car, his standard procedure, Andy turned the ignition key and started the engine. He would be in New York by morning.

***

It was the following morning just about 6 AM. Raymond Luca sat in Andy's office at the diner. Andy had just returned from Atlanta on an early morning flight. Raymond sat in Andy's big chair behind Andy's desk. Andy sat on the opposite side. Raymond was going through the files that Dr. Rouseau had furnished. "Good work Andy."

Andy said nothing but he was very gratified that the boss was pleased. "Mary Harrison had a daughter. Foster Harrison claims that it wasn't his. The early blood tests from Atlanta seem to prove him correct. The daughter's name is Crystal and she's an anchor for the evening news at WSAV Channel 3 in Savannah."

Raymond Luca leaned back in the chair. "Any doubt in your mind that this is Denton Wellbon III's daughter?"

"None Boss. Who else could be her father?"

"I tend to agree. While it's certainly possible that someone else could be the father we only know of two people that Mary was involved with at that time and these documents seem to eliminate one of them. Are you certain that Denton is unaware of her existence?"

"He hasn't got a clue."

"Does she know who her father is?"

"That's a little harder to figure boss. She somehow made it to my diner."

"Her grandparents?"

"They are about the only way she could have found out about me. Foster never knew, but he did admit to meeting with her earlier this year. But I sure never mentioned the diner to the grandparents. How she got here is a real mystery. You want me to pay them another visit?"

"No, the old man is dying it will serve no purpose. Actually we should thank them. Because of what we believe they told the girl, however they gained that knowledge, we became aware that a daughter exists."

"What do we do now Boss?"

The old Don folded his hands on the desk. He appeared lost in thought for a moment but only for a moment. "Our objective is to renew the association we once enjoyed with the Atlantic Corporation. If Trevor Mason and Abe Rueben succeed we'll have to kiss Atlantic off and start from scratch with another company. In light of that we have to make certain that Denton continues to believe that it's to his benefit to renew this relationship. It's time you meet again with Denton and inform him of what we now know."

"I'll set it up right away boss."

"Also, see who we know in Savannah. I know how Rueben operates. This girl gives him a major opportunity to apply leverage on Denton. We need someone watching Crystal Harrison."

"You think Rueben knows about her?"

"We have to assume that he does."

"You think he'll try blackmail?"

"No, he's already doing that. I know him. He would do exactly what you and I would do. If he thinks this deal is in jeopardy he'll threaten her life and he's quite capable of making good on that threat."

"Should we be considering that?"

"Not yet. I prefer the type of relationship that we had with Denton's father. Let's just keep an eye on Crystal for now."

Andy rubbed his chin. "We still don't know why Denton's father had all trace of the girl removed from the Court House or who did the job for him."

"No we don't and it seems like whoever did it is still out there somewhere. That's why we have to be very careful." With that the old Don rose and walked around the desk. "Come my friend let's have Connie get us some of that greasy breakfast that your diner does such a good job on."

***

There was all of the official hoopla that the opening of any trade show brings, a pre-show breakfast, speeches by officials of the National Kitchen and Bath Association, Kitchen and Bath Industry Show, and anyone else who could make it on the dais. Then finally at ten o'clock on Friday morning the ribbon was cut and thousands of professionals involved in the industry went streaming into the cavernous McCormick Center to peruse the hundreds of booths that were erected by the manufacturers who serve the industry.

The first shift of Tony's troops were ready and manning the booth. Mac, Tony, Carroll, David, Dale and Sarah had toured the booth at nine AM and were very pleased with how it presented their company against the other exhibitors. Mac gave Jake and Matt, the two Fox technicians that were in charge of and did the majority of the work setting up the booth, the next three days off to relax and have fun in Chicago. Mac only asked that they keep their cell phones on in case they would be needed to make an unexpected repair. Sarah informed them that this time would not count against their vacation time.

Much earlier Mac had a breakfast meeting with his entire staff and Roberts from Futures Unlimited. The sun was barely coming over the horizon on Lake Michigan when they met in the Regency Club on the thirty-fifth floor of the Hyatt. Tony used his member key and had everyone listed as his guests. The first order of business was to inform them as to how the meeting with Trevor Mason had gone. Roberts was very optimistic. He wasn't intimidated by the fact that Mason was meeting with another interested party today. He believed that their first offer was a good one and if they were forced to go higher the other party would have to jeopardize the future profit picture to beat their top offer. Roberts felt that because the proven management team was in place their group could afford to bid higher than what might be wise for anyone else. He was very optimistic but warned that sometimes smart people have other motives rather than profit for wanting to purchase a company, so he didn't want to hold out false hopes. But, all in all he felt their chances looked good. Everyone was pleased with his comments. Mac was the only one at the table that realized that there were two more options if the Futures Unlimited gambit failed. There was the possibility of dealing directly with Denton and his mother or of enlisting his old friend Ray Luca in the fight. However, Ray was the least appealing of those options. Mac maintained silence on these other two avenues.

Mac invited Roberts to remain for the conclusion of his staff meeting and Roberts accepted the invitation. Mostly it was housekeeping. Like the sales force, management had a schedule for manning the booth as Tony and Mac wanted senior staff to be present to meet Fox dealers when they visited. In addition Mac wanted them all to see Tony's sales force in action as they tried to attract new dealers in geographic areas where Fox was lacking representation.

Tony then assigned what he referred to as an entertainment schedule. Tony had selected some of the top ten accounts in sales that he knew would be in town for the show. He assigned a member of the senior staff to accompany the appropriate Regional Sales Manager in dining the dealers. Tony had already made reservations at the best restaurants in town for each of the staff. These private dinners were scheduled for tonight and Sunday night, the last day of the three-day show. Tony also reminded all of them that the Fox reception for all Fox dealers would be held in the Grande Ballroom of the Holiday Inn at the Mart Plaza tomorrow, Saturday night. Tony reserved the ballroom six months ago so that the Fox reception would be just across the street by overhead walkway from the Merchandise Mart's gala event of the same night. That event would feature an open house of all cabinetry and accessories showrooms on their home furnishings floor. This event was in coordination with the show and Tony reminded them to pay a visit to Fox's newest flagship showroom that just opened under the ownership of Glenn Glen and Mark Markel. "If you thought that you were going to have a vacation in Chicago, my apologies. My staff will be working their butts off so I thought that we should too." No one argued, but each realized that the next three days would be exhausting.

To Catch a Fox

Dale Hershey commented on what a coup it was for Tony to have Fox's dealer reception so close to and in conjunction with the Mart's open house. "My compliments Tony, how did you pull that one off?"

Tony smiled, "A good friend with connections tipped me off to the Mart's plans very early in the game." As he made the statement his stomach twisted into that increasingly active knot as he recalled that the friend was Blair McManus.

Mac and Tony covered a few more details. Some tips on how to man a trade show booth that those not in sales might not be aware, along with show shuttle bus schedules from the hotel to McCormick Center and the availability of Tony's rental car if they were quick enough to beat Mac and Tony to it. Everyone had a good laugh at the last and then adjourned to make their walk through of the booth before the official show opening. After that each was responsible to pursue their individual schedules.

Now it was fifteen minutes after ten on that first morning of the show and Mac and Sarah were standing in the aisle across from the Fox booth watching as the first of the attendees began entering and inspecting it. "Thanks for bringing me along Mac," said Sarah.

"No thanks are necessary Sarah. As you can see Tony puts the senior staff to work when he has us out here and I needed you to give your Human Resources report during our annual meeting with Corporate yesterday. By the way, if I didn't say so before you did a damn good job."

"No you hadn't mentioned it, but thank you. I worked hard on it and it's good to hear that you were pleased."

"More than pleased, I was relaxed."

Sarah gave him a quizzical grin, "Now what does that mean?"

Mac gave her his wry smile in return. "When Dennis would stand up to give those reports I was always on the edge of my seat. I never knew what he was going to say or how he was going to present it. With you, I never had a doubt that you would make a professional presentation or that it would be in sync with our other projections."

"Dennis' reports weren't 'in sync' with the others, how could that be?"

"Damned if I know Sarah. He would sit there week after week listening to us hammer out a business plan. Dale would ask him if the rising costs of our benefit package would fit in with our assumptions of increased overall costs and Dennis would assure us that he was on top of it and in negotiations with our insurance carrier to make certain that any increases would fit the plan."

"So what happened?"

"Well we would all give our reports with Dale doing as he did yesterday presenting the financials. Then Dennis would stand and give the Human Resources report. Last year he announced an increase in health care costs that was twice what the plan could cover. The price increase that Dale and I put together wouldn't cover it not to mention the number of units that Tony forecast to be sold. Both should have been increased."

"He did this at the annual meeting without warning all of you before hand that some adjustments had to be made?" Sarah was astonished.

"Yep."

"What happened?"

"All Hell broke loose. Trevor was a pussycat yesterday because we were fortunate enough to have all the numbers going in the right direction. We had a year like that last year too, until Dennis gave his report and blew all of the strategic planning the rest of us had done out of the water. It made us appear incompetent. Now Trevor and I had several disagreements in the past at these meetings and when you disagree with him he can get pretty loud and radical, but before I could justify my position with numbers even if he didn't agree with me. But last year Dennis left me to hang out to dry. The numbers didn't add up and Trevor finally had a right to be upset and he didn't waste it."

"I shudder to ask what happened?"

"Well Tony, Dale and I all expected to be fired on the spot. Carroll and David would have probably survived because it falls more to the CEO, CFO and VP of Sales to put together the numbers. Trevor went through the roof. He made us all get out our calculators and demanded that we show him how our numbers could possibly work. None of us did because we knew that it was impossible with Dennis' report. He turned to Dennis and asked if Dennis was certain that his numbers were correct?"

"What did Dennis say?"

"I recall his exact word: 'absolutely' and he said it as if he was somehow justified. Like the rest of us knew of this and ignored him."

"But wasn't he aware that the number in his report didn't agree with the number in the strategic plan?"

"He should have been. Dale gave us all preliminary copies to review a week before the meeting with corporate. When Dale questioned him again during our final run through Dennis assured us that while he still didn't have a final number the one we were using was close enough and should have us covered."

"You're kidding!"

"Nope. Then Trevor went into a rage like I never saw before. He literally tore one of our annual report books apart and threw the pages all over the conference room. Remember, unlike this year last year was a typical year and we had the meeting in Goodville. Even Denton Wellbon, John Hogg and Betsy Michaels, all of whom you met yesterday, looked terrified and they weren't the people that the tirade was directed against."

"Well obviously none of you were fired."

"No we weren't, although I'm not certain why. However, it was a Friday afternoon and Trevor gave us until seven o'clock the next morning to come up with new numbers that would work. Trevor had Betsy cancel their flight back to New York and make other flight and hotel arrangements. Usually we all went out to dinner before they left, but not that night. The folks from corporate went out themselves and we all worked through the night. All except Dennis, there was nothing for him to contribute as we were now all working around his numbers."

"How did you make the numbers work?"

"The only way we could. We knew that we couldn't get away with cutting benefits so we upped the price increase and increased the number of units that we had to sell to cover the increased costs. You've worked with us enough to know that those calculations are easier stated than made to work on paper."

"Oh yes. What happened on Saturday?"

"Trevor was deadly calm on Saturday morning. Unlike the day before he never raised his voice. He allowed Dale, Tony and me to present the revised report while all of the others, both our staff and corporate, sat silently and watched. When we were finished and sat down Trevor rose, walked to the front of the room and addressed us. He took the revised report, the one that we worked all night on and calmly threw it in the wastebasket. Well this is where we expected the axe to fall, but it didn't. He then pulled out a copy of our original report. Told us that we were going to live by our original numbers and he was going to teach us how to do just that. He went on to explain how we were going to cut benefits. Trevor and I had an ongoing argument ever since he became president of Atlantic Corporation because Fox's benefit package was considerably better than the other division's packages. I've always felt that we needed to offer more so that we could have a low turnover as we hire artisans as opposed to factory workers. Trevor never saw it that way and now he had the perfect opportunity to force me to reduce the benefit costs."

"So that's how we wound up with the sudden unrest that allowed the union to get its foot in the door."

"That's how. Dale and I took a chance. We cut the benefit package but compromised by increasing the hourly rates across the board. We expected another explosion in New York when we sent in the revised copy, but Trevor never said a word. However, as you know it wasn't enough to appease the work force. Ironically, we wound up restoring the benefits and keeping the wage increase. Our current plan is even more ambitious than either of the plans that we put together for last year's meeting. We would have never dared to present a plan like the current one to Trevor either as the original that Dennis sunk or the revised that Trevor threw in the wastebasket. We should have had more confidence because as of today it's working."

"What did you say to Dennis after this was all over?"

"Well before I talked to Dennis both Dale and Tony came to me and announced that they wouldn't go into another corporate meeting with Dennis as part of the team. This wasn't the first time Dennis had been out of sync with us, but it was by far the most outrageous. The previous times we were able to cover in the meetings so that it didn't become an issue."

"What did you do?"

"Well I'm certain that you noticed that Dennis retired early. He is eligible for both Atlantic Corporation benefits and Social Security, but I know that he was planning on working until he was seventy-two. I asked Dennis for an explanation as to how he got so far off the mark or why he didn't inform us about it. He said he didn't think that it made that much difference." Sarah just shook her head in amazement as Mac continued. "I told Dennis that he had a choice. Either he took early retirement and we throw him a wing ding of a party and wish him well or I fire his ass right there on the spot."

"He wisely chose retirement."

"Yes, but he wasn't very happy with me and I'm certain he will hold it against me until the day he dies. By the way that was a great retirement party that you threw for him."

Sarah blushed. "I now think that I probably went overboard."

"Oh no, it was perfect. His family was very happy. I don't think he explained his sudden 'decision' to retire to them. Forgive us but we all decided not to give you the background before Dennis left. We didn't want you to be prejudiced against him. We decided that if he wanted to tell you he could, but we weren't going to until he was gone. The party's over so you've now been informed. I hope that you're not upset with our decision."

Sarah thought for a moment. "On the surface I think that I should be upset, but then I suppose that what happened between all of you and Dennis before I arrived is really none of my business. No I agree it was best. I gave him a party that was appropriate for the number of years that he was with the company. As you just heard when you made me aware of the circumstances I had second thoughts, but I'm guessing that I did what you wanted."

"For his family's sake yes, I truly adore his lovely wife and I wouldn't hurt her for the world."

"It does explain your rather brief remarks."

"I didn't want to lie. Now you understand why I wasn't the least bit concerned about your report yesterday. I knew that it would be professionally prepared and presented with an eye on the overall business plan and I wasn't disappointed."

"Thank you again, anything else that you have collectively decided to keep from me?"

Mac put on a thoughtful look and rolled his eyes toward the ceiling as if in deep consideration. "Nope, nothing more, you are privy to all of our dirty little secrets."

"Good. I do have a question though."

"Fire away."

"I notice that on Tony's schedule for the senior staff to help entertain our top dealers your name and mine are conspicuously absent from tonight's schedule."

"So far I've not heard a question."

"Why is that?"

"Why is what?"

Sarah laughed softly, "Don't get cute with me Boss you know what I'm asking. Why are we not helping to entertain tonight?"

"Well as I recall last week you agreed to go out to dinner with me while we were here in Chicago. It looks like tonight is open and I made reservations for two at a very fine restaurant. Am I presuming too much? Aren't we still on?"

"Yes we're still on. May I ask the purpose of this dinner?"

"Strictly social, must it have a greater purpose?"

“How will that look to the others?”

“Oh, that concerns you?” Mac put a mock incredulous expression on his face.

“Appearances always concern Human Resource types.”

“Well it doesn’t concern me. What I do on my own time and who I do it with is my business.”

“For the benefit of the others we should have a legitimate reason why we are skipping out on the entertainment schedule. After all, the others are working and we are socializing. What reason did you give Tony for us skipping out?”

“I told him I was going to review you.”

“But my first review isn’t due until I’m at Fox for six months.”

“How long have you been with us Sarah?”

“Only about three and one half months.”

“Okay, this will be your three and one half month review.”

Sarah laughed. “You are something else William MacLode.”

“Meet me in the hotel lobby at seven this evening. We’ll take Tony’s rental car. I have it reserved for us tonight.”

“We’re skipping out on Tony and we’re taking his car too? You’re bad Boss.”

“Yes I am, but you are correct. Until Trevor says differently, I am the boss.” They both laughed and then Mac motioned toward the Fox booth. “Let’s go meet our customers.”

“I would be delighted Boss,” responded Sarah.

***

To Catch a Fox

The small conference room was well above the convention center floor at McCormick Center. It had a large window that looked out over the show booths and the thousands of people moving among them below. Clint Matthews had reserved the room for just this purpose, his meeting with Trevor Mason. The two men were the only representatives from their respective companies present. Both men were domineering CEO's, combative by nature to the extent that each sought not just to be victorious, but also to vanquish the opposition. There was hardly room enough in one room for both egos at the same time.

Trevor was standing with his back to Matthews looking out the window. Matthews was seated at the small conference table in the center of the room. There were several high backed executive style swivel chairs placed around the table that had laid upon it two bound copies of Matthews proposal for the purchase of Fox Cabinetry. Trevor was not happy, he had never met Matthews prior to this meeting, but already he disliked him. Trevor thought he was an arrogant son of a bitch. Matthews held a similar opinion of Trevor Mason. The main problem was that they were both very much alike. Cut from the same pattern. Trevor puffed on one of his Cubans, it didn't escape Matthews that Trevor failed to offer him one.

"Fifteen million is your offer?"

"Not a nickel more Mason, the place is only worth twelve." Matthews could stand it no longer and reached in his coat pocket for a pack of cigarettes and his lighter. While he extracted a cigarette from the pack and placed it in his mouth he continued to talk. "The money is there. You can see that in the prospectus. 20% is cash, the balance is a combination of loans that I've secured against corporate assets that I currently own and a loan against assets that you list for Fox in that monstrous report you commissioned from Bertrum & Bertrum. I have letters from the financial institutions involved and we've spent the last hour going over the fine print. I've got a letter of intent that states that this offer is good pending the outcome of the due diligence that my investors will conduct. What more do you need? Three million more than the net worth is pretty generous."

"So you say, did your calculator break before you came up with that number?"

Matthews lit up his cigarette. "Come off it Mason, that's the best offer you'll get and you know it."

Trevor took another puff and blew a cloud of smoke toward the ceiling. “That’s not what the other guys said.”

“Get out Mason, you don’t think I’m gonna fall for that do you?”

“You don’t have to fall for anything Matthews you can do nothing and lose this company.”

“There’s nobody else and you know it!”

“Really? Okay, if that’s what you believe we’re finished here.” With that Trevor walked toward the door.

“What, you’re gonna walk out? Okay there may well be another offer on the table but I guarantee it’s not as good as mine…you’re bluffing!”

“You don’t have to guarantee anything Matthews.” Trevor opened the door.

“Mason if you walk out on me I won’t guarantee that the offer will remain on the table!” Matthews was standing now. Trevor tipped his cigar toward Matthews and saying nothing left the room closing the door behind him.

“Damn,” swore Matthews. He stamped out the cigarette in an ashtray then pulled out his cell phone. He called up a number from the memory.

“Hello Mitchell? Matthews here. He walked out. Yeah you heard me he walked out! Walked on my offer of 15 million. 15 million! That’s 25% more than we figured its worth. You told me I wouldn’t have to go over 20%.”

“What? I’m not putting up any more of my own money! Well then you come up with more money. The deal we had doesn’t go far enough to cover this…then you find a legal way!” Matthews snapped the phone closed and put it in his pocket. “Damn” he swore again. He wanted Fox, but not at any cost. His only hope was that Mason really was bluffing or that Mitchell Green could locate some legal cash that could be funneled into the effort. The union could not be financially involved with the management of a company that it would attempt to organize after the purchase.

Outside the conference room, striding down the carpeted hallway Trevor Mason smiled. He might have just thrown away a cool million but the look on Matthews' face was priceless. Besides John Hogg's research had revealed that Clint Matthews' had the same union in his companies as Mac believed was attempting to organize Fox. "Bastard!" he muttered to himself. That couldn't be coincidence. Williams wanted to get the union in before he made his offer so he could use that to force the price down. That's where his 12 million numbers came from. Trevor's smile broadened he may have underestimated MacLode. Mac made a gutsy call that stopped the union dead in its tracks. He even risked being fired by reversing Trevor's direct order. But Tony Conocenti seemed to be pulling the sales numbers out of the fire. If he were planning on keeping Fox, he would have to take a second look at Mac and his team. There may be more there than what he previously thought. Trevor's cell phone vibrated in his inside breast pocket. He extracted it and flipped it open.

"Mason here."

"Trevor, this is Carlton Smith." The voice on the phone was the silky smooth voice that characterized Trevor's boss. "How's the show going?"

"Very good Carlton. We can be proud of Fox they represent us well in these events."

"Yes, Fox always puts the best foot forward at trade shows and the like. Mac and Tony do a good job."

"What can I do for you Carlton?"

"Nothing really, I just needed to inform you of a change in dates."

"What date is that Carlton?"

"The annual meeting it's been moved up to the middle week in November as opposed to the customary time of the middle week in December."

Trevor had approached an elevator and had pushed the down button, but when the car arrived and the door opened he ignored it and stepped to the side. "What…how can that work? We won't have the numbers ready by then. I can only speak for Atlantic but I'm certain that none of your other corporations can have final numbers by then. Who decided this?"

"As to the numbers, you can go with the rough preliminary numbers at the November meeting and turn in the final exact numbers to the Board in December. As to who decided, that's a little strange. Apparently there was an emergency meeting of the Executive Council yesterday in Manhattan. It was held with only those members who could assemble quickly; those being the three of the four that live in the city."

"We're you there Carlton? You're on the Executive Committee."

"As Chairman of the Board I'm on the committee and I usually attend the meetings, but when it's not my day to be in the city I sometimes skip them. This was one I missed."

Trevor was getting suspicious. "Was Mary Wellbon there?"

"No she was out of town doing charity work I understand. It was just the three others that live in the city, less Mary of course, but there is only five total so three makes a quorum. As I said before since I live outside the city they often meet in an emergency if I can't make it."

"What possible emergency could require changing the date of the annual meeting?"

"I don't know. Sam Henley called me and he was very vague about the whole thing. He said he would explain it to both Mary and me when I come into the city on Monday. Well Trevor you were my first call, as I knew you were out of town and I didn't know what your schedule might be. I must call the other corporate CEO's now. Have a good show and give my regards to your man Mac and his crew."

"Yes, I will. So long Carlton."

Trevor was dumfounded. What was going on? What would make an emergency meeting of the Executive Council necessary? More important, how would the change in dates affect his plans? Trevor flipped open his cell phone again and called a number out of memory.

"Abe Rueben," said the voice on the other end.

Trevor quickly explained what Carlton had just told him. “I don’t like this Abe. Do you think they suspect something?”

“Well there’s no reason to panic Trevor, but I’m very suspicious of this.”

“They can’t know about our plan can they?”

There was a long pause and then Abraham Rueben spoke again. “We have everyone covered. If any of them talk they know that they would lose a windfall profit and in all cases suffer embarrassment at the revelation of something that they did in the past. Some of them could even go to jail if we reveal what we know. Was Mary Wellbon at the meeting?”

“I asked Carlton the same question and he told me she was off somewhere doing charity work.”

“I know that you think we have Mary and Denton under control Trevor, but to me they are unknown quantities. I think we can control Denton, but Mary Wellbon is unpredictable. Who else besides Carlton Smith has the clout to call an emergency meeting of the council?”

Trevor sighed, “No one except possibly Mary Wellbon.”

“Right or someone on her authority, and by his own admission, unless he lied to you, Carlton is as puzzled by this date change as are we so he certainly didn’t call the meeting.”

“Why would she risk Denton’s secret being revealed?” Trevor moved further away from the elevator as the door opened again and numerous people got off. He didn’t want this conversation overheard.

“Maybe she doesn’t care. Maybe she’s willing to let her own son hang out to dry.”

“What about her charity work and her husband’s reputation?”

“I don’t know Trevor. She’s a tough old bird, maybe she’s decided to play like she’s aligning with us and fight this out at the annual meeting. She might be willing to gamble that she can win by her shear force of will at the board meeting."

"Why push up the date?"

"To give us less time to prepare."

"You think Denton's with her?"

"Who knows? But Trevor, remember I said not to panic. We still have something that neither of them is aware that we have."

Trevor smiled. "We know that Denton has a daughter. That could make all the difference."

"Exactly. Tough old Mary Wellbon is a grandmother, but she doesn't even know it."

"We could go several different ways on this. How do you suggest that we play it Abe?"

"You're coming back to New York when?"

"Sunday night."

"Let's meet first thing Monday morning. I don't want to talk about this even on a cell phone."

"Meet me in my office Abe." With that they both hung up and Trevor took the next elevator down to the show level. He didn't like this but still remained confident that he and Rueben had the situation covered. He had to continue with the plan. Now he wanted to set up another meeting with Mac and his potential partner Roberts.

Chapter 20

Duke Winston sat at the end of the bar in the establishment that he owned. He was watching as his bartender Marvin served the regular clientele. Bunch of losers he thought. They were vets from various wars and police actions. They gathered at Duke's bar because of the military theme he employed. Lots of vets either had made a career of the military or they returned home, put the experience that they gained in uniform to good use and went on with their lives. But not this bunch, they never got over it. Either they came to bitch about things that happened years ago or they came to exaggerate about things that happened years ago. The worst part was that it was only three in the afternoon. Most of them were either underemployed or unemployed. They represented an assortment of failed marriages, failed business ventures and failed careers. All came to Duke's bar to forget. They forgot their current troubles by drinking too much and living in the past, no matter whether that past was good or bad. Oh well thought Duke as long as they could pay for their drinks they were a constant source of revenue for the bar.

Sometimes Duke told them some of his own war stories, but he had to have a couple of beers in him before he would entertain them. They hung on his every word. Duke himself was in the military. He was in Army Special Forces, better known as the Green Berets. He served several tours of duty in Viet Nam and when that war ended he remained in the Army for several years as part of the "black ops" Delta Force. On one of their super secret missions Duke did permanent damage to his left leg. He still walked with a slight limp. That was enough for a medical discharge and a pension from the Army. Duke never married and he was frugal by nature, preferring the Spartan life he had adopted in the military. He had more than sufficient savings and had invested his money wisely over the years.

Upon his return to civilian life he purchased this bar and was able to live quite comfortably on his business revenues, investment income and Army pension. But it wasn't enough. He missed the action that he had experienced in the military. Duke soon became bored. Then, by chance he met Abraham Rueben. They became friends and one night when the two of them were drinking together, Duke was lamenting about how boring civilian life was. Abe questioned Duke about the various black ops skill sets that he had acquired. After Duke answered the questions, Abe asked if he would be interested in making some very handsome money on the side. Duke responded in the affirmative and then questioned what type of work it would be?

"Discrete work," was the answer, "but not always legal. Does that pose a problem for you?"

"Hell no," was Duke's response.

"Could Duke assemble a team of professionals like himself if the job required?"

"If the pay's right," was the answer.

"The pay will match the difficulty and risk of the job. Could this team keep their mouths shut?"

"They wouldn't work for me if they couldn't."

On that particular night the two men were drinking in Duke's bar. Abe looked about at some of the customers then back at Duke. "None of these I trust."

Duke laughed. "Oh god no, I know other pros like myself that are just itching for some action, any action."

That's how it started. Abe would call two or three times a year and ask Duke to assemble his team to do some clean up work. The work ranged from strong-arming and beating people up like the job last year that they did for Abe in Chicago, to clean up work with a body like the one Duke removed from Abe's office and relocated recently. In addition the team made arrangements with local contractors to repaint the office and install new carpet the following day. The money was extremely good and Abe paid all of his people quickly. Duke had assembled a very talented team, adding members and skill sets as needed. He had a computer expert on the team so it was possible to do a professional job of editing the surveillance tape that was monitoring the side door of Abe's office the night the body was removed. Abe increasingly came to rely on Duke's team and not only did they perform at the highest levels but they never asked any questions.

Duke and his team were not typical of special ops people. All had run afoul of military justice at least one time in their careers. Duke himself had been busted from captain to second lieutenant twice, both times for using excessive force against innocent natives in the countries that he was operating. There were other charges that resulted in lesser retribution, usually involving disobeying orders. Duke personally felt that the higher you went in rank in the military the more you were forced to deal with a bunch of ass-kissers that had little or no field combat experience. He had no respect for half measures or human life when it got in the way of achieving his objectives. The objectives were usually more in Duke's mind than in the orders that he was given. Duke suspected that his injury had come at a convenient time for the Army. He believed that they were looking for any excuse to get rid of him. With the numerous decorations he had won during his career the Army wanted to avoid any appearance of canning a hero. Then came the leg injury and Duke was mustered into retirement and returned to civilian life so fast that it even caught him by surprise. Duke had become an embarrassment from which the Army wanted to distance itself.

Duke surrounded himself with ex soldiers that shared his resentment of the military. Their reasons were slightly different from Duke's. All had been convicted of violent crimes and spent time in prison at Fort Leavenworth. All, including Duke, believed that they were the only people that truly understood the situations that they were thrown into. All resented civilian oversight and the ass-kissing wimpy officers that catered to the politicians. Indeed whenever Duke said the word politician he almost spit it from his mouth as if it had a sour taste. Although Duke and his buddies nearly all had at least two years of college in their backgrounds, their intelligence and education were never enough to remove two fatal flaws that all shared in their personalities. They could never see the possibility that they could be wrong and they simply got high on violence. While most professional soldiers see violence as a necessary tool to achieve their missions, if given an alternative they would choose to avoid it. Most human beings chose self-preservation if their objectives can be achieved with minimal risk. Duke and his buddies went out of their way to take risks. Recklessness and brutality was a way of life for them. They would call themselves realists or pragmatists, but the rest of the world saw them as severely lacking in morals and judgment, loose cannons that defied all attempts at control. Perhaps the worst of all was that they all thought that they were somehow "getting even" for injustices committed against them.

To Catch a Fox

Duke wasn't surprised by the phone call he had received from Rueben just ten minutes ago. Abe had another job for them. This time it was a real black ops type said Abe. He told Duke to assemble his team and have them ready to leave for another state at a moments notice. When Duke requested a description of the work and a time frame for "jump off," Abe promised to meet with him on Monday afternoon to determine what equipment would be required. They then selected a remote spot where both could meet without the fear of being observed. Sounds interesting mused Duke and after hanging up with Abe, Duke began calling his team and whetting their appetites. Another fix for their addictions was imminent.

***

The table in the dimly lit corner of the cozy Italian restaurant had proven conducive to conversation. They were hungry so Sarah and Mac both ordered a full meal including soup, appetizers, entrees' and dessert. Neither had eaten since Tony's early morning breakfast at the Hyatt. The steady pace of dealers and prospective dealers through the Fox show booth had made it impossible to take a break. The popularity of the booth, like nothing else, was evidence to Sarah that Fox was very much a leader in the world of luxury custom cabinetry. In their industry Mac had likened them to a BMW or Mercedes. Sarah was impressed that many of the Fox dealers congregated at the booth whenever they took a break from walking the show. They would meet other dealers there and renew old acquaintances. It was obvious that they wanted very much to feel a part of the organization. Tony's well trained troops were ready and able to accommodate those desires.

The leisurely pace of the meal gave the two Fox executives a chance to converse and really get to know each other beyond the typical relationship of two coworkers. As the meal progressed Sarah and Mac reminisced about their native land of Scotland and their diverse backgrounds. While they came from opposite ends of the socioeconomic spectrum, they did find much common ground to discuss. Both had studied in and received their degrees in the United States and both had a close relationship with their parents.

Even though it was years ago, the accident that abruptly took her parent's lives remained as an unhealed wound for Sarah. Because of his recent experience of losing his father and before that his mother, Mac could identify with her emotions. Perhaps it was the evening or perhaps the wine, but soon both were speaking frankly about their parents and what the loss of them had meant. Indeed Sarah's retelling forced Mac to remove the tight "lid" that he had imposed on those emotions since his return to the states. Suddenly they both found themselves sharing feelings that they had not confronted or revealed to anyone else. As the meal and the evening wound down they were silently looking into each other's eyes over after dinner drinks. Mac stared into Sarah's soft brown eyes. She returned the gaze with a faint quizzical smile tugging at the corners of her mouth. "What is going on behind those unreadable eyes of yours Boss?" She asked softly.

Mac smiled and dropped his gaze to his glass of Amaretto. He left out a quiet sigh. "It has occurred to me that I've never spoken so frankly and honestly with a woman before, as I have tonight." He raised his eyes to see the impact of his response, but Sarah's expression hadn't changed.

"Does that bother you?" she asked.

Mac was thoughtful, "normally I think that it would but somehow tonight it doesn't bother me at all."

"I'm glad that it doesn't bother you. I want you to feel comfortable talking to me."

"I do. I feel very comfortable talking to you. I suppose that you 'Human Resource people' are accustomed to baring your souls to others, but I'm not."

Sarah laughed. A delightful laugh thought Mac. "Whatever gave you an idea like that? Actually Mac, I'm usually a very private person. This was a bit out of character for me also."

"Does that bother you?" asked Mac as he turned the tables.

Sarah's smile broadened. "No, no it doesn't bother me at all. I suspect that it's the company that I'm keeping on this evening."

"I'm glad that you too feel comfortable talking candidly with me." What a sexy smile she has thought Mac. Why haven't I noticed it before now? She was lovely in a simple black form-fitting dress with a neckline that almost but not quite revealed cleavage.

The waiter presented an unwelcome intrusion. "Will there be anything else?"

"No, I believe that we're ready for the check," was Mac's reluctant response. Suddenly he didn't want this evening to end. Mac returned his attention to Sarah and found that she was still gazing at him with that rather mysterious half amused look on her face. "Now what's going on behind your lovely brown eyes? For me they are equally unreadable."

Sarah shifted slightly in her chair. "Well I was just thinking that you aren't anything like I imagined you to be."

Mac raised his eyebrows. "Ooh, that could be bad, very bad indeed."

Sarah laughed, "No actually it's good, very good."

"How so?"

"Well, forgive me but I have to be honest. From the coverage that the local papers give you when you are involved with some community event or another I've noticed that you are always accompanied by a different female companion."

Mac smiled a slightly guilty smile and confessed, "I've been fortunate that numerous young ladies have been receptive to my invitations."

"Well it left me with the impression of, and forgive me for this, an aging playboy who was too immature to make a commitment, a chauvinist who was fighting desperately to maintain his youth."

Mac feigned mock pain, "ouch!" He exclaimed.

"I'm sorry, that was brutal and out of line."

Mac laughed, "Don't apologize for a single word of it. There's enough truth there to make me wince."

"Well by working along side with you, observing your management style and now being with you tonight, I find you to be quite different from what I imagined."

"I'm nearly afraid to ask how you do find me."

"Don't be, it's all good. I see a man that cares for his associates and his fellow management team members. I see a man whose top priority is to preserve Fox Cabinetry as a place where people may earn a fair wage to buy their homes and put their kids through college, a place where they may have a career if they chose. I see a man who instructs his Human Resources manager to find the best health care that the company can afford and then to back it up with a tough safety program to protect everyone. I see a man that places these things ahead of profits and satisfying the nearly impossible demands of the people that 'own' Fox. Although the man I see is well aware that profits have to be made in order to achieve all that I just mentioned…in short, a man that can make the tough decisions. Tonight I saw a different side of this same man. Tonight I saw a sensitive person who has a strong sense of family and loyalty. I saw a man who can be vulnerable concerning his fears, but not afraid to share them with another human being." Sarah paused considering if she should say what else was on her mind. She decided to venture forth. "I see a man I like."

Mac was slightly overwhelmed. "Well, I must admit that if I was prone to blushing I would be red as a beet right now. I do try to do and be all of those things, but I'm well aware that I fall way short of my goals far too many times. Thank you Sarah, those were very kind words."

"Mac you should know me well enough by now to be aware that I don't say things to get brownie points."

"Oh yes, you tell things as you see them, even when it's not flattering and makes me uncomfortable. I always admire your honesty."

The waiter brought the check and Mac gave him his credit card. The man disappeared again. Mac finished the last of his drink and then engaged Sarah once more. "I too have been pleasantly surprised as we've become more acquainted. I expected a shrill women's libber that would be a stern disciplinarian in the shop. I expected a person of nearly intolerable ambition, one that it would be necessary to 'ride herd' on to keep her reasonably under control. But that's not what I found. I found a gentle but firm master of communications. I found a person that enables me to communicate with the people in the shop far better than ever before. I found a person with strength, intelligence and compassion, a person that has rapidly gained the trust of the people on the shop floor. I found the person that I need to finally round out this staff. As his final act was hiring you, I suppose that Dennis finally got it right…I too have found a person that I like."

"I thank you. Those are truly kind words." Sarah did blush just a tad.

The waiter brought the slip for Mac to sign and then they both got up and left. Both were silent during the short ride back to their hotel in Tony's rental car. After giving the keys to the valet service Mac escorted Sarah into the cavernous lobby. Mac paused near the base of the escalator that rose from the street level to the upper lobby level where the main desk and the elevators were. "I guess we've already had our after dinner drinks. Can I interest you in a night cap at the hotel bar?"

Sarah considered this. She too was reluctant to see the evening end, but looking at her watch she smiled and declined. "I'm afraid I can't Mac, although I would love to, it's nearly midnight. You know that Tony wants to walk the show with us before it opens tomorrow morning." Exhibitors were allowed on the show floor at any hour in case there were repairs that had to be made on the booths.

Mac looked at his own watch. "My word, you're right. Yes, Tony will be ready to go very early. I suppose we should call it a night."

Sarah smiled, "Thank you for a beautiful evening Mac."

"You're quite welcome Sarah. I surely hope that we can do it again in the near future."

"I would like that." She hesitated and during that hesitation Mac was deciding if he should kiss her, but she suddenly stepped on the escalator and said "good night Mac."

"Good night Sarah" he said to the still smiling figure as she ascended to the upper level. Mac watched until she disappeared above. He took a deep breath. The evening had progressed much further than he usually allowed or that he had planned. But he was very pleased. So pleased he decided to celebrate by himself with a nightcap. With that he headed for the bar.

To Catch a Fox

Mac ordered a Canadian Club on the rocks from the bartender when someone sat down on the stool beside him. It was Trevor Mason. "Mac my friend, how are you doing?"

Mac turned and found that Trevor was not alone. Betsy Michaels took the stool on the other side of Trevor. Both held drinks in their hands. Mac could tell by their eyes and manner that they had both been drinking for some time, but Trevor always amazed Mac at his capacity to hold liquor. Several Atlantic Corporation executives had previously spent evenings drinking with Trevor, thinking that he wouldn't remember what they said or what they did. To their chagrin the following morning he recalled every word and action in greater detail than did they. Mac decided that he would avoid drinking with Trevor at all costs.

Mac's drink arrived and he raised the glass to both Trevor and Betsy, "To a good show."

"To a good show," responded Trevor.

"To a gud sow," echoed Betsy.

Mac had no reason to think that there was anything improper going on between these two. Given that Trevor's other two traveling companions were Denton Wellbon III and John Hogg, two very moderate drinkers. Mac suspected that Betsy was the only one who would be interested in hanging out in a bar with Trevor. If Trevor had considered making improper advances, she wasn't unattractive; he was smart enough to have made his move while she was still sober enough to reward him. Betsy had passed that point more than an hour ago.

"Mac I again want to tell you what a good job you're doing fending off a union and holding a decent margin."

"Thank you Trevor."

"No thanks necessary you deserve it… Mac about our other business." Trevor glanced at Betsy who seemed transfixed by her glass. "Betsy's not aware of our talks are you Betsy?"

Betsy stirred from her near stupor. "What dud you shea Trevor?"

"Nothing doll, go back to your drink."

"Oookay."

Trevor smiled then turned back to Mac. "We can talk," he said. "I've received another offer."

"More or less?"

Trevor chuckled. "Now Mac you know I'm not going to tell you that. You have to decide if you want to risk losing the company or do you want to better your offer to be safe?"

"How long do I have? You know I'll have to consult our backers and my other partners."

"I can give you a few days."

"Honestly Trevor it's hard for me to imagine that you got a larger offer."

"Imagine what you want Mac. But I suggest that you offer as much as you're able. I would really like to see you get Fox, but you know I have to look out for our investors…I would hate to see you suffer regrets if you lost the company when you could have afforded to offer more."

"I'll let you know Trevor."

"Good, don't take too long." Trevor rose from the bar and took Betsy by the arm. "Come on Betsy, I'll escort you up to your room." With that the two slowly left the bar. Trevor walking straight and tall while Betsy leaned against him her arm in his.

Mac sipped at his drink. "Damn," he said under his breath. While it was expected that Cab Corp would make an offer here at the show Mac was hoping that something would happen and they would change their minds. He would have to check with Denton to see if he had any knowledge of the offer. But Denton, like Trevor, would be bound by ethical considerations not to reveal the amount if an offer was received. That would not be in the interests of the investors. Mac smiled to himself. Trevor Mason being bound by ethical considerations suddenly seemed amusing to him. Then the smile faded. It's down and dirty time thought Mac. We'll have to go with our gut.

Mac sat at the bar nursing his drink, then he pulled out his cell phone and called Tony's cell number. Mac knew that it would be turned off as Tony was most likely in bed after a long evening of entertaining dealers, but he left a message. He told Tony to leave for the show without him in the morning and he would catch up later. Mac decided to meet with Mr. Roberts of Future's Unlimited as early in the morning as possible to discuss their next move.

To Catch a Fox

PART 4

Chapter 21

The last two days of the show were as hectic as the first. Indeed they were every bit as hectic as Tony had promised, the continuous flow of dealers and prospective dealers through the booth asking repetitious questions concerning a new door style that Fox introduced at the show. Explanations to prospects about various support programs available to dealers and the constant need for glad handing existing dealers. At one time or another all of Fox's major players made an appearance. When they did they received concentrated attention from their Regional Sales Manager and Fox top management. John Malicki, Tony and David Elliott greeted Glenn Glen and Mark Markel from the local Chicago flagship warmly. Ed Clancy, from Milwaukee received polite attention by John, but the show yielded several candidates to replace him. It had been obvious to Malicki for some time that Ed was pushing his other lines harder than he pushed Fox. Fred Balderson from L.A and Bonnie and Brad Klein from San Francisco spent a considerable amount of time with Ralph Sinclair, Tony, Carroll Brubaker and David Elliott. Terry Barlow, Fox's number one dealer from Atlanta was seen in deep discussion with her Regional Manager Danny Meck, Tony, Mac and Carroll Brubaker. Sarah and Dale Hershey floated in and out of these groups as necessary.

The Saturday night Fox reception at the Holiday Inn Mart Plaza had been an overwhelming success. After visiting the open house at the Merchandise Mart the Fox dealers all gathered to eat, drink, socialize and dance to the tunes of a band that Tony had hired for the occasion. Tony had gambled that he wouldn't offend any of his dealers and sent out R.S.V.P. invitations declaring this to be a black tie event. Tony was big on pushing the image of Fox as a truly exclusive high end line of cabinetry. It worked. All the Fox dealers at the show attended the Fox reception. If they didn't own a tux they rented one. The ladies arrived dressed as if this was opening night along the walk of the stars at Grauman's Chinese Theater in Hollywood.

Trevor Mason and his entire staff made an appearance along with members of the local media and industry trade magazines. Trevor, a drink in one hand and a hors d'oeuvre in the other, gravitated toward Mac and Tony. "You guys throw quite a party," he exclaimed smiling.

Tony smiled, "We must represent Fox and the Atlantic Corporation as the class acts that they are boss man."

"Just keep those sales coming in Tony, if this is what it takes then more power to you." As he spoke Trevor popped the hors d'oeuvre into his mouth and grabbed another off a tray carried by one of the catering staff. "Do you have an answer for me Mac?"

"I'll have a firm answer for you by Monday morning. I've discussed the situation with our investors and I need to touch base with my staff. You noticed that we've been a bit busy the last couple of days."

"Hard work is good for you. Monday morning is time enough, but don't wait much longer. The other party is getting antsy." Trevor emptied his wine glass, placed it on a nearby table and took another from a different waiter. "See you boys."

"What's that about?" inquired Tony of Mac.

Mac informed Tony of the other offer. "We expected this, but it means that to insure our position we probably have to up our offer. The question is by how much?"

"What did Roberts say?"

"He claims we can afford to offer more and he's spending the weekend going over the numbers to determine just how much."

"But, for all we know we could be the high bid already."

"That's right Tony. The question is do we want to gamble that we are?"

"Damn!" exclaimed Tony. "Trevor always makes certain he wins."

"He certainly tries to. Can you arrange for the entire staff to meet for breakfast again in the Regency Club tomorrow morning? I need to brief them on what I just told you."

"Consider it done Mac."

As Mac moved away to begin working the room a hand caught Tony's arm. Tony turned to see Blair at his side. In answer to his surprised look Blair said "I'm media remember. You had Brady send out a bucket full of media passes to this event."

Tony smiled. "Whatever I'm glad you're here." Her hair was up in a formal do and she was resplendent in a simple but elegant low cut black evening dress.

"Are you Tiger?"

Tony found it comforting that she referred to him by that nickname. "You know I am."

"I hope so."

"Will you accompany me as I work the room or must you cover other manufacturer's parties tonight?"

"No, I covered the Merc Mart event across the street earlier and your party is the last on my list for tonight."

"Does that mean that you'll stay with me?"

"Yes, I'll stay with you through the evening as long as you realize that our personal issues are not resolved."

"I'm very much aware of that fact Blair; painfully aware."

"Do you plan to resolve them? They aren't going away." The green eyes darkened again.

"Yes I plan to resolve them, but this isn't the time or the place. We have one more day of the show and I'm scheduled to take several of our dealers out for a night on the town tomorrow night. The entire Fox staff is flying home on Monday morning, everyone that is except me. I thought if you could spare some time we could meet for breakfast on Monday and talk things out."

"Sounds like a plan Tiger."

"You have any preference?"

"That restaurant out at the end of the Navy Pier where we had breakfast before, let's meet there."

"That works for me Blair, how about a late breakfast, say 9:30? I'll have a pretty late night."

"They serve breakfast until noon so let's make it 10:00. I have the whole day off because I'm working the weekend here at the show. Give yourself a little more sack time."

"Ten it is." With that Blair linked her arm to Tony's and the two of them began circulating through the crowd chatting with dealers. David Elliott, whom Tony had kept abreast of recent developments with Blair, noticed the pair walking together. He hoped they were resolving their differences. From what David could determine the two of them were meant for each other if only that blockhead Conocenti could realize it.

Another couple was circulating the room only under the guise of introducing a new member of the Fox team. Mac and Sarah were walking together, although not arm in arm, as Mac introduced his new Human Resources V.P. to the dealers. As they moved between groups Sarah looked at Mac. "I was worried when you missed Tony's early morning 'walk the show' tour for the senior staff. I was afraid that I kept you out too late last night."

"No not at all Sarah." Then Mac related to her his chance encounter with Trevor Mason in the hotel bar after they parted.

"What do you think we should do?"

Mac was thoughtful as he told her that Roberts was in favor of upping the offer. The only question was by how much?

"Mac you know that none of us can stretch any further. Dale has set up financing for me so that I can be a part of this. I can't borrow any more. If any more money is offered it will have to come from either you or the Futures group."

"It would come from Futures it just means that the more we borrow the longer it takes to pay them off so that we own the company entirely ourselves. It also makes it harder for us to show a profit. We need to decide this as a group. That's why I have Tony getting us together for a meeting tomorrow morning." As Mac finished the two approached Carroll Brubaker and Dale Hershey. Dale had a worried look on his face.

"What's wrong Dale?" asked Mac. "You don't look like you're enjoying yourself. You have that look on your face that a CFO gets when an expense account looks suspicious."

Dale looked about the room critically as the band began to play a slow dance tune. "I'm enjoying myself Mac I'm just worried about how much Tony spent on this shin dig?"

"He's spent more than we allotted for this event, but he's postponing the expense of a new brochure until well into next year, so it will all pretty much balance out."

Dale smiled that 'good guy' smile of his. "That makes me feel better Mac."

"Good, now have some food and wine and circulate Dale. This is a good chance for you to meet more of our customers." As Mac was speaking Carroll touched his arm and indicated the dance floor with his wine glass. All looked in the direction that he was pointing and they saw Tony and Blair dancing in the middle of the circling couples.

"Is that the girl David told me Tony was seeing?" asked Dale.

"Apparently so," answered Carroll.

"They dance well together," remarked Sarah. "She's beautiful."

Mac watched for a long moment then turned to the others, "Try to be extremely considerate of Tony right now," he said.

Carroll looked puzzled, "Why now more than any other time?"

"It's no secret although I'm probably the only one that is aware of it, Tony's divorce papers came just before he left for the show. Everything is worked out and all he has to do is sign them. The trouble is that he's been carrying them around in his jacket pocket for the best part of a week and he hasn't signed yet. Between that, the show and some sort of problem he's having with the pretty redhead it's been a tough week for him."

Sarah shook her head slowly. "That's too bad. He's a good guy."

"Yes he is and that's why we need to be considerate of his feelings just now. However, none of us standing here created any of these problems for him. So Ms. Fraser; May I have this dance?"

"Why certainly Mr. MacLode, I would be delighted to dance with you." With that the CEO of Fox and its Human Resources V.P. took to the dance floor.

Dale Hershey and Carroll Burbaker watched as Mac and Sarah swirled about amidst the throng of couples. Dale turned to Carroll, "Is there more going on here than meets the eye, something that we may not be aware of?"

Carroll took two glasses of wine from a passing waitress and handed one to Dale. "I hope you like red." Dale nodded in assent. Carroll then contemplated Mac and Sarah. They seemed to be dancing a bit closer than you might expect a boss and one of his female executives to dance. "Maybe and maybe not, you know the boss has always been a bit of a ladies man. However, he usually keeps a proper distance from those that work for him…"

"A bit of an age difference too don't you think? I mean it doesn't take an accountant to figure that Mac is old enough to be her father."

Carroll gave Dale an amused look. "That never stopped the boss before."

"Your right, nor did it stop the ladies from accepting his advances. Maybe I'm just jealous."

"Oh well, they're big boys and girls. I'm not going to worry about any of them. I'm going to concentrate on producing all those units that Tony's people are sending into the shops and I suggest you concentrate on keeping the numbers straight."

Dale clinked his wine glass to Carroll's, "Good advice my friend. Good advice indeed."

The party finally wound down around one in the morning. That was when the last of the dealers left and the Fox staff could finally return exhausted to their hotel. Tony had chartered a bus for any dealers that felt too inebriated to drive or even hail a cab. Fox's lawyers recommended this so as to limit the possibility of liability if some misfortune befell any of the guests as they returned to their hotels.

***

Morning came early for Mac's staff as they met with him and Tony for breakfast on the top floor of the Hyatt Regency Hotel. After hearing of the other offer all gave Mac permission to raise their offer based on the recommendations that Roberts would give them by Monday morning. Then all headed to McCormick Place for the last time.

The final day of the show passed slowly. The crowd had thinned slightly and the pace was beginning to show on both the Fox senior staff and the sales force. Nonetheless if a prospective dealer looked promising Tony's people overcame their exhaustion and rose to the occasion. Around three in the afternoon Jake and Matt and the suspicious subcontractors that Mac had hired arrived at the booth to begin packing the loose items. The show rules prohibited them from starting the tear down until after the show officially closed at five in the afternoon. Upon the close of the show each of Fox's senior staff returned to the hotel to freshen up for their last round of entertaining the "high rollers" as Tony called them. These were the last of the Fox dealers that consistently led the pack in sales.

***

The Chicago morning was cold and gray. The wind whipped in off Lake Michigan giving all who braved it a taste of the winter that was fast approaching. Tony pushed against it as he pulled the collar of his leather jacket higher around his neck. After being "imprisoned" in suits and ties for the last several days Tony wore a black turtleneck pullover and blue jeans under his black car coat length leather jacket. A shiver surged through his body and he was glad that he was approaching the restaurant located near the end of the Navy Pier. He was not able to “sleep in” as Blair advised. Dale suggested that they save the outlandish cab and only slightly better shuttle bus fares by having Tony shuttle the senior staff out to O’Hare with his rental car. That meant that all had to leave at a time that would accommodate those leaving on the earliest flight. Tony was up at six after finally getting to bed at two. The entire staff, all six of them with luggage and briefcases crammed into the trunk and piled on their laps, stuffed themselves into the supposedly six passenger car. Tony remembered thinking it was no wonder CFO’s were usually the least popular of corporate officers. Dale was the only one who seemed cheerful during the trip.

Tony entered the restaurant. The blast of warm air that met him felt good on his face and hands and the breakfast aromas reminded him that he was hungry. Tony checked his watch it was ten AM. As the hostess approached Tony spied Blair sipping coffee and sitting in a booth next to a window that looked out on the end of the pier and the lake beyond. He indicated that he was with Blair and as he made his way to the table requested his own cup of coffee from the waitress. Blair too was casual as this was her day off. She wore a gray hooded sweatshirt with the word ‘CHICAGO’ written on it in large blue letters. In addition she was also wearing blue jeans, but it was Tony’s opinion that she looked much better in jeans than he did. Her hair was swept back into a long red ponytail that was tucked through a scrunchie; on her head was a Cubs baseball cap. A blue ski type jacket hung on a coat hook near the booth where she was seated. It was obviously Blair’s.

“Good morning,” said Tony as he removed his jacket and then sat down across from her.

Blair looked up from her steaming coffee cup. “Good morning Tiger,” she said softly.

“It’s cold out, it feels like winter will soon be here.” responded Tony.

“Yeah, but I like winter, especially in Chicago. I think it makes us tougher than most folks.”

Tony smiled, “I don’t think I’m into tough anymore.”

Blair briefly smiled that dazzling smile of hers then she indicated her cup of coffee. “I’m sorry, but I couldn’t wait for you. I got here early and I needed a cup of coffee badly.”

“No problem. I have one on the way.” Damn thought Tony, how can she look so sexy in a baggy sweatshirt and jeans? The waitress arrived with coffee for Tony and took their order. Then silence befell them as the low-pitched breakfast noises in the restaurant began to surround them. Finally Tony broke the silence. “I’m sorry Blair, but I don’t know where to start. I’ve been a foolish jerk.”

Blair grinned, “Calling yourself a jerk sounds to me like a good place to start.”

“Okay I deserved that, but you’re correct we have larger issues to discuss and until you pointed them out to me the other morning I was blind as a bat to them. Why don’t you open with your perception of our problem?"

Blair took a deep breath, “Okay, I can do that.” She mentally warned herself to be cautious, as Tony could be quite charming while being contrite. “Your reaction to seeing me on T.V. with another man is just a symptom of the problem. I know that you’re sorry, but I’m concerned that you’re sorry for the wrong reasons.”

“Blair, you must know that I care for you. I was jealous. I reacted badly I know. I should have called you as soon as I could and get it all straightened out, but I was hurt.”

“So you just blew me off? You were prepared to dump our relationship, a relationship we both had invested time into over the past several months. Dump me on the trash heap without even talking to me? Without even hearing my explanation?”

“I was afraid.”

“Afraid, afraid of what?”

“Afraid that you would reject me. Afraid that you would just laugh that ‘I don’t take anything serious’ laugh and tell me that our casual thing was over. I didn’t think I could take that on the heels of my separation and impending divorce.”

Blair was quiet for a moment as she studied Tony's face. He was looking at the table while he was talking. Now he raised his gaze and met her eyes directly. This wasn't an act, a tactic to calm her down and smooth things over. No Blair saw truth in Tony's eyes. He was being straight with her. "Blair I know that I've never told you how I feel, but even when it sounded as if you were expressing your feelings you were so flip about it that I never knew if you were serious or not. I never had the confidence to tell you my feelings. So when I saw you with Andersen my worst fears seemed to be realized."

Blair exhaled. She wasn't certain if she had been holding her breath or not. Then she began, slowly and deliberately, choosing her words carefully. "First I want to make a point so that there is no misunderstanding. I want to repeat what I said the other morning. I know that previous to that morning I've only hinted at or coyly acknowledged it in the past... Okay, I have to admit I was a tease." A pause and then, "I love you...There, I've said it again. I've said it without wrapping it in some joke or outlandish remark or flirtation. You've right, I've been very flip about saying this. But the simple fact is that this woman seated before you, who has dumped men in the past because they couldn't match shirts to socks and ties or because she was offered a more lucrative job in another city. This woman has fallen in love with you...I apologize for not sounding more serious when I spoke those words before. Maybe I too was afraid. "

"What were you afraid of?"

"The same thing as you! Do you think you're the only one afraid of rejection? At least you can claim to have been married. I've had numerous relationships but they never went anywhere. Then I met you and everything seemed different. I guess it seemed too good to be true. I guess I too was afraid that if I totally allowed you inside my feelings for you I would be way too vulnerable to being rejected."

Tony was almost beside himself with joy. She actually said it out loud. Twice! She actually stated it like she meant it. He opened his mouth to respond, but she held up her hand and stopped him. "Let me finish. It would break my heart to end this now, that's why I was so furious with you when I thought you were giving me the brush off. But it would eventually hurt us both even more if I allow this to continue under false pretenses."

"What do you mean 'false pretenses'?"

"I mean if we allow ourselves to operate under the false assumption that this relationship will operate like your previous one with your soon to be ex wife."

"But it won't! You understand about my career."

"Yes, but do you understand about mine?" Blair's look was intent and her jaw suddenly set.

Tony knew that his answer to this question was fraught with danger. He decided to side step. "Since I've recently been nominated for jerk of the year, I best keep my mouth shut and listen."

"Smart move I never said you were stupid Tiger." Blair finished her coffee. "I'll try to explain. I have to be equal in any relationship with you. I can't survive as an individual any other way."

"I think I treated Shelia as an equal in our marriage."

"You did not treat Shelia as an equal, not when it came to career choices. You've told me enough that I've surmised that, but I thought we were different until the incident with Andersen."

A look of apprehension crossed Tony's face. "Are you going to think I'm hopeless if I say I'm not quite certain what you are telling me?"

"Not if you tell me you will listen and consider what I have to say."

"I will Blair, I promise."

"Okay, I know I'm venturing into sensitive waters here, but I think our future is at stake so I must. Your first wife was a stay at home mother and I admire and respect that. That's a tough job. I'm not a stay at home woman. If I find the right guy I plan on getting married and hope to have children, but I'll tell you now that I have to be a working mom. I need that. I thrive on the work place. I have to be in the game. Could you live with that?"

Tony remembered the pressure that was on him after Shelia gave birth to their daughter Sharon. It was tough being the only breadwinner, but Shelia wanted to stay at home with their child and Tony supported that decision. Could he support the exact opposite? It suddenly seemed very attractive. "Yes, I could live with that as long as we, ah my wife and I, found day care with the proper atmosphere for learning and play. I think playtime is important to a child. We would also have to divide our time with the child and that can be tough with two careers. I've always felt that I shortchanged my daughter. Sharon and I have a good relationship, but it's not as close as the one she has with her mother. But I'm still confused. Shelia and I both agreed on her being a stay at home mom. This was not some Chauvinistic notion that I forced on her."

"That's not the part I have a problem with. I wouldn't be surprised if Shelia introduced the idea."

Tony shrugged. "I think she might have raised the topic."

"And what did you do when she did?"

"I did what I had to do. I worked my butt off so that I could support her in that role."

"Did you ever tell her what that might involve? Did you tell her you might be away three weeks out of four, leaving her to manage the home and a child herself?"

"I figured she knew that."

"Tony don't get angry with me, but I think you were already on a mission, an ego trip. You were going to take Fox Cabinetry from a sleepy southeastern Pennsylvania cabinet shop and turn it into the leading manufacturer of luxury cabinetry in the nation. Now with your wife wanting to stay at home with your daughter you had the perfect excuse to throw yourself selfishly into your career. I'm certain that when your wife protested your long absences from home you cast it up to her that she wasn't bringing in any money. Did you?"

Tony shifted in the booth. "I might have. I suppose I did… How should I have handled it? What should I have done?"

"When the topic initially surfaced you should have sat down with her as an equal and discussed the ramifications. She worked outside the home before she had the baby. She was making a serious career choice. You both should have shared in this decision. The two of you should have determined what was best for your child and your relationship. Determined what was best for your joint goals. Perhaps through dialog you may have been able to reach a compromise. Something that would have worked for you both, instead you said okay and went charging off into the wilderness of business, the man warrior supporting his family. You expected nothing more from the home front than for your wife to be grateful at the largess you supplied. You were then shocked when she was anything but happy about the existence she was living. Why? Because you were never home to help. You were doing it in the manner that you wanted to do it, not in a manner that was best for your family or in a manner in which your wife had input. You used what you certainly called 'her' decision to justify your mission for Fox."

Tony rubbed his eyes with both his hands. "I never thought of it that way."

Blair plunged ahead, afraid to stop and assess if she was making any progress. She was going to see this through to the bitter end. "Now you're in a relationship with a woman that has a career in the world of business. As soon as that career required something that didn't fit into the world, as you believed her world should be, you are so threatened that you're ready to cut and run."

Breakfast came and provided Tony a brief bit of cover. He immediately busied himself with spreading jelly on his toast and applying pepper to his omelet. Then he quickly filled his mouth to avoid speaking for just a bit longer.

"Tiger, am I totally off the mark? Am I making sense to you? I don't think all things should be the woman's way, I think that in an equal relationship all decisions should be shared. All options examined and every choice made jointly. Most of all both careers and all that they entail must be viewed as having equal importance."

Tony swallowed. He could no longer avoid responding. "Well, I have to confess that I hadn't thought much about these things until our little encounter over at the Hyatt the other morning, but you pointed out some severe flaws in my thinking. Perhaps I shouldn't glorify it that much. Rather I should describe it as flaws in my assumptions."

"Tiger do you see my point? Is there any common ground for us here?"

"Yes there is. After the other morning I've been giving this a lot of thought. I was beginning to see what you were upset about and just now you have confirmed my conclusions and given them new depth."

Blair allowed herself a small smile perhaps it was even a smile of relief. Tony hadn't dismissed her as out of hand and he showed no signs of stalking off. "One comment you made is interesting. Tell me more about your thoughts on dividing your time with the child in light of dual careers." She felt hope and she wanted to plumb his thoughts further.

Tony thought for a moment. "Oh what I said earlier? If two people have careers and they are equally important, then it seems to me that you have to take turns. By that I mean when the child gets sick and can't be left in day care then the parents have to take turns staying home to care for the child."

"Even if your turn comes up when you are preparing to leave for an important contract signing with a potential flag dealer in a market like Chicago?" There was a wicked smile playing at the corners of Blair's mouth.

Tony swallowed hard. "I might ask you if taking turns is okay when you are preparing to leave for the coast to do a series of columns on important celebrities."

"A typical salesman trick! Answer a question with a question. I asked you first!"

"So you did." Tony thought for a moment. "That's tough isn't it? Honestly."

Blair raised her eyebrows in thought and sighed loudly. "Yeah it is Tiger. It really is. But as the mother, and bear in mind I've not been a mother to date, I think I could do it." Tony tactfully did not mention that she had answered first anyway.

Tony looked out at the Lake. A small squall was coming ashore and suddenly rain pelted against the window. It made the warmth of the restaurant feel even better. The waitress appeared and inquired if they needed anything else. Tony asked for another order of toast. He marveled that he could be this hungry after the heavy meals he had consumed while entertaining dealers this past weekend.

He made a mental note to resume his exercise routine as soon as he returned home. The waitress departed and it was obvious that Blair expected his answer. "Wow. I guess that I could do it too. If you think about it, neither of us is in a business that is life or death. What I mean is, and I'm not making light of our career choices, but we aren't brain surgeons. Not even those things that the people around us place life and death emphasis on. In reality they can usually wait for another day. It may be inconvenient but they really can wait. Would anyone have died if you didn't get that interview with Dirk Andersen? Would the world come to an end if it had taken another week to get Glenn Glen and Mark Markel to sign their contracts with Fox? The answer is no in either case."

Blair smiled the warm smile that Tony was accustomed to seeing, not the smirk she had affected ever since he had stupidly brushed her off. He was glad to see it return. "But Tony would you and I be willing to pay the price of telling those people around us, my editor and your fellow corporate officers that our child and our obligation to each other came first? After all you could lose the prospective dealer and my paper could send someone else in my place. Our decisions could have a severe price tag on them."

This time Tony didn't hesitate. "Now I can speak from experience. As someone presented with the choice of putting my relationship with my wife and daughter ahead of my career and failing to do so, the results of putting the wrong one first aren't desirable. I'm living proof of that. I've achieved nothing in business that has been worth having the time I spend with my daughter rationed out."

Blair was thinking that in spite of her best efforts she might be falling even more in love with this guy. Then Tony spoke up again. "But we may have allowed the interjection of a child in the equation to sidetrack us. A more immediate question is would I understand when the demands of your career clashed with my career or would I respect the instances when you have to do something like accompany a handsome movie and TV star to some gala event? Would I understand when you have to do something that for whatever reason, I'm not comfortable with? On the other side you mentioned before that I might end up taking strange women out to lunch and dinner when I'm traveling. We both know that my job requires that I do just that. Are you comfortable with that?"

"Now you're addressing the heart of the problem." Blair put her elbows on the table and laced her fingers together to form a support where she placed her chin. She cocked her head slightly and fixed her stare on Tony's eyes. "Please continue

Tiger. I'm very interested in what you have to say." She decided to hold her answer for a bit longer.

"Well I'm going to make a point here too." Tony felt that they were now plumbing the very mechanics of their future relationship, if indeed there was to be one. For some unknown reason he was no longer afraid. "You went out on a limb earlier and stated flat out that you are in love with me. That's a bold and yet vulnerable position to be in. I'm going to say this to you. I'm in love with you too Blair."

Blair's smile was as wide and beautiful as Tony had ever seen it. "Thank you Tiger, I'm thrilled to hear you say that," she answered in a voice barely above a whisper.

"I'm very glad that you are thrilled, because I've never been more serious about anything in my life. But so far we have been speaking hypothetically. Now let's consider a real problem." Even with his hectic schedule of the past few days Tony had spent a great deal of time thinking about Blair, the manner in which he had acted and her comments that morning in the Hyatt Regency. He had also taken a new harder look at his failed marriage. He had come to the realization that it was more than Shelia not understanding the demands of his career and his neglect of her. Listening to Blair this morning he began to see that it ran much deeper than that. The more he listened to Blair the more he was coming to grips with his own failures. He meant what he just said; he really did love Blair and he was determined to make this relationship work. He mentally crossed his fingers and plunged ahead. "Our declared love for each other is not hypothetical and neither are the circumstances we live in. You work and live in Chicago and I work and live in Lancaster Pennsylvania. So far we've carried on a remote romance, but suppose we take the next step. Just suppose we decide to get married. I'm not a casual live together kind of guy. I believe that people should make enduring commitments to each other." Tony knew just how ironic that statement was because unknown to Blair he had his unsigned divorce papers in his jacket pocket. "How do we reconcile the geographic distance between our homes and jobs?"

"I've thought about this, probably long before you and I have some ideas, but this time I really want to hear yours first." Blair felt her stomach become all tingly. Up to this point Tony seemed to be making an honest attempt to meet her halfway. She really wanted this to work but she wasn't going to accept almost but not quite.

"Well, I must first give you some background on the current situation with Fox." With that Tony brought Blair up to speed on the Fox management team's attempt to buy the company from Atlantic. He also told her about the other offer and even if that offer wasn't good enough and for whatever reason Mac's team failed, someone new was going to own the company and that made his future uncertain."

"I'm impressed you actually have an opportunity to be part owner of Fox Cabinetry."

"Yes. Now back to our situation. I think we have to evaluate each of our jobs and locations in terms of what they mean to a combined future and then we have to choose."

"Okay Tiger, this is critical. What do you mean when you say choose?"

"Well, I'm not certain but we have to have some criteria. Maybe we simply have a pact that whoever has the best job and by that I mean the job that has the most potential to benefit the overall relationship or perhaps I should say the overall goals of the relationship. It could be determined by opportunity or by the size of the salary, but we have to agree on those criteria in advance." Tony paused for a moment in thought. "I'm not certain that the size of the salary should outweigh any other factors, but the important thing is that we establish the criteria in advance of the decision. Then we can arrive at a decision based on those criteria and we both have to honor that decision. The location of the job that we both decide is the one best preserved is where we live and the other person moves there and finds work there. No matter how long the other person has worked at his job or the level of involvement."

"You would be willing to leave Fox if we determined that my job was the better of the two? You would leave even if you were a part owner?"

"Yes Blair, I've come to see that in a loving equal relationship I have to be willing to do that if your job is the most important to us." Tony looked out the window again, but he wasn't really looking at anything in his line of site. Instead he was seeing Shelia the night she told him she wanted a divorce. "As I just told you, I've learned the hard way which is the most important, career or the relationship with someone you love."

"Well Tiger if I told you that I wasn't touched by what you just said it would be a lie. My thoughts were that it might not be necessary for you to give up your job with Fox. Look how often you are on the road anyway. You could live here and fly back for meetings or whenever you felt the need. Working for the paper I have to stay closer to home. However should we decide that salary is the critical criteria, I only make $150,000 a year at the Tribune, I'm sure that you make more. We may decide that your job is best for us because of your earning power. I wouldn't like leaving, but I'm certain I could find an equally good job closer to yours if, and I must interject that is a big if, if that's what together we determined. The important thing is that we make the decision together."

Tony swallowed hard. He made $125,000 in salary and bonuses at Fox. He never suspected that Blair outscored him on that front. That was a revelation best left for another day. "Yes, well we aren't at a point that we have to make those decisions, but it's important that we agree in principle on how we make them." Tony found himself hesitating once again. "Am I pushing too far if I say I think we agree in principle?"

"Tiger, we agree in principle. If you can assure me that what you just suggested would be the model for all of our decisions. That we start with the basic principle that I'm your equal partner in this relationship and that as such my career and the part of my life that is separate from yours is equally important as your career and independent life, then I think that we should continue exploring this relationship. That is if you still want to."

Tony leaned across the table, took Blair's hand and kissed it tenderly. "I love you Blair. I want to continue this relationship more than anything else in the world. More than career, more than anything."

"I love you too Tiger. That all goes ditto for me." Tony thought that he might have detected a tear in Blair's eye, but he made no mention of it.

They finished their breakfast and after the empty plates were removed Blair excused herself and went to the ladies room. The rain had stopped and they decided that they would just, as Blair described it, "take the remainder of the day off and bum around town together." Tony got on his cell phone and changed his flight arrangements until late tomorrow afternoon. When Tony was alone he reached for his jacket that he had hung on the hook over Blair's. From the inside pocket he pulled out the divorce papers that he had been carrying around all week. Well, he thought, Sheila found someone else and maybe he had too. It was time to close this chapter, mistakes and all, and move on. Tony pulled out his pen and signed at every place that his lawyer had marked for him. He took a deep breath, carefully folded the papers and returned them to his pocket. He would mail them later today. Fortunately Blair wasn't here to see the small tear in his eye.

Then Blair returned all tricky smiles and flirtatious remarks. She was the "old" Blair again and ready to go. She quickly donned her jacket and linked her arm to Tony's. Tony paid the bill making some comment that if they were in a truly equal relationship it should be her turn to pay. "I'll decide when I'm equal and when I need you to be more equal," she grinned.

"I trust you'll keep me informed as to when you are and when you aren't?"

"You'll be the first to know Tiger."

As they walked out into the cold she pulled closer to him. Tony liked the feel of her close to him. He liked the feel of their being together again. Things were always exciting and unpredictable with Blair and, as he discovered these last few weeks, she could also be a little dangerous. He realized that he liked that. It added a certain zest to the relationship. Then sporting that impish grin she focused those enchanting green eyes on him and said, "Hey Tiger, if you're nice to me and buy me something pretty, I might make you dinner at my place tonight. Who knows you might get lucky."

"Ah, lucky as in how?"

"Lucky in that I might not make you do the dishes afterward."

"Do dishes enter into this equality thing? I didn't know it was going to be this tough."

"Shut up while you're ahead," replied Blair and they headed toward Tony's rental car parked just off the Navy Pier.

***

To Catch a Fox

It was the Monday morning after the KBIS show. Trevor had taken a late Sunday night flight home to New York. Now Abraham Rueben and Trevor Mason sat in Trevor's office. The door was securely closed and Trevor told his secretary that he must not be disturbed. Trevor informed Rueben of the two offers that were on the table for Fox.

"What a surprise MacLode and his team want to buy Fox; how about that. Where do they stand in the bidding?" asked Abe.

Trevor smiled. "They're actually a million low, but they don't know that. I think I can squeeze a little more out of them."

"The financing is solid?"

"Very solid and I actually prefer to sell to them over that ass Matthews."

"What do you care?"

Trevor smiled. "Actually I don't, I'll go with the high bidder, but I don't like Matthews. I think he tried to sic the union on Fox to push the price down. Lucky for us Mac decided to show a flash of brilliance at just that moment."

"The combination of selling Fox and the financing you obtained from those Far East bankers means that we can cover our immediate financial obligations."

"It sure does, but now I'm worried about Mary Wellbon and moving the annual meeting date forward."

A frown crossed Abe's face. "Have you talked to Mary?"

"Just this morning."

"And?"

"She claims that she was as surprised as we were and although she makes it clear she doesn't like our tactics or us personally she is with us. She pointed out that she wasn't at the meeting either."

Abe snorted. "I think she's lying. I think she's decided to fight us. I think that even if she didn't attend the meeting they were doing her bidding. She's attempting to force our hand gambling that without her votes we can't pull it off."

"You think she would hang her son out to dry? Damn the negative publicity?"

"She did the first time otherwise you, my friend, wouldn't have your ass parked in that chair. If Denton had been made chairman then I doubt if he would have hired you."

"I hate to admit it but you're right about Denton not hiring me. However, I still can't imagine Mary Wellbon accepting her son being exposed as guilty of statutory rape and the repercussions that may have on Denton's wife and Mary's social standing."

Abe shook his head. "You might be right, but you might not and we can't take the chance that you may be wrong."

Trevor slammed his fist onto the desk. "Damn it! Without Mary's vote we don't get Denton's and without either of the Wellbon's proxies we don't get the company."

"We also assumed that if Carlton Smith saw the way Mary Wellbon was voting he wouldn't buck her and would go along, even if he didn't agree. With Smith that puts everything over the top. However Mary goes so will Smith and right now, denials to the contrary, we have to assume that Mary will desert us."

"So what do we do?"

Abe had a wicked smile growing on his face. Trevor had seen Rueben smile so seldom that he realized that the smile was crooked and no smile seemed to go with the hard eyes. "Remember Trevor we know something that neither Denton or his mother know. We know that Denton has a daughter. Now I'm betting that information can get both Denton and his mother back in the fold."

"How do we break the news?"

"I'll break the news Trevor. I'll talk to Denton. While I do that you open our battle on a new front."

Mason frowned. "What front is that?"

"Carlton Smith."

"The only thing we have on him is that he had to have knowledge about Melissa Kensington's nephew bilking Wellbon – Smith companies out of over a million dollars."

"That should be enough."

"But unlike the others including Melissa's pulling strings to protect her nephew, we can't prove Carlton's involvement."

"He doesn't know that. Do you think you can pull that off Trevor?"

Mason smiled. "You take care of Denton and his mother I'll take care of Smith."

Rueben shook hands with Trevor and left the office. What Mason didn't know was that Abraham Rueben's plans to 'take care of Denton and his mother' included far more than the revelation of Crystal Harrison's parentage.

***

Sam Grabowski and Harry Sigfreid stood behind the seated technician. The NYPD lab was stumped. They couldn't explain how the small patch of orange light came to be in the upper left corner of numerous frames in the surveillance tape, the tape taken from Abraham Rueben's office building. Sam then called on his old friend Harry and the FBI for help. Harry had them come to the FBI labs to use their software. "Well?" asked Harry of the technician.

"Wow, this is state of the art," replied the technician.

"What's that mean?" asked Sam.

"This tape is really a copy in the strictest sense of the word."

"You mean that there is an original somewhere?" asked Sigfreid.

"Yes and no."

"Just tell us for god's sake! I hate playing twenty questions with you smart guys!" Sam Grabowski was his usual impatient self. Harry Sigfreid couldn't suppress a smile.

"What I'm saying is that this surveillance system is digital. You know like those new digital cameras." The technician was unruffled by Sam's comment.

Sam's brow furrowed. "They have that in video too?"

"They sure do."

"Okay," said Harry in his lets cut to the chase tone. "How did the orange light get there?"

"Well you've told me that there is an orange light from a neighboring establishment that could possibly shine in the window on the opposite wall."

"Yeah, but it is turned off every night before the time period that this tape was made." Sam's voice still held the edge of impatience. He hated wasting time going back over already established facts.

"What I believe you have here are segments from an earlier period implanted or superimposed on segments from the later period. Notice that the light only appears in frames from 11:05 through 12:30. That is after the restaurant has closed and the light being on a timer has turned off. The light is clearly visible at the same location on earlier tapes. However the appearance there is quite natural as those time periods are during the time that the light is normally on."

"You obviously don't believe that the light was mysteriously turned back on during the time frame it appears." Sam was slightly puzzled.

"No I don't think so Lieutenant. Besides you had one of your men check to see if the light had experienced any malfunctions during that time period and the answer was no."

"That's correct, now explain what you mean by superimposed."

To Catch a Fox

"Do you watch much football?"

"All the time during the season."

"I think it first appeared on Monday Night Football, I'm not certain. Do you recall that yellow stripe that the network superimposes on the field to show the TV audience where the ball has to move to make a first down?"

"Yeah how do they do that?"

"Well the stripe isn't actually on the field. Neither the players or the fans in the stadium can see a yellow stripe, but the TV viewer can."

"That's superimposed."

"Yeah, but it's a little more complicated than that. You see TV has a three second delay on live events. That allows them to transfer the image to videotape before transmission. Now somebody got the idea to run the images through the computer during this time frame. Computers take images, words, pixels what have you and reduce them to numbers or x's and o's. Once you reduce an image to numbers and symbols you can alter it any way you desire. The networks chose to add a yellow stripe where the first down marker is located. Now they got real cute with it. They want it to appear to the TV audience as if it actually exists on the field so they developed software that automatically 'pulls' the players and officials from the image of the field and puts them back on 'over' the stripe after the stripe is imposed. That makes it appear as if a player, official or the ball is on top of the line when any of those cross over or lie on it. That is why it appears as if a player's foot is resting on the line and not the line crossing over the player's foot."

"That's pretty clever," said Sam. "But how's that principle working on our surveillance tape?"

"Well since this began on a video card in a digital video camera, if someone wanted to block out an image they didn't want to appear all they would need to do would be to take the 'code' from one set of frames and replace the code for the original frames with the transposed code."

Sam was getting excited. "That's why we're seeing the light in a time period that we know it was turned off. Someone took the codes from earlier images and transposed them into the later time frame."

"You got it lieutenant, but they were either in a hurry or they got sloppy. It would have been just as easy to eliminate the small patch of orange light," said the technician.

"How can we prove that?"

The technician turned away from his computer screen. "That's tough. This is why photo or video evidence is no longer allowed in court. It's too easy to alter. When you alter a digital image you in a sense create a new original. But you may not have to prove it lieutenant. It all depends how smart the person was that did the tech work. To create this tape you would have to download from the video chip in the video camera, run it through a computer software program to alter the image, just like the networks, and then print the altered image on a tape. If the person doing this forgot to erase or destroy the original video chip the original images may still exist on that chip. With the existence of the orange light we know they are at least a little careless."

Sam and Harry suddenly looked at each other, the same thought on both their minds simultaneously. "We need a subpoena for that entire security system," yelled Sam. With that he burst through the lab doors on his way to talk to the DA and find a judge.

***

Denton Wellbon III was speechless. He was seated in Andy's office at the diner. He suddenly felt a wave of nausea sweep over him. Andy sat behind his desk and watched Denton closely. He had just revealed the existence of Crystal Harrison, Denton's daughter to Mary Johnson Harrison. Denton closed his eyes and leaned forward, his head nearly between his knees. Andy thought for a second that he was going to throw up and he definitely didn't want that happening in his office. But then Denton sat upright again although he immediately seemed to slump in the chair. His face was pale as he almost whispered, "Are you certain?"

Andy pushed the medical files across the desk and explained what they were. Denton slowly opened the folder and scanned every detail. Then he closed them and raised his eyes to meet Andy's. "All this proves is that Foster Harrison isn't her father," he said hopefully.

Andy held his gaze. "Do the math Denton, she's twenty six years old. Who else did Mary Johnson – Harrison have sex with twenty six years ago?"

"Denton sighed, "Mother, thinks that I was too drunk to have had sex with Mary that night and I can't remember if I did or didn't."

Andy sat up straight. "You've told your mother about all of this?"

"Yes, and Susan too."

"What did they have to say?"

"They are very supportive of me."

"Did you tell them about Trevor Mason and his plan to take over the company?"

"I told them everything."

"What was your mother's reaction?"

"She wants to fight."

"Great! The don will be happy to hear that." Andy realized that he had slipped as soon as he had referenced "the don", but Denton didn't seem at all surprised or puzzled.

Denton smiled a faint smile. "Relax Andy mother told me all about the relationship between my father, you and Raymond Luca."

Andy permitted himself a smile. "So your mother knew all along. The boss and I often suspected that she did. How does she feel about our renewed relationship?"

"Surprisingly she said that 'you can be very useful at times'. I'm learning a lot about mother that I never suspected."

Andy laughed. "Very useful that's rich. I'm glad that your mother appreciates the concept of you scratch my back and I'll scratch yours."

Denton stared at the ceiling. "Should I have a blood test done to remove all doubt?"

"Denton we don't have time for that. Your daughter has already been to this diner."

"What? How?"

"Damned if I know, but she's the spitting image of her mother, that's what got my attention. That's what got us to checking up on your one night stand." Andy related the details of his sighting of Crystal and the aftermath. He left out the strong-arm methods that the 'research' involved.

"Please don't call her a 'one night stand'."

"Sorry, but that's what she was. Hey, I've had hundreds of them." Andy then filled in the details concerning the marriage to Foster Harrison, Mary Johnson-Harrison's suicide and the fact that foster parents adopted Crystal. Denton for his part decided to keep silent concerning the fact that Mac had made him aware of some but not all of these details. "Okay Denton what's your plan for fighting Trevor?"

Denton then related their strategy. Denton's mother telling Trevor that essentially she hated his guts, but he left her no choice but to protect herself and her son by going along. This was a tactic to give Trevor and Abraham a false sense of security and perhaps stop them from taking any further more drastic actions. He explained how his mother called in favors on the executive council and got the annual meeting moved forward by nearly a month giving Mason even less opportunity to gather insurance votes. He also explained how Mary Wellbon would wait until the very last second to persuade Carlton Smith to vote with her, then surprise Trevor during the meeting and vote his proposals to take over the company down. Denton briefly allowed himself to ponder how it was that two women with the first name of Mary had dominated his life and decisions to date.

"Sounds good Denton, but by my count you're still short on votes, even if Carlton Smith votes with you. Remember Trevor has acquired all of those proxies. Sounds like a standoff. That's not a good outcome, as you don't have the votes to get your ass into the Chairman's chair. Without you gaining control, Trevor is free to wreak havoc as revenge for you and your mother double crossing him." Without going into too much detail, Denton explained about the off shore funds and that he and his mother had acquired those votes. Andy had purposely played dumb concerning the off shore funds. He didn't want Denton to know of the don's involvement. "I'm impressed. That concentrates the battle on Carlton Smith. I'm certain that Trevor believes that however your mother votes Carlton will do as he's always done and vote the same way. If Trevor truly believes that you and your mother are voting with him he's no doubt assuming that Carlton will follow. Are you certain that your mother can convince Carlton to once again follow her lead?"

"I believe so. I'm counting on it."

Andy lit up one of his smelly cigars. He offered one to Denton, but Denton declined. Andy puffed a cloud of smoke toward the ceiling. "You may have Trevor fooled, but I know Rueben. He'll have a backup plan ready in case you and your mother defect. But we'll discuss that later. Right now we need to discuss another aspect of this. I just told you that you have a twenty six year old daughter. You've told me that you informed mother and wife of your little tryst and they are supportive. What would this new information do to that support?"

Denton swallowed hard. "I don't know."

"It means that your mother has a grown granddaughter that she's never met and your wife has a stepdaughter."

"Good lord, you're right! That hadn't occurred to me." The two sat in silence as the implications of this turn of events sank into Denton's very being. "You have no idea how she found your diner?"

"At first I thought it could only have come from her grandparents on her mother's side, although I thought I was careful never to leave a trail back to here. But then it occurred to me that her mother, your one night stand, might have told her about her heritage. Mary Johnson–Harrison is the only person that knew everything, including your father, you and me. The fact that she found her way to this diner probably means a combination of the two. I don't know. It was a long time ago and I might have screwed up somewhere."

"If she found you, it's entirely possible that she could find me!"

"But the fact that she hasn't shown up on your doorstep already tells me that for whatever reason her information is incomplete."

"You say she's a news anchor on TV in Savannah?"

"Yeah, she's the most popular local TV personality."

"How about that," Denton suddenly and unexpectedly felt a surge of pride.

"So what are you going to do Denton?"

Denton hesitated, "For now nothing."

"You're not telling anyone?"

"Not immediately. I have to absorb this new twist myself. I don't know how I feel about this. Not yet at least…I don't know Andy…I can't believe that all these years I've had a daughter and never knew it."

"Okay, I guess it can't hurt. You have to know the right time to tell your mother and wife. I'll tell you what I'm doing. I've already flown a couple of my cousins down to Savannah to find her. I'm flying down to join them tonight."

"Cousins?"

"Yeah, real cousins, I'm a nephew of the don himself. We keep as many of the top echelons of the family as blood relatives as possible, that way it protects us from betrayal."

"Oh, and what are you going to do when you find her? That shouldn't be too hard by the way as she's no doubt on TV every day."

"Just keep an eye on her. We have to assume that Rueben also knows that she exists."

Suddenly the possibilities became clear to Denton. "My god he could try to harm her or threaten to at the very least!"

“You’re getting the picture Denton. He could hold her hostage for your vote and your mother’s, sort of an insurance policy. With those two blocks a given, it makes Carlton Smith’s vote much easier to attain. Rueben doesn’t like to play a hand unless it’s a sure thing. Rueben doesn’t trust anybody. He’ll assume you and your mother will double cross him and are pleading with Smith not to vote with Mason. Knowing this do you doubt that he’ll use Crystal to assure your vote? Of course all of this assumes that you actually care what happens to little Crystal. Up until twenty minutes ago you didn’t know that she was alive.”

Denton tried to keep emotion from his face, but inside deep in his heart he was appalled at what he believed Andy was suggesting. “You mean if Rueben grabs her and threatens her I should call him on it by essentially telling him to do what he pleases with her. Tell him he’ll find out how I vote when I vote?”

“That’s what I mean Denton.”

Denton felt another wave of nausea roll over him but he was able to control it. “I couldn’t do that. Even though I’ve never known her she is here because of me. I’ve already had enough negative influence on her life. I can’t allow her to be harmed because of me. Andy, I want you to do everything in your power to protect her.”

Andy smiled, got up and walked around the desk. “That’s exactly what your old man would have said. Family was all-important to him too. Just like in our business. We keep the blood relatives close around us.”

“Can you protect her?”

“I told you, we’re already on it. Now go back to the office and act like nothing happened. Can you do that?”

“I’ll try, yes I can do that.”

As Denton rose to leave Andy stopped him at the office door. “Denton, the next time you decide to tell your mother and wife something, I would like to know about it first. I thought we trusted each other.” There was suddenly a change in tone and demeanor. Andy’s voice was no longer friendly.

Denton picked up on the change. "I'm sorry Andy, you're right. The time was right and I did it, but I should have called you first. It won't happen again."

Andy's smile returned. "That's good Denton, that's good."

Denton had his hand on the doorknob, but before he opened it he turned back toward Andy. "What would you say if I told you I think I should tell Susan and mother about Crystal?"

Andy thought for a moment. "The don and I talked about this after we traced Crystal's whereabouts. The don says that if she found the diner she will eventually find you. If you tell your family about her first, it takes away any chance, short of physical threats against her of Mason and Rueben blackmailing you."

"Okay I'm thinking straight now," said Denton. The initial shock was passing. Now it was Denton's tone and demeanor that was changing. Denton locked his gaze on Andy's eyes. "You see to it that nothing happens to that girl and you and the don will enjoy the same relationship that you enjoyed with my father. I like you Andy, and I appreciate your help, but if that girl is harmed in any way our arrangement is off."

Andy took the measure of the man standing in front of him. He was changing. He was discovering who he was. He was beginning to act and talk like his father. "Understood Denton," was Andy's reply. Then he added. "Spoken like your father. The don will be glad to hear this." A week ago Denton would have probably allowed himself a small smile at hearing that, but not now. Denton stared into Andy's eyes for a long moment. Andy met the gaze and held it. It was clear that Denton was serious and would back up what he said. Then suddenly Denton turned and walked briskly through the kitchen toward the entrance. Andy marveled how Denton suddenly even seemed to walk like his father.

To Catch a Fox

Chapter 22

Trevor Mason sat impatiently in Carlton Smith's outer office located three floors above Mason's own office in the Wellbon – Smith Building. Smith's secretary informed Trevor that "Mr. Smith is sometimes late in the morning depending on traffic." Trevor was not accustomed to waiting on others. Even others like Smith to whom he had to report. Trevor glanced at his watch. They were supposed to meet at 10 AM. Smith was 18 minutes late. Finally the outer door opened and in walked Carlton Smith, seemingly in no particular hurry. "Good morning Trevor."

"Good morning Carlton," Trevor strained to keep the irritation out of his voice.

Carlton then turned his attention to the pack of messages that his secretary handed to him. Trevor felt that he spent an inordinate amount of time going through them, especially when he was already 18, now nearly 20 minutes late for their appointment. Finally Smith turned to Trevor and motioned him into his office. Carlton closed the door behind them and moved to his chair behind his huge deck. "I wanted to compliment you on the numbers that the Atlantic Corporation turned into us for the first half." Trevor noted that there was no apology for his tardiness.

"Thank you Carlton. We'll soon have the third quarter together and it should look even better. I truly believe that the changes that I've instituted at Atlantic are finally having an affect on the bottom line."

"It would seem so. Please have a seat." Carlton motioned to one of the two overstuffed chairs positioned in front of and facing his desk. Trevor settled into the chair in response. The chair allowed one to sink deeply into it. Trevor always suspected that behind the desk Carlton Smith's chair was adjusted to seat the occupant as high as possible, thus forcing the visitor, when seated, to look up to Smith. "What brings you up here Trevor?" Trevor noted that Smith was using that patrician voice that he sometimes affected. Not much in this world irritated Trevor Mason more than the suspicion that he was being treated in a condescending manner. Of course Trevor never hesitated to do the same to people that reported to him if he felt it worked to his advantage.

Trevor came up from the street and Carlton came from extreme wealth. With the exception of their work the two barely had any common ground on which to build a conversation. However, Smith recognized Trevor's ability to energize a company. His methods were heavy handed and didn't create the best morale among the managers that reported to him, but his string of successes was unbroken. Trevor Mason could take a sleepy or even a sinking company and drag it kicking and screaming into a state of profitability. He had definitely improved the financial picture at Atlantic and that was exactly the reason that Carlton had hired him. It was a bit of a bruise on Smith's ego that Trevor was having success where he personally had failed, but Atlantic's recent performance also improved the bottom line of Wellbon – Smith's earnings sheet and that made Smith look brilliant to the board. The fact that Smith considered Mason to be an uncouth braggart and a bully did nothing to enhance their personal relationship.

"I'll be brief. Carlton you've made it very clear to the board that you are anxious to fully retire. Am I correct?"

Carlton Smith's brow furrowed. This was the last topic he expected Trevor Mason to bring to his attention this morning. He was curious as to where this was going. "Yes you are correct. I've made no secret of my impatience with the board to select my replacement."

"I'm going to make several proposals at the annual meeting that will permit you to retire. I would like your support on those proposals."

Carlton leaned forward in his chair. "What type of proposals Trevor?"

"My proposals will allow the board to select your replacement at the meeting."

"Trevor, much to my displeasure the board is still procrastinating. They haven't even appointed a nominating committee."

"The proposals that I will put forth will in themselves nominate a candidate for your position."

Carlton's facial expression became more puzzled. "Trevor what the hell are you talking about? Are you thinking of sitting in this chair yourself? If you are you are delusional. There are other subsidiary presidents that have far more tenure and have earned the right to be considered for this position sooner than you."

Trevor chuckled, "No not me Carlton. I know that I'm the relative new boy on the block. There would be no support for me among the board members."

"That's certainly true. While the results that you've produced have been noticed and even admired by the board, you certainly haven't cultivated the alliances that are required to catapult over your contemporaries into this chair."

"I'm aware of that Carlton." Trevor's voice was tight. He was going to enjoy cutting this overstuffed windbag down to size.

"Might I inquire who you may be considering?" Carlton spread his hands in a magnanimous gesture. "Assuming that you actually had the power to be a king maker." The voice oozed with sarcasm.

Trevor smiled, "Denton."

"Denton?" Carlton laughed a hearty artificial laugh that Trevor thought lasted too long to be authentic. "I know you weren't here at the time Trevor, but his mother could have pushed to have Denton awarded this chair when her husband died, but she chose not to do so. Mary Wellbon would never approve of that! She sat on the sidelines then and I see no indication that she would change her mind now. Why would she? Denton is still Denton, Trevor."

Trevor stopped smiling. "Times change Carlton, you still see Denton as he was. Under my tutelage Denton has matured. He's ready to take over."

Carlton stood up and walked over to the floor to ceiling window to gaze out at the New York City skyline. From this side of the building the twin towers of the World Trade Center gleamed in the late morning sun. "Trevor, what kind of fiasco are you thinking about? You know how things are accomplished in this corporation, especially the replacement of a retiring chairman. The board appoints a nominating committee that goes searching for candidates. When the committee believes that it has found one that will please the board, the board interviews that person and then votes on him. If a majority of the board approves, we have a new chairman. Sorry, I've not yet mastered the habit of calling that individual a chairperson. Now don't misunderstand Trevor I have been hearing good things about young Denton recently, but none so improved as to hand him my chair."

"Mary Wellbon has already agreed to support my proposals. Those proposals will propel Denton into the chairman's job. We need you to agree to support us." Trevor enjoyed dropping that bomb. He sincerely hoped it to be accurate.

Carlton turned around to face Trevor, the smug look gone from his face. "I don't believe that. Support what?"

"I'm not going into any detail now Carlton."

"How can I promise to support you if I don't know what you are going to propose? Tell me why I should do this? Oh and by the way, I don't believe that Mary has so drastically changed her opinion since you arrived at Atlantic."

"You'll support me because it's the smart thing for you to do."

"Why is that Trevor?" There was irritation in Carlton's voice.

"Donald Kensington-Cramer."

Carlton Smith slowly returned to his chair and sat down, a bit heavily thought Trevor. Now not only was the smug look gone but a look of apprehension was crossing his face. This was the last name he expected Trevor to mention. "Poor Donald is dead. What does he have to do with all of this, this proposal you're talking about?"

"He hasn't anything to do with the proposal Carlton, but I believe he had quite a bit to do with you."

Now Carlton's face grew pale. Trevor's gamble had paid off. Smith was hiding something. "Trevor I think I only met the man once when I was visiting his aunt. I really know nothing about him. Why would you say something like that?" In spite of the body language that spelled discomfort, Carlton Smith's voice remained quietly calm.

"I've discovered that Donald worked for the Atlantic Corporation for nearly a year and yet I can't find anyone who can remember him. He apparently also worked for other Wellbon – Smith companies at one time or another, but no one seems to remember his being at any of them either."

"I really don't remember Trevor. If you say he worked for us, perhaps he did some consulting work."

"Nope, I checked."

"Your point Trevor?"

"My point is that Donald collected a lot of money from companies owned by Wellbon – Smith, yet no one seems to be able to document what if anything he did to earn it."

"Go on Trevor."

"Donald couldn't have collected the amount of money he did unless people in very high places in this corporation either made it possible for him to do so or they simply looked the other way. Either way, it's fraud."

Carlton exhaled rather loudly. "Who exactly do you suspect are these people 'in very high places' Trevor?"

"My suspicions aren't important. What is important is that Melissa Kensington, Mary Wellbon and Denton Wellbon have all decided to vote for my proposals…I would say that this is a wise decision on their part. I'm certain that you will make a similar decision too. Feel free to call any or all of those people if you doubt what I say." Trevor rose and walked toward the door.

"Are you threatening me Trevor?"

Mason turned with a look of mock surprise on his face. "Why would I threaten you Carlton? I've simply pointed out that someone has perpetrated a serious white-collar crime in our company. I'm certain that the board is not aware of this. Of course, if someone like Denton were to assume the chairmanship, he would no doubt make certain that this type of information would never come to light. Now someone from the outside may feel differently."

"What about you Trevor? How do you feel about this type of information?"

To Catch a Fox

Carlton Smith's voice was suddenly subdued.

"Carlton, I understand that things happen. Denton's been a loyal assistant to me. Should he become chairperson, I would follow his lead and do whatever he asked. I'm certain that he would never want to see anything happen to someone that he refers to as an uncle."

"You're obviously referring to me Trevor. Do you believe that I had something to do with this Donald Kensington-Cramer thing?"

Trevor smiled what he sincerely hoped was a condescending smile. "Company records are company records. I have them in a safe place." Before opening the door he turned back to Carlton Smith. "I would recommend that we keep this discussion private Carlton. Do you agree?"

Carlton stared at Trevor for a long moment fury in his eyes. "Yes Trevor I agree."

"Let me know what you decide Carlton." With that Trevor Mason departed.

When the door closed behind Trevor, Carlton Smith stared at it for a long time. "Damn!" Carlton cursed. Why did he allow Melissa to talk him into this? Now it's turning into a huge mess. Carlton was very familiar with this situation. Years before his wife died, Carlton had a brief affair with Melissa Kensington. She persuaded Carlton to hire Donald to help him get back on his feet after one of his numerous stints in rehab. The problem was that Donald could never bring himself to show up for work. Melissa then used her charms to have Carlton "move" Donald from company to company payroll. They never kept him in any one company too long so as not to arouse suspicion when he never showed up. When questioned Carlton explained that Donald was doing consulting work for the parent corporation and all the subsidiaries were sharing in the cost. Unfortunately if pressed today Carlton could not produce proof of Donald's consulting. Because Carlton said it the CFO's bought it and simply found a way to deal with the accounting in individual ways. That should have made detection even harder. How could Trevor discover this?

Carlton told his secretary to see that he wasn't disturbed. Then he picked up the phone and dialed Melissa. He damn well sure was going to talk to everyone that Trevor mentioned. He had to find out what Trevor was planning with these mysterious proposals and how he was going to have enough votes to pull this off.

Could he have something on all of these people? Carlton didn't care about the others, but there was enough money involved in the Donald Kensington – Cramer affair to merit serious jail time. Carlton felt perspiration forming on his forehead as he punched in Melissa's number.

Trevor Mason returned to his office after his meeting with Carlton Smith. He was thinking about Carlton's office suite and made a mental note that when they took over the company he would find another office for Denton because Trevor wanted Carlton's for himself. He also smiled because he planned on finding a way to replace Denton as chairman within a year of his assuming that office. Trevor wanted the luxurious office and the title. What could Denton do? Nothing, with knowledge of the Wellbon family's secrets Trevor owned him. As he was passing his secretary's desk she took an outside call. "A Mr. Roberts of Future's Unlimited on the phone for you Mr. Mason."

Trevor stopped at his office door a smile began to cross his face. "Yes, I'll talk to Mr. Roberts." Inside his office Trevor picked up the phone. "Hello Mr. Roberts how are you today? Good, good, have you decided to change your offer? Good are you putting the new offer in writing? Excellent. I look forward to receiving the revised letter of intent. Yes send me a fax immediately and a courier would be the best for the original. Thank you, I'll let you know as soon as possible. Yes, you have a good day too sir." Trevor never hung up the phone but hit the speaker button for his secretary. "Get Clint Matthews on the line." Trevor waited impatiently until the phone buzzed. Trevor put the hand set to his ear. "Trevor Mason."

"What do you want Mason?" the voice was Matthews and it sounded irritated.

"I'm going to do you a favor Matthews."

"Why because you love me, fat chance, what's the game Mason?"

"I'm serious Matthews. It's down and dirty now and I'm going to tell you what you have to beat. Of course if you have no more interest in purchasing Fox I won't annoy you any longer."

"You always annoy me Mason, but I am interested. What's the number?"

"Fifteen point five million."

To Catch a Fox

"You gotta be kiddin' Mason. You expect me to believe that someone is offering you 15.5 mil for Fox? You think I'm that stupid?"

Trevor laughed. "You really want me to answer that Matthews? This has more to do with your balls than your intelligence. You know that Fox is worth it. The question is do you have the guts to do what you have to do to own it?"

"You son of a bitch!"

"I may be a son of a bitch Matthews, but I'm the son of a bitch that can decide who gets Fox."

"You have a firm offer of 15.5?"

"The fax is on its way and a courier will deliver the letter of intent no later than tomorrow."

"Don't accept the offer until you hear from me Mason. I'm working on additional financing."

"You have until noon tomorrow." Trevor heard Matthews begin to protest as he hung up on him. I love this job he thought to himself. Then he considered how much fun he would have when he controlled all of Wellbon – Smith and not just Atlantic Corporation. Trevor looked out the window at the Manhattan skyline. He had complete confidence that Abe Rueben could keep Mary and Denton Wellbon in line. If Mary Wellbon wanted to move the date of the annual meeting forward that was fine with him. That meant that his dream of controlling Wellbon – Smith would be realized even sooner. This was going to be a great day.

***

Denton Wellbon met his mother and Susan at The Brasserie at five in the evening. He needed to tell them the shocking news that Andy had revealed to him about Crystal Harrison. Abraham Rueben had called several times through the day, but Denton had managed to avoid him. Denton didn't know what Rueben wanted, but whenever Abe talked to Denton one on one without Trevor present, it wasn't good. Denton assumed that if Andy knew of Crystal then in all probability Abe did too. Denton ordered drinks and told the waiter that they would summon him when they were ready to order the meal.

Susan was concerned about the distracted expression on Denton's face. "What's wrong Denton?" she asked.

Denton shook his head. He didn't know where or how to begin. Mary Wellbon knew her son. Whatever he had to tell them it wouldn't be good. "Out with it Denton."

"Yes mother. I met with Andy this morning."

Susan looked momentarily puzzled, but then recognition spread over her face. "Oh, the…" She paused and then lowered her voice. "The mob guy."

"Yes, that's the one. He had some shocking news." Denton was finding it difficult to come up with the proper words. About this time the waiter arrived with the drinks. When he had departed Denton continued. "I don't know quite how to say this."

Mary Wellbon took a sip of her martini. "Spit it out Denton," she said with an edge of irritation in her voice.

"Yes mother. The girl that I had the indiscretion with, Mary Johnson Harrison, she, she…"

"Denton, please," glowered his mother.

"She, I, we, had a daughter."

"What?" Susan was aghast. Mary Wellbon took another sip of her drink, her expression unchanged.

"Apparently I got her pregnant."

"What makes you think that the child is yours?" It was Denton's mother asking the question.

Denton explained about the medical report that Andy had shown him. Mary Wellbon considered this for a moment. "That only proves that it wasn't

Harrison's child."

"That's what I said mother, but Andy did the math. Mary Johnson Harrison had dated Foster Harrison previous to our liaison, but had broken it off about two months before. Then we had our little tryst. Andy claims that she wasn't with anyone except Harrison immediately after that and the medical report proves that it wasn't his child. That only leaves me."

Mary Wellbon said nothing. Susan wanted to know all of the details. Denton told them everything that he knew concerning Crystal. When he had finished silence engulfed the table. Mary signaled the waiter for another martini.

"My word, she's my stepdaughter!" This realization had a profound impact on Susan. Denton couldn't tell if this was good or bad.

"She's also your granddaughter mother."

Mary Wellbon didn't acknowledge her son's last comment. Instead she ate the olive off of the toothpick that came with the martini. After she had savored the vodka soaked morsel, she leveled her gaze on Denton. Her next utterance was not at all what Denton expected. "Does Andy think that Mason and Rueben know?"

"Mother! I just told you that you have a granddaughter in her early twenties."

"Answer my question. What about Mason and Rueben?"

Incredulous Denton stammered his reply. "Andy says that we have to assume that they know about her."

"Andy's right. What are you doing about it?"

"I sent Andy and his soldiers to Savannah to keep an eye on her. I think that's what you call them. I told him if any harm came to her our arrangement would be off."

"Good. You understand that the don will expect a favor in return for their services?"

"I understand mother. I can live with that."

"Excellent. We mustn't allow Rueben to harm her or be in a position to harm her. If he succeeds in that, he can blackmail us out of this company."

"This could explain why Abraham Rueben has been attempting to contact me all day." Denton was still in a mild state of shock at how his mother was taking this news.

"I'm certain it does," agreed Mary Wellbon. "They no doubt suspect that we were behind having the date of the annual meeting moved up, even though I told Trevor differently."

Denton decided to raise a subject that had been laying on his mind all day. "Mother, do you think Andy would use force to protect Crystal?"

"If necessary, but Denton you must remain totally ignorant of the tactics employed by Andy and his boys down in Savannah. Do you understand?"

"Yes mother." Once again silence. Susan seemed to be far away and lost in thought. Mary finished her second martini. Totally puzzled by his mother's reaction to this news Denton ventured onto thin ice with a question. "Do you think we should all make an effort to meet Crystal some day? Andy has seen her in person. She found his diner. The fact that she found Andy's diner opens the possibility that she may eventually find us." Denton glanced nervously in Susan's direction; she was again looking directly at him. "I've been thinking about this all day and I might like to meet her sometime. What do you think?"

"Not now Denton. We have too much going on already." Mary Wellbon's answer was quick and sharp. Susan appeared as if she was about to speak, but when hearing the tone of her mother-in-law's voice she remained silent.

"What do I do if Rueben informs me that I have a daughter?"

Mary considered this for a moment. "Turn his world upside down. Really give him a shock and tell him you already know where she is and who she is. But don't, I say don't tell him how you know. Got that?"

"Yes mother, if you think that best."

"I think that anytime that we can keep them off balance it's to our benefit." Mary suddenly looked sharply into her son's eyes. "Listen to me Denton. This changes nothing. We are in a battle to retain control of our company. The company that brought this family out of the ranks of poor immigrants, the company that has provided for our family over the years. We will win! No matter what dirt they throw at us, weather it is fact or fiction. Do you understand?"

"Yes mother, I understand." Denton motioned to the waiter. "Are we ready to order dinner?"

Mary Wellbon rose from her chair. "You two order. I'm certain that you have much to talk about. I have other things that I must do tonight. I'll see you both later. Denton we must forge ahead. No looking back now."

When she was gone Denton turned to Susan. "Honey, I don't know what to say. What are you thinking now?"

"I don't know what I'm thinking. This week has been unreal." The waiter arrived. "No," said Susan. "I'm not hungry. Could we just have coffee?" Denton ordered two black coffees.

Denton took Susan's hand and cradled it in his. "Susan, I never meant to cause you such pain. I can't believe how much impact one stupid decision could possibly have on the remainder of my life. Susan I love you. Don't ever think that I don't."

Susan placed her other hand around Denton's. "Denton I love you and I always will. Your mother is right, 'we must forge ahead' I don't want to look back either."

"I don't understand my mother's apparent callous reaction to this news but I am grateful for your understanding. I love you so much." With that, Denton was forced to release Susan's hands and wipe a tear from his eye. Susan placed her arm around him as the two coffees arrived.

***

Mary Wellbon sat in the big leather chair behind what was once her husband's desk. Carlton Smith was pacing back and forth in front of her. It was nine in the evening. The same evening that Denton had revealed the existence of his daughter. She had left Denton and Susan earlier in the restaurant not only because she believed that they required time to discuss this new development but she had previously agreed to meet Carlton at her penthouse. Carlton quickly downed the Scotch that Mary had poured for him. Mary, by contrast, hadn't touched her Scotch.

"Well Carlton, you screwed up this time." If Carlton Smith was expecting any sympathy out of Mary Wellbon he now realized that it would not be forthcoming.

"I know that you must be shocked that I once had an infidelity with Melissa Kensington. I loved my dear departed wife. I don't know why I was so weak. But it was the only time. I swear."

"Oh spare me that shit Carlton. I knew about your affair with Melissa. I also know of at least five others over the years. I think your wife knew of most of them too. Why she didn't kick your ass out and take you for all you are worth will always be a mystery to me."

Carlton's face drained of color. "You knew? My wife knew?"

"Oh hell, I think everyone knew. You couldn't cover your tracks with a dump truck full of gravel. No your tendency toward adultery isn't what shocks me. What I can't believe is that you allowed Melissa to talk you into putting her bum of a nephew on our payrolls. You had to know that the kid never did a day's work in his life. How much money did you allow him to collect from our companies in return for nothing?"

Carlton hung his head. "More than a million dollars in a little over a year."

"Over a million dollars! I should have you thrown in jail!"

"I'm sorry Mary. I really am."

"I want an honest answer to this next question Carlton. Should I ever discover that you've lied to me I'll throw you to the hounds personally. Do you understand?"

“Yes Mary, I would never lie to you.” Mary considered that statement long enough to make Carlton squirm. “Honest Mary! For god’s sake!”

“Carlton did you ever take any of that million dollars yourself as a kickback from Donald?”

“No, not a cent.”

“Carlton?”

“No Mary, so help me God! I swear! I’ve done a lot of despicable things in my life but I’ve never stolen a single penny from our company. You’ve got to believe me.”

Mary Wellbon finally took a sip of her Scotch. “Pour yourself another glass if you want Carlton.” Carlton Smith went to the bar and refilled his glass. Mary noted that his hands were shaking. “I believe you Carlton.”

The look of pure relief that immediately sweep over Carlton’s face was genuine. “Thank you Mary. I appreciate that.”

Mary considered the situation. It was obvious that Trevor Mason now suspected that her vote at least and Denton’s at worse were no longer secure. That’s why he was going after Carlton’s vote. Carlton’s vote along with the proxies that Trevor already held in his possession wasn’t enough to complete the coup without either Denton’s or her own block of votes, but it could certainly keep Mary from getting a majority. Mary’s thoughts were interrupted by Carlton.

“Mary, what is Trevor up to? Could he really take over the company?”

“Yes he could, if certain votes fall into place for him.”

“He said that he was going to put Denton in my chair. Now, it won’t upset me to retire. You know that I’ve wanted to retire ever since my wife died. What I need to know is: are you backing this move?”

“Trevor thinks that I’m going to vote with him. I’ve even told him I am, but I have no intention of doing so. I know that Trevor would replace Denton within a year of his taking the chairmanship. Offering your job to Denton is just a way of securing his vote."

"Why didn't you just tell him no in the first place?"

"You've obviously been to see Melissa. I suspect you high tailed it to her place right after Trevor left your office, so you must know that Trevor is blackmailing her just as he's black mailing you."

"Yes, yes, is he blackmailing you too?"

"He thinks that he is."

"But you're not going to cave in to him?"

"No," was Mary's curt reply.

"Why is he coming after me?"

"I suspect that originally he didn't think it was necessary. He assumed that if he secured my vote you would follow blindly along as you usually do Carlton." Carlton Smith made no response, but he did admit to himself that it was true. "Now, since I got the annual meeting date moved up…"

"You did that?"

"Indirectly."

"Why?"

"So Trevor would have less time to blackmail shareholders out of their proxies; he has quite a few more than you, Melissa and I already lined up."

"So if he loses your vote he needs me to pull it off."

"I think that he's a little shy, but if he isolates me he expects that I'll cave in so Denton can replace you as chairman."

"He has Denton's vote?"

"Again he thinks so."

"But Denton may vote with you?"

"I expect that he will, but I believe that Denton is about to come under some very intense pressure in the next week or two. I believe that Denton is strong enough to resist it. In fact I'm betting the company on it."

"Mary, I'm sorry but we're talking Denton here. He's never been the determined fighter that his father was."

"You may be underestimating him Carlton. He's grown a lot in the last couple of years. While you were telling me that he was a good kid but would never be able to fill his father's shoes, Trevor Mason was teaching him quite a bit. In addition, Denton learned enough about Trevor Mason to determine that if Mason installs him as chairman, Mason will be running the show and Denton will just be a figurehead."

"If you defeat Mason do you plan on installing Denton as chairman yourself?"

"That's correct Carlton, but Denton will have the real power. No matter who wins you will have your wish of retirement fulfilled at this year's meeting. Will you vote with me Carlton?"

"If I do Trevor Mason will reveal the fraud Melissa and I committed to the finance committee. You know that they will press charges against us!"

"If you vote with Trevor I'll do the same!"

"Come on Mary! What am I supposed to do here? I can't win. I'm damned if I do and damned if I don't! I'm too old to go to jail Mary!" Carlton's voice was quivering along with his lower lip. For a moment Mary Wellbon thought that he might cry.

"Get hold of yourself Carlton! My husband always thought you to be gutless. Now sit down and brace yourself on the arms of that chair. Your hands are shaking so much that you're about to spill your Scotch on my throw rugs." Carlton sat down, but his hands were still shaking as he raised the glass to his lips and took a large gulp. "First off Carlton, don't you get angry at me I didn't get you into this, you did it to yourself! I certainly hope that Melissa was good in bed because you're paying a steep price for her past favors. It all comes down to trust Carlton. If Trevor wins he will always have your secret to hold over your head. Even in retirement. Hell he could cut off your retirement and you wouldn't be able to say a thing concerning it." Mary allowed that possibility to sink in for a few long moments.

"If you win how will you stop him from ratting on me?"

"If Denton sits in your chair by virtue of my support for him, I'll have him see to it that all records that would implicate you in fraud will disappear. I have no need to hold an axe over your head Carlton. That way when Trevor drops his bombshell on the finance committee, there will be no records to back up his charges."

"How can you guarantee that to me?"

"I have my ways, but you will have to trust me. Do you believe that Trevor will leave you off the hook?"

Carlton ran his fingers through his white shock of hair. Mary thought that this was probably the first time in their long personal history that Carlton looked a bit disheveled. "Okay Mary. You've made your point. You can count on my support at the annual meeting."

"Carlton does that mean that you'll vote with me?"

"Yes, of course that's what I mean."

"I was just checking. Your answer sounded a bit noncommittal the first time. Thank you Carlton, now go home and get a good night's sleep. Everything is going to be all right. "

Carlton Smith finished his drink, placed the empty glass on the bar and assured Mary that he could find his way out. "Good night Mary and thank you."

"You're quite welcome Carlton. Now just live up to your promise and you may retire and live happily ever after." Carlton nodded his head to Denton's mother, pulled on his coat and found his way to the elevators in the hall.

To Catch a Fox

When Mary was certain that Smith was gone she picked up the phone and began punching in a number. Then thinking better of it, she cleared the number and selected one from her autodial. It only rang twice when Denton answered. "Denton, it's your mother." With that opening she launched into an explanation of how Trevor was attempting to blackmail Carlton Smith in an effort to secure his vote. When she had finished she paused and then asked the critical question. "Denton I don't trust Carlton. He could go either way no matter what he is saying now. What should we do?"

Denton was in his study. Susan was upstairs getting a shower. They had decided to turn in early. Denton thought for a moment then answered. "Call Paul Henley mother, He's already proven that you can trust him by moving the date for the annual meeting and not telling anyone that you were behind it."

"Paul is trustworthy. What should I tell him?"

"Tell him to begin quietly trying to enlist support among the board members to vote with us. Give him the list of names that I gave you of the people that Trevor has in his pocket. Paul must not call any of them or Trevor will find out for certain that we plan on a fight."

"What should Paul tell them?"

"The truth mother, tell them that someone is attempting a hostile take over. Tell Paul to call in all of the markers that he has out. Tell him to imply without really stating it that he is supporting you in this attempt to thwart the takeover."

"All right Denton, but are you certain that you want to do this. If someone tells Trevor about this we lose the element of surprise and tip Trevor off that he may need more votes."

"I'm aware of the risk mother. We can't even be certain that Carlton won't tell Trevor, but we are only two weeks away from the meeting. We have to play every angle now. I don't want to lose and still have some arrows left in my quiver. It will be all right. Paul has always been loyal to you and father when father was alive. He's a good man. He can pull this off. Tell him how many votes we need to win without Carlton. If anyone can get them Paul Henley can."

"I'll get right on it Denton." With that Mary Wellbon replaced the phone in its cradle. A smile crossed her face. This is exactly what she was going to do before she decided to see what Denton would suggest. Maybe he does have the guts and determination it will take to run this family empire. Mary picked up the phone again and called Paul Henley.

***

Over at Central Park West Susan was just coming down the circular stairs from the upper level of their co-op. She was dressed in a white soft terry cloth bathrobe with her hair wrapped in a white towel. She could hear Denton talking on the phone. He was slowly walking around the large living room. His voice held a tone that she had never heard before. It was the soft tone of authority. Denton was apparently speaking to Andy, the strange man that the Wellbon family all seemed to know from the diner. Then Denton ended the call and placed his cell phone on the hall table near the door. He looked up and spied Susan. He opened his arms and Susan moved to give him a reassuring hug. "That was Andy. He and his men are in Savannah. They will move to protect Crystal immediately."

"How will they do that?"

"Keep an eye on her as she goes about her daily routine, but if anyone makes a move to harm her they will do what's necessary."

"What does that mean?"

"They will use whatever methods are required to protect her."

"Even force?"

"These are violent men Susan, but they are on our side." Denton paused and then spoke again while Susan was considering the fact that she and Denton suddenly found themselves employing thugs from organized crime. "I told Andy that when this is over and we're certain that Crystal is safe, I want a meeting with the don."

Susan pulled back slightly. "Why?"

"I'm finding that father and grandfather were right. You can't always play by the book. When you are in a position like we are in there is always someone that wants to take away what you have. The only way that you stop them is by being stronger or by having friends that are stronger than your enemies are, Father always had something that men like these want. In that fashion he controlled them. I want to meet with the don and find out exactly what he wants. It's obvious that we control whatever it is."

Susan buried herself in his arms again. "I don't like the idea of you dealing with people like this Denton."

"Don't worry Susan. I'm beginning to understand how and why my grandfather and father, and yes even my mother was successful. They understood power and used it. Now I understand it too." Denton kissed the top of her head as he cuddled her in his arms. Denton was thinking that he was beginning to enjoy the way people were suddenly listening to him and giving deference to his suggestions, even his mother. He could hardly believe it. Yes, he would win this battle and he would run Wellbon – Smith as his father and grandfather had before him, with an iron hand and a will made of steel. Susan was thinking other thoughts, she was not certain that she liked this new found assurance that she heard and felt in her husband. He looked at and loved her the way he always had, but there was something new. A hard edge was creeping into his personality and it left her a little afraid. Not that she was afraid of Denton. She knew that he would never harm her. No for the first time in their life together she was afraid for them and their future.

Chapter 23

Duke Winston stood beside the battered pickup truck parked to the side of a dirt road on a remote part of Tybee Island. Tybee was twenty some miles from Savannah. Duke was on the mainland side. The Atlantic side had the beaches where all the resorts, beach houses and people were located. The dirt road where Duke found himself was surrounded by swamp and scrub pines. Civilization was the last thing that Duke wished to encounter on this night. The yellow harvest moon was rising off the Atlantic and cast odd shaped shadows across the roadway. Strange living sounds occasionally drifted up from the swamp but none of them bothered Duke. He had survived in the jungles of Southeast Asia and in truth the living creatures of the swamp that were making those sounds probably had more to fear from Duke than Duke did from them.

Duke straightened slightly as a pair of headlights rounded the bend that was about a quarter of a mile from his location. The headlights approached cautiously as if they weren't exactly certain where this road was going. Then about twenty yards from Duke's pickup the vehicle behind the lights pulled to a stop on the opposite brim of the road. The lights remained on for a few minutes after the motor had stopped. Then finally they too were turned off and the door on the driver's side opened. A tall lean figure in jacket and slacks approached. The figure stopped about 15 feet from Duke.

"Would you happen to be a man named Duke?" inquired the figure.

"I might be and who are you?"

"Albert Bernard."

"Well Albert I'm pleased to meet you. Yes I'm Duke, Abe Rueben sent me."

"I did as Mr. Rueben asked me to do. I pulled the private detectives I hired off Crystal Harrison."

To Catch a Fox

"Good job Albert."

"I hope Mr. Rueben wasn't displeased with the work we were doing for him down here."

"Not at all, he was very pleased with the way you kept track of Crystal twenty four hours a day without her getting suspicious."

"Is the job finished?"

"It is for you and your men Albert. I have other specialists with me to pick it up from here. Albert, Abe Rueben wanted me to make certain that he sent you enough to pay your men and give them a bonus to boot."

"Yes sir, he was very generous."

"Well Albert he asked me to give you your bonus personally."

"Mr. Rueben has done quite enough for me. Why did we have to meet way out here?"

"I won't bullshit you Albert. You and the people you hired were simply keeping an eye on the lady. In order to protect her, my people may have to break the law. Rueben didn't want you to be involved in that. We figured that the cops only come to this side of the island when they have to. As for your bonus the man insists on you having it Albert." Duke reached into his leather jacket pocket pulled out a manila envelope and tossed it to Albert. Albert caught it and opened the flap. He looked up at Duke and even in the dim light of the moon the surprise showed on his face.

"It's all cash! How much is in here?"

"Ten thousand, I told you Rueben was very pleased with your work."

"I don't know what to say. Tell Mr. Rueben thank you for me."

"I'll do that Albert. I surely will. Now you best be on your way. I suspect that even out here the cops show up once in a while and we don't want them asking us too many questions."

"Right, nice meeting you Duke."

"My pleasure."

Albert turned and began walking toward his car. Albert didn't hear the sound behind him, not that there was much to hear. He probably barely felt the three quick sledgehammer blows as the nine-millimeter slugs passed through his heart and out his chest. In one fluid motion Duke had filled his hand with the Walther nine millimeter semi automatic and the swip, swip, swip sound of the rounds leaving the silencer was all that disturbed the night. Just that quickly Albert lay dead in the middle of the dirt road, a pool of blood spreading around him.

Three other figures dressed like Duke in dark clothes emerged from the shadows. Duke strolled over to the crumpled body and removed the manila envelope that Albert still clutched in his right hand. Duke straightened up and turned to the others that had accompanied him to this desolate locale. For a few moments the sounds of the swamp had ceased, but now they were resuming again at their previous low level. "Everybody wearing gloves?" All responded in the affirmative to Duke's question. "You know what to do. Put the body in the car and push it off the edge over there into the swamp. We know that it's deep enough to be totally submerged there. Sweep away any trace of the tire tracks leading off the side of the road. By the time they find him the swamp critters will have pretty much made a meal of him. "You all got hairnets on? I don't want no DNA left behind," again a positive response. "Okay, get with it."

Duke returned to the pickup truck, climbed in behind the wheel and watched as his men worked quickly and efficiently. Rueben leaves no trail back to himself thought Duke. None of the private "dicks" that Albert hired had ever seen Rueben or knew who he was let alone who was meeting their payroll. He briefly speculated as to if or when Abe would think that he Duke knew too much. Would he be considered an expendable liability? Well, if and when Mr. Abraham Rueben tried that move he better be mighty quick and smart or Duke just might have a surprise for him.

Duke turned on the walkie-talkie feature on his cell phone and called another of his team. "Duke here. You got the girl under your watchful eye?"

"Roger, she just turned in for the night," was the reply.

To Catch a Fox

Duke tucked the semi-automatic pistol back into his jacket. The serial numbers had been filed clean. Later in the night he would dispose of the weapon miles from this location and in a manner that would probably assure it never being found. There was a large splash from beyond the bank on the other side of the road as Albert's car sank slowly out of sight in the dark inky black water. Duke lit up a cigarette.

***

Abraham Rueben's secretary burst into his office. "Mr. Rueben, the police are here."

"Yeah, Mr. Rueben and we brought you a present." Sam Grabowski was on the secretaries' heels with a paper in his hand. Abe Rueben said nothing, raised his left eyebrow and took the paper from Grabowski's outstretched hand. He examined the search warrant silently for a long moment.

"Everything seems in order officer. What is it you expect to find?"

"Oh, you never can tell."

"Well, according to this you are still investigating Donald Kensington Cramer's death."

"Yep."

A uniformed policeman was waiting at Abe's office door. Sam turned to him, "Start with the security system. I want everything, cameras video chips everything."

"Don't let us bother you Mr. Rueben, we won't mess anything up for you. You just go right on with whatever it is you do here." Sam turned and followed the uniformed officer out the door.

Rueben watched Grabowski leave and stared at the open door for a long time. Then he turned to his secretary who was still standing beside his desk. "You may return to your duties Ms. Bauman, and please close the door on your way out." Ms. Bauman, looking very annoyed, did as her boss instructed. When he was alone Rueben looked again at the search warrant. What could they possibly want with the security system? That tape Duke worked over was clean they couldn't have found anything. Rueben pulled his cell phone from his jacket pocket. Soon there was a voice on the other end.

"Yeah Abe." It was Duke Winston's voice.

"Everything go as planned last night?"

"Like clockwork. We disposed of the excess baggage and have your 'bird' covered like a blanket."

"Sounds good Duke."

"Yeah."

"However, I have a problem on this end."

"What's your problem?"

"The police are here with a search warrant."

"Really?"

"Yeah really, they seem interested in the security system. Why would that be?"

"Did you give them the clean tape I gave you?"

"Yes, I thought that was supposed to remove all suspicion."

"Should have, but maybe they got lucky."

"What's that supposed to mean Duke?"

"Sounds like they might think we tampered with it."

"I thought it was clean Duke?"

"Nothing's perfect Abe."

"What the hell are they looking for Duke?"

"The original video chip I would guess. They want to see if we were smart enough to erase the original data."

Rueben was beginning to get angry. "Were we smart enough to do that Duke?"

"We were smart enough but I told my guy to preserve it in the original format."

"You what? You mean they're going to find a chip that shows all the activity that took place at that exit that night? You know what that links me to Duke! Duke I swear if I go down I'll take you down with me!"

"Relax Abe they're not going to find the original chip."

"What makes you so sure? They're taking the entire system."

"You think I'm stupid Abe?"

"I didn't no, but I just might be having second thoughts." Abe was becoming very irritated with his number one mechanic.

"I told you to relax. They're not going to find it because I have it Abe."

"Then destroy it immediately!"

"Sorry Abe, that chip is very incriminating for you. I plan to keep it in a safe place as insurance."

"What is it Duke? Suddenly you don't trust me?"

"Now Abe let's just say I want some insurance to be certain that I don't become excess baggage like Albert Bernard some day. Now you relax Abe, as long as you're straight with me you can trust me completely. I'll see to it that I'm the only one that knows what's on that chip. When you want us to make the next move on the bird, let me know." With that Duke was gone. Damn! Thought Abe. He's black mailing me! But I need him, especially now. Then with further thought Abe smiled. Of course Duke kept the chip. That's exactly what Abe himself would have done if he were in Duke's shoes. Besides he was relieved that officer Grabowski wasn't going to find what he was looking for.

He needed Duke to finish the Crystal Harrison affair for him. After that, well after that he would see if Mr. Duke is excess baggage. It was Abe Rueben's custom to deal with one situation at a time. Abe considered the immediate concern, that being the police in his building looking for anything that would put Donald Kensington-Cramer in this office the night of his death. He didn't know exactly what put them on to the security system. If Duke had the original video chip and Abe had the office redone in its entirety, Abe was convinced that the search and impounding of his security system would not present a problem. Ironic, thought Abe, this was one death that he was involved in that was truly self-defense. Because he didn't want to have to prove it he simply moved the body to point the investigation in a different direction. Now the police were in his building with a search warrant.

Having mentally dealt with the immediate problems Abe prepared to leave for his first appointment. It was with Denton Wellbon. After a day of not being able to contact him, he made an appointment with Denton's secretary for this morning. He had a bit of a surprise for Mr. Wellbon.

***

"Good morning Abe," Denton greeted Abe Rueben at the door of his office.

"Good morning Denton."

"I apologize that I couldn't get back to you yesterday Abe, but I was very busy."

"Think nothing of it Denton, your secretary was kind enough to block out some time for me this morning."

"I hope I haven't caused you any inconvenience Abe."

"Oh some inconvenience Denton, but nothing serious. Unfortunately I'm afraid that I'm the one that is about to inconvenience you."

"Interesting, have a seat Abe." Denton offered Abraham Rueben one of two matching leather wingbacks that sat flanking an antique coffee table in the corner of his office. The set was away from Denton's desk and the two chairs for guests that sat before it. Denton used this corner for a more intimate one on one meeting when he didn't want a desk between he and his guest. "How is it that you fear you will inconvenience me?"

"Well, I've discovered some information that you may find distressing and ultimately dangerous if it fell into the wrong hands."

"I appreciate you coming to me Abe. Ultimately I'll have to be the judge of how distressing and dangerous the information."

The tone of confidence in Denton's voice was new to Abraham Rueben and it caught Abe by surprise. He hesitated for a long moment while evaluating Denton. This was a different person than the one that had picked Abe up for his first New York meeting with Trevor Mason that rainy night back in June. Denton now met you eye to eye and didn't flinch. "Yes, that's correct of course Denton." Abe suddenly had an uneasy feeling. This visit was designed to put enough fear in Denton's mind to assure that he and his mother voted with Trevor. So why did Abe feel as if he should be on the defensive?

"What is it you have to tell me Abe?"

"There's no point mincing words. I've discovered that the girl that you had a one night stand with had a daughter." Abe opened his briefcase and pulled a manila envelope out. He started to open it to show Denton the birth certificates and make his case for Denton's parentage when Denton reached across and calmly took hold of his hand.

"I assume that you're going to tell me about Crystal Harrison." Abe was nearly speechless, a condition in which he seldom found himself. "I already know about Crystal Abe. She is a T.V. news anchor in Savannah Georgia. I'm convinced that she is my daughter, you don't have to make the case." Denton held Abe's hand in a firm grip for a long moment before releasing it. Abe had to regroup under the now withering gaze of Denton Wellbon.

"How did you know Denton?"

"After you and Trevor demonstrated that my secret was no longer a secret I decided to do a bit of research on my own. I do have a few resources you know.

I'm not penniless."

"No you certainly aren't Denton. May I ask how you discovered her existence?"

"No."

"Pardon me?"

"I said no Abe, my resources are my business." Denton's eyes narrowed and his gaze became cold. Had his mother been present at this moment she would have been shocked and then pleased as to how much he resembled his father.

Abe cleared his throat. "Of course Denton, of course, however, knowledge doesn't take away the risk. If those who we've determined are your enemies should ever discover this they would use it against you."

"No doubt Abe," Denton demonstrated little concern in his voice making Abe's level of concern elevate.

"Denton if this information fell into the wrong hands not only would it become public knowledge but your mother and your wife will also find out." Denton said nothing. Abe's suspicion began to grow. "Denton you told Trevor and me that you managed to convince your mother to vote our way for your benefit. You told us it had not been necessary to tell your mother the entire story."

"And so I did Abe. However, when I became aware that it's fairly certain that I have a daughter, I determined that it was only a matter of time before she decided to seek me out. Therefore it follows that my mother and wife will eventually learn the truth. I have to be ready for that and whatever consequences are a result."

Abraham suddenly had the sinking feeling that everything that he and Trevor had worked for was now spinning out of control. "Denton, are you telling me that you no longer care if your secret becomes public knowledge? Are you telling me that it no longer matters to you if your family learns the truth?"

"Oh it matters very much Abe. If I could somehow avoid all of this I would, but it seems highly unlikely to me that indefinite avoidance is possible."

To Catch a Fox

"Well it is Denton, it is."

"How so Abe? Explain this to me."

Abraham Rueben thought that he detected a patronizing tone in Denton's last comment. This conversation was becoming increasingly annoying and threatening. "I have a lot of influence Denton. You've committed the support of your mother and yourself to Trevor and me at the annual meeting. In return for that I can make certain that your secret remains a secret."

Denton broke off his intense scrutiny of Abraham Rueben and stared across the office and out the window for some time. Long enough that Rueben began to fidget, "Denton, trust me on this."

Denton jerked his attention back to Rueben. "You want me to trust you did you say? No Abe, I don't trust you because what you really meant just a moment ago is if I vote your way you wouldn't reveal my secret. You are blackmailing me in the same fashion as you are the owners of several of the other proxy votes that you've accumulated."

Abe's voice now dropped to a threatening growl. "Let's not forget Denton that you provided the information necessary to blackmail those people. You aren't exactly an innocent lamb in all of this. Don't force me to take drastic actions."

"Relax Abe. Mother and I are in your camp. Tell Trevor that plans are progressing as he envisioned them. I plan on being chairman of Wellbon – Smith after the annual meeting and of course I'll owe an eternal debt of gratitude to Trevor for putting me there. Translation: Trevor will be vice chairman and the power behind the throne. Furthermore we are all safe."

"What do you mean by 'we are all safe'?"

"Just like the recently ended cold war Abe. We both have enough knowledge that each of us possesses the ability to destroy the others. Therefore it doesn't make sense to betray one another. I just don't want you, Abe to think that I don't know what you are all about."

Abe Rueben hesitated and then stood up. "I think we are both clear on how things stand now Denton. Your family has many secrets. You know what you must do to keep them secrets. Am I correct?"

"You are correct Abe. And on your side you and Trevor now know that you must accommodate mother and me by living up to our agreement. You must do this because you both wish to stay out of jail. Is there anything else you wished to tell me?"

"Only that you remember that we would not be the only ones going to jail."

"As I stated before Abe, it would be mutual destruction and no one benefits from that. Would you like to say more?"

Nothing at all Denton," and with that Abraham Rueben left Denton alone in his office. Denton picked up the phone to report on the meeting to his mother.

***

"Denton knows of the girl? He knows she's his daughter?" Trevor Mason was incredulous. He was up out of his chair and around his desk in an instant to meet Abraham Rueben face to face. Upon leaving Denton's office Abe went immediately down the hall to Trevor's.

"Yes he knows. He even knows where she lives and works."

"How Abe? How could he have found out?"

"I'm not sure, but I have a hunch. Funny, I never thought that young Wellbon would have the nerve."

"What are you talking about?"

"I'll tell you when I find out for certain, but it doesn't matter now. Anyway, I'm not all that concerned that he already had knowledge. After all I went there for the purpose of telling him the exact same thing."

"So what are you concerned about?"

"His attitude. He's confident and self-assured. He acts and sounds like he's in control. He avoided me for a whole day and then through his secretary he chose the time and place of our meeting. I actually think that I was ambushed."

Trevor moved to the bar and considered what drink would be appropriate for ten thirty in the morning. He reached for the vodka as he decided on a Bloody Mary. He offered to mix one up for Abe, but Rueben declined. Abe had related every detail of the conversation to Trevor. "Well he's correct about the mutual destruction aspect. It behooves him as much as us to keep our mouths shut." Trevor finished mixing the drink and took a long sip. "Are you convinced that he is serious about continuing with the plan?"

"I'm suspicious about his mother being in our camp."

"You think he lied to us when he told us that she decided to support him when she realized that we nearly had enough votes and it wasn't necessary to reveal his secret to her."

"I think he told her everything. I think she's the source of this mutual destruction idea and she told him to be certain that he let's us know they are aware of it."

Trevor took another long sip. "Well all along we've known that Denton posed as much of a threat to us as we do to him. Unlike the others that we had secrets on, Denton was in on the scheme. If he blows the whistle on us he will surely do some time along side of us. But I never expected him to have the moxie to cast it up to us like that."

Abe stuffed his hands in his pockets. "As I said, I think the credit goes to Mary Wellbon. Now that is a problem. She could be a formidable adversary."

"Your suggestion is?"

Abe was silent for a moment and when he turned toward Trevor his eyes were like two dark voids. "I'm not allowing you to go into that board room in two weeks without having an edge."

"What kind of an edge?"

"Remember Chicago Trevor. Just like then you leave the details to me. The less you know of my actions the safer for us both."

"Abe, you know I didn't like what came down in Chicago."

"What do you think came down? You saw a few headlines, some people wound up in the hospital and you jump to conclusions."

"Those people just happened to be stockholders that planned to vote against my plan to sell the company."

"Yeah Trevor, lucky for us they changed their minds. I guess their close brush with death put a new prospective on things. But you made some big bucks off the deal and it got you noticed by Wellbon – Smith. I wouldn't complain about the circumstances if I were you."

"Okay, okay do what you think best, but I don't want any knowledge of your plans whatsoever…just one more thing. Keep yourself as distant from whatever happens as possible. I don't want anyone to work their way back to you or they'll eventually suspect me."

"Have I ever failed you Trevor, or for that matter, have I ever left a trail back to you for the cops to follow?"

"No Abe, you haven't."

"Then relax, we'll get what we want and Denton and mommy will be following along right behind us like sheep. I'll take care of everything Trevor. You just keep Carlton Smith on our side." Abraham Rueben left the office as Trevor was giving him a nod of reluctant permission.

***

Andy Bevilaqua sat in the atrium restaurant in the Savannah Marriott. Ironically he sat only two tables away from the table where Crystal Harrison met with Foster Harrison for the first time just five months ago. Of course Andy had no knowledge of this fact. He slept in this morning after arriving in Savannah late last night. His cousins, all soldiers for Don Luca, had arrived earlier and had set up a "command post" in a block of rooms at this hotel. They had reserved the largest room for Andy.

To Catch a Fox

Andy sipped his coffee and read the morning paper while he waited for his scrambled eggs and sausage to arrive. He knew it wouldn't taste nearly as good as Sid's back at the diner. But then Sid cooked everything in lard. The news was the same. Y2k everywhere you looked. Andy chuckled to himself. People buying generators, stocking up on canned goods, even buying chickens to lay eggs and to eat for god's sake. What was this world coming to? Denton had sent two of the Atlantic Corporation's programmers down to the diner and they set his computers up so that they could survive the turn of the century just fine. If Andy could survive it so could everybody else. Of course he did have some help, but everybody has to have a friend somewhere.

The cute young southern belle brought Andy's breakfast. "Here y'all go Hon," she drawled.

"Thanks," replied Andy. He admired her shapely behind as she sashayed away from the table. She can call me 'Hon' anytime she wants thought Andy.

Just then a commotion near the door caught Andy's eye. It was his cousin Tommy hurrying past the hostess toward Andy's table. Andy pulled out a chair for him and he quickly sat down. Tommy was short and lean. His thick black hair was slicked back in a D. A. hairstyle. He wore a black leather jacket, white tee shirt, black slacks and white socks with black loafers. The only thing missing were pennies in the loafers. Andy figured he was either imitating the Fonz from the old TV series or he was stuck back in the fifties. Andy was jealous of that thick head of hair, but he had no desire to copy the style.

"What's up Tommy?"

Tommy looked nervously back and forth in the crowded dining room. "She's already covered."

"What do you mean 'she's already covered'?"

"There's already guys on her."

"What guys?"

"How should I know? But they're out there and they got her covered with a freaking blanket."

"She doesn't know that she's being followed?"

"As near as I can tell she doesn't have a clue."

"Okay who are these guys? Did you or any of the boys recognize anyone?"

"No one. These are either local or they come from way out of town. I mean not even New York. These guys are mechanics. You can tell that by the way they run their stakeouts. When she's driving their tails switch off smooth as shit."

"How many?"

"We count ten."

"Ten? That many?"

"Yeah Andy. That many."

"No wonder the switch off on the tails is smooth, they got a freakin' army out there, and we don't know who they are." Andy paused in thought. "Shit!" Tommy just sat quietly as his superior and mentor considered the implications. "That means Rueben knows about the girl. They have to be his men, but where did he get them?"

"Chicago?"

"Maybe, but we pretty much know who's out there. If it were Chicago one of our guys would recognize somebody. I can't think the Chicago family has suddenly added ten new soldiers."

"What should we do Andy?"

Andy furrowed his brow in thought. "Pull back and you guys keep your distance from these operators. But don't let them out of your sight! Be sure to call me if anything happens. I'm callin' the boss. He's gonna be freakin' pissed." Tommy nodded and left to organize his troops. Andy pushed his eggs around on the plate. This is just great he thought. We got freakin' tails on tails. All we need to make this a real freakin' circus is to fall over the cops. This broad has more people interested in her than flies on a piece of shit. With that poetic thought Andy took his cell from his belt and placed the call that he dreaded. He punched in the don's number.

***

Duke Winston sat sipping a beer in his room. He and his men were staying in a Comfort Inn just off Interstate 95. He had ten men beside himself. They were split into three shifts of three each with one floater. The current shift had covered Crystal Harrison on her way to work and at this moment Duke was watching the lady herself present the evening news. Suddenly his ears perked up. Crystal's co-anchor, a man, was saying something more interesting to Duke than the news:

"Well Crystal I hear that you are going on vacation next week. Where are you off to?"

"I haven't decided yet, but wherever I go I'm going by myself and I plan on catching up on my reading. I may not even turn on a T.V."

"How long will you be gone?"

"Two weeks. Debbie Hilton will be sitting in for me." The banter continued but Duke had heard all that he needed to hear. He hit the mute button on the remote and grabbed his cell phone. Soon there was a voice on the other end.

"Evenin' Abe, I just stumbled onto a valuable piece of information. Thought you might be interested. Our 'bird' is going on vacation by herself for two weeks beginning next week. Isn't your meeting next week?"

"Close enough. If we want to make a move this couldn't come at a better time." Abe hesitated in thought for only a second. "Okay, it's a go."

Duke finished his beer. He would meet each shift as they came in to go over the plan. This had to work like clockwork. He took a deep breath. Damn it felt good to be back in action.

In New York, Abe Rueben snapped his cell phone closed. Good, he thought, we're nearing end game. With that he summoned his secretary on the intercom.

To Catch a Fox

"Send the gentleman in Ms Bauman." Ms. Bauman was working late once again. The firm paid her very handsomely but she did wish that her boss would keep more regular hours.

A tall man with an excellent tan and close-cropped white hair entered Rueben's office and closed the door behind him. Abe offered him a chair but he declined. "I'll stand, thank you."

"Very well, I appreciate you flying in from Chicago on such short notice."

"Not a problem. Your friends in Chicago send their regards."

"You can tell them that I have the highest regard for them also." The man nodded a silent response. With that Abe handed him a manila envelope. The man opened it and removed a photo and several sheets of paper. "All the information you need is there, including the location of the job that he is doing for me at this very moment."

"Looks complete."

"You must wait until this task that he is doing is completed."

"How will I know that?"

"I'll tell you."

The man reached into the envelope again. This time he extracted a neat bundle of cash, "Twenty thousand?"

"Yes," replied Abe. "As usual you'll get the balance upon completion. You may count it if you wish."

The white haired man replaced the contents in the envelope. "You never cheated me in the past. Any special requests this time?"

"No, I just want him dead. Quick and clean."

"It will be done." With that the man turned and left Abe's office. As the NYPD had essentially dismantled the building's security system after the Donald

Kensington-Cramer intrusion, Abe had little concern of people remembering this visitor over the many that entered the building and his office on a daily basis. Well, thought Abe, all that will remain to be done is to acquire and destroy the video chip, and that would soon be attended to. This turned out to be a very productive day.

***

“Okay Mason, you win. Sixteen million for Fox, but that’s it. I’m done. Not a penny more.” Both the resignation and irritation in Clint Matthew’s voice were more than evident. On the other end of the phone Trevor Mason smiled and took the time to put both feet up on his desk before answering. “Mason, did you hear me?”

“I hear you Matthews,” was Trevor’s calm reply. “I want details of the financing and I want a letter of intent.”

“Both are on the way. Will you at least give me a verbal agreement in principle?”

“Hell no not until I examine your proposal.”

“Okay, it’s my turn now Mason. You have twenty-four hours to respond to me as to your acceptance.”

“The hell I do. I’m the one selling. That puts me in control. I’ll take as long as I damned well please to look over your proposal.”

“Listen up Mason, if you don’t get back to me within that time frame the offer may expire!”

“Shit you say! Don’t threaten me Matthews. You and I both know that this offer is open as long as you want Fox. If you decide you don’t want it, then I just sell to someone else. It’s always nice talking to you.” With that the phone went dead and Clint Matthews was left with yet another reason to dislike Trevor Mason.

***

The year-end annual board meeting of Wellbon-Smith at its advanced date was just three days away. As Thanksgiving was only a week away New York City was already preparing for the Macy's Thanksgiving Day parade and the holiday season to follow. This year being the turn of the millennium would add to the excitement and the anticipated crowds that New Year's Eve would bring. But on this morning those events were the furthest from the things that were occupying the attention of the small group gathered in the combination den and office of Mary Wellbon's penthouse. The group included Mary, her son Denton and his wife Susan, William McLode and the addition of one Paul Henley. Mary explained the now critical role that Paul was playing in the fight for corporate control to McLode. Mac signaled his approval and asked Paul Henley directly how the vote count was shaping up.

Paul Henley was a slight bookish looking man. His fair hair was thinning on the top to the extent you could see right through it to his slightly tanned scalp. He adjusted his large horn rimmed glasses before answering. Mac did not need to be told that Henley was an accountant by profession. He somehow looked the part. "Actually Mr. MacLode it's about even by my estimate. That's assuming of course that everyone in this room will vote together."

"That's more than an assumption Mr. Henley," interjected Mac.

"Very well then, I have managed to secure enough additional votes for our side that we can win outright if Carlton Smith votes with us. I should tell you Mr. MacLode that I am also voting my considerable shares with you folks."

"I certainly appreciate that Mr. Henley and I'm certain everyone else in this room does also," responded Mac.

Mary Wellbon spoke up. "We all appreciate your loyalty Paul. I know that you didn't have much time, but you've done a bang-up job. Mac, I'm certain that you are wondering about Paul's comment that we are about even. I have Carlton Smith's verbal commitment to our side, but I quite frankly don't trust him. I told Paul to try to make up that short fall just in case Carlton bolts to the other side. I'll spare you the gory details, but Trevor and Abe are blackmailing him also."

Henley spoke again. "I've fallen just short of making up Carlton Smith's vote. If he goes with us we are way over the top."

"Suppose he doesn't go with us." It was Mary who inquired.

"Then we fall just short. Ironically, you are both in the same situation. Mason and Rueben have been continuing to buy votes with promises of buying all or a large portion of shareholder's stock back at above market value after they win control. They apparently believe that both of the Wellbons will bolt and they like you have been trying to make up the difference. Apparently they have been more successful than me as they are offering cash and I'm appealing to loyalty. It's good that we were able to shorten the time in which they have to work."

"No more blackmail Denton?" asked Mary.

"Apparently not, since my meeting with Abe we are all on a cordial basis, but have not discussed the takeover in nearly a week."

Mary looked at Mac. "They don't know which way your funds are voting because they haven't a clue as to who controls them."

Denton spoke, "They assume that the fund vote will go against them."

"So would I if I was them," answered Mary. "They also assume that both of us are lost no matter what we told them."

Henley responded. "As you are short without Carlton, Mason is just a little short with him but without one of you."

Mac smiled and shook his head. "So it all hinges on Carlton Smith."

"Yes," said Mary, "or on one of us bolting."

Denton looked shocked, "Mother, why would you say such a thing? Mac isn't going to bolt, I know you won't and you certainly don't think that I will do you?"

Mary looked at Denton. "I think you need to fill Mac in on the discovery you made this past week Denton."

"Is that absolutely necessary mother?"

"Yes." She gave no other explanation.

Denton sighed. He might as well assume that he had no privacy any longer.

To Catch a Fox

"Here's the story Mac."

When Denton finished Mac leaned back in his chair in thought. After a few moments he turned again to Mary. "Knowing Abe Rueben's past I assume that you expect a threat on the girl."

"Yes."

"Mother, Andy has her covered."

"I know that's what he's told you, but I trust no one when it comes to maintaining control of the company in this family."

Suddenly Denton was out of his chair, his face suddenly flushed. "Mother, you expect me to bolt?" Susan reached for Denton's arm, but he yanked it away.

Mary remained calm as she stared up at her son, the son who was beginning to remind her more and more of his father. "No, but I want you to be aware that Rueben and Mason now realize that they are in a fight. It's obvious that between Paul, at our instruction, and Abe on the other side, that most of the major stockholders have been contacted. Neither side has the element of surprise available. They can do the math as well as we can. They no doubt know that I will go down fighting; therefore you are the only one who they may be able to get to. Just be aware that they will try son."

"They can't get to me. I have complete confidence in Andy and his men." Denton turned to Mac. "Mac, you've known the don. Do you believe they will fail?"

Mac turned to Mary, "Much as I love the old man, I have to admit that violence is not beneath him. I agree with Denton that I feel better that he and Andy are on our side."

"Just be aware Denton," was all that Mary Wellbon would say.

Across town another meeting was taking place in Trevor Mason's office. It was once again between Abe Rueben and his client Trevor Mason. The purpose was the same, to count votes. "Damn, all the work we've done and if one of the Wellbons fail to vote with us we fall just short."

"I've tapped out all of the shareholders who are willing to trade shares for an inflated stock value Trevor."

"Yeah and each one means we stretch our credit line even further, but we have to play to win. Losing isn't an alternative. Damn it Abe, we've got to have at least one of the Wellbons vote with us."

"That will be Denton."

"I'm convinced it won't be Mary."

"She may come along when she realizes that we're going to win. She will want to be on the winning side."

"How can you be so sure of Denton, after the meeting you had with him?"

Abe smiled his crooked smile. "Are you certain of Carlton Smith?"

"Yeah, he's scared stiff of going to jail."

"Well I'm certain that I'll have Denton in my pocket by Thursday morning when the meeting begins. With Smith and Denton we're over the top."

"How?"

"Leave that to me Trevor."

"I have no choice do I?"

"Like you said, losing is not an option."

***

Crystal Harrison had her bags packed and loaded in her Jaguar convertible. The car was parked down on the street on the northeast corner of Lafayette Square outside the house where Crystal lived. Crystal loved the second floor apartment she found in this beautiful old Victorian style mansion. Lafayette Square was one of twenty-two picturesque historic squares in the heart of Savannah's historic district.

To Catch a Fox

After her trip to New York she returned to Savannah and decided to focus on the life that she was building for herself and put the past behind her. Her producer told her that she was now doing the best work of her career. She found this new apartment and she was enjoying an occasional luxury like the new convertible parked outside. The mysterious trust fund allowed her to indulge. Whatever her mother's mysterious past, whatever her real father's identity, Crystal was coming to grips with the fact that she may never know the truth. She was no longer certain that she wanted to know her father's identity. It was obvious that he was very powerful and from what her grandparents told her not very nice. He would go to any length to protect himself. Crystal decided to occasionally spend some of the money he gave her and move on with her life. She was so looking forward to this vacation.

She was going over her checklist for the last time to make certain that there was nothing that she forgot to do before leaving for the airport and her two weeks on one of Mexico's sunny beaches. She had the post office hold her mail, she stopped the newspaper; she was working her way down the list when suddenly the front door bell rang. Who could be calling now? All of her friends and co-workers knew she was leaving today. Whoever it was she couldn't waste time, she really had to leave for the Airport.

Crystal opened the door into the hallway and discovered a deliveryman with a large box on a bag wagon. "Yes?" she asked her puzzlement sounding in her voice.

"I'm looking for a Ms. Crystal Harrison."

"I'm Crystal Harrison."

"Delivery for you ma'am."

"Delivery? I don't think so there must be some mistake. I've not ordered anything."

"This is the address and you just told me that you're Crystal Harrison."

"Who's it from?"

To Catch a Fox

"L.L. Bean."

"I haven't ordered anything from L. L. Bean."

The man looked slightly exasperated. "Ma'am please, I have other deliveries to make. How about if you and L. L. Bean argue this out later and let me make my delivery and get on my way. There's no money due."

Crystal looked at her watch. "Very well, bring it in I have to be leaving for the airport. Where do I sign?"

The man pushed the bag wagon into the apartment. "Right here ma'am," he said and handed her an electronic clipboard. "Just use this stylist and sign your name anywhere on the bottom section." As Crystal turned her attention to signing her name the hypodermic needle plunged into her left shoulder. Shocked she cried out as she instinctively tried to pull away. But strong hands held her until the contents of the needle emptied into her body. "Now that wasn't too bad was it little lady?" The fake deliveryman had a broad smile on his face.

Crystal twisted free clutching her arm. "What? Who are youuu?" she cried out just before crumpling to the floor unconscious.

"I got her, get up here and give me a hand." The deliveryman spoke into a walkie-talkie that he pulled from his belt. Soon two other men appeared at the apartment. They opened the large empty box and carefully placed Crystal's limp form into it. They then systematically went through the apartment until they found her purse. In her purse were her car keys and her airline tickets. Being careful to leave everything as they had found it, they locked up the apartment and using the bag wagon took the box and its contents down the combination freight / handicapped elevator in the rear of the building. That way they avoided the front staircase where they might run into the owner or another tenant.

Duke Winston sat across the square in his pick up truck. Beside him was a young woman who from a distance bore a remarkable resemblance to Crystal Harrison. They watched as the three men brought the box out from the alley and loaded it into the delivery truck parked in front of Crystal's Jaguar. "What's in the box?" asked the girl beside Duke.

"Just some stuff we had to pick up here." Duke answered rather off handedly.

The girl correctly figured that it was none of her business. When the box was loaded and the truck secured, one of the men walked across the square to Duke's pick up. Duke rolled down the window on the driver's side and without a word the man handed Crystal's purse to him. Then the man joined the other two in the delivery van and they drove off down the street.

The girl watched Duke as he rummaged around the purse. He located Crystal's wallet, removed her drivers license and passport, replacing them with another of each. He then replaced the wallet in the purse and handed the purse to the girl. "The wallet has a Georgia driver's license with your photo and the name of Crystal Harrison on it. It also has a passport made the same way, don't worry they are perfect fakes. No airline check in person will be able to detect any problem with it. There are also several legitimate credit cards under the same name. If I were you I'd practice a signature similar to the real Crystal's on the back. Few people compare but it pays to be careful. Close should be good enough. There are airline tickets in the purse, hotel and rental car reservations and a car full of cloths that should fit you sitting across the street." Duke handed over the keys to the Jag.

The girl checked out the airline tickets. "I'm going to Guadalajara, Mexico for two weeks?" she squealed.

"Yeah, stay out of trouble."

"And that's the car?" The excitement in her voice raised another octave as she noticed the Jaguar emblem on the key chain and realized it must belong to the car across the square.

"Yeah and make certain that you put it in long term parking at the airport. I don't want it getting towed away before you return."

The first expression of concern began to cloud the girl's face. "Is this the Crystal Harrison I'm impersonating? The one on Channel 3?"

"That's the one."

"But what if someone asks me if I'm really her, I can't pass for someone that everyone sees on the television every night."

To Catch a Fox

"Just tell them that you get that a lot. That's why I had the license made with your picture on it. Tell them you just happen to have the same name. Look here's the scoop, but you've got to keep this a secret. Understand?" The girl nodded her head. "The real Crystal is going undercover to get a story, a big story. You have to keep her cover by making it look as if she really is going on vacation like she's been telling all her listeners on T.V. Got it?"

"Wow, yeah I got it. Wow! All I have to do is go on vacation?"

Duke grinned. "That's all you have to do. Okay now here's some spending money." Duke gave her a sealed envelope. "There's five thousand in cash in there. I'll give you five thousand more when you return in two weeks. I'd use the cash before I use Crystal's credit cards. Use the cards for the hotel and rental car only. Got it?"

"Yes sir and thanks, thanks a lot!"

"Get going now, you need to get to the airport with plenty of time to check in. The flight leaves at eleven this morning."

"I'm on my way!" With that the girl sprang from Duke's pick up and ran across the street to the Jag. Duke watched as she drove away. She was a stripper that he found in a joint out in Chatham County. She's a good-looking girl he thought. It's a shame I'll have to kill her when she gets back. Duke pulled a pack of cigarettes from his jacket and lit one up. Blowing smoke out the still open window, he started the old truck and slowly drove away. Everything was going as planned.

***

Andy's cousins and they were all his legitimate cousins, stood before him in his suite at the Marriott. No one wanted to look Andy directly in the eye. "Let me see if I understand this. A girl that looked like Crystal Harrison got out of a pickup truck that was driven to Crystal's apartment by one of Rueben's mystery operatives."

"We don't know for sure that they work for Abe Rueben Andy."

"Shut up when I'm talkin'! Who else would they work for?" Andy let out an unintelligible growl that made his companions huddle even closer together. "This ringer for Crystal then gets into Crystal's car and drives away…Well, yes or no?"

"Can we answer?"

"Oh hell yes, that's why I asked a question because I want the damn answer you dip shits!"

Tommy spoke up. "That's the way it happened Andy."

"How do you know it wasn't Crystal?"

"Because we saw Crystal go into the house after she put her luggage in her car and she never came out."

"How do you know that she's not still in her apartment?"

Tommy looked nervously at his fellow soldiers and then answered Andy. "Because we went into the apartment after everyone else left." Tommy waited for Andy's wrath to befall him.

"Did you break in?"

"Well, we picked the lock, we didn't break anything honest."

"You're sure you didn't leave any prints?"

"Come on Andy, we're not stupid. We wore gloves."

"What did you find?" Andy's voice was more civil once again.

"The apartment was empty. I mean there was furniture and stuff but no one was there."

Andy ran his hand back over the top of his bald head. "Tell me about this delivery truck that stopped in the middle of all of this."

"It was just a delivery van with a package on a bag wagon. We don't even know if it was going to Crystal's apartment or to another in the building."

To Catch a Fox

"Bag wagon, it took a bag wagon to handle this package?" Andy suddenly believed that he was on the trail. "How big was this package?"

Tommy indicated a size by extending his hand at least 50" above the floor. Andy looked at the hand for a long moment. "How big around was the box?" Tommy indicated by forming a rough circle with his arms. "Give me a size!" Andy's voice was rising again.

"Okay Andy, about 24" x 24" and at least 60" high."

"They brought the box back out to the truck without delivering it?"

"Well yeah, I guess they did."

Andy muttered to himself. "That's big enough to have Crystal Harrison inside. They snatched her. Did anyone follow the delivery truck?"

"Ah, no Andy."

"No? You freakin' guys! Did anyone follow the pickup truck?"

"Yes," said Tommy. "It went to a motel outside of town."

"You have someone watching this guy that drives the old truck?"

"You know it."

"Then let's hope and pray that this hot shot decides to pay a visit to the place where they've stashed Crystal. Don't you guys dare leave this jerk out of your freakin' site. Understand?"

"Understood boss."

"Good, now get out of here!"

Tommy got some of his courage back. "Should we try to find the girl that left in Crystal's car?"

"Why? You already told me that you are certain she's not Crystal so who cares where she went. She's just a decoy! We're here to keep Crystal safe and so far a troop of Boy Scouts could have done a better job! Now go!" Everyone scrambled to get out of Andy's room. Andy shook his head. How was he going to tell the don about this?

***

The figure dressed in dark sweat pants and sweat shirt had an equally dark ski mask pulled over his head. He moved silently and cautiously through the tables and chairs that were evenly spaced around the bar room. The large room was totally dark except for the light from the street lamps that streamed through the windows casting eerie shadows along the floor. It was three thirty in the morning. The bar had been closed since two and the bartender had locked up a half hour later. Now the building was totally deserted. When he reached the bar he placed his hand on the smooth molded edge and followed it through the gloom until he came to the wall. He felt along the wall until he found the doorway that he had remembered from past evenings spent in this establishment. This was the office door and like the side door that opened into the alley it was locked. But the door to the alley didn't keep the intruder at bay for long and neither would this door.

Pulling a leather case from his pocket he removed some slender tools from it and inserted them in the keyhole. The lock yielded without a struggle. During his college days he had a summer job with a company that sold and installed safes and were also locksmiths. The tricks that he learned there proved to be valuable on certain occasions. This was one of those occasions. Unlatching the door he moved to the hinge side and pressed his back against the wall before cautiously pushing the door open. A single loud snap echoed through the building. In the center of the doorway there was now a one-inch diameter wooden spear with pointed end sticking about four feet out of a hole in the threshold. The spear was spring loaded so that it shot upward out of the floor when the door was opened. The man walked cautiously around the spear noticing that he shuddered slightly as he passed it. He was aware that the owner of this establishment was well schooled in the art of setting booby traps. That's why he was watching unseen from a sky light in the roof as the bartender, a loyal friend of the owner's, locked up and set the traps. He had already disarmed one at the door he used for entrance. That one was particularly nasty as a trap door in the floor opened up to reveal several daggers pointed toward the ceiling with their handles firmly secured in wooden planks. The unsuspecting intruder would have fallen through the trap door onto them. This one made two and he knew there was one more.

Moving slowly and deliberately across the office he came to the desk. In the same manner in which he worked his way around the bar the intruder moved around the desk. Behind the desk was a large portrait of a naked woman lying on a sofa. He carefully removed the painting from the wall. This revealed a flush mounted wall safe. Now it was time for a little light on the subject. Taking a pen light from his pocket he aimed the small beam of light at the safe. Being very familiar with safes he recognized that this model was rather old with a combination lock. The lock would be no problem. These old safes had noisy tumblers. He continued to shine the pen light over the surface of the safe door when he spied it. A small caliber hole was just below the combination lock dial; that wasn't supposed to be there. The man expertly and carefully felt around the outside edge of the safe door. There it was a small notch along the right side large enough to get your one finger in. If you didn't feel it you might think it was a knot in the paneling.

The intruder took a deep breath and carefully put his finger in the hole and pulled. The small section of paneling came out revealing a small compartment with a stainless steel pin extruding from the side of the safe. The man studied the pin carefully, he pulled on it but it would not move. Then he pushed on it and it slid nearly flush into the side of the safe. That must be it. Pulling out a stethoscope he pressed the face against the door and slowly turned the dial while listening for the tumblers to fall into place. When the last number clicked in it was the moment of truth. Keeping his head below the level of the safe door he very carefully began opening it. When the door was entirely open he ventured a look inside. There pointed directly at him was a small caliber gun attached to a very complex mechanism. When the door was closed the barrel lined up exactly with the hole under the combination lock dial. The intruder inspected the set up and determined that on the second spin of the dial the gun should have fired. It would have except that the steel pin that was hidden behind the paneling disarmed the mechanism.

It didn't take long to find the video chip. Duke Winston was so confident that his booby traps would catch any trespasser in his bar that he made no attempt to conceal the chip inside the safe. The intruder smiled to himself and tucked the chip safely in his pocket. Taking Duke's friend and bartender out on the town one night was one of the smartest things he ever did. When the man got a few drinks in him you couldn't shut him up.

To Catch a Fox

By four forty five the intruder had all of the traps reset, the doors locked and he was out in the alley where he entered. At nine the bartender would return, disarm the traps and never know that anyone was there. After making certain that there was no one around Abe Rueben removed the ski mask from his head and strolled down the alley toward the street. He had carefully parked his car several blocks away, but it was beginning to get just a little light in the east and the walk would be pleasant in the cool autumn air. Abe seldom did his own dirty work, but he had trusted too many people of late. That meant too many people knew too much. That was all about to change and this little escapade was the first step.

Chapter 24

Denton Wellbon stopped at the coffee machine on his way to his office. As he filled his cup he noticed an overnight deliveryman at his secretary's desk. She was signing for a package. As he passed her desk she handed it to him. "Good morning Mr. Wellbon, this just came for you."

"Thank you and good morning to you too Emma." Denton entered his office and tossed the packet on the desk. He booted up his computer and sat down sipping his coffee. After answering a few e-mails he listened to his messages on the answering machine and made notes as to which he must return calls. He checked his appointments and discovered that his day was fairly free with the exception of a morning appointment with Abe Rueben. His secretary had filled it in and Denton couldn't help wondering what Abe wanted after their last meeting. This would probably be the last minute pressure that Denton's mother had warned him about. If so he was prepared for it. Strange, he expected both Trevor and Abe to make a double barrel assault. Anyway he would find out soon enough. He wondered if his mother was making any progress on cementing Carlton Smith's vote. Then he remembered the packet.

He opened it and dumped the contents out. What was this? There in front of him were several photos of a young woman bound, gagged and blindfolded. A copy of yesterday's Savannah newspaper was draped over her. "What is this?" Denton called out loud. Then the last item to fall out of the packet caught his eye. Denton picked it up "Oh my god!" Denton's hands began to tremble. He suddenly felt sick to his stomach. The item in his hand was a Georgia driver's license. The photo on it was obviously the girl that was bound and gagged. If that wasn't disturbing enough the name on the license was, Denton swallowed hard as he broke out in a cold sweat, it was Crystal Harrison's. He dropped the license on the desk as if it had burned him.

"Mr. Wellbon." It was Emma on the speaker. Denton didn't hear her or rather it didn't register. "Mr. Wellbon, Mr. Rueben is here to see you."

"What? Oh yes, send him in." Denton answered absently, not realizing what he was actually saying his mind was racing still looking at the license that lay before him. He checked the envelope there was nothing else in it. He had to think.

"Denton?" Abe Rueben was standing over Denton's desk. When Denton looked up it was obvious that he was flustered. That's more like the Denton I know thought Abe. "What's this on your desk?" Denton didn't answer he was still reeling. Where was Andy? He was supposed to keep an eye on her. Rueben picked up the photos and the license. "Denton," he said. "This is your daughter."

Denton gripped the arms of his chair. He slowly raised his eyes and met Rueben's. "Abe, if you had anything to do with this, I swear I'll…"

"You'll what Denton? First don't jump to conclusions. Where did you get these?" There was nothing sympathetic in Abe's voice as he tossed the photos and the license back onto Denton's desk.

Denton glared at Abe. "They were delivered this morning by a parcel service. How do I know that this is my daughter?"

Abe opened his briefcase and took out the envelope that Denton wouldn't look at the other day when they met. "If you look in here you will see that the photos that I had to show you are of the same girl, besides there is the driver's license."

Denton riffled through the contents of Abe's envelope. It was obvious that it was the same girl. Suddenly Emma was calling again. "There's a strange call for you Mr. Wellbon."

"Not now Emma."

"It's a man who won't give me his name. But he said to tell you that he just wanted to verify that you received that package I gave you this morning. He has a very strange sounding voice."

Denton turned pale. He looked at Ruben whose face held no emotion. "I'll, I'll take the call Emma."

"Put it on speaker," said Abe.

Denton determined that wasn't the best idea so he picked up the receiver. "Denton Wellbon."

"Listen good Wellbon because I don't take questions I ask questions. You got the packet?" The voice sounded slightly metallic so Denton decided that the caller was using some sort of device to disguise it.

"Yes."

"We know Harrison is your daughter. We know that isn't common knowledge. We want five million in thirty-six hours. I'm certain that you can figure out what will happen if you fail to meet our demands."

"I can't get that…" Denton's voice was hoarse.

"Shut up! I told you to listen, five million in thirty-six hours! Don't call the cops because we've arranged it so that she doesn't appear to be missing. I'm sure that neither of us wants the kind of media attention that her abduction would generate. Now you get the money and I'll contact you and tell you what to do with it. If you don't, well I'll say it again; you can figure out what will happen to your daughter." The phone went dead.

Abe tilted his head slightly to the side as Denton slowly hung up the phone. "Well?"

Denton closed his eyes. "They want five million in thirty-six hours."

"You've got it."

"Not in cash!"

"You've got enough assets to borrow against." Abe paused for affect. "Of course you don't have to do anything. You don't know her and she has no idea who you are. You just asked me how you could be certain she was your daughter. This isn't someone that you raised. You only recently discovered that she exists at all. You can tell the kidnappers to go to hell."

"She'll eventually find out who I am, then what will she think of me?"

"If you don't pay the five million those idiots could solve the whole problem for you." Abe was gambling. He was aware how the Wellbons felt about family.

A stunned look of disbelief appeared on Denton's face as he realized what Abe was suggesting. First Andy and now Abe. "You, you mean I should let them kill her?"

"She's an attractive girl. They'll probably entertain themselves with her as a consolation prize for the risk they took. Her last few hours won't be pleasant but what do you care?" Abe wanted to paint as horrible a picture in Denton's mind as possible. In that he was devastatingly successful.

Abe's face was as cynical as Denton had ever seen it. The fact of the matter was that in the short time since he had learned of Crystal's existence he really had come to care. He found himself doing homework to find out as much as he could about Savannah's number one evening news anchor. She was quite the young lady. Denton had already acquired several promotional photos from the television station's web site of Crystal. He was certain of her identity even before his inquiry. Denton was surprised at the feelings of pride and more that had been stirring in him over the past twenty-four hours. The knowledge of paternity stirred some instinctive primeval desire to protect in normal human beings.

"No Abe, no! It was the result of my careless fling that she exists at all. She hasn't a mother to turn to, and I could have had a hand in her mother's suicide without even knowing. Besides if I weren't who I am these hoodlums never would have kidnapped her in the first place. I've failed her all my life without ever knowing it. I won't fail her now. Now that I know who she is and that she's my daughter. How could these thugs know?"

Abe ignored that question and satisfied that Denton was in the proper frame of mind sat down in one of the chairs across from Denton's desk. "So you want her freed?" His tone was nonchalant.

"Yes, unhurt if possible. Abe, planned or not even though I've known nothing of her all these years, she is still my daughter." Denton couldn't say it enough.

Abe reached inside his suit jacket and rubbed his ribs. Even though some time had passed they still bothered him on occasion. "Very well, if that's what you want I might be able to help you Denton."

"How?" Denton's thoughts were clearing slightly from the initial shock. He was extremely suspicious of Rueben.

Abe settled back in the chair. "I know you don't like me Denton. I know that you think I'm behind this. I'll be honest with you, I won't hesitate to use this as leverage to get what I want, but I can help you free Crystal safely and you won't have to part with the five million."

"It's not the five million I'm worried about. Again I ask how?"

"From the moment that I discovered you had a daughter I've had her watched by an ex cop friend of mine."

"You had her followed?" Denton was getting confused and irritated. Why did he have to play twenty questions? Why couldn't Rueben just tell him what happened?

"Yep, he and some local help that he recruited. We watched her round the clock."

"Then they saw her being kidnapped?"

"That's right."

"Why didn't they stop it?"

"They tried. At least my friend tried to stop them."

"What happened?"

"I think they must have killed my friend and disposed of the body. I haven't heard from him in two days."

"Good grief!"

"Yeah he was a good guy. He worked out of Baltimore."

Denton shook his head. Now someone had died. "Have you called the local police?”

“Yeah, I reported him missing.” Abe certainly didn’t seem too overcome with grief thought Denton.

“If your friend is dead how can you help?”

“I know you think this hard to believe but I have other friends. My friends are the kind of men that know how to play rough.”

Denton’s frustration level was rising. “Again I ask; how can you help?”

While it never showed on his face, Abe was smiling inside. He was playing Denton just the way he wanted. “My friends know where they have Crystal. That's why I'm here this morning.”

“We should call the police!”

“Denton! Do you have a brain? Hello! You and I are both tangled up with Mason in a corporate take over that involves blackmail. Blackmail is illegal. Must I remind you of your ‘mutual destruction’ comment? Did it ever occur to you that I might not be responsible for this but one of your other enemies might be? Someone that figured out that you are the only person that had any dirt on them for us to use, someone that might be out for money and revenge. If I could find out about Crystal why do you think no one else could? If I’m right and the cops bust them, guess who they’re going to take down with them?”

Denton held his head in his hands. Until thirty minutes ago he thought that he had things under control but now everything seemed to be spinning in every direction. “So what will your friends do?” He finally asked.

“Simple, they’ll free her.”

“Won’t that involve violence?”

“Well gosh Denton it might!” Abe’s voice was mocking Denton. “But won’t letting them rape and kill her be a bit violent too? I suspect these people aren’t into being humane.”

Denton sat up straight again and stared at the nonchalant figure seated across from him. From the first evening that he and Rueben met, Denton had disliked the man. Now the longer he knew Abe the easier it was to despise him. "And the price that I have to pay for this rescue is to vote with you and Trevor at the meeting tomorrow."

"That's what I meant by getting what I want. It's an ill wind that blows no one good Denton." Abe smiled his crooked smile.

"I already told you that's how I was going to vote. Mother too."

"Yeah well Trevor believes that, I don't. But if you were actually being straight with us then this is really a freebie."

"How do I know that you didn't set this whole thing up so that you could pressure me? That this is just an insurance policy for my vote."

Abraham Rueben stood up and began to laugh. "You really are the suspicious one aren't you? Okay Denton, I'm not going to justify that question with an answer. But let's be realistic. The bottom line is what difference does it make? Your options are such. One: You don't pay the ransom and allow them to kill your daughter. Two: You trust me and allow me to have my friends rescue Crystal. Three: You pay the ransom and hope these thugs keep their word. In most cases they don't. In most cases they would rape and kill her and run with the money. Why risk the possibility of her being able to identify them? It doesn't matter who's behind the kidnapping Denton the options and results for you are the same. Now which option makes the most sense to you? Play ball with Trevor and me tomorrow, I see to it that we rescue your daughter from the bad guys, she still is ignorant of your identity and you become chairman of Wellbon – Smith. Now to me that sounds like a win, win, win Denton."

"When will you do this?"

"Right after you vote the correct way."

"Damn you Abe! You could have your friends free her now couldn't you?"

"Sure but I'm not stupid! The thirty-six hours won't be up when we vote tomorrow. As soon as we have the company locked up I'll make the call."

"How will I know that she's safe?"

"When I tell you so! Later when she reappears on Savannah's six and eleven o'clock news. Who knows she might even do a story on her mysterious abduction and rescue. It could all turn out to be good for her career."

Denton's mind was racing. Surely Andy was on top of this, but if for some reason he wasn't then what? He told Abe and Trevor that he was voting with them anyway. It was a lie of course so what's the harm in one more lie, especially if it could save Crystal? Denton shook his head slowly back and forth. "Okay Abe, I have no choice. I've already told you that I'm voting with you and Trevor, but you won't believe me. I'll state it again. Mother and I are voting with you, but now that this issue has come up I'll only vote your way if you rescue Crystal."

"I like the terms." Abe allowed himself another smile.

"Abe if I ever find out that you had a hand in this, I'll…"

Abe lunged across the desk as quickly as a mountain cat brings down a deer. He grabbed Denton by the lapels.

"That's the second time you've threatened me this morning, so now you listen up!" Abe was nearly pulling Denton up out of his chair. "Threats mean nothing to me Denton, only deeds. So far you don't score too high on the deed meter. The next time you even think about threatening me you better check out if you have the guts to take me on. Don't talk about it do it! Are we clear on that point Denton?"

Denton pried Abe's clenched hands from his lapels. "Yes Abe, quite clear. Just get Crystal back alive."

Abraham Rueben released Denton and straightened his tie for him. "It will be done Denton when you vote correctly tomorrow." With that he turned to leave but on an impulse he paused and turned back before opening the door. He wanted this last comment to be private too. "I don't know how much you know about me Denton, but my firm has always practiced in New York. My recent hiatus in Chicago was a temporary interruption to my personal practice."

Denton wondered where this was going. "What has this to do with anything Abe?"

"I'm a New Yorker, it's my home town. I know a lot of people here."

"Me too, I'm missing your point."

"My point is that in the past I too have worked with Andy down at the diner." Abe noted that Denton's face seemed to tense, the kind of tense that you demonstrate when you're trying hard not to show any emotion. That alone was enough reaction to answer the question that had been haunting Abe.

"Andy?" Denton replied hoping that his tone conveyed ignorance. In Abe's mind it did not.

Abe smiled. "I found him and his don to be grossly incompetent. I certainly wouldn't bet the farm on them." With that Abe left and closed the door behind him.

Denton stared after him for several minutes. He picked up the phone on his desk and then thought better of it. Putting the receiver back on its cradle he opened his cell phone. "Mother, we need to talk. Your place as soon as I can get there." Upon ending that call Denton grabbed his briefcase and as he passed Emma's desk he told her to have his driver meet him in front of the building and that he was out for the day.

"Yes sir, Mr. Wellbon." Emma was indeed puzzled. Denton Wellbon put in more hours behind his desk than any other executive in the Atlantic Corporation. She was also mystified because she was certain that she heard muffled yelling behind the closed door of Denton's office when Mr. Rueben was in there. She hoped that all was well for Denton. His face bore the expression of a troubled man just now. The administrative staff all agreed that he was the nicest of the executives at Atlantic. Only John Hogg was any competition for that title. Certainly not Trevor Mason or Betsy Michaels; she sighed and returned to typing letters.

Denton's driver had the car in front of the building by the time he reached the ground floor. It was a standard Lincoln limo wheelbase. Not a stretch. After giving his driver his mother's address he closed the privacy window between the driver's compartment and the rear section and got on his cell phone. Soon it was

Andy on the other end.

"Andy what the hell is going on?" Denton then explained about the packet that arrived, the phone call from the abductors and the visit from Abe Rueben.

Andy sighed. "They were here when we arrived. They're pros all right. They ran the snatch like a military operation."

"Did anyone try to stop them?"

"You mean any of my guys? I'm telling you Denton it was so slick that we only realized what had happened after it was over and they were gone."

"No one was killed during the kidnapping?"

"Not that we know of, why?"

"No reason. Do you know where they are hiding her?"

"We're on top of that Denton."

"What does that mean Andy? Do you know or don't you?"

"Not yet but we should know tonight."

"For sure?"

Andy swallowed hard. That was the exact question the don asked when the two of them had this same conversation. "For sure Denton."

"Can you rescue her safely?"

Again Andy paused while thinking of the skilled mechanics that he was apparently up against. "Yes Denton we can and we will."

"Andy the annual meeting is tomorrow at ten in the morning. You have until then. Otherwise I'll have to vote against mother and with Trevor Mason so that Abe Rueben will rescue her."

"Denton these are Rueben's men for god's sake. Of course he can rescue her. All he has to say to them is 'let her go.'"

"Even so I have no choice. If I don't vote with Mason they'll surly kill her. Remember Andy you and the don want to renew the relationship that you enjoyed with my father. I'm telling you that to do business again with Wellbon – Smith you have to get me good results tomorrow. I'll never be able to reactivate that arrangement if I have to deal with Mason and Rueben."

Andy paused for a long moment. He knew that Denton was right. The don and Rueben would never work together after Rueben aligned himself with the Chicago mob. The only thing that kept the don from having Rueben eliminated was Rueben's supposed "files" on the don's family and it would have started a war with the Chicago family. It was bad enough having to make commitments to the don; this was like having two bosses. "I'll do whatever I have to do Denton."

"I know that you will Andy." Denton snapped his cell phone shut. Rueben's last comment was laying on Denton's mind. After a few moments he decided to call Paul Henley. Not only was Paul a close family friend and ally but he also advised Denton and his mother on their investments and did their taxes. Paul was a CPA by trade. "Paul, Denton Wellbon here… no this is concerning my private financial affairs. I need you to put together a package that will allow me to borrow five million dollars by tomorrow night… That's right you heard correctly, five million. I don't care how many of my properties and other assets you have to use as collateral. Understand? Trust me Paul, I'll explain everything to you later… No, again this has nothing to do with the meeting tomorrow, at least as far as you are concerned… Yes and say nothing about this to anyone." Denton ended that conversation knowing that Paul was shocked and had many questions, but being a loyal friend he would do what he was asked and hope that Denton knew what he was doing and would explain soon.

Denton stared out the window at the passing New York City scene. It was a mostly cloudy day with the sun making only an occasional appearance from behind the clouds. The canyons between the high-rise buildings took on that peculiar gloom that can cover the city on a morning like this. Denton felt that gloom in the very depths of his soul. He wondered how he was ever going to get out of this mess. He didn't know if he could save Crystal's life let alone ever meet her and explain that he was her father. He wondered how she would accept that news. Would she be resentful? Would she even care? How could one poor decision on one night of a person's life have so many repercussions in so many lives? The obvious impact was on Crystal and her mother, but there was also Susan. Denton still wasn't certain what the long-term effect would be on his marriage. His mother? As it had been through his entire life, Denton's mother was always a mystery to him. Her reaction to this whole affair wasn't anything like what Denton expected.

There was his life. If he voted with his mother he could be responsible for the violent death of his only child, a child that he never knew. He was not concerned about Trevor and Abe implicating him in blackmail. If they did that they knew that he would bring them down also. Mutual destruction would keep all three of them safe from each other. But what if Abe had been straight with him, as unlikely as that possibility seemed? What if one or more of the people that they had blackmailed realized that Denton could be the only source of information used against them? Would the possibility of mutual destruction protect him then? Would he be exposed to more attempts at revenge for the remainder of his career and life?

What if Andy failed to rescue Crystal? Denton would certainly have to vote against his mother and Mac in order to assure Crystal's safety. He would betray Mac and his mother would no doubt disown him. How would he face Paul Henley and all of the shareholders that were siding with his mother never considering the possibility that Denton would desert her or them? With either vote Denton would no doubt ascend to the chairman's position tomorrow but if Trevor won Denton was certain that it wouldn't be long until Trevor gathered enough votes to remove him from the company altogether and take over sole control. Abe made it clear enough where he stood on that issue and it wouldn't be long until he convinced Trevor that he could no longer trust Denton. Denton took a deep breath. He was certain that his father and grandfather faced many tough times like this while building their empire. If he was to inherit it he couldn't panic or shirk his responsibilities. He had to succeed. He didn't know how but he just had to.

***

Crystal Harrison lay blindfolded, bound and gagged on the musty mattress of a creaking cot. She had been here since she awoke from her drugged sleep. It seemed that she had dreamed of being in a small cramped area and later sitting upright in a chair. There had been several bright flashes of light and then darkness again. But it was all a blur and she couldn't determine if that had actually happened. She believed it was several hours ago that she slowly began to regain full consciousness. It was difficult to fathom the exact passage of time. Her arms and legs were numb. Earlier she attempted to call out, but with the gag in her mouth all she could manage was some muffled grunts, far too quiet for anyone to hear.

Panic set in as she tried to remember what happened to her. How did she get here? Would anyone be looking for her? No they would not! Everyone thought she had left for vacation in Mexico! She began to sob softly, but then the reporter in her personality took a firm grip on her very soul. She had to remain calm. She had to make sense of all this if she was to escape and survive.

She began to test her memory. She remembered the delivery man and the box. He must be the one that abducted her. She tried to burn his face and his voice in her memory. Why had he done this? What was he after? It was then that she heard the sound of a door opening and footsteps came near. A new male voice spoke to her. "You need food Ms Harrison. I have some soup in a bowl for you. You are at a location where it is impossible for anyone to hear you should you call out. I expect you to behave when I remove the gag. If you don't believe me when I tell you that I'll knock some of those pretty teeth out if you make a sound. Do you understand?"

Crystal nodded her head in the affirmative. Strong hands sat her up roughly. The gag was removed from her mouth. She opened and closed her mouth in relief. "Thank you," she whispered. There was no reply. A spoon touched her lips and she opened her mouth. Beef noodle soup. It tasted good as she realized that she was hungry. It was a large bowl and the man silently and patiently fed her all of it. When he had finished Crystal decided to risk a question. "Why have you brought me here? What do you want?" There was no answer as the gag was placed in her mouth again. Her captor then lay her down on the cot and she heard the door close behind him. Now she knew that there were at least two captors.

Later she could hear low conversation from the other side of the door. Several voices now, she could not tell how many there were in total. They seemed to be playing cards. This was what she had to concentrate on. She had to try to keep track of passing time and listen for any clue or information that may allow her to discover what this was all about and hopefully present her with an opportunity to escape. She was well aware that she was on her own with no one looking for her.

To Catch a Fox

If she were to escape it would have to be from an opportunity that she herself created. If she failed, well she wasn't going to allow herself to think about that.

Chapter 25

It was now early afternoon on the eve of the Wellbon – Smith annual meeting. After Denton explained to his mother what had occurred in his office this morning, she had insisted on bringing Mac and Paul Henley on board. Mac was in town for the meeting even though his presence was not mandatory. The various divisions gave their reports to their corporate presidents and then the presidents reported to the board of directors at the annual meeting. In this case Mac and his team made their report in person to Trevor Mason and his staff in Chicago. Mason made his rounds to the other divisions of the Atlantic Corporation and Mason would then give the report for Atlantic at the meeting. The other corporations would do the same.

Paul Henley was the last to arrive. All day he had been dividing his attention between making certain that they could count on the votes that had given them verbal commitment and attempting to raise the five million that Denton told him he required. This was the earliest that he could make it to Mary Wellbon's penthouse co-op. Paul looked tired and slightly haggard when he entered Mary's office - den. "I'm sorry I'm late. I've been very busy."

"We totally understand Paul," said Mary. What have you to report?"

"The votes are solid. We stand as we did the other day. We simply need Carlton Smith's vote." Paul paused and looked at Mary. "Do we have Carlton's vote?"

Mary gave a slight smile. "Yes, if I can guarantee that Denton will destroy all records pertaining to the Donald Kensington-Cramer labor scam."

Paul turned to Denton. "Can you do that Denton?"

"Yes, no question. I know where all the related files are located. I plan on giving Carlton a list and allowing him to destroy them himself before he departs the company." Mary gave an approving nod.

“Then we have it wrapped up.” Paul Henley permitted himself a smile.

“Not quite Paul. If we look like we’re going to win tomorrow Carlton will vote with us, but if we show any signs of losing crucial support Carlton will jump. He’s made that abundantly clear.” Mary’s face was devoid of emotion as she spoke.

Paul frowned, “I just told you our support is solid Mary. We win.”

“We have a problem Paul.” Mary then went into great detail for Mac and Paul Henley concerning the abduction of Crystal Harrison. She pulled no punches. When she finished she asked if there were any questions.

MacLode looked at Denton. Denton was staring at the floor. “Denton, I understand that you have to do what you have to do where your daughter is concerned.”

“Thank you Mac. I appreciate that.”

Mac continued. “However, I’ve known Don Luca ever since college. I’ve not known him to fail. If his man Andy tells you he will rescue your daughter, I believe it will happen.”

“I agree Mac.” It was Mary Wellbon speaking. “My husband worked with the don for many years. He found him to be extremely dependable. If he or Andy told us they would do something, it was done…I don’t care what that ass Rueben told you Denton.”

“I certainly hope that you are both correct.” Denton was staring at the floor again.

Mary turned her full attention on Denton. “Listen to me Denton, you are voting with us as planned tomorrow morning whether you hear from Andy or not. Andy will succeed, and we will not make any assumptions if we don’t hear from him before ten.”

“Mother we can’t take the chance.”

“Yes we can and we will.”

Denton could not believe what he was hearing. "Mother, like it or not this is your granddaughter we're talking about. I have to know that she is safe before I cast my vote."

"Denton she will be safe. You cannot risk everything that this family spent three generations building because you expect a rescue to occur on schedule. This is the type of pressure that I was warning you about."

Denton rose from his chair and walked to the window. He gazed out but wasn't actually seeing anything. What he was seeing was a young woman that he had never met. At this very moment she was alone and scared and she had no idea that her fate rested in his hands. The father she never knew, the father that she sought but so far hadn't found. A large part of the family she never knew was present in this room and they were deciding whether she was more or less important than the family's financial empire. Denton shivered when he considered what her fate might be if he gambled and was wrong.

Mary continued her argument. "Denton, from what you have come to know about Abraham Rueben what makes you think you can trust him over your mother and Mac your long time business associate? What makes you think that after you vote his way that he'll keep his word? Why would he want to take the chance of the possibility that Crystal could identify her abductors and ultimately have the trail lead back to him?"

Denton shook his head. What should he do? "A valid observation mother, you are correct. There is no good alternative. Damn it! There is no good choice!"

"There is only one choice Denton. You have to have the courage to vote what's best for the company and your family and trust the people we have working for us to do what they say they can do." Mary Wellbon, as always, was emphatic.

Denton grabbed his coat and headed for the door. "Denton," his mother called after him, "Where are you going?"

"I have to discuss this with Susan mother." The door in the entrance foyer slammed closed behind Denton. Mary Wellbon collected her thoughts and then turned to Paul Henley.

"Paul, Denton told me he has you setting up financing for the five million ransom the kidnappers are asking for."

"That's right Mary."

Mary Wellbon scribbled a series of numbers on a piece of notepaper. "Here, this will save you some time. Pull the money out of these accounts. They are my personal accounts. Get the money in small bills. If the banks give you any flack about thirty days notice remind them how much of their stock I hold."

"You're going to pay the ransom?"

"Yes, if that's what Denton decides to do. Take a couple of Wellbon – Smith security people with you. I don't want you getting mugged along the way." Mary nodded to him and Paul knew that was his signal to depart. After Henley left just Mac and Mary remained in Mary's office.

"Has Trevor given you an answer on your offer to buy Fox?"

Mac shook his head. "Not yet, we're definitely in a bidding war with Cab Corp."

"Where do you stand?"

"We don't know, we've submitted a 15.5 bid, but we don't know where Cab Corp is."

"Trevor will have to nail it down soon. He needs to go into that meeting tomorrow knowing how he's going to pay for all those proxies that he bought."

"He's not given us any indication. Roberts is contacting him sometime this afternoon to see if he's made a decision."

"He'll have to get approval to sell tomorrow so he has to make a decision. I'll do all I can to block the sale if he goes with Cab Corp."

"I know that you will Mary and my staff and I appreciate that…I have to return to our original topic. Do you have a sense of how Denton will vote tomorrow?"

Mary raised her line of vision and stared into space. "I think he'll do the right thing."

"Forgive me Mary, but it's hard for me to determine just what the right thing is in this situation."

"He'll vote with us Mac."

"Regardless of whether he knows that the girl is safe or not?"

"Yes because that's what his father and grandfather would have done. I believe that after all of these years his bloodline is stirring within him. He will do what he has to do and he will be a great chairman for our company."

Mac was impressed. "You're that certain?"

Mary smiled, stood up, walked over to where Mac was seated and placed her hand on his shoulder. "Unless that is, he doesn't." Mac was mildly surprised at her good natured demeanor while speaking of the possibility of her own defeat tomorrow. "Mac, my maid has a light lunch prepared. Would you care to join me? I want to discuss Fox."

"I would love to Mary."

***

Trevor Mason was putting the finishing touches on the Atlantic Corporation's annual report. He had elected to work at his home today so as not to be distracted. The phone on his desk rang, as he was proof reading. "Trevor Mason."

The voice on the other end was that of Abe Rueben. "Good afternoon Trevor."

"You're late. I expected a call before lunch."

"I was busy."

"You better have been working to secure the vote for tomorrow."

"I was."

To Catch a Fox

"How do we look?"

"We're in. I secured Denton's vote this morning. If you have Carlton Smith's there's no way we lose."

"I just got off the phone with Smith. He again committed to us. He's scared stiff that he'll go to jail if he votes any other way. You're sure you have Denton?"

"Yeah, I'm sure."

"I suppose I don't want to know the how and why behind that?"

"Definitely not Trevor, I know that I can't come into the meeting tomorrow, but I'll be in the building with my phone on in case you need me for anything."

"Good, you can wait in my office. I'll have some champagne there so we can celebrate afterward."

"Sounds good, I'll see you in the morning Trevor."

Trevor hung up the phone. There was only one more thing to do to complete preparations for the biggest day in his business career. He picked up the phone and punched in the number for Clint Matthews.

Chapter 26

The phone in Andy's hotel suite rang but one time and Andy grabbed it. It was Tommy on the other end. "We got it boss. You were right. The guy in the pickup led us right to it. We had to follow him in shifts so that he didn't get wise. We used three rental cars. He did a lot of double back before finally going to their hideout. They work shifts. They all stay in that hotel out by I-95 and do twelve hour shifts, five guys each."

"Where is it Tommy?" Tommy gave Andy the detailed directions. "It's a mobile home out in the boonies boss."

"You and the guys stay put. Give them space. We don't want to tip them off that we're there. I'll bring the rest of the guys."

Andy hung up and grabbed his Glock automatic from the desktop. He gave the weapon a quick once over, made certain he had a full clip inserted and one round in the chamber. He tucked it into his shoulder holster and after slipping on his jacket he put six additional loaded clips in his pocket. He then called the remainder of his men and told them they were leaving in five minutes. Next he called the don. When Don Luca answered Andy said only: "We know where they are and we're going to go get the prize."

"Good work and good luck Andy," the don paused for effect. "Andy."

"Yes Boss."

"You must not fail," with that the phone went dead.

Leaving his room Andy collected the remaining cousins and they headed for the parking garage. No one spoke. They were the most heavily armed guests to depart from the Marriott that night and they were grimly expecting that they must fight a small war.

To Catch a Fox

***

Denton Wellbon was in the back seat of his company limo when his cell phone vibrated in his pocket. "Denton Wellbon," he answered.

The metallic voice spoke quickly. "I know that you have a good memory so I'll only say this once."

"Wait," exclaimed Denton. Good lord, they even have my cell phone number he thought. "Give me proof that Crystal is all right!"

"You have my word and that's all you get. Now here is the bank account number that I want you to wire the money to at precisely 5 PM Eastern time tomorrow night. When you do I will notify you where you can find your daughter." With that the voice rattled off the number and Denton repeated it after which the phone went dead. Denton pulled a small notebook and pen from his inside jacket pocket and wrote down the account number. Well they are very careful thought Denton. If I had gone to the FBI there would be no time to trace that call. He supposed that the money would bounce around the world several times to avoid tracing and eventually wind up in a Swiss Bank account. The kidnapper would be relatively safe because of the Swiss' reputation for maintaining the anonymity of their customers. These were not small time punks.

My office number, my cell phone number and the knowledge that I'm purported to have a good memory. Damn Abe, thought Denton, if he's behind this he's so confident that he isn't even trying to hide his trail. If I exposed him, which he knows I won't, he'd just point out how many others have this same information. Denton realized that he could never prove anything.

Denton then called Paul Henley and gave him instructions that unless he heard differently he should wire the ransom money to the account number that Denton gave him at exactly the appointed time tomorrow. In addition he instructed to have security personnel from a nearby Wellbon – Smith company in South Carolina prepared to pick up Crystal. He prayed they would find her alive.

***

It was two-thirty in the morning and it was a very dark and moonless night. The old mobile home sat in a small meadow approximately two hundred feet off the brim of the narrow gravel road. The meadow was ringed with tall pine trees and the side of the road opposite the mobile home was actually the edge of a pine forest that stretched for miles. The mobile home was dark and appeared deserted. It in fact wasn't deserted at all. It was a minimum of five miles in any direction before one would encounter a farmhouse or any other sign of civilization. The near isolation was the reason that this old mobile home was chosen.

A mild autumn breeze whispered through the towering pines as dark shadows moved along just inside the edge of the ring of trees. The shadows swept silently among the brush and bushes, ghosts in the night that required no light to navigate by. The first perimeter guard was seated beside one of the pine trees, his position hidden by foliage that was piled randomly around him. He had a clear view of the rear of the mobile home and it was his responsibility to respond with his modified M-16 at the first indication of an intruder. The shadows seemed to glide to his position and converge on him. There was no sound, no bright muzzle flash from the M-16, no muffled scream, only the wind blowing through the trees. After the briefest pause the shadows moved on. In their wake the first guard lay dead or soon to be so, a gaping wound in his throat from which blood was gushing forth that pooled on and then soaked into the soil on which he lay. A second cluster of shadows swept out of the pine forest, crossed the road and then disappeared in the waving meadow grass. One by one the three guards on the perimeter fell suddenly into the clutches of the shadows. One by one they were left grasping their throats in an instant of silent horror as in mere seconds their life gushed out of them. Then all of the shadows disappeared into the shifting tall meadow grasses.

***

Andy stopped his rental car behind the rental that Tommy was driving. They were parked on the side of the gravel road about a mile from the old mobile home. Tommy and the men that were with him approached Andy's car as Andy doused the headlights. Andy rolled down the window. "Tommy, where are the other two cars?" He kept his voice low.

Tommy responded in the same subdued fashion. "Over there in the trees. We only kept my car out so you could see it."

"The ground solid over there? I don't want to get stuck. We may need to make a quick exit."

"It's good. It looks like the state highway guys use it to park equipment when they are working out here."

"Okay, let's you and I put these cars over there too. That way they're hidden in case anyone comes down this road."

"Ain't nobody been down here since we been here Andy."

"Shut up and humor me."

"Right boss."

After the cars were sufficiently out of sight, Andy assembled his men. Tommy had three guys with him and Andy brought two along with him. That made seven total the entire group that Andy brought to Savannah. "Tommy you're sure there are only five of them out here?"

"Yeah boss. Like I said, we think they work in twelve-hour shifts because we know that the other five are back at their hotel. That leaves five here."

"So all five are in the trailer?"

Tommy hesitated. "We think so."

Andy briefly looked toward the heavens for help, a gesture that went unnoticed in the dark. "What the shit does that mean?"

"Well we know that the guy in the pick up brought five out and took five back, but we couldn't tell where they all came from. Hey Andy, you told us not to get so close that they would know we were around."

"Yeah Tommy. Yeah I did. Okay, everybody give your pieces one last check. Tommy how far is it to the mobile?"

"About a mile Andy." Tommy gave them all a brief description of the lay of the land and approximate distances.

Then Andy's soldiers gathered around him. "When we get within sight of the mobile home I want Spuds and Turk to move out around those pine trees. We can't take a chance on them having lookouts posted."

"What do we do if we find them?"

"Kill 'em stupid. We all got silencers. The goons in the mobile home won't hear you. After you get all the way around we'll all surround the trailer and bust in. Remember, we don't want the girl getting hurt."

Spuds and Turk seemed a bit uneasy concerning their role in the rescue, but they feared Andy more than anyone hiding in the bushes. After a few questions about the procedure for breaking into the mobile home the group drew their weapons and proceeded to walk down the road. The walk was quiet with only the faint sound of their footfalls on the gravel mixing with the wind in the pines. As they neared their objective the pace slowed and they became even more conscious of any noise they were making. Suddenly a blinding flash burst forth up the road near the location of the mobile home. Andy and his men all took cover in the bushes along side of the road.

***

The two dark forms in the meadow grass peered at the small screen that the one held in his hand. The other held a device that was pointed directly at the mobile home. The screen showed three infrared forms within the trailer. One of the forms was reclining toward the south end of the structure. The other two forms appeared to be sitting toward the north end near the door. They shut the device down and returned it to the pack on the one individual's back. Then the one figure spoke softly into a microphone on his headset. The advance began immediately.

The two men from Duke's team that were assigned to watch Crystal inside the trailer had blackout curtains covering the windows so that no light from inside would escape and reveal their presence to any passer by. They felt secure knowing their perimeter was covered by their teammates in the circle of pines surrounding the trailer on three sides. "How was our guest when you checked her?"

"She's okay. I took her gag off and fed her."

"You kept the blindfold on her didn't you?"

To Catch a Fox

"Yeah, you think I'm stupid?"

The first man ignored the question. "Did she try to kick and hit you?"

"No she seems to have accepted that she can't overpower us. She's just scared."

"She should be. Nothin' good is gonna happen to her."

"Shut up she can hear you!"

"So what?"

"Just shut up that's all. You want to play some cards?"

At that moment there was a loud explosion outside and the single light bulb hanging from the ceiling went dark. With the curtains on the windows the interior of the trailer was pitch black. "What was that?" There was concern but no fear in the query.

"How the hell would I know? Find the door and check it out while I raise the outside guys." With that the speaker began calling on a walkie-talkie to his perimeter guards. The other man groped his way to the door. Upon finding it he cautiously opened it to the outside, dropped to the floor and with his M-16 pointed toward the outdoors rolled across the threshold. His plan was to stop for only an instant, try to pierce the darkness and determine what took place. However it was lighter than he expected. Atop a telephone pole out along the road a transformer was smoking and spewing sparks. Trying to determine what was the cause he lingered longer in the open doorway than what he originally planned. He never saw the red laser dot on his forehead and was dead an instant after the silent projectile followed the light beam into and through his skull.

"I can't raise anyone. What do you see out there?" The only answer from the motionless form on the floor was silence. In the dim light from the door it was apparent that the back portion of the his partner's head was gone. Realizing what happened the man instinctively turned the table over for cover and dove toward the outside wall. Plink, plink, plink, plink, plink, plink, plink, plink a hail of rounds tore through the thin wall of the trailer all confined to the area that the men were occupying. The rounds entered from both the front and the rear.

Several caught the man diving for cover, and the impact threw him to the floor. He knew that his unseen adversary would be coming through the door any second. He struggled to point his M-16 toward the doorway, but the bones in his one arm and his one leg were shattered. As he strained through increasing pain to aim his weapon a dark figure with what appeared to be faintly glowing green eyes burst through the opening. That would be the last image he would see as the dark green-eyed figure pumped several more rounds into his body.

Crystal Harrison lay bound and blindfolded on the mattress in one of the mobile home bedrooms. She had been straining to hear the faint conversation between what she had determined were her two guards. At times there had been more voices and at other times the voices changed. She had been unable to determine how many abductors she had. She could no longer feel her arms and legs. She believed she had been held for about a day and a half. Did anyone know that she was missing? Was anyone looking for her? Did anyone care? Get hold of yourself she thought. Everyone where you work would care if they knew. Her newly discovered grandparents would care. She was not alone in the world. She was not! Crystal briefly allowed herself to wonder if Foster Harrison would care, but than decided there was nothing positive in thinking about that. She was frightened, but managed to keep a firm grip on her emotions. It was like a nightmare, but she never awoke from it. One minute she was about to leave on vacation and the next this! She had to stay calm and keep her fear under control if she was to have any hope of surviving this ordeal.

Then she heard raised voices in the other room followed by a commotion followed by a sound like stones hitting metal in rapid succession. Suddenly she heard the door open and there was movement in the room where she was being held. Strong hands helped sit her up on the mattress and began to unbind her hands and feet. A voice that she had not heard before spoke softly and reassuringly to her. "Everything is okay. You're safe now." The gag was removed from her mouth. "Are you Crystal Harrison?"

"Yes," was all that Crystal could manage to say. Her throat was dry and her voice was hoarse.

The voice spoke again. "I'm going to leave the blindfold on you for just a few minutes more. I'll lead you outside. There are things in the other room that you really don't want to see."

"Okay," replied Crystal. She had no choice but to trust this new voice. She was keeping a tight grip on her emotions, afraid to hope in case this was some sick cruel trick that her abductors were playing. However, this was the first friendly voice she heard since the deliveryman came to her door yesterday morning. Or was it the morning before that, she wasn't certain. She just knew it was the longest period in her life. Now there were strong hands on either side of her, hands that helped steady her as they raised her to her feet. She discovered that her legs were very weak and she leaned on these strangers for support. They led her out through the now bloodied main room of the mobile home, guided her steps so that she didn't trip over the bodies and helped her to the ground outside. There they removed the blindfold. It was night and very dark. As her eyes adjusted to the dim light she looked at the men who had helped her. She gasped at what she saw. Two tall figures on either side of her dressed all in black with some type of helmet and green eyes that glowed faintly.

"Oh, sorry," said the one who had been speaking. "These are night vision helmets. They make us look kind of weird. They both pushed the special goggles up onto the top of their helmets. This revealed two very human faces, albeit covered with camouflage paint. She now noticed that they were heavily armed with automatic weapons and body armor. Other dark figures now walked out of the night. Most of them had leaves and portions of bushes attached to their clothing. It was easy to imagine that in the dark if they simply knelt down on the ground they would seem to disappear.

"Who, who are you?" Crystal was still skeptical, but very happy to be standing on her own two feet, unbound and able to see, even though that was very difficult in the night.

"I can perhaps answer some of your questions Crystal." Crystal peered into the gloom. Another figure was emerging from the darkness. The voice that accompanied it sounded familiar, but Crystal couldn't quite place it. As the owner of the new voice approached she could make out the form of a large and even under these circumstances, a very well dressed man.

"Mr. Smith!" Crystal cried out and surprised even herself by running into his arms.

"I've told you before to call me George," said Smith as he returned her grateful hug.

Suddenly Crystal truly believed that she was safe in the arms of this mysterious man who perplexed her as much as anyone these past several months. But he had never done anything to harm her. Indeed he had done several things that helped her. There was no reason to believe that he would harm her now. She buried her head in his arms and began to cry. Smith stroked her long auburn hair. "It's okay now Crystal. Believe me when I tell you that everything is okay and there is no one left to harm you." Crystal continued to sob. Smith kept his arm around her and began to slowly guide her across the meadow toward the gravel road. "My men will clean up, let's you and I get out of here. We have one stop to make before I take you home." Crystal said nothing but continued to cling to this mystery man who had played such a major role in her life long before she even knew of him. She cared not where he was taking her. At this moment with Smith's arm tightly around her, she never felt safer.

***

Andy and his men remained in the cover of the roadside bushes for several minutes after the bright flash up ahead. They could see sparks sputtering through the trees in the distance. Then the sparks slowly began to fade and Andy signaled for everyone to follow him.

"What was that?" asked Tommy.

"How should I know? But we're going to find out," was Andy's gruff reply.

The small, armed contingent continued down the gravel road through the dark night. Just before the trailer came into view the group was surprised when a solitary figure stepped out of the bushes and into their path. All seven weapons immediately came to bear on the dark form. "Hello Andy, I see you brought some friends," said the large man.

"Who are you and how do you know my name?" asked Andy as he aimed squarely at the stranger's chest. Andy didn't like this one bit. He wanted to be the one with the advantage of the surprise.

"It's not important who I am, but if you must have a name you may call me Mr.

Smith."

"Okay Smith, what do you want? This better be good."

"I want you to leave your boys here and take a little walk with me Andy."

"Fat chance." All seven weapons cocked nearly simultaneously. "Say what you got to say real quick Smith before we waste you where you stand."

"I wouldn't do anything stupid like that Andy." As Smith calmly replied the bushes along the roadside stood up to reveal figures in black with automatic weapons trained at Andy and his men. All seven of them immediately noticed the red dots of the laser targeting devices on them.

"Now, everyone remain calm and holster your weapons." After a moments hesitation Andy indicated that they all do as they were told. The weapons were immediately, if reluctantly holstered. Smith continued "Andy come over here before I lose my patience." Andy walked to where Smith was standing. "You men with Andy, nothing will happen to you as long as you stand quietly." Then Smith indicated to Andy to follow him and he walked off the side of the road and into the bushes. As Andy followed the circle of dark figures tightened around Andy's soldiers.

About ten paces off the road Smith stopped. Andy stopped beside him. "Andy I want you to meet someone. I think that the two of you passed briefly in your diner a few weeks ago. Andy this is Crystal Harrison." Crystal, still fearing Andy, moved out of the bushes and quickly to Smith's side. "He won't hurt you Crystal in fact his life probably depends on keeping you safe. I am right aren't I Andy?"

Andy looked at Crystal and then toward Smith again. "Smith, do you work for Abe Rueben?"

Smith laughed. Crystal realized that this was the first time she heard him laugh. It was a nice laugh she thought, sort of grandfatherly. But the words and the tone of his answer to Andy were anything but. "No Andy, I don't work for Rueben. There are five dead men up the road at the mobile home you were headed for that did work for him. I can introduce you to them if you like."

"No, no I don't need to meet them. So who are you and how do you fit into this?

I know that Rueben's men snatched Crystal, so the fact that they are dead and she's with you means that you and your men must have sprung her."

"Nothing gets by you does it Andy?"

"Look you got the drop on me I figure that even though you don't have a gun in your hand someone has me in his sights. But you don't have to be a smart ass."

"You're right on both counts Andy. I apologize. However, I think it's ironic that the man that beat up Crystal's grandfather now desperately needs to prove that she is safe. Crystal, Andy and his gang that can't shoot straight were on their way to rescue you. The only trouble is that they were in way over their heads. The team and it was a well-disciplined team that was holding you would have cut them to pieces before they even got close to that ramshackle mobile home you were a prisoner in. Those guys were all renegade heavily armed special ops guys, accustomed to unconventional warfare. That's why my guys had to use high tech stuff they couldn't get their hands on nor ever suspected that they would need. That was the safest for you and the most efficient way to stop them. Had we not been so equipped, we would have had a real firefight on our hands. But we outnumbered them more than two to one, so we would have prevailed… So Andy, 'who am I?' I'm the guy that saved your life by doing your work for you."

Andy wisely knew it was time to keep his mouth shut and listen. Smith continued, as Crystal again was amazed at the confusing and mysterious story that kept unfolding around her. Who was she that all of this was happening. "Now I'm going to save your life again. I'm going to allow you to take the credit for saving Crystal's life. That should appease the don, which will keep you alive, and Denton will again allow you and your boss to have a, shall we call it a business relationship with his company?"

Andy shook his head. "How do you know all this?"

"I know a lot of things Andy. I know more about this whole situation then either you or your boss."

"You're turning Crystal over to me?"

Crystal grabbed Smith's arm. "No please George. Let me stay with you."

To Catch a Fox

"Don't worry Crystal I would never turn you over to this thug."

"Who you callin' a thug?" Andy raised his voice in indignation.

"You! That's who! If I had my way we would waste you like we did those real soldiers back there." Smith thought about that for a moment as he glared through the darkness at Andy. "On second thought they're no better than you, just better trained. They like you prey on innocent people that can't defend themselves... Now listen close because I'm only going to say this once. Tomorrow morning..." Smith looked around. The inky darkness was giving way to the gray gloom of pre dawn. "This morning as soon as I release you and your wise guys, you call Denton and tell him Crystal is safe. Got it?"

"Does she know?" Andy indicated Crystal.

"Shut up! It's not important for you to know what she knows and what she doesn't, just do as I tell you!"

"Okay. I'll do just like you say."

"Of course you will, it's your neck if you don't. Go back to your guys. When my people see you return they'll release you all. Return to your cars and go back to Savannah. If you don't try anything stupid, my people won't kill you. You may tell your guys anything you want. Make yourself look like a big man." With that Smith took Crystal by the hand and led her back into the bushes leaving Andy alone. Andy was furious and thought briefly about pulling his weapon, but wasn't certain what he would do with it if he did. He looked around as he remembered the hidden gunman that Smith referred to, and then he turned and went back toward the gravel road. Back to where his cousins were forced to wait.

Duke Winston got concerned when he couldn't raise his field crew on either his cell phone or the radio. It was six AM, the normal shift change came at ten, but Duke had his crew loaded in the pickup truck and was headed out to the boonies toward the mobile home. His guys were pros; he couldn't imagine what could possibly have happened. But he also couldn't imagine two equipment failures, the walkie-talkies and the cell phones simultaneously. He wasn't certain what he would find, so during the entire trip he had two of his men still trying to raise the field crew by both methods. They had no success, all of which raised Duke's level of anxiety.

To Catch a Fox

As they approached the meadow, Duke spotted a truck in the road ahead of them. He immediately pulled off to the side and sent two of his men to investigate. They leapt from the truck with their rifles at the ready and disappeared into the forest. Long minutes passed until Duke's radio crackled. "It's a power and light crew. They're working on a transformer on a pole. Looks like they're replacing it."

"Can you see the trailer from your position?" Duke's voice had an urgent sound.

"Not yet, we'll have to give the power crew a wide birth so that they don't see us. As soon as we're out of their line of vision we'll be able to get our heads high enough out of the tall grass to check it out."

"Do it, we'll hold this position until you report. Don't let yourselves be seen in case we no longer control the trailer." While Duke felt that last statement unlikely, he decided to be cautious. After all there was no good reason why his field crew didn't answer their calls. Time passed. Duke knew that his scouts would have to move slowly as they would be crawling on their stomachs through the tall meadow grass. Finally the radio crackled. "Duke."

"Yeah what do you see?"

"You got to see this for yourself."

"What the hell are you talking about?"

"Just drive up the road and you'll see what I'm talking about."

"That will blow our cover!"

"We don't need cover boss."

Duke slammed the truck into gear and lurched off with the tires throwing gravel twenty feet in the air. What the hell was going on? Duke charged past the power and light truck leaving them in a cloud of dust. He pulled into the old driveway leading to the mobile home and slid to a stop. "Son of a bitch!" Duke yelled. There in the meadow before him was, was NOTHING! The trailer was gone! There wasn't even a break in the grass! The old dirt driveway led to nothing and then stopped!

Duke and his men got out of the truck and approached the area where the trailer had been. His two scouts were already standing there. Duke turned to his men. "Fan out, cover the perimeter and see if you find any trace of our guys." Duke watched as his men began to cover the area. He then inspected the portion of the meadow where the trailer sat. It was on this location as recently as last night at ten o'clock when he brought out the next shift. He noticed that the sod had just been laid. The sod obviously came with the tall meadow grass already rooted. It was shorter than the surrounding grass, but that wasn't noticeable from the road. The driveway had signs where heavy truck tires had pressed the grass down and there were areas off the driveway where the grass was pressed or broken. Duke surmised that the truck that carried the mobile home away did this. The same truck probably had a forklift on the rear to unload the sod and a crane behind the cab to lift the trailer on. Possibly there was a second flatbed truck. By this time the remainder of his team returned to the pickup.

"Nothing Duke. No spent shell casings, nothing. Just three different spots that look like the soil is soaked with blood, other than that the area is cleaner than when we came here."

"Where are these spots?" asked Duke.

"About the exact positions that we placed the perimeter guards," answered one of his men.

"Damn! Okay, lets get out of here."

"Duke, what about our guys?"

"I suspect that they are under that new sod, whoever rescued Crystal Harrison put them there. We're going back to the hotel, get our gear and get the hell out of here. Rueben never told us we would be up against this level of enemy. I assumed we might have to tangle with the police or even the FBI because this was a kidnapping. But these bastards were running a paramilitary operation. They weren't concerned about reading anyone their rights, they just hit and hit hard." Duke looked around the meadow. It wasn't long ago that his men and he had been here with the Harrison girl. They selected this meadow because no individual owned it. Until recently it belonged to someone up north, but that individual sold it to the state of Georgia so that it was annexed into the state forest across the road. Duke had done his homework. The state didn't have removal of the trailer scheduled for another year. No one ever came out here. Who were these people? How did they know the location?

Duke and his men wasted no time getting into the pickup. Duke now feared that whoever did this knew where they were staying and might be out to eliminate the entire team. However, they had too much incriminating equipment back at the hotel. They had to risk return so they could disassemble it and take it with them. Duke decided to play it as safe as possible and so he chose an alternate route of return.

***

While Duke and his men were making their discovery Denton Wellbon III and his wife Susan were meeting Denton's mother and Mac for an early morning pre-meeting breakfast. Because of the early hour they met at a corner restaurant not far from Mary Wellbon's penthouse co-op. Mary knew the owner and arranged for a table in a section well away from the restaurant's regular breakfast clientele.

Denton was anxiously waiting to hear from Andy concerning Crystal's safety and Mary being prepared for any last minute report from Paul Henley concerning possible critical shifts in the voting blocks had laid her cell phone on the table. Denton laid his cell phone beside Mary's so he wouldn't miss a call. Mary looked at Denton. "Denton I gather that you haven't heard from Andy as of yet?"

"Nothing, no."

"What are you going to do if you hear nothing by voting time?"

Susan spoke up. "Mother Wellbon, we've been up most of the night discussing this and really haven't arrived at a decision." Denton nodded in agreement. He looked exhausted and haggard.

"What are your feelings on this Susan? I value your opinion." Mary as always was direct in her inquiry.

Susan hesitated for a long moment before answering. "Neither of us wants to see anything happen to the young woman. We determined that if Andy fails in his rescue attempt we will notify the FBI before we deliver the ransom money."

"What about the vote?"

"Mother! Does nothing matter more to you than the future of Wellbon-Smith?"

"I'll answer that question in a minute Denton right now I want Susan's opinion."

"I know this will sound like a cop out Mary, but I really don't know what I would do in Denton's position. Therefore I'm leaving that decision to him. He will have to live with the outcome no matter what it is."

Mary nodded in agreement. "That was an honest answer to a difficult question Susan. I appreciate that, your honesty is one of the reasons I love you very much."

Susan blushed slightly, "Thank you, I love you too."

Mary reached across the table and squeezed Susan's arm. "Now Denton I'll answer your question. You father and grandfather built this company out of nothing. I'll be the first to admit to the people at this table that they did not always play by the rules. They did what immigrants had to do in what was then a WASP controlled world. You should all be aware that Wellbon was once Welbonski when your grandfather and grandmother entered this country through Ellis Island. Our real family name was not one that you could do business with on the level that your grandfather intended to play, so he officially changed it. Sacrifices were made and yes Denton, some people even died along the way. Mac is familiar with some of the people that we do business with and the tactics they employ." Mary glanced in Mac's direction. Mac nodded silently as Denton looked to him for an answer. "I'm not going to justify those acts or even tell you that I would agree with them if I had been a part of those decisions, but our history is what it is. If I was in your position Denton I know what I would do."

Denton jumped in, "And what would that be mother?"

"I would never give this company over to scoundrels like Trevor Mason and Abraham Rueben, period! Certainly Rueben can rescue the girl. He's the one who kidnapped her!"

"That would be your decision even if it meant sacrificing my life? That's what this is equal to mother! Crystal is my daughter even if I've not been aware of it and have never met her!"

"Are you convinced she is your daughter Denton?"

"It doesn't really matter does it mother? She's a human being and I hold her fate in my hands."

Mary took a sip of her coffee. "Denton this is one of those epochal moments in your life, and no one can make this decision but you. You've chosen wise council in your wife. She is correct you will have to live with the results no matter what they may be." Mary paused and looked around the table, and then she returned her gaze to Denton. He met that gaze and held it defiantly. "Whatever you decide I will support, you will never hear a complaint from me from this day forward. You know how I feel, but I am not you. This is your time Denton, it is no longer mine."

Denton's eyes softened as the implications of his mother's answer sunk in. "Thank you mother. I truly appreciate that."

Mary Wellbon reached across the table and squeezed Denton's arm in the same fashion as she had his wife's. "I love you both you know," she said softly. Denton's eyes misted over. He couldn't remember when his mother had last spoken those words, if ever.

"Excuse me I have to visit the men's room for a moment." With that Denton, overcome with emotion, rose and left the table.

The conversation continued concerning the voting procedure that Wellbon-Smith's corporate rules dictated. Unnoticed by anyone but Mary, Denton's phone began to vibrate. Mary picked it up and looked at the screen. It was a text message from Andy. Mary accessed the message. "Crystal safe – call you later. Andy" Mary looked around the table. All including Susan were engrossed in conversation. Mary made a decision and tucked Denton's phone in her purse.

When Denton returned he looked around at his companions. "Are we finished?" All nodded in agreement. Without really looking at it Denton scooped up the phone that lie on the table and put it in his pocket. It was nearly identical to the one Mary had just put in her purse, as they were standard Wellbon-Smith corporate issue. Denton picked up the tab and all left for what may become the most important meeting in company history. Mary had an important piece of information that would definitely affect the outcome of that meeting. She decided to keep that information to herself.

***

Crystal Harrison was home in her apartment. She had just taken a long shower and finally felt clean. Her hair was wrapped in a towel and she wore a soft terry robe. The events of the last two days almost seemed like a bad dream except that the man she knew as George Smith was napping in her living room. When they returned to Savannah Smith told her that they had tickets for a nine o'clock flight this very morning to New York City. Then in his usual cryptic manner he told her that "nearly all" her questions concerning her family would be answered there. After the events of the last several days Crystal again wanted those questions answered.

She paused on her way to her bedroom to look in on the mysterious Mr. Smith. He sat dozing in an easy chair with the morning paper askew on his lap, the morning sun shining brightly through the tall bay window. The morning paper contained not a single word about Savannah's well-known news anchor being abducted. Everyone incredibly still believed Crystal to be on vacation. Smith instructed her to allow that fiction to continue. He informed her about the girl that her abductors were using as a ringer for her. He said that he would arrange for the local police to pick her up for credit card fraud upon her return. Smith was a large man with thick curly dark hair with a touch of gray around the edges. He was not fat; in fact he appeared to be incredibly fit. Crystal judged him to be somewhere in his fifties. She smiled; looking at him asleep just now he once again appeared to be anyone's image of a grandfather just taking a morning nap. But his expensive tailored suit jacket was pulled slightly to the side revealing an exotic automatic weapon in a shoulder holster. Crystal could not allow herself to forget that no matter how grateful she was and how safe she felt in his company this was a very dangerous man. She was not certain how many deaths he was responsible for early this morning in the Georgia countryside. For that matter, she wondered how many people he personally killed. She didn't for a minute believe that his name was George Smith. Still he had almost certainly saved her life. Now he seemed to be the only key to ever knowing who her father was and her real family, if any existed. She would go to New York with this man. She would learn the truth.

She decided that before she put on clean clothes she had better awaken Smith. She approached and gently touched his arm. The barrel of the automatic weapon was in her face so quickly that she never saw Smith's hand move! Crystal gasped and jumped back. The cold eyes behind the gun sights softened as they recognized Crystal. The weapon dropped and Smith, chuckling, replaced it in its holster. "I'm sorry Crystal. There are certain instincts that you have to have in this business."

Crystal took a deep breath and removed her hand from her mouth. "My heart is slowing to about 200 beats per minute. I'll be okay soon…I didn't mean to startle you…" Crystal's breathing returned to normal and with her other hand on her chest she determined that the pounding of her heart was subsiding.

"Allow me to apologize Crystal. After the experience that you had I certainly did not intend to scare you."

"By the way, since you brought it up, exactly what business are you in?" queried Crystal.

"Why Crystal, I would have thought that a smart girl such as you would have figured that out by now."

Crystal was calmed down enough to give Smith a slight smile. "Well I'm sorry to disappoint you, but I haven't figured it out Mr. Smith."

"Why I'm in the business of saving fair damsels such as you that are in distress." Crystal shook her head her smile broadening. "Now you get dressed Crystal we don't want to miss our flight." Crystal nodded in agreement and disappeared into the bedroom.

Chapter 27

The annual shareholder meeting of Wellbon-Smith got underway at eight AM. The meeting was held in a theater style room adjoining the boardroom on the top floor of the Wellbon-Smith building. Carlton Smith sat in the most central chair on the raised dais and as chairman of the board conducted the meeting. Mary Wellbon sat to his immediate right as vice chairman and the remainder of the executive council including Paul Henley filled the other seats. There was a central table that faced the raised dais with two chairs behind it. This was where the individual corporate presidents gave their reports for their respective conglomerates. The remainder of the board of directors sat directly behind this table and the major shareholders filled the raised theater type gallery behind them. As Wellbon-Smith was a privately held company the number of people in attendance was relatively small. No more than sixty.

Carlton Smith called the meeting to order. The first items of business were the reports from the corporation presidents. These were greatly abbreviated because of the advanced date of the meeting. The understanding being that the final numbers would be delivered to the board by the middle of December. The reports given today were limited to projections and each corporation's three-year plan. Occasionally an individual division that had exceptional performance or there were problems that were being addressed were highlighted. Old and new business would be brought up after these reports. The reporting order was according to the seniority of the corporation with Wellbon-Smith. Because the Atlantic Corporation was the flagship and the original company that the holding company of Wellbon-Smith grew out of it had the most seniority of all. The sequence was Atlantic, Sterling International, Williams Manufacturing, Global Industries and finally Pfeiffer International Trading Company. Because of this Trevor Mason and Denton Wellbon III went first.

Atlantic had a stellar year so there were few questions concerning their projections. The report went smoothly and both Trevor and Denton were the recipients of several accolades. Trevor and Denton took their seats in the gallery while the other presidents gave their reports. Trevor leaned over to Denton. "As soon as these reports are over we can force the vote. We'll soon be able to install you as chairman and me as vice chairman Denton."

"Yes, I can hardly believe it Trevor." Trevor thought that Denton seemed a bit distracted, but Trevor also knew the intense pressure that Abe could apply. Abe had never failed him so Trevor was certain that Denton would vote with him when the chips were down.

Denton quickly checked his cell phone but there was still no message. What was going on? Denton told Trevor that he had to use the men's room and left the auditorium for the hallway outside. As soon as he was in the hall he pulled out his cell phone. He did not want Andy's number stored in his memory, so he had it memorized. Denton punched in Andy's number, but only got Andy's answering machine. (Andy was flying in route from Savannah to New York and was not permitted to turn on his cell phone after take off.) Denton left a message asking what was happening; was Crystal safe or not? He refrained from thinking about the possibility that Andy and his men were dead.

During the ten o'clock break the entire group adjourned to a room adjoining the auditorium for pastries and coffee. Denton met with Paul Henley downstairs in Denton's office. Henley had the five million ready and deposited in several individual accounts that he could wire the money from quickly if necessary.

As Denton made his way toward the elevators to return to the top floor and the meeting, Abraham Rueben emerged from Trevor Mason's corner office. He stepped directly into Denton's path. Abe kept his voice low so that only Denton could hear. "It's all up to you now Denton. Your future, your daughter's life, you vote with Trevor and all your problems go away. As soon as I hear your vote I call my people and they rescue Crystal. Everything's up to you Denton."

"How can you be so certain that your people can rescue Crystal?"

Abe noted the suspicion in Denton's voice. Nothing wrong with that he thought. He had no concern for Denton's suspicions. Denton could prove nothing. "I only hire the best people. You cast the correct vote and Crystal will be safe."

"Thank you Abe, I was aware of the importance of my vote; if you would kindly step aside." Abe did as requested and Denton walked the remainder of the distance to the elevators. When Denton turned and pushed the button to the top floor, he saw that Abe Rueben was still standing watching Denton as the doors closed.

After the break everyone returned to the auditorium for the final report from Pfeiffer International Trading. Denton still had no message from Andy. Mary Wellbon took the opportunity of the break to check Denton's cell phone which she now possessed. Andy had left two more messages assuring Denton that Crystal was safe. She returned Denton's cell phone to her purse and returned to her seat as vice chairman.

After confronting Denton in the hall Abe Rueben returned to Trevor Mason's office. Although he didn't like the tone in Denton's voice a moment ago, he was certain that Denton was in his hip pocket. Denton was a decent person and he wouldn't risk his daughter's life for this or any company. He simply couldn't live with himself. It would have been a totally different situation if the vote depended on Denton's mother. Abe smiled to himself as he thought of Mary. That bitch was tough. She played the game the way he and Trevor played. Abe was grateful that they were dealing with the younger Wellbon. Abe could smell victory; this was going to be a great day. Just then his cell phone rang. Abe checked the screen. It was Duke Winston.

"Yeah Duke?"

"You son of a bitch! You filthy son of a bitch!" Duke's voice sounded like a guttural growl.

"What's wrong with you?"

"You set us up you son of a bitch!"

"What are you talking about?" Abe raised his voice to match Duke's.

"You said the most we would have to tangle with was the local cops and maybe some wise guys or the FBI!"

"Yeah and that's all you should have to tangle with. What's the complaint?"

"Half my crew is missing and no doubt dead. We're packing up at the hotel now to get the hell out. I just hope they haven't followed us here. I don't want to shoot my way out!"

"Who's following you? What the hell are you talking about Duke?" This couldn't be the result of Andy and his boys. Duke's men could take care of them easily.

"You didn't tell us that this gal Harrison was so important that her rescuers are black ops guys! Who the hell is she anyway and what kind of people have you tangled with?"

"What are you talking about Duke? What black ops?"

"Abe, they not only killed my men, they took the mobile home that we were hiding Harrison in. It looks as if the mobile never existed. Grass growing where the trailer was less than six hours ago, half my men vanished and we're getting out of here before they catch up with the rest of us! If all of us had been out there at the same time I think we would all be dead! Abe, if you had told me what the hell to expect we would have been ready for them. As it was we weren't anywhere near prepared for this type of, of warfare! That's the only word that fits what happened to my men. These guys don't play by any rules. We were out manned and out gunned thanks to you!"

"Duke, where's the Harrison girl?" Abe's voice was suddenly desperate. What the hell was going on?

"Who knows? The black ops guys have her, whoever they are. Listen and listen good Abe. My men and I can fight black ops with the best of them, but we need to know that's what we're up against. I equipped my men to take on the kind of adversary you told me to expect. Not this. I'm gonna make you pay for this Rueben!" The phone went dead.

Abe sat stunned in Trevor's chair. What was going on? Duke and his men were the toughest, smartest fighters he had ever met. This couldn't be Andy's gang. The only thing they were good at was strong-arm tactics and catching an adversary outside his favorite restaurant and spraying him with lead. The M-16's Duke said he needed should have been plenty of firepower to take out Andy's bunch. Did Denton get gutsy and call the FBI? No the FBI doesn't work like this, besides how could they have found Duke so quickly? Who? Who did this? Why did they do it? Abe thought briefly of the exceptional cover up of Crystal Harrison's existence.

Suddenly Abe came back to the situation in New York. Was Denton aware of what took place in Savannah? There was no way of knowing. He grabbed his cell phone and punched in Trevor's number. He had to warn him that Denton's vote might be in question. While not desirable, it might be wise to try to postpone the vote until the board meeting in December. Abe wasn't certain of the mechanics of doing that but he didn't want Trevor to go into this with the key block of votes in doubt. Damn! Abe got only Trevor's message that he was unreachable and did Abe desire to leave a voice message.

The reason Abe got those results was that at this moment Trevor was on his feet before the dais making his proposal. He had shut off his cell phone before taking the floor. "Mr. Chairman, Executive Council, Directors and shareholders, I propose the following."

After a lengthy tribute to Carlton Smith that was frequently interrupted by applause Trevor dropped his bombshell. "Carlton, I know that you have been impatient with the pace that the search committee has been moving in finding your replacement. I know that you are anxious to enter a well deserved retirement."

"I am that Trevor," interjected Carlton from the dais, to the scattered laughter of the assembly.

"Well because of that Carlton, I'm proposing that we nominate Denton Wellbon III to replace you as Chairman of the Board of Directors of Wellbon-Smith." As Trevor expected, a gasp went up in the auditorium. However the only people surprised were Trevor's fellow corporate presidents, especially those who believed themselves to be in serious consideration for the position. As none of the presidents held significant blocks of stock they were never contacted by either Abe Rueben or Paul Henley and were some of the few in the room that were unaware of the takeover battle that was now officially in progress.

The president of Global Industries, who happened to believe that he held the inside track when the search committee met rose and called the motion out of order as the search committee was the designated body to recommend Carlton's replacement. Carlton Smith informed the gentleman that there was nothing to stop a proposal such as Trevor's from being made from the floor, but all holders of voting stock could take the point made into consideration when voting.

Melissa Kensington rose from the rear of the room and came forward to one of the numerous microphones placed around the room. As planned beforehand she seconded the motion that Trevor Mason placed on the floor.

Carlton opened the floor to debate and again the president of Global doggedly brought up his point about the search committee. This time Paul Henley, who always made certain that the meetings followed not only Robert's Rules but also Wellbon-Smith rules as outlined in the corporate charter again shot the suggestion down. Most of the shareholders were aware of the struggle for control of Wellbon-Smith. As expected there were questions and discussion appropriate for a motion of this magnitude. One of Mary Wellbon's supporters asked Trevor who would be on the executive council if his proposal, now motion passed. Trevor replied that he believed that the new chairman would select a new executive council. Did he have any names to share with the meeting? Trevor's ego got the best of him and he mentioned that he might be under consideration as vice chairman. The current executive council had several outside directors. Would the new council have any outsiders? Yes, at least one. Who might that be? Possibly that could be prominent lawyer Abraham Rueben. Why didn't Mary Wellbon place her son's name in contention for the chairmanship? Trevor told the questioner that he would have to ask Mrs. Wellbon that question. Mary nodded to Trevor, but made no move to answer the question. The fact that Trevor was taking all questions and not referring any to Denton spoke volumes to many of the shareholders. The questions continued from Trevor's supporters and adversaries alike. Someone finally called for the question and the voting began.

***

William MacLode rode up to the top floor on the same elevator as Abe Rueben. Paul Henley had called Mac to inform him that voting was about to begin. The two men, both aware of who the other was by name, had never met in person. Because of this both were unaware of who they were sharing the car with. Abe hurried off ahead of Mac and made his way to the security guard at the entrance of the meeting room. Abe had no credentials that would allow him to enter and was refused entry over his protestations. Mac presented identification as the owner of the Southern Cross Investments, Caribbean Fund and Commonwealth Fund. Mac was allowed to enter the meeting, as he was a voting shareholder. Abe stood staring after the tall man with a slight, was it an English accent? The very man he had attempted to meet in London and had failed. The funds had never sent an actual representative let alone the owner being present. They always voted by mail proxy going along with the majority. What was going on here?

Abe pulled a business card from his pocket. He scribbled a note on the back and asked the security guard if he would at least deliver this message to Trevor Mason. The guard agreed to do it at the first opportunity. Abe pulled out a one hundred dollar bill. "I need it delivered now."

The security people at the Wellbon-Smith building were very well paid and had excellent benefits. "I'm sorry sir, even if I accept your generous offer I can't deliver it now. Mr. Mason is in the process of presenting a proposal to the shareholders."

Abe put the card back in his pocket, the note that he had scribbled said only to delay the vote and call Abe. It was too late for that now. Abe took the elevator back down to Trevor's office. He had no idea how Denton would vote now. He had no idea what was happening. After some thought Abe flipped open his cell phone again and called a different number other than Trevor's. A voice answered almost immediately.

"This is Abe. The job is finished. The subject is now expendable. Attend to the details that we discussed as soon as possible."

"It will be done."

Abe sank into Trevor's chair. Abe was in possession of the security system's original digital chip. Duke had failed him and was of no further use.

***

When Carlton Smith called for the vote Trevor again took the floor and presented a folder filled with the proxy votes that he had gathered along with the documents authenticating them. Trevor could cast votes for all names in the folder. Another protest came from the president of Global, but it also was to no avail. The Corporate Secretary began checking the documentation.

Denton sat like a zombie in his seat. He was the object of much discussion around him, but he wasn't aware of any of it. He would soon have to vote and he had to assume that Andy had failed. Denton opened his cell phone and called up the address book, strange he thought Susan's number was always the first name on the list. Now it was third. Denton was too preoccupied to realize the implications of this and selected Susan's number.

"Susan Wellbon."

"Susan, Denton, I need you to proceed with our alternate plan."

"No word from Andy?"

"None, he might even be dead. I have no way of knowing."

"Oh my!"

"Just do as we discussed Susan."

"I will. I love you Denton."

"I love you too." Denton snapped the phone closed.

***

George Smith and Crystal Harrison sat side by side in first class on their flight to New York City. Crystal sat by the window and Smith on the aisle. Suddenly something crossed Crystal's mind and she had to ask. "When did you make these flight reservations?"

Smith smiled. "Immediately after you were abducted."

"You knew when I was kidnapped?"

"Yes, in fact I watched it happen. It was a slick operation. Those guys were good."

"Why didn't you stop them?"

"I wasn't prepared. I was alone at the time. I was reasonably certain they would try, but I had no idea when it would happen until they did it. Besides it happened in broad daylight. My people and I work best at night and I didn't want a fire fight in the middle of Savannah."

"You had enough confidence in your ability to free me that you made these reservations even then?"

"I never plan on failure Crystal."

"How did you know they wouldn't hurt me?"

"Well eventually they would have. Eventually they would have killed you. But that wouldn't have happened for oh…" Smith looked at his watch, "probably not for another hour."

"You know exactly when I would have been killed?"

"An educated guess, you see there are events taking place in New York as we speak that you are having a very big impact on. However nothing is ever certain in this world, so we rescued you as soon as we could get ready."

"Me? I'm having an impact on events in New York?"

"Yes, that's why we're at 30,000 feet and on our way there. You're a very important person to quite a few people."

"Mr. Smith…"

"I thought you were calling me George."

"George, you've become very important to me in the last few hours, but I must tell you that every time we meet you provide more questions for me concerning my life than you answer."

"Yes I do Crystal and you've been very patient with me. I will tell you that today most of your questions will be answered."

"Really? You promise?"

"I promise."

"Why now? You made this sound nearly impossible the first time we met."

"Then it was, but certain events now make it unnecessary to keep secrets. In fact there are certain advantages to getting some things out in the open."

"What did you mean by most of my questions will be answered and some things out in the open?"

"The only real question that won't be answered is who I am and why I've taken such a large interest in you all of your life."

"As of this morning, I think I would like to know the answer to that as much as I would like to know who my real father is."

Smith smiled. "I bet you would, but remember Crystal 'curiosity killed the cat'."

"Yes, but 'satisfaction brought it back' George."

"Not in this case Crystal. I have one more very important instruction for you and I'm going to trust you. Can I trust you Crystal?"

"You saved my life. Of course you can trust me."

"You must never mention me to anyone. Anyone no matter what, do you understand?"

"I understand. You have my word," Crystal answered reluctantly.

"Good, because you of all people know that I'm a very dangerous man."

For just an instant Crystal saw that cold soulless look in George's eyes, but then the friendly grandfather returned.

***

The voting took place in order of the size of the shares owned progressing from smallest to largest block of shares. Trevor was voting for all of the shares that he had a proxy. The voting on Trevor's proposal was nearing an end and the tally of 'yeas' and 'nays' that Paul Henley was projecting on a large screen behind the dais showed Trevor's proposal well in the lead. But the three largest voting blocks were yet to cast their votes. Together they accounted for over a third of the voting shares. They would decide the outcome. In the order of voting that would be Denton first, Carlton Smith second and Mary Wellbon last, as she held the largest block of stock. By that order Mac voted "nay" for the funds just before Denton's name was to be called. This no longer concerned Trevor. He knew he was covered.

The Secretary called out Denton Wellbon's name. "How do you vote Mr. Wellbon yea for the proposal or nay against it?" Denton failed to respond and a silence fell over the room. Trevor turned to look back at Denton, a frown on his face. Mary Wellbon, who was neither superstitious nor inclined to prayer both crossed her fingers and said a quick prayer. "Mr. Wellbon?" The Secretary's voice was the only sound to be heard.

"I hear you Mr. Secretary," responded Denton. Denton's expression was totally blank, revealing no emotion. He was staring straight ahead. All eyes were fixed on Denton. Trevor's supporters, willing or not, all had much at stake with this motion. If this motion passed it was either the first step to cashing in on exorbitant capital gains or hopefully having Trevor destroy any proof that he might have as to some wrong doing they may have done. Paul Henley made certain that Trevor's opponents were all aware of the buyout deals that Trevor had cut. Passage of this motion would put Wellbon-Smith into financial jeopardy paying off those exorbitant capital gains as the outstanding shares were returned to treasury status.

"Mr. Wellbon?" The Secretary called again for Denton's vote. Everyone in the room was on the edge of their chairs. Did Denton support Trevor's bid to take over the company? Would he turn down the position of chairman? The president of Global Industries was totally confused. He and his fellow corporate presidents were about the only people in the room that did not understand the battle that was in progress.

"I vote nay Mr. Secretary!" Denton folded his hands on his lap and bowed his head. "Please forgive me Crystal," he whispered to himself… "God please don't allow any harm to come to that innocent young woman."

A crescendo of voices erupted, some ecstatic and some distraught. Trevor was up out of his seat. "Denton, what the hell?" Trevor expected Carlton Smith to vote with him. Smith had committed to Trevor because he was afraid of prosecution for the Kensington-Cramer scam. He was now certain that Mary Wellbon would vote nay. Even with Smith's support, without Denton's vote Mary's vote would end his dream of taking over Wellbon-Smith. It would leave both sides short of a majority.

Mary Wellbon closed her eyes, said another unaccustomed prayer of thanksgiving and then turned to look at the tally on the screen behind her. Denton's vote put the nays well out in front. Carlton would be the next to vote. He had also promised his vote to Mary. Carlton's vote would clinch it if he kept his promise, but Mary didn't trust her long time associate. Mary put her hand over the microphone in front of Carlton and leaned over to whisper in his ear. "Trevor's defeated without Denton's vote. You know I'm going to vote with Denton and now so does Trevor. We need your vote for a majority. If I were you I'd go with the winners."

Carlton turned toward Mary. "They say I could go to jail as an accessory Mary!" As much as a whisper could be desperate, Carlton's was. "Win or lose if I cross up Trevor he may go to the auditing committee with what he knows about the Kensington-Cramer thing."

"It doesn't matter to Trevor now. Without a clear majority he's lost. You know I'm going to make my own proposal as soon as this one is defeated. If you go with us, I'll keep you from going to jail. You be loyal to me and I'll be loyal to you."

"Can I count on that? What if I don't vote with you? Trevor promised not to turn me in if I vote with him."

"Carlton we've known each other for years and you ask me if 'you can count on that'? You bastard! If you don't vote with me I know what Trevor doesn't know. I know that you lied to me Carlton. I know you were taking kickbacks from Donald Kensington-Cramer. And I can prove it! That would make you more than an accessory. You couldn't claim that you were ignorant of what Donald was doing. You vote with me now and on the proposal that I'm about to make and I'll see that you get to retire happily. If you don't I'll put you in jail for the rest of your life! Who are you more afraid of Carlton, Trevor or me?"

The Secretary called out "Carlton Smith, how do you vote sir, yea or nay?"

Carlton removed Mary's hand from the microphone, took a deep breath and in a hoarse voice said "nay."

Trevor Mason had left the microphone on the aisle and was now seated beside Denton. He could really care less how either Carlton or Mary voted. Like Mary he knew that the game was over with Denton's vote. "What did you just do Denton?" Trevor's veins were bulging he was so angry that he could hardly speak. "I was going to make us great together! We could have taken this company to new heights! Didn't you talk to Abe?"

Denton looked Trevor square in the eye. "Enough Trevor, you and I know that you were only using me. First you threatened me with an old secret from my past. Then you threatened to harm someone important to me. You threatened to harm my daughter for god's sake!"

"I don't know anything about that."

"Of course not, you let Abe do your dirty work while you keep your hands clean."

"I expected possible betrayal from your mother, but I didn't expect it from you Denton."

"I don't see it as betrayal. You ask me what I did? I did the right thing Trevor. I did what I did because it was the right thing to do for the most people involved. I didn't do it because I was threatened, or because I was blackmailed, or out of self interest. I did it because it was the right thing to do. I don't suppose you would understand that." Denton excused himself and headed for the dais.

As he moved down the aisle Denton heard his mother make a similar proposal to the one that was just defeated. She also proposed Denton for the chairmanship, but assured everyone that the management team that had been so successful under Carlton Smith would remain in tact. She assured the shareholders that Wellbon-Smith would remain financially solid. She also assured everyone that under her proposal the company would remain in the control of the Wellbon family. She reminded them that under her family many of them had become wealthy.

By then Denton had reached the dais. Mary turned the microphone over to Denton. Denton proceeded to take questions from the floor after Mary's motion was seconded and discussion was opened. Yes, the executive council would continue to include his mother as vice chairman.

One of Trevor's supporters asked about the commitments that were made to buy back stock for the treasury. Denton assured the shareholders that signed agreements with Trevor Mason to sell their stock in exchange for their proxies that those promises would be honored. The company would buy the stock back and it would become treasury stock. However the company would only pay the value as determined by the method outlined in the articles of incorporation. This would not make everyone happy as this method guaranteed a value far less than what Trevor and Abe agreed to pay. Some would elect to hold their shares while others would realize that to sell now would net them more than they would ever get from Trevor Mason and Abraham Rueben now that their scheme to take over the company had failed. When Denton was asked why Wellbon-Smith wouldn't honor Trevor's agreements to the letter, Denton pointed out that these agreements held no legal weight because they violated the company's articles of incorporation that required the board to approve any sale of stock. This was not done. A follow up question from another shareholder pointed out to Denton that the clause he just invoked applied only to sales between a current shareholder and a person who was not currently a shareholder. Although the amount of stock that Trevor Mason personally held was small he was indeed a shareholder. Denton smiled and answered. "Sounds like an excellent court case to me." It was clear that Denton wasn't afraid of a court fight on this issue.

Amid cheers and some laughter the question was called for and the voting began. This time the proxies were released and it was apparent that many of them would now support this motion. Several of the minor shareholders including the corporate presidents who entered the session with dreams of becoming chairman voted yea and then departed in total confusion.

As soon as she made the proposal Mary Wellbon left the dais. She went down several floors and waited for Denton in his office. When he was finished speaking to the shareholders Denton again tried to call Andy. Finally Andy answered his cell phone. As he entered his office Mary could hear Denton say, "She's okay? She's safe?"

"That's what I said Denton. Didn't you get all those messages I sent you?" Andy was wondering if nothing could go the way he wanted today.

"No, not a one."

"Well I left the first one around seven this morning."

"I'm complaining to the wireless company. Not getting your messages put me through hell this morning! But she's okay."

"Honest Denton, I saw her with my own eyes. She's safe."

"Where is she? Is she with your people?"

"No, ah we found it necessary to hire some local talent. They are familiar with Savannah and they took her home."

"So she's home. She wasn't harmed."

"She wasn't harmed and your secret is apparently safe."

"What about the people that were holding her?"

Andy was hedging. "Let's just say they won't bother you or your family any more."

"Oh, I understand." Denton closed his eyes for a moment. He told himself this was the only way that he could have been certain that Crystal would be safe. "Andy, forget about the message problem, whatever it was. You, the don and I will all sit down and discuss future arrangements when you think the time is right. Yes, we won the vote I'll soon be chairman. I'll be the real chairman."

"Mason won't be a factor?" Andy was beginning to feel pretty lucky. Considering the way the day began. He had gotten away with a very sketchy report to the don this morning, but he would have to come clean with him later. He figured it would be okay as long as Wellbon-Smith fell into their laps. That meant keeping Denton believing that the don and Andy were responsible for Crystal's safety.

"After today Mason won't be a factor. I'll see to that."

"Congratulations Denton. The don will be glad to hear that Mason isn't a problem anymore."

"Thanks again Andy." Denton closed the cell phone. He turned to his mother with a huge smile on his face. "She's safe mother." He took a huge sigh of relief. "She's been safe all morning!"

"I know."

Denton frowned. "How did you know?"

Mary took Denton's phone from her purse. "Here's yours, now give me mine."

Denton looked at the phone that Mary laid on the desk. Then he pulled the phone he had just used from his jacket pocket. "Mother you had my phone! No wonder I didn't get Andy's messages. How long did you have it?"

"Since breakfast."

"How long did you know she was safe?"

"Since breakfast, if you check your phone for messages you'll see that Andy did inform you early this morning as to Crystal's rescue. I suspect that's what he was telling you. He wasn't lying."

"Mother, you knew and you didn't tell me?"

"That's right."

"Do you know you put me through hell?"

"I can imagine."

Denton wanted to be furious with her, but he was still feeling the euphoria of knowing that Crystal was safe. A great weight had been lifted from his shoulders. He sank back in his chair. "Mother why on earth would you not tell me that Crystal had been rescued? Not only was I worried about her, but I agonized over how to vote."

“Why? Why, you ask? I wanted to see if you would make the right decision under duress. Not knowing if Crystal was safe or not. I wanted to see if you would take the long term view of what would be best for all of those people that depend on Wellbon-Smith companies to feed their families. I wanted to see if you could trust the people that you sent to do the job you sent them to do. I wanted to see if you could risk your personal interests and concerns for the interests of the group. I wanted to see if you had enough confidence in yourself to truly run Wellbon-Smith without someone like Trevor Mason behind you actually calling the shots. Lord knows I’m not going to do that for you. Most of all I wanted to see if you could make the tough calls like your father and grandfather did.”

“You think I made the right decision?”

Mary smiled, “You made the decision that I would have made.”

“Was that the right decision mother?”

Mary laughed. “Alls well that ends well Denton.”

“Did I make the decision that father and grandfather would have made?”

“How should I know? I could never predict what those two renegades would do!”

Behind them Mac and Paul Henley broke into laughter and applause. “Forgive us for eavesdropping,” said Paul. “We came down to get you two. It will soon be time for you both to vote. Your motion is well on the way to passing. Everyone in the room knows that Denton will take over for real and the company will once again truly have Wellbons at the helm.”

“I have one more thing to take care of.” Denton opened his own phone this time and called Susan. “Did you contact the FBI Susan?”

“Yes answered Susan.”

“We don’t need them now. I just talked to Andy. Crystal is safe.”

To Catch a Fox

"Thank God Denton!"

"Whom did you talk to at the FBI?"

"Special agent Harry Sigfreid."

Denton took down Sigfreid's phone number. "I'll take care of it Susan."

Mac and Henley had already left for the boardroom, but Mary remained. "You called the FBI." It was not a question.

"Yes."

"I know that you were prepared to pay the five million.'

"Yes."

"You're a good man Denton Wellbon."

Denton called agent Sigfreid and identified himself. "My wife called you earlier concerning a disturbing phone call I received about a woman named Crystal Harrison of Savannah. We have no connection with this woman, but they asked us for ransom. We're you able to find out anything concerning this? We found it very disturbing."

Harry Sigfreid sat in his office looking at his cluttered desk. "Yes Mr. Wellbon, we checked into this for your wife. The Savannah office confirms that Crystal Harrison is simply on vacation. We believe this to be a hoax."

"Thank God," answered Denton. We thought it must be as we've never met the young woman."

"Well, the pranksters simply used the name of one of Savannah's television personalities."

"Really, then I guess it was all a prank. I apologize for putting you to this trouble agent, but it was very upsetting."

"I understand Mr. Wellbon. No problem. Please call us if these pranksters call again, if they do try to get as much information from them as you can."

"Yes, I will. Thank you again." Denton closed his cell phone.

Denton turned toward the door. "Let's get back to the meeting mother. I have some important items to address as soon as I'm voted in as Chairman."

Mary followed her son out of the office. She had never been more proud of him.

On the other end of Denton's phone call Harry Sigfreid slowly returned the receiver to the cradle. What are the odds thought Harry? Sam Grabowski observes Denton Wellbon at an old mob front called Andy's Diner, rekindling suspicions that there is a connection between the Atlantic Corporation and the underworld. Then the nephew of a major stockholder of Wellbon-Smith the parent company of Atlantic is the victim of an apparent homicide. The circumstances point Grabowski's homicide investigation toward one Abraham Rueben, lawyer to Trevor Mason the president of Atlantic Corporation. Now Denton Wellbon and his wife call the FBI concerning what is almost certainly a kidnapping hoax involving a person that they don't even know. All of these events centering on the Wellbon-Smith Atlantic companies within the last six months.

Harry picked up the phone again and called Sam Grabowski. When Sam answered Harry said; "Sam, Harry. Let's meet for a beer after work. I think we need to talk."

***

Down the hall from Denton's office in Trevor Mason's corner office, Trevor and Abe Rueben were both having a scotch. "What happened Abe?" Trevor's face was ashen.

"For the first time in my life Trevor, I haven't a clue."

"You haven't got a clue? You haven't got a clue? I thought you had Denton locked up!"

"I thought you had Carlton Smith locked up!"

"Smith didn't matter once Denton jumped! What went wrong?"

Abe let out a long sigh. "Trevor, we stumbled onto something a lot bigger than we ever imagined."

"What are you talking about?"

"I don't know who this Crystal Harrison is, but she is somehow involved in something bigger than our plan to take over Wellbon-Smith. We just tripped over this by accident. The people that came to her rescue were…"

"Denton mentioned kidnapping! What did you do?"

"Relax, you weren't involved and neither was I for that matter."

"You're sure this can't be traced back to you. For god's sake, they execute people for kidnapping Abe!"

"I just told you that we aren't involved. Do you want to know more than that Trevor?"

"What? No! I don't want to know. I don't want to know! You just better be right!"

"Trust me Trevor."

"I trusted Denton to you and look what happened. Six months of work down the drain."

"Shut up Trevor."

Trevor drained his scotch. "What's the fallout?"

Rueben took a sip of his scotch and thought about the current situation. A situation that he never believed they would find themselves in. "Well because we had to guarantee the purchase of the stock to get the proxies. That is the proxies that we couldn't blackmail into our possession, we had to personally guarantee those agreements so we still owe those people the money. The people that we blackmailed did what we asked and will hope that if they keep their mouths shut we won't bother them anymore."

Trevor loosened his tie. "Without the chair and the council under our control we can't sell any companies. Without the power to sell the Far East financing evaporates. We can't make good on the contracts." Mason walked over to the bar and refilled his glass. "Abe, are we ruined? Before I left the board room I heard Denton promise to honor our contracts only at the standard company determined value."

"Really? Good old Denton. Maybe we aren't ruined after all." Abe laughed, "For those that don't take Denton's offer and chose to pursue us in court I may have to argue that the contracts are invalid because we were violating the Wellbon-Smith articles of incorporation."

"That's the same argument Denton used upstairs when someone asked why he wouldn't honor the value we put on the stock. You think that will work?"

"Who knows, this is America? It would actually help if Wellbon-Smith sued us for violation of corporate rules. That would give our argument credibility." Abe began to laugh uncontrollably.

"What's so damn funny?" Trevor wasn't in a mood for humor.

"I just realized that we might wind up on the same side of a lawsuit as Wellbon-Smith claiming that what we did was in violation of company rules."

"You think that it will work!"

"It might. It will at least stall things long enough for us to both get our personal assets out of the country. But you Trevor, Denton will almost certainly fire you as soon as the meeting is over. I still have my law firm."

"Yeah, Paul Henley already informed me that the executive council wants to meet with me as soon as the meeting adjourns. But I have a greater concern Abe. I'm still worried about jail or worse. We didn't exactly play by the rules."

"Like I said, the people that we blackmailed are all fearful of going to jail for one reason or another so they will keep their mouths shut hoping that we'll leave them alone. Then there's Denton's 'mutual destruction' theory, which really does protect us both."

"The other stuff Abe."

"Oh you mean the stuff that you don't want to know anything about?"

"Yeah."

"That's been taken care of."

Trevor looked at Abe. "I guess I have to trust you. Oh, you're coming with me to the meeting with the executive council. I may need my lawyer."

***

Denton accepted the chairmanship of Wellbon-Smith when the final vote tally showed that his mother's motion won by a wide margin. He became the third Wellbon out of four chairmen to hold the position. The retiring Carlton Smith being the only exception. Denton was unique in that unlike the previous three chairmen he didn't run unopposed but he did run against himself. As Denton and Susan would later tell friends that were unfamiliar with the battle for control of the company "you had to be there."

Denton made a brief acceptance speech to the shareholders. When finished he opened the floor to questions. A board member asked how Denton intended to pay for the shares that he promised earlier to purchase back as treasury stock. Denton answered that he planned to sell off a very profitable division, Fox Cabinetry of his own Atlantic Corporation. He explained that by doing that there was a consortium of Far Eastern banks that would finance the remainder at reasonable interest rates. Denton called John Hogg to come up to the dais and explain the two offers that they received. After hearing the offers, Denton recommended that the board approve the sale to the Fox management team over the Cab Corp Group even though the Cab Corp offer was $500,000 more. Hogg explained that the Fox team offer was backed by a solid group of investors called Futures Unlimited and was 100% payable upon settlement while Cab Corp asked that one million be left in the company to be paid off in three years. Denton requested that the board approve the sale before adjourning. That would allow them to honor the first requests for buy backs. The board quickly approved the sale to the Fox team.

Then Denton had Paul Henley take the worst possible buy back scenario and show the impact the loans from the banking consortium and the interest rates would have on the company. Because they would go with the company's value of the shares the impact was far less than what it would have been under Trevor's plan. Denton explained that they could not overextend themselves by acquiring more companies for several years. Privately he and Paul were certain that most of the shareholders would choose to keep their stock.

***

Mac was sitting in the back row when the proposal to sell Fox to his team was approved. He was on his cell phone to his team back in Pennsylvania. They had Mac on a speaker in the conference room at Fox. Mac's voice came in loud and clear. "They approved it! We're going to own Fox Cabinetry!" The conference room erupted in unbridled cheering. Mr. Roberts from Futures Unlimited was also on site and joined in the celebration.

Tony Conocenti picked up the phone cutting off the speaker. "Mac, you did it."

"No, we did it Tony. We did it."

"We couldn't have done it without you Mac."

"All we have to do now is keep it profitable and pay for it."

Tony laughed. "Don't bring us back to earth just yet Mac. Let us enjoy the moment."

"Okay, Tony you've got a deal. Is Sarah there?"

"Yeah, hold on and I'll get her."

As Mac waited for Sarah to come to the phone Mary Wellbon stood to be recognized. Then Sarah was there. "Mac, congratulations, you pulled it off!"

"You're as bad as Tony. We pulled it off. We all did it."

"Mac everyone feels bad that you're not here to drink champagne with us."

Mac could hear the cheering and laughter in the background. "Yeah I can tell they all miss me. Sarah, if I'm on speaker please take me off."

"We can talk privately now."

"If you really feel badly that I'm missing the celebration you could make it up to me."

Sarah smiled, "How could I possibly make it up to you?" she said naively.

"Have dinner with me tomorrow night. I'll be home in the morning."

"You've got a deal Boss."

"I'll pick you up at seven."

On the dais Mary Wellbon paid a brief but touching tribute to Carlton Smith, as this would be his last meeting as chairman of the board. Carlton got a standing ovation and then he adjourned the meeting for the last time.

To Catch a Fox

PART 5

Chapter 28

They were all gathered in the cherry paneled, richly appointed conference room on the top floor of the Wellbon-Smith building. This room was just off the mini auditorium where the annual board of directors / shareholders meeting had just concluded. There was a large solid cherry table in the center surrounded by green leather upholstered high back swivel chairs. All manufactured by Fox Cabinetry. The view of the city was fantastic. This was the room where the board normally met for their monthly meetings.

The executive council was not present, as Trevor expected, at least not all of it. Mary Wellbon, Paul Henley and the newest member and now chairman Denton Wellbon were the only council members in attendance. In addition there was William MacLode. Trevor knew Mac, but Abe only recognized him as the owner of the off shore funds. "Mac, what are you doing here?" asked Trevor.

"Denton and Mary invited me Trevor."

Abe had a puzzled look on his face. "Trevor you know him?"

"Of course I know him, he's William MacLode president of our Fox Cabinetry division."

Abe just shook his head. "He also owns or controls the offshore funds that I went to London to get their proxy votes."

Trevor turned on Abe. "What? When did you discover this?"

"Earlier this morning Trevor, he produced his voting credentials while I was in the hall."

"This is just great!" said Trevor to no one in particular. "You go to London and the owner works for us in Pennsylvania." Trevor turned to Denton who took his place at the head of the table for the first time. "Abe's here as my lawyer, although after this morning I'm beginning to wonder why."

"Shut up Trevor," replied Abe. "Why is my client here Denton?"

"We have a deal for you Trevor."

"What kind of a deal Denton?"

"It's simple really. If we ignore the fact that you attempted to take over the company by illegal methods including blackmail and kidnapping…"

"I had nothing to do with kidnapping Denton," interjected Trevor.

Abe spoke up, "I told you Denton you were jumping to conclusions. I'm the one that offered to rescue the lady Denton. By the way, are you paying the ransom or are you taking my other advice?" Abe wasn't allowing his loss today to rattle him. Trevor gave Abe a sidelong look as he definitely decided that he didn't want to know any more about Abe's methods to secure Denton's vote.

"Abe I'm sure you know that Crystal Harrison is safe. Apparently Andy isn't as inept as you thought." Denton couldn't resist the dig. Trevor rolled his eyes and sat down in one of the high backed chairs.

"That wasn't Andy," muttered Ruben almost to himself.

A slight frown crossed Denton's face, but he ignored Abe's comment and continued, "As I was saying; other than those unsavory actions Trevor, you've done everything that Wellbon-Smith hired you to do. While I might question your general attitude toward your employees, you did turn Atlantic into a very profitable corporation again. In addition to that I learned a lot working with you."

Trevor's face showed mild surprise. Abe took the chair next to Trevor. Mary, Mac and Henley were seated at various locations around the conference table. Trevor hesitated before answering. "Thank you Denton."

"You're welcome Trevor."

"What's the deal Denton? Cut to the chase." Abe was his usual direct self.

"The deal Trevor is this," Denton addressed Trevor and ignored Abe. He slid an envelope across the table to Trevor. "In that envelope is the first installment check in a series of checks that will come to you each business quarter for the next three years."

Trevor opened the envelope. He raised his eyebrows and showed the check to Abe. "Every business quarter for three years?"

"That's right Trevor."

"What do I have to do?"

"Resign."

Abe narrowed his eyes. "You're not firing him?"

"Not if he resigns. If he resigns he's eligible for this, what should I call it? This golden parachute."

Trevor looked confused. "What do I have to do in return Denton?"

"Simple. Keep your mouth shut. We all have dirty hands in this thing Trevor. Keep your mouth shut. At your age, combined with the pension that you are eligible for in a few years as a former executive in the Wellbon-Smith world; you shouldn't have to work for the remainder of your life. You won't be as rich as you might have become as chairman of Wellbon-Smith but you will be able to keep your big house in Connecticut, the membership in the country club, you're 60' yacht that you keep out at the marina on the sound and continue to drive expensive cars. That is if you resign and sign a nondisclosure form that our lawyers are drawing up now."

Trevor looked at Abe Rueben then back at Denton. "Your theory of mutual destruction?"

Denton smiled. "You could call it that. Of course if you ever violate our agreement and talk to anyone about our activities, go to work for someone else or start your own business the money and the pension stop."

"Of course that's understood."

Abe sat up straight in his chair. "When will we have this document to review?"

Denton turned to Abe and his eyes turned cold. "First thing tomorrow morning, I'll expect it signed and hand delivered to my office within twenty-four hours or the offer is rescinded and I'll go to the police personally."

Abe laughed. "You wouldn't dare. You're as guilty as us Denton."

"I'm not afraid to call Crystal Harrison in my defense. I'm betting that I can make a jury see that all of my actions were aimed at protecting her. You think you can justify your actions as anything more than greed?"

Trevor interrupted. "Denton, this is a generous offer. I expect that we won't find anything objectionable in the document. I fully expect I will be able to sign it."

Denton and Abe Rueben were still locked in a cold stare as Denton spoke. "That's great Trevor. Enjoy your retirement." Denton paused, "of course as Abe isn't an employee of Wellbon-Smith but is your lawyer, you will have to take care of him. That will be all."

Trevor and Abe rose from their chairs and left the room. Everyone was quiet as they all looked at Denton. Denton was still staring at the closed door when Mary broke the silence. "You're a pretty tough egg Mr. Chairman."

Denton turned to his mother and smiled. "I have one more piece of business before we adjourn. I just vacated the position of vice president of the Atlantic Corporation and the president just resigned. We can't allow our flagship corporation to drift without a skipper and first officer." Denton turned to Paul Henley. "Paul I know that you don't need the job, but could I impose on you to take my place as Vice President at Atlantic?"

"Wow Denton, I hadn't planned on a regular day in day out position."

"Help us out will you Paul?"

"As long as it doesn't last too long I'll do it." Paul had a history of being the Wellbon family's Mr. Fix It."

Then Denton turned to Mac. "Mac, we couldn't have won without you."

"We couldn't have won without any of us Denton. By the way, my team told me to give you their congratulations and well wishes. They also thank you for choosing us as the successful bidders."

"Just a sound business decision Mac. Tell them for me that I thank them for the well wishes, but they'll probably wind up hating me."

"Why would they hate you Denton?"

"They'll hate me because I'm offering you the job of President of Atlantic Corporation."

Mac was speechless and the expression on his face left no doubt about it.

"You don't have to answer me now. Take a couple of days to think about it, but I warn you Mac, I'm not inclined to take 'no' for an answer."

Mac managed to speak. "Denton they expect me, I expect to continue as president of Fox. Wouldn't that be some kind of conflict?"

"Well you couldn't continue as president of Fox, because there aren't enough hours in the day, but you could continue as an investor in Fox. Most of our executives have investments outside of Wellbon-Smith. I know I do."

"But Futures Unlimited may not permit it. After all they backed us with the idea that I would continue as the CEO."

Denton smiled. "You'll still be a Board member of the new Fox Corporation. You'll be available to advise them at any time. I suggest that you ask them."

***

George Smith stopped the black Mercedes along the curb at the Manhattan high rise. He and Crystal Harrison landed at Kennedy around noon. Crystal was amazed that he had this beautiful car waiting in long-term parking. Not to mention the black Hummer he used to drive her around Savannah earlier, the same Hummer that he left in long term parking at Savannah International. After they picked up the Mercedes, Mr. Smith took Crystal to the Brasserie for a fantastic lunch. He told her that after what she had been through she deserved it. Crystal didn't argue.

They chatted, mostly small talk and mostly Crystal answering questions that Smith had concerning her job. He did speak briefly about himself, but only to tell Crystal that he had a daughter just about Crystal's age. Crystal asked where she lived and Smith said simply that she "passed away." Crystal thought that Smith's eyes became moist for just an instant and then he changed the subject and that was all she learned about the man who seemed to know more about her than she did.

"Why have we stopped here?" asked Crystal. Smith didn't turn the engine off. Instead he reached into his inside jacket pocket and produced a business card. He gave it to Crystal. It had a woman's name on it. A name that Crystal didn't recognize, "What's this?" she asked.

"When you get out of the car give the card to the doorman over there. When he sees the card he will allow you to go up to the penthouse."

"I'm going to the penthouse, what for?"

"You wanted answers. That's where you have to go to get them."

"Why would whoever lives there let me in?"

"Because you're expected," Smith reached across Crystal and motioned to the doorman.

"You're not coming with me are you?"

"No, and remember; not a word or question about me to anyone. Anyone. When you leave this car it's as if I didn't exist. That includes the trust fund. Say nothing about it either. Do you understand?"

Crystal took a deep breath. "I understand." She glanced at her watch. It was three in the afternoon. This was so unreal considering where she was twelve hours ago. "Will I ever see you again?"

"Probably not but life takes strange turns."

Crystal had only met this man twice in her life, but he was responsible for her being alive now. Had it not been for him she suspected that she would already have died a very unpleasant death. Were it not for him she suspected that she wouldn't be in New York now possibly to have many of her life long questions answered. Were it not for him she would not be the wealthy young woman that she was today. Without warning she threw her arms around his neck. "For a woman that likes to think of herself as independent and not needing anyone's help, I kind of like the idea of you watching over me. You're sort of my Daddy Warbucks."

George Smith accepted the hug and then firmly but gently unwrapped her arms from around his neck. He smiled his grandfatherly smile. "Remember I'm in the business of saving fair damsels in distress. Who knows, you may need to be rescued again some day."

The doorman was standing beside the passenger door. He waited discreetly until the emotional scene inside the Mercedes was completed and then he opened the door. With tears in her eyes Crystal handed him the business card. "Oh yes, I was told to send you up immediately." As Crystal was about to enter the revolving entrance door she looked back toward the curb. The black Mercedes had already disappeared into traffic.

***

Harry Sigfreid sat alone at the corner bar on Lexington and 138th street. He checked his watch. It was nearly 3:30. Sam should be here shortly. Sam's watch was over and he was seldom late for their beer and conversation sessions. Harry looked around the room where a few people were seated in booths. The establishment was typical. The building was long and narrow. There was a bar along one wall, booths along the other where high windows with thick impenetrable glass bricks stood guard over each booth. At one end of the room facing Lexington was a storefront window with various brewers' neon advertisements hanging in it. The entrance was in that end. At the other end was a space for the obligatory billiard table and dartboard. The old heavy oak paneling was dark as was the entire room. Harry and Sam chose this bar for their regular sessions because it was midway between both of their offices. As Harry sat contemplating the days events Grabowski settled down on the bar stool beside him. "Harry," was his only sign of recognition.

"Sam. Is the bar okay with you or would you like a booth?"

"We're the only ones at the bar right now and we have this end pretty well nailed down. It suits me fine."

They both ordered beers. It was the second for Harry as he had consumed one waiting for Sam to arrive. After a few silent sips Harry opened the conversation. "How did you make out with the video equipment that you confiscated from Rueben's law office?"

"Not good. We looked at everything. We checked video chips until we were sick of looking at doorways where no one came through all night. We found nothing."

"So the chip from the camera at the side entrance, the one that you thought was tampered with, revealed nothing?"

"Well that's the only straw that I have to hang onto. That chip was missing."

"Did you ask Rueben about it?"

"Sure, of course he knows nothing. He claims what we already have is original. He sent me to the head of security for the building, the man seems like a competent straight shooter, but the security guy had no idea what could have happened to that chip. Strange huh, the one chip that could verify that the tape was tampered with turns up missing. One other odd thing, the security guy told me Ruben had him fire all of the guards the other day. He said he was advertising for new personnel. I think I need to talk to those fired guards."

Harry lifted his bottle of beer, replenished his glass and contemplated the bubbles. "Not as strange as what I'm about to tell you." With that introduction Harry proceeded to relate to Sam the events of the day. Susan Wellbon's strange reporting of a possible kidnapping, the victim being someone that neither she nor her husband has any connection and lives in Savannah Georgia.

"What? The Susan Wellbon? The one married to Denton the third? The same Denton who's a big shot in the Atlantic Corporation? The same Denton Wellbon that I've seen down at wise guy Andy's diner?" Sam was incredulous to say the least.

Harry smiled. "That's the Susan I'm talking about. By the way, Andy is only a purported wise guy. No one has ever been able to prove anything."

"The hell you say!"

"It gets better. It turns out that the purported victim is a local Savannah television personality, but when the Savannah office checked it out she's in Guadalajara, Mexico on vacation."

"Savannah verified that?" Sam was suspicious of anything that involved the Wellbon family.

"Yup, she's checked in at the local Hyatt and has been either on the beach or shopping since she got there. The hotel people say she has a driver's license, passport and credit cards."

"What made the Wellbons think this person was kidnapped?"

"Ransom phone call."

"Did you check their phone calls?"

"Yeah, as much as we could on such skimpy information, but this is a family that does business all over the world. Their incoming calls at the office, home and cell phones for the last three days came from everywhere."

"So you think it was a prank." Sam lit up a cigarette and offered one to Harry. Harry reluctantly rejected the offer as he was attempting to quit. "I wish I could quit," muttered Sam.

"Back to your speculation on it all being a prank. I have to believe it was given the facts. Especially the fact that there seems to be no connection between the purported victim and the Wellbons. But what are the odds? You are investigating a possible homicide that also has ties to Atlantic Corporation via Wellbon-Smith. It's all very strange."

To Catch a Fox

Sam drained his beer and signaled for another. "Damn, what was that theory some egghead scientist came up with several years ago?"

Harry smiled this should be good he thought, "I have no idea what you're talking about."

"It was about chaos yeah that was it, chaos."

Harry began to chuckle. "What does chaos have to do with anything?"

"You know, nothing in the universe is orderly in spite of the way things appear. All is chaos and things for the most part happen randomly even though the fact that they are unrelated is pretty hard to accept. Chaos."

Harry too required another beer. He decided that this should be his last as he consumed those pretty fast. Or, maybe he should get something in his stomach. "You want dinner? I'll buy."

"If you're buying I'll eat with you."

They ordered burgers and fries from the bar menu. Then Harry picked up the conversation again. "So you think that all of these strange events that just smack of being tied together somehow is really random because of some theory concerning chaos?"

Sam grinned. "Hell no not for a second! I would bet a paycheck that all this is tied together somehow, but I'm no where near knowing how."

The T.V. above the bar was turned to a news channel, as there were no sports to watch at this particular time. The announcer was turning to business news as the burgers and fries were placed before the two friends. "In the world of business today, one of the oldest and most venerable firms in this city has a new chairman tonight. The shareholders of Wellbon-Smith elected the grandson of the founder Denton Wellbon III to be the new chairman of the privately held conglomerate. Mr. Wellbon's mother Mary said that…"

Sam sat back from the bar folded his arms and shook his head. "Will the coincidences never end?" Harry simply stared at the T.V.

To Catch a Fox

Unnoticed to both Sam and Harry a large well dressed man with thick curly hair had seated himself at the opposite end of the bar. In fact the man had followed Sam from the Manhattan South Division when Sam left work. He had finished his beer and was leaving a tip for the bar tender. As he rose to leave he handed a manila envelope to the bartender and pointed toward the two men at the other end of the bar. The bartender dutifully carried the envelope to Sam.

"Hey Sam, that guy at the other end said to give this to you." As Sam looked toward the other end of the bar all he could see was the back of a large man in a dark expensive looking overcoat walking out on the street. The envelope was sealed.

Harry looked at Sam. "Open it."

Sam took out his pocketknife and cut open the end. Harry looked over his dinner as the contents spilled onto the bar. "Holy shit!" exclaimed Sam. There on the bar were 8 x 10 photos with the time and date they were exposed recorded in the lower right hand corner. The pictures were in sequence and showed Donald Kensington-Cramer getting out of his car. The time and date were the night that Donald died. The car was parked at the exact location as Sam's people had discovered it after it was stripped, that being across the street from Rueben's law office. The remainder of the photos showed Donald crossing the street, walking along the front of Rueben's law office, turning down the alley past the entrance to the underground parking garage and finally from another angle, entering the side door of the office, the very door that the camera with the missing chip was covering. The light from the neon sign on the restaurant was off essentially validating the time in the lower right hand corner.

"Stop that guy!" yelled Sam to Harry, but until they got out on the street the large well dressed man had disappeared into the sea of humanity that was flowing on the sidewalk.

Harry shrugged. "We'll do a complete lab workup on the envelope. We'll find whatever other prints, threads you name it, anything that doesn't belong to you that's in or on that envelope." That proved to be wishful thinking as the envelope and the photos were clean except for Sam's and the bartender's prints. The bar tender could have saved them the trouble. He noticed that the man never took his gloves off the entire time he was in the tavern. It was cold enough outside to warrant gloves, but few people kept them on inside and never to drink a beer.

To Catch a Fox

***

Duke Winston pulled the old pickup into the rest stop off I-95 just north of Rocky Mount North Carolina. He and his men had split up when they left the motel. Duke had pulled off the interstate several times to determine if he was being followed, but there was no sign of a tail. He had been driving since early morning, but because he had made so many stops he was still nearly forty miles south of the Virginia state line.

Duke needed a break. He parked the truck, pulled his baseball cap down over his eyes and zipped up his jacket. It was late November and there was a definite chill in the air. Duke walked to the restroom in the main building. When he came out he realized that he hadn't had anything to eat since some coffee and a donut at the hotel that morning. He decided to pay a visit to the vending machines in the small open pavilion next to the main facility. There was no one at the vending machines so Duke took his time to make his decision. He finally selected some peanut butter crackers and coffee. Choosing a picnic table he sat on the table section and put his feet on the bench.

The sun was setting and there were the typical gray autumn clouds streaked across the sky. Winter was coming thought Duke. When he drove into the rest area there were three other vehicles in the lot. Now there were four. He had accounted for the owners of the original three vehicles but not the fourth, but then he spied them, a young couple walking their dog in the pet area. Duke's table sat among the shadows of the tall pines that covered the rest area. Duke turned to check the landscape behind him. From this angle he could see the big rig parking area. There were several sitting there with their engines running. Then Duke noticed another rig apart from the rest near the exit to the lot. A tall man with a dark complexion and close cropped white hair climbed down from it and began walking up the path to the main building. Duke turned his attention back to his crackers and coffee.

***

Mary Wellbon's maid greeted Mac at the door of Mary's penthouse co-op. She took his overcoat and escorted him into the living room. Denton and his wife Susan were already there and were having drinks. "Mac come in, we've been waiting for you." Mary rose from her chair and extended a hand to Mac who accepted it graciously. It was now five o'clock in the evening of the day that the Wellbon family reasserted their control of Wellbon-Smith.

"I apologize for being late Mary. I have a new friend named Sarah that I value her opinion. I couldn't wait to inform her of Denton's job offer and get her advice."

"I hope her advice was positive Mac." Denton spoke up from the love seat where Susan was seated close to him.

Mac smiled. "Like me, she wants to consider it for a bit."

Mary smiled. "No wonder you trust her judgment. Could this new friend also be a romantic interest?"

"Possibly, one can hope."

"Then we wish you all the luck in the world Mac."

"Thank you Mary."

"Fix yourself a drink at the bar Mac. Get whatever you want. I've invited the three of you here tonight for a two fold purpose; first to celebrate our victory today with a sumptuous dinner, and second to tie up loose ends."

Mac fixed himself a Canadian Club on the rocks with a splash and a twist. Looking around he inquired, "Is Paul Henley going to be late?"

"He's not coming. We'll celebrate with him at another time. He's frankly not involved with the loose ends that I want to tie up tonight. These loose ends are long overdue to be dealt with."

"Well mother you certainly have raised my level of curiosity, are we eating first or are we tending to these loose ends as you put it?"

"We'll do loose ends first Denton."

Mac took a sip of his drink and moved to an empty chair, the same wing back that he sat in during his first visit to Mary's home. All were seated now except Mary, who sipped her whiskey sour and gazed at each of them individually before speaking again. Silence hung over the room as the anticipation rose. Mary took a deep breath. "After I left all of you at the office this afternoon I met someone who I've known indirectly for many years, but never met face to face until today." Denton frowned as Susan turned toward him, a quizzical look on her face, but said nothing. Mary continued. "She arrived here at the penthouse sometime this afternoon and was patient enough to allow Maria, my maid, to entertain her until I arrived home to introduce myself. Like all of you she has many questions, questions that will soon be answered."

"What questions mother? I have no questions."

"You will soon." Mary walked to the door leading to her office / study. Looking into the softly lit room she beckoned someone to come forward. A neatly dressed very professional looking young woman with long auburn hair falling loosely onto her shoulders entered the living room and stood next to Mary Wellbon. Mary put her arm around the young women's shoulders. "May I introduce to you Ms. Crystal Harrison?"

Denton's mouth dropped open, but he seemed unable to make any sound. Susan's eyes widened as she caught her breath. Mac studied Crystal for a long moment and then calmly took another sip of his whiskey. Mary squeezed Crystal's shoulder and smiled at her. Crystal returned the gesture. "Crystal and I have passed the time getting to know each other. She has many questions and I told her that I would answer as many as I could as soon as you all arrived. Crystal this is my son Denton and his wife Susan."

"Hello Crystal," Susan regained her voice before Denton and rose to shake Crystal's hand.

Denton struggled to his feet, his legs suddenly extremely weak. "Ah, um, I'm pleased to meet you." Denton managed to shake Crystal's hand after she steadied his.

Mac got to his feet and moved across the room. "Delighted I'm certain," said Mac as he bowed and kissed Crystal's hand.

"This is William McLode Crystal, he's president of our Fox Cabinetry division.

Fox is a company that Mac and his associates are about to purchase from us."

"I'm pleased to meet you all." There was just the ever so faint hint of a southern accent.

"Please everyone be seated and I'll begin my story." Mary waited until Crystal selected a chair and accepted a glass of wine from the maid.

Mary remained standing and began her tale. "Quite a few years ago Crystal's mother Mary, a name I shared with her, was a student in a pilot vocational-technical program. The program allowed students to work as interns in various businesses while completing their high school education. Crystal's mother was working at Pfeiffer International Trading Corporation. As both you and Mac are aware Denton, Pfeiffer's main facility is in Baltimore and is one of the Wellbon-Smith companies."

"Of course mother," Denton had regained his composure but he couldn't take his eyes off Crystal. She sat silently sipping her wine. She looks tired thought Denton, but then who wouldn't. She had been kidnapped, rescued and Denton assumed that Andy or one of his cousins or an associate had seen to it that she was brought here, but why here and on whose authority? Once again it seemed as if his mother was in charge so he had to assume that she was the instigator of this gathering. Why would she do this without consulting him? Denton glanced at Susan. How was she taking this he wondered? Susan had a look of concern on her face as she studied Crystal intently.

Mary continued. "Crystal's mother was working in Pfeiffer's office and was assisting several of Pfeiffer's customhouse brokers. This is one of the services that Pfeiffer offers to its clients. A customhouse broker takes care of all of the paperwork for shippers that are either exporting or importing into the United States. Mary Johnson was a natural not only at administrative work in general, but she took a particular interest in the paperwork surrounding customhouse brokering. Her supervisors at Pfeiffer were extremely proud of her work and enthusiasm and made certain that she was introduced to the "brass" from the parent company, Wellbon-Smith, when they came to visit."

"Where is this going Mother?" Denton wasn't certain how large an audience he desired. Today's events had produced about as much stress as he had ever experienced and actually meeting Crystal Harrison for the first time, well his nerves were threadbare.

"Trust me and indulge me Denton, you'll see." Mary Wellbon's tone was neither threatening nor condescending. She continued. "Let's skip forward in our saga to the night when Mary's mother was invited to a frat party at Princeton. It was no coincidence that she was there. The "brass" at Wellbon-Smith, after meeting her and reviewing her work, were also impressed with her abilities and they applied for a scholarship to Princeton on her behalf. She won the scholarship and she was on campus for an applicant weekend. This is where all perspective students get to come and live on campus to get a preview of college life. As she was an extremely attractive young woman, the frat house that you Denton belonged to invited her and several of the other high school students that were present to the party. The counselors approved, as their goal was to give the applicants a well-rounded view of campus life. After all, they believed that because of the presence of high school aged students chaperones would be at the party all evening. Something got fouled up, or was purposely fouled up or someone was simply asleep at the switch but that never happened."

Denton definitely didn't like the direction this was taking. Mary paused and stared directly at Denton. "It was at this very party that you Denton decided to do something totally out of character for you and you made drunken advances toward Crystal's mother Mary Johnson." Mary turned to Crystal. "I'm afraid dear that your mother accepted the offer extended by my son while he was under the influence and felt a need to demonstrate his manhood to his frat brothers."

"Mother!"

Mary turned to Denton with one eyebrow raised. "Did I say anything that wasn't true Denton?"

Denton couldn't believe that this was how this incredible day was going to end. "No Mother!" He turned to Susan. "I have to be the one that ends this," he said. Then turning to Crystal he forced himself to look directly into her eyes. "Crystal I have a confession to make." Crystal's eyes held apprehension.

"Denton!"

"No Mother she has to hear this from me!"

To Catch a Fox

"Denton, before you say anything you must hear me out."

"No Mother, I have to do this!"

"Hear what?" asked Crystal softly. Was this it? Was this the missing part of her puzzle, her life? She was suddenly afraid of what she might hear. This day might be more than she could handle. Now she was about to hear…what? "Whatever you want to tell me please tell me Mr. Wellbon. This summer I met with the person that I've always thought was my estranged father to discover that he wasn't my father at all. I've learned that my personal history is nothing like I had been told all of my life. This means that my own mother was lying to me. As I told your mother earlier, I now believe that I understand why she lied, but it's getting scary. I have been abducted for no apparent reason, rescued thank God and now I find myself here among strangers. Strangers who seem to know a great deal about me, I've been promised the answers that I seek and I intend to finally get them. I can't go on living out this mystery that I had no hand in creating without some reasonable explanation."

All in the room were silent. Mary Wellbon apparently decided to see what would happen next. Denton stood up and walked across the room to stand before Crystal. He hung his head and clasped his hands in front of him. "No Crystal, you don't deserve any of the heartaches or the events that you have been subjected to. Lord knows you've just been trying to live your own life, but the sins of others, of the past have interfered with that up until now."

Crystal sat her glass of wine on an end table, being careful to place it on a coaster. Strange she thought, at a time like this she was conscious of not marking her hostess's furniture. She took a deep breath and looked up at Denton. "Tell me what you want me to know Mr. Wellbon."

Denton's mouth and throat went dry. "I…I'm…what I'm trying to say is that… I'm your…your…I'm your father."

Crystal finally heard someone speak the words. She had wondered how she would react if she ever heard those three words. Now that she heard them she felt strangely devoid of emotion. Too many things had happened too fast. She was still just grateful to be alive. She had no idea why her life had been threatened, but she knew it was and at this moment just being alive meant more to her than hearing those words. Perhaps she was just too tired to be able to absorb the implications.

"And he truly believes that Crystal. He truly does. But he's wrong. He's not your father." Mary Wellbon finished her whiskey sour and returned the empty glass to the bar. All eyes were on her. Denton's mouth was open again, his face incredulous.

"Mother, how can you say such a thing? We have to be honest with this young woman!"

"That's precisely why I can't allow either one of you to believe a fiction. I'll say it again Denton. You are not Crystal's father."

"Mother, why? You've seen the evidence. While I admit it isn't conclusive, who else could possibly be her father? This can't be helping Crystal." Denton's emotion was so intense that he was truly short of breath as he spoke. The words seemed to be forced from his body between gasps.

"Because I know who her father is!" Only her unblinking eyes matched Mary Wellbon's level tone of voice as she focused on her son.

"Mother?"

"Please sit down Denton and allow me to finish what I've begun." Mary's tone now became patience mixed with concern. Mary sat down in a chair next to Crystal. She took Crystal's hand in hers and looked directly into Crystal's eyes. "Darling what I'm about to tell you may be as difficult for you to hear as it is for me to say."

"Mrs. Wellbon you've been vary gracious to me since I came here. You've inquired about my situation and you've listened sympathetically as I've related my story. I appreciate your sensitivity toward my feelings, but nothing can compare to what I've been through the last forty-eight hours. I need to finally know the truth, no matter what it may be."

"Yes dear and you deserve to know that truth." Mary took a deep breath. "Let's return to the so called 'brass' that came to visit Pfeiffer. The people Pfeiffer's executives showed off Crystal's mother to were none other than one Carlton Smith and Denton Wellbon II, your father Denton."

All eyes were on Mary except Denton's. He was struck as to the resemblance between Crystal and her mother. Denton would not admit it but he would have had a hard time remembering exactly what Mary Johnson looked like until Crystal walked into the room. Then Mary's image came flooding back to him. Like her mother she was beautiful.

Mary Wellbon laughed a soft ironic laugh. "Just a few hours ago I upbraided Carlton for his infidelities. He should hear me now. Anyway, like you Crystal your mother was very beautiful."

Crystal blushed slightly. "Thank you Mrs. Wellbon. You're very kind."

"Not at all, I'm merely stating the truth and it happens to be pertinent. Knowing that her bosses wanted to show her off to some people from corporate Mary Johnson was dressed very professionally and she probably used a bit more make up that day than she would have if she were just going to high school. She apparently looked far more mature than her seventeen years. Mature enough that the two big shots from corporate were not only impressed with her skill sets but also with her beauty. Now my husband had a nasty habit of not paying attention to what was being explained to him. He always had his mind in two places simultaneously, first he was concerned as to what was going on around him to the extent that it interested him and second his mind was focused on whatever money making scheme he was currently playing around with. This means that sometimes, if his interest wasn't peaked, he missed some very important facts effecting the current situation. On the day that he and Carlton paid a visit to Pfeiffer he somehow missed that this was a vocational technical program for high school students. He missed that fact and assumed that Mary Johnson, by her appearance, was older than her actual age; in his mind that made her old enough."

His mother's words finally tore his attention from Crystal. "Mother what are you saying, old enough for what?"

"Unfortunately old enough to have an affair," Mary turned back to Crystal. "Crystal I'm certain that your mother was swept off her feet when my husband paid attention to her. He was quite handsome. Lord knows he had the same affect on me when I was just out of college. He was older now but the addition of a touch of gray hair made him look very sophisticated even though his overall appearance was younger than his years. Being rich didn't hurt either. I'm certain it wasn't hard for him to make a young girl fall in love with him."

"Mother, you…you're saying that…"

"I'm saying that Crystal's mother and my husband had a brief but torrid affair. Denton, my husband Denton, found some excuse to bring her to New York in connection with her job with Pfeiffer and, well there's no fool like an old fool."

Denton stumbled to his feet once again. "You're saying that…" Denton couldn't get the words out.

"Crystal is your half sister Denton."

Susan gasped and reached for Denton's hand. Denton was standing and swaying slightly. His knees were really rubbery now. "Then my father is actually her father?"

Mary smiled a sardonic smile. "That's generally the way it works when two people share one parent. I suppose that makes me sort of her stepmother, hell I don't know."

Denton now sat down on a hassock, his elbows on his knees and his head in his hands. "My god!" was all he could manage. Susan left the loveseat and knelt beside him gently running her hand up and down on his back.

"Crystal by the time that my husband realized just how young your mother was she was already pregnant. Imagine, he was brilliant enough to build an industrial empire but couldn't think to use protection. I suppose it was a macho thing."

Crystal like Denton III was shocked, but for some unfathomable reason this had the sound of truth to her. She couldn't explain it but Denton's "confession" just didn't ring true. Mary Wellbon had told her earlier when they were alone that her husband was deceased. Together with the information that the elusive and mysterious Mr. Smith had given her this all sounded like something that a wealthy man like Mary Wellbon's husband could pull off. Mary also informed her that her son had just today risen to take his father's place in the family business. Only now did he possess the power to have a man like George Smith working for him. But, there was the night her mother spent with Denton III.

"Mrs. Wellbon, forgive me, but even you admit that my mother spent a wild night partying with your son. How can you be certain which one is my father? How do you know all of this?"

"First because my husband confessed the affair to me; he had to when he discovered your mother was pregnant. You have to understand my husband. Family was very important to him. Even, and please forgive me for this Crystal, even illegitimate family. Abortion was never considered, neither by my husband or your mother. Thank goodness. You are a beautiful talented person. Second, that confession took place before the night she spent with my son, that night in which he was so drunk that he doesn't remember anything. I can assure you that absolutely nothing happened between them. Thank God!" Denton no longer desired to protest this point.

Crystal realized the implications. "I believe you as to who is my father, but how can you be certain nothing happened between my mother and her, her…"

"Her lover's son," Mary completed Crystal's thought in her usual unflinching manner. "Because after the dust settled and after I came to grips with my hurt, I went to see your mother. I lied, I did meet you before today Crystal, but you were barely two years old then. I no longer felt animosity toward her. She was just a child when all this happened. My husband bore responsibility. Your mother filled in the missing pieces that my husband couldn't bring himself to tell me."

"Your mother loved my husband. I truly believed that after I met her. I believe she loved him until the day she died. Perhaps that unrequited love was the reason she took her own life. I don't think that she ever got over losing Denton." Mary stared into space with unseeing eyes for a moment. Then she continued. "My husband did truly love me, even though he committed this mistake. He confessed to me and begged my forgiveness. I didn't give it to him for several years, but finally I relented. He desperately wanted to stay with me. I wasn't sure and several times I considered divorce, but although I had the papers drawn up I never had them filed. Anyway, my husband informed your mother that he would always support her and their child, but he wouldn't leave me. Your mother being a child herself and grievously hurt made an immature decision. She didn't want to marry the boy Foster Harrison that she recently broke up with." Mary looked at Crystal. "From what your mother told me of Foster and what you told me earlier today I believe I understand. Your mother decided to get revenge on my husband. She wasn't thinking of the future, she was hurt and she wanted to strike back. Love does that sometimes. She accepted the invitation to the weekend at Princeton knowing that several of the frat houses were having parties at the same time. She verified which fraternity that my Denton's son belonged to and made sure she attended that party."

"Our getting together was planned? Planned by Crystal's mother?" Denton was beginning to think that everyone involved knew what was going on except him.

"Yes and you were her target. Crystal's mother had no idea once she got to the party how she would manage to get you alone. As a plan her revenge was strictly high school. She had seen your photo. I suppose my husband showed it to her at some point. Lord knows why. She just wanted to strike back at the man she loved but who had just broken her heart. She believed that sleeping with his son would hurt him severely. As to the mechanics of actually accomplishing what she set out to do, well she was running on raw emotion. There wasn't a lot of planning. She never dreamed that you would cooperate and make it easy. We humans discount how random many of the events in our lives are. We try to see logic that sometimes isn't there. You Denton deciding to hit on this beautiful girl while having no idea as to who she was and her connection to you was certainly one of those random events."

"So mother was actually looking for your son that night?" Crystal wasn't certain how this would lead to revenge. "What made her think that Denton, this Denton, would tell his father? Young boys don't usually call home to tell their parents about their conquests."

"Well your mother, being older and more mature when I met her, admitted to me that it wasn't one of her better ideas. I'll explain how that little miscalculation backfired."

Denton moaned. "Why did I decide to approach her?"

Mary Wellbon looked at her son. "Denton, look at her daughter. Crystal is the spitting image of her mother. Her mother was no doubt the prettiest girl at the party that night. I doubt that you were the only boy who wanted to hit on her. You were simply the only one who had enough guts and the only offer she planned to accept."

"Oh." Denton looked around the room at his mother, wife, business associate and apparently his half sister. This was not the celebration that he imagined would top off this extraordinary day.

“Fortunately you were too drunk to do anything. I know this because…”

“Because Mary Johnson Harrison told you,” would this never end thought Denton.

“That’s correct Denton, thank you.”

Crystal was still puzzled, “I’m still not certain where the revenge was supposed to come in. I understand that she wanted to hurt your husband, but short of her telling him, how was he to find out?”

“Your mother expected young Denton to let it slip that he had been with her. She made certain that he knew her name. She even wrote it on a piece of paper and put it in his pocket. She expected to get a call from my husband. That never happened as my son never told a soul until his father confronted him. You probably lost the note she left Denton.”

Denton simply made a shrug of resignation.

Crystal frowned. “So what did she do?”

“She first attempted to contact my husband one last time. He would no longer answer her as he broke it off and didn’t want to prolong it any longer. So out of frustration she told her father, your grandfather that she had slept with young Denton. She didn’t reveal the affair with his father. I suppose that somehow in her love torn mind she still held out hope of them getting together. That somehow thinking that she slept with his son would hurt him and simultaneously make him jealous so that he would return to her. She also needed to admit to and explain the pregnancy to her parents. She was starting to show. She expected her father to call young Denton’s father and raise cane. That was the extent of her plan for revenge. Your grandfather did more than that. He attempted to blackmail us. He threatened to have Denton, our son, charged with statutory rape unless my husband paid him off.”

“My grandfather would not have done that! He told me he didn’t know your name, that your husband’s representative contacted him.”

Mary studied Crystal for a long moment. "I'm told that you met your grandfather for the first time only a few weeks ago."

"Yes," Crystal wondered how Mary Wellbon knew this but said nothing.

"Did he tell you about the nasty affair at the bank?"

Crystal hung her head for a moment. Mary Wellbon seemed to know everything. "Yes he did."

"I told you that this could be as hard for you to hear as it is for me to tell. It's true that my husband sent his emissary to contact your grandfather, but only after your grandfather contacted us and threatened to go to the police if we didn't pay him. Your grandfather may be a very different man now. Facing death tends to change us. But is it all that large of a stretch to imagine that he would attempt blackmail? Back then when he had no qualms about embezzling the bank?"

Crystal didn't answer. Denton shook his head. "Mother, you knew all of this all along?"

"Of course Denton, I told you the other night that your father told me everything. Besides you work with Andy. I work with his boss the Don."

"So that's how Crystal arrived here." Denton stood up again and walked to the bar. He fixed himself another drink. "Anything else you would like to share with us mother?"

A slight frown passed across Crystal's face after Denton's comment. It was obvious that Andy was the family's emissary and met with her grandfather. Mr. Smith had explained to her that Andy was a mobster and it sounded as if Mary Wellbon and her son were also very familiar with him. But Smith seemed to hold Andy in low regard. It was hard for her to put these two factors together.

Mary returned her attention to Crystal. "Are you all right dear?"

Crystal smiled a faint smile. "I suppose so. This all seems to make sense and mesh with what I've learned recently. My father was your husband. This is a bit overwhelming. Excuse me Mrs. Wellbon, but there is one more very large missing piece to this whole affair."

"That would be your abduction."

"Yes Mrs. Wellbon."

Mary turned to her son. "Why don't you fill your sister in on how it came to be that she was kidnapped by these hoodlums?"

"Yes mother." With that Denton told Crystal Harrison about the struggle for control of Wellbon-Smith.

"My life was the threat that they were holding over your head to get your vote?"

"Yes Crystal." Denton stared at the floor. "Now I really must confess something to you. Something that even mother won't argue with. I put your life in danger by voting my own and my family's interest. I didn't give in to this blackmail. Can you forgive me?"

Mary interjected. "Crystal, Denton sent Andy and his men to rescue you and was prepared to go to the FBI if they failed. He was very brave today and I'm proud of him."

Crystal wanted to say that it wasn't this Andy that they spoke of or his men that rescued her, but Smith's final words were burned into her brain so she made no comment on the rescue except to ask exactly who Andy and his men were?

Denton smiled. "If you decide to become more involved and want to get to know your family better, well maybe some day I can tell you about Andy." Then he turned to his mother and his face became serious. "Mother, you knew Crystal wasn't my daughter when I discovered what I thought was proof positive that my one night stand produced a child." His tone was bordering on anger.

"Yes I did. I told you that you were too drunk to perform that night."

"No you told Susan and me that you believed me to be too drunk to perform. That's a hell of a big difference from actually knowing because you talked to the other party involved!"

Mary Wellbon rolled her eyes slightly toward the ceiling. "Well yes, yes it is."

"Why Mother? Why did you let me go on believing and agonizing over the possibility of my having a daughter?"

"Well I had kept the secret for so long, I guess that I wanted to preserve the status quo if at all possible."

Denton's face was getting redder as his voice rose. "You and father also knew that I wasn't Crystal's father and you both determined to simply shut her grandfather up. Father could have owned up to the truth. Instead he made me the fall guy. His fall guy!"

"I told you the other night that I didn't agree with your father's methods."

Denton was getting angrier by the moment. "You knew this morning that Andy had already rescued Crystal, but you said nothing to me!" There it was again thought Crystal. Everything meshed together perfectly except this one point. This Andy could not have succeeded in a rescue attempt. Not against her captors. Yet her new found family obviously believed that he was responsible. Who was this Mr. Smith?

"I already explained that to you Denton. I wanted to see if you were man enough to make the right decision under pressure and you did." Mary's voice remained patient.

Susan moved to Denton's side and put her arms around him. "Denton, all is well that ends well. Crystal is safe and you have expelled Trevor Mason from the company. Because you are clever no one is going to know of the methods that were used in the takeover attempt. The attempt failed and you are finally legitimately in the chairman's chair, the chair that your grandfather and father occupied. You couldn't be there without your mother. The family once again controls Wellbon-Smith. Let's keep everything in perspective."

Denton sighed and looked back toward his mother. His voice softened. "I assume that you requested Crystal's presence here tonight."

"Yes, as I told you I deal with Andy's boss."

"I have to ask mother. After keeping this secret all of these years, why did you change your mind?"

"A fair question that I know must be on Crystal's mind also so I guess it's time to explain. Several things changed my mind, first our friend Mr. MacLode over there."

Mac smiled. "How so Mary?"

"At our first meeting you stated that 'blackmail only worked as long as you were afraid of the truth.' I considered all of those shareholders that Trevor and Abe had terrified. What were they terrified of? The truth. Crystal was placed in foster homes and later adopted because I was afraid of the truth. I decided that I was no longer afraid of that truth. Crystal was placed in danger because this family couldn't face the truth. We had a purpose for hiding it years ago. Keep my husband out of jail. But he's been dead for years now. The truth could no longer hurt him. I finally decided that it could no longer hurt me either, but hiding the truth could hurt Crystal. It almost did." Mary turned toward Crystal again. "Crystal welcome to the family, this family is not like the family you thought you had. And we're certainly not like your adopted family. We seem to be forever fighting with someone to protect what we worked for and built. We may employ some questionable people and means at times but we do stick together. It wouldn't surprise me if after what you went through you would tell us to shove it and walk out of here. After all, by yourself without any help from us you created an excellent career. You're quite capable of taking care of yourself. You really don't need us. But if you can forgive us for past sins and decide to stick around, and I for one hope that you do. You are welcome to be a full participating member of this family. Please let us try to make amends for the problems that we've caused you."

Crystal looked at Denton. "Are you prepared to have a half sister?"

Denton looked at Susan who still had her arms around him. Susan's smile was warm and inviting. "All things considered Crystal, I think it works much better for you to be my sister than for you to be my daughter."

"Amen," sighed Susan softly.

Mary came and put her arm around Crystal. "Is that a yes? Are you going to stick around and get to know us?"

"I think I will Mrs. Wellbon. You'll excuse me if it takes me some time to adjust to this new situation. I'm a bit overwhelmed and I have to be honest, I'm not certain how I feel about this whole thing. I've spent all summer wondering who my father and family really were. Now that I know who and why I have to spend some time mulling this around in my mind. I don't know how I feel about any of this. I'm sorry but I don't know how I feel about any of you. I need time to think."

"I totally understand Crystal. At least let us begin by giving you dinner."

"I will accept your invitation to dinner but afterward I'll probably be exhausted and go right to bed. I think I'm running on adrenalin." Crystal realized that she had no hotel to spend the night. "Oh, I'll have to call for a hotel room."

"Nonsense, I planned on you staying here tonight. Maria already has a room made up for you. You are welcome to stay as long as you like. I have plenty of space it's just me here rambling about."

"I was supposed to be in Mexico on vacation, but you know how that turned out."

"Stay here for the remainder of your vacation then you can return to your job in Savannah. It will give us a chance to get to know you better."

"I may take you up on that. I have to sleep on it so I'll decide in the morning. If nothing else you folks are certainly interesting. It's just that whatever happens next I'd like to be an observer and not quite as close to the action as I was this time."

"No guarantees in this family and please call me Mary."

"Okay Mary."

Mary turned to the others. "The cook has been holding dinner for us. I'm certain he'll be upset with me if he believes it to be too cold, so everyone shower him with compliments. It will spare me a long conversation later. Now follow me to the dining room and let's eat!"

As the little party moved toward the elegant dining room, Mary was considering what she was to Crystal "I guess I'm sort of your stepmother even though your mother and my husband were never married. Oh hell, I don't know what I am, but I'm glad you decided to stay."

Crystal smiled in answer, but her mind was still filled with questions. Questions about the things that were not explained tonight, the mysterious Mr. Smith and the trust fund that he attributed to her father. The incorrect impression about her rescue, none of these subjects had been addressed and Smith had made it clear that his name was never to surface. In the dining room Crystal accepted the chair offered to her next to Mary Wellbon.

To Catch a Fox

PART 6

Chapter 29

It was three thirty in the afternoon on the day following the Wellbon-Smith annual board meeting. Sam Grabowski sat in assistant district attorney Tamara Wilson's office. Scattered on her desk was Sam's report of the investigation into the suspicious death of Donald Kensington-Cramer. Along with the report were photos. First of Kensington-Cramer's car, the photos showed the condition that the car was found in, but more importantly the location. The location verified by the photos as directly across the street from Abraham Rueben's law offices. Next were the sequential photos of Kensington-Cramer getting out of his car, which although in far better condition than the previous photo is seen parked at the same location where it was discovered later by the police. The sequence of photos showed Kensington-Cramer crossing the street and walking toward Rueben's office building and turning down the alley near the entrance to the underground parking garage and entering the side door to the office off the alley. Next was the F.B.I. lab report on the confiscated surveillance cameras. The report stated that there was reason to suspect that the camera positioned to observe the door where the photos showed Kensington Cramer entering the office was altered to erase his entrance. The report went on into great detail as to why the lab reached that conclusion. Ms. Wilson studied all the reports and the photos carefully. After completing that review she reread the coroner's report.

"I admit it looks incriminating Lieutenant, but it is all circumstantial." Tamara Wilson was a thirty something strikingly beautiful blonde. She had a cool air of sophistication aided today by the fact that she was very professionally dressed in a dark pin stripped suit with a formal looking silk blouse under the jacket. Sam liked Tamara, but he knew her to be one tough cookie. She had an outstanding win / loss record as a trial lawyer, but she maintained that record by not prosecuting cases with what she called 'pie in the sky evidence.' Sam needed to convince her that this case was not that flimsy.

Sam cleared his throat before he spoke. "Yes, but the dates and times on the sequential photos show that Kensington-Cramer entered Rueben's office building at or near the coroner's estimated time of death. That gives credence to the lab's opinion that the surveillance tapes were altered. In addition, I believe something happened in Rueben's personal office because it reeks of fresh paint and new carpet."

"That all sounds good detective, but on the one hand you're going to want me to demonstrate in court that the surveillance tape could be technically altered to erase any image of Kensington-Cramer entering the building and on the other hand I'll have to prove that the date and time on the sequential photos are authentic. A jury could easily determine that if one could be a fake so could the other. Not to mention the fact that you received these photos from a mysterious man in a bar, a man that you can't produce to testify how he acquired the photos. In addition the body was found across town at Kensington-Cramer's apartment."

"But the coroner's report states that he didn't die in the fall and that he died at about the time that the photos were taken at Rueben's office. Doesn't that give credibility to the photos? What about the car? Why was the car there if Kensington-Cramer didn't drive it there? Why was it abandoned there? Why didn't he drive it home? How did he get home?" Sam was getting irritated. Was he the only one that could see that Rueben was involved in Kensington-Cramer's death up to his eyeballs?

Tamara looked at the photos one more time and when she raised her gaze her icy blue eyes bored into Sam. Sam couldn't help it. Even with all his years on the force facing the bad guys, this woman intimidated him. "Okay lieutenant, I can't go to a judge on the strength of this and ask for an arrest warrant, let's at least bring him in for questioning. Something stinks here and I want to be an observer when you put your questions to him. But mark my words you better get me more than this. I agree with you, he's involved in this somehow, but I need more. Understand?"

"Yes I do and I'll get it for you. I'll bring him in this evening for questioning. I'll call you when we pick him up." Sam gathered up his files and hurried out the door.

Tamara watched Sam go. Sam was a good detective and his strongest suit was that he was tenacious. He would have to be very tenacious along with being very clever to nail Abraham Rueben. She was very familiar with Abe Rueben. He was a mob lawyer with a long unsavory reputation. He was also rumored to have run afoul of the New York families when he went to work with the boys in Chicago.

However, because he knew too much and had the evidence well documented and hidden, he was apparently untouchable. The word was that if anything suspicious ever happened to him certain documents would wind up in the hands of the F.B.I. Even more obscure rumors hinted that he ran his own operations and he wasn't above brutality and murder if it served his purposes. None of this could be proven of course. She would love to get this very dangerous man off the streets and out of action. But she also knew what a tough nut he would be to crack.

A prime element missing in Grabowski's case was motive. Sam had found nothing linking Kensington-Cramer to Abe Rueben with the odd exception that Rueben was one of the people that attended Kensington-Cramer's funeral. Tamara picked up her copy of Sam's report and thumbed through it. There it was. Rueben attended the funeral with one Trevor Mason. The report listed Mason, as president of the Atlantic Corporation and the Atlantic was an integral part of the larger conglomerate Wellbon-Smith. Wait a minute. Donald's aunt was Melissa Kensington, New York society dame. What else should she remember about Melissa? Tamara called her secretary, "Hugh, come in here a moment please."

Hugh entered his boss' office with a quizzical look in his eye. "Yes Boss?"

"If I said the following what do you think of? Wellbon-Smith, Atlantic Corporation, Trevor Mason and Melissa Kensington."

Hugh thought for a moment. "Well let's see, Wellbon-Smith owns the Atlantic Corporation and Melissa Kensington is a prominent New York society dame. I have no idea who Trevor Mason is. Oh! Melissa Kensington is also a major shareholder in Wellbon-Smith."

"Hugh you are amazing. How do you keep up on all of these so-called celebrities in this town?"

"I read all the gossip columns, right after I read the financial pages of the Times and the Journal."

"Okay that's all I needed." Well there was a connection of sorts. That explains why this Mason guy was at the funeral but why was Rueben there? "Hugh." Hugh returned carefully concealing his irritation. "Yes Boss."

"Call around to some of your friends on the street and others that might work for the papers. Call anyone you can think of but find out if Rueben is Mason's lawyer.

"Rueben who?"

"Oh, I'm sorry Hugh. Of course you have no way of knowing what I'm talking about. Abraham Rueben is a trial lawyer with the firm of Murray, Marx and Rothmere. Trevor Mason is president of the Atlantic corporation."

Hugh grinned. She was tough to work for, but he actually liked her, sort of. "Most of the time I don't know what you are talking about."

"Go back to work. I promise not to bother you again."

"Yes Boss." He sincerely doubted that would happen.

This is really weak she thought. I don't even know what I'm looking for or why I'm bothering. Grabowski is working on instinct, and he's probably right, but without some kind of break... "Good luck Sam," she said to herself. "Good luck."

Hugh returned to his desk in the outer office and began typing up a deposition on his desktop computer. Beside his desk on the credenza in front of a window was a small portable television set that he kept tuned to CNN. Hugh Becket liked to keep up on current events. The volume was turned down so as not to disturb anyone. If the picture looked interesting he would turn it up to determine what was happening. Just now he noticed one of the talking heads standing in a wooded area with several big rigs parked behind her. The caption under the picture stated that he was looking at a scene somewhere near Rocky Mount North Carolina. Hugh turned up the volume. His sister lived in Rocky Mount. "The body was discovered by one of the workers at this interstate rest stop. The worker noticed that this particular tractor-trailer had been parked here since she had come on duty at seven o'clock this morning. It's not unusual for drivers to sleep in their sleeper cabs at rest stops, but they seldom remain this long. Thinking perhaps the driver was ill she investigated and discovered the body with two bullets in the brain. The State Police are investigating..." Hugh turned the volume down again and resumed typing.

***

To Catch a Fox

Abraham Rueben looked at his watch and decided to call it quits. It was seven in the evening. Earlier he had reviewed the document that Denton had given Trevor. Trevor signed it and returned it to Denton personally.

Denton Wellbon III that little shit! Abe warned Trevor about him. But Abe thought he had Denton covered; he had his daughter for god's sake. But somehow Denton trumped him. He must have sent Andy Bevilacqua as a decoy, but who actually freed the girl? If he believed Duke they had the firepower of a small army. They had to be working for Denton, who else could have sent them? Remembering the professional way that Crystal Harrison's true identity had been hidden Abe shook his head. An amateur had outflanked him. During his long career, Abraham Rueben had taken on some of the smartest, toughest opponents this city and Chicago had to offer. Now he was beaten. For the first time in his life he was beaten, beaten by whom? A wimp born with a silver spoon in his mouth beat Abraham Rueben. A wimp had been tougher than Abe when the chips were down. A wimp had been more ruthless. Damn!

Suddenly Abe was weary of thinking about Denton, although he knew that it would eat away at him until he was able to get revenge. He promised himself right then and there that he would indeed get vengeance for the potential fortune he lost and the humiliation that Denton had forced him to suffer. Oh yes Abe thought, Mr. Denton Wellbon III would be very sorry that he ever decided to take on Abraham Rueben, very sorry indeed.

With that settled he chose some files that required his attention and placed them in his briefcase. His firm did have clients other than Trevor Mason. Then he looked out the window at the dazzling city lights. He thought that he heard the wind whistling about the building and he went to the closet and took out his heavy overcoat. After all it was nearly Thanksgiving and the weather in New York City had been seasonal.

Taking his Colt .45 semi automatic from the drawer he clicked off the safety and tucked it into his waistband. Abe only carried it there when traveling between the office and his car. Over the years he had accumulated quite a list of potential enemies and he wanted to be able to access his weapon quickly should the need arise. Once in his car he would place it in his shoulder holster. Abe's car was equipped with bulletproof glass and reinforced body panels. Abe locked up his office and walked through the rows of cubicles where the paralegals and the associates worked until he arrived at the elevator in the wall opposite his office. After pushing the down button the elevator arrived and the doors opened. Abe entered and pushed the button for the ground floor. This was one of the perks that went with owning the building. The underground garage went five levels down. The quarters were close and the ramps narrow. Abe parked just outside the side door on the ground level. Ground level but still under the enclosure so that he didn't get wet leaving his car when it was raining.

While descending Abe thought of the news item that he heard on CNN today. At an I-95 rest stop near Rocky Mount North Carolina a worker found a man's body in a tractor-trailer. It was murder execution style with two bullets in the victim's head. Abe smiled. He knew that his hit man was going to use a big rig for cover and then abandon it when the job was finished. Making certain that it was perfectly clean. He wasn't certain as to how he planned the escape. That bit of information was never revealed. The two 22 caliber slugs in the brain were a bit of a trademark for his hit man. That way if it were too "hot" to make a contact with him, Abraham or any of his other clients would know that the job was completed and that his man did it. Even though the victim's name was not yet public knowledge Abe knew that Duke Winston was dead.

Ah Duke, too bad you became expendable thought Abe. It would be difficult to find anyone of Duke's caliber and skill sets to replace him. It was hard to find people that weren't burdened by conscious and could be totally brutal. Even the mob soldiers found it hard at times to kill one of their own, but not Duke. If the "mission" as he called it required killing his grandmother he would have done it. Replacing Duke would not be easy. It occurred to Abe that his requirements called for someone like himself.

Then Abraham thought of Duke's bartender. Ironically the very same bartender that tipped Abe off to the numerous booby traps present in Duke's bar would also be the person assigned the task of getting the video chip out of the safe and mailing it to the FBI. Abe laughed out loud as he pictured the surprise in the bar tenders eyes as he realized that the chip had been stolen.

None of Duke's team, half of which was now apparently dead, ever met Abe or even talked with him. All instructions were given and payrolls were met through Duke. When a job was completed no one except Duke knew Abe's identity. Now all evidence pointed toward Duke being dead. They would eventually figure out who the body was and then and only then would Abe pay his assassin. As for the video chip, Abe destroyed it the same morning that he stole it. Abe knew that Duke trusted no one, so even the bartender wouldn't know what was on that chip. He would just have instructions to mail the chip. Abe felt that he was covered.

Well thought Abe, I may have lost the takeover bid to Denton, but everything else was cleaning up fairly well. The doors opened and Abe moved through the main lobby toward the door leading to the parking garage. On his way out he passed the security guard who was monitoring the screens that held the images transmitted by the surveillance cameras. The man was one of the new team he had his Security Chief hire.

"Good night Mr. Rueben," said the guard.

"Good night," answered Abe. He was still wondering if the security guards were a cost-effective expense. Judging from the experience of a few weeks ago they weren't.

Abe pushed through the parking garage door and emerged out under the enclosure. He began walking toward his car. He reached in his pocket, pulled out the key and pressed the button. The horn beeped one time and the turn signals flashed informing him that it was now unlocked. Then Abe stopped. He pressed another button on the key fob and the engine started. No bomb this time thought Abe. Early in his rather dark career a car bomb had nearly killed him. Actually it probably should have killed him, but he proved to be very lucky. The individual that had wired the bomb had proven less than competent and the position of the bomb worked in Abe's favor. However, his legs still bore the scars of the burns that he acquired as a result of the blast. Soon after he emerged from his stay in the hospital, Abe determined who the bomber was and had him run over with a truck. The police thought it to be an accident. It was after that incident he acquired the additional remote control to start his engine; long before the auto manufacturers offered it as an option. He was amused at how tiny a unit it now was. His first one, that he had specially made, looked like he was flying a remote control model airplane. Not only was it handy to warm the car on a cold morning, but also he could start the engine from a remote distance, far enough away that if a bomb detonated he would be safe.

"Mr. Rueben." The voice came from behind him. Abe turned expecting to see the security guard he just spoke with. The man probably thought of something that he deemed important and wanted to relate it to Abe. But all he could see was a dark figure in the shadows of the garage.

"Yes, who am I talking to?"

The figure took two steps into the light, "Just me."

Abe blinked in his surprise. It can't be. Abe's hit man had never failed him in the past! But, there was no mistake it was Duke Winston standing there. "Hello Duke, I'm surprised that our security people didn't come out here and hassle you."

"I've studied the system. There are numerous 'holes' where you can walk undetected."

"Is that so, I'll have to have that changed. It's good to see you Duke."

"I expect that you are a bit surprised Abe."

"Why would that be Duke?"

"You probably thought I was dead."

"I spoke with you yesterday morning. Why would I think that?"

"Because you sent that white haired son of a bitch to kill me, that's why! The dumb bastard had no idea how many gooks in Nam tried to sneak up behind me and kill me. I broke his neck. He was dead before he hit the ground. Then I put two rounds in his brain from his own weapon just because he pissed me off!"

"I don't know what you're talking about Duke."

"The hell you say! You're the only one that had reason to have me killed. All the others with reason I've already killed. I also found my photo in his truck cab."

Abe wasn't going to fool around with this crazy any longer. In one quick movement Abe hit the panic button on his key fob, dropped both the keys and the briefcase that was in the other hand, drew the Colt from his waistband and dove toward the nearest car for cover. While raising the Colt to fire at Duke, Abe managed to get off one round before he landed behind the car. Split. But Duke was lightening fast himself, simultaneously moving to his left while his weapon came out from under his fatigue jacket in a blur spitting lead through the silencer as it moved. Split, split, split, split. Abe hit the concrete and slid behind the parked car. Then there was only the continuous honking of Abe's car horn. Duke dropped to one knee and grasped his weapon with both hands as he watched for Abe to emerge. Because of Duke's quick move Abe's only shot missed him clean. The door to the interior of the office beside Duke began to open. Duke spun and fired three more rounds through it. Split, split, split. The door wavered for a second and then the security guard pitched face forward out of the opening. After hitting the concrete he didn't move. Even though his clip held ten rounds, Duke had already ejected the first clip and replaced it with a full one.

Duke remained crouched and cautiously approached the car that Abe had disappeared behind. Because of the dim light, Duke couldn't determine if Abe was still at this location or had moved off into the shadows. He was certain that he had hit him. Moving around the rear fender Duke saw Rueben. He was sprawled on the parking garage floor lying in an ever-increasing pool of blood. Duke stooped over to inspect his work. Damn he thought I haven't forgotten how to lead a moving target. All four rounds had found their mark, but one had entered Abraham Rueben's temple.

Duke rose, casually gathered up the discarded magazine and the spent shell casings and walked off down the alley. Again carefully avoiding the security cameras. In the distance he could hear sirens over the annoying honking of Rueben's car. The guard probably pressed some button that alerted the cops. Halfway down the alley Duke stopped before an open manhole cover. He lowered himself down in and replaced the lid. Then pulling a flashlight from a pocket he began making his way through the underground labyrinth from which he came. His pickup was many blocks away, much further than what the initial search and seal off would cover. One of his team worked for the Department of Water and Sewers and had provided Duke with the map of the city's system. Duke always knew that it would come in handy sometime. Then he remembered that this was one of the team members that didn't return from their most recent mission in Savannah. Damn Rueben he thought, pitting us against a full-blown military operation. He expected that he would never know who ran the rescue or why this one kidnapping required such firepower. But Rueben had to know and he committed the ultimate sin in combat. He downplayed the threat and sent them in without the proper tools to fight the kind of adversary they would eventually have to face. At least he just had the pleasure of killing Rueben.

***

When Sam Grabowski discovered that Abe Rueben wasn't at home in his co-op, he posted one of his detectives at the residence and headed toward Rueben's office building. While in route he heard the radio chatter about an intruder alarm at the very address that he was headed for. What the hell is going on thought Sam as he pushed the accelerator down and switched on the flashing lights? He kept the siren off so as not to warn the intruder and began to weave through traffic.

Upon arrival Sam found two patrol cars parked at the entrance to the underground parking garage over which Rueben's office building stood. Sam hung his badge around his neck and walked over to a group of officers standing beside a car. "What's up?"

"Good evening detective, what brings you out so fast?"

"I was on my way here when I heard the call. What do we have?"

"Two dead in what appears to have been a shootout. The security guard over there never got a shot off, looks like he was shot through the door as he attempted to come out here. He apparently set off the alarm that we responded to before he left his post."

"Where's the other one?"

"Over there behind that car."

Sam walked to the car, "Son of a bitch!" Sam couldn't believe his eyes, it was Abe Rueben. He stared at the body in the pool of blood before him. One of the officers approached.

"Do you know him sir?"

"Yeah, I know him. I was coming here to take him in for questioning. He's got a handgun clenched in his right hand, but he surely wasn't the one that shot the guard. The guard worked for him."

"We're not sure how it came down detective. We think there was another shooter."

"Looks that way."

"What do you want us to do sir?"

"Carry on with your investigation. Touch nothing until the CSI unit gets here." Sam turned and walked back to his car. He didn't feel like answering a patrolman's questions just now. He would wait for the CSI team and see what they could come up with, but he couldn't help feeling discouraged. Now more than ever he believed that his hunch was correct. That Rueben was somehow linked to Donald Kensington-Cramer's death. But he also couldn't help thinking that so much more must be going on here. He believed the mob was somehow involved. Especially the way this crime scene looked. This appeared as if someone was waiting to gun down Rueben. That wouldn't surprise anyone. But Rueben was a savvy old soldier; he wouldn't be taken down without a fight. The gun in his hand proved that. It would be interesting to learn if he got a shot off and if the slug could be found.

Sam opened the door and settled in behind the steering wheel of his car. He was suddenly very tired. It seemed that things hadn't changed at all since he and Harry Sigfried were both rookies. Damn! How could he be so close and yet so far! Somehow this was all tied together with the fact that old Denton Wellbon's kid was now hanging out down at Andy's Diner. That had to mean that old Don Luca out on Long Island was involved somehow. No matter how legitimate he now claimed to be Sam still believed that Luca was running the mob and somehow involved with the Atlantic Corporation. If that was true Atlantic was being used as a cover for mob operations, but as Harry continually pointed out that had never been proven. Sam felt like he was starting all over again. He could only wait and see where this investigation led. Even then he could come up empty. He hoped that someday, somehow he could discover what really happened here and why. Maybe then he could break this whole thing wide open. Until then he had no choice but to wait and bide his time. That was something at which Sam was good.

Sam picked up his cell phone and dialed ADA Tamara Wilson, no point in her hanging around the office waiting for him to pick up Rueben. She probably had some high-powered date that she would rather be with anyway. As he listened to the phone ring he wondered if Harry might be up for a beer or two later tonight.

Chapter 30

Thanksgiving came and Tony Conocenti met Blair McManus in New York City for the Macy's Parade. Because Blair had connections through her previous job with the New York Times, they got seats in the V.I.P. viewing stand. Tony made reservations at an excellent restaurant called The Manhattan Grill for a leisurely Thanksgiving dinner afterward. Tony had the traditional turkey and filling and Blair had grilled salmon. It proved to be a perfect day. In the evening Blair talked Tony into taking her dancing at several of the current "in" clubs. It had been years since Tony had been dancing, but Blair was very good and she made Tony look like he knew what he was doing. They danced until the last club on Blair's "must see" list was about to close down. Afterward, in the early morning hours they decided to walk the ten blocks back to the Marriott in Times Square rather than take a cab. They walked most of the way in contented silence. The night was cool. Tony was very conscious of the fact that Blair had her arm linked with his and was walking very close. He thought he felt her shiver slightly so he put his arm around her shoulders. As they neared the entrance to their hotel Blair broke the silence.

"This was a great day Tiger, thank you."

"Yeah it was wasn't it?"

"I almost forgot. You said earlier that you had something to tell me. What is it?"

"Oh, yeah, that's right. Well, it turns out that since Mac helped the Wellbon family retain control of their company they offered him the position of President of the Atlantic Corporation. That position is currently vacant with the departure of Trevor Mason."

Blair looked surprised, "Wow! But I thought Mac was a partner with you guys in buying Fox?"

"He is. I mean he still is. He's decided to retain his shares in Fox and accept the position at corporate. He'll remain on our new board of directors. Thank goodness because the rest of us couldn't pull it off without him."

"What about the outside investors? How do they feel about this?"

"Mac talked it over with them and told them that if they were uncomfortable he wouldn't take the position at Atlantic. Apparently they told him that as long as he retained his shares and his seat on our board of directors, permitting him to be an active advisor, they were okay with it."

"So if Mac is the new President of Atlantic, who will run Fox?"

Tony hesitated for a few moments. "Well we took a vote and the rest of the staff unanimously voted for me."

Blair stopped in her tracks. "Did you just say what I thought you said?"

Tony grinned. "What did you think I said?"

"That you, Tony Conocenti, my Tiger, are the new president of Fox Custom Cabinetry!"

"I guess that's what I said."

Blair squealed and threw her arms around Tony's neck. Then she pressed her lips tightly and sensuously against his. When the very passionate kiss softly ended she stared up at him with those beautiful green eyes. Even in the dim light of the streetlights they seemed to shine. "I'm so proud of you Tiger."

"It's a little scary. Mac's a hard act to follow."

"You can do it."

"I definitely want to try. I won't be taking over until the first of the year. That's when the deal will be finalized. Because we worked there and ran the company for so many years, we breezed through the due diligence."

"What's due…what?"

“Due diligence. When you purchase a business you have a period of time to examine the books, interview key employees and in short turn over all the ‘rocks’ looking for any horrors that might be hidden there. If you find any that really scare you, you may back out of the deal. We figured we already know what’s under the rocks. The Futures people simply went over the books with us. That was really a vote of confidence from them.”

Blair frowned and tilted her head slightly to the side. “What? You have something else to tell me?”

“I can’t keep any secrets from you can I?”

The ornery grin returned to play at the corners of Blair’s mouth. “You better never. Out with it.”

Tony looked up and realized that they were standing at the entrance to the Marriott. “I’m cold, how about you?”

Blair shivered again. “Yeah, I could stand to be inside right about now.”

“Let’s go in and see if the hotel bar is still open. If it is let’s have a nightcap and warm up before turning in.”

“When do I get to hear whatever it is that you still haven’t told me?”

“Over the nightcap.”

“Suppose the bar is closed.”

“Then you may never find out.”

Blair took a playful swing at Tony. He ducked and ran into the hotel. Blair was close on his heels. The bar remained open and the two settled down at a table near a window. The bar was on the fifth floor and the view was partially of Times Square and partially of the Great White Way. When their drinks were served Blair raised an eyebrow and gazed at Tony. “Okay let’s hear the rest of it.”

“Well this has nothing to do with Fox Cabinetry or my new position.”

"Okay…"

"I did some shopping in Lancaster yesterday before I came over to the City."

"What did you buy?"

"Well that's just it. For this kind of shopping I would have liked to have you along for an expert opinion, but you were still in Chicago."

"What did you buy, clothes, something for your apartment?" Blair considered herself to hold a PhD in shopping, so she was getting excited just contemplating Tony's purchase. "I know! You bought a new car! You were celebrating your promotion."

"I don't need a car the company supplies me with a car."

"Yeah, if you like a four door Buick or Pontiac. Mac has a company car but he also has a classic T-Bird. What did you get? Tell me?"

Tony grinned. "I didn't think that your imagination would escalate the price tag so rapidly. I mean you went from clothes to a classic car in less than four seconds."

Blair grinned sheepishly. "I'm sorry Tiger. Now what did you buy?"

"Well after your expectations, I hope you're not disappointed."

She was bouncing up and down in her chair now. "I still get excited on Christmas morning now tell me what you bought!"

Tony pulled a small box from his jacket pocket. "Just this," he said. As he spoke he opened the box and placed it in Blair's hand. Blair stared at the contents of the box. It was a beautiful diamond ring with the crystal clear stone placed exquisitely in a delicate setting.

Her eyes were open wide with surprise as she raised them to meet his. Her mouth was slightly open, the smile of anticipation gone. "This is a ring," she whispered.

Tony's expression was a combination of seriousness and apprehension. "Yes it is."

The silence lasted but a second, but to Tony it seemed an eternity. Damn, had he misread her again? Was he pushing too fast too soon?

Blair swallowed, but her mouth felt dry. She believed that her hand was shaking, although it didn't appear to be. "Tiger…is this what I think it is?"

Oh to hell with it! Thought Tony, here I go! "Blair, will you marry me?" He blurted it out.

Blair looked down at the ring again. It was beautiful she thought, and so was this man who just gave it to her, although at the moment he seemed a bit pale. "Yes, yes, yes! Of course I'll marry you Tiger." Blair stood up and looked around the establishment. There was an older couple at a table and a lone man at the bar. A young girl was working behind the bar. Blair grinned at Tony. She knew how conservative and straight-laced he had become since living in Lancaster County Pennsylvania for nearly twenty years. Then she turned toward her audience.

"Blair no," said Tony as he reached for her, but it was too late.

"We're going to be married!" yelled Blair. He's my Tiger and I'm his girl and we're getting married." The few people that were in the bar immediately stood erupted into spontaneous applause and showered them with congratulations. Who says New Yorkers are a hard uncaring bunch thought Blair. Tony stood up beside her and caught up in the moment grabbed her and gave her a long passionate kiss, much to the delight and further cheers of the patrons.

When the cheering and congratulations finally stopped and everyone returned to their previous locations, Blair placed the ring on her finger and reached across the table to take Tony's hand in hers. "You didn't really think for a moment that I would turn you down?"

"Well, it was pretty scary. I've been thinking about this for weeks. Then suddenly when you hesitated I was forced to consider the possibility of rejection for the first time."

"Well I didn't reject you and I never ever plan on doing so."

To Catch a Fox

"I love you Blair."

"I love you too Tiger. More than you'll ever know."

"Blair, if our getting married creates a problem. I mean a problem for your career then I'll turn down the position at Fox and I'll find a job out in Chicago. We can live there."

Blair stared at him for a long moment. Once again Tony had no idea what to expect when she spoke again. "You're serious aren't you Tiger?"

"Yes of course. I've been doing a lot of thinking about the conversation that we had out on the Navy Pier. You're more important to me than any job."

Blair's eyes softened and they were in danger of overflowing with tears. "That's the sweetest thing," she said. "It won't be necessary Tiger. I talked to my editor. He's been pushing me to move much closer to New York's style center. He believes that I can retain my position and file my work via e-mail from a home in someplace like Lancaster. Lancaster is only a couple of hours from New York and there are daily flights to Chicago so I could make meetings if necessary."

"So, you're saying that you can move to Lancaster and keep your job with the Trib?"

"Yes."

"Who initiated this conversation, you or your editor?"

"Me, but it's an idea that he's floated to me before."

"When did you rekindle this conversation with your editor?"

"Oh it was right after our breakfast meeting on the Navy Pier."

"But you had no idea that I would ask you to marry me then. I had no idea that I would ask you."

Blair was grinning that ornery grin once more. "A body has to be prepared. Didn't they teach you that in Boy Scouts? Besides, we gals are always way ahead of you guys when it comes to the state of a relationship."

Tony laughed. "I don't remember what I did in grade school let alone Boy Scouts. But I'll tell you one thing that I won't ever ever forget."

"What's that Tiger?"

"That I love you!"

"Oh Tiger, I will always love you too." With that they drank a toast to themselves, left a generous tip and slowly made their way arm in arm to their room. Blair thought that this had to be the happiest most romantic day of her life.

***

Mitchell Green waited in Jerome Jefferson's outer office. He sat silently fidgeting while Jefferson's secretary worked on her computer. It was the day after Thanksgiving and Green had to catch a flight out of Vegas last night because this same secretary called him and told him to be in Jefferson's office by nine this morning. Now he was here and cooling his heels, he checked his watch for the fifth time in the last five minutes, it was now nine fifteen. Jefferson's secretary continued pounding her keyboard. After she instructed him to be seated she apparently became oblivious to his presence.

Suddenly the phone on the secretary's desk rang. She picked it up, listened for a second and then turned toward Green. "Mr. Jefferson will see you now."

"Thank you." Green approached the door and hesitated, he had no idea what to expect. He wasn't returning to the home office as the conquering hero. If anything he was the field general who had to explain why he lost the battle. He summoned up his courage, turned the doorknob and entered. Jerome Jefferson sat behind his desk reading some reports. Mitchell stopped in front of the desk and stood silently waiting for Jefferson to finish his reading. After what seemed like an eternity, but was barely thirty seconds, Jefferson put the reports down and looked up.

"Wellbon-Smith voted to sell Fox to the management team and not to Clint Matthews." There was no good morning or other greeting; in fact Green noted that there was no emotion what so ever in Jefferson's voice.

"I know."

"Why?"

"Trevor Mason failed in his attempt to take over Wellbon-Smith. The Wellbon family is once again in control of the corporation. Denton Wellbon III is now chairman and his mother is vice chairman. Instead of Mason becoming vice chairman and the real power, as was his plan, he is out entirely."

"Out entirely? They fired him?"

"The official word is that he chose to take advantage of his stock options and severance agreement."

Jefferson looked back at the papers on his desk, but he wasn't reading them. "You live by the corporate sword you die by the corporate sword. However, in this case I'm certain my old classmate Trevor walks away with a sweetheart package."

"Yes, it seems so. Because Denton Wellbon attained the chairman's position with the help of his mother and her allies, he was not beholden to Trevor Mason. It seems that our old nemesis William MacLode somehow wound up in control of a large block of voting shares. He aligned himself with the Wellbon family and helped them block Mason. Out of gratitude Mary Wellbon swung the vote MacLode's direction and sold Fox to him and his team."

Jefferson shook his head. "So Denton Wellbon emerges as a skillful corporate player that can play both sides and be victorious, no one that I know ever expected that. I'm certain that Trevor Mason didn't see it coming. Incidentally MacLode has certainly given us problems hasn't he?"

Mitchell wasn't certain where this was heading. He feared that this could be scapegoat time. "Yes, he has. He seemed to know what we were doing before we actually did it."

"Yes he did didn't he? Where is Matthews now in all of this?"

"I explained to him about MacLode and the Wellbon family and why he lost Fox even though he offered more money. He was upset about losing Fox, but I think he took pure joy out of hearing that Mason not only lost his takeover bid but his job as well. I gather they don't like each other."

"Does Matthews blame us?"

"No, he realizes that we were way out on a limb as it is and could offer him no additional support."

"Way out on a limb may be the understatement of the year Mitchell." Jefferson was contemplative for a moment. "Any chance of a shareholder suit against Wellbon-Smith because they accepted a lower offer when they could have sold for more?"

"I don't think so since Matthew's offer required Wellbon-Smith to leave money in the deal and the Fox team offer didn't. The board could argue that cash at settlement without the risk of financing was the more prudent offer. Wellbon-Smith is a privately held corporation. Class action suits are nearly impossible. You would have to have a few disgruntled shareholders file suit and Denton Wellbon all but took that threat away by offering to buy up any of the shareholder's stock that Mason had agreements with at the official value per share. Not the lucrative capital gains most had sought, but probably good enough to take away the threat of a suit."

"I suppose you are right. Denton again demonstrates surprising skill."

Mitchell decided to bring this to a head. "Where do we go from here?" He was quietly hoping that "we" was an accurate description of the future.

Jefferson looked up at his young lieutenant. "Keep working on the other companies that we've targeted and keep your contacts within Fox."

Mitchell Green felt a great feeling of relief inside, but he didn't show it. "You still think that there's hope for Fox?"

"You never know." Jefferson returned to his reports. It was clear to Mitchell Green that the meeting was over. He turned and started for the door. "Green."

Mitchell froze and turned. "Yes Boss?"

Jefferson looked up once more. "Mitchell, I've probably led you astray."

"I'm not following you Boss."

"I've had you concentrate totally on organizing enough companies so we can be eligible for the merger."

"But that's of utmost importance."

"Yes it is Mitchell, but something else is important."

"Sir?"

"Let's not forget why we got into the union movement to begin with. We wanted to make the work environment better for the worker."

Mitchell was silent for a long moment. "I guess if we concentrate on that the other falls into place."

Jerome Jefferson smiled. "Yeah, I'll find a way to stall the merger. I've discovered that they want us as badly as we need them. From now on we go into a company's work force with a positive program and not just a negative look what the big bad company is doing to you. Got that?"

Mitchell Green returned the smile. "I got it Boss."

***

Trevor Mason sat in his study sipping his morning coffee and looking out through the French doors at his five-acre estate. The team of gardeners that he employed was busy gathering the fallen fall foliage. The Thanksgiving holiday was over and for the first time since college he didn't have to return to work. It felt strange. On his desk before him lay the Wall Street Journal and the New York Times. He was an avid reader of both. Normally he was looking for political and business trends that would affect the companies of the Atlantic Corporation. But today and apparently for undetermined days to come, his only interest would be the trends that might affect his personal portfolio.

He still found it hard to believe that he had lost not only his takeover bid, but his job as well. He really felt that he had every base covered going into the annual meeting. The only loose cannon was the unexpected one, Denton Wellbon. The plan was to have Denton so convinced that his personal future, family reputation and marriage would be ruined by the revelation of his secret one night stand; that both Denton and Mary Wellbon would grudgingly come to realize that the only way they could maintain their privacy and reputations was to put Denton into the chairman's chair with Trevor as the power behind the throne. With the committed votes that Trevor had locked up and Abe Rueben's assurance that he could keep Denton and thereby Mary Wellbon under control, just as he had those shareholders in Chicago, Trevor never expected what actually occurred.

MacLode was an unexpected factor. Trevor assumed that the offshore funds would vote against him, but he never suspected that they were controlled by one of his division presidents. Now in the aftermath it was apparent that Mac had approached the Wellbons and Trevor believed, convinced them to fight. Mac promised his support for the Wellbon family in return for their support for his team to purchase Fox, even though he was the low bidder. Trevor glanced again at the open Wall Street Journal in front of him. This morning it was announced that Mac was named the new president of Atlantic Corporation. Trevor's old job! If there was a bigger winner than Denton and Mary Wellbon in all of this, it was definitely MacLode.

Trevor turned his attention to the Times. On page three was an article about a possible gangland shoot out. Trevor poured himself another cup of coffee from the thermos type container that the cook had left on his side bar along with his favorite mug. The first time he read it the news about Abe Rueben came as a shock. "Prominent New York lawyer with suspected mob ties found gunned down outside his office." Trevor couldn't believe it. Abe was killed the same day that he delivered Denton's severance document to Trevor with the recommendation that he sign it. After the initial shock subsided Trevor began to think about Abe's murder and the implications for him. He decided that there were no negatives for either Trevor or his family. What the hell thought Trevor; Abe's mob ties and the fact that he had played the New York family against the Chicago boys had finally caught up with him. Then Trevor's lips began to form a rather perverse smile. Rueben was the only link between him and the shady activities that he and Rueben had participated in both in Chicago and New York. Well I'll be damned thought Trevor. Someone did me a big favor. While he would miss the services that Abe could supply, he wouldn't miss Abe. Now he could truly enjoy his forced retirement. There was nothing or no one left to actually tie him to Abe's dirty work or for that matter, to Abe's murder.

His wife Julia quietly entered the room. "How are you?" she inquired.

Trevor looked at her, realized again how beautiful she was and smiled a thin smile. "Okay I guess. I just realized that this is the first time since we moved here that I've sat behind this desk and had nothing to do."

Julia sat down on the soft leather couch across the room. She was an elegant lady in her early fifties. "Is that a bad thing?"

"For me it is."

"Trevor, you did a good job at Atlantic. You did what you always do you made more money for the shareholders."

"I did that."

"It's not your fault that the Wellbon family decided to put their own people into power after Carlton Smith retired." Trevor made no response so Julia continued. "It upsets me that Denton Wellbon showed no loyalty to you. Especially after all that you taught him."

"I did teach him a lot. He should actually make a decent chairman for the company now."

"He wouldn't have if you hadn't taken him under your wing. I despise him."

"What?" Trevor brought his eyes back to stare at his wife. He had once again begun to follow the leaf gathering process. She was of course ignorant of the plan to take over Wellbon-Smith that he and Abe Rueben had attempted. "No Julia, don't be angry with Denton."

Julia was surprised. "Trevor, I don't care what the press release is calling it, he fired you. That's the most ungrateful thing I think I've ever seen in my life."

"Actually Julia I was extremely angry with him at first, but now I realize that he was only doing what I would have done in his position."

"What do you mean?"

"There was a press release early this morning from Wellbon-Smith to the Wall Street Journal. Denton has promoted William MacLode to my old position."

"MacLode, he was president of the Fox division wasn't he?"

"That's right."

"I thought you told me that you believed him to be less than ambitious as a manager. Not hungry enough I think is how you put it."

"I did, but I think I was wrong. He saw an opportunity to support the Wellbon family in a crucial vote at the annual meeting and he made the most of it. I think I may have underestimated Mac."

"Why does that make you feel any kindness toward Denton Wellbon?"

"I feel no 'kindness' as you put it. I simply have grudging admiration for Denton. He learned his lessons well from me. Mac allied with Denton and his mother when it counted so he rewarded Mac. I would have done the same."

Julia thought about this for a moment and then dismissed it as a man thing. She would hate Denton Wellbon III as long as she lived for what he did to her husband. Then she put that distasteful thought out of her mind and changed the subject. "Well your severance package is very generous. It will allow you to take early retirement. So let's begin acting like retired folks, how about a round of golf with me this morning?"

Trevor smiled. "You know I think I'll just take you up on that."

Julia was obviously pleased. They hadn't had much time to golf together in recent years. "I'll go change and we'll leave immediately. You better get a warm jacket dear; it's a bit cool out this morning. Afterward, if you like, we can have lunch at the club house."

"Sounds good to me said Trevor." Julia left and Trevor picked up the remote for the television and switched on the morning news. Even though he was "unemployed" he still wanted to hear the Bloomberg financial report. Then he reconsidered and turned off the television. To hell with the financial report, after golf and lunch he just might take Julia to look at that new yacht that caught his eye at the marina. With Denton's severance deal he could easily afford it. Maybe this retirement thing wasn't as bad as he had imagined. Trevor went to the closet to pick out a warm jacket that would not impede his golf swing. He would put his dream of running a corporate empire on hold for the immediate future.

***

The three men sat silently in the office of Andy's Diner down by the Fulton Fish Market. Don Luca sat behind the desk in what was normally Andy's chair. Andy sat across from the don beside Denton Wellbon III. The old don leaned back in the chair and folded his arms across his chest. He smiled a warm smile. For anyone that wasn't aware of his position in the world he appeared to be a benevolent old man. "Congratulations on your new position at Wellbon-Smith Denton. May I call you Denton?"

"Of course you may Mr. Luca, and thank you. I couldn't have accomplished it without the help of your very capable lieutenant, Andy." Denton noticed that the don didn't offer to put him on a first name basis.

The old don's smile broadened. "We are honored to have been of service to the son of our old and trusted friend, your father. Before he died we promised him that we would look out for your interests. We are honorable men and we keep our promises."

"That you do," replied Denton.

Andy sat quietly beaming. The old don took a cigarette from a silver case and lit it up with a very expensive looking lighter. He took a deep draw and then blew smoke rings toward the ceiling. "I read in the Wall Street Journal that you have promoted William MacLode to the position recently vacated by Trevor Mason."

"Yes, both mother and I believe him to be quite capable."

"Quite capable indeed, you are aware that he was my son's roommate in college?"

"Mother informed me so."

"Mac is like a second son to me."

Denton was not aware that the ties between Mac and the don were that strong, but he always seemed to learn something new with every visit to the diner. That fact explained how Mac gained some of his knowledge concerning the Wellbon family.

"Now Denton I'm certain that you are aware that your father and I had a…what should I call it…an arrangement."

"I've gathered as much although I'm not exactly certain of the details."

"The details are simple. Occasionally my business may require the use of some trucks from one of your businesses. I'm not talking drivers; I have plenty of capable drivers. Just the trucks, we will request that they be parked in a specific parking lot and inform you that your drivers may pick them up in twenty-four or forty-eight hours. You bear no risk. In a different vein, we may require some blank invoices, statements and bill of lading forms. You know the type of document I'm looking for, from one of your companies."

Denton thought this over for a moment. "I see no problem with that. However I do have one question; what if one of the rigs has an accident while your driver is behind the wheel?"

The old don blew more smoke rings. "That's why I'm recommending that you change insurance carriers to the carrier that we use. It happens to be a small insurance company that I use personally." The don handed over a packet of papers to Denton. "You will notice in there that my family owns this small company. If we control the insurance claim and it happens while one of my men is driving, we'll keep the costs under control and there will be a minimal amount of investigation."

Denton hesitated for a second. "That sounds acceptable, but I have another question."

"Denton my friend, you may ask all of the questions that you want."

"How can I ask this? Suppose one of your drivers is in possession of one of our trucks and the police stop it. Suppose there is some sort of ...contraband found inside."

The old Don smiled at Denton. "In the unlikely event that should happen and I want to stress the word unlikely, you have nothing to worry about. You see if that ever happens you will have filed a stolen vehicle report before the police will have stopped the truck."

"How will that be possible?"

"Denton, we have friends everywhere. Even in the police department."

"Oh, I see...very good."

The Don paused. "In return for these favors that you will do for us, we are at your disposal for anything that you may need. Such as a cover-up like your father had us do for the unfortunate incident with Crystal's mother, or a random rescue." The don smiled. "Usually your father used us mostly for how shall I put this, you know, persuasion."

"I understand. I appreciate the extraordinary measures you have gone to for our family. Is there anything else that Wellbon-Smith may assist with?"

"I'm certain that there will be, but for the moment that will be all. You will find that we need few favors and are not demanding at all."

Denton rose from his chair. "Wellbon-Smith will be as loyal to you as you have been to us. I can't thank you enough for rescuing Crystal." Denton had explained Crystal's true identity to Andy and the don at the beginning of the meeting.

Andy grinned. "I told you we wouldn't fail you Denton." The don simply smiled.

"You didn't." Denton reached across the desk and shook the old don's hand. He was surprised at the strength in Luca's grip. "Good day gentlemen."

"Good day Denton and happy holidays to you and your family. Tell your mother I said hello," replied the don.

"I will and happy holidays to you both." With that Denton left the tiny office and closed the door behind him.

Andy and the don sat silently for a few moments. "Good work Andy. We're right back where we were before Denton's father died."

"Yeah it all worked out."

"Sort of Andy, sort of…" The don took another long draw on his cigarette and then crushed it out in the ashtray. "It appears that the Wellbon family has no knowledge of those paramilitary types that stopped you. You did a good job of faking it."

Andy looked sheepish. "Yeah I know." Andy found out years ago that it was better if he leveled with his boss because the boss always found out the truth. Those guys that tried to feed the boss a line, well they weren't around anymore. Andy had survived as the don's right hand man longer than anyone else. He believed that his honesty was the reason why. He gambled on being up front with the don immediately upon his return from Savannah. So far it had worked.

The don continued. "From what Denton just told us they, whoever they are, brought Crystal Harrison to New York. She's apparently here now and staying with Denton's mother. Denton acted as though we knew about it because he seems to think that we arranged it."

Andy rubbed his bald scalp. "I don't get it Boss, why didn't Crystal blow the whistle on me? She was with the big curly haired guy. She knows that I didn't have anything to do with her rescue. Shit Boss, we know that wasn't the first time she saw me. She was here in the diner the other week."

"I know Andy and I don't know why she is protecting us or how long she will continue to do so." The don stopped and stared at the ceiling for a moment. "Maybe she's not protecting us maybe she's protecting them, the military types. Who decided to bring her to New York? Was it Denton, his mother or someone else? Did she make that decision herself? Who? I don't know. Find out who these people are. Find out who that big guy is with the dark curly hair that stopped you. But the most important thing is to find out who they work for and what their interest is in all of this. We found out that contrary to what we believed Denton's father was not above concealing things from us. We now know that he allowed us to believe that Crystal was young Denton's daughter when she was actually his. How do we know that his son won't do the same?"

Andy blinked. He hadn't considered this. "We don't know."

"That's right. We don't know. For the first time I'm not certain if I can trust a Wellbon. Find out who those people really are and if they work for the Wellbon family. If they don't work for the Wellbons find out who they do work for and what their interest is in Crystal Harrison." The don paused for effect then he changed the subject. "However there's something else we need to do first."

"What's that Boss?"

"Abe Rueben was killed last night."

"Yeah I heard it on the news. It couldn't have happened to a nicer guy."

"I'll shed no tears for him. But remember his threat when he returned to New York?"

"Yeah, he sent us all letters before his return stating that he had preserved copies of all of the incriminating documents that his law firm had on us over the years. Then he said that if he should ever die mysteriously or violently those documents would be sent to the F.B.I. immediately." Andy suddenly had an uncomfortable look on his face.

"We know that we didn't have him killed." Luca said absently.

"Hell no Boss, none of our people was involved. It would have been stupid unless we knew where all those files were."

"Well we need to know now. Find the files Andy. Right now you have no greater priority. This is even more important than finding out who those guys are that rescued Crystal Harrison." Luca's face was the most serious Andy had ever seen it. They had tried before to find the files and failed. It would be harder now.

"Boss, I'm on top of it. As soon as I heard Rueben was dead I had some of our friends in the police department check the report after the CSI unit covered the crime scene and Rueben's office. They didn't find anything. Even the wall safe was empty."

"How about his co-op?"

"Same thing, the cops found nothing. After they left I took some guys there personally and we tore the place apart, we didn't find a freakin' thing." Andy was starting to sweat. "He had a secretary boss do you want us to lean on her?"

"Are you watching her?"

"I got three of the boys on her around the clock."

"Good. Andy, did you know she was Rueben's lover?"

"Hell no! Really?" snorted Andy.

Luca smiled. "Yeah really, but she seems too obvious. Rueben was too clever for that. He knew she would be the first one we would think about. But watch her just the same. If she mails anything or puts something in a locker in the next several weeks, get your hands on it, I don't care what you have to do. If she goes anywhere near the F.B.I., the D.A.'s office or the cops.... Kill her. You know how to make it clean so that it doesn't point toward us."

Andy swallowed hard, his mouth went dry. "She's already talked to the cops boss."

"When?"

"They must have called her to identify Rueben. They had her come down to his office building even before the body was removed. But our contacts on the force said she didn't tell them anything concerning us and she didn't give them anything either. In fact some detective named Grabowski was there but he was asking her questions about that Kensington-Cramer kid that took a dive off his balcony."

"I know of Grabowski, he's a good cop but he can't be bought. He's in homicide now, so he has no reason to be interested in us. That's good." Luca was silent for a few long moments. "Grabowski would have provided the perfect opportunity for her to drop the hammer on us, but she didn't. That could be a sign that she knows nothing." The old don looked thoughtful. "On second thought just keep a watch on the secretary and don't lay a hand on her for now. We can always get her if warranted. Let's not muddy the waters."

"Are you sure boss?"

"Yes, I'm sure for now."

The don got up, put on his overcoat and started for the door. Before he opened it he turned back to Andy.

"There is one other place the damned files could be," he appeared thoughtful as he stared at nothing for a long moment.

"Where's that boss?"

"Never mind, we can check on that later. In fact, it might be for sale soon." Luca appeared lost in thought again. Then he spoke. "For the moment keep in touch with our people inside the force and stay close to Ruben's secretary. If that information exists and gets in the wrong hands we could all be looking at prison or worse!" On that note Luca left and slammed the door behind him.

"Right boss," replied Andy to the closed door. He was alone now and he had a feeling he would have to work through the holidays.

Outside in the parking lot the don's car and driver were waiting for him. The driver held the door open as the old man got in. When he was sequestered inside he lit up another cigarette. Exhaling the smoke he contemplated the recent events. He was no longer thinking about Rueben and his cache of incriminating documents. He had confidence that Andy would take care of that. Maybe Rueben was bluffing all these years and there were none. After all they had looked everywhere, bribed everyone they could think of and beat a few people up, but still no papers. They could never touch Rueben for fear that the files did exist and he had a friend that would drop the files in the mail. However, every minute that went past that the Feds weren't on his doorstep the safer it became. Luca had people on his payroll in the federal building. They were waiting to intercept anything that looked incriminating. If the other location and Rueben's secretary lover were the keys, then the old man had a plan. Luca was probably the only person who knew of the other location. What was the old saying? Keep your friends close and your enemies even closer.

The Wellbon family and the association that the don's "family" had enjoyed with them over the years had been quite beneficial to both. Each had needs that the other could fulfill. He had worked long and hard to renew it. Now with the successful reunion of the two complete he was suddenly uncomfortable. Could he trust Denton Wellbon? After all Denton had double-crossed Trevor Mason and outsmarted Abe Rueben. Hell, he might have been behind Rueben's murder. Was that possible? Could he trust any Wellbon? If this paramilitary group, whoever they were, worked for Wellbon he and his family were immune to intimidation. Denton could certainly afford to hire people with those talents. Intimidation was the don's stock and trade. Without it the Luca family would be powerless.

As the car pulled into traffic Luca contemplated the silver cigarette case for a moment and suddenly smiled to himself. What irony, Denton had presented him with a safety net, an alternative. He stared out the window at the passing scene. Yes, the possibilities made him smile even broader. William MacLode, the man who was like a second son to him was now president of the Atlantic Corporation. What a perfect situation. Mac even owed him a favor. The old man chuckled out loud.

***

Denton Wellbon entered the front door of his co-op. Susan was waiting for him. "Hi honey," she greeted him.

"Hi Hon," Denton took her in his arms and kissed her. He held her close and looked into her eyes. They had been through so much the past six months. "I love you," he whispered.

"I love you too Denton."

Denton frowned. "What's wrong?"

Susan smiled. "I worry about you."

"You don't have to, I'm fine."

Susan took a deep breath. "I called your office earlier and they said that you were out for the afternoon. They said that you didn't tell them where you were going."

"If you needed me why didn't you call me on my cell phone?"

"You were down at that diner near the fish market weren't you?"

Denton's frown grew deeper. "Why do you ask?"

"You're doing business with those mobsters."

Denton smiled. "We have an arrangement, nothing that you have to worry about."

"I don't like you doing business with those people."

"Relax dear, mother told me how father kept his distance and still kept them under control in case he needed them."

"How would that be?"

"Keep them off balance, so that they are never totally certain that they know where you are coming from."

"I don't understand you or your mother when it comes to those people. I thought I knew you both."

"Just don't worry. They can be valuable friends at times. They certainly helped us out with Crystal."

"I know, but they scare me."

"Don't be afraid. My father managed them and I can manage them. Trust me."

Susan took a deep breath. "Okay, she said. Okay."

Denton held her close. "Let's go out to dinner. What do you say?"

"Okay, let me change clothes. Where do you want to go?"

"I don't care, you pick it."

Susan squeezed him tight. "I'll make up my mind while I'm changing," she said. Then she went upstairs. At the top of the open stairwell Susan stopped and turned back to Denton, her face and voice serious. "I don't trust them Denton and worse, I fear them. Be very careful, if not for yourself then for me." With that she disappeared into their bedroom.

Denton turned and walked to one of the living room windows. He pulled back the drapes and looked out across Central Park. While Susan's comments disturbed him, he still felt good. He was finally running the company that his grandfather and father founded and built. He would build it even larger and if sometimes he had to manipulate the don and his boys, he would find a way. Just like his father and grandfather. Denton finally felt like he was where he was supposed to be. Running Wellbon-Smith was his destiny.

Chapter 31

It was two weeks before Christmas and the Fox management team was having their annual private Christmas party. It was now Friday evening, that same afternoon the factory shut down and the management team hosted a catered luncheon for all the employees of both shifts. Carroll Brubaker and his wife had flown out to Vegas to host the party at that plant with Tom Erving. Mac, Tony and Carroll rotated this task. This year it was Carroll's turn... Various awards were given out and each year everyone got a present. This year it was a hooded windbreaker in the company colors with the Fox logo on the left breast. The two parties were linked for the first time through Fox's computer system. Except for the time difference, the entire company was celebrating Christmas together.

It was at this party that the team announced their purchase of Fox Cabinetry to the employees. They assured everyone that the company organization, policies, pay schedules and benefits would remain the same. The surprise to Mac and everyone else in management was that there was unbridled celebration. Apparently the employees linked the parent corporation with the reduction of benefits and Mac and his team as restoring those benefits.

After the party for all employees was over, the management team had their own party at an exclusive restaurant. They all went home dressed up, and had an evening together. This year they rented a second floor room in the Log Cabin, one of the finest steak houses in the county. They often brought visiting dealers here to entertain and were well known by the staff and the owner.

Sarah Frazer pulled her Trans Am GTA into the restaurant parking lot. The Log Cabin sat on top of a hill amid tall pine and fir trees. As Sarah got out of her car the wind sighed through the boughs and Sarah pulled her coat tighter around her neck. Winter had definitely arrived. She looked around the lot. Amid the regular patrons cars she spotted all of the Fox team's cars except Mac's and of course Carroll Brubaker's. Neither Mac's company car nor his classic T-Bird was in evidence. She wondered where he was.

To Catch a Fox

Sarah liked this old place. It truly began as a log cabin in the woods, except that it was not built during frontier days but during prohibition. It was originally a speakeasy with a rather shady past. Upon entering the establishment the mater de recognized her and escorted her upstairs to the room where the Fox party was being held. Everyone turned to welcome her as she emerged at the top of the steps.

Dale brought his wife, Tony brought Blair McManus and David Elliott brought his wife. Dennis Morton and his wife were invited back for one last Christmas party. Sarah Fraser came alone and she was curious as to whom Mac would show up with. After all he was widely acknowledged to be one of the county's most eligible bachelors. While she didn't really want to admit it even to herself, she was a bit disappointed that Mac had not mentioned anything to her about the two of them coming together. They had such a wonderful time together while in Chicago for the show and at their celebratory dinner when he returned from the meeting in New York. She had sort of expected it to continue. True, Mac had been heavily involved in the effort to purchase Fox and additionally in the fight for control of Wellbon-Smith. When he was offered the position as president of the Atlantic Corporation, she was the first one that he told and the only one that he sought an opinion from. But other than that it had been business as usual upon their return. Finally at this moment, standing here amid all the trappings of joy, she was forced to admit to herself that this is probably the reason that Mac remained on the most eligible bachelor list. That thought took the wind out of her sails and left her feeling a bit down.

The waiter took her coat to the cloakroom and returned with a glass of Chablis wine for Sarah. She looked puzzled as she accepted the glass. She had not requested it. The waiter smiled. "Your boss, Mr. MacLode instructed me to see that you had a glass of wine if you arrived before he did. I believe that this is your preference?"

Sarah smiled. "Yes, yes it is. Thank you."

Sarah was puzzled and intrigued. What made Mac think that she would arrive alone? She was alone of course, but what made him assume that she would be? Maybe he didn't care if she had brought a date. Maybe he would do the same thing even if he knew she had an escort. Knowing Mac's reputation as a lady's man she was anxious to get a look at his date. He would not miss this event.

Dale and his wife Edie drifted over and after Dale introduced Sarah to Edie they began talking about the employee reaction to their announcement that afternoon. After that Dale excused himself and went to congregate with the "boys". Sarah and Edie began talking about their respective jobs. Edie was a CPA and working at a male dominated firm. She and Sarah had much in common since Sarah was the only female on the new Fox board of directors. Dale's wife was quite interesting and charming and she possessed a wicked sense of humor. They were reveling in telling "war" stories. Swapping tales of the battles and predicaments female professionals face in the male dominated professional workforce. Sarah decided that she liked her. Edie made her laugh and that helped to pull her out of the funk that she found herself in.

"Excuse me, do you need a refill?" The familiar voice was directly behind Sarah. She turned to face Mac.

Smiling, Sarah noted that Mac was his usual immaculate self in an expensively tailored suit. "I'm good for a bit. Thank you for the first round."

Mac acknowledged Edie with a hug and a kiss on the cheek. "Merry Christmas Edie, it's good to see you again."

"Merry Christmas Mac, and congratulations on your new position."

"Thank you Edie. If I couldn't remain involved with Fox, I don't believe I would have accepted it. We'll just have to see how the future works out."

"The future will work out fine for both you and Fox. Tony is a good selection to replace you. He understands both manufacturing and the retail end of this industry. Now if the two of you will excuse me, I have to greet the other ladies in the room. I'm dying to meet Tony's girlfriend." With a knowing smile Edie began to circulate about the room. She had known Mac for a number of years and sensed that this would be the time for her to depart.

Sarah looked around beyond Mac. "Looking for something?" asked Mac.

"Well, I wanted to meet your date. When you were late I expected the two of you to make a grand entrance. Where is she?"

"Where's your escort?"

To Catch a Fox

"Well if you must know Boss, I have no escort tonight."

"Really? Well I have no date either." Mac stepped back and admired Sarah in her elegant yet simple black sheath dress. The neckline was tastefully low cut and there was a split up the right leg. "You look great," he beamed. "You really do like black."

"You noticed."

"Well I've seen you in it several times now and I think you do wonders for the color."

"Why thank you. You don't look bad yourself."

"Well," said Mac, "I can solve our mutual problem."

"We have a problem?"

Mac's face turned serious, "Oh yes, a rather large problem."

"And that might be?"

"Two top executives at the management Christmas party without dates. That's not good. Our partners might think no one would have us."

"And your solution to this 'large problem' would be?"

Mac offered his arm. "I know it's a bit last minute, but would you accompany me to the Fox Christmas party?"

Sarah smiled. "I think I might like that."

"I'm taking that as a yes."

"It is a yes." With that Sarah placed her arm in Mac's and they moved off to mingle."

With the success of their bid to purchase Fox so recently behind them, this was a joyous Christmas party indeed. There were many toasts to continued success and to each other. Then there was the exchange of gag gifts. Immediately after Thanksgiving each member of the senior management team drew a name from a hat. That was their secret partner. Each one then left anonymous clues as to their identity on the desk of the person whose name they had pulled. They attempted to guess who their secret partner was up until this Christmas party when the partner brought a gag gift and revealed his or now her identity. Before opening the gifts, all were placed under a Christmas tree that the restaurant included in the decorations, the individual had to guess who the partner was. Since the clues were meant to confuse rather than help solve the mystery, no one guessed correctly this year. To everyone's delight that broke Mac's string of three consecutive correct guesses. Dennis was included in this game for one last time.

Sarah had Tony's name and presented him with a bound book that had every reason or outlandish excuse that Dale and Mac could remember Tony giving as justification for giving dealers special credits against their invoices. The cover inscription stated that it was a training manual for the new V.P. Sales and Marketing. When Tony took his new position as president he would have to hire or promote someone to take his old position. Tony loved it and thanked her as he claimed that he had long forgotten many of them. Sarah received a round of hearty applause in this first attempt. With Brady's help she had managed to solicit this information from Dale and Mac without revealing her identity to either of them. By successfully doing this she kept her own name in the running as a potential partner for everyone. Dale had Sarah's name and presented her with a baseball bat with an inscription. The inscription read: "To be used on blockheaded male partners when they fail to recognize the genius of a woman." Sarah gave Dale a big kiss on the forehead and warned them that she would not hesitate to put it to use.

The bar was open and everyone could order from the menu. All had a sumptuous meal and just before the dessert tray was brought around, Tony and Blair gained everyone's attention and announced their engagement. The announcement was met with cheers and best wishes, starting another celebration accompanied by another round of drinks. As things quieted there was the traditional time of reminiscing and the telling of company lore. Sarah was seated beside Mac and was amazed at what a humorous and skillful storyteller he was. The team hung on his every word. While this was her first Fox Christmas party, she was certain that these folks had heard these stories before, but they all seemed to relish them as if it were the first telling.

To Catch a Fox

Looking about the rustic setting, lavishly decorated for Christmas, and noting each of her new partners and friends, Sarah was quietly pleased that she had accepted the job offer from Dennis Morton this past summer. Who could have foretold that barely six months into the job, her male peers would accept her and she would be a shareholder in the newly independent company of Fox Custom Cabinetry. With a seat on the board of directors no less. Dale and Mac had come up with a plan where by she was able to borrow money from Futures Unlimited and pay it back with deductions from her paycheck. She was very grateful for this opportunity.

The party slowly wound down and the participants wished each other a Merry Christmas and began to drift home. Mac had the bar tenders watch for anyone that they deemed not fit to drive. This year there weren't any as everyone drank moderately. We must be getting older and wiser thought Mac. Should someone have had too much, Mac would have called a cab to take them home and Mac himself would have made certain that the person's car made it home in the morning. As Tony and Blair said their good nights Mac and Sarah became the only party goers left. Mac turned to Sarah. "I'm not ready to end this wonderful night just yet. Are you?"

Sarah smiled. "What do you have in mind big guy?"

"How about joining me for a nightcap? The bar's still open."

"You talked me into it, you sweet talker."

Mac escorted her downstairs to the bar. There was no one else seated there. They sipped on their drinks and made small talk. Mac was fascinated by the doomsayers that were convinced that civilization would melt down at the stroke of midnight on New Year's Eve as the century turned. Fox's I. T. System had passed its final testing of program adjustments at the end of October, so there were no fears that their system would fail to reboot when they returned to work after the holidays. Sarah asked how it was that programmers in the late seventies and eighties could have been oblivious to the threat of the turn of the century to their programs. Mac explained that in college he had studied two of the main business languages of the day, IBM's RPG II and COBOL. He explained the fact that these were basically linier languages, not easily adapted to the current concept of modular programming. Modular programming saved valuable storage space because if a routine could be used over and over again in a program you could code it one time and simply route the data and operation through it as many times as required while the program was running. With linier programming you had to duplicate the same code as many times as required, thus using up valuable storage space. Even the COBOL "go to" command saved only a small amount of space. Compared to contemporary systems the storage available at the time was far more limited. It took less programming and therefore less storage space to create a fixed field like "19" as opposed to a data entry field, so in the tight environment of the time every savings counted.

Sarah questioned their thinking suggesting that surly they realized the problems this would create down the road. Mac countered that the thinking of the day stated that all the programs that were being written would be obsolete and therefore replaced in no more than three years. No thought was given to the possibility that any of these programs would still be in use at the turn of the century.

"Wow," said Sarah. "The programs were more durable than anyone imagined."

"Well they worked. They did their job and it became easier and far less expensive to simply modify them and add to them rather than scrap them and install or write new programs from scratch. The patches became more elaborate than the original program."

"Eventually everyone forgot about the fixed date field?"

"Yeah until faced with the turn of the century and then one day it was sort of 'holy shit!'"

Sarah was amazed. "Well thank you, I have a lot more respect for the programmers of the day after this discussion than I previously held."

"I'm glad to hear that, as I was one of them. In college and for a while afterward I hired out as a programmer to several small businesses to earn extra money. I was one of those COBOL cowboys that the world credits for forgetting that the year 2000 would eventually come around."

Sarah laughed. "I see. Does this mean that I can believe what you just told me or was that all an elaborate excuse concocted to excuse you from your share of responsibility?"

Mac put on his best serious face and intoned in the most sincere voice he could muster. "Oh, Ms Fraser, you can believe every word of it as gospel."

Sarah placed her hand on Mac's arm. "Now I'm really not sure." They laughed together and Mac gave no more assurances.

They sipped on their drinks for a while. Then Mac turned to Sarah with a smile. "I'm going home for Christmas this year."

"To Scotland?"

"Yes, Scotland, where else would I call home? You too for that matter."

"You're going to spend Christmas at your father's castle, how exciting."

"Yes, well I guess it's mine now. I thought it would be good to spend the holidays with what's left of my family and the household staff. My father always hosted a party for the staff and their families on the day before Christmas. You know a large traditional feast in the grand hall and presents for the children. Everyone would be disappointed if I didn't continue the tradition. I promised them I would do the same."

"That's sweet Mac, I wish I could be there to see it."

Mac's face lit up. "Well then, go with me."

"What?"

"You heard me. Come along back to Scotland with me for Christmas. I'll pay all your expenses."

"Gosh, I…I don't know Mac. How would it look?"

Mac grinned. "This isn't a proposition. The castle has over one hundred rooms. Remember it's a glorified bed and breakfast, you can sleep as far away from me as you want."

It was Sarah's turn to smile. "I meant how will it look to the people at Fox? You know the employees and our partners."

Mac finished his drink. "Are you blushing?"

Sarah shook her head. "I hope not, it's probably the wine."

"Yes no doubt… Sarah, a long time ago I stopped worrying about how things looked. I work at Fox and I'm dedicated to showing a profit and giving those people a secure place to work. Beyond that my life is my life. For your sake I suggest that you take the same approach, no matter what your decision concerning my offer."

Sarah smiled and took a deep breath. This was something that she definitely should not do. The red flashing warning lights were going off inside her brain, but just as she did during the lunch at Morgantown she heard herself say: "Okay, I accept. When do we leave?"

Mac flashed a broad white smile. The biggest smile Sarah had ever witnessed from him during her tenure at Fox. "I'm planning on December 20t. I need some time to oversee the preparations for the party. Can you be ready by then?"

"Let's see that's eight days, sure no problem."

Mac was truly in a celebratory mood now, "Another round?"

"No, thank you I've had enough for one night."

"And so have you Mac," interjected the bartender who had been standing discreetly by in case they required his services.

Mac smiled, "You're right, that's what I'm paying you to do. Will you call a cab for both of us? I don't want to risk a DUI or worse." The bartender nodded and disappeared into the back.

"How will we retrieve our cars?" asked Sarah.

"This is a secure lot they'll be safe here tonight. I'll pick you up late tomorrow morning with the T-Bird and we'll take turns ferrying them home."

"Call me before you come over and don't make it before ten."

"There's no way I'll call you before ten," promised Mac. "If you can spare me the time it's a great excuse to have breakfast together."

"Offer accepted," responded Sarah.

The cab arrived and the two Fox executives climbed into the rear seat. Mac's condo was the first stop on the way. Before opening the door Mac leaned over and gave Sarah what could only be described as a long passionate kiss. When it was finished Mac smiled, "When you give a kiss like that it's always gratifying when the person you are kissing kisses you back. Thank you." Sarah smiled her best demure smile as her response.

"I'll see you in the morning dear," Mac said just before exiting and closing the door.

As the cab carried her away Sarah was left to contemplate the events of the evening. It had started out on an emotional downer. But it definitely ended on a high note, higher than she could have ever expected or hoped for. He called me 'dear' she thought and she touched her lips where he had kissed her. She wondered how many women in the past he had called by the same term. Many no doubt, only the future would tell how seriously Mac himself took that word. The cab soon stopped on the street outside her home. Mac had already paid the cabby generously enough that the fare was covered and the cabby was compensated with a very nice tip. Sarah thanked the driver and got out on the curb. As the cab drove away she decided not to fall into the trap of over analyzing the situation. For now she would just be very happy that Mac had included her in his immediate plans. She would go down this path one step at a time.

***

Crystal Harrison returned from Christmas shopping. She took several trips to ferry all of the shopping bags from her car to her second floor apartment. She had returned to Savannah the first full week of December after spending more than a week visiting with Mary Wellbon in her penthouse co-op. After completing her task she settled into her favorite chair in the living room and surveyed all of her presents. She was amazed. She never had this many gifts to purchase. She always bought presents for her adopted family, but this was the first Christmas that she was aware of her real family.

She had decided to accept her family, even though there was much to have reservations about. First was her father. Mary Wellbon told her much about her husband Denton Wellbon II. Crystal still held mixed emotions concerning him. There was no longer any doubt in her mind that Mary's husband was her father. For that knowledge she was grateful. Her father's identity was no longer a mystery that plagued her and his wife gave her detailed information concerning what he was like. True, he was dead. She would have liked to have met him and questioned him about his torrid relationship with her mother, but that was not to be.

Crystal determined that her father was a paradox. On the one hand he had his mob "friends" terrorize her grandparents to protect him from blackmail and from going to prison for statutory rape. He had protected himself at all cost. Even at the potential expense of his son. This was something for which she had a hard time forgiving him. Her grandfather proved to be something less than a saint when he blackmailed her father. Also it was now obvious that even near death her grandfather had lied to her about his knowledge concerning the identity of her father. Crystal forgave him this lie, as she believed that her grandfather thought he was protecting her. On the other hand her father had taken responsibility for his actions. While he broke her mother's heart, he never deserted her or their child. He always made certain that they were provided for and even now she had her father to thank for the fact that she was a very wealthy young woman.

Crystal thought of her newly discovered brother and his wife. While in New York she spent some time with them. They were a truly devoted couple. She could tell that they had a great relationship because whenever they were together they were subtly but constantly touching each other. She admired Susan because she apparently planned to stand by her husband even when she discovered what they both thought was the existence of her husband's illegitimate daughter. Crystal developed a soft spot for her much older brother. Denton sent in the "cavalry" to rescue Crystal even though he believed that it might jeopardize his family's business and if all the facts as he understood them came out, he might face criminal charges. That took guts as far as Crystal was concerned, considering that he had never met Crystal and might have been safer if he had let events play out.

If the kidnappers had killed her, there would have been no evidence concerning that night at the frat party. But her brother chose to attempt a rescue.

Then there was Mary Wellbon. During her stay at Mary's penthouse she and Crystal had agreed that Crystal, when asked, would refer to Mary as her stepmother. Neither of them knew what the correct title would be for a lady in Mary's position. Dynamic, determined and tough were words that came to mind whenever Crystal thought of her. It took guts to go and meet the woman that had an illicit affair with her husband, even several years after the fact. In her crash course to Crystal on the Wellbon family Mary Wellbon had pulled no punches. She shared much knowledge with Crystal, some of it flattering to the family and some of it not so flattering. Crystal had grown to like the head of the Wellbon clan very much. Mary Wellbon truly made Crystal feel welcome. She introduced Crystal to "her" New York, even taking her to the Wellbon-Smith building to show her the nerve centers of the far flung family empire. The only thing that Crystal couldn't understand was Mary's hesitation to contact Crystal after both Crystal's mother and father had died. What harm could it have done then? She put that question to Mary Wellbon point blank. The response was just as direct. Pride. At that time in her life she was too proud to admit that a young woman, barely more than a child could have tempted her husband to cheat on her. No excuse, just the facts. That was Mary Wellbon.

Then there was the family business. No one could argue that it was immensely successful, but even though her newfound family avoided discussing it, Crystal had observed more than enough to determine that the Wellbon family still freely associated with the mob. She already knew of Andy from the diner and the role that he played in keeping her grandfather silent for so many years. She recalled her fear at her surprise encounter with Andy the morning after her visit to her grandparents. Then ironically brother Denton sent Andy and his "wise guys" to rescue her. They never got the chance, but they certainly took credit for it. Crystal was amazed that Andy was able to dupe both Denton and his mother concerning her rescue. It was apparent that the family maintained a continuing relationship with these questionable characters. She was aware of what the Wellbon side of the arrangement got from it: strong-arm. She was afraid to speculate what the mob side extracted in return. Crystal was not comfortable with the fact that her family's business interests sometimes required the services of thugs. The less she knew of this part of her new family's affairs the better. Crystal determined that she could maintain a relationship with her family without becoming involved in the family's businesses. Certainly that was the prudent course to take.

The most puzzling character in this new family line up was the mysterious Mr. Smith. He approached Crystal with the first sketchy information about her then unnamed father. Smith revealed this information only after he was reasonably certain that Foster Harrison admitted to Crystal that he wasn't her father. Smith revealed the existence of the trust fund, a fund of which Mary Wellbon and her family seemed to have no knowledge. He also disclosed that he had been the administrator of that trust fund to her adopted parents, and Crystal had to assume, her mother before them. Smith was the person that informed her that the trust fund was now being turned over to her, with certain conditions. Crystal noted that events had made those conditions moot with the exception of the condition of silence.

Smith was the one who really rescued her from the kidnappers. Smith and his amazing army! Crystal lacked a more appropriate word to describe the force that Smith commanded. Crystal also believed that if her rescue had truly fallen to Andy and his gang, both she and they would be dead today. Crystal, even though terrified, drugged and blindfolded remained a reporter at heart. She listened carefully to the kidnappers. Their way of talking, their movements, the military like discipline that they exercised in taking her prisoner and in guarding her. She heard them refer to a perimeter guard and the changing of that guard. They worked in shifts with military precision, something of which Andy and his wise guys were ignorant. The kidnappers, whoever they were, came from a military background. Only people like those Smith commanded could defeat the kidnappers, and that they did with deadly efficiency.

Who was the gentle acting but extremely dangerous Mr. Smith? Mary Wellbon and Smith credited Crystal's father for providing for Crystal and her mother, which logic dictated he surly did. But Mary seemed ignorant of the existence of Smith and the fund. She like Crystal's brother Denton seemed convinced that Andy was responsible for Crystal's rescue and neither of them ever mentioned the mystery man who called himself George Smith. From what Crystal had personally observed Andy hadn't a clue as to the identity of Smith and his men. For his part Smith despised Andy.

Did Smith actually report directly to Crystal's father? Was this yet another layer of deception and protection that her apparently clever and devious father had set up to provide for Crystal and her mother while further protecting himself from discovery? It seemed logical. Not his wife, not Andy, perhaps not even Smith knew the whole story. Only Denton Wellbon II, Crystal's father was privy to everything. If this was the situation, then there were provisions that if Crystal's father died before the trust fund was turned over to her, Smith would continue to be employed to see the whole thing through to the finish. What finish? Was it all finally over? Finished? Was that what Smith was referring to when he left her on the street? Was his job finally over? Was he moving on? Did all this make sense?

Crystal grew weary of the speculation. She would pursue it no farther. Whoever he was, Smith had saved her life. He made her promise that she would never reveal his existence to anyone and he made a point of including the Wellbon family, however indirectly, in that promise. He could rest assured that she would keep that promise. She smiled as she suspected that he had no fear about that.

Crystal returned to the task at hand and began getting her presents out of the bags. Crystal bought wrapping paper and she would take great joy in wrapping each present. This year there were a lot. She had the normal gifts for her adopted family and now she finally knew her real family. Her real family was far from perfect and a little scary but then no one's family was perfect. The important part was that they had extended the welcome mat to her and she had accepted. Crystal finally belonged. She wanted to finish wrapping presents today so she could ship them to New York. That way they would be there when she arrived.

Her holiday plans consisted of visiting her adopted family the weekend before Christmas and her grandparents on her mother's side on the day before Christmas. That was the earliest that she could get away from the station. She would fly to Baltimore immediately after her last telecast. Crystal was in daily contact with her grandparents. While no one expected her grandfather to achieve any significant longevity, he seemed to stabilize after finally meeting his granddaughter. On Christmas Eve she would fly from Baltimore to New York. Brother Denton would meet her at Kennedy and take her to a late family dinner at Mary Wellbon's penthouse. The next morning they would exchange presents over a Christmas brunch. Crystal arranged to spend the week of Christmas with her "stepmother" in return for covering the turn of the century celebration in Times Square for her news team. She was as excited about this Christmas as any since she had been a little girl.

Suddenly Crystal stopped wrapping as she experienced an epiphany of sorts. She sat completely still and gently bit her lower lip. She may not know Mr. Smith's true identity but she now realized to whom he must report! There was only one person who could have coordinated all of this!

***

It was late in the evening of the day before William MacLode and Sarah Frazer planned to leave for Scotland. Mac was packed and ready to leave. He would pick up Sarah early the next morning and they would drive to Philadelphia where they would catch their flight. Mac wasn't concerned about the lateness of the hour as he planned on catching a nap during the long flight across the Atlantic. There would be no Concord jet this trip. Mac was seated in a booth in the rear of Portifino's Restaurant in the City of Lancaster. He was alone and was sipping a glass of Chardonnay. The late evening diners were scattered about the establishment and none of the nearby tables were occupied. The waitress approached and asked if he was ready to order. Mac hesitated and started to explain that he was waiting for a friend when he spied a familiar figure entering the front door. "That's the party I've been waiting for," he explained as he indicated the new patron. "If you would be so kind as to escort her to this booth and give her a menu we can begin."

The waitress smiled and proceeded to fulfill Mac's request. As his guest arrived at the table Mac stood and the two embraced in what the waitress noted was about two seconds too long for the normal casual greeting between two friends of the opposite sex. When they were seated the waitress laid the menu on the table and told them she would give them a few moments to decide. Mac's guest looked up at the waitress, "I know what I want if he's ready to order."

Mac smiled, efficient as ever he thought. "I'm ready also." With that the two proceeded to order two tempting pasta dinners. The waitress took the order and left. Alone now the two old friends looked at one another and smiled. Mac was always amazed at the transformation that occurred with this woman. The work place persona, the hair pulled back in a tight bun, the school marm clothing and the rimless glasses gave way to the evening and weekend persona. The long light brown hair flowing down over her shoulders, the very expensive and chic clothing, the contact lenses and that very feminine figure that she somehow managed to conceal during the day. Mac knew from experience that there was nothing fake about it. She had always been and remained one of the most amazing and intriguing women that Mac had ever known.

To Catch a Fox

"How are you Brady?" Mac broke the silence.

The wide white smile that no one at the office ever imagined to exist spread across her face. "I'm fine Mac and you?"

"I've never been better."

"I would guess not. You are now the largest minority shareholder in the 'new' Fox Custom Cabinetry LLC, not to mention the fact that you've replaced your nemesis Trevor Mason as president of the Atlantic Corporation. It stretches my imagination to see how it could get much better for you…Oh wait! You're whisking your new and very attractive young V.P. of Human Resources away to Scotland for a holiday tryst in the family castle. God, this sounds like one of those yucky romance novels!"

"Now Brady, you're the only person other than Sarah and me that knows about that."

"That's because you haven't a clue how to make airline reservations online."

"Well yes, that's true but Sarah and I would appreciate it if you kept that knowledge to yourself."

Brady shook her head. "Translation: Sarah has no idea that I booked the flights and know of your little adventure."

"Yes Brady, once again you are correct."

"Relax Mac. This is me, Brady, your secret is safe."

"I have no doubt that I can trust you. But I want you to know that this isn't a 'tryst' as you so crudely called it. This is two native Scots going home for the holidays and staying in a glorified bed and breakfast. In separate rooms I might add."

Brady laughed that husky laugh that Mac loved to hear and seldom did. "Like the separate rooms at a certain bed and breakfast in New England some years ago?"

Mac chuckled. "Did we make it through the first night?"

“Oh hell no! We were young and in heat for god’s sake. It only lasted until we met in the hall going to the community bathroom. You were only wearing your pajama bottoms and I had on a too short too transparent negligee. We were in your bed in a fit of passion before we even knew what hit us!”

“We were young and foolish weren’t we?”

Brady sighed wistfully. “Yeah we were. You were the new young president of the Fox division and I was your young infatuated secretary. If anyone had ever found out…now we’re older…but only one of us is wiser!”

“What’s that supposed to mean?”

“Sarah Frazer, she’s half your age. Aren’t you ever going to grow up?”

Mac smiled an impish smile. “I hope not.”

“That’s exactly my point. Even our friend Tony has grown up and found a lovely woman to share his life with.”

“Blair is younger than Tony,” retorted Mac.

“Oh stuff it! She may be five years younger but not half a lifetime!”

Mac shrugged. “Maybe you’re right. We’ll see…”

“Good lord you’re blushing! William MacLode is actually blushing! I never thought that I would see the day, there is hope after all.”

The waitress brought the meals and a glass of wine for Brady. When she left Mac raised his glass. “To us, two former lovers, two life long friends, may we always be here for one another.”

Brady raised her glass and touched Mac’s. “To us…that’s sweet Mac,” she said in that low sexy voice of hers.

They ate in silence for a while. Finally Mac spoke. “What happened to us Brady?”

To Catch a Fox

"What happened to us? What happened to me is the more appropriate question."

Mac stopped twirling a fork full of penne pasta and stared across the table at Brady. "Okay what happened to you?"

"I wanted a commitment from you. We were an on again off again item for nearly four years. You spent more time during that period with me than anyone else that you dated. I wanted you to commit to our relationship once and for all so that I didn't have to worry about every skirt that crossed your path. You have apparently forgotten that you just couldn't bring yourself to do that…you still can't!"

"I've made lots of commitments in my life. I'm committed to Fox, my work, the people that work for Fox, our customers; I've made lots of commitments and seen them through." Mac knew that this answer wasn't going to get him off the hook.

"But not the big one. The one where you personally commit your life to another person usually defined as a spouse."

Mac finished twirling and put the helping of pasta in his mouth. Silence reigned for a few minutes more as Mac considered Brady's comments. "You never married me," he countered.

"You never asked."

"True, but you knew I loved you."

"Just how would I know that? You never actually said the words, you never asked for my hand and when I forced the issue of commitment you looked as if you were having a stroke."

"I did not!"

"You did too! You grew pale, you stuttered and you looked so distressed that I actually was afraid that you might throw up. That's when I decided to not waste any more time on you."

"That's why you never accepted any of my invitations and brushed off my advances after that?"

"That's why. I can't believe that you're only now figuring this out. For a brilliant man you can be incredibly slow when it comes to understanding relationships."

Mac decided to change the subject. After all these years it was impossible for them to pick up where they left off. "How's your husband?"

"Committed to our marriage!" was Brady's sharp reply.

Mac laid his fork down and spread his hands wide. "Are you through beating me up? I asked you here so I could say thank you for all your help these past months. Not to rehash my past mistakes."

Silence again as Mac summoned the waitress to refill his glass of wine. Brady indicated that she was "good for now."

"I could make a commitment now, if I were to find the right woman." Common sense told Mac to drop this subject. He never intended the conversation to follow this route, but he just couldn't let it die.

"You sure?"

"Yeah, I know what I'm looking for now. I didn't for a long time."

Brady tore off a hunk of freshly baked bread, dipped it in olive oil and slowly spread some of the restaurant's trademark condiments on it. Each small loaf was accompanied with assorted grated cheeses and whole roasted garlic. It was the main reason Brady loved this place. "If I may pry; exactly what are you looking for in a woman?"

Mac lifted his wine glass, passed it under his nose several times and then took a sip. He swished it around in his mouth briefly getting the full effect of the flavor before swallowing it. Then he looked Brady straight in the eye. "Someone like you," he said and turned his attention to his meal once more. Brady was shocked. She had long ago given up hope of hearing anything like this from Mac. She smiled an ironic smile. Now that it's way too late she thought. Now that it's safe to say it out loud.

Mac raised his eyes once more. Brady thought that they seemed to be misting over. "That's strong garlic," said Mac. He pulled out his linen handkerchief and dabbed his eyes.

"Yes. Yes it is Mac," answered Brady softly. "Mac… You know that I'm committed to Harvey. He really is committed to me."

Mac waved his hand. "Of course I know that. The two of you have been happily married for what? Five years now?"

"Six."

"Okay then six. Don't misunderstand Brady. It may take me a while to realize my mistakes, but when I do I can live with them. Harvey is a great guy. I like him. I wouldn't do anything to hurt either of you." They both returned to their meals.

Mac eventually looked up again. He wanted to get this conversation back on track. "How is Harvey? It's been a while since I've talked to him."

Brady looked at her boss with soft eyes. "My husband is fine. He's at a union meeting tonight."

"How does he feel about you helping me bust the union organization attempt at Fox?"

"He doesn't know and he better never find out."

"I suspected as much. Don't worry he won't find out from me."

"I'm not worried. I trust you completely. After I met Harvey you never gave him any indication that you and I were ever lovers; even though that took place long before he arrived on the scene."

Mac sipped the fresh glass of wine. "If it wasn't for your husband's connections Mitchell Green would never have enlisted your aide in the organization attempt. He assumed that you share your husband's views on unionization."

"Actually I do share his views, but I also believe that a union is not right for Fox.

First, these are artisans not strictly assembly line workers. I'm not certain that union leaders would be sensitive to the difference. Second you Mac have always been sensitive to the employees needs. Now Sarah Frazer is having regular communication meetings between management and all of the employees. In addition you folks in management actually admitted making a mistake with the benefit package and then corrected that mistake. I'm more than ever convinced that Fox is better off without a union."

"Well I couldn't have beaten back the threat if you hadn't told me that Green recruited you to act as the inside spy and suggest people to help with the card check. You kept me informed concerning every move they were making and you gave me a conduit by which I could feed them what I wanted them to know. By the way, it didn't hurt that you suggested some of the most inarticulate people that we have working for us to be their recruiters."

"Well I didn't want to give him the names of respected charismatic people."

"In addition your friendship with Tom Erving's spy out in Vegas helped keep Tom informed too. Your previous high school relationship with her was a stroke of luck."

"After I talked to her she kept both Tom and me informed of the union's every move out in the desert. Tom never knew that I recruited her."

"You did well." Mac nodded in appreciation, "Thank you sounds inadequate."

Brady smiled. "My very generous end of the year bonus was appreciated."

"That had nothing to do with this. That was purely because you are the best executive secretary I've ever seen. I'm afraid a good dinner at a good Italian restaurant is all I can offer you in return for your 'cloak and dagger' work."

"It works for me Mac. It's been a long while since you and I spent time together away from the office."

"Does Mitchell Green suspect that you were a double agent?"

"No in fact he contacted me yesterday to tell me to lie low. They were calling off the campaign for a while, but they weren't giving up on Fox."

"Interesting, I thought that their interest in a small company like Fox was only to get their foot in the door with Atlantic and Wellbon-Smith companies. Now that we are truly autonomous I imagined we would hold no interest for them."

Brady frowned. "You're right. That is puzzling. Fox by itself is too small and the way you've split up the manufacturing facilities even make it less desirable to organize… Do you want me to keep contact with him?"

Mac exhaled wearily. "Yes you best do that. I really thought we were finished with this. I must warn Tony."

"You're not going to tell Tony about my role in all of this are you?" Brady trusted Mac, but she knew that if he told Tony about her role as a double agent, Tony would tell Blair and Blair would have a trusted friend and soon a host of people would know. Perhaps including her husband and that would be a disaster. One advantage to Mac's inability to make interpersonal commitments was that there was no one that he trusted enough to share secrets. All secrets were safe with Mac.

Mac shook his head, "No of course not. I'll still be involved with Fox as a member of our new board of directors so you and I will keep this as our secret. Just keep me informed if anything develops."

"I will Mac. I promise. Our failed romance not withstanding, I've always considered you my closest friend. I may give you a rough time on occasion, but you can count on my loyalty."

"I've never questioned it Brady, never once."

Brady gave him a warm inviting smile in response. They chatted about numerous things during the meal. Brady inquired as to what Mac intended to do with the home estate in Scotland and Mac explained his desire to keep it and maintain operations. Other topics came up and they passed a pleasant evening, two old friends simply catching up. After dessert and coffee Brady looked at her watch. "I have to go. I told Harvey we were meeting to tie up loose ends before you turned the company over to Tony. I'm not certain how long his meeting will run, but I should be going home."

"Of course, I'll walk you to your car." Mac paid the bill, helped Brady with her coat and they walked out into the cold December night together. The street was deserted as they crossed to the other side and walked the half block to the restaurant's parking lot. The row houses in this end of town were decorated with bright blinking Christmas lights. Brady unlocked her car door then turned to Mac.

"Thanks for dinner."

"It's the least I could do for you Brady. Thank you again for your help."

"Mac, whenever you need help with anything you can call on me."

"The same goes for you too Brady." They stood looking at each other in the darkness then without warning Brady threw her arms around Mac's neck and gave him a long passionate kiss. Surprised, Mac kissed her back. When it ended, Mac could only say "Wow!"

Brady laughed. "Mac, forget what I said about Sarah earlier. If she turns out to be 'the right woman,' go for it. You only get a few chances in life. Don't miss out." She squeezed his hand, got in her car and quickly drove away.

Mac watched until her taillights disappeared around the corner. Then he walked across the lot to his company sedan. Mac never drove the T-Bird if there was any chance of inclement weather and tonight there was the possibility of snow flurries. He got into his car and started the engine. While waiting for it to warm up he reflected on the past six months. The death of his father, fighting off a union, the successful battle to purchase Fox, indeed the related battle for control of Wellbon-Smith and his unexpected promotion to president of the Atlantic Corporation. Mac shook his head in wonderment. You go along for years working at the same things and then suddenly everything changes. With the exception of the loss of his father everything eventually worked out for the best. Upon further reflection, even through his sadness, he saw opportunity in his father's death. I suppose that's the way it should be he thought. The passing of the torch, the chance to carry on, maybe some day he would return home and pick up where his father left off in the political arena. For the first time it occurred to Mac that he had no heir to carry on the family name or its proud traditions. That thought both sobered and saddened him.

Mac's thoughts then turned to Brady and he felt an old ache return to the pit of his stomach. Why had he been so stupid? Why had he kept putting her off when he knew that she wanted to get married? What Brady didn't know was that when Mac realized that she was getting serious about Harvey he almost ran to her one night and begged her to take him back, asking her to marry him! But he didn't. He stood silently by, attended their wedding and gave them a lovely gift with his best wishes. He even took some strikingly beautiful fashion model, whose name he could no longer recall to their wedding and reception. He supposed that he did that just to show Beady that he was doing okay without her. Mac shook his head. He really was without her. Even though they had maintained this close friendship over the years, they certainly weren't sharing their lives. It was probably a blessing that he was taking the position in New York. Finally he and Brady wouldn't be working side by side every day. Was that why he had never married? Was he subconsciously still hoping that he and Brady would get together? Mac let out a long sigh. It had been over for Brady for years, maybe now it would finally be over for Mac.

The car was warm and the heater was expelling warm air. It felt good. Mac put the car in gear and moved out into the street. His thoughts moved to Sarah and he smiled to himself in the dark. In just a few hours they would be together, together for more than a week in one of the most romantic settings in Scotland. Maybe Brady was right. Maybe God was giving William MacLode one more chance to come to his senses and be truly happy. Mac took a deep breath. Suddenly he was really looking forward to Christmas!

THE END

To Catch a Fox

Epilogue: January 1, 2000

They were watching the television in the large luxurious living room. Dick Clark was counting down the seconds as the huge bejeweled ball descended in Times Square. As the ball touched the bottom the words "Happy New Year 2000" flashed on and off across the screen. The large man with curly black hair dressed in an expensive immaculately tailored suit turned to his companion and smiled. "You know it's customary to kiss the one you're with at this moment."

The woman returned his smile. "One usually knows the name of the person that they are kissing," she said. "What are you calling yourself today? Smith? Jones? What?" She was teasing him of course as she was one of the few people that actually knew his real name.

The large man laughed that friendly grandfatherly laugh. "I don't know I'll have to check my most recent driver's license. However, for the moment I suppose Smith will suffice."

"Okay Smitty, let's kiss!" Mary Wellbon moved across her living room to where the mysterious Mr. Smith was standing and planted a big kiss on his mouth. "How was that?" She asked before removing her arms from around his neck.

"Tastes like more," he replied.

"In your dreams!" They both had a good chuckle. Mary looked around her penthouse. The lights were still on, the T.V. was still playing and on the street far below the New York City traffic was rumbling along at its usual pace. "Well, imagine that. Apocalypse has been delayed."

"Once again," smiled Smith. "May I?" he asked as he removed his jacket and loosened his tie.

"Certainly, we've known each other too long for you to think that you have to ask permission for such a trivial thing."

"Well you are the infamous Mary Wellbon."

"I'm the same Mary that The Company recruited on campus so many years ago. I'm the same Mary that The Company assigned a young overachiever as my coordinator. After completing training I managed to marry into the target family that they selected for me. You sir, are that same coordinator. I remember thinking how young you were when we first met. You are the only person on the face of this earth that knows all of my secrets; by the way what was with that 'infamous' comment?"

Smith ignored the reference to his use of the word infamous. "We've been a team for a long time Mary."

Mary nodded in agreement, "Langley tells me that we've worked together longer than any other team that they have in the field; world wide."

"There aren't many teams left," commented Smith with a tone of concern in his voice. Then as an afterthought, "Since we know each other so well I'm going to have more of your whiskey."

"Help yourself. You can get drunk if you desire. We're the only ones here."

"I might crash here tonight."

"You know that you are always welcome, we just can't ever be seen together."

Smith laughed. "You think you need to coach me on the rules?"

"I'm sorry, Of course not." Mary shook her head. "I've got a bad habit of telling people what to do."

"You aren't having guests over tomorrow? No family?"

"No, I'm meeting the family at a restaurant for a late afternoon meal tomorrow and the hired help have the day off. Crystal is flying back to Savannah tonight after she finishes her reporting assignment in Times Square, so the place is yours if you like."

Smith looked around the penthouse, "I've always liked this place. The Company allows me to stay in good hotels, but this beats them. I'll take you up on that invitation."

Mary sat down on the love seat. "Good, now come sit beside me and we can reminisce about the past year. Isn't that what normal people do on this night?"

Smith poured his drink and joined her. "Are we normal?"

"Not hardly…All things considered I think we've had a successful year."

Smith looked around the penthouse living room. "Are we secure?"

"Yes, I sweep for electronic bugs twice a week. The window glass, floor, ceiling and the walls have protection against long distance listening devices. We're as secure here as we would be at CIA headquarters out at Langley."

Smith appeared to relax. "Yeah we did have a successful year. Things could have gone south at any point, but we managed to avoid disaster. In fact Crystal seems to be ahead of schedule. I thought that was brilliant, a bit dangerous but brilliant of you to have me bring her here immediately after her rescue. It paves the way for our next step."

"It was a calculated risk."

"What made you so certain that she could keep my role in her life a secret?"

"She's my husband's daughter. If he couldn't keep secrets he would have been in jail years ago. Also, after having met her mother, I knew there must be a bit of the romantic in her. It's been terribly exciting having a mysterious stranger in her life. Especially after you rescued her from the most terrifying and traumatic event she had ever experienced. After all of the years that you and I have been watching her, I felt confident that I could predict her actions in this situation."

Smith sipped his drink. "Your idea for the additional trust fund was a master stroke."

"I could afford it. My husband provided for Crystal quite well through college, but the funds were just about exhausted. If you remember having you administer the original fund wasn't the easiest to set up."

Smith smiled, "No it wasn't, but you were very clever. It would not have been a good thing if that were left to anyone else. Left to himself your husband might have chosen Paul Henley. How did you ever get him to agree to me, someone he never knew or met?"

Mary smiled. "I used my feminine charms. Besides at that time he was working hard to get me to forgive him for the affair." Mary continued, "I figured that creating a new fund for her now would only make her more indebted to us if we ever need to apply leverage on her."

Smith sighed "at first I thought she wasn't going to use it, but she's started to tap into it now. On a related subject, your husband sure threw us a curve twenty some years ago when he shacked up with Crystal's mother."

"Yeah and he managed to break my heart too."

"I'm sorry Mary. That was crude and inconsiderate of me. I know how you felt about your deceased husband."

"It's okay Smitty. Your statement was accurate. That really was a curve…Ironic isn't it, Denton told me everything. He kept all of those secrets from everyone else yet he shared everything with the one actual spy in his life."

"He never knew that. Besides you're good."

"I know. I suppose a broken heart was fair trade, as I was never honest with him. He never suspected that our meeting was not by chance, that my assignment was to make him fall in love with me and marry him. What I never suspected was that I would actually fall in love with him."

"You know Mary, when I realized that you actually loved Denton I almost recommended that our superiors at the CIA cut you loose. I was afraid that your emotions would stand in the way of you doing your job."

"Really? You never told me that!"

"I never made the recommendation to the Company either."

"Why not?"

"I got to know you better. I realized that you were the consummate professional and that you could finish a mission no matter how it interfered with or messed up your personal life."

Mary reflected on what Smith had just said. "That's either the biggest compliment I've ever received from a fellow professional or an indictment on being certifiably nuts. How did you mean it?"

"I'll never tell," laughed Smith.

"But the curve my husband dealt us presented us with our greatest opportunity."

"Yes, Crystal was a blessing in disguise. I have to admit that I had doubts when you first mentioned her as your eventual successor in the Wellbon family empire. I always favored young Denton."

"How do you feel about her now?"

"I'm 100% behind her. Denton, like his father will be an excellent front. Crystal, can take your role and as his half sister pull the strings as the CIA requires."

"What about Langley?"

"I've filed our reports and they are in agreement. They think that Crystal has a lot of potential. They've given us the green light to go forward with her."

"Good…Without knowing it Wellbon-Smith has served this country well Smitty."

"Yes, thanks to you Mary. Your family business owns companies that do business all around the world. Small companies, but aggressive nonetheless. While our enemies in the cold war suspected all of the large U.S. companies like IBM, your companies provided cover for our operatives to recruit and run spy networks wherever we required. None were ever suspected or uncovered."

"We did okay huh Smitty."

"Yeah and Langley acknowledges that fact."

"In reference to your earlier comment that there are few teams like us left, I'm almost surprised that we have the green light to recruit Crystal. Do they really want to continue this operation since the cold war is over?"

"Well it's been tough since the Congress has essentially reduced intelligence gathering to listening posts and spy satellites. It hasn't budgeted for human intelligence, 'humit' for the past several years. Fortunately there are those in the CIA that realize how short sighted this strategy is."

"Smitty I know that an operation like this is relatively inexpensive compared to spy satellites, but how are we maintaining funding when Congress has such an aversion to 'spooks'?"

Smith laughed. "Our operation is kind of off the books. You didn't really think that we spent $500 on hammers and $1000 on screw drivers did you? Only Congress believes that we're that stupid. Besides, it's Company policy to appear stupid every couple years. It keeps the real bad guys from taking us seriously. In addition the civilian hierarchy at the top is always changing, so few ever stays long enough to figure out what we're really doing."

"Okay we preserved our secret operations at Wellbon-Smith by covering up my husband's indiscretion. We even managed to eliminate the threat that Abe Rueben and Trevor Mason presented with their attempted takeover. The loss of Fox is no problem. Since it basically operates in the continental U.S. we never utilized it for spy operations. It's too bad that we couldn't have prevented the kidnapping of what has to be our most promising future asset, but we got her back without a scratch."

"If I could have moved faster Mary we could have blocked the kidnapping before it happened, but our superiors insisted that I assemble an international force from other agencies. Special Ops people that didn't know each other, and would never work together again. Since it's illegal for the CIA to operate within the borders of the United States it had to be impossible to trace this operation. That took a little time and I was forced to run a rescue rather than the more desirable preventive mission."

"Well the whole thing fell together when Denton came to me and explained that Trevor was planning a take over. I knew that Mason was up to something because he was preparing to market Fox; I just didn't know what it was. Crystal would be Rueben's logical target to put pressure on Denton to keep him in line. That didn't allow you much time to set up protection for Crystal. But to quote my daughter in law, "All's well that ends well."

"Yeah, I really like Crystal. I'm glad we got her back unhurt. I wish I could have eliminated the don's boys too while I was at it. I've no time for those predators even though we were on the same side this time. "

Mary smiled. "Smitty, remember they have come in handy in the past. We'll let Denton continue to deal with them."

"I know Mary, I know. I just worry that the FBI will stumble across this operation some day and we'll get crucified for looking the other way concerning the don and his illegal activities."

"Don't worry, I won't let that happen. On a different topic; how did you know exactly how the kidnappers would be set up to defend their hiding place? I hear that not only did you eliminate them swiftly, but you even removed all trace of their having been there."

"Simple, Rueben hired Duke Winston. I followed his gang to Duke's bar the night that Donald Kensington-Cramer was killed. I knew Duke when he was a Special Forces team commander in Nam and I was on my first assignment as an agent. This was before I was assigned to you. I know how he thinks. He's a nut case; they finally drummed him out of the service because of it. Fortunately today the Army does a better job of screening these types out of Special Forces."

Mary Wellbon contemplated the man seated next to her, "Smitty, we're old friends, may I ask you another question?"

Smith smiled, "Of course you may. You're my closest friend. You may ask me anything, I've never kept secrets from you."

"Did you eliminate Abe Rueben?"

The large man contemplated his glass, smiled and shook his head, "No, no I didn't. I tipped off the NYPD to the fact that Donald Kensington-Cramer entered Ruben's office building the night of Donald's death, but I did no more. It wasn't necessary. Thanks to your son he was no longer a threat to our operation." Smith returned his attention to the television. The network was party hopping from coast to coast. Then he added in a low voice, "The bastard deserved to die, his life simply caught up with him."

Mary watched her long time partner and friend closely; she was concerned for him. "I know that you are a professional but he was indirectly responsible for the death of your daughter. I thought you might have done a little freelance work."

Smith turned back to her, emotion showing on his face. Mary could count the number of times on one hand that she had witnessed true pain in his eyes. She was with him when he had received the news of his daughter's death and she had attended the funeral incognito. This was the third time. "It crossed my mind more than once, but as you said he was 'indirectly responsible'. I'm looking for the actual murderer. One of these days I'll find him. One of these days…" Smith's voice trailed off.

"Who do you think killed Rueben, the New York crime families?"

"Your old friend don Luca? No, I suspect that the don has Andy and his boys scrambling to find whatever Rueben had on them that kept him alive this long. If he hadn't had something big on them he would have been dead the moment he returned to New York."

"Then who did it?"

"A rumored long time Chicago hit man was found dead at a North Carolina rest stop along I-95. Word is that he worked for Rueben more than once over the years. I think Abe was trying to knock someone off and they turned the tables on him."

"Who do you suspect?"

"I can't be certain so this is pure speculation, but my old friend Duke Winston wasn't at the trailer when my special ops guys rescued Crystal. I suspect that he was high tailing it home when he tangled with the hit man. Abe didn't like failure and Duke tends to get pissed off if you try to kill him."

"Interesting," satisfied Mary changed the subject again. "What does the

Company have next on our agenda?"

Smith took another sip of his whiskey. "Ever hear of a guy named Osama Bin Laden?"

"No, I've never heard the name."

"That's the problem. You should have and you should be very afraid. He's putting together a loose knit terrorist organization in the Middle East. Some people at Langley see him as the next big threat to U.S. security, but nobody is doing anything about it. Part of the reason is that even at the Company not everyone agrees on the threat he represents."

"Why is that?"

"No human intelligence on the ground. We have no operations in the Middle East. As some previous friends went by the way side and as our Congress developed an aversion to spook networks we lost our window to this shadowy world. Our allies in that part of the world tend to be two faced and even Israel's Mossad has been known to spy on us."

"How does Wellbon-Smith fit into this?"

"Denton will soon become aware of some lucrative contracts that will be up for bids in various countries in the Middle East. They are legitimate contracts, some government and some private. It will look like an excellent opportunity for skill sets possessed by your Sterling International and Global Industries. Make certain that Denton insists that companies from these two Wellbon-Smith conglomerates bid on these contracts. I assure you they will get their share. These contracts will be very profitable for your companies."

"They always are."

The contracts will require Sterling and Global to set up facilities in several Middle East countries. You will have to hire a lot of locals. Once there we can begin our usual task of recruiting and running a local spy network that operates within your businesses."

"What's the time frame?" asked Mary.

To Catch a Fox

"Completely operational networks by 2005."

"Is that fast enough?"

"I hope so, because of the language and cultural differences we can't hope to infiltrate any faster."

"You'll give me details on these contracts so that they don't slip by unnoticed?"

"Absolutely. Now Mary, as the Company has only had to keep members of your family safe and out of jail in exchange for all of this, our superiors are curious as to the time table you have in mind for Crystal."

"Please Smitty, I find it embarrassing that the Company had to go to these extraordinary measures to maintain our cover and our operations."

"Don't be ashamed Mary. As you stated before, even with the problems we had keeping your husband's secrets an operation like us that provides, operates and maintains cover for spy networks around the world is far less expensive to support than the launching and maintenance of spy satellites."

"My time table for Crystal; as I suspected she has already linked me to you. She's a bright girl and she dropped a few hints to me while staying here over the holidays. I didn't take the bait. I've neither confirmed nor denied her suspicions. You need to know that the hints that she dropped never broke her promise to you. If I wasn't who I am and know what I know I would have had no clue as to what she was referring."

Smith smiled, "She's a smart girl. The fact that you let it slide probably makes her even more suspicious."

"I hope so. I will be going south to Savannah sometime during January. I'll be visiting her. Since we have the green light to go forward that will be the time that I will begin recruiting her to take my place."

"You think she will go for it?"

"Not at first but then neither did I."

"But you're convinced that you can recruit her."

"Yes, unlike me she won't have to marry into this family and we will have the trust fund if we need leverage. So you don't have to consider replacing her with my son. He's fine where he is. We just have to keep him out of trouble with the don."

"It's agreed that we don't tell young Denton?"

"Agreed, he'll make a fine chairman for Wellbon-Smith and he will be an excellent front just as his father was. Meanwhile unknown to him we will train Crystal to be an agent just like me. Just as his father before him, Denton will never suspect a thing. He will use Andy and the boys very sparingly but I'll keep my eye on them."

"If you recruit Crystal, she will have to go into training and after that you will have to find some position for her in the business."

"Don't worry; I already have that worked out. Because we removed all trace of her origins from public records we can create any background for her that is necessary."

Mr. Smith finished his whiskey. He looked at Mary Wellbon and smiled. "Yes Mary I think we had a good year. I feel good about the future also."

"Me too Smitty. You know as soon as I have a fully trained Crystal in place at Wellbon-Smith I'm going to retire."

"I suspected as much."

"I know that you aren't as old as I am Smith, but you are way past being eligible to retire yourself. When do you plan on getting out?"

Mr. Smith contemplated his empty glass then rose and moved toward the bar where he filled it. "When do I plan to retire you ask? When there are no more dragons to slay or fair damsels to rescue…Happy New Year Mary."

Mary Wellbon smiled, "Happy New Year Smitty."